**DREW PEARSON'S INSIDE STORY OF
WASHINGTON IN ITS GREATEST CRISIS!**

The President of the United States is elected by
33% of the vote. Taxes are the highest in history,
bitter racism rages across the land, a riot at a
leading university sends hundreds to prison camps,
National Guardsmen supplement the local police
in America's major cities . . . and the President
proposes the most startling solution ever heard of
to save the country—a solution which could
obliterate the country itself!

Highly disturbing and as current as this morning's
headlines, THE PRESIDENT is the brutal inside
truth behind the power at the very top!

The President

DREW|PEARSON

AVON PUBLISHERS OF BARD, CAMELOT, DISCUS AND EQUINOX BOOKS

All of the characters in this book are fictitious, and any resemblance to actual persons, living or dead, is purely coincidental.

AVON BOOKS
A division of
The Hearst Corporation
959 Eighth Avenue
New York, New York 10019

Copyright © 1970 by Luvie Moore Pearson as Collector
of the Estate of Drew Pearson.
Published by arrangement with Doubleday & Company, Inc.
Library of Congress Catalog Card Number: 73-113074.

First Avon Printing, January, 1972

AVON TRADEMARK REG. U.S. PAT. OFF. AND
FOREIGN COUNTRIES, REGISTERED TRADEMARK—
MARCA REGISTRADA, HECHO EN CHICAGO, U.S.A.

Printed in the U.S.A.

CHIEF CHARACTERS

Benjamin Bow Hannaford, the President, formerly the senator from Ramada
Fern Cudder Hannaford, his wife

AT THE WHITE HOUSE

Edward Deever, special assistant to the President. The narrator
Evangeline Boswell ("Vangie"), secretary to Mrs. Hannaford
Cleo Watterson, secretary to the President
Matthew Fixx, special assistant to the President, congressional liaison
Dalton Warfield, special assistant to the President, minority problems
Fred Goldstein, press secretary
Verne Latour Sparrier, the Vice-President, former governor of California

THE CABINET

Burke Boswell, Secretary of Defense. (Vangie's father)
Walter Edgerton, Secretary of State, former senator from Ohio
Margaret High McNally ("Meg"), Secretary of the Treasury
Homer Murphy, Secretary of Health, Education and Welfare

5

Samuel Moscowitz, Attorney-General, former director of the FBI

General Dudley, Chief of Staff, the Army
Admiral Strang, Naval Chief of Operations
General McTaggart, Chief of Staff, the Air Force
General Clyde (Nuke the Chink) Upshaw, retired
Pvt. Moses Mulford, Chemical Warfare Service

THE PRESS

Lou Parente, syndicated columnist
Bates Pendragon, syndicated columnist, the Pringle news-
    papers
C. C. Pringle, publisher
Mona Varnum, United Broadcasting
Larry Hosmer, United Press

OTHERS

Marsha Treadway Parente, Lou Parente's wife
Minerva Boswell, wife of the Secretary of Defense
Judy Stapp, Senator Stapp's wife
Carla Foraker, former wife of Congressman Lance Ruck-
    ett
Arvid Farbelman, a poet-playwright
Kakamba Jones, black militant leader, vice-presidential
    candidate, Black-and-Tan Party
Augie Baldini, cousin of Lou Parente
Merton Huckerby, Board of Directors, "DOOR"
John Laurens Early, Chief Justice, the United States Su-
    preme Court

PART I

In this country the right things always get done for the wrong reasons.

—BENJAMIN BOW HANNAFORD

Sunrise comes gently in the southwestern desert of the United States. Even in early November when the air is chilled, the first light of dawn has a marvelous power to restore, to heal, to replace night's gloom with morning's optimism.

As I strolled the rolling hills of Ramada Ranch, I needed that reassuring golden glow of the sun as badly as I have ever needed anything in my thirty-five years. I had been awake for forty-seven hours. Gingered with Dexedrine and vitamin pills, I moved shakily across the crunching sands, admiring the changing colors of distant Ramada Range—purple-gray to violet-green to a lavender-gold, as the sun worked magical brush strokes on the spare hills. I could have wandered through that parklike setting, amid prickly pear, cholla, paloverde and mesquite for months, living off the land and becoming a friend to lizards and cactus wrens.

But a retreat to nature was not in the cards for Edward Deever, aide and confidante to former Senator Benjamin Bow Hannaford. To begin with, I am a city man (the city is Washington, D.C.) even though I was born in Indian Mound, Ohio, population 795. I doubt I would survive one night in the desert. My pointed black shoes were unequal to the rough footing. My neutral gray suit was too thin and I shivered. Beyond any of these considerations (my hands are soft and my wind is meager) loomed the future.

But what kind of future? I would know soon enough. At least I hoped I would. My passage through a creosote thicket flushed a covey of Gambel's quail. Reluctantly I turned on the tiny transistor radio I had taken along on my morning constitutional.

" . . . Vice-President Beldock is holding a small lead over Senator Hannaford in California. Mr. Beldock is picking up votes in Orange County and he now leads the Hannaford-Sparrier ticket by three thousand votes. . . ."

I switched stations. There was no balm in Gilead, as Ben Hannaford would have said. " . . . California will hold the key to this presidential election. If Smead Beldock holds on to his lead there, the election will be inconclusive. No candidate will have the needed 270 electoral votes and the election will go to the House of Rep—"

Click. Again I switched stations.

" . . . a win in California would give Senator Hannaford that state's 45 electoral votes, and would also give him a total of 271, making him the next President of the United St—"

Click. Resentful of reality's intrusion into my desert idyll—a chuckwalla peeked at me suspiciously from behind a rock—I turned the radio off. But if I were apprehensive, what about my boss, Benjamin Bow Hannaford, late of the United States Senate, the greatest man I have ever known, our party's candidate for the highest office? I had seen him a half hour ago and he had been unnervingly composed. "Edward," he said, "get out of the house and take a walk. You look pale, and you're talking damn foolishness. Not like you, son."

No, it was not like me. I am a cool customer. *Bloodless, nerveless*, the Washington reporters called me during the time of the Big Scandal. Unmarried. Uncommitted—except to Ben Hannaford. I'd been through the fires with Ben, and both of us had emerged burned, scarred, calloused. How else explain our incredible political comeback?

Right hand trembling, I returned to the radio. It was no help. " . . . 88 per cent of the California vote is in, and Vice-President Smead Beldock is holding grimly to a four-thousand vote lead, hardly a lead at all in California, but significant in that . . ."

There was, I'm told, a French writer, fashionable after World War II, who had a theory of human life as *absurd*. My education was limited to Ohio Normal College (A.B.) and I scarcely qualify as an intellectual, but I did not need a smart Frenchman to tell me this. Six years in Ben

11

Hannaford's employ, six years on the inside of the Washington scene, the whole colorful, corrupt, chaotic circus of our political life had told me this years ago.

Absurd. How else describe my boss's candidacy? Two years ago Senator Benjamin Bow Hannaford, the big man from Ramada, multimillionaire builder, operator, buddy to oilmen, compromiser, arm-twister, Bible-quoter, old-fashioned liberal-populist, the richest and most potent man in the United States Senate, that wildlife refuge on the Potomac, had been shamed and brought to earth in a "scandal" that still set tongues wagging in the capital. Ben had been censured by the Senate. Ben had resigned and gone back to Ramada City, to his ranch house and to his vast corporate enterprises. I, Edward Deever, ageless boy-wonder of his staff, tarred and dirtied during the hearings, had lingered quietly in Washington as his confidential man.

I need not be modest. I had done my job magnificently, helped by the limitless sums of money Hannaford could deploy. And now he might—or might not—become President. I thought of those Orange County voters in California—decent Americans, if a bit puritanical and superpatriotic, rejecting Ben's reasonable view of the world, in favor of Smead Beldock, or worse, for the Save America candidate, General Clyde (Nuke the Chink) Upshaw and his running mate, an old associate of ours in the Senate, the Honorable Gabriel T. Tutt of Alabama.

It seemed incredible to me that we had done as well as we had—226 electoral votes already. Virtually all were from industrial states, where the Upshaw-Tutt ticket had bled away much of Beldock's conservative support. *Absurd.* The whole election had an absurdity about it. Consider the *fourth* party—Congressman Angel Lopez Garcia and Kakamba Jones, running for President and Vice-President, on the Black-and-Tan ticket!

The sun warmed my bones, cleared my sinuses, endowed my Dacron-clad limbs with new vigor. Somehow, I assured myself, we would win California—although as I turned off the transistor I found it hard to accept the fantasy. The truth was we were licked in California. All that remained to be counted were some mysteriously delayed ballots in central Los Angeles, including the feverish black district of Watts. Every poll had predicted that the Garcia-Jones slate with its anti-white racist appeal, would sweep those precincts, or at least so erode our strength, that Smead Beldock would squeak through.

So it would be on to the House of Representatives for more trading, bickering, spying, arranging, wheeling and dealing. Of course Hannaford was superb at this sort of thing. But I wondered if I had the strength to go through with any more of it. Entertaining these notions, I at once realized I could not refuse him. Just as I had labored through the chaotic Chicago convention of last August in his behalf, performing missions never mentioned in any political science textbook. Never.

Again the notion of the *absurd* titillated me. In photographic clarity, I found myself recalling the manner in which Ben and I had swung the convention away from the conservative forces of the young governor of California, handsome Verne Sparrier, our current running mate. I rested on a rock. A jack rabbit bounced by.

"Edward," Ben Hannaford had said to me three months ago in our headquarters in the Sheraton-Blackstone Hotel, "If we can shake Kentucky loose, I think we can cash in all the border states. They like me, but they're waiting for someone else to make the first move."

"Why Kentucky?" I asked. "Our polls show they lean toward Verne Sparrier. They appreciate that law, order and a billy-club pitch."

"Hell, nothing to do with ideology. Or principle. I just think that the vice-chairman of the Kentucky delegation, Judge Jervis Kickley, is ready to be convinced."

I was on guard. "Kickley? That old cross burner? Sir, he has fought us down the line. He's the core of Sparrier's strength in Kentucky."

"I said to hell with ideology," Senator Hannaford said. (All of us kept referring to him as senator, even after his resignation. In my mind he will always be The Senator.) Ben handed me a slip of paper, and I felt a tremor in my gut as I saw his childish scrawl. Ben's formal education ended when he was fourteen and went to work as a rigger in the oil fields of his native Ramada.

"What does this mean?" I protested. "Room 1516, Hotel Overlook, Ohio Street?" I had a pretty good idea what it meant, but I wanted him to explain.

"Judge Kickley is being entertained at the hotel this very moment. You are to pay him a visit. Make sure that Brother Goldstein and his camera accompany you."

I frowned. "Senator, do we have to do it this way?"

"I'm afraid so. We can't let the convention drag on any longer. Someone's got to get the nomination and it might as well be me."

"Can't we work on delegates? I mean, pose the issues again, convince them you're the moderate voice here, that you're the man who can get enough black support, hold enough suburban people, and—"

Ben shook his handsome, square face. He had aged since the censure two years ago—grayer at the temples, the lines around his mouth and chin deeper. But the eyes were still an alert, dark brown. His tread, his handshake were those of a young man.

"No, we have to start playing rough. I've looked over the lists, and the vice-chairman of the Kentucky delegation, old Judge Kickley may be our man. Let him move the Bluegrass State, and maybe we can move three or four fence sitters."

"I don't like it," I protested. "The last time you sent me on one of these errands we got into terrible trouble."

Ben Hannaford waved me off. There was no denying him when he wanted something done. " 'In the mouth of two or three witnesses shall every word be established.' "

I knew what he meant by that. Fred Goldstein and I would be the witnesses. Judge Kickley would have a grave decision to make.

The absurd charade proceeded. Fred, a former television network newsman who was our efficient press secretary, got his tiny camera, loaded it with high-speed film, and we arrived at the Hotel Overlook, a decaying dump redolent of Lysol, at dusk.

"Cheer up, Fred," I told our press secretary. "You'll never get a Pulitzer prize doing this, but think of the memoirs you'll be able to write."

"You and that goddamn crazy Indian." Fred scowled. He has frizzy red hair (a Cossack somewhere in his Semitic ancestry?) and is a sour, loyal and talented young man. The term "Indian" referred to Hannaford, who bragged frequently about his Kiowa grandmother.

One five-dollar bill got us to the house detective, another to the elevator operator, a third to the bell captain. The latter—a stooped skid-row sort—took us to the dingy door with the number 1516 on it. Gently, he inserted a master key in the door, turned the knob and then vanished into the Overlook's murky corridors.

"It's do or die for dear old Rutgers," I said.

Goldstein readied his mini-camera. I raised high a battery-powered bulb much favored by newsfilm cameramen called a "sun-gun." Then I opened the door and the two of us strode in.

Like Jove hurling a thunderbolt, I pressed the button on the sun-gun and drowned the dreary room in a blinding white glow. Fred, sullen and businesslike, was taking photographs before Judge Kickley and his two—*two!*—companions had any idea what was happening.

"Whuh? Whuh? What the hell is goin' on?" the jurist cried.

"Ah, Jesus Christ, ya lousy bastids," one of the girls exclaimed.

"We deh masseuses, das all," the other said. She was a coffee-brown Negro girl in a starched white uniform. Masseuse, indeed.

Although I have since studied the photographs several times (the negatives were destroyed in the presence of the judge after he saw things our way) I still am not certain what was going on in room 1516.

Judge Kickley was lying on his back, clad only in an undershirt and his socks. The Negro girl in the white uniform was kneading and stroking his corpulent torso—for all I knew she *was* a masseuse—and the other lady, a seedy blonde was crouched further up on the bed, engaged in some other activity. If she *also* were a masseuse, she practiced her profession in an odd manner. She was naked.

Goldstein danced around the room clicking away as I kept the sun-gun burning. I had to give the judge credit; he was not frightened. He assumed, of course, that we were the Chicago vice-squad. Police posed no threat to him. He handled police with natural grace. (The girls were of a different mind, especially the black girl. They protested, squealed, and kept producing identity cards, medical reports and certificates proving they were practitioners of naturopathy, muscle tone and spinal manipulation.)

"Dang, a man cain't git him a little poontang no more," Judge Kickley protested as he struggled into his underpants. He had a round cherubic face and a fringe of white

15

hair. I knew him as a pillar of the old guard in Kentucky, a mortal foe of school integration.

The blond girl had dressed; the Negro girl had gotten her shoes on. I dismissed them. "You ladies may leave. We have business only with the gentleman."

They flew out the door. The judge looked puzzled. "Whut in hell goin' on? Don' they git arrested? Ain't done nothin'. They bust in hyeah claimin' they masseuses . . ."

I sat down on a hard-backed chair and crossed my legs, letting Judge Kickley sputter. With the ultra-bright light turned off, he now got a good look at me, and after studying me with reptilian eyes, he recognized me.

"You . . . you . . . Hannaford's boy? Deever?"

"That's correct, Judge. I am not a Chicago police officer. I'm Deever. The photographer over there is another of Hannaford's boys, Mr. Goldstein."

"Oh, pretty tricky ole Hannaford." The judge drew on his trousers, then fell back on the bed, where so recently he had brimmed with passion. I am no prude or bluenose and I was sorry I had interrupted his pleasures. Would he get a refund from that odd medical team? Or a rain check?

"Your Honor," I said carefully, "back in the thirties the FBI once raided a whorehouse in Washington known as the Hopkins Institute. Mr. Hoover's efficient agents got the names of two hundred members of Congress who patronized the institute. Do you know, sir, that from that day on the FBI never had any trouble with financial appropriations for the bureau?"

Judge Kickley sat up and began to puff. "Goddamn Hannaford. He don't hold no purse strings. Y'all don't scare me."

"Fred," I said to Goldstein. "I suggest you have that roll of film developed just so we make sure we will get a clear set of prints." Fred nodded and left.

"It isn't money we are talking about, Judge," I said. "Senator Hannaford and I feel you are making a grave mistake in refusing to vote for his nomination. There are fifteen members of your delegation who'll move if you move, and then maybe the whole gang, and then maybe a bloc of border states. Now would you want those photographs circulated back home? Especially since you've started the Church, God, Country, Home and Flag Crusade for Young People?"

16

To my surprise, a ragged smile pushed Judge Kickley's purple cheeks upward, twisted his moist lips. He knew a political operator when he met one. "Tell Hannaford okay. He's a good ole boy."

I reported our foray to Ben. He rubbed his huge knuckled hands—the hands of a high steel man, a crane operator—and laughed softly. "Edward, I think we got us a nomination," he said. "I'm sorry for old Kickley, but we had to move. Couldn't let Sparrier take over this fine political party."

"I'm sorrier than you are. I got to like the judge. He took it all with a lot of dignity."

Ben waved his hand in appreciation. "We did the old man a favor. Saved him from wasting his substance with riotous living." He reached for a phone. Oh, we had work ahead, a convention to win. "Edward, start on the top floor of the Conrad Hilton Hotel and work your way down—you and Brother Goldstein and our allies. As St. Luke put it, 'Go out in the highways and hedges and compel them to come in.'"

I do not suggest that *all* political prizes are won in this manner. But Ben Hannaford was far and away the best of the candidates, a stronger, more intelligent, more humane man than Governor Verne Latour Sparrier of California could ever hope to be. The opposition party already had a flinty conservative running for President—Vice-President Smead Beldock, a man so enamored of the tobacco industry (he was a millionaire farmer) so zealous of protective tariffs, so opposed to medical warnings on cigarette packages, that he had been nicknamed "Smokey Smead" by columnist Lou Parente. The growing third party movement, Save America, had nominated General Clyde (Mad Bomber) Upshaw.

It was in the nature of things that our party should look for a tough-minded liberal. Ben filled the bill. No misty-eyed theorist, he was a practical, compassionate and open-minded man. If he operated in a highhanded, sometimes brutal manner, he did so with an eye on a noble goal—a decent life for all Americans.

We had run a shrewd campaign—attacking General Upshaw as a dangerous military crank (the country had long grown accustomed to the spectacle of criticizing Army officers; it was no longer deemed unpatriotic to do so) but only in localities where he was *already* so regarded. Quite frankly we did not want Upshaw and his running mate Gabe Tutt rendered impotent. The nation had grown markedly conservative, notably in domestic matters, and it was Ben's strategy to keep Upshaw and Tutt sufficiently strong so that they might eat away at Smead Beldock's vote.

From the start Ben had discounted Angel Lopez Garcia and Kakamba Jones. "Those people delude themselves. They can't win. They can't hold a balance of power. Because they offend everyone, as soon as they unite, everyone else unites against *them*. They won't take a single state. There is no vast hiding vote of young kids, radicals, professors, and there's just so many blacks who get out to vote." He scowled and made an impatient gesture. "A damned pity, too, because those black people have all the *real* grievances, not the nuts like Upshaw or the bigots like Gabe Tutt."

Once more I turned on the radio as I walked toward Hannaford's sprawling ranch house.

" . . . definitely a minority president, elected with the lowest percentage of the vote since Woodrow Wilson's 41.9 per cent in 1912 . . . "

At first I thought Ben was in, that California had miraculously gone to us. But no. The commentator was merely saying *whoever* became President—Hannaford or Beldock—would rule with a thin mandate, if mandate it were. Ben and Smead Beldock were now virtually even in the popular vote, both somewhat over twenty-five million, both with about 33.7 per cent. General Upshaw, whose response to questions on foreign policy was, "It's us or them, and I choose us!" had, with such weighty pronouncements, convinced seventeen million Americans that he was fit to run the nation. Angel Lopez Garcia and Kakamba Jones had never been factors, although they had gotten over six million votes. Truly, the party claiming to represent Negroes, Latins, Indians, the angry children and the rebellious academy, had done poorly.

If we lost, there was still the House of Representatives. But the prospect would be grim. Beldock would come into the peculiar contest—each state delegation voting as a unit after a poll of all members—with a 244–226 lead in electoral votes. General Upshaw, with his bloc of 68 votes would be inclined to help Beldock. They were quite close in philosophies. If Beldock believed in "law, order, jails and the death penalty," General Upshaw swore by "law, order, bayonets, machine guns and detention camps."

No prospect pleased me as I approached Ramada Ranch House from the rear. In the corral, two of Fern Hannaford's bay geldings enjoyed a morning romp with a pinto pony. Thinking of Ben's wife—quiet, ladylike, sensitive Fern—I found myself looking up to her second-story bedroom window. A light had just gone on. The shades were up.

I saw Fern, in a pink dressing gown, looking as if she had just risen. She was shaking her head slowly. Then I saw Ben Hannaford, in shirt sleeves, approach her and take her in his arms. I felt guilty observing my boss and his wife in private affection. In their attitudes toward one another they were always formal, polite, reserved, behaving with the dignity of two African lions. One did not observe the love play of lions.

Of course, from my vantage point at the corral, I could hear nothing. But I noticed Fern's blond head shaking rhythmically. She was crying. Once her face turned toward the window and I saw her gentle features distorted, the mouth awry, the eyes agonized. This upset me. Fern Cudder Hannaford was a woman of great wealth and status in Ramada. Her family, the oil-rich Cudders had run the state house for years; Ben was a Johnny-come-lately, a poor boy who had made his fortune with his brawny hands and his shrewd brain. What distressed me?

I suppose I resented her sorrow, since it destroyed a great American myth—the one which assures us that wealth brings happiness, and that vast wealth brings *un-limited* happiness. Ben was stroking her back, patting her cheeks with a handkerchief, his dark face tender and concerned. They loved one another deeply. The money had something to do with it, I'm sure. But that was no reason for me to doubt the sincerity and warmth of their love.

As I grew guilty with my Peeping Tom-ism, I saw Ben kiss Fern on the cheek, on the neck, and then lead her away. His powerful right arm was around her waist as they departed; her honey-blond head rested on his iron shoulder.

Was she weeping because of his imminent defeat? Or because she was terrified by the prospect of becoming

19

First Lady? It could have been any of several things. Of this I was certain—more and more, Fern Hannaford had come to hate and fear the public life. A woman of painful shyness, almost inarticulate, possessing no ambitions for herself or her husband, other than to live quietly at Ramada Ranch with her dogs, horses and millions, she had become paranoid on the subject of public abuse. And Ben had been wickedly abused in the campaign. To the Upshaws and the Tutts he was "Bolshevik" Hannaford for having built supermarkets (at a huge profit) in the Soviet Union. To Kakamba Jones he had been "that honky pig fascist mother-lover with his greasy oily wife."

Fern herself was not spared in the savage campaign. Not only suffering insults from the lunatic left like Kakamba Jones, but from *her very own family*. The Cudders, oil people to the marrow of their bones, had disowned Ben as a radical, a meddler, a coddler of Communists and a nigger-lover. As a result, Fern was now *persona non grata* with them. This familial rupture tormented her. But she never uttered a word of her hurt to anyone. Except perhaps Ben. And perhaps that was what had made her weep. Childless, she had been very close to her brothers and sisters, nieces and nephews, especially Miles J. Cudder, reputed to be the richest of them all, a young man who had unsuccessfully tried to take over Ben's seat in the Senate.

Ah, nephew Miles. Is that why you chose to donate millions to Save America and Defenders of Our Republic (DOOR) and their mad leaders? These were people who referred to Ben Hannaford as "Big Chief Traitor" and in obscene letters, informed him that he was "in the cross hairs." Translation: *he was within the sights of a rifle and would be killed.*

Judy Stapp's harsh voice—totally out of place in the redwood-and-sandstone interior of the ranch house—drifted into the corridor.

"What is with those goddamn voting machines in Los Angeles?" I heard Senator Sidney Stapp's wife ask irritably. "Sid, can't we get any kind of word from LA? I thought we had friends there. Some lousy friends."

I walked into the arena-sized sunken living room, bright with hunting prints, antelope horns, bearskins and a Viking's fireplace of native red stone in which a mesquite fire

20

crackled. Fred Goldstein had set up three color television sets, on which he switched channels with a remote-control gadget.

Frank McGee, on NBC, was explaining that his network's computer, BRAINAC, refused to make a prediction on California. "It is too close to call," Mr. McGee was saying. "BRAINAC won't commit itself. Vice-President Beldock's lead is now about thirty-five hundred, and twelve per cent of the state's vote, most of it in central Los Angeles, is still uncounted."

John Chancellor broke in. "Frank, isn't it true that the polls showed that those districts which are largely black and Mexican-American, will go heavily for the Black-and-Tan ticket? And if so, won't that eat into Senator Hannaford's vote?"

The camera switched to McGee, adjusting one of those small earpieces. "Yes, John, that was the prediction. But Senator Hannaford has been running strongly in such places as Harlem, and the Hough district of Cleveland and other black ghettos, so well in fact that he has taken industrial states like New York, Pennsylvania, Ohio. . . ."

Chancellor again: ". . . of course, Frank, the big votes —backlash votes if you will—piled up by General Upshaw in those states had much to do with Senator Hannaford's victory. Another way of putting it is that General Upshaw's conservative vote had a far greater eroding effect on the Beldock vote, than did Angel Lopez Garcia's vote on Senator Hannaford's. . . ."

But we were losing in California. I slumped into a wicker chair at the rear of the living room, too exhausted to man one of the private lines that Fred Goldstein had set up on a Spanish table. There was only a handful of people at the ranch house. Ben did not want his home overflowing with friends and advisers. He liked a small, tight, efficient team. Governor Verne Sparrier of California, our vice-presidential candidate, that cheery, smiling, praying, young Jaycee, was holding the fort at our downtown headquarters at the Ramada Stockman's Inn. He was an organization man from his blond crew cut to the points of his J. C. Penney shoes; he would handle the crowd.

Charles Kuralt appeared on CBS. "CBS's CEREBRO, Walter, refuses to make a prediction in California. It's just too close. So we're watching and waiting. Again, if the

21

Golden State goes to Senator Hannaford, he'll have 271 electoral votes, one more than needed for election. If it goes to Vice-President Beldock, he will have 244, and the result will be inconclusive. . . ."

Senator Sidney Stapp of California, our campaign manager, an old friend of Ben's, paced nervously. Normally Sid was not a pacer. Now, he was worried stiff. In his early fifties, Sidney Stapp was an alarmingly handsome man, lean, wasp-waisted, his silvery hair lovingly waved. A former theatrical and motion picture lawyer of considerable wealth, he had grown weary of creating careers for actors who then went on to public office. Sid decided he wanted a political career of his own and was now in his second term in the Senate. He was a moderate voice in the Senate—no activist, but no obstructionist either—and he had worked smoothly with Ben for a long time. (If he had one failing, it was his penchant for the boudoir; to all on the Hill he was known as "Swinging Sid," a lecher of prodigious appetite, willing to share his bounty with friends and colleagues.)

"What does Warfield report from LA?" Sid asked Fred Goldstein irritably.

Fred was cradling a phone between ear and shoulder, like the trained journalist he was, riffling through a phone book with his hands. Cigarette smoke wafted up to his grape-green eyes and he blinked. "Can't even get to him, Senator," Fred said. "Warfield's under orders to report only to the boss."

Dalton Warfield was a black man, a social worker, a courageous leader in Watts who was committed to Ben's candidacy. He had worked the past two years with Hannaford-Western on ghetto construction programs in Los Angeles.

"Good God, why the hell are those machines still out of whack?" Judy Stapp cried. She bounced up from the couch, a leggy, full-bosomed, well-rumped woman possessed of a flamboyant sexiness. In deference to the subdued frontier atmosphere of Ramada Ranch, she had eschewed her normal far-out garb—pantsuits, outsized jewelry, boots—for a sedate gray wool dress. Still, she flamed and heated the air by her very presence.

In addition to the Stapps and Fred Goldstein and myself, the only other person in the room was Cleo Watterson, Ben's private secretary, a calm woman in her fifties.

She was extremely attractive, gray-haired, firmly girdled, smooth-limbed. It had long been rumored that Cleo was "an old flame" of Senator Hannaford's. I never believed it. She was an efficient and diplomatic woman, utterly loyal, a Ramada City girl who had never married. That she was able and faithful and intelligent was sufficient; Ben rewarded these qualities.

"Where's the chief?" I asked Cleo.

"Upstairs. Communing with the Great Spirits." Cleo enjoyed these references to Ben's Kiowa blood. It amused her—the notion that this rich, powerful, ambitious man was part Indian.

"And Mrs. H.?"

"Doing poorly, Edward. Poor thing. I wish we could help."

"I'll never forgive Congressman Ruckett for what he did to her. Nor will Ben."

Cleo Watterson adjusted her eyeglasses. "The little bastard was re-elected. Better than two to one. I hope the chief makes it to the White House just so we can go to work on that weasel."

During the long, embittered election campaign, Congressman Lance Ruckett of South Dakota, a founder of Defenders of Our Republic (DOOR) and a fanatical right-wing zealot, had led a spitting, cursing mob of his adherents out to the Mitchell, South Dakota, airport, where Ben was making a speech.

I recalled the day in terrible clarity—the sun scorching the rubbery asphalt beneath our feet, the air breathless, the snarling mob shimmering in the heat. As Ben and I tried to move through the crowd, each of us protecting Fern (later we agreed it would have been wiser to return to the plane), Lance Ruckett and two of his female disciples broke through, brandishing placards. With an insane burst of energy, the women, two well-dressed young matrons, began cursing at Fern and striking her several times with a large sign reading TREASON IS HANNAFORD'S GAME.

"I will never forgive that slimey son-of-a-bitch Ruckett," Ben said to me grimly. "He and I got an account to settle."

The attacks on him he did not mind; Ben was born to a life of struggle. Fist fights in the boondocks in his youth were no different to him from political abuse. But the outrageous assault on Fern was more than he could bear. (To Ruckett's credit, he tried to apologize later; Ben refused to see him.)

"We figured Ruckett would win big," I said. "He's a whole backlash movement by himself."

Cleo frowned. "Taken a good look at the way the new House shapes up?"

"I'm not happy. We still have a majority, but what does it mean? The old conservative coalition is stronger than ever."

"Anyway, the Senate doesn't look too bad," Judy Stapp offered, as she took a cup of coffee from Sarah, the Hannaford's Apache Indian maid. "We still have friends there."

How odd, that the mighty Senate, which in its righteous anger had censured Ben two years ago, still leaned toward him. It was understandable. He had been the force there for many years—chairman of the Interior Committee, a key seat on the Finance Committee, chairman of our own party's campaign committee, a man skilled at manipulation, kneading, bending and convincing people. How often had I seen him prowl the maroon carpeting of the great semi-circular chamber, tugging one man's elbow, embracing another, whispering in a third's ear. Yes, he had been a king in the Senate. Deposed, he now sought a higher throne.

" . . . most incredible comeback in the history of American politics," Walter Cronkite was saying. "Eric, as we all know, Senator Hannaford left Washington two years ago under the cloud of censure, rumors, all sorts of complex dealings. Yet somehow he got his case across to the people, to a deadlocked convention last August, and now he may very well . . ."

"Come on, fellahs," Judy Stapp shouted. "Cut out the history lesson. What the hell goes in California?" She wheeled on her husband.

Senator Stapp did not seem to hear his wife. Inured to Judy's assaults on his ears, dapper Sid had developed a talent for tuning her out.

"Sidney, get on the phone and give 'em hell out there!" Judy shouted. "Jesus, we got you as a campaign manager, and the governor as our vice-presidential candidate, and we can't shake loose a couple of thousand votes . . ."

But now neither Sid, nor I, nor Fred Goldstein, nor

24

Cleo Watterson was paying any attention to Judy's angry words, issuing from her mobile red mouth. Fred had switched up the audio on ABC, and a young commentator, who was unfamiliar to me, a bespectacled boy, was pronouncing words of doom.

". . . almost complete returns from the state of California according to ABC's computer LOGOS give that state to Vice-President Beldock, which means that the electoral totals of no, we repeat, *no* candidate will . . ."

"Bastards," Fred said.

"Oh God, no," Swinging Sid murmured. He started to walk swiftly to the stairway leading upstairs to Ben's private study. Cleo dissuaded him. "Better let the chief commune, Senator. If it's true he'll want to mull it over."

Furiously, Fred switched to NBC. BRAINAC wasn't committing itself. Nor was CBS's CEREBRO. They refused to state that Beldock had licked us in California.

"Damn machines," Fred Goldstein muttered. "They lie in their teeth." He was dialing frantically.

"A correction, Eric," Cronkite was saying. "CEREBRO now states that if the present trend in Los Angeles County's central districts continues, then Vice-President Beldock will win California. But it will make no flat declaration, so for the time being, Senator Hannaford is in the running . . ."

Grimmer and grimmer. At least NBC wasn't writing us off. How dreadful for us to be at the mercy of these machines! (I refer to the computers, of course, not the networks and their people, all of whom had treated us generously in the campaign. They had been monuments of fairness to Ben, more than I could say for a lot of newspaper publishers who had felt more at ease with the likes of Smead Beldock. On balance, the TV commentators and producers are probably the most unbiased people in journalism.)

" . . . can only repeat, John, that NBC's BRAINAC is playing it cozy and refuses to give California . . ."

Amid sighs of relief, I tiptoed out of the living room. Cleo Watterson may have cautioned Senator Stapp, our campaign manager about disturbing the boss. But no such warnings could keep me from his side when he was in trouble.

I found him on the phone in his small pine-paneled study. He was in shirt sleeves, tie-less, looking fresh and relaxed. The man was indestructible, as resilient as the ocotillo bushes that waved in the desert wind outside the house. Apart from some faint smudges of fatigue beneath his mahogany eyes, his skin was ruddy, his voice firm. "Yes, Doctor, sometime this morning," he was saying. "She seems to feel those green and black pills helped her last time. You know, she refuses to take anything to make her sleep, since she's always depended on exercise and fresh air. But this election business . . ."

That would be like Ben. We may have lost California, and the election, and the White House, and all of his dreams, but he was worried about Fern's health.

"Mrs. H. is feeling ill again?" I asked.

"Maybe we can arrange a tropical vacation for Mrs. H. once we are settled in the White House," Hannaford said easily.

The galling confidence of the man! "Senator, have you heard the ABC prediction?" I asked. "They have given California to Smead Beldock."

The phone buzzed. He hadn't even been listening to me. He picked it up—a secret number that only he and a handful of others knew about. "Ah, Dalton, I was wondering what was keeping you."

Ben indicated that he wanted me to listen in. I picked up an extension.

"That sounds splendid, Dalton," Ben said. "Unfreeze the machines when you are ready."

"We're ready," I heard Warfield say in his weary voice. Who could blame Dalton Warfield for being weary? He had seen a brother shot dead by white night-riders, his house bombed five times, his store-front office destroyed, and the extremists of his *own* race turn on him when he helped end the bloodshed of second Watts.

"Then go get 'em," Ben said cryptically. They exchanged a few more words. Ben hung up.

"I don't know what you're going to get, sir. ABC says we've lost California. The polls showed we'd lose it. We are losing it. . . ."

My voice dwindled. I hadn't realized how drained I was. On a small black-and-white TV set on the senator's desk I read the latest popular vote figures.

| BELDOCK | 24,991,807 |
| HANNAFORD | 24,845,322 |

UPSHAW	17,824,560
GARCIA	6,701,944

"Good Lord," I murmured. "Even if you win, you'll be the first man to lose a popular vote and win the electoral total since Rutherford B. Hayes. And with just thirty-three per cent of the vote, at that."

" 'Suffer it to be so now,' " he said. "For thus it becometh us to fulfill all righteousness."

"I've had my share of suffering. I don't know how much more I can take."

"Try this, Edward. 'Gather up the fragments that remain, that nothing be lost.' That's what we are after, Edward. Fragments, mere fragments of votes."

Ben Hannaford was much given to these biblical quotations. Rumor had it that his father, an itinerant oil-field rigger, was a self-taught lay preacher in the Church of the River Brethren. Ben had been steeped in the Book; he had learned to read and write through Scripture. Yet he uttered the holy words with no high-blown pomposity but in a familiar, droll manner.

"Fragments may not be enough. I don't like the look of the new House of Representatives. Eight more John Birchers. A strong lurch to the right. Old Emmett O'Boyle, our senile Speaker, won't lift a finger to help us. I read the House as going for Smead Beldock."

"Cheer up, son. Rutherford B. Hayes may have been a minority President, but he was a good one. Reformed the civil service, as I recall."

"It was pure luck he got in. The commission decided, after much argument, he had won the electoral vote 185 to 184 and the bitterness haunted him all his life. The politicians never got off his back."

Ben squinted at the TV monitor. Beldock's people were claiming we had stolen New Jersey, and we were charging that Beldock had robbed us of Kentucky.

"I have a broader back than Rutherford B. Hayes, Edward," he said to me. "If I'm elected by five million, or if I trail Beldock by a quarter of a million, I'll be the President. He'll be out, and I'll be in, and that's what matters. Once a man gets in the saddle, it's the poor sucker on the ground has to worry."

"It sounds to me as if you're falling back on your

27

Indian fatalism. We'll be in the saddle . . . but barely. For the life of me, sir, I can't figure out who voted for us."

"Lots of decent Americans," Ben said. "Those as don't have murder in their hearts."

"You're pretty confident for a man who has been declared a loser by the ABC computer."

Ben took another call. It was his running mate, the youthful governor of California, Verne Latour Sparrier. Again I listened in. I was distressed by the similarity between Sparrier's voice and that of certain Sunday night radio preachers—the gentle ranting, the undercurrent of revelation. No wonder Ben had left him at the Ramada Stockman's Inn. Sparrier may have had charisma, but he did not wear well.

"Senator, I am uneasy," young Sparrier said. "I called Louisville an hour ago, and one of Mr. Beldock's people said they were preparing their victory statement."

"Don't fret, Verne," Ben said. "Lots of votes are being counted right now. We're still in it."

"Not according to my people in Los Angeles." Ben looked bored. Why? The man *was* governor of California. Surely his sources were good.

They chatted on—Ben soothing his running mate, calming the younger man, and I reflected on the ironies of our political system. Why was Verne Sparrier on the ticket at all? Bluntly, he was the price Ben had to pay for nomination. Sparrier had been his main opponent—a far more conservative man, a slick young operator. It was felt by the bosses, the hacks, the precinct captains, the more sour elements in the party, that this was a conservative year, a very conservative year. Who was a liberal any more? And where did they have to go? The party had long lost much of its southern support; the labor unions, furious over black agitation, had drifted off to listen to wilder music; the middle class was uneasy. And Ben understood too clearly that one could not, despite the arguments of the "new politics" and the "new left" elect a President with college kids, blacks, Jews, academics and other minorities. There weren't enough of them.

"In a sense," Ben said to me one hot night in Chicago, "I'm the great deceiver. I'll come on like a rich man, frontier wheeler and dealer, maybe a little dishonest—"

"A little!" I protested. "After the censure—"

He held up his hand. "Everyone's forgiven us that. At

least they understand our position. I can talk tough, act like an uneducated roughneck out of the prairie, quote the Bible, and when everyone is convinced I'm a basic American, I can stop spending money on bombs and start building schools."

Enough delegates finally agreed with Ben. Or, as he put it, were deceived by him. Not to mention those who followed Judge Jervis Kickley's lead.

But it had turned into a package deal: the regulars, the conservative delegates, the South, *demanded* that Verne Latour Sparrier, the man who had crushed second Watts, get the vice-presidential nod.

"Hell, it won't hurt long," Ben told me. "We'll stick him in a small office somewhere and let him award scholarships."

I wondered. Governor Sparrier was a shrewd cookie, an effective speaker, and although he was not personally wealthy, he had a lot of backing from California's oil, farming and defense industry millionaires. What bothered me about Sparrier, quite simply, was that he was unpeggable. He dealt in mushy generalities.

"If it is all right with you, Senator," Sparrier was saying, "I am making plans for a recount. I'm not without friends in Los Angeles. I intend to show that Garcia and that crazy African running with him stole the votes in LA and—"

"Slow down, son," Ben cautioned him. "We'll worry about recounts when we need 'em. Besides, Beldock's already asked for recounts in three states we won. Let *him* do the hollering for a while." He hung up.

On the TV monitor, there appeared now the angry faces of Angel Lopez Garcia, and his side-kick, Kakamba Jones. The Black-and-Tan Party had erected a huge tent in an open lot in South Chicago, in the middle of a black slum. This was their election headquarters. All white reporters and TV technicians had been barred. Newspapers and networks had emptied the high schools and colleges for any black with the smallest interest in a writing career and hired them. It wasn't a bad idea, and I gave old Garcia credit. He was no fool and he was really not a bad man.

Garcia was accusing everyone of stealing votes, and promising to run big in Los Angeles. Kakamba was raging. Waving his gnu's tail fly whisk, raising high his robed arms, he screamed at the world: "Genocide is being committed. Blacks are being murdered. Today you have our blood, but tomorrow we will have yours! White pigs, your day has come."

Grimacing, Ben switched channels. "Damn fool. His own worst enemy. We got to save people like that from their own stupidity."

On another channel, Beldock's backers in Louisville were being interviewed. Yes, they had high hopes of taking California. Votes were being counted in Los Angeles, and while they did not think they would take the city, Senator Hannaford would not run well enough to win California.

"Said what, Dalton? Opening some of the machines to check the results? Oh, that's fine. Yes, right here. . . ."

Ben asked me to start calling some Washington contacts—old friends in the press, congressional chums, merely to express our thanks for their support. I left.

Entering the corridor, I saw the door to Fern's room open. She appeared in the doorway. Fern was in her late forties, but she always looked younger; now she looked her age. There was an unsteadiness about her that disturbed me.

"Can I help you Mrs. H.?"

"No . . . no thank you, Edward. The senator is . . . is he—?"

"He's taking a call. But I'm sure he'd be delighted to see you. He's alone."

"Oh. No, I won't bother him." She seemed to sway, and I moved toward her. Fern reached for the doorknob and braced herself. "Edward, please ask Sarah to bring me some hot tea. Thank you."

Poor woman. She never had made demands on anyone. Now she found it difficult even to summon a maid! For a fleeting moment I hoped that, for her sake, Ben would be defeated; that he would retire to Ramada Ranch and let Fern rest.

As I reached the living room, Fred Goldstein handed me a piece of wire service copy. He had installed all the press services at the ranch.

"Read this," he said.

Washington, D.C., Nov. 7—(AP)—Negro leaders charged today that Negro voters in five northeastern cities were forcibly kept from the polls by armed groups of whites, in some instances aided by local police.

The Justice Department said it was investigating the charge, which was made jointly by the National Association for the Advancement of Colored People, the Southern Christian Leadership Council, the Urban League and the Student Nonviolent Coordinating Committee.

Reverend Henry Esmond, speaking for the black organizations claimed that the cities involved were Newark, New Jersey; Waterbury, Connecticut; Hazelton, Pennsylvania; Beacon, New York; and Newport, Rhode Island.

Dr. Esmond said that an organization called the "White Guards" were responsible for the incidents. In at least one city, he said, fighting erupted between blacks and whites, while police stood by. "Our reports are incomplete," he said, "but we are getting eyewitness testimony and will have a full report for the Justice Department in a day or two.

"Ye gods," I said. "Can this be our America?"

"If anything," Fred said. "It was worse than they let on. Yesterday the media agreed to lay off, at the request of the Attorney General. Kretz, our beloved President, didn't want anyone to make waves. But you can't sit on a story like this."

"Northern cities," I said. "Not Alabama or Mississippi."

We had run well in the South—but it was a polarized black vote. Southern Negroes tend to be thoughtful. They had preferred Ben Hannaford to the Garcia-Jones ticket, but we had failed to carry any southern states.

" . . . first results from Los Angeles have failed to cut into Vice President Beldock's lead appreciably . . . votes split about equally four ways. . . ."

I heard the TV commentator's voice and I was overwhelmed with gloom.

"That bastard Upshaw," Judy Stapp was saying. "If we manage to sneak in, we'll have him to thank—for splitting the conservatives. Is that to laugh?"

"I'll get on my hands and knees and thank him," Sid Stapp said. "If we make it."

They were whistling in the graveyard. The LA returns were going sour.

" . . . cut into the Vice-President's lead slightly, Senator Hannaford now trailing him by 3570 votes . . . and must do appreciably better among black voters in Watts . . ."

It was now past nine in the morning. The desert sun had turned half of the huge living room a red-gold. Distantly I saw the television mobile units, parked beyond the split-rail fencing of the ranch house lawn. I saw the huge rotating dishes, the booms, the electronic gear that would cover Ben's departure for downtown Ramada City —either as the next President or as a *possible* President.

Just outside the porte-cochere were parked the official limousines, and around them lounged a half-dozen secret service men, shave-headed young fellows in gray suits, augmented by a party of Ramada state troopers in broad-brimmed khaki hats, sand-colored suits, laced boots. They all seemed remarkably calm. Why not? They were nonpolitical men. Only fools like myself had chosen the nerve-racking uncertainties of politics for a career, and then inadvertently. For all my cold-blooded equanimity, for all my neutral coloration, the veneer of blandness I present to the world, I wonder sometimes if I am equal to the life Ben Hannaford more or less forced upon me. I hate to lose.

I walked outside again. One whiff of that creosote-scented perfume was enough to revive me. I nodded at the secret service chief—his name was Markland—and the captain of state troopers. They were listening to the car radio.

As I walked by I saw pasted to the side window of the state police Ford, a small sticker—a white cross on a light blue field, a sort of simplified Greek flag, I knew what it was. It was the emblem of the White Guards, our newest national lunacy. They had made enormous inroads into police forces. More secretive, more violent in their aims, they had long replaced the relatively mild Birchers as an underground force among many underpaid, hard-working cops.

"What's that insignia, Captain?" I asked.

The officer studied me with the beefy face of the law, a lord of the earth. "Cain't say, sir. Some fella pasted hit on. Sort of patriotic club. Church and so on."

How many policemen, law enforcement officials, probation officers and the like, were reading White Guard

32

leaflets, disgusted, infuriated by the Kakamba Joneses, by the indecent shouts of "Pig" and "mother-lover"?

Luis Ramirez, the Hannaford's gardener, an old friend of mine, had his wheelbarrow set up at a bed of exotic cacti. A brown, gnarled gnome in his sixties, Luis had that innate dignity that so many Mexican-Americans in Ramada possess. *"Que pasa, Luis?"* I asked.

"Nada, señor." In the breast pocket of his sweat-stained, tan work suit was a transistor radio. He had plugged it into his bronzed ear and was listening to the returns as he loosened earth around a particularly handsome organ-pipe cactus. *"Cabrón,* that Garcia," Luis said. "He takin' the boss's votes in California. If not for him, we be big winner."

He squinted up at me. His seamed, leathery face told me of another America—different from that of my state police captain with his uncooked sirloin of a face and his sneaky White Guard emblem. Wasn't there a novelist who wrote, after Sacco and Vanzetti were executed, *"All right, we are two countries?"*

"You see this leetle guy?" Luis asked. He pointed to a curious carrotlike plant, about three feet high, pale green in color, sprouting spiked branches.

"A cactus?"

"No. Very rare thing. We got as present from governor of Baja California. Boojum tree."

"Boojum? That's from a poem, Luis." I recalled the Lewis Carroll poem, and the line, "the snark *was* boojum."

"Luis don't know poetry, *señor.* But he knows a good plant when he sees one. Down in Baja they grow thirty, forty feet high. Local people say they live forever, good-luck plant . . ." Suddenly he stopped digging and was squinting at me. "Jesus Chris' . . . Jesus Chris' . . . the boss winning . . . the boss gonna win . . ."

Luis yanked the earplug out and with a fumbling hand pulled the radio out of the breast pocket. He turned up the volume.

" . . . going heavily for Senator Hannaford, who is now leading Vice-President Beldock by twelve hundred votes in California."

The two of us began to giggle, like schoolboys preparing a prank. Then Luis started to rise, his sun-seared

33

bones creaking, and I rose with him, and we shook hands, as the smiles on our faces turned into broad grins.

"El Presidente, verdad?" he asked rhetorically.

"It looks that way, Luis."

The radio shrilled on. " ... a stunning upset in the Watts district ... where the Garcia-Jones ticket was supposed to run ahead of the major parties ... Senator Hannaford showed amazing strength, piling up majorities in Watts and the surrounding districts ... Olivera Street ... East Los Angeles ..."

I pumped Luis's hand and hurried to the house. The car radio was going in the state trooper's Ford. But he and the secret service agents maintained a discreet silence.

"It looks like we have a winner, gentlemen," I said as I hurried by.

For this I received one smile—sincere I am sure—from the federal man. From the captain, that displayer of white crosses on his car window, I got nothing, not even a friendly nod.

In the house Judy Stapp was weeping hysterically. Her husband Sid had collapsed into an easy chair, stunned, deflated. Cleo Watterson and Fred Goldstein were manning telephones—a few favored newsmen and friends had the ranch number, and they were eager to be in on our apparent victory.

Goldstein shoved a phone at me. "Schwab, Associated Press," he said. "Wants to know will we claim victory on the basis of the network predictions?"

"Of course," I said into the phone. "This is Ed Deever, and you may quote me."

The newsman's loud voice withered my ear. "Beldock's people say you stole California. His guy says you rigged the results in Los Angeles. Some dirty business in Watts with those broken-down voting machines . . ."

"We deny it categorically. Who stole Kentucky?"

"Come on, Deever. Kentucky is a lousy eleven electoral votes and it's Beldock's home state. California was all the marbles."

"Well," I said, "never let it be said that Senator Hannaford didn't have all his marbles."

"That isn't funny. Look, we don't have anything against Hannaford, but this California business stinks. It smells bad, Deever."

34

I wanted to respond with Dr. Johnson's witticism, but memory failed me. Besides, Ben was making his appearance. Buttoning his double-breasted blue jacket, he was descending the stairs, looking calm, rested and cheerful. "Sorry, Mr. Schwab," I said, "but the senator calls. As far as we are concerned, he is the President-elect."

We formed a worshipful mob at the foot of the stairs— Judy Stapp and Cleo hugging and kissing the boss, the servants coming out to applaud—Sarah, the Apache girl, Travis, the butler, Pilar, the cook, Jack Lightcap, the ranch boss and a tearful Luis, who had come in smelling of sun and earth and sweat.

"I hope this isn't premature," I said shakily to Fred. "Beldock won't concede. He says he'll demand a recount, that there were irregularities in Watts. . . ."

Fred scratched his frizzy red hair. "Last minute votes are in. They say we carry the state by four thousand four."

Ben Hannaford raised a hand. "My calculation is a bit different . . . exactly four thousand seven hundred and twenty-two."

I stared at Fred, as Ben shook hands, laughed with his friends, asked Sarah to look after Mrs. Hannaford. She was not feeling up to the motorcade and the public appearance in Ramada City. "How the hell does he know the exact figure?" I asked Fred.

"Instinct," said Goldstein.

"Instinct, hell." I followed Hannaford's broad blue back across the room and out to the limousines. The high-powered engines were gunned. Distantly the television trucks were preparing to move off, like a file of mechanical elephants and follow our victory ride across the desert to election headquarters at the Ramada Stockman's Inn.

"Edward," Ben said at the door. "Ride with me."

The party paused at the door. Ben had turned to catch a last look at the television sets. The networks had switched to the Black-and-Tan headquarters in the tent in Chicago. Kakamba Jones, in a lion-skin cloak and a yellow yarmulka, was waving his fly whisk.

"Genocide has been committed! Race murder! Oh, the blood will flow, *keena-bwana!* The pig Hannaford and his white pig facists has stolen our victory! We will have our terrible vengeance!"

"Some victory," Ben said. "We saved the damn fools from their own folly."

Then a curious thing happened. Congressman Angel Lopez Garcia, our chief opponent in Los Angeles, appeared and elbowed Kakamba Jones away from the microphones.

"Is too early to tell, Kakamba, *amigo*," Garcia said, in his most clownish manner. "We got to get more evidence, you know? I mean, for my part, I concede, and I congratulate Senator Hannaford. I mean, somebody got to ween . . ."

Kakamba now shoved Garcia away. Clearly, the Black-and-Tan party was undergoing inner turmoil. "Away, you lousy mongrel, you lick-spittle! Genocide will be avenged!" And with that Kakamba Jones pointed his fly whisk at the camera, and at all of watching America. His liverish lips curled and his beard bristled and he unloosened the ultimate battle cry: *"Up against the wall, mother-f——"*

The networks caught him on the "f" and the Chicago scene vanished, replaced by a black, silent screen.

Sirens screaming, we roared away on the twenty-two-mile blacktop road that led to Ramada City. Two years ago, when Ben was in the Senate, he had *forced* Presiden Hayward Kretz to come down to Ramada on a muggy August day to cut the tape dedicating the new road. Wha⁺ powers he had wielded! Even when columnist Lou Parente had revealed that the highway ended at Ben's garage, that it was Hannaford's private trail, built with federal funds, the public only laughed.

As the TV trucks pulled alongside—despite angry gestures from the secret service men in front and in back of us, and the ubiquitous Markland riding with the chauffeur —I closed the soundproof partition.

"We did it, Edward." Ben winked at me.

"Yes. Just the way you got this road built two years ago."

A TV technician wanted Ben to lower the window and to wave. Ben did not lower the window, but he lifted a hand. I shrunk back against the gray upholstery. For some reason I was feeling queasy. The President-elect perceived my discomfort.

" 'Behold, I make all things new,' " he said. " 'He said unto me, write for these words are true and faithful.' "

"Save that for the press conference, Senator."

We zoomed down Ben's private highway, sirens screaming. A handful of ranch hands waved to us. Some Indians emerged from their hogans to hold up their coppery arms in greeting.

"That will be one of our first orders of business," he said. "Help the red brothers. Yes, Edward, we are going out among 'the poor, and the maimed, and the halt and the blind.' "

I was bursting with indignation. "Senator, no one admires knowledge of the Scripture as much as I do, but there are times when it makes me sick to my stomach. What does the Bible say about stealing forty-five electoral votes? Do you have anything appropriate from Kings or Prophets?"

Ben waved at a family of farmers perched on a rail fence. "I am afraid not, son. You see, elections were a lot simpler among the Chosen People. The elect were the anointed of the Lord, touched and elevated by the divine fire."

I was not amused. I stared at him, trying to make him admit something—anything. Then I noticed that he was making a supreme effort to keep from bursting into laughter. My offended honesty tickled him. Riding parallel to us, a TV mobile unit had fixed its probing camera on us. I prayed that the images were blurred and that there were no lip readers in the audience. For what I had to say was of an exceedingly private nature.

"Senator, you stole those Los Angeles votes. You have robbed your way into the White House."

Hannaford raised his right hand to greet a lonesome Indian standing outside a ramshackle general store. "You've hurt me, Edward. You've hurt the old man."

"Dammit, you knew right down to the ten-group, as they say in the new math, what your edge over Smead Beldock would be."

"An educated guess, son." He turned his handsome, graying head toward the opposite window. A crowd of small school children waved back at the President-elect.

"Tell that to Beldock. He'll contest the election."

"Do you really choose, Edward, to side with that to-bacco farmer? That mealy-mouthed clown who took two hundred thousand dollars in farm subsidies last year—while the colored people in his district don't get enough protein in their diets?"

"I detest Smead Beldock," I said, "but I have better evidence than anything his flunkies have to say. I just wanted to see if you would admit right off that you rigged the vote."

"You know the old man better than that," Ben said happily.

Huge billboards loomed around us as we approached Ramada City. They broadcast sour messages and presaged trouble for us.

IMPEACH MOSCOWITZ
SAVE OUR FBI FROM REDS

This was a reference to the director of the Federal Bureau of Investigation, Judge Samuel Moscowitz of New York, one of the country's leading civil libertarians and a close friend of Ben's. Ever since the jurist had taken over the bureau, it had become a model of legal probity and had zealously prosecuted civil rights violations. Thus it had earned the undying hatred of the True Believers.

"By God, I'll get you to admit it," I went on. "You not only gave Warfield the signal to get some kind of sneaky operation going, but you fixed our opponent out there, Congressman Angel Lopez Garcia.

"After the NBC computer decided you'd won California because of that upset in LA, there was nary a peep out of Garcia. Normally he'd be up there screaming foul, murder, robbery and genocide."

"Edward, the big spick believes. He trusts me."

"I can smell the deal. You promised Garcia you'd get him his seat in Congress back, if he kept his big mouth shut about the vote count. Maybe even his seniority. But I gather you couldn't buy off that African witch doctor who was his running mate."

He began to laugh. "Say, you're a pretty shrewd analyst, aren't you, Edward? If I ever decide to fire you, I bet *Newsweek* would take you in a minute."

"I may resign before you get a chance to can me. You will be pilloried for this. It will cast a shadow over your
38

Administration. Even before you take the oath on January twentieth, you will be condemned."

He dabbed at his eyes with a handkerchief. I could see an announcer, riding in the mobile unit, reporting Ben's laughter, his tears. It was too bad he could not pick up our conversation. There we sat, the next President and his closest aide, confidante, stooge, discussing the theft of Los Angeles.

The billboards waxed bigger, more frantic.

> NUKE THE CHINK!
> VOTE UPSHAW AND TUTT

> "I WILL HANG ALL TRAITORS AND
> HANG THEM HIGH."
> —GENERAL CLYDE UPSHAW

We were on the outskirts of Ramada City—the usual day-glo mélange of any American city—Big-Boy Hamburgers, Johnny-on-the-Spot Cleaners, Bowl-a-rama, Mobil, Esso, Chevron, Citgo. The ugliness was appalling. No self-respecting rattlesnake would want to be seen in such surroundings.

"Edward, you must take the long view," the President-elect said. "Did I steal votes in Los Angeles? Not too many. Enough to give us California. Did I steal them from Garcia? I guess I did. But don't shortchange me. Some blacks voted for me honestly."

"You are condoning theft, corruption and all the dirty things that should be eliminated from American political life."

"I'm not condoning them. I merely say let's use 'em, if the other fellow insists on using 'em. Look at it this way. It's about time that an honest black man like Dalton Warfield gets a chance to steal an election. The Irish and the Italians and the Jews and the Poles have been rigging local votes since they got a smell of the power. They have been cheating on ballots in the white southland since the Civil War, not only votes but birthrights."

"So Garcia and Jones, and the people who wanted them were innocent victims?"

"Garcia knows he's better off with me in the White House. And Jones will learn it someday, if he ever keeps his trap shut long enough to hear someone else talk."

The crowds were larger now—casually dressed Americans, women in cottons, men in jeans, kids in shorts. A huge sign greeted us:

RAMADA CITY
WHERE THE WEST IS BEST

The motorcade slowed as we moved on to George S. Patton Memorial Highway. People leaned from hotel and office windows. The streets were crowded. Ben was a Ramada City boy, and they were out to pay him homage. That his politics were considered much too leftish by the powers in Ramada—the oilmen, the cattle barons, the bankers—did not affect the enthusiasm of the welcome. It was Ramada City's day.

"Edward, I think I've educated a lot of black people today," the President-elect explained. "I want them to understand that they must play a vital role in our national corruptions, such as rigging elections. No one raised much of a fuss when Illinois got swept into John Kennedy's column in 1960. I'm told they voted every tombstone in Cook County. But Nixon didn't holler too long. His people figured it was a standoff. They'd done some juggling of their own in California. It's just that Kennedy's people juggled a little better. Now I want our blacks to have the same kind of leverage—rig elections, steal votes, make deals under the table. They can't get what they want by committing crimes of violence and scaring white folks with their threats of racial wars. That only gets people angry. They have to do it the way we have been doing it all these years."

He raised his noble head to greet the sunlit crowds. Was he joking with me? No. There was always a germ of truth in Ben's hyperbolic outbursts, these fits of plain speaking that so infuriated his colleagues. How could I forget that memorable speech of his on the floor of the United States Senate, after his fellow club members had voted to censure him, fifty-two to forty-five for certain dealings with the mortgage-and-loan lobby? There stood Big Ben Hannaford, *primus inter pares,* ticking off all *their* petty finagling, expense account padding, free airplane trips, nepotism, favors for friendly corporations and unions and other special interests, their monetary windfalls and convenient legislative boons!

40

"You can't mean that," I said. "That's un-American. You want to corrupt black people."

"No, elevate them. Get them away from crime in the streets, to crime in the office."

The crowds poured into the street, pressing around our slow-moving limousine. They were happy, but not exuberant. To be candid, I had difficulty figuring out who were the 33.7 per cent of the voters who had chosen Ben. Surely not many of those friendly, clean people pressing around the car, to the distress of the secret service.

But *someone* had voted for Ben. Somehow he had gotten twenty-five million Americans to register their approval of his progressive program. I thanked God for the electoral college. Infirm, rickety, antiquated it may have been, but it had elected us. It was a freakish win.

I consoled myself with the vision of Ramada City's high pastel-colored office buildings and hotels that rose around us, a sunny canyon of glass and brick, most of it erected by Hannaford-Western. Ben was a builder, a doer. He had met payrolls and deadlines and he was a political animal down to his toes. At least he would enter the White House unafraid, unhesitant, grasping the nettle with a calloused hand.

"Ray for Ben!"

"Y'all showed 'em, Ben!"

"We got us a President, we got us a President!"

Ben waved back. I suppose some people wondered why Fern wasn't with him.

The car rolled past Smead Beldock's local party headquarters. HONESTY IS MY POLICY read a sign over the store front. No doubt it was.

"Edward, honesty is a grand policy," Ben said, waving vigorously from behind the bullet-proof glass bubble of the moving car. "But it sometimes has to be spiced with a little crookedness. Not a lot. Just enough to give the chili some taste. Nothing worse than chili without a tangy bite to it."

Our limousine pulled up to the curb in front of the red carpet rolled at the entrance of the Ramada Stockman's Inn. Security had gone haywire. The crowd surged behind a wavering cordon of local police in powder-blue uniforms. But it was a good-natured crowd.

"I'm beginning to believe you," I said.

"I am serious, son. I propose that the Congress enact a

depletion allowance for human beings. Why not? A man's resources diminish as he ages. Their resources are depleted every bit as much as the oil in the ground. I'll work something out, maybe better than that 27.5 per cent the oil companies get."

He *was* serious. During the campaign Ben had burned his last bridge to the fat cats of oil.

Arms outstretched, smiling slightly (Ben never overdid these public appearances) he got out of the car and greeted his supporters. The crowd applauded, whistled, cheered. At once the security people formed a protective ring around him—secret service chaps in their gray suits, state policemen in Smokey Bear hats, local cops. Ben reached over their broad backs to "press the flesh"—a handshake here, a tap there, a shouted greeting to some old worker or retainer.

Around us I saw the telltale red lights gleam on four TV cameras. There were two mounted on wheeled tripods on the sidewalk, a third, stationary, on a wooden platform at the entrance to the Ramada Stockman's Inn, a fourth, handheld, a "creepy-peepy," operated by a sweating cameraman bearing the power unit on his back.

The reporters pressed forward at once. I recognized most of them—Larry Hosmer, of United Press, network men, some local people, and standing out like a black swan amid the rather disheveled group, a young Negro woman named Mona Varnum, who worked for a network. She was one of the first black women assigned to major political coverage, and Fred had told me she was as intelligent and sharp-tongued as she was pretty: Afro bob, huge gold earrings, flashing eyes, skin the color and texture of a coffee mousse.

Ben halted amid the circling ring of out-thrust microphones, to the distress of Markland, our shepherd. I studied the opened windows of the hotel. Don't ask me why; I'm hypersensitive to all that coverage. In 1968 I stood in front of the Conrad Hilton in Chicago when the police battered and bloodied the foul-mouthed kids (some of them good kids with good hearts) and for some reason I've been wary of TV exposure ever since. I don't imply that the cameras *incite* riot; rather I suspect they have a nose for it. Yet on this sunny, bracing November morning in the pale city in the desert, I detected nothing but happiness.

"Yes, I would call the result conclusive, Mr. Hosmer," Ben was saying. "If you win by five votes or five million, you've won."

"The Beldock people say you stole California."

"Unproven."

"They say there were voting irregularities."

"I'm horrified. I've made no such charges."

Mona Varnum thrust the mike at Ben. Willowy, I believe is the appropriate description of her figure. Had she taught it, I would have majored in Swahili at Ohio Normal.

"The polls said you could not possibly win California," Miss Varnum said huskily. "Congressman Garcia was supposed to win much more of the vote in Los Angeles. What happened?"

Markland was muttering in Ben's ear. "Let's move on, Senator. The crowd is getting too big." And it was. A vast sea of sun-splashed, smiling Americans.

"I tell you, Miss Varnum," Ben said, ignoring the secret service man, "I had polls of my own taken, and I always knew California was mine—one way or the other."

They roared: that was the old Ben Hannaford. Just enough of a rogue to get a laugh. I rotated my head, looking at the opened windows of the old hotel. On the second floor, a TV technician had moved into view with one of those huge round microphones, that all but hid him. I believe they are called "parabolic" microphones and are used for picking up crowd noises.

"General Upshaw's campaign manager just released a statement calling for an investigation of the whole election," a man from Ramada Radio said. "He claims Congressman Garcia made a deal with you. That a lot of his backers were told to support you at the last minute and that they co-operated in falsifying the counting."

Ben cocked an eyebrow and raised his handsome head. " 'I giveth the cheek to him that smitheth me.' " He tapped the man gently on the chest. "But not forever, eh, brother? The general better have evidence. Better than he had when he laid that egg in front of the Foreign Relations Committee. Any man who could accuse NATO of being a Communist plot had better be careful about making *any* kind of accusation, hey?"

"Let's move it on, sir," Markland muttered peevishly.

"Senator Tutt says you can't possibly govern," a man

from NBC said. "He says you should resign or consent to another election."

"I have these words for dear old Senator Tutt," Ben said. " 'Do they provoke me to anger? Do they not provoke themselves to the confusion of their own faces?' "

Everyone laughed. I heard the crowd voicing their gaiety. "You tell 'em, Ben!" "That's our Ben!"

I felt reassured. Ben still had the touch, could still reach people. Many of the people on the sidewalk, surrounding us on the red carpet, would have disapproved of Ben's course, his sense of social justice. But they'd follow him, because they liked him and trusted him.

"That'll be all, gentlemen," Markland said. The lack of security was upsetting him.

Ben stepped forward. The reporters edged back respectfully. Only Miss Mona Varnum, the Queen of Sheba herself, stayed close, insisting on one more query. "Senator, how do you intend to get the support of ... of ... people? ..."

I heard firecrackers. Short, snapping reports, ridiculously small explosions. Then I saw Mona Varnum's face contort in agonized surprise, and heard her voice dwindle into a pained gasp, almost an embarrassed sound, as if she hated the thought of betraying weakness in front of all these whites.

There was a mad frenzy at the hotel entrance. People shrieked and ran toward the lobby. Plate glass crashed. Markland and his aides were surrounding Ben. The state police shoved reporters away—all but Mona Varnum, who had collapsed into Ben's arms. She had fallen against him, her eyes glazed and her jaw slack, and he had lifted her off the ground, carrying her in his mighty arms. In horror I saw that there were two wide, dark red splotches on her upper arm and shoulder. She was bleeding profusely.

People were being driven from the streets, running into stores, escaping to office buildings. I followed Ben through the churning, screaming mob, and as I approached the shattered glass doors of the hotel, I noticed that the huge parabolic dish was missing from the window. If it were there to pick up crowd noises, it should have stayed there during the dreadful incident.

"Up there! Up there!" I shouted. But no one heard me. Markland and his men had forged an iron ring around

Ben, and Ben still bore the semi-conscious black girl in his arms. Before us, inexorably, timing our progress, moved one of the tripod-mounted cameras, its red light gleaming, as it transmitted the awful moment.

The lobby had been emptied by the police. Only Matthew Fixx, our top legislative aide, a Ramada City boy, well known to everyone in town, and a platoon of cops, were in evidence. Matt, paler than tree fungus, his waxy face melting, his tan suit sagging on his spare frame, rushed toward us. "Okay, okay? Is the senator okay? Oh, Jesus, Jesus, God . . ."

"Matthew, call Mrs. H. at once and tell her I am all right, the son of a bitch missed me," the President-elect said.

Matt nodded, his ears flapped and he vanished.

"For God's sake, Mr. Markland—you, officer—anyone," I yelled. "There was one of those big microphones in a window . . . it's gone. . . ."

The hotel manager guided us to his office, where Ben set Miss Varnum down on a couch. A doctor had been summoned, a small, fussy, but competent-looking little fellow, who, it developed, had been one of our leading party workers in Ramada County.

"They appear to be flesh wounds," he said. "Thank goodness, they're high on the shoulder and the upper arm." He busied himself with a hypodermic needle, a patch of gauze, kneeling alongside the black girl. Mona Varnum moaned; her eyes were closed, her mouth partly opened. In agony, she was more of a stunner than ever.

"You're gonna be okay, little girl," Ben said to her. "You hang in there. Doctor, can she be moved?"

"Yes. We'll get her to St. Mark's Hospital as soon as I give her a sedative."

I was staring at Ben's white shirt. It was adorned with huge maroon splotches—Mona Varnum's blood. There was a small, ladylike cry from the girl reporter as the doctor jabbed his needle into that tantalizingly smooth arm. It seemed horrid to me that such perfect flesh should have to be subject to insult and abuse. But then, black flesh—of all shades, of all textures—had a long history of being injured.

"Put her in a suite," Ben said. "Bill me for it. Anything that's got to be done, do it. I want reports twice a day on her condition."

The physician nodded. "She'll be fine in a few days," he said. "She's in shock now, but as soon as she's stronger we can probe for the bullets." He felt her pulse. "Strong, steady," he said.

Assured that Miss Varnum was in good hands, Ben nodded at me. "Let's go. Got to show the people the bastard missed me. Or maybe give him one more crack at the old man if he's still around."

Matt Fixx was standing at the door, his jaw trembling. "I spoke to Mrs. Hannaford, sir . . . she's okay . . . assured her . . ."

Somebody had to assure Matthew Fixx, I thought. Somehow, despite all the police frenzy (I have learned through experience that for all their professionalism, policemen, from rustic sheriffs to the FBI, can behave like horse's asses in a crisis) the knot of reporters had reassembled. Some had bluffed their way through the cordon, others had sneaked through. Among them was Lou Parente, the syndicated columnist, who had once been our scourge. His swarthy broken-nosed pugilist's face towered above the others.

"You okay, Senator?"

"What about Mona?"

"How badly hurt is she?"

"She's fine," Ben said. "Flesh wounds. I wasn't touched." He moved out of the manager's office into the dim lobby. As he did, I saw Markland hurry toward us with two of his gray-suited aides.

"Stay right in the office, Senator," Markland said. "I've called for a car, and we're going to go back to the ranch until this blows over."

Ben looked wrathful. "The hell you say. I'm going out to talk to my folks."

"No, sir, I can't permit it. We may be dealing with a conspiracy—more than one man involved. I can't let you out there in the ballroom in full view of that crowd. The local people have not co-operated in security and—"

"Son, if it is a conspiracy, the only way you'll find out is by giving 'em the target again. They won't waste shots on anyone else."

A state police colonel loomed in back of Markland. "We can't take the risk, sir."

A whistle blew out in the street; sirens; shouts. Evidently the police were racing through every room of the hotel.

Guests were being ousted, belongings searched. I could see an IBM salesman, with his blond, culotte'd wife, and their three blond chicks being detained at the door and ordered to one side.

"I forbid it," the secret service chief said.

Senator Sidney Stapp and a weeping Judy appeared among the crowd outside the office. "Mr. Markland is right, Ben," Sid said. "I'd advise you to lay low. You can make your victory statement from the TV studios around the corner. I've already asked the colonel about securing the studios and it's no problem at all ... we can set up lines in a minute."

"No, dammit. How does it look to the rest of the world if the President-elect can't get up in front of his friends and thank them? What will our allies think?" Good God, he was joshing them; kidding them about their fears for his safety. "Why the dollar may collapse, the German mark go under."

Sidney Stapp came forward and looked into Ben's eyes. "I beg of you, Ben. Let's go to the studio. The people in the grand ballroom won't feel let down. They'll understand. My God, an attempt made on your life, a reporter wounded. Besides, Governor Sparrier is doing a terrific job of calming everyone."

Ben's eyes widened. "What?"

"Verne has been superb," Sid said. "He's calmed everyone, kept them in their seats, talked to them, explained that you're okay and that everything is under control and that—"

That was all the boss had to hear. He raised his broad shoulders and edged forward. "Sorry, Markland," he said. "Number One has got to get out there and make himself available. If you're President, by God, behave like one."

Markland and the police colonel exchanged grieving looks; they knew when they were licked. They moved aside to let Ben pass.

We emerged into a huge pantry, where the help, most of them blacks and Mexicans, stared at Ben, and many applauded him.

"Mira, mira, el sangre ..."

"Good goin', Mr. President."

"We all vote for you, Senator."

A transistor radio blared from a steward's table, and we could hear Verne Sparrier's nasal, ministerial voice. " ...

not been hurt ... urge you all to remain here ... it is unlikely that the President-elect will be able to appear publicly ... until security measures have been taken to—"

I could see the sour scowl on Ben's face. The governor of California had never been one of his all-time favorites. Emerging from the pantry, we walked through a storage area and ascended another flight of service stairs, stepping carefully around thick cables that coiled and snaked their way to the roof of the hotel.

The police shoved open a door flanking the stage of the ballroom (it was known as the Fiesta Room, inevitably), and our party entered. Police, the Stapps, Matthew Fixx, myself, Parente and the other reporters who had sneaked by the haphazard security arrangements, shouldered their way through—and amid us strode Ben's resolute figure.

A great cheer went up from the people in the ballroom. I saw the TV cameras swing their snouts away from the rostrum to point at Ben, and I heard the cheering grow to a rising relieved roar, as the crowd got to their feet to give Ben a standing ovation.

Governor Sparrier sensed what was happening and halted his peroration in midsentence, to turn and shout, "And here, in God's hand, saved for the republic by a bountiful divinity, is the President-elect of the United States, untouched by the assassin's bullet ... Benjamin Bow Hannaford. . . ."

I was at Ben's side, and I heard him growl under his breath, as he waved to the crowd, "If Sparrier calls me His Only Begotten Son, I'll punch him."

"The governor gets carried away," I whispered.

"Can't get carried far enough away to suit me."

Then the old tiger himself was on the stage, shaking hands, waving his arms, his jacket opened so that all could see the gory stains, acknowledging their support, their good wishes.

"Nobody has been seriously injured," Ben was saying. "Miss Varnum, a reporter, was hit in the shoulder. I am told she sustained flesh wounds and is in shock. She had come forward to ask me a final question when the shots were fired, and moved into the assassin's field of vision. But she'll be fine. Every effort is being made by the police to track the criminal down. All I can say is, he can't be a Ramada boy with rotten marksmanship like that."

There was a prolonged wave of laughter, of cheering,

of applause from the throng. This was Ben Hannaford—indestructible, kidding, making them feel secure because of his own native strength.

"What just happened out there in front of the hotel," Ben was saying, "is the kind of thing that has got to end in this country. Let's put down the guns and start talking, one to the other. . . ."

More applause. I was standing at the edge of the stage, marveling at the man's composure, his fatalistic acceptance of the terrifying incident. A few inches higher, and those two bullets would have plunged into his unprotected head.

"I got to hand it to the Master Builder," Lou Parente was muttering to me. The columnist, a hulking presence was edging up to me. "It's his day, all right. Steals California. Makes it to the White House with a third of the popular vote. Gets shot at and is missed. And ends up carrying a beautiful spade reporter into the hotel lobby. Blood on his shirt and everything."

"You sound as if you think we staged it."

"Christ, no. It's Hannaford's luck. They'll probably discover the guy who shot at him is both a Minuteman *and* a Communist. So he'll win every which way."

Ben was saying generous things about his opponents—Smead Beldock, General Upshaw, Congressman Garcia—and Parente exhaled into my ear, a moist blast of coffee-scented air. "How can he put out such crap, Deever?" the columnist asked. "He hates their guts, and they hate him."

I couldn't resist a barb. "As much as you hate his guts?"

A hurt look clouded Parente's eyes. "Me? Me hate him? You're wrong, Deever. Sure, I blew the whistle on the big guy two years ago when he was trying to buy everyone in Washington. But it's a different ball game now."

"We cannot let the cities wither and die," Ben was saying. "I know something about building. And you can't just put up buildings and expect a new city to arise. You have to build *people*. You have to give them work, and education, and pride and a desire to see their children succeed where they failed . . ."

"How different?" I whispered to Parente.

"Jesus, he's all we got left." And coming from him, the man who had launched the assaults on Ben Hannaford, this was a rare and touching tribute.

"You say *we,*" I said. "Am I to conclude that you are now among our hirelings in the press?"

Parente glowered at me. "You know me better than that, Deever. Not even Hannaford is rich enough to buy me. But whether I like it or not, I'm gonna find myself on the same side as you guys."

"Really?" I asked.

"Yeah. You people are in worse trouble than you know. Why anybody would want to be President at this time, beats me."

I raised my head, affecting a superior attitude. It was good to be able to do this to Lou Parente, a man few could outstare, outtalk, outbluff. "That remark shows you don't know Hannaford as well as you claim to."

"Maybe so, Deever. I just hope his back is as broad as all you stooges of his seem to think. He's gonna need all the *coglioni* in the world to face up to what's waiting for him."

Later I asked an Italian journalist what the word meant. Ben had that quality, in large measure. In a figurative sense, of course.

"I ask your help in getting us back on the track," Ben was saying. "I want us to simmer down. Stop the shouting and the shooting. We're poisoning the good American air not only with pollutants and industrial waste, but with words. Too much talk, my friends, and not enough action. Whenever a country gets taken over by talkers, instead of doers, it is in trouble. I have been a doer all my life . . ."

"Can't stand much more of this," Parente said. His morose eyes darted around the huge room. Then he turned to leave. "Call me when you get to Washington. I got some stuff you should know about." He moved heavily, a bulky, independent man, to the rear of the ballroom.

"I don't care who the talkers are, they're all talking too much, too loose and too wild—whether they're black students carrying guns on college campuses, or businessmen joining crackpot outfits like DOOR, and drilling in their back yards on Saturdays. They've got to stop."

The applause was not nearly so enthusiastic now. There were very few blacks in the audience. And a lot of our local backers, while perhaps not as fanatic as the fearful businessmen who backed the militant demands of Defenders of Our Republic, they still felt a kinship with these ardent protectors of private property.

"Building takes money," Ben went on. "I know all of you are asking, where are we going to get it? I know something about finance and budgets also, having run our party's campaign committee for a long time." He paused, letting a naughty smile crinkle the corners of his mouth. "Maybe too long, some people in Washington thought."

"And maybe too good, Ben!" someone yelled from the back of the ballroom.

This set off more laughter. Parente had paused at the rear of the ballroom. I could see him shaking his head in wonderment.

"Yes, we'll find the money to build our new Jerusalems," Ben said. "I'll just hint where I think it can come from. You know one of my esteemed opponents, a famous general who served his country well, was asked why he wanted us to have twenty times more bombs than we really needed to kill every Russian and every Chinese in the world—and lots of others who aren't Russian, Chinese or Communists, just plain people. And the general replied, 'I want to make the rubble dance.'"

A gasp went up; a few murmurs. This inelegant remark by General Clyde (Nuke the Chink) Upshaw was what had probably kept his vote down to seventeen million and had restricted his electoral total to sixty-eight. After all, most people really do not want to be incinerated or to incinerate the other citizens of the world.

"Well, friends, here is a President-elect, who with all due respect for the military, doesn't want to make the rubble dance, but wants to make *people* dance. I don't hold with those long-haired kids who are raising cain at the colleges, but they know one thing. They know we spend more on death—bombs, missiles, planes, ships, poison gas, chemicals, bacteria—than we nearly get around to spending on schools and libraries and hospitals and homes. Yes, they know something's out of joint, and I mean to talk to them and find out . . ."

This didn't set too well in a state where student demonstrators had been dealt with fiercely and swiftly.

But Ben was a master of timing. He'd told them a lot of things they really didn't want to hear—because he'd set them up for it. I kept thinking of the brilliant manner in which Charles de Gaulle conned, deceived, hoodwinked the Algerian white colonists into thinking he was on *their* side, with his patriotic, jingoistic generalities, and then,

51

when they were convinced, freed Algeria from France. "I have understood you," was the enigmatic way De Gaulle put it. And sensing now that they didn't like his kind words for student rebels, or blacks, or his wariness of the military, he let them have the King James version, full blast.

" ' . . . to bind up the brokenhearted, to proclaim liberty to the captives, and the opening of the prison to them that are bound. To proclaim the acceptable year of the Lord and the day of vengeance of our God, to comfort all that mourn. To give unto them beauty for ashes, the oil of joy for mourning, the garment of praise for the spirit of heaviness.' "

I waited at the side of the stage for the boss. As soon as he had left the lectern, our running mate, Governor Sparrier, was at it. His plastic face beamed.

"Do not be alarmed if you are asked for credentials at the door as you leave," the Vice-President-elect was saying. "This is a routine check and the police assure me everything is in hand. Now if any of you were witness to the tragic incident of a few minutes ago, please go to room 207 at once and report . . ."

He seemed to be enjoying himself. There was a good deal of the policeman in Sparrier—the young, clean, honest, college-bred kind of cop.

Now began the crucial two months of waiting, the so-called "interregnum," the period of planning, programming, analyzing until January 20 when Ben would take the oath of office from Chief Justice Early. He approached the tasks calmly and we set about interviewing and hiring people at once.

Our command post was two floors of the elegant Hotel Manger Hay-Adams, just across the President's Park and Lafayette Square from the White House. From his suite in the Hay-Adams, Hannaford could look out at the executive mansion. As I recall this period, however, he did not spend many hours gazing wistfully, mooning, at the mansion. It did not especially awe him. During the term of the outgoing President, the amiable (and lazy) Hayward Kretz, Ben had spent many hours in the White House. He understood that the tradition of the place was far greater than any one man, that its history represented the accumulated words and deeds of many men—some noble, some frail, some active, some indolent, but all basically good men. I believe one of our academic experts on the presidency has written that although we have had a few inefficient and uninspired presidents, this country has never had an out-and-out scoundrel in the office. And many men, coming to power with little to recommend them, have risen admirably to the job and performed with a wondrous regard for their country's estate.

"It is not a home," Lyndon Johnson once said. "It is a place you go when you finish work." And dear Harry Truman, who was one of our heroes, once commented with his customary candor, "It's a great white prison."

Jefferson didn't like the size of the place. It was big enough, the great democrat said, for "two Emperors, one Pope and a Grand Lama." Perhaps. To my mind, however, there is something appealingly down to earth about the White House. I like the way tourists roam freely through the public rooms. Actually, its 132 rooms, 20 baths, 18 acres and 400 trees are not all that lavish when compared, for example, with the country homes of certain European nobles and oligarchs—English lords, Greek shipping tycoons, German industrial barons—most of them knaves, fools and tyrants. And I like the way in which the mansion combines comfortable living quarters with efficient, rather modest office facilities. I think it is peculiarly American—charming, spacious, livable.

Soon the Hannaford team would take over. Not just a residency, but a temporary four-year lease, by the good graces of 33.7 per cent of the American people. Every time I thought of that figure I shivered. Had any President ever come to office on a more fragile, suspect basis?

Seated at a small desk at one side of Ben's hotel office—he was at his own desk, telephoning his aides in Ramada City to make sure they were placing all of his stock in Hannaford-Western in a charitable foundation fund—I studied the final figures. They drowned me in gloom.

HANNAFORD	25,967,231	33.7 per cent
BELDOCK	25,998,876	33.8 per cent
UPSHAW	17,678,450	23.1 per cent
GARCIA	7,109,986	9.3 per cent

The polls, which had refused to pick a winner, had not

been far off. They had tended to underrate General Upshaw's strength, and had overrated that of the Garcia-Jones slate. It was only a last minute switchover of Garcia voters— blacks, Mexicans, disaffected young people, academics—that had put us over, notably in California (with help from Dalton Warfield's poll watchers) and in other big states.

I pointed this out to Ben.

But he was less concerned with our narrow victory than he was with the Congress. The new House of Representatives was full of avid right-wingers, law-and-order types, sleek, small-town lawyers and businessmen who were "sick and tired" of coddling criminals, hippies, student rioters and most of all the raging blacks. The Senate—well, the Senate was Ben's old home and hunting ground.

Lou Parente summed up our precarious condition in his syndicated column, "View from the Hill."

If ever a man deserved the prayers of ordinary Americans, it is the President-elect. Mr. Hannaford is now striving to put together an Administration for this divided, angry nation. We've raked him over the coals in the past for his highhanded dealings in the Senate, but right now he gets nothing but our good wishes.

Consider if you will the fact that his 33.7 per cent of the popular vote—.1 per cent less than Smead Beldock's —is by far the lowest in history. Mr. Nixon's 43.3 per cent looks huge by comparison.

What is even more alarming is the seventeen million votes run up by General Clyde (Nuke the Chink) Upshaw and his running mate, Senator Gabriel T. Tutt of Alabama, who deserted Ben Hannaford and their party to go his own way with the advocates of a first strike against Red China, and detention camps for rioters. This is double the vote that George Wallace—a flaming liberal by comparison—got in 1968.

We have to be realistic. The Beldock vote is a conservative vote. The Upshaw vote is reactionary. Add them up and we get 56.9 per cent of the electorate who really aren't much in accord with Ben Hannaford's reasonable attitude. He wants to recognize Red China, spend billions in the cities, cut the defense budget. But a lot of our people don't seem to react favorably to such a program. They want blood, and Hannaford, for all his faults, is not a bloody man.

But he is a tough man, a resourceful man. The way he bounced back from scandal and censure two years ago to capture his party's nomination and sneak in under the wire in the election, must be admired. At the moment it is this resiliency, this ruggedness, this power to command and control—and yes—connive, that he will need if he hopes to ease the country's agony.

Ben was delighted with the column. "Bygones are bygones, Edward," he said. "You go have a long talk with the big wop. He's on our side now. No time for grudges these days."

The Cabinet would have to be carefully chosen. Ben was less interested in paying off old debts—a standard practice of his in the Senate—than in getting top-notch men for the posts. Right off, he angered the right-wing by naming Senator Walter Edgerton of Ohio, a pipe-smoking Rhodes scholar, to be Secretary of State. Edgerton had been chairman of the Senate Foreign Relations Committee, a balky, recalcitrant group which was said to have nineteen members and twenty-one and one-half separate opinions. A free and independent thinker, Edgerton had led the opposition to our country's ill-starred attempt to intervene in the "outrageous Communist invasion" of the Arab principality of Djarak on the Persian Gulf.

To those who have forgotten this footnote to our recent history, let me remind them, that it was my boss, the President-elect B. B. Hannaford, who had tried to foist a two hundred and fifty million dollar rider on the Foreign Aid Bill, for the benefit of Djarak and its bloated ruler, Prince Omar Aziz.

Ben had overreached himself. You simply did not make end-runs around Senator Walter Edgerton. This mess helped bring about Ben's fall from grace in the Senate. In the process of "educating" certain other senators about the crying need for financial aid to Djarak, Ben made lavish "campaign contributions." Parente found out. The "contributions" were publicized. Our enemies called them bribes. And eventually the censure vote came about.

And yet, there was a curious concurrence of attitude on foreign affairs between Walter Edgerton and the boss. Neither like the *armed* intervention in Djarak. President

Kretz, in one of his rare decisive moods, had despatched several thousand Marines to the fly-blown, sand-whipped desert to help Prince Omar Aziz "maintain freedom." "All we ask," Kretz's Secretary of State kept intoning, "is that north Djarak let its neighbor alone." But there was no north Djarak. Just several hundred barefoot tribesmen armed with Czech rifles. A tribal revolt suddenly became a test of freedom around the world. However, Senator Edgerton had gauged the disgust of a good many Americans. Conservative and anti-Communist the people may have been, but they no longer had the stomach for endless adventures among half-naked illiterates who had no concept of freedom, or liberty, or anti-Communism. They understood food and land and camels.

So the great Djarak adventure withered away. Eventually our Marines were pulled out. A United Nations force (twenty Swedes, a Nigerian officer and five machine guns mounted in Jeeps) were despatched to the burning spit of sand. Ben's grandiose "Djarak Amendment"—to make a suburban, barbecue-tending, golf-playing Babbitt out of every Djaraki Arab—foundered of its own weighty ambition.

The truth was Ben no longer cared. A major factor in the Djarak affair was Ben's closeness to the Longhorn-Middle East Oil Corporation, which was owned by his in-laws, the Cudders. They were locked in with Hannaford-Western in a variety of ways. But ever since Ben's Chicago speech and the campaign, in both of which he had put himself down squarely on the side of black power and a detente with Russia and China, he had alienated the Cudders.

"Same thing happened to Lyndon," Ben said to me. It was the morning we had just learned of Senator Walter Edgerton's acceptance of the post of Secretary of State.

"What is that, sir?"

"You can't expect any good out of oil companies. They are the biggest bunch of four-flushing greedy bastards God ever suffered to walk the land."

"That's pretty strong talk from someone who has been up to his knees in oil since he was fourteen."

"Oh, they'll earn money for you. But cross them a teeny-weeny bit, and they'll get the knives out."

"What about Lyndon?"

Ben swiveled about in his high-backed chair and stared

across the greenery to the White House. "No man did more for the oil people in Texas and Oklahoma than Lyndon. When he was a congressman, and a senator, and Vice-President. Went down the line for 'em. Then he became President. There was one thing Lyndon understood, and it was that civil rights legislation, a break for our Negro citizens was long overdue. So he put through more and better civil rights laws than all the Presidents that preceded him, *combined*. And that includes Jack Kennedy, whom the liberals love, while they seem to go on hating Lyndon forever."

"But what about the oil people?"

"They never forgave Lyndon for those civil rights laws. And what raises my blood pressure is the simple fact that not one of those laws in the slightest way infringed on their right to make money. They wrote vile books about him. Told lies about his wife, one of the finest women ever was our First Lady. And it hurt him. 'I've he'pped them all my life,' he told me. 'Now look.'"

"And you think they'll treat you the same way?"

"I don't give a damn if they do, Edward. I welcome their hatred. I was of their persuasion—up to a point—once."

"I'd say more than to a point. You once battled to raise the depletion allowance to 33⅓ per cent . . ."

"Well, watch me battle to knock it down, way, way down."

I had to admire him. He was approaching the greatest job on earth with brimming confidence, his sense of history and of purpose.

Thus, Walter Edgerton, a man denounced in the editorials of our oil-funded press, by their paid scriveners, on their ranting radio broadcasts, as a traitor, an appeaser and a homosexual (all lies) was to be our new architect of foreign policy.

His other choices were equally imaginative—able, independent people, the very best he could find. He showed me his proposed list of key cabinet officers one morning.

Treasury—Mrs. Margaret High McNally, vice-president of the New York Stock Exchange.

I thought this was sheer genuis. Mrs. McNally was known

slightly to me—an attractive gray-haired grandmother, a widow, a financial wizard. "Great choice, sir," I said.

"Why not? Why not a woman to run the country's finances? They manage the household budgets and they do it damn well. It's always the wife who knows how far the checking account will stretch. She knows where the bargains are, she knows how to make do, when to buy, when to save. Meg's got family down here, and she'll love it."

The next name was a natural.

Health, Education and Welfare—Homer Murphy

"On the nose," I said. Homer Murphy was a black man, the mayor of Washington, D.C. Recently, he had been pleading with the Attorney General to take the National Guardsmen off the street. In an effort to reduce crime, an understandable concern, the guard had been stationed on street corners, on foot patrol for the past six months. Crimes were still committed; the black people of Washington seethed.

"Homer will be fine," Ben said. "He can go up to the Hill and talk to the Congress and they will listen. You tell me why, Edward."

"Because he is a famous athlete," I answered. "We're still a celebrity-mad nation. Homer was front-page when he played middle-linebacker for the Washington Redskins. They all remember him in his helmet and cleats stopping the Green Bay Packers four times in a row inside the five-yard line four years ago."

Of course Murphy—a supporter of Ben's city-building program—had a lot more going for him than his past as a national football hero. He was an intelligent, persuasive, compassionate man, born to a life of slum poverty, one of seven sons of a Virginia dirt farmer. Congressmen would listen to him—less for the good sense he spoke, I understood, but more in terms of his past glory as a Washington Redskin. There is a little bit of "jock" in most politicians. How accurately Ben had put it—*the right things getting done for the wrong reasons.*

I glanced at a few other names. Particularly was I impressed with the choice of Professor Abraham Dent of Arizona Institute of Technology as Secretary of the Interior.

"I admire Professor Dent," I said, "but what will the

Senate think?" Abraham Dent was a militant, acid-tongued conservationist. His motto was "Less Progress, More Parks." In his CONSERVATIONIST NEWSLETTER he had outraged and attacked every land developer, oil driller, road builder and industrial power in the country. Professor Dent was an advocate of redwoods, whooping cranes and alligators, and an implacable foe of industry.

"The Senate will have to chew on Professor Dent for a while," Ben said. "I learned a lot during that debate on the New Wilderness Bill. What was it that Johnny Lord kept saying at the hearings?"

Johnny Lord was Senator John Tyler Lord of Vermont, an aristocratic New Englander, all Harvard and genealogical tables, who had battled Ben on his bill to permit "multiple use" in the national parks and wilderness areas.

"Senator Lord said that if we do not permit the earth to produce beauty it will not produce food either. Only it isn't his line. He was quoting some professor."

"I can't get it out of my head. We need a man like Abe Dent there to stop us from poisoning ourselves."

"Dent will embarrass you. He is widely hated by the industrial fat cats."

"No, they can't lay a hand on him." Ben laughed. "He is a conservationist, he believes in the American wilderness, in God, the sky, the animals and the birds. You don't dare holler Communist at a man like that, or socialist, or pink, or anything else. The patriots know deep down that he's a better American than they are."

The Cabinet was shaping up splendidly. The biggest job that remained unfilled was that of defense. Ben insisted that this post was the cornerstone of his Administration, and he wanted a strong, independent and unflappable man for the job.

"Know what I want, Edward?" he asked me, as I departed to meet with Matthew Fixx on hiring staff personnel. "I want a man who can sit in front of admirals and generals and tell 'em the party is over. No more blank checks."

"Too bad you can't handle the job." It was odd that a man who had made millions out of defense contracts should have so little respect for the military. Perhaps the brutal manner in which General Clyde Upshaw and his fellow war horses had savaged him had made him vindictive.

"I would love to," Ben said. "And I intend to. But I need a front man. Someone who won't start saluting and bowing in front of brass. Keep your eyes open."

"That is a vague mandate, sir. I hardly know where to start. What kind of a man do you want? Rich? Poor? Industry? Government? University?"

Ben beamed at me. " 'Clothed, and in his right mind.' "

"St. Mark," I replied. "I'm afraid he isn't available."

It was too bad, I mused, as I sat in my private office in the Hay-Adams, that Mr. Clark Clifford was no longer around. There was a man! I recalled those uneasy last months of Mr. Johnson's stewardship, when Mr. Clifford, singlehandedly turned the Administration upside down on the Vietnam issue. What a performance that had been!

"You have got to understand how Mr. Clifford was able to do that," Ben explained. "You see, he is not a liberal, or any kind of political dogmatist. He is basically a lawyer, a rich one, a smart one, a professional. He doesn't have any burning need to prove to the world that he is a one hundred per cent anti-Communist crusader, the way people like the Rostows and the Bundys always have to. He is rich, influential, secure, happy, and practical. So he could get the President moving on peace, and talk back to those generals when they demanded another two hundred thousand of our boys to do their dirty work."

How shrewdly Ben had analyzed the man, the task, the need for the right kind of agent at the right time. We would need a secretary of defense as courageous and as able and as shrewd as the man who had forced a President to make a 180-degree turnaround on Vietnam.

Recruiting activities—"head-hunting" Matt Fixx called it in his relentless Washingtonese—took up all my time. I ate hurried dinners in my hotel room, and found myself sleeping five hours a night. It was something of a relief, therefore, to get a dinner invitation from Lou Parente and his wife. I recalled the columnist telling me he had important information for us, that he was no longer the enemy he had been two years ago.

The only embarrassment about the evening was the fact that Mrs. Parente was an ex-mistress of mine and a key

60

figure in the censure matter. Her maiden name was Marsha Treadway, and she had been our chief mail clerk when Ben was running the Senate. I'll skip many of the details. Suffice it to say that Marsha and I shared a comfortable bed for about six months, she gratified all my sexual needs, I hers, the two of us discreet about our affair. Then I decided to end the matter. In a fit of pique, she stole a sheaf of compromising documents from our office. Out of this theft, the censure hearings grew.

She was fired, testified against us and later married Lou Parente, the beneficiary of her treasonable behavior. Oddly, Hannaford did not have any vindictive feelings about Marsha's betrayal. Nor did he ever allude to the fact that had I not terminated our love-making, she might not have decided to avenge herself in such a destructive way. In any case, I was glad for Marsha that she had married, and now had a baby son, and another child en route. She was a rather bland, good-natured girl, from western New York State, a typical pretty, not-too-bright, Washington office type. She had had a few affairs before meeting me, including one with her current husband. So, in a sense, she had come home.

The Parentes lived modestly in a split-level house in Bethesda, just over the district line. The small lawn, the cramped rooms, the one-car garage did not mesh with the public image of Lou Parente as a high-priced journalist. I realized part of the answer was that Parente was paying alimony to two prior wives. But beyond this, he was a rare man, a fellow who had little interest in material things. He would not have known what to do in a historic Georgetown town house, shooting his gold-linked cuffs at assorted Alsops and Restons and the like. He was an old-fashioned, hard-nosed, ill-tempered newsman, a vanishing American, and where he lived and the style in which he lived scarcely interested him.

Nor did his mode of dress. He was wearing a soiled sweat shirt when he received me in their tiny living room (shrunk even further by the baby's playpen in the middle of the carpet) and was sipping beer from a can.

"The Big Indian say anything when I asked you out here?" Parente asked.

"He approved."

"Natch. He needs any friend he can lay his mitts on. Boy, do you guys have troubles."

Marsha Treadway Parente came in from the kitchen. Beneath her checkered apron, she bulged with life. I rose and I kissed her gently on the cheek. A pained sense of loss shivered me. Bachelorhood would surely be my fate. I like women; I like sex; but I recoil from any sort of lasting commitment. Bloodless, Marsha once called me. She may have been right.

"Well, Eddie, you don't change much. Same general store stay-comb on your hair? Why don't you grow sideburns or a beard?" She gave me an extra hug.

"You know me better, Marsha. I am Mr. Square."

"Deever knows what's good for him," Parente said. "Hannaford'll have him running all over the Hill planting microphones and twisting arms. Sideburns don't help in that line of work."

Parente, I noticed, had let *his* grow—iron-gray, thick—down his leathery cheeks. Lou was a rugged-looking man given to coarse speech. But this was a cover-up, a false front to disarm the unwary. I'd run a check on him, and knew that he was a graduate of Brooklyn College, had a master's degree from Fordham and had taught government for several years.

We enjoyed a quiet dinner. Marsha had been thoroughly domesticated, I was pleased to note. Like many girls who marry a bit late after a good deal of tumbling in and out of beds, she had taken eagerly to domestication. The food was simple—lamb chops, spinach, a green salad, and a red California wine—all of excellent quality.

I was pleased that Marsha bore no attraction for me now. Her reddish hair was undone, and her normally plump figure was considerably heavier due to the burden she bore. I tried, as she served the cheddar cheese and water biscuits, to recall the gasping nights of lust we had enjoyed in my bachelor quarters. It seemed a century ago with someone else.

We took our coffee into the cramped living room, where Parente, with contempt for his property, put his suede boots on the coffee table and let cigar ash fall on the sofa and the carpet. Oddly, Marsha did not seem to care. She brought us a brandy bottle and excused herself to do the dishes and watch television.

"Yeah, Deever," Lou said, "you guys are about to walk into a bear trap. I hope Hannaford is as tough and as smart as people like you keep insisting."

"I thought he proved it with his comeback."

"A political freak. Saved by a third party lunatic and a split on the electoral vote. Come on, Ed, you really have to count Beldock and Upshaw's vote as *one*. Nobody wanted a reasonable man this time. Most people wanted a hard ass."

"You underestimate Hannaford."

"The hell I do, Ed." Parente lumbered up from the sofa and located a thin book on the shelves on either side of the tiny fireplace. "Listen to this, pal." He began to read. " 'Viability in policy has three ingredients. First is a purpose that moves with the grain of history, a direction consonant with coming needs.' "

"Yes, that's Neustadt," I said. "Do you deny that Ben, who wants to spend billions to build the cities and elevate the poor and the blacks, and cut the defense budget, do you deny that such a direction is in line with this country's needs?"

"Yeah, you and me and Reston and Lippman think so. But we ain't the fifty-six per cent that voted for the cavemen," Parente said. He resumed reading. " 'Second is an operation that proves manageable to the men who must administer it, acceptable to those who must support it, tolerable to those who must put up with it, in Washington and out.' "

I paused before responding. "Well, that's a little tougher."

"You damn said it. You taken a look at the new house of Representatives? Sure, Hannaford can stock the executive branch and the courts and the regulatory agencies with nice guys. But he isn't going to get the time of day from those shit-kickers in Congress. Tolerable? Manageable? Acceptable? You know what Congressman Lance Ruckett is after—pre-emptive strikes against the Chinese, detention camps for *schwarzers* and a law forbidding the teaching of evolution in public schools."

"I don't see the national picture as quite that gloomy."

Parente scowled and read on. " 'Timing can be crucial for support and acquiescence; proper timing is the third ingredient.' "

"I admit the time may not be quite right, but it is a President's job to lead—to bend and shape the electorate."

Parente slouched back to the sofa and sipped at his

63

cognac. "What if they won't bend? What if they tell the President to go piss up a rope with his reform plans? What if the majority of Americans are so fed up with black wildmen like Kakamba, or hairy foul-mouthed college kids, that they won't accept *any* program except one to suppress, confine and maybe knock off some of these noisy bastards?"

"I don't think that most Americans feel that way."

"Think again, buddy."

He opened a manila folder on the coffee table, spilled some cognac on it, wiped it off with the sleeve of his sweat shirt and handed it to me. It was a four-page printed newsletter, smartly gotten up in two colors, on the order of I. F. Stone's Weekly. As I read it, however, it became apparent that its editorial position was light years removed from Mr. Stone's.

It was headed: DOOR TO FREEDOM.

Under that enigmatic title appeared the explanation: *A Newsletter of Fact and Opinion, Published by the Defenders of Our Republic. NOT FOR GENERAL CIRCULATION.*

I began to read an article entitled "The Stolen Election."

B. B. Hanaford, a sly and treacherous man, has stolen the presidential election. Conniving with the mongrel swindler Angel Lopez Garcia and the black savage Kakamba Jones, he has contrived to rob the American people of their real choice.

DOOR would have reluctantly settled for Vice-President Smead Beldock, even though he is not a true bedrock patriot. Our choice was that great American patriot, General Clyde Upshaw and his courageous running mate, Senator Gabriel T. Tutt. Hannaford represents a cunning, dishonest and utterly untrustworthy tradition in American political life. A careful study of his career in and out of Congress leaves no other conclusion than that he has been, and is now, a *conscious, functioning member of the international Communist conspiracy.*

"Oh, for goodness sake, Lou," I protested. "This garbage has been floating around for years. The Birchers called Eisenhower the same thing, and it made him stronger than ever. I don't want to read any more."

"Eisenhower wasn't elected by the lowest popular vote in history, kid. Eisenhower didn't have to contend with the dirty-mouth kids and the darkies and the AFL Polacks and CIO Italians who wanna kill 'em all."

"You think that this sort of drivel can become a mass movement, create a great country-wide surge of feeling?"

"It has already," Parente said ominously. "Read on."

I skipped some mouthings about Ben's sinister dealings with the Eastern European countries—building supermarkets in Hungary and Romania, pipelines in Bulgaria and so on. All old stuff. Then there was this paragraph.

Hannaford had better tread warily. Let him examine the make-up of the new House of Representatives. Patriotic groups like DOOR and Save America have never been better represented in that esteemed body, which more accurately reflects the national will than a President freakishly and dishonestly elected by a one-in-a-million chance. Let him watch his step. Or perhaps it would be best for him to get it over with quickly—let him try to bull through his socialist schemes for wasting the national treasure on black killers and their illegitimate spawn. Let him try, so that the national outrage will be loud, clear and immediate.

"They're challenging him," I said. "But for the life of me, Lou, I can't get alarmed. They've always been around."

"Not in such numbers, buddy."

"What makes you think they're smart enough to . . . to . . . hurt Ben?"

"They're learning, Deever. Look at the back page."

I found an article headed "Recruitment Proceeds," just over the mail-in coupon for the "Impeach Moscowitz Kit."

DOOR is pleased to report that twenty-two more urban police chapters have been formed since the election. Progress is also being made in enlisting the help of major newspaper publishers, since the television networks, with their usual talent for flirting with socialist plotters, continues to ignore DOOR's pleas for co-operation. The DOOR committee on the judiciary is now operating in thirty states.

"Threats, threats," I said. "I'm not frightened." But I was—just a little. I stared at an advertisement.

SEND IN $1.75 AND RECIEVE YOUR
"IMPEACH SAMUEL MOSCOWITZ KIT"
Stickers—Buttons—Leaflets
Petitions—Pamphlets
"GET THE GOVERNMENT OUT OF THE RED,
AND THE RED OUT OF THE FBI"

Could this kind of low-grade comic stumbling pose a threat to the President, to the fabric of our society? I rejected the notion out of hand.

Disturbed, I got up and paced. "But dammit, what can these people do? Suppose they get a mass following, all of the people who voted for Upshaw and Tutt, and many of those who voted for Beldock. ... Ben's in, and they're out. All they can do is work on Congress to kill his legislative program. And Hannaford knows something about Congress himself."

Parente sighed and walked to the television set to turn on the eleven o'clock evening newscast. As the picture unscrambled and the voice of a laundry soap commercial trickled forth, he turned to me grimly, "Kid, you better warn your boss."

"Of what?"

"They are going to get rid of him."

"How, how?"

"I dunno. I only know they figure they were robbed. If it went to the House of Representatives, Beldock would have won, but only with the support of Upshaw and Tutt, which would have meant cabinet posts for the general and all the other lunatics. At long last, they would have been in charge. So what does Hannaford do? He steals it from under their nose. They'll get your guy, Deever. Or they'll wreck the country trying."

"I don't believe you. You underestimate Hannaford. You always do."

The newscaster came on. President Kretz had moved more National Guardsmen into Cincinnati, Omaha and Phoenix. The Russians, the Chinese and the Mongolians had started preliminary talks in Stockholm over the Mongolian War, but were arguing over the seating arrangements. A judge in Pasadena claimed he had irrefutable evidence that black poll watchers in Watts had tampered with voting machines, and he intended to submit his evidence to the Justice Department. There was speculation that Ben would name Senator Maury Eisenberg of Illinois, the millionaire realtor, to be Secretary of Defense.

I listened with half an ear. Parente was no fool, and no alarmist, and a man with excellent sources. He knew, I was certain, a lot more than he was telling me. But he wanted this information conveyed to Ben. I would draw up a memo for the boss tomorrow, I assured him.

"It's strange," I said. "You were once our worst enemy, Lou."

He waved away my attempt at camaraderie, as Marsha, in a blue chiffon robe, joined us. I was pleased with myself—not the slightest spark of envy.

"Christ, you guys are all I got left," Parente growled.

I tried to get Hannaford's attention riveted on Parente's report, particularly the warning that *they*—some kind of cabal of the paranoid right, with allies in more respectable places—were after his hide.

"Parente shouldn't be taken lightly," I said.

"We've learned that the hard way," Matt Fixx said. Matt had not been involved in the "scandal" that resulted in Ben's censure. He had acted as Ben's counsel during the hearings, and the poor young fellow had been somewhat dazed by the revelations. He and I had at one point been at opposite ends of the spectrum.

"They can't hurt us once we're in *there*," Ben said. He pointed out the window to the White House, serene in a wintry haze. It was a few days before Christmas. A spindly Christmas tree concocted of plastic glittered in a corner of the hotel room, set up by faithful Cleo Watterson. Fern had wanted to go to Ramada Ranch for the holiday, but Ben could not spare the time. He was not an avid vacationer, like some Presidents.

"I am to do nothing about Parente's report?" I pursued.

"Talk to the wop now and then, Edward. Keep him on our side. We'll feed him stuff as it suits us. He'll be used, and he won't mind."

"Don't delude yourself. No one uses Parente. The only

thing is, he's convinced there are a lot worse elements in public today than you, truly dangerous people. So he'll be good to us—for a while."

The buzzer rang. It was Cleo, advising Hannaford that his nephew, Miles J. Cudder, heir to the Cudder oil millions, board chairman of Longhorn-Middle East was in Washington and wished to see him. "Not available," Ben said.

"You should talk to him, sir. It wouldn't hurt to bury the hatchet." I was disturbed by the way Fern's family, powers in the southwest, had turned against Ben.

"They'll come around." He pointed to the White House across the park. "That's the power, over yonder. And they know it." Ben leaned backward, bracing his corded hands behind his head. "By God, I've studied the last few presidencies, and I'm amazed at how the office gives the man a kind of glory and a power he never dreamed he had. Not a selfish kind of power—but a power for the general good."

Matt Fixx and I listened attentively. For all his lack of schooling, there was a native wisdom in Hannaford. He had ended his education at the age of fourteen, but his education had never ceased.

"I tell you boys what intrigues me the most," he went on, "is the way Presidents pull off the damnedest surprises."

"A sort of reverse English?" Matt ventured.

"You might call it that, Matthew. Let's start with Harry Truman. Inexperienced. Scared stiff. Absolutely no knowledge, the wiseguys said, of foreign affairs. He'd wreck us, people warned. So what is Harry best remembered for? Why, the Marshall Plan and NATO—two of the most constructive programs we ever undertook. Saved Europe. Maybe saved the world. But that was little Harry, who didn't know France from Brazil."

"I'm not sure I buy that thesis, sir," I said. "Mr. Truman was following certain historical imperatives. And he had superb men around him—Marshall, Acheson, others."

"But he had to make the decisions. Only he was President. Look at Eisenhower. Military man. Brought up in army camps. Now what are the two things Ike will be most remembered for?"

"That's easy," I said. "Ending the Korean War—"

"Under terms that would have gotten a liberal like Adlai Stevenson lynched," Matt interjected.

"—and warning the nation about the military-industrial complex."

Ben grinned. "See what I am getting at? The last two things you'd expect of a five-star general in the White House."

"What about Jack Kennedy?" I asked.

"Well, he's a tough one to figure," Ben said. "Maybe the exception that proves the rule. Peace Corps ... sort of in keeping with what he was before ... young, bright, imaginative fellow. I'd say he went against his grain when he let the military talk him into the Bay of Pigs."

"Exception!" I cried. "You said, sir, that all these programs of the Presidents, policies that went against their predicted behavior, were for the general good. Do you think the invasion of Cuba was in that vein?"

"Hell no," Ben said. "I said Kennedy was an exception. Which brings us to Lyndon. Southerner. Big hat, boots, the accent. Elected by the oil people, they used to say. So what does Mr. Johnson do in office? Why, he only puts through the greatest social reforms, the greatest civil rights measures we have ever witnessed. *Some Southerner!*"

"And Mr. Nixon?"

"Tax reform," Ben said easily. "Everyone saw him as a creature of the big money, the corporations. Well, he enacted the best tax reform this country had in years. Finally closed some loopholes and gave poor folks a break."

"Hayward Kretz?" I pursued.

"Now don't back me into a corner, Edward," the boss said. "It's only a theory. President Kretz is a newspaper publisher, and they are the most predictable people in the world. He went into office without an idea in his head and he's going out no wiser."

"And leaving us with a god-awful mess," I said. "That man must have idolized James Buchanan. Postponing, temporizing, putting everyone to sleep with his platitudes. Imagine being remembered as the President who posted National Guardsmen permanently in ten American cities."

"There's my thesis proven," Ben said. "Hayward Kretz was elected on a platform that said he aimed to get the Federal Government off people's backs and out of their lives. So he ended up siccing the soldiers on us."

"And how will you surprise people, Senator?" I asked. "How will you go against your grain?" Matt Fixx looked aghast. He would not have dared talk to the boss in so cavalier a fashion.

"I've done that already. Hannaford, the old schemer, the lobbyist, the friend of the oil people and the special interests. Here I am trying to redistribute the national treasure." He gazed past the two of us, at the painting of John Adams on the wall. "We have to get our hands on all that defense money, boys. Got to tell those generals off. Party's over. People are sick of being taxed to death for more death."

Our conversation was interrupted by an urgent phone call from Judge Moscowitz, the director of the FBI. As Ben betrayed not a flicker of emotion, no sign of caring one way or the other, Moscowitz revealed that they were now looking for a man named Henry Kaspar as the suspected would-be assassin, the man who had wounded Mona Varnum outside the Ramada Stockman's Inn six weeks ago.

"Any sign of a conspiracy?" Ben asked.

"None," the judge replied. "Kaspar is a loner. A long record of mental disturbances. Two arrests for arson. Two more for exposing himself in public. Born in Manhattan, Kansas, raised in several places in Colorado and Utah. Finished school in the tenth grade, average intelligence. Kaspar was last employed as a steam-fitter's assistant in Midland, Texas. A drifter, a man on the fringe, Senator. God knows where he got the notion that it was incumbent upon him to assassinate you. We've checked his last lodging, in Ramada City, and have found nothing at all to indicate any right- or left-wing associations. We're working on family, people who knew him and so on. . . ."

"Where do you think he is now?" Ben asked.

"I have to be honest. We haven't the faintest notion."

Ben paused. "You releasing all of this, Sam?"

"I'm afraid we have to. The wanted flyers are going out to post offices this afternoon. We have more than enough information to go on."

Ben thanked the FBI chief. Then he stroked his chin. "I had hoped they'd catch the bastard before releasing all that stuff."

"Why?" Matt asked.

"Mrs. Hannaford worries a good deal lately," he said.

"This sort of thing—that fellow being on the loose—won't help her any."

It was a rare revelation of his deep feeling for Fern, his concern about her. When Matthew Fixx had gone, Ben suggested I pay an occasional visit on Fern, who remained in their hotel living quarters, inaccessible to the press, silent, withdrawn.

I knew why he was upset. He did not merely love his blond, statuesque wife. He worshiped her. One had to keep in mind that money and power and success were important things to Ben Hannaford, no matter how much he jested about them. Fern, with her oil inheritance had helped him achieve his lofty status. I am not suggesting for a moment that it was his wife's fortune and family that made Ben. Anyone with his drive and intelligence would have made his millions and his mark, sooner or later. It was simply that Fern Cudder's connections hastened Ben's rise. And Ben was a grateful man. He never forgot a favor or a friend. Loyalty to, and love for, Fern ran deep and true in him.

I purchased some magazines and some Washington guide books and histories for Mrs. Hannaford, hoping that Fern would not interpret my gesture as a comment on her unfamiliarity with print. But candor forces me to state that both she and her husband were strangers to books—and even magazines. They both glanced at the daily newspapers and the news magazines, but I daresay there were not a dozen books in the Ramada Ranch House.

"How nice of you to think of me, Edward," Fern said. It was two-thirty in the afternoon and she was in a dressing gown—this one a lush maroon velvet, buttoned from her throat to her toes, giving her more than ever the look of a dowager queen, a big-boned, firm-bodied, blond Juno.

"Well, I imagined this period can't be too much fun for you," I said. "With the senator up to his neck in work."

"Oh, I don't mind."

I wondered what she did to keep busy. There was another small Christmas tree in the corner of the room, a cluster of brightly wrapped packages at its base. On a kidney-shaped desk I saw an opened box of stationery. Fern had been answering mail.

"It's a shame we couldn't find the time to go back to the ranch for Christmas," I said.

"Yes, that would have been pleasant." She ushered me to a green plush hotel chair—I think living among hotel furniture, temporary objects, that had no meaning for her, upset the poor woman—and she sat opposite me, her hands folded in her lap. "Of course, Christmas is a time for children. And perhaps it is best that we be here. . . ."

"I'm sorry. I mean, all your nieces and nephews . . ."

Fern smiled sadly. "Yes. I doubt that they would be allowed to visit us." She looked grave. "Edward, I am not very good at these feuds and family intrigues."

I tried to change the subject by chatting about past First Ladies, how they had all emerged as personages in their own right, women who became loved and respected by the people. I told her about Abigail Adams hanging her laundry in the East Room; of Dolley Madison cutting the Gilbert Stuart portrait of Washington from its frame the night the British burned the capital; of Mrs. Lincoln distressing poor Abe by overspending on refurbishing the East Room; of Mrs. Coolidge's sky parlor, later used by Mamie Eisenhower as a sitting room, where she could watch her parakeets and canaries; of Mrs. Johnson's thoughtful work in improving the public tours, collecting American art and landscaping the grounds. Perhaps I talked too much, because Fern was markedly unresponsive.

Eventually, she got up and walked to the window. Distantly, the White House beckoned. To her it was a castle of terrors. "Mrs. Kretz has been so sweet," she said. "She has twice asked me to come to visit and to show me around, but I have had to invent excuses."

"You must go, Mrs. H. It will take some getting used to, but you will learn to like it there. You know Mrs. Ulysses Grant once wrote that her life in the White House was 'a bright and beautiful dream.' "

"It shall be a nightmare for me."

"No, you mustn't think that way, Mrs. H. You will find that Americans will respect you and will wish you nothing but good. They are a warm and grateful people—where First Ladies are concerned. For all the political rancor that can surround a President, all the attacks and charges, none of this touches the First Lady. At the height of Senator Joe McCarthy's attacks on Mr. Truman, the senator found some nice things to say about Mrs. Truman. And she *was* a wonderful person, and the public knew it.

"Look at Mamie. It was really a shame the people never got to know her better. Yes, she was shy, and frail, and always took a back seat to her husband, but those who knew her, knew her to be a witty and gracious and truly dignified person. You know, she practically never said a word in public, and then some time after Ike's death, I heard her being interviewed, and I was amazed to discover what a delightful, articulate person she was."

"All of what you say is true, Edward. But the fact remains that I am a person who cannot abide being *hated*."

I was stunned. "But Mrs. H., what I am saying is that despite all the bitterness in American politics, a special niche is set aside for First Ladies. They are immune to assaults . . ."

"As immune as I was at the airport in South Dakota?"

"I know. It's not easy to shrug your shoulders at these things. There's a wild strain loose in the country these days. But if any man can handle it, it's the senator."

Fern held out her palms in a helpless gesture. "But why should he want to? He could have stayed out of politics after the censure. We had everything we wanted. He could have continued his work with Mr. Warfield in the cities as a private citizen. . . ."

"No, ma'am, excuse me for correcting you. He did not have everything he wanted. He wanted the power. Not really for himself, but for what he could bring to it, for the good things he could do for this country."

Fern walked—stately, dignified—to a small portable bar which the hotel had furnished. "Goodness, I am a poor hostess. Would you care for a drink, Edward?"

"Just a soft drink, Mrs. H. A Coke or something."

She served me, then poured herself a staggering belt of bourbon and sipped at it. As I had suspected for some time, she was at the bottle. Ever temperate in her habits, this new taste was not in character. No wonder Ben was disturbed.

"You'll get to love it in the White House," I said. "History is a wonderful companion."

"I am not so certain about our current history," Fern said. "I sense that this country is filled with angry people, who seem to have nothing better to do than hate."

I shook my head and started to interrupt.

"No, let me continue, Edward. I have the feeling that

73

my husband is standing on a small sandy island, the kind we find in the Ramada River when the floods recede, and that on either side of him are these hissing, coiled rattlesnakes, so filled with venom that they strike out blindly. And although the senator tries to keep the mail from me, Miss Watterson inadvertently let me see some of the appalling letters he is getting. Oh, the anger, and the disgusting language, and the threats, and the vicious insults . . ."

"It is part of the price we pay for being public figures."

"I am very reluctant to pay it." She sighed. "However, I shall try."

"And we will all stand ready to help you. Now suppose I telephone Mrs. Kretz's secretary and arrange for a visit."

Fern did not seem to hear me. At length, she replied, "In a day or two, Edward. Perhaps after the holiday."

Leaving, I commended to her the fine book, *The Living White House,* one of several I had purchased for her. "You'll find a lovely quote by Abigail Adams in it," I said. "Nothing to do with her laundry. As a matter of fact it's carved on the mantel in the State Dining Room. Mrs. Adams said, 'I pray Heaven to bestow the best of blessings on this House and all that shall hereafter inhabit it. May none but honest and wise men ever rule under this roof.' "

"I'll study them, Edward," Fern said weakly. "Perhaps if I were as bright as you, or the senator, this would all be easier for me."

On leaving her, I decided it was mandatory that I hire a young lady of unusual talents to be Fern's secretary. She needed someone youthful and compassionate at her side, someone to keep her *au courant* with the Washington scene. In the frenzy of putting our own staff together, we had let Fern flounder. And she was hardly the type of aggressive woman to have started hiring people on her own.

I was discussing this with Ben in his hotel office—he approved and gave me *carte blanche* to start interviewing girls—when Cleo buzzed, to announce the arrival of Congressman Charles (Chuck) Gantry of Missouri, a bright, progressive, energetic young men slated to be our Secretary of Housing and Urban Development.

"First Lady's problems will have to wait," Hannaford said. "This is real trouble."

Gantry entered. I knew him only slightly, more by

74

reputation than by personal contact. And his reputation was a formidable one. A St. Louis lawyer, he had been a leader in improving race relations in the ghettos and had worked out a viable formula for low-cost housing units on a "scattered sites" basis. Lanky, rather slovenly and offhand in manner, thick-maned, and articulate, he was of the new breed of urban lawyers, public servants, reformers. A devout Roman Catholic, Gantry had worked closely with progressive elements in all the churches.

The President introduced us. "Explain to Edward what this is all about, Congressman," Ben said. "I know the details already."

Gantry ran his hand through his thick brown hair: he wore it long, and with sideburns rather too long for a midwestern legislator. Then he seemed to hesitate.

"It's all right," the President-elect said. "Ed is my eyes and ears. And he can be useful in these ticklish matters."

Gantry looked at me quizzically. I suppose I am something of a rare bird. The first notion that comes to the minds of altruistic men like Gantry is probably, *Deever: corrupt sycophant*. They're wrong of course. I'm a functionary; a catalyst.

"Well, for the past four years," young Mr. Gantry said, "I've been a consultant to the Schlammerstein Foundation in St. Louis. Old Mrs. Schlammerstein gives scholarships to black children and has financed study groups on ghetto problems . . ."

"Sounds most commendable," I said.

"It is. But Senator Tutt hardly thinks so." Gantry frowned. "In any case, the foundation was paying me twenty-five hundred dollars a year as a consultant. I'll be frank with you, I needed the money. We're broke all the time. And I did a hell of a lot of work for them. Not only did I get these fees, but the foundation picked up my tab now and then when I traveled—small stuff—hotel rooms, airplane tickets."

"Mr. Gantry has resigned from the foundation," Hannaford said. "Obviously he couldn't work for them and serve as Secretary of HUD."

"What's the problem?" I asked.

"Gabe Tutt," the Missourian said, "has gotten hold of photostats of the bills paid by the foundation and the checks they sent me. One of his aides, that young fellow Eustis, has also dug up some ancient discredited stuff

75

about Mrs. Schlammerstein. Good God, she's a saint, that old woman. But back in the thirties she had the usual intellectual flirtations with front groups. Her name on letterheads, newspaper ads."

"I see the picture," I said. "Gabe will attack you as having been in the pay of the Communist conspiracy."

"He has so advised the Majority Leader, Senator Hopewell," Ben said. "Gabe says he's going to make this a test case."

"Test case?" I asked.

Hannaford's jaw was set. There were glints of fire in the Indian eyes. "The senator from Alabama is of the mind that if he can rally the Senate to block my appointment of Mr. Gantry, then he can stymie our whole program. In short Gabe has gone on notice that the knives are out."

Gantry looked flustered. "Mr. Hannaford, please let me ask you again, in front of Mr. Deever. Do not offer my name. I want to serve in the Cabinet, but why should I be an albatross around your neck? You can get some other experienced man to head up HUD. Why make me an issue with Senator Tutt? You'll need his support. He can make more trouble for you, than I can do good."

Hannaford rubbed his chin. I could see that Gantry knew him only slightly. When you challenged Ben Hannaford—as Gabe Tutt had done—you got a fight. If there was anything that could be said about the boss, it was that he was no coward. Or, as athletes used to say, there was no ki-yi in him.

"No, Mr. Gantry," Ben said. "With your permission, we'll go to the mat with Senator Tutt on this. Give me a chance to test the powers of the presidency early in the game. Besides, I want you for the HUD job. I know all about your work in scattered site housing, in community control, local police forces."

"I don't see . . ." the congressman said. "I mean, sir, I was badly advised to have that connection with the foundation."

"Not at all. It was peanuts. Piddling stuff. That's why you got in trouble. If you'd taken a hundred thousand dollars from the oil lobby nobody would give a damn. But it was just a few dollars a year from a do-good foundation. That, son, is a damned crime."

Gantry smiled. "All right. Can I do anything to make

this easier for you, aside from severing my connections with the foundation?"

Hannaford got up and ushered the legislator to the door. "No, Mr. Gantry. This sort of diplomacy is something that your President and Mr. Deever regard as their specialty. Fellow with a Ph.D. like yourself, who writes articles for *Harper's*, you'd be out of place trying it."

When Charles Gantry had left, Hannaford issued my orders. In fact, I had them before the big man had returned to his desk.

"Senator Tutt is running a private screening at the Barristers' Club, Edward," he said. "Get over there right now, and offer him a modest proposal."

As I rode a cab to the club, I mulled over Gabe Tutt's seemingly immortal powers. How we had suffered his alcoholic breath and rancid temper over the years! A reeking vat of old hatreds and senseless greed, he had demanded flattery, accommodation, conciliation—and gotten it. Sworn enemy of pornography, socialism, welfare, mongrelization and disarmament, he was himself one of the most corrupt of men. His native Alabama groaned beneath the weight of munitions factories for obsolete shells, air bases peopled with ghosts, naval depots crammed with rusting junk, all bestowed on the state by Gabriel T. Tutt, Chairman of the Senate Armed Services Committee. And as this government largess descended on Alabama—factories, bases, shipyards—Gabe made damned certain that not a dollar of federal money went to hungry black children. That, he shouted, would be *communism!*

"The moral is clear, Edward," Ben had once said to me. "If you are a southern bigot with strong ties to the Pentagon, you can do anything you please and nobody will call you, because you are, by definition a *patriot*. But Heaven help you if your skin is off-color and your accent strange, like old Garcia."

Yes, the mighty Congress had chastised, humiliated and ousted Congressman Angel Lopez Garcia (who was in fact a bright legislator with a deep if sometimes askew social conscience), but old Gabe Tutt charged ahead—spending, cheating, roaring and damning his critics as Reds, traitors, socialists and pornographers.

A Negro porter advised me that Senator Tutt was

entertaining a private party, and that admission was by invitation only. But I bluffed my way in. He knew who I was. Black people respected Senator Hannaford and anyone associated with him. The papers that morning had carried the story that Homer Murphy, the Negro mayor of Washington, would be our Secretary of Health, Education and Welfare.

The door to a private room was opened for me, and I slithered into darkness. Not total darkness. A projection machine was whirring away, and on the white wall behind the luncheon table, a curious motion picture was being shown. The cone-shaped beam of white light illuminated swirls and clouds of cigar smoke. An audience of about a dozen men sat in heavy silence watching the black-and-white images on the wall.

On the wall, faintly out of focus, a naked man wearing a mask, sideburns, black sox and his shoes, was performing an unnatural act on a stringy woman of indeterminate age. She was on her knees. He was in back of her. No one, I thought, could be driven to sexual acts by such garbage.

"This vile thing has been shown in regular picture houses in New York," I heard Gabe croak. "Damn critics in New York claim it's art. Art, y'all heah?"

A second woman entered the scene. She was a stout lady, naked as a herring, and she sort of plopped herself on top of the masked man. All three bodies fell on the bed and commenced to work on one another. A good deal of stroking and licking was going on, but none of the participants appeared to have their hearts in their work.

The audience, Gabe's guests, were captivated. I studied the faces—eyes goggling, half-smiles on rubbery lips, cigars being chomped moistly, here a sweating forehead, there a trickle of saliva on a fat chin. Gabe knew how to hold his audience.

"We gonna suppress this," Senator Tutt rasped. "We gonna git all them pornographic peddlers, all them corrupters and Communists and perverts, and squash them lak you squash a boll weevil."

As my eyes grew accustomed to the gloom, I was able to pick out members of the luncheon group.

Item, there was General Clyde Upshaw, recently the presidential candidate of Save America. His eyes were like two points of ice and his back was ramrod straight. The hard lines of a frustrated military career—or was it constipation?—formed a fretwork around his neck and cheeks. Breathing deeply, he stared at the three actors, now lumped in a mish-mash of arms, legs, behinds and breasts on the bed.

Item, Congressman Lance Ruckett of South Dakota, clear-eyed, white-skinned, his boyish, chubby face gleaming with perspiration and sanctity. No cigar gleamed in his mouth. I knew him to be abstemious and exceedingly polite. He smiled too much, but he had a scorpion's sting and an air of ecclesiastical certitude. He would be a power in the new House of Representatives.

Item, Bates Pendragon, syndicated columnist, the gutsy, two-fisted, word-cracking hero of the far right. Pendragon was an odd bird—tweedy, mustachioed, broad-shouldered, a sort of conscious mimic of the young Hemingway, whom he imitated in his lust for shooting birds and small animals.

Item, his publisher, Cosmo Carl Pringle, old C.C. himself, white-thatched and ruddy-faced, a supporter of Save America and DOOR, who had personally written the scandalous editorials that depicted my boss as "a conscious, crafty, clever confidence man, catering to Communists and conniving with Kremlin criminals."

There were others—a retired admiral who had gotten rich by lobbying for "defense" contractors, a professor from Texas who had "proved" the biological inferiority of blacks, a fundamentalist preacher named Bewley who ran a prosperous mail-order prayer service, a superintendent of schools from up-state New York who had burned all the sex-education manuals in the county publicly.

A group, as Lou Parente would have put it, of "nice customers."

Yet they could not be dismissed lightly. General Upshaw and Senator Tutt had convinced almost eighteen million Americans that they were fit to govern the nation.

"Oh, I say, I say, look at that," boomed Bates Pendragon. The writer had a stentorian bellow of a voice. The accent was strongly eastern seaboard—good prep schools, Ivy League college. "Say, they really go at it."

"Filthy scum," Senator Tutt mumbled.

"Mongrels," General Upshaw hissed. I was surprised to hear his voice—a tight, reedy noise. During the campaign he had rarely spoken, just glowered and frowned.

"I say shoot them," the admiral suggested.

And the preacher: "Without benefit of trial."

"Well, you understand," Pendragon boomed. "This is a direct result of progressive education—John Dewey and the pragmatists, as well as gnosticism, eclecticism and the whole Galilean fallacy."

"We've got to get after the Supreme Court," Congressman Lance Ruckett said chirpily. "No reason why we can't impeach any man who votes to permit this sort of degrading filth. He turned to C. C. Pringle. "Say, that could be a darn good campaign for you fellows in the press. I'm very bullish about the make-up of the new House. I'm organizing a conservative study group to move things along."

"Sounds splendid, Lance," the publisher said.

"Impeach, hell," General Upshaw said. "I would like to get the people who produce these alone in a room, with a slippery elm club."

The admiral piped up. "In the old days, in the Navy, we got these sorts naked in the shower room and worked over them with wire brushes."

The grand finale: the three actors, having presumably consummated some kind of team orgasm (it had not been apparent on the screen) now turned to the audience and displayed their private parts, while sticking their tongues out at us.

The lights went on. Senator Tutt's aide, the young chap named Eustis, began rewinding the film. Gabe Tutt, lighting up a fresh cigar, espied me at the rear of the room.

"Who . . . whut?" he coughed. "Deever . . . whut the hell."

"Good afternoon, Senator. And gentlemen."

"You not invited."

"Oh yes. Your office phoned to say you wanted me here."

"Hunh. Don't recolleck." Gabe was thoroughly pickled, deep in booze.

"This has been a most instructive demonstration," I said.

A miasma of suspicion settled over the room. None of these people had any use for Ben Hannaford. To them he was the traitor personified, a man who should have been one of them—rich, puissant, plain-talking, hard as nails, a meeter of payrolls and a builder of cities. Yet he had chosen to run with people like Dalton Warfield and Maury Eisenberg and had even been tolerant of Angel Lopez Garcia.

"Senator Tutt," I said brashly. "I need a minute of your time. The President-elect has asked me to convey some information to you. Perhaps Mr. Eustis has a selected short subject he would run while you and I meet—Mickey Mouse or Bugs Bunny."

This got no laugh. The guests, resenting my intrusion, began to leave. Hands were pumped (no one sought mine), backs patted, belches smothered. Eustis packed up the screen and the projector. Then, with sneaky, self-conscious manner, he hastily collected some mimeographed sheets that lay about the lunch tables. I decided I wanted one. He left; Gabe and I were alone.

"Hunh, Deever, you still a putty smart li'l coon hound," Gabe said. The bourbon vaporized from his maw, assailing my nostrils. I marveled at his constitution. "But yew cain't fool Gabe. You not invited hyeah."

I tried my boyish grin. "True, Senator, but I figured you aren't quite ready to start taking on the President-elect. Or the President-elect's number-one boy."

"Now look, son. Yew go tell Hannaford whut you seen heah. Thass commonism. Thass whut the radical, bearded intellectuals are makin' of this country. Me and young Ruckett, we gonna git laws passed 'gainst this. We gonna end obscenity in this country."

"I doubt that the President-elect will want to give such laws top priority."

"He better," Gabe said menacingly. "He ain't such a big coon. We gon' git him up a piney tree with a pack o' mean ole hounds. Yeah."

"Well, maybe I spoke too soon. The senator does have strong feelings on obscenity in public life, sir."

"Yeah, now you talkin'."

"Yes. Mr. Hannaford feels that it is obscene for ten per cent of the farmers of your native Alabama to suck five million dollars a year in federal subsidies from the government, while the poor blacks of your state get less than two hundred and fifty thousand dollars a year for food assistance. That is the sort of obscenity that Mr. Hannaford does not intend to tolerate."

As I spoke, I had a sense of liberation, exhilaration. To

be candid, I had always feared Gabe Tutt. Now I was more or less telling him to go to hell.

"Whuzzat? Whuzzat 'bout food 'sisstance? Damn lie. Only people hongry in Alabama are shiftless niggers."

"Well, we can debate that later, sir. Perhaps with Congressman Gantry."

His eyes brightened. "Yeh, yeh. Gantry. Damned radical."

"Senator, I am here to discuss Congressman Gantry with you. We are advised that you intend to launch a campaign in the Senate to have Mr. Gantry's appointment to the cabinet rejected, on the basis of some trivial matters. Is that correct?"

Gabe's rheumy eyes vanished in the wrinkled folds of his eyelids. "Hee-hee. You damn said it. Ah got that Commie-lovin', sweet-talkin', skirt-chasin', race-mixin' Gantry where Ah want him. Playin' around with communist foundations. He ain't gon' be in no President's cabinet."

"Mr. Hannaford does not want you to oppose him."

"Cain't stop me."

"I would not be so certain, Senator Tutt."

"Hannaford threat'nin' me?" Gabe growled.

"This is no threat, sir," I said. "You know how Senator Hannaford works. He makes accords with people, agreements."

"Me 'n' Hannaford parted ways. Tell 'im."

"I think he knows that. You called him a coddler of Communists during the campaign."

"Ole Gabe is a plain speaker, boy."

"Then I'd best resort to some plain speaking of my own. You deserted our party. You chose to run on the Save America ticket with Upshaw. You insulted and abused my boss, and many of your associates came out flatly and called him a traitor. I don't recall you ever dissociated yourself from those remarks."

"Didn't have to, damn it."

"Perhaps. Now according to the hoary traditions of the Congress, any Southerner who runs out on the party and works against it, does so in the full conviction that he cannot be hurt. He will not be punished. He will not be reprimanded. It is simply assumed that the *heart* of our party, in the Congress at any rate, is the southern racist."

Tutt struggled to his feet. Cigar ashes cascaded down

82

his white shirt and his black tie. "You damn said it, Deever! Ain't no one gonna git Gabe Tutt off'n Armed Services or any place else! I been chairman Armed Services twenty years, and aim to stay theah! Goddamn and little fishes, I run the United States Senate, me and my friends!"

Palsy shivered his right hand. It shook so violently it knocked a glass of water from the soiled table. I slid him gently into a chair. His breath fluttered his lips.

"Don't count on it, Senator Tutt," I said.

"Don't count on whut?"

"On keeping your seniority and your committee plums. The President-elect has authorized me to inform you that his first order of business after inauguration will be getting you thrown right the hell out of the party."

"Whut? Whut? Hannaford said whut?" His eyes were blazing.

"You are to be stripped of all seniority. You will not only no longer be chairman of the Armed Services Committee, but you won't even be on it. In short, Senator Tutt, your number is up. The President-elect is a forgiving man but there are limits to his compassion. You will be just one more aging, corn-pone-chewing rustic, shorn of your power."

"Aaargh . . . aargh . . . aaargh . . ."

"My boss means every word of it. You will be lucky with a seat on the District of Columbia Committee. Or, if he feels kindly, Post Office and Civil Service."

"Goddamn Hannaford and goddamn you," he croaked. "Sunsabitches. Ain't you ever heerd of separation of powers?"

"That will get you nowhere. Hannaford has decided that this business of protecting you confederates has got to end. You're no better or worse than the Garcias. You have to take your medicine. When you stab your party in the back, you have to be punished."

Again his right arm began its palsied dance. I almost felt sorry for him. Gabe was in his eighties. I certainly did not want to hasten his end. "Aaaagh . . . kaaaagh . . . kraagh . . ."

"Now then, Senator," I said. "The President-elect is a reasonable man. If you will give me, here and now, your pledge as an honorable senator, in *writing*, that you have no intention, now or ever, of opposing Congressman Gantry, he will relent."

"Whut? Howzat?" Shrewd old owl; he saw the deal. "Ah keep mah seniority? Chairman Armed Services? Ever'thin' else?"

"The works. You will remain our beloved, respected and powerful chairman of Armed Services, with all the rights and privileges thereto pertaining."

Oddly, the quivering stopped and his right arm was still. "Hee-hee-hee. Ole Hannaford, he a feisty ole boy."

"Yes or no, Senator? I need a firm statement from you and a note in writing." I took a small white pad and a ball-point pen from my picket.

"Hee-hee . . . damn Hannaford . . . ole possum . . ."

"Here, I'll write it, and it will merely need your signature. You abide by it, and you will remain a tower of strength in the world's greatest deliberative body."

"Mebbe yes, mebbe no . . ."

"If it's mebbe no, Senator, you will be as naked as newborn shoat in a red dirt pigpen in the piney woods. Naked as an ole catfish strung up on a hookful of sowbelly."

"Dang, Deever, you put it jes' right. Gimme that ole paper." He didn't even bother reading what I'd written. Of course, he'd deny the whole thing if it ever came to a showdown. What we held over him was the massive power of the presidency, and he knew it. "Yeah, ole Hannaford, ole Ben. Used to be one of us. But he sold out. Thass whut he done, sold out."

"I suggest you keep those sentiments to yourself." I pumped Tutt's flaccid, freckled hand and left him slumped in a chair, his eyes closed.

"We ain't through with you, Deever," he rasped. "We ain't through with Hannaford neither."

I believed him. On the way out I noticed that Gabe's aide, Eustis, had failed to collect one of those mimeographed sheets he had seemed in such haste to harvest. I took one and stuffed it into my pocket.

Ben explained to me that his tactic with Gabe Tutt grew out of the fragile nature of our mandate. "We can't antagonize anyone at this stage, Edward. We got to make friends."

"You didn't make one of Gabe."

"No, but we shook him up. He'll move a little more carefully from now on."

"Hannaford spoke in more detail about how we had to move slowly, appeasing some people, shutting others up, accommodating, persuading. As he spoke a disturbing piece of newsfilm appeared on the evening TV news report which we were watching. On the Columbia campus, Kakamba Jones, recent candidate for Vice-President on the Black-and-Tan ticket, was haranguing a small crowd. "Genocide!" Jones screamed. "Race murder! This university is a white racist extermination center, no better than Auschwitz. This university has one purpose—the mass murder of black people!"

"How will you accommodate *them?*" I asked.

"Those people will be tougher," Ben said, as Kakamba Jones roared on. One got the idea that the trustees of Columbia were reincarnations of Himmler, Goebbels and Eichmann. What fills me with despair about these spokesmen for the angry minorities—and dear God, I know they have hundreds of burdens—is that they can make no gradations of evil, let alone good. If you dare to disagree with me, you are Hitler.

"Nothing seems to work with them," I said.

Ben got up and turned Kakamba Jones off. "They don't understand one essential fact of life. They have no mass support. They don't even have support in important places, like government, the press, the schools. Not only that, they managed to get Upshaw and Tutt close to eighteen million votes. They holler revolution, but the only revolution they'll bring about is the other kind—Hitler's kind."

"Many years ago, Senator," I said, "a fellow named Lewis wrote a novel called *It Can't Happen Here*. It was about the way fascism came to America. Do you think it could happen here?"

He looked grave. "Not so long as I'm in charge it won't. But we're in for some close calls, Edward."

Our staff work proceeded swiftly. Fred Goldstein had selected his press staff. Matthew Fixx had gotten together some able people to work on legislation, speech-writing and congressional liaison. Cleo Watterson had hired Ben's personal staff. It occurred to me I had been delinquent in finding a companionable young lady to help Fern. Several were interviewed, but none seemed to me sufficiently

85

genteel, yet interesting, to rouse Mrs. Hannaford from her querulous state. Until Vangie arrived.

To begin with, I liked her name—Evangeline Boswell. It summoned up all sorts of literary associations for me. I liked her nickname even better—Vangie.

"And of course, you're a direct descendant of James Boswell," I said.

She was impressed neither by my attempt at high-blown literary knowledge nor the flattery. "Daddy claims we are," she said. "All kinds of genealogical evidence, Malahide Castle papers and so on. But I don't believe it."

"Daddy?" I asked. I studied her résumé in front of me. "How obtuse of me. You're Burke Boswell's daughter."

"Golly, you make it sound so corrupt."

We both laughed. Burke Boswell was a wealthy Washington lawyer-cum-lobbyist, a remarkable fellow who had made a reputation for himself as a shrewd, sagacious pleader for a variety of awesome clients ranging from cosmetics and drugs manufacturers to missile makers.

"Why do you say that?" I asked. "You are his kin."

"Yes, but I don't want it to influence you. I know I might prove an embarrassment—the way Daddy wheels and deals and operates."

The act of crossing her long, hairless limbs excited me—the plaid miniskirt climbed and I saw a good deal of healthy thigh.

"Miss Boswell, if we decide to hire you, your father's eminence will have no bearing one way or the other. The President-elect and I are noted for our talents for doing what we think is right and caring very little for gossips and scandalizers."

"Oh, I know. I was in Kenya when you and Mr. Hannaford got involved in that mess with the money. But I read every single word in the overseas editions of *Time* and *Newsweek*."

Most girls would have been wary of mentioning the censure hearings. A spunky, outspoken type. "Kenya, yes, that's interesting." I glanced at the résumé. "Smith. Graduate work at NYU. Two years as a Peace Corps volunteer in Kenya, teaching English in a Luo village. Some office work, some teaching in Harlem."

She laughed. "Age twenty-five, single, health excellent.

It doesn't say that I led the occupation of the admissions office at Smith and was severely reprimanded."

"We certainly won't hold that against you. The President-elect is not intolerant of the views of young people."

She cocked her blond head. Her hair was straight, long, held in place at the side with a plain gold clip. "I get that song from Daddy a great deal. But the truth of the matter is, he and I are on different wave lengths. He's fine on generalities, but he won't come around when there's a showdown."

"Does your father know you are applying for a job with the new administration?"

"I'd never tell him. Let him read about it in the newspapers."

"Yet you seem to like him."

She shook her head at my apparent lack of perception. "Burke Boswell is a hard man to dislike—as his opponents in court find out. They start adoring him, and when he's got them melted, he socks them with everything."

"You're unfair to him. He's a widely respected lawyer."

"My father is a *lobbyist*. He makes millions by frightening foolish rich men that he, and only he, can worm his way into committees, courts, executive agencies and get them what they want—whether it's a rise in freight rates or a contract for GI underwear or a tariff on Japanese steel."

"But he gets the job done. And he seems to be a most honorable sort of man."

Vangie sort of whooped or guffawed. "Oh, Mr. Deever! My father is as full of stuffing as a Christmas turkey! He claims he's not a lobbyist, that he doesn't get millions for his fat cats. Well, if that's the case, he's sure as hell cheating *someone*. Those idiots who *employ* him, like Hasluck Cosmetics or Holyrood Paper Products."

Her sassy attitude captivated me. I had the notion that she would be good for Fern. And she would be fun to have around. When she moved her legs again, I stared. Panti-hose, I believe they call those odd garments. I had a thousand things to do that afternoon, but I was enjoying myself, and I kept her.

"Those huge bracelets," I said. "They're unusual."

"From the Masai. My friends in Kenya. Here, smell."

I sniffed the multicolored beaded hoops on her strong wrists. "Odd. Sort of a gamey odor."

"It's rancid sheep fat," Vangie informed me. "The Masai rub it on themselves to keep bugs away."

"And I take it you've used it to keep the wolves away."

"Wolves don't bother me." She paused and stared impudently at me. "Nor foxes."

This was a hit, a palpable hit. Because of my rather sharp, small features, *Time* magazine had often referred to me as "fox-faced Edward Deever" or the "foxy aide to Ben Hannaford."

"You're hired," I said. "But you should know what you're being hired for."

"I'll take anything—press staff, Congress, I'm not choosy."

"We want someone like you to be Mrs. Hannaford's social secretary."

Vangie turned her long head sideways. The lamp on my desk glinted in that single gold clip over her ear. *"Mrs.* Hannaford?"

"That's the idea. The First Lady is in need of a good right hand. Someone poised, and well-connected in town, and efficient. You score high on all three."

"It's not what I had in mind."

"Sorry, Miss Boswell. I advise you to accept the offer. You will find Mrs. Hannaford a gracious, sweet and undemanding person. Too much so, I fear. She needs someone like you to talk to, to confide in." I reached across the desk and touched her firm hand. "You'll be doing me a big favor. I know you're right for the job."

"You mean . . . right in the White House? In and out of all those private rooms?"

"That's the idea."

Again she guffawed—that upper-class whoop, which in women of lower social rank would be considered rude, but in model WASPs has a certain charm. "If the SDS mob at Smith could see me! And what will my Afro-American buddies say?"

I handed her a form to fill out. "They will no doubt try to infiltrate, which would please us no end. Answer everything, including the loyalty oath, Miss Boswell. You are on staff."

Cleo Watterson peered over her spectacles at me, after I'd introduced Vangie to her. Ben's secretary and the young lady chatted briefly, then Vangie departed. "Too pretty," Cleo muttered. "She should lower her skirts and muss her hair."

I knew what was bugging Cleo. The last good-looking girl I had hired was Maria Valdez. Ben had become infatuated with her, and the saucy girl had encouraged him. There had been no affair; I was sure of that. But he'd teetered on the brink. Cleo did not want a repeat performance. Nor did I.

"I think Miss Boswell is a cool customer," I said. "She's one of those political, sharp-tongued types. Used to occupy buildings at Smith. Peace Corps, that sort of thing."

Cleo just shook her pretty gray head. If she was worried about Ben having another of his rare, rare flings, I was not. After all, he was to be our President, and as we all know, Presidents are all moral, faithful, sexless, impassive men, impervious to the flesh and its temptations.

I had forgotten about the mimeographed sheet that I had stuffed into my pocket after my confrontation with Senator Tutt. Alone with Fred Goldstein, we studied the paper. It was headed simply WEEKLY STRATEGY REPORT. There was no indication as to who had issued it, whose strategy was involved, or anything else to indicate its origin.

"These guys are getting secretive again," Fred said gloomily.

I told him who had been present at Gabe Tutt's screening of dirty movies, and he pursed his lips. "A convention of ball-breakers. Tutt, Upshaw, C. C. Pringle, Pendragon. The one I can't stand is Congressman Lance Ruckett. Where the hell does he get his dough? How dumb can some millionaires be, forking money over to that grinning little putz?"

"This damn thing is fascinating," I said. "It explains a lot."

"Yeah, and it has a helluva logic to it. Those hard-noses are a lot smarter than the hairy kids and the Afros."

The strategy sheet read as follows:

Concerned conservatives may well ask why our organizations are not engaging in public protests or counter-demonstrations over the recent acts of violence by student radicals against the universities.

89

The answer is very simple: the SDS vandals and terrorists, the black savages, are *doing our job for us.*

Strange as it may seem, that is the case. It behooves every patriot, every conservative, every believer in the republic, to remain *neutral* and *silent,* while the bearded Communists, traitors, cannibals and pornographers bring the universities to their knees.

Why is this our strategy?

Because these very universities—the Harvards and Berkeleys and Columbias and CCNYs are the real enemies of patriotic conservatives. It is in our direct interest to see them nullified, weakened, shattered, if necessary, *burned to the ground.*

Every un-American, radical, socialistic notion in currency in this country today was nurtured and disseminated at some university. Yes, the faculties of Columbia and Harvard and CCNY and Berkeley are the real guilty parties. They sowed the dragon's seed; the dragons are now destroying them. And all to the good. Let them devour each other.

Once the wild radical students, and the "Afro-Americans" have successfully weakened and gutted these so-called halls of learning, reduced them to chaotic slums, the time will be ripe for the patriots to move against them.

We repeat: *Conservatives should sit back, wait and say nothing.* Make no protest when these wild-eyed children barricade some dean, beat some professor, burn another's research. They are bringing down people who deserve to be destroyed. Let the black lunatics scream genocide and brandish shotguns and threaten faculties; the more these two groups assault one another, the better the climate for the eventual triumph of patriotism.

Please advise your local conservative groups, your strategy committees, your neighborhood associations to remain neutral and uncommitted as these depredations continue.

"I didn't think they were that intelligent," I said, after studying the sheet.

"How smart do you have to be to figure that out?" Fred asked rhetorically. "You'd think those jerky kids and those *schwarzers* would understand it also?"

90

"It's the Weimar Republic all over. The Communists attacking liberals and socialists and trade unions, battling them to the death, calling them 'social fascists.' And guess who was waiting in the wings, ready to pick up the pieces."

Fred ran a hand through his kinky orange hair. "Fellow with a little black mustache? Hollered a lot? Had funny ideas about Jewish persons?"

We could still joke about it. But both us knew it was far from a humorous situation. I decided to prepare a memo for Ben. The more I thought of Congressman Lance Ruckett and the Conservative study group he was going to organize, the less happy I was.

A few days after I had hired Evangeline Boswell as Fern's social secretary—she had not yet come to work, since she had some loose ends to take care of in New York—her father came to our attention. The Boswell family was destined to play a major part in our Administration.

It started when Ben roused me from a weary sleep. (We had been putting in fifteen-, sixteen-hour working days.) "Edward, turn on your television set to the 'Today' program. That fellow Boswell is on. He's debating Gage on that atomic testing business."

Yawning, I called for my morning coffee and switched on the hotel TV set. In glorious scarlets and greens, the "Today" Washington studio bloomed before my blinking eyes. On either side of an NBC commentator sat Burke Boswell, lobbyist and lawyer, and Senator Gage (Honey-Tonsils) Hopewell, our beloved Majority Leader, and an old associate of Ben's. Senator Hopewell was the Hill's leading character, and he wallowed in his role, intoning his pompous speeches as if each word were coated with margarine. He had a round face, a bulbous red nose like W. C. Fields, and two bushy sprouts of cottony white hair above each ear. His eyes popped, and he could enlarge them to frightening size to express shock, outrage, fascination, disapproval or disbelief. Truly an old hambone was Honey-Tonsils, but also a cunning, shifty, treacherous and extremely conservative man—who had to be watched at all times. I wondered how Mr. Burke Boswell would fare with him.

"Mr. Boswell," the NBC moderator began, "is it correct

91

that you, on behalf of your client, Hasluck Industries, intend to sue the Atomic Energy Commission to force it to stop underground testing in Nevada?"

"That is correct, sir," Boswell replied. "My client has millions of dollars invested in factories in Nevada. We cannot have that investment jeopardized by repeated underground blasts. We cannot be victimized because the Pentagon and the AEC feels it has to destroy the air, the water and the very earth on which we walk. We intend to fight it right into the courts."

"Senator Hopewell, as chairman of the Joint Senate-House Atomic Energy Committee, you must feel rather differently than Mr. Boswell," the commentator said. "Would you care to comment?"

Here it came—the wind, the gas, the big blow. "Yaaaaas," Gage chanted. "I must perforce deplore Mr. Boswell's rash and precipitate action. He is trifling, may I say, with our very security, our survival, indeed, the survival of the free world. Yaaaaas."

Only an old blowhard like Gage could still invoke that catch-all "the free world" with a straight face. How free? As free as Greece? Or Nicaragua? Haiti?

"The senator doesn't have to lecture me on national defense. Those big bombs could be set off somewhere else. They're polluting the air, poisoning the springs, causing nervous breakdowns among our workers, and worst of all, ruining millions of dollars worth of merchandise."

"What might that merchandise be, Mr. Boswell?" the moderator inquired, glinting, as if he had the lawyer trapped.

"No secret. Various cosmetics. Deodorants. Mouthwash. Perfumed soaps. Shampoo. Hasluck makes a varied line of goods. What is happening, as our scientists tell us, is that every time one of these underground blasts goes off, the structure of the polyesters is altered, and the basic amalgam, the congeners and chemical cognates, are disordered, so that a deodorant that is supposed to smell like attar of roses, comes out more like rotting mackerel. This is, I must stress, a very serious matter for a company that has invested millions in the manufacture and marketing of scents."

This was a truly remarkable speech. It marked a turning point in America's attitude to the various lords of the A-bomb, the AEC, the Pentagon and the Senate-House

92

Atomic Energy Committee. In effect, what Boswell was saying was that his client's underarm sprays and oral rinses were *far more important than the perfection of the mighty instruments of megadeath.* Though it was a bold position to take, I had the feeling that Boswell was on strong ground. And I sensed that old Hopewell understood this, and was wary of his opponent.

"Mr. Boswell," chimed Gage, "Mr. Boswell, how can you sit there and maintain that Mr. Hasluck's perfumed toiletries, yaaaas, those various unguents and sprays and lotions, are of greater import than the defense of our beloved land?"

"I'm arguing facts, Senator," Boswell said in a loud voice. "This country needs deodorants as much as it needs atomic warheads."

Of course. I should have remembered. The stress on deodorants should have tipped me off. This man was the one Lou Parente had written about some months ago, dubbing him "Armpit" Boswell because of his tenacious and dedicated lobbying for the cosmetics industry. To me, he looked like the kind of fellow we needed in the Administration.

Boswell was an odd-looking man. He was seated, but he obviously was a soaring giraffe with endless legs and arms. He had a large-featured, mobile face—a long nose, a prognathous chin, and wide, vivacious eyes. His hair was wheat-blond, and he wore it long and lank (like his daughter) and his skin color—even making allowances for the livid television hues—appeared to be a rich scarlet, a true bourbon blush.

"Senator, you and I know that those tests are nothing but more of the same," Boswell went on. "I've had AEC scientists admit to me that one blast is the same as another. Why keep it up? They aren't even aimed at anything—just big blowups under the ground. Someone has to speak out against this, and I'm glad to do it, in behalf of my clients."

"Well, let me state," Honey-Tonsils choraled, "no man is more friendly to the great creative, yaaaas, productive boons of our free enterprise system, and that would include the Hasluck Corporation and its many profitable ventures. But really, Mr. Boswell, how can you and your esteemed client be willing to place yourself in the same boat, the same leaky craft, so to speak, as the bearded radicals, the fuzzy-headed intellectuals, the friends of Red Russia and Red China, the appeasers and coddlers and disarmers who are blind to the mad depredations of the Communist beast? Is that any place for a wealthy corporation to be?"

Boswell shifted his stork legs, smiled—with great warmth I thought—and responded. "We don't care who is in the boat, Senator, and what their reasons are. But if there is a leaky craft around, it's the AEC and the boys in the Pentagon. They keep telling us those tests are safe. We don't believe it. We have proof they're not. I refer to the last issue of the *Bulletin of the Atomic Scientists.*"

"Well, now really . . ."

But Boswell was no man to be deterred by Gage's gonging voice. From his pocket he took out a magazine and began to read. "A committee of our top physicists have raised these questions," Boswell said crisply. "First, why has the government put a lid of secrecy on the official report of a marked rise in tritium, or radioactive water, in the area of the test site? Second, why has the committee of which, you, Senator, are chairman, refused to vote for a new and improved monitoring of installations in Nevada? Third, why are repeated demands from the public for information on this year's underground megatonnage repeatedly ignored? Fourth, what safeguards are being taken to prevent accidents like the recent underground slippage of a six-mile-long, twenty-foot-high escarpment, which geologists are certain was a result of last June's one megaton test? And fifth, what is being done, first to investigate, and second to prevent outbreaks of diarrhea, skin rash and loss of hair among thousands of sheep at the Mormon Mill Crossing Ranch, sixty miles south of the AEC test area? Now, Senator, until some responsible agency of the government responds to these questions, we will have no choice but to take you people to court."

No one—or very few people—dared use the rude expression "you people" in referring to senate gods like Gage Hopewell, not to mention the Department of Defense and the Atomic Energy Commission. *You people,* indeed. But there was something so boyish, so charming, so outgoing about Mr. Burke Boswell, that Honey-Tonsils took it without even a nod of his cotton-fringed head.

"Mr. Boswell, walk softly," Senator Hopewell oozed.

"Yaaas, I too respect the scientists, but they are, in effect, special pleaders. I have faith abiding in our military men."

"Did you say special pleaders, Senator?" the lobbyist asked. "There are no more special pleaders and self-serving operators than our generals. Senator, you and your pals may as well face up to it. The day is long gone when the American people will accept on face value anything the generals tell them. That goes for airplanes costing a half a million dollars each, when a civilian firm can buy the same darn crates for a hundred thousand bucks, or for phony information about those atomic explosions in Nevada."

Gage turned in his seat. His rotundity weighed him down, and made an odd comparison with Boswell's skeletal figure. "Sir, you are mouthing sentiments that will give aid and comfort to our enemies."

"Sorry, Senator," Boswell said joyfully, "but that scratched old record has to go also."

Now it was understood in Washington that nobody talked like that to Senator Gage Hopewell of Wisconsin, Majority Leader, medicine man, vendor of Indian vegetable oil soap, and defender of every railroad, dairy, tool-and-die works and cement factory in his state. His esteemed law firm represented many of these. And funny old Gage saw to it that nothing bad could happen to them in Congress. Petty monarch, old wiseacre, Falstaff with a strong sense of double-entry bookkeeping, Honey-Tonsils was not a man to be crossed lightly.

"I put it to you, sir," Senator Hopewell pumped. "Your patriotism is in question."

"Senator, what could be more patriotic than a free enterprise corporation giving jobs to thousands supplying goods for millions, insisting on its rights? No, sir, we will not tolerate contamination of our mouthwashes and deodorants by underground blasts. I wish I could make you understand that this has nothing to do with morality."

"What indeed, has it to do with?" Gage sang.

"Money."

There was a tense pause; Hopewell with his mouth agape, unable to respond to this ultimate truth. The NBC moderator had no more questions. Mr. Burke Boswell had brought the discussion around to a theological climax, an apogee of revealed faith. Indeed, what could be more

95

American and patriotic than his concern for his client's money?

A few hours later Matthew Fixx and I stood in Ben's suite and nodded our agreement—Fixx somewhat less enthusiastically than me—as the boss announced that he had found a Secretary of Defense.

"That Boswell will do fine," Ben said. "He treed old Gage like a smart hound on a fat coon. Did me good to see Gage squirm, the old rogue."

On the way to see Hannaford, I had pulled some old Parente columns on Boswell from my file, and I now referred to them. "Sir," I said to Ben, "do you really think the Administration can sustain a man who has been dubbed 'Armpit' Boswell?"

"That doesn't bother me. That lanky galoot can charm a buzzard out of a paloverde tree. Notice how he smiles when he lets the zinger loose? He'll stand the Armed Services Committee on its ear."

" 'Armpit' isn't all," I went on, studying the clippings. "Last year Boswell lobbied before the Interstate Commerce Commission to raise the rate at railroad restrooms from a nickel to a dime. He won, of course. Parente nicknamed him 'Pay-Toilet' Boswell."

Matt Fixx looked horrified. "Goodness. A Defense Secretary known as *Pay-Toilet?*"

Ben was convulsed in laughter; Matt Fixx was shocked. "Can't wait to get that man on the team," the boss laughed. "He's too damn good." He wiped his eyes and pounded the desk with his huge fist. "Boys, do you realize what that string bean got away with this morning? Now, just think about the opposition to A-bomb testing in this great land. Who has led it? SANE—intellectuals, eggheads, a sort of mousey group. Mothers March for Peace. Scientists. Dreamers. Whole bunch of *outsiders*."

"Old Gage would eat them alive," I said. "And the generals wouldn't even listen."

"You know it for the truth," Hannaford said. "Now along comes this spindle-shanked high-pockets Boswell, this money man, this smart-ass lawyer who scares the dumb corporations into paying him off for conning the government, and he says, 'Stop blowing your damn bombs, you're ruining my client's mouthwash!' And you

96

know something? He's going to *win*. Oh, he'll make 'em listen."

"Well," Matt offered, "it will be a fascinating interface. I mean, if we can get Mr. Boswell in a one-to-one relationship with the Pentagon."

"Proves Hannaford's First Law of Politics," Ben said.

Matt and I exchanged tolerant looks; the boss had to be afforded his idiosyncrasies.

"Don't ever forget it," the President-elect said. "In this great country, all the right things get done for the wrong reasons."

Two days later, a second member of the now famous Washington Boswell family joined our Administration. All that was necessary was a single private meeting between Hannaford and the lobbyist; they chatted, liked one another, and the offer was accepted.

Boswell's parting gift to Hasluck Industries was a restraining order from the federal court in Nevada ordering the Atomic Energy Commission to cease and desist at once all underground testing until such times as proper safeguards and monitoring devices were installed. For these services, I later learned, which involved about three days' work, Boswell received a fee of sixty thousand dollars. I learned about it through Lou Parente's column. The newspaperman (like myself) was intrigued with Boswell and appeared to have some kind of pipeline to his office.

President-elect Hannaford has picked himself a winner in his Defense Secretary, the millionaire lawyer Burke (Armpit) Boswell. Boswell is the man who forced the Atomic Energy Commission to halt their underground blasts in Nevada because the contamination and reverberations were ruining his client's mouthwash, underarm deodorants, shampoos, and assorted cosmetics.

Said client, the terrifying Alden Hasluck, the cosmetics tycoon, screamed bloody murder when Boswell submitted his bill for three days' work—a neat sixty thousand dollars. Boswell then snapped back at Hasluck's Washington man:

"You tell Hasluck to pay up in a hurry. It'll give him a little class. He can sit around the Fontainebleau in

Miami Beach and boast to his gin rummy pals how he paid Burke Boswell sixty grand for three days."

The money came through. We can't wait to see Boswell go to work on the generals and the admirals.

The press appeared to be confused by the Boswell appointment to a job so close to the nation's security, but they refrained from criticizing. After all, the man's prime interest was money and big business. How could he be all bad? Only Bates Pendragon, the new right-wing belleletrist, writing for C. C. Pringle's chain, had expressed doubts.

But Pendragon's was a lone voice. Just about everyone was ready to accept the tall fellow with the frank, manly grin. He was too American, too much in the grain, not to be trusted.

A few days later, Henry Kaspar, the man sought in the attempted assassination and the wounding of Mona Varnum, was gunned down by Mexican federal police, in Baja, California.

Judge Moscowitz, the FBI director, at once reported to President Kretz, and the latter, a model of consideration where Ben was concerned, summoned the boss to a special briefing at the White House. I went along at Ben's invitation.

How odd it all seemed, sitting there in the pleasant oval office, with its high scalloped niches over the bookcases, as President Kretz nodded fitfully at Moscowitz's narration.

Here were three totally different men—Kretz, a North Carolina newspaper publisher who had accidentally become President, Ben Hannaford, a vigorous multimillionaire who had brawled his way up from tar-paper shacks to the high office, and Judge Samuel Moscowitz, a Jewish tailor's son, who by dint of brilliance and dedication had become one of our chief law enforcement officers. Their backgrounds were utterly dissimilar, yet all three had that consciousness of service or working in the public weal.

"I am sincerely sorry that our agents were not able to stop the Mexican federal police from killing the man," Judge Moscowitz said. "Our people were arriving by chartered flight to Punto Chivatos, and as you may know, airfields down on the peninsula are less than adequate—

dirt strips, if you're lucky. They had to circle the strip twice at Punto Chivatos, and while they were, the Mexicans returned Kaspar's fire. He was holed up in a fishing lodge and was well armed."

The judge showed us a radiophoto of the dead man. Ben and President Kretz studied the photograph and were silent. I knew what they were thinking. There was, if truth be known, something so pathetic about Henry Kaspar, that it aroused their pity—as it did mine. There seemed a total shaming in his violent end.

"I still can't understand how he got through all the security in Ramada City," President Kretz said.

"I have investigated that matter thoroughly," Judge Moscowitz said. "And as I have pointed out to Senator Hannaford, it is a price we pay for permitting such wide coverage of public events. I don't know the answer. We can't restrict the media. Kaspar simply stole a set of television credentials, decked himself out in three or four badges, picked up one of those microphones and walked, unmolested into a hotel room. We can count ourselves lucky that he couldn't manage the apparatus and his .38 at the same time."

Ben clasped his hands and looked pensive. "You, of course, won't close the files on this."

"No, sir," Moscowitz said. "Every clue that Kaspar left will be tracked down. We've interviewed over two hundred people already, and these will continue. But I am convinced we are dealing with a single individual. If we study the history of these assassinations, we have found that almost always to be the case. There simply is no organized conspiracy at work."

"Sometimes I wonder," Hannaford said. "I don't argue that these assassinations are connected. But it seems to me the people who get killed or shot at all have one thing in common."

"What is that?" the President asked.

"They want to help black people."

Hayward Kretz, as I believe I have pointed out, was from North Carolina, but he was anything but a racist. Tolerant, wishing all men well, he had a fair-to-middling record on civil rights. I think he felt hurt that blacks didn't like him better, that they were somewhat ungrateful. Ben's remark seemed to rouse some mild sense of guilt, of chores undone that disturbed him. "I don't quite follow you, Senator," he said.

"But look at who we've murdered," said Ben. "The Kennedy brothers, Martin Luther King, Medgar Evers. No one's ever taken a shot at Gabe Tutt, or Lance Ruckett, or anyone who thinks black people should be kept in their place."

President Kretz remained silent; he did not like the calm waters of his mind ruffled by waves of doubt.

"You see, the tradition of killing people and getting away with it, is an old American one," Ben said. "Let's be honest. You and I are both Southerners, Mr. President. And that's where the conspiracy has existed for a long time, as well as on some good northern police forces. I don't have to recall 'em—Emmett Till, those four little girls blown up in Birmingham, that black army colonel in Georgia, those two white boys and the Cheney boy in Mississippi. We could run down to the NAACP right now and get a list three blocks long."

"And of course," Judge Moscowitz said, "the blacks now feel that it's a two-way street. What are street crimes, but a kind of blind vengeance? Read the psychology of muggers—they do it less for the money, which is often trivial, than for the satisfaction of humiliating a white face. Carl Sandburg put it aptly, gentlemen, when he told us that the slums take their revenge."

But President Kretz, dreaming of his acres of pines and his clear trout streams in the Great Smokies, had lost interest. His sea-blue eyes drifted toward the window and he brushed back his snowy hair. We understood the interview was over.

As we rode in the limousine back to the Manger Hay-Adams, Ben told me that he had already received fifteen hundred threatening letters since the election. "I'm doing better than Lyndon already," he said. "He got twelve thousand in four years. Looks like we'll break the record."

It was dusk. The lights of Washington were fuzzed with a wintry haze. The National Guardsmen directed traffic on corners where no police were on duty. It was a dreadful thing to see in the capital city.

"Edward, somehow, we have to lower the national boiling point, get people talking to one another again," he said. "That professor at Harvard was right. You keep talking bombs and death and body counts and kill ratios and you create an atmosphere in which kids think nothing of slitting an old lady's throat for her purse. And the brighter kids want to bring everything down because they're disgusted. And the blacks are violent because they know the historical truth."

"I wish I had some bright ideas," I said gloomily.

"Oh, we'll come up with some. People like Boswell will help."

I suppressed a laugh. "Really, Senator . . ."

"Don't laugh, Edward. You'll notice how nice the press was to us on the appointment. Even that fellow Pendragon couldn't insult us. Boswell is a fixer, a trimmer, shrewder than an old coyote. We can't use zealots these days, we need accommodators."

"I am to assume that Mr. Boswell's fixing and trimming will be purely in the public interest?"

"Purely."

I now had the job of introducing Evangeline Boswell to her mistress, Fern Hannaford. Vangie had shipped her belongings from New York and was living with her family until she would move into the White House as a member of the official family.

"She's more than welcome so long as she doesn't smoke marijuana in the Red Room," Ben said. "Or plant the damn stuff in Jacqueline Kennedy's garden."

I assured him that Vangie, who had surely inhaled her share of grass, was nonetheless a model of middle-class virtues. His approval secured, I told Mrs. Hannaford, and she invited us to tea that afternoon.

For a while nothing was said. These two women, it seemed to me, were separated by a grand canyon of age, background, ideas, prejudices and tastes. Fern seemed to have declined since I had last spoken to her. The books I had given her rested on a lamp table where I'd left them. Again, I sniffed that minty odor, the sign of the private drinker.

I was terribly sorry for her. All her money, her horses, her land, her oil, her pure-bred dogs, all these seemed irrelevant to the world into which she would be hurled in less than a month. I realized that aggressive young people like Vangie Boswell, who were in tune, engaged, activist, had the right idea. You had to get into the thick of things;

if you didn't, you wallowed about and eventually disintegrated. I could understand those surveys showing why wealthy suburban wives became boozers or had dismal affairs.

"Perhaps Edward has told you, Miss Boswell," Fern said, after she had, with natural elegance served the tea, "I shall not find this life easy. All during the years we lived in Washington, I did not entertain much, and then only for a few select friends. We were not party-givers or party-goers."

"I can understand that, Mrs. Hannaford," Vangie said. "Washington parties are the most overrated affairs in the world. The men all stand in a group talking politics, and the women are left alone to gossip."

"How accurately you put it, dear," Fern said. "I am not one for gossip, or carrying tales, or . . ." Abruptly, she touched her throat—she was wearing a sensible high-necked maroon dress—in a gesture suggesting fatigue, or confusion. "I'm not too well today, Edward. Staying cooped up here is not good for me, but I don't feel like going out."

We said nothing. Vangie darted a puzzled look at me—as if to say, *I was not hired as a nurse.*

"The weather has been miserable," I said. "Ramada weather, all that sunshine, spoils us, Mrs. H."

Something more affecting than Washington's chills and vapors was disturbing the woman. For a moment I was desperate. I seemed to have ended up handling another of Ben's problems, but one I could barely manage. Was Vangie Boswell really the person who could arouse Fern, cheer her up? Could anyone do it?

"Do you ride, Miss Boswell?" Fern asked.

"Yes, I love to, but I haven't for some time."

Ah, ah, common ground. I uttered a small prayer of thanks for Vangie's patrician mother, the kind bred in the saddle.

"I do miss the horses," Fern said wistfully.

"Maybe we can go out together," Vangie said. "I used to own a bay gelding and a roan mare."

Dull-eyed, I sat there sipping my hot orange pekoe. There I was, fox-faced, slick-haired Eddie Deever, the bright boy from Indian Mound, Ohio, who could not ride.

"English or Western?" Mrs. Hannaford asked.

"Mother was a firm English saddle advocate."

"Well, my dear, we'll change that. We are Westerners, tried and true."

It was decided that the wet, cold weather was not conducive to riding, but that with the first sign of spring, they would don jodhpurs and boots, saddle up and away. Meanwhile, Vangie would report every morning to Mrs. Hannaford, and they would plan a social schedule.

"The first big affair after the Inaugural," I said, "will be the reception for the Daughters of the American Revolution. About sixteen hundred of them. I'll get some information on it from Mrs. Kretz."

Fern turned pale. The notion of receiving sixteen hundred women stunned her. Then Vangie laughed and broke the tension.

"Golly, Mrs. Hannaford, if two good horsewomen like us can't ride herd on the DAR, who can?" she asked.

Fern afforded us a wan smile; she could still smile.

"I've got a suggestion," Vangie said. "There's a special exhibition of Winslow Homers at the Corcoran, and maybe Mrs. Hannaford would like to see it. We could leave right now and still make it before closing. It shouldn't be too crowded."

Again, that pained blankness marched across Fern's face. "Corcoran . . . ?"

"Do you like Winslow Homer as much as I do?" Vangie asked. "Those Maine coastlines, and those Gulf Stream pictures! They make you feel you're there."

By God, it worked. Fern was on her feet, kneading her hands, smiling. "I am not certain I can recall Mr. Homer's work," she said. "Perhaps I've never seen it, to be honest."

On the way out I squeezed Vangie's hand and whispered in her ear: "Good girl, good thinking. Keep her at it—museums, parks, the works. She's got a lot on the ball, but she has to be pushed a little."

I left them at the elevator as the secret service man approached them. Fern was smiling. I wondered how long it was since she had been through an art gallery. In my mind's eye I saw her progressing from the traditionalist Winslow Homer up through de Kooning, and on to Warhol and Oldenberg. But fantasy is not my strong suit, and I watched them depart with a sense of achievement; Fern was coming out of her shell.

The New Year came, not reviving "old desires" as the *Rubáiyát* tells us, but filling me with a sense of dire events in the making. In the winter months, the American tradition has it, riots do not erupt, cities and universities remain quiescent, hibernating until the sun warms the streets and renders mob action pleasurable. But such was not the case in January. President Kretz, in the waning days of his authority, appeared determined to make Ben's assumption of power extremely difficult.

I have already mentioned that National Guardsmen were now permanent fixtures on the streets of a dozen American cities. How appalling that a rational man like Hayward Kretz was forced to draconic measures! There were shooting incidents daily—a black teen-ager here, a drunken Negro laborer there, pot-smoker on this coast, a Mexican agitator on the other. We had, it seemed, settled down to a modified siege. The poor, the black, the young, were learning the grim truth—they possessed no real power. The power lay elsewhere. And it could be a cruel and repressive power, one which drew nods of approval, of certification from millions of work-a-day, wage-earning Americans. Time and again I was reminded of Ben's perceptive comment when, in 1968, we had watched on television as the Chicago police bloodied and battered the youngsters in front of the Conrad Hilton Hotel.

"The whole world is watching!" the kids had chanted—assuming that their martyrdom would stir the minds and hearts of America, and perhaps the world. "Yeah," Ben growled in disgust, "the whole world is watching and *approving."* While the liberal commentators, and the well-educated élite prophesied that police brutality would sway millions to the side of the long-haired children, Ben knew otherwise. He knew the heart of his country. He did not need the pollsters to tell him a few weeks later than 71 per cent of the nation *approved* of what the cops had done with their clubs and their mace and their fists.

For all of President Kretz's kindliness, he, too, was aware of the bald facts. The mass of Americans were not wild-haired, pot-smoking, visionary youngsters, ready to make common cause with, and excuse the extravagances of, aroused blacks. Hardly. Not at all. The bulk of Americans wanted these disturbers of the peace suppressed. And so, in January, the President, upset by what appeared to be a new rash of outbreaks on the campuses, signed into law the Emergency Riot Control Act—to the applause of a sympathetic Congress. In a day or two, thanks to the efficiency of Attorney General Fawcett ("Those who impede others from their education, should be rounded up and sent to detention camps until they learn to behave") the first mass arrests were made at Columbia, CCNY, Berkeley, Wisconsin and, of all places, Texas Christian University, where a small, vocal SDS unit had been formed.

So swiftly did the Federal Government move under the ERCA, that local authorities, the arrested demonstrators and their lawyers were left agape and confuted by the actions. Public opinion polls taken at the time showed that 68 per cent of the American people approved of sweeping roundups of the occupiers and demonstrators.

I asked for, and received, a background report of what was happening at Columbia from a distraught Judge Moscowitz. The account was in dry, bureaucratic language, but it augured ill for Ben and for the problems we would face.

With Fred Goldstein present, I studied the report. Later, we could huddle with Matt Fixx and draw up recommendations for the President-elect. But what kind? What roads were open to us to reach the infuriated, alienated young? God knows they had a lot to be angry about. But what distressed me was that they refused to understand the depth of the national hatred they had aroused. I was convinced at that time that a good portion of the American people were quite ready not only to arrest them and stick them in "detention camps," as the Attorney General indicated, but *to shoot them out of hand*.

One may wince. One may call me a Cassandra. One may say that Deever underestimates the compassion in most Americans. But such doubters do not know, as "The Shadow" used to tell us, "What evil lurks in the minds of men." I know. I have been close to the centers of political power. I try not to think about how we flirt with danger, how thin is the ice on which we walk, how close we are to the brute, the ape man with the bone club.

The FBI director's report began as follows:

Last November, that part of Columbia University north of West 120th Street, known as Teachers College, was forcibly occupied by extremist black groups headed

105

by the Afro Avengers. It was renamed Lumumba University. After much debate the Board of Trustees of Columbia voted to turn all of Teachers College over to the black groups, who then formalized their seizure. The buildings are now ruled by an *"Indaba,"* a Zulu word, meaning a council of wise men.

The area has become self-governing, bristling with arms, and, according to our informants, split into factions, too complicated to describe here. Essentially— Lumumba University is separated from Columbia, run by its own council, headed by Kakamba Jones, with its own curriculum. It has no accreditation with any university association, and has awarded no degrees.

Because of the success of the Afro Avengers in bending the trustees to their will, radical white groups on the campus have grown more militant. They feel they have been "up-staged" by the blacks, who have literally revolted, seized and held part of the university.

At a meeting of white radical groups between Christmas and New Year's, a parallel action was decided upon. Unlike previous campus occupations, which had to do with specific programs, this seizure would have an "existential goal." The students would occupy a building, arm themselves, hold off police and declare themselves a separate, independent school. The university would be faced with this dilemma: if blacks could be permitted to seize and keep and run a segment of the school, why not a coalition of the leftist whites—SDS, Progressive Laborites, Mao-ists and Third Worlders?

The report went on to indicate some of the leaders of the new coalition. Among them was a man I had met some years ago in Washington, a poet-playwright named Arvid Farbelman, a bearded, foul-mouthed, publicity-seeking fellow, who at the age of forty-four, was still regarded as a "youth" leader, a guru to the young.

In early January, when President Kretz enacted into law the Emergency Riot Control measure giving the Federal Government new powers of law enforcement, the white coalition at Columbia decided the time had come to confront the government. Up to this point, it is important to note, the student rebels' main target had been the university *itself*, and its attendant activities—ROTC, defense establishment research, black studies, student participation in university affairs.

But with the passage of H. Res. 987 in the waning weeks of President Kretz's term, any disturbance at a university that interfered with the rights of others, could be declared a state of insurrection. It was no longer a game of "get the guy with the glasses," the fat, soft, bookish university. They were going after the toughest guy on the street.

Thanks to what Senator Tobey used to call "this mystical television," we were able to watch the steps leading to the ultimate tragedy at Columbia, the holocaust that greeted Ben's first week in office and presented him with a crisis that had been years in the making.

We watched as Arvid Farbelman, that forty-four-year-old "youth leader," burned a copy of H. Res. 987 on the steps of Low Library and proclaimed:

"What we do now will be an existential act. Action first, thought later. We have no program, only ideals."

At once, the Attorney-General Fawcett issued a warning. The law would be enforced. Let the judges and courts decide on its merits later. "We warn those who would interfere with the actions and desires of others," Attorney General Fawcett announced in his quavery voice, "they will be dealt with immediately, under powers granted me by this new law."

"Bullshit," responded Arvid Farbelman.

With only token resistance from the meager force of elderly university policemen, the coalition of white students marched on and occupied Schermerhorn, Fayerweather and Avery Halls on the Columbia campus. It was 1968 all over again, but with certain crucial differences. They were *armed* this time. Rifles and shotguns were carried into the buildings. Four mildly dissenting professors were beaten, in a rash of moral certitude. Research files of Professor Demmering, an expert on Locke, were disgustingly desecrated. These expressions of intellectual purpose culminated in the draping of a banner from a high Schermerhorn window, which proclaimed: F--K KRETZ.

Occupations were nothing new at Columbia or at a hundred other American campuses. Since the termination of the Vietnam War, and the establishment of the volunteer army, together with the appointment of the civil libertarian Judge Moscowitz to the FBI directorship, much of the edge had been taken off the demonstrations. But with the signing of H. Res. 987—the last flutter of the dying swan—old angers were aroused. And, as the reporters on the scene at Morningside Heights observed, this occupation had a different odor about it—guns, sleeping bags, food supplies, two-way radios, the impedimenta of a long siege.

There followed the usual negotiations. But the radicals were adamant. If Kakamba Jones and his black rebels, his Afro Avengers could be given—*given!*—Teachers College to create their own Lumumba University, why not the rebellious whites? Why not indeed? There was a logic to their argument, and President Miklos Voss of Columbia, who had been successful at calming student tempers before was now faced with an insoluble problem.

But with the passage of H. Res. 987, one swift flick of President Hayward Kretz's pen, all discourse, polite and otherwise, was suspended. Arvid Farbelman would now have the privilege of saying "bullshit" to a bayonet.

In our headquarters at the Manger Hay-Adams, Fred Goldstein and I, and Vangie Boswell, and a few of the girls watched with hideous fascination as the National Guard—with the New York police held in reserve— stormed Schermerhorn Hall with tear gas and new riot guns which sprayed salt and bird shot. After a short, one-sided war, they cleared it.

On the television screen, we saw the occupation was coming to an end. I must say, the Guard performed excellently. I made a note to get the commanding officer's name and keep it on file. There was no resistance from the students (and nonstudents, since a third of the demonstrators were outsiders like Arvid Farbelman) as the guardsmen herded them into waiting trucks. I suspect a few blasts of the riot guns had taken the fight out of many of the rebels. It had become, I am grieved to relate, a commonplace for an occasional rioter to be shot dead. The public did not care. The public *approved* the heavy hand. As for the black community, they offered not a word of sympathy when some middle-class white liberal arts major would be peppered with bird shot while fleeing a burning classroom, at, let us say, Wisconsin.

As we watched the roundup of the dissenting young from the Columbia buildings, I pondered their isolation, their lack of support in the nation. Would they ever learn? Would they ever understand the pitifully weak minority they represented? Many of the reforms and changes for which they agitated (I do not mean the hard-core revolutionaries, but the average involved students) were long overdue. God knows the depletion allowance was a scandal, that the defense budget and the billions wasted on death and the "defense of the free world" were shocking, that expenditures and programs to elevate black people, and Latins and Indians were shamefully inadequate. Our priorities were insanely wrong. We celebrated death. We spent billions on useless hardware, some of it useful only in its capacity to kill. Ben knew this. Liberals knew it. Professors knew it. And I suspect, many Americans knew it. But one simply did not effect these changes by attacking Harvard, or Oberlin, or Columbia. Blacking the eye of the fat boy with the bag of jelly beans (the universities) while the bullies ran wild (the Gabe Tutts, the Lance Rucketts and their ilk) hardly was a means of effecting reform. Somehow, when the boss moved into the White House, we would have to show them by immediate example how to get things done. *For the wrong reasons,* as Ben always said.

The new mass arrest had one notable difference. There was virtually no violence—a lot of the fight had gone out of the youngsters—but that is not the difference to which I refer. Instead of being booked before a magistrate, and released on bail, these 427 demonstrators, under terms of the Emergency Riot Control Act, were herded into a vast detention center on Ellis Island, a "correction camp" surrounded by barbed wire. Not a single member of the press was permitted to embark for the island in New York Bay, where the students and their allies were taken. Press boats took off from the Battery and from the New Jersey side, and were ordered away by the Coast Guard. Helicopters zoomed and dipped over the barracks, but photographed very little. The demonstrators were kept indoors. Neither lawyers nor relatives nor friends were allowed to visit them.

"For Chrissake, it can't go on like this," Fred protested. "They've violated every article of the Bill of Rights and all the Supreme Court decisions of the last fifteen years."

There were protests. Senator John Tyler Lord of Vermont, a courageous New Englander, was the first to cry out against "This outrage, this desecration, this denial of every American legal procedure." He was joined by twenty-eight other senators including Maury Eisenberg of Illinois and Royce Henshaw of Montana. Congressmen were less quick to react. The Speaker of the House, the ancient, doddering Emmett Brian O'Boyle of Rhode Island, stammered that "he would have to examine the details of the law to see if it had been properly executed." To people like Lance Ruckett of South Dakota, the Ellis Island prison camp was "long overdue."

What distressed us, as we gathered that evening in Ben's office to discuss the untoward turn of events, was the *indifference* with which millions of Americans appeared to greet this ominous development. No sooner had we sat down around the oval table, than Fred Goldstein, transistor pressed to his ear, brought us word that National Guardsmen in Berkeley had arrested three hundred young people and detained them in a hastily erected "camp" on the site of the old Presidio.

There were more alarming portents. When rioting students at C. W. Post College, Long Island, were rounded up by the National Guard and packed off in army trucks to a temporary "compound" at Roosevelt Raceway, crowds of ordinary Americans turned out to *cheer and applaud* the arrests. Fred Goldstein telephoned one of his contacts with the Long Island newspaper *Newsday*, and learned that the mob was not a casual gathering, but an organized show of support for the guardsmen. "A blue-collar and lower middle-class bunch," Fred said. "Guys from Grumman, Republic, the electronic factories on the island. Beer drinkers and bowlers. They came in caravans. Most of the cars had those blue and white flags stuck on the windshields—the Save America insignia."

Now, faced with hundreds of "detainees," young people herded to the courts behaved in a predictably confusing manner. Some judges issued writs of *habeas corpus,* set bail and freed the prisoners. Others refused to do so, pending clarification. At Ellis Island, for some odd reason, about half the Columbia demonstrators were freed—and were greeted with showers of garbage and bricks by an irate mob of union members, the very proletariat these young idealists intended to uplift.

"Tiger's out of the cage," Hannaford said to me. "Not those crazy kids. They're kittens. The big tiger is in the unions, the PTA, and the Grange Hall. We're going to have us a time getting him back in."

Before meeting with the President-elect, I huddled with Senator Maury Eisenberg of Illinois, a liberal and an expert on big-city problems. "A dreadful state of affairs," he said mournfully. Senator Eisenberg is a rather droop-faced, bloodhound of a man—fearless, incorruptible.

"But why did Kretz do it?" I asked.

"Edward, he read the election returns. He added Beldock's vote to Upshaw's, looked ahead to his party's future and decided it was what the country wanted."

If Eisenberg upset me, it was nothing compared to what I experienced in the cab back to the hotel. Oh, I had sniffed the prevailing winds. But the cabdriver, a certain Salvatore Melfi, confirmed my gloomiest sentiments. This Melfi had no forehead, scant hair, and tattooed forearms. There was a plastic Virgin atop his dashboard, a magnetic Christopher on the panel, and a large blue and white sticker on his front left window. The car radio blared a newscast, and the announcer was informing us of the latest mass arrests—at Swarthmore College, that fine old Quaker school, 123 students had been driven from the Admissions Office by a special National Guard unit and were now being held incommunicado in a nearby armory.

"Serves the fuckers right," Melfi snarled.

"I beg your pardon?"

"Those college fuckers. Serves 'em right. Shoot 'em all. Kill the pricks."

We stopped at a red light on Pennsylvania Avenue. As we waited, two odd-looking people crossed the street in front of the cab. They were hippies, or students, lost souls, God knows what—a black youth in an Afro bob and a khaki cape and sandals, walking arm in arm with a scrawny, young blond girl in jeans.

"See dat?" Melfi growled. "I'd take those two fuckers and shoot 'em in the head. You can do it now. We got 'em all in one place. Like a stadium or a big hall, or like the armory they just put those bastards in. Then open up with the machine guns. That's all. That's what they need."

I sucked in my breath. But I realized I was listening to no fanatic, no madman, no violent fascist, but a devout, loving father and family man. "Yes, I suppose you could. But all those bullets flying around. The damage to property would be considerable."

Perhaps this sobered him. But he said no more. The message came to me loud and clear.

"There will be no inaugural parade next week," Hannaford said bluntly. "And none of those damn foolish, useless balls."

It seemed a sensible idea. With the country riven, with mass arrests mounting and arguments about the Emergency Riot Control Act rife, demonstrators and counterdemonstrators parading around the "detention centers" and "compounds" that had so swiftly arisen, it would have been difficult to justify nubile baton twirlers and peau de soie evening gowns.

"The society columnists will raise hell," Margaret High McNally, our Treasury Secretary-designate said.

"Not to mention the American Legion posts and high schools sending their kids here for the parade," Matt Fixx added.

"Sorry," said Ben. "We'll have a big wing-ding on July Fourth, some kind of national event. That parade is a bore anyway, and lots of people know it. The President stays warm in his little coop, with the electric heaters, while those poor kids in tights and panties freeze out there in the street."

"But, sir," Matt Fixx said in a pained voice, "the planning for the parade has been an on-going affair for several weeks. All the reviewing stands are up . . . all that lumber . . . I mean, there's been a huge input . . ."

Input. On-going. Pure Washingtonese. Ben Hannaford hated these locutions but he tolerated them because Matt was a crackerjack on legislation and had high acceptance in both houses of Congress.

"Well, there's going to have to be an out-put," the President-elect said. "Give the lumber to Secretary Murphy here. He can see that some of his friends in the city put it to good use."

Homer Murphy, the huge black man, who was to be our Secretary of Health, Education and Welfare looked grim. "In the mood they are in, Senator, they'll burn it. They're in no mood to build anything."

"Do you hear anything from Columbia?" I asked Murphy. "I got a call from one of my people at Lumumba University this morning. A bad scene."

We all turned to listen to Homer. His was a commanding presence, the Chicago Bears and New York Giants had learned.

"Fellow who works for HEW tells me the National Guard is getting ready to clean the place out."

Ben pursed his lips. "Have the Columbia people requested this?"

"No, sir. This is coming right from the Attorney General's Office. Columbia very reluctantly turned those buildings over to Kakamba Jones and his crowd, but they're willing to let it simmer along that way. The word is, they're improving discipline there, got a new curriculum and have brought in a lot of kids from Harlem to take special courses. So it just might work. I know Kakamba Jones is a fake and a loudmouth, but he isn't *all* fake and *all* loudmouth."

"When is this supposed to take place?" I asked.

Homer Murphy raised his eyebrows. "Day or two. They'll get the same treatment as the white kids. Detention centers until they learn to behave."

"This is all regrettable," Vice-President Verne Sparrier said. "But I think they brought a good deal of this on themselves."

There was truth in Governor Sparrier's righteous attitude. But the more one examined our national sickness, the harder it became to settle on causes. Yes, the blacks' outrages were going to bring on a terrible vengeance—or an equally destructive indifference on the part of whites. But if blame were to be affixed, what about the four-hundred-year-old crime? What about the historic abominations against black people—the unspeakable malignancy of the slave trade, the traditions of repression, the formalized lies and frauds and deceits and tyrannies, and the ultimate threat of noose, gun and fire, used to crush these innocents?

"Yeah, on themselves," Homer Murphy said. "If the bust takes place, if the guard moves in to clean out those buildings, there'll be worse than an occupation."

"How do you mean, Homer?" Hannaford asked.

"When those white students were rounded up, the protests were mild. Lot of cheering. But if the black brothers get hit, watch out. Harlem is waiting."

For some reason, I longed for the presence of Burke Boswell, our Defense Secretary-designate. But he was not involved in urban matters. At the moment he was over at the Pentagon, conferring with the generals and admirals. With the eye of a shrewd lawyer, he was checking their books. A few surprises lay waiting for the inviolate military. Boswell was needed over there, although his agile mind would have helped us at the moment.

"Can't another appeal be made to President Kretz to reverse himself?" Meg McNally asked.

"Too late," Ben said. "I spoke with the President this morning. He feels the country waited too long to get tough with these rioters. Mr. Kretz told me that he leaves office with a clear conscience."

"What about the Attorney General?" Homer Murphy asked.

"Even less interested," Ben said. "Judge Moscowitz intends to submit his resignation tomorrow as FBI director. He says he can't face himself if he has to enforce ERCA. I shall appoint him my Attorney General. The only question, as he sees it, is how soon can a case be gotten to the Supreme Court so it can be declared unconstitutional. But until then, it will play hell with the universities and the cities." The President-elect hunched his huge shoulders. I saw the pain in his dark face. Whatever might be said of Ben Hannaford—cunning, tough, manipulative—he was not a cruel man. "That damn law is a shooting license for every police force in the country, for any damn fool in charge."

"Sir, we can unwind the machinery in a week or so," Matt Fixx said. "These arrests are taking place only on direct orders of the Attorney General, with or without the request of local officials. Once we get Judge Moscowitz in office, I think we can activate a destruct mechanism on the Emergency Riot Control Act. The Congress will scream, but that law is so ambiguously worded, that we can survive the interface. I think we'll be in a better than one-to-one relationship."

Ah, if only the world were as easy to mold "nearer to the heart's desire" as Matthew Fixx with his "destructs" and "interfaces" imagined. I heard Matt droning on, calling for a "feasibility" study of the law, a "restructuring" of the Justice Department, and, worst of all, "a new scenario." The kid had picked up a lot of student jargon; it did not mesh with his farm boy's face, flapping ears and mobile Adam's apple.

"The damage may have been done," Homer Murphy

said. "Yeah, once we are in, the President can put the brakes on these arrests. But the law will be on the books. Bad taste still in everyone's mouth."

Silently, I thought of my sullen cabdriver, Salvatore Melfi. *Kill 'em! Kill 'em!*

"We have got to give those youngsters and those black people some hope," Ben said. "More than hope. Programs. Action. Keep 'em busy, so they don't want to riot. Otherwise, the rest of this country will show 'em what's in their hearts."

"Not really in their hearts, Ben," Senator Royce Henshaw said. "I cannot lose faith in our people."

"Neither can, I, Royce," the President-elect said. "But they have to be calmed down. Not just that fifty-six per cent that went for Beldock and Upshaw, but those hairy children and Homer's soul brothers."

"Who can blame them?" asked Royce Henshaw. The senator was a youngish man with a great mop of wavy brown hair. He had taught history and political science in his native Montana. Dreamy, sentimental, he seemed an anachronism in the halls of the Senate. "Look at us. Just look at us. A budget of two hundred and twenty billion dollars, of which one hundred and twenty billion is for . . . for . . ."

"Death," Homer Murphy said.

"Yes, death," Senator Henshaw repeated. "Cities rot. Babies die. Schools are crowded. Hospitals crumble. The bottom fourth of our people are condemned to the treadmill of despair, poverty, broken homes, hunger, welfare, and more despair. And we, the lords of Congress vote every dollar that is asked for death. Missiles. Warships. Giant planes. Ben, in the Vietnam madness, the loss in American aircraft came to *eight billion dollars*. Eight billion. I awake in the middle of the night and I find myself repeating the figure."

Murphy rapped the table. "For eight billion we could fix up every school district in America and build junior colleges in our twenty biggest cities."

"It is beyond belief," Henshaw went on. "Eight billion dollars in burned, wrecked, crashed airplanes, technical monsters—not to mention the good men who die with them. And for what? For stopping Communism? For those bloody dominoes we kept hearing about? For surrounding a China, already surrounded by our armed islands? Or was it worth eight billion dollars to burn those thatched huts, those rice paddies and banana plantations, and make homeless wanderers out of millions of Asian peasants?"

"That war ended," Ben said.

"It ended, yes," Henshaw went on. "But the psychology stays with us. We are an armed people. We are governed by machines, by a cruel technology, by a self-perpetuating lunacy that pronounces all engines of war excellent. I know damned well what impels those unwashed children to occupy university buildings, and Kakamba Jones's friends, no matter how misguided they may be, to seize a university."

"I don't blame them," Hannaford said. "I only wish they'd realize they have some friends and give us a chance."

"They've been sold down the river too often," Homer Murphy said. "Kretz did nothing in four years. Except start a fifteen billion dollar program to develop the Iron Ball."

The Iron Ball was a supersecret multiwarhead anti-anti-antimissile. Seventeen separate "defense" contractors shared in the bonanza. It was reputed to be the last, final, unbeatable "defensive" weapon in our arsenal, although many scientists called it the "Edsel." It's full military name was "Manned Orbiting Multiple Satellite Entry Relay," or MOMSER.

"Precisely," Henshaw said. "*Death.* You can't keep creating death with a nation's wealth and not pay the price. And these kids, the blacks, the protesters are powerless."

"I'll tell you what their trouble is," Hannaford said. "They tell us 'Give us all or nothing.' You know what they get. Nothing. Not a damn thing."

There was a prolonged silence at the conference table. Outside the hotel windows dusk was settling over the troubled city. On the sidewalk beneath us, a duet of embarrassed National Guardsmen walked back and forth, protecting us from the wicked poor, the malevolent black man. *The slums have their revenge.* But those who live beyond the filth and misery and despair of the slums, are capable of greater vengeance.

"All right," Ben said. "All right. I have heard enough of despair and gloomy counsel. Any man who gets elected

116

with a third of the popular vote has a right to be an optimist, to do any damn thing he pleases." He turned to Fred Goldstein who had been taking shorthand notes. "Fred, issue a statement for the morning papers. As soon as I am in office, I will have the Attorney General review every arrest made under ERCA. Every one. The arrests will be viewed not only in the light of this law, which I find ambiguous and controversial, but in the light of judicial tradition, and the Bill of Rights. I will instruct the new Attorney General to permit the issuance of habeas corpus writs in all, I repeat, all arrests, and the immediate setting of, and granting of, bail."

Fred was scribbling madly. "Anything else, sir?"

"You'll be asked about an Attorney General. Call Judge Moscowitz and determine exactly when he intends to submit his resignation, then get his okay on an announcement that he's our new boy. The judge has got a lot of leverage with the press and liberals."

Homer Murphy smiled cynically. "Sorry, Senator, that won't help any more. The kids hate liberals more than they hate people like Kretz and Gabe Tutt."

"Then I say, they deserve everything they get," Governor Sparrier said tautly.

"Afraid it doesn't work that way any more," Murphy said softly.

I studied Verne Sparrier narrowly. He was getting more and more "liberal" by the day, by the hour. As a young congressman he had made a career by attacking "liberals, pinkos and bleeding-heart socialists." Had he really changed? Or did it matter? The man was a chameleon, unlocatable, without fixed notions on anything—except perhaps his career. And odd duck, our Vice-President-elect.

"Well, I don't want people on their knees," Ben said, folding his arms on the table. "I just want 'em all to calm down for a few weeks, so we can get something started. 'Envy and wrath shorten the life.'"

He was feeling better. The press announcement about a review of arrests made under the new law, the granting of bail and habeas corpus would do much to assuage the outrage in liberal quarters. (*A descent into legal darkness*, The New York *Times* had editorialized. *The courts must act at once to test it and to throw it out*.) A buzzer on the desk announced that he had "visitors." Warming to the occasion, he was polishing up biblical quotes. That was a curious trait of Hannaford's: when distressed, he seemed to forget all those fine scriptural phrases. Only when he was optimistic and yeasty, did the holy words pour forth.

The door opened. In a swirl of color, Angel Lopez Garcia and Kakamba Jones entered. Garcia had gotten fat and looked old. His usually impeccable tailoring was a thing of the past; there were gravy spots on his lapels and his maroon tie was indifferently knotted. But he was as jaunty as ever, puffing on a foot-long brown cigar from his Cuban admirers in the Communist state. As for Jones, how can I do justice to his flamboyant garb? A purple yarmulka perched on his mahogany head. His shimmering robe was of swirling green satin, shot with gold and silver. In his long ebony hand, he waved the ivory and gnu's-tail fly whisk of high office.

" 'Who is this that cometh from Edom with dyed garments from Bozrah?' " asked Ben, as he rose to greet them.

"Ha jambo keena bwana," Kkamba Jones said loftily. Disdaining Ben's proffered hand, he raised the whisk. Behind smoked glasses, his eyes were secretive, mystic.

"Why don't you junk that Swahili?" Homer Murphy said. "You know, Jonesy, Swahili is an *East* African language. We're West Africans, all of us."

Kakamba spun, pointing the whisk at Murphy. "The curse of M'Junga on you, house nigger."

The Secretary-designate of Health, Education and Welfare, I am certain, could have cracked Kakamba Jones in half, but he chose to keep his cool. "Swahili, yeah. It's East Africa, man, a language full of Arabic, Hindi and English. You keep teaching it in schools, you'll have to institute *remedial* Swahili next year."

"White man's coon, is what you are, Murphy," Kakamba crooned. "I have the power, not you. You are doomed, rejected, an Uncle Tom, jiggled on strings by white masters."

Everyone in the room watched this duel between the two black men with varying reactions. Senator Henshaw appeared to be unnerved; Treasury Secretary-designate Meg McNally, horrified; Governor Sparrier enraged; Ben amused.

"Still got your contacts on the New York police force, Jonesy?" Murphy teased. "The brothers tell me that every

118

time you stage a riot or a march you make a deal with the cops—so many paraders, so many sit-ins, so many busts. They say you get a special rate for hospital cases."

I had heard this before. Jones was not entirely a wildman. He was a shrewd, calculating politician. His costume and his outbursts were theatrical effects. Actually, he was a man who could sometimes be dealt with, and Murphy knew this. In fact, I sensed a sort of "soul" camaraderie between the two.

"Beware, Murphy," Jones warned. "Hannaford will dress you in a jockey's uniform, turn you to stone and stick you on the White House lawn."

Governor Sparrier started to rise. His face was ashen. "Now that is quite enough. Mr. Murphy, why you sit there and take this abuse from that rabble-rouser . . ."

Homer merely smiled; Kakamba ignored Sparrier. This was part of militant strategy. The intransigents, the hard conservatives, the reactionaries, the southern despots were almost always ignored. The strategy was to assault and abuse the *center* and the *liberal left*. Thus, Columbia, Berkeley and all the colleges could be attacked. But Senator Gabriel T. Tutt and General Clyde Upshaw and *Save America* were rarely engaged. Curious. I wondered if these people—Kakamba Jones and Arvid Farbelman and all the angry children had ever read their history books. The Communists in Germany after the First World War pursued that same ingenious strategy—attack and weaken the liberals and the left, but never a hand lifted against the Nazis. And so Communists, socialists and liberals perished in the same fire. . . .

Ben told Garcia—the ex-congressman was subdued, and I felt he was tired—and Jones to sit down. Garcia obliged; Jones squatted on the floor. Then he outlined his plans for halting arrests under the emergency measure that President Kretz had signed. There would be a review of all cases, bail would be granted, roundups terminated.

"You will be too late," Kakamba said. He affected a clipped accent, a sort of West Indian-cum-Mayfair delivery. "We know that massed units of the National Guard, including tanks and artillery are moving on Lumumba University. They will besiege us and commit genocide on us. You cannot stop them."

Hannaford eyed him warily. "Mr. Jones, you sound as if you're anticipating the event with pleasure. Why don't you

119

fool everyone by moving out of Teachers College? Those buildings aren't yours. You stole them from Columbia. What's more, that separate studies deal of yours is discredited with every black educator in the country. All your smartest professors say it's for the birds. Go on, move out."

"I am not one to deny the white devils their acts of genocide," Kakamba sniffed.

"By God, you won't give me a chance," Ben said. "You won't give anyone a chance. I tell you, I'm going to take the teeth out of that law in a few days. I want people like you, and Garcia and those kids, whose language I don't even understand, to come to Washington and talk to us. Now Senator Henshaw here, together with Secretary Murphy and Congressman Gantry, who'll head up Housing and Urban Development, and a few other top people are working out a *ward* system for the cities. Decentralization. Community control. Let you folks elect your own people in small units. Your own police. Your own teachers. Give you some power, some say over your own destiny, how you want your kids raised. I want all of you to help. But dammit, if all that's on your mind is attacking colleges and cursing, and screaming genocide, nothing will get done."

Kakamba Jones, arraying his long black legs, scrambled to his feet.

"Race murderers," he said, sweeping the room with his fly whisk. "Slave masters. Lynch mob. I know your community control. It is a plot to perpetuate ghettos. To keep us herded into our prisons so we can be more easily gassed and burned."

Verne Sparrier had turned to a block of ice. Who could truly blame him? There was no reasoning with Jones. Only Homer Murphy and Ben seemed unmoved by his outburst. Murphy understood him: it was part of Jones's "scenario"—to outrage, insult, abuse, and then *settle*.

"Mr. Jones," Royce Henshaw said with marked emotion. "The ward plan is quite the opposite. It is aimed at a genuine reform of—"

At the sound of that word, Kakamba began to leap up and down in his gold-sandaled feet. "Reform! *Reform!* That is what I was waiting to hear! Mr. President-elect B. B. Hannaford, millionaire builder, let me tell you that we will fight your reforms to the death! We preach revolu-

120

tion, not reform! You give us a bowl of watery soup, when we want the whole dinner. Our first priority is to destroy the reformers! We will fight you, and fight your ward system, and your white schemes to subdue us!"

Angel Lopez Garcia appeared mortified. His dusky face flushed crimson, and he shifted his bulk in his plush chair. "*Bastante,* Jonesy, *bastante.* You gotta excuse heem, Mr. President-elect. He lose his head sometime'. He don' really mean all that, he say it to make an effect, you understan'?"

The old fox, once one of the Hill's most effective legislators, did not want Jones to destroy his own comeback. Like Ben, Garcia was a trader.

"Mr. Jones," Ben said, ignoring Garcia's effort at peacemaking, "you knock off us reformers and you'll have to deal with General Upshaw. And Congressman Lance Ruckett. And lots of other mean folks."

"And Senator Tutt?" Kakamba asked slyly.

"And him."

"Aha!" Kakamba crowed. "Hypocrite! I am informed that you have made a secret pact with Senator Tutt, assuring him he can keep his seniority and his chairmanships—Tutt, the vilest bigot of all! You have run true to form! Why should we fear the wolf, Tutt? It is the fox Hannaford we must fight!"

With that, Kakamba Jones, borne aloft on the billowing robes of his green, gold and silver cloak, swept through the door.

"Apologies," Garcia said softly. "You know .. he gets excited . . ." Poor Garcia. He had no stomach for violent confrontations. I had the feeling throughout the campaign, that the shouting mobs that came to cheer Kakamba Jones frightened him—just as the wildmen of the right often alarmed Verne Sparrier. There is a lot to be said for our public servants. They seem, on the whole, to exercise more restraint than many of their constituents. There is something about holding public office that teaches a man that life is not all a matter of absolutes; that there is a give-and-take, a need for conciliation that makes progress possible and problems soluble.

I noted that Senator Henshaw and Homer Murphy were taken by surprise by Kakamba's revelation that Gabe Tutt had been spared presidential punishment.

"He was bluffing about Tutt, I gather," Homer said gently.

"No, I'm afraid not," Ben said. "I had to shut Gabe up. Keep him disgruntled but not mutinous. Too early to start picking fights with entrenched powers like Gabe."

Henshaw understood. He was a senator, and he knew that old tigers like Gabe, with his power in Armed Services, Finance and the party caucus could ruin or badly cripple a President's program. Of all the people in the room, it was Angel Lopez Garcia who looked most thunderstruck by Kakamba Jones's revelation. (Evidently these former running mates confided in one another not at all. I suspected they detested each other.)

The meeting came to an end, and Ben told Fred to contact Judge Moscowitz at once. He wanted to confer on the mass arrests and how to redress the balance. In three days he would be President and would have the power. (Moscowitz, and the other secretaries-designate, would of course need senate confirmation. But there would be acting secretaries holding over and Ben could effect changes at once.)

"Angel, stay a moment," Ben said. Garcia lingered as the others left.

"I work on Jonesy on thees community control deal. Jesus Chris', las' week he was hollerin' how he was gonna inseest on community control, decentralized police force, everything you mention. Now you tell heem you gon' shoot for it, and he hollers genocide. *Carai.*"

"That's why he hollered, Angel. He didn't like the idea of me suggesting it. Let him simmer down, and he'll come around."

Angel's tan face grew solemn. A truly mixed man. ("Chico," he once told a reporter, "you try to figure out wha' I am. I am part Negro, Spanish, Indian, Dutch, English, Hindu and maybe a leetle Jewish on my mother's side. But you don' have to be Jewish to hate me.")

"He never come around if they bust Lumumba University, Ben," Angel said. "That place scare the hell outa me. They got guns, bullets, the whole thing a damn arsenal. ..."

"We'll work on the Attorney General," Ben said. "And you talk to your people in Harlem."

Garcia waved a pudgy hand. I wondered just how much cachet he still had with the people of the slums. "Ben ..."

122

He looked embarrassed. "You know, Angel not gettin' any younger. Or prettier."

"You look *muy toro*, Angel."

"Yeah, *muy toro*." He relit his dark brown cigar. It filled the suite with the odor of the moist Cuban earth, the gold island sun. "You know, Ben, I reesk my ass for you in Los Angeles."

"I know you did, Angel."

"Yeah, I go along with that theeng ... the voting machines ... the poll watchers. You know, if Kakamba's crowd ever get the goods on me, they make it rough for Angel."

My suspicions had been right. Ben had rigged something with his opponent in Los Angeles. Garcia and Jones, on their Black-and-Tan ticket were supposed to carry the central districts. And then—the upset.

"I appreciate what you did for an old friend," my boss said.

"As much as you appreciate Gabe Tutt?"

"Every bit, *amigo*." Ben got up and sat on the edge of his desk. Night had settled over the city. Beyond, we saw the gleaming white facade of the President's mansion. In a few days, it would be ours.

"I've been in contact with Speaker O'Boyle, Angel. You will get your seat back. The House will vote narrowly to reseat you. And I will see to it that your seniority will be restored. As well as your chairmanship of the Public Works Committee."

"*Con mucho gusto, viejo amigo*," Garcia said.

"*Por nada*," Ben replied.

"Oh, for sometheeng. Never *por nada* with my old friend." Beaming, tears rimming his dark eyes, Garcia walked over to Ben and embraced him. The President-elect peered at me over Garcia's bear hug and crinkled his nose—the congressman's cologne was an affront to him.

"I be a good frien' to you in the Congress, Ben," Garcia said tearfully.

"I'll need every friend I can get," the boss said. "Now, Angel, go talk to Kakamba and tell him to roll with the punch. If they clear out Lumumba University, tell them to go quietly. I'll start changing things in a few days."

When he had left Ben asked me to draw up a memo, with Fred Goldstein's help, on the status of the arrests under ERCA.

"That was generous of you," I said. "What you intend to do for Garcia."

"I have to do some balancing. A favor to Gabe Tutt. A favor to Garcia. You notice, Edward, I didn't lose my temper with Mr. Jones, either. I'm on a narrow piece of middle ground."

I thought of Fern's nightmare—her dream of Ben isolated on a strip of land, with venomous snakes on either side. "It seems to get narrower every day," I said.

"I have faith unbounded in the people. 'As one to whom his mother comforteth, so will I comfort you.'"

I shook my head. "I have a dread feeling that the House doesn't want comfort. It wants blood. Worst of all, so do the people. What's happened to this country, sir? A cabdriver told me today he was in favor of killing those students who have been rounded up. If you turn those kids loose, what then?"

"Nothing. Nothing at all."

"They'll start demonstrating again. People will ask why aren't they back in compounds, the way President Kretz promised them. And you'll be accused of coddling Communists and perverts."

"I will have to persuade a lot of people I'm doing the right thing. Edward, Harry Truman once said that the presidency's biggest power is the power to *persuade*. I intend to be persuasive. With the people. With the Congress. Anyone who'll listen."

Ben stood at the window and gazed across the park. Night in the revered city—the lights, and the dark skies of winter, and all the hopes and the great promises of a mighty land of endeavor, and creativity, and joy and brotherhood. . . . How had the dream soured?

"Edward, I don't deceive myself. We eat the bread of adversity today. We are in the furnace of affliction." He rubbed his square jaw. The man was troubled. In all the years I had known Ben Hannaford, I had never seen him so shaken. There are limits to a man's confidence, to the resolution he brings to his efforts. And I wondered now, if deep in the night, at that dread hour of three in the morning, when the human spirit flags, whether Ben awakened, Fern's silent form beside him, and wondered what had driven him to seek the presidency, and whether now that he had grasped it, the magic would elude him?

"I'll get you that report on the arrests. I'll check Fred

124

on the inaugural arrangements—as simply as you indicated. I'll be at the Boswells tonight in case you need me." I wanted desperately to do more for him, to ease his burdens, to come up with some miraculous scheme, some grand plan, some magical formula to right the land again.

"Cheer up, Edward," he said, as I dolefully collected my papers and stuffed them into a brief case. "You and I have been through the fiery furnace. We'll survive. And we'll do better than that."

"With the Lord's help, sir."

He winked at me. "Wouldn't think of doing it any other way, son. 'In the wilderness shall waters break out and streams in the desert.' "

Two nights before inauguration, Vangie Boswell invited me to her parents' home for dinner. I was anxious to meet the man who would head up the defense establishment, and I relished the thought of being alone with Evangeline— if only in my bright red Triumph sports car—for the drive out to Wesley Heights, where the family lived.

A light snow was falling as we drove down Constitution Avenue. Ben had ordered a radical departure from precedent for the inauguration. He would take the oath from Chief Justice John Laurens Early not on the East front of the Capitol, as is traditional, but on the steps of the Lincoln Memorial. There would be no parade, no band, no music, just a simple prayer, and a brief presidential address. That was all.

We drove by the memorial. A platoon of National Guardsmen stood at parade rest around the base of the inspiring marble monument. Ben had specified that he did not want any scaffolding, any seats or any platforms erected, except for a small press stand. "We'll just stand on the steps," he said. "Cabinet, Supreme Court Justices, the rest of us. And the people can stand also."

As we rode by, I thought of a summer's night two and a half years ago when I had driven around the monument with another lovely young girl who had joined the Hannaford team. Maria Valdez, the supple, young Mexican-American maiden, whom I might have loved, had not Ben fallen for her. Ah, the lost chances. Maria had been a wide-eyed innocent, a child just out of Ramada University, in Washington for the first time. I had quoted to her the inscription inside the Lincoln Memorial. Now, with Vangie at my side, I found myself saying it again.

" 'In this temple, as in the hearts of the people for whom he saved the Union,' " I said softly, " 'the memory of Abraham Lincoln is enshrined forever. . . .' "

"It's beautiful," Vangie said. "I wonder if your boss didn't have some flattering comparisons in mind when he decided to take the oath there."

"No, not Ben. He'd be the last man to compare himself with Lincoln. He's not that kind of self-worshiping peacock. But I do know what he had in mind."

"Explain." She nestled closer. Or did I imagine it? Heaters in small foreign cars generally throw about as much warmth as a candle. The windshield was thick with frosted flakes, and the going was skiddy.

"Ben is aware that the Union is splitting wide open again. He hopes that people will understand that we're one country, the way Lincoln envisioned it and maintained it."

Two National Guardsmen, directing traffic at the corner of Wisconsin and Reservoir Road, halted us, for a spot check. Who knew but that we might be dangerous enemies of the republic? I was furious, but I realized my anger was wasted on these shivering, snow-flecked young boys. (I had heard some confidential reports that there were instances of young guardsmen throwing down their rifles and refusing to participate in the campus roundups.)

"Routine check, sir," the boy said. "Because of the inauguration. Sorry. Y'all can move on."

"Our beloved President Kretz," Vangie said bitterly. "No more money for schools and the poor and hospitals. But lots of money for soldiers on the streets and the Iron Ball missile system."

I drove into the tree-shaded undulating streets of Wesley Heights. "We're depending on your father to help the President change all of that. New priorities."

As we walked up the snow-covered path to the large, ungainly, white stucco house, its sides flanked with sculptured yews and hemlocks, Vangie laughed. "Don't set your hopes too high. I've got the usual quota of parental respect. But old Dad has no principles. The only morality he knows is the kind that comes out of a checkbook."

"I'll settle for it," I said as Vangie opened the door with a key and we walked into a warm, brightly lit foyer. "It

126

beats the political power that grows out of the end of a gun."

Mrs. Boswell greeted me. Truly, they were a family of basketball players. I gauged Mrs. Boswell to be about five foot eleven inches, a lean, straight-backed woman with plain blond hair and a good face—large featured and mobile like her daughter's, and possessed of a warm smile. She wore no jewelry and a simple beige knit dress.

"Now, isn't it odd that we've never met before, Mr. Deever?" she said. I took her to be in her early fifties. Her face was seamed and tanned—skiing, sailing, tennis, riding. People like Mrs. Boswell seemed to be tanned all year round. I think they kept a place in the Virgin Islands. She was quality folks, of a breeding infinitely more elevated than her husband's. Vangie had told me that her mother's family were Washington society, old "Cliff Dwellers."

"One of my maternal ancestors," Vangie said, "sold green lumber to Major Ellicott—Pierre L'Enfant's surveyor. Warped all his models."

As Mrs. Boswell ushered us into a vast, gloomy living room, I reflected that the *real* money of the marriage had been brought to it by the man of the house, Burke Boswell. Minerva's donation had been "class"—good breeding, a disarming frankness, good works, the right friends and a congenial superiority of manner that offended no one and impressed all.

"I've been a bit out of touch with the Washington scene," I said. "That is, ever since Senator Hannaford departed two years ago."

"But you've been *living* here," Mrs. Boswell persisted. Her voice was loud and assertive.

"Yes. I've been Senator Hannaford's confidential man."

"Not *confidence* man?" Vangie giggled.

"Vangie, please," her mother cautioned—but she, too, was laughing at me. I didn't mind. There was no malice in their attitudes.

"I have his confidence," I said. "But, not in the sense you indicate, Mrs. Boswell. I must tell you, you needn't walk around the censure and my role in it."

"Oh, that is precious," Mrs. Boswell said. "I mean, if you don't mind talking about it . . . did you and he really steal all that money from those mortgage people? For a

127

bill that was already dead in committee? And was it a half a million dollars?"

"Mother, why don't you get Edward something to drink and stop this baiting?" Vangie protested.

"Please, I'll tend bar." I got up and went to a walnut bar in the corner of the huge, gray-green room. They were both scotch drinkers. I settled for a half glass of beer. As I age, alcohol does less and less for me. "Mrs. Boswell, it was only a quarter of a million . . ."

"Only!"

"Yes. And it was actually a contribution to the campaign funds of several senators."

"Edward, don't fake," Vangie said. "Your boss never reported it as such. It was given to him. Then he decided to dole it out to some pets who could help him ram some disreputable bills through Congress. Including one that would have desecrated the national parks. I've read about the whole sorry thing. Don't minimize it."

I served them each a scotch on the rocks. "It's history," I said. "You have to understand Ben Hannaford to know why he took it. It was a test. To see if he could get away with it. To keep in shape, as it were. I know that sounds dreadful. But he's changed a good deal. The way things are going in this country, I think the President has to have a bit of the con man in him."

Mrs. Boswell let out a happy *whooop!*—the same equine whinny I had heard Vangie utter in my office. "That's grand, Mr. Deever, grand!"

Vangie rolled her eyes in mock horror. "Good God. The country going up in flames—and we have a confidence man as President, and a lobbyist as Secretary of Defense!"

"That's your undergraduate idealism showing, Vangie," I said. "The times demand not only pragmatists, but a certain cunning in our leaders . . ."

"Say," Mrs. Boswell interrupted, paying no attention to my attempt at Hannafordian rationalization, "wasn't there some juicy scandal, I mean a *sexy* scandal connected with that whole affair?"

I admitted that Marsha Treadway, now married to the columnist Lou Parente, had stolen documents from us, which had led to the censure action. Parente had published them, and a scandal ensued. But I said nothing about my affair with Marsha. It was irrelevant.

128

Mrs. Boswell enjoyed this morsel. "It all had a good result," she said loudly. "It made your boss President, and I sort of like him."

I looked puzzled. *"Made* him President? Mrs. Boswell, Senator Hannaford had to battle every inch of the way to overcome the onus, the shame of those charges—"

Again, that horsey *whooop!* cut me off. "Come off it, Mr. Deever! It helped nominate and elect him! Half the people who backed him thought he was a martyr, and the other half admired him for being a slick crook."

"I should have warned you about Mother," Vangie said. "She's a notorious plain speaker."

"I'm on guard. Mrs. Boswell, I'm glad you like the President-elect. But I must assure you he is more than a power-hungry schemer. He has a genuine awareness of the social problems threatening this country, even though his *modus operandi* may smack of the rigged wheel."

"Sounds like Daddy," Vangie laughed.

"What sounds like Daddy?"

Burke Boswell had entered the room. Or rather, he had glided in. In the flesh, he was even ganglier than on television, a truly lofty man, in a maroon velvet smoking jacket and matching slippers. In his left hand he held a champagne glass filled with what appeared to be a painfully dry martini. As he pumped my hand I had to stare straight up, like a child peering up a skyscraper. Above me I saw a long, crimsoned face, loose-featured, lantern-jawed, a lock of gray-blond hair falling over the forehead. Had he worn a cardinal's ring, I would have knelt and kissed it.

"Welcome, Edward," the tall man said. "Your boss said we should know each other better. Seems you're his *Numero Uno.*"

As he spoke, his mouth seemed to form a natural smile. Now I know this sounds foolish, but for a man of obvious intelligence, force, wit and character, it was the strangest of smiles—almost *moronic.* Then I realized it was part of the man's guile, a sort of boyish earnest of good intentions, of small-town innocence. One had to look above that smile to the gooseberry-green eyes to understand that too much trust in that dopey smile could leave the viewer with an empty wallet.

"Edward was just saying that the President-elect's style

is a mask for high purpose," Mrs. Boswell commented. "How say you, Burke?"

"Hell, I'm sure of it," the Defense Secretary-designate said. "Ben Hannaford is a magician at that sort of thing. Thank God he's on our side."

What side? I wondered. Hasluck Industries, awash in deodorants? North Central Railroads and its ten-cent pay toilets? I watched this string bean drain his double martini, and I realized we not only had a king lobbyist on our team, but a king boozer. His face had that rich ruby coloration not from skiing or horseback riding, but from long hours with John Barleycorn.

"Yes," Boswell went on, as he settled his sticklike figure into an easy chair, "high public office in this land requires a high talent for moving the pea under the shells."

"That's horrid," Vangie said. "No wonder the kids at the colleges hate all of you. No wonder they want to burn the places down."

Boswell sucked the dregs of his drink, and waved the empty glass at his wife, who, with no sign of the protest which many women convey to hard-drinking husbands, took it, and refilled it from a glass pitcher on the bar. "Daughter dear, those children don't understand how things work in this country."

"I've heard this before." Vangie pouted. "Everything's a big fake, a fraud, a show."

"Not quite," Burke Boswell said. "It's a matter of making the public approve of action A, which is something they'll tolerate or even, applaud—and meanwhile sneaking in B, which is what you really have to get done, but which they don't care for at all."

A man after Hannaford's heart, I could see. He had even added a few variations to Ben's theories.

"You're saying that the American people have to be *deceived* into accepting the right things," Vangie protested. "That's appalling."

Boswell gulped down half of the new martini, as easily as if he were drinking a vanilla milk shake, and smiled his foolish smile. "Daughter dear, Franklin Delano Roosevelt was the master of all con men, and thank God for him. The majority of Americans had no desire to fight the Nazis in World War II. That is a sobering fact. German-Americans, Irish-Americans, Italo-Americans. Native fascists, naïve socialists, pacifists, Quakers, and the basic

130

isolationist sentiments of most people. No one had any real quarrel with Hitler and Mussolini—except the Jews. Lots of folks would have been willing to let Hitler run Europe. There's still a strong school of right-wing philosophers who'll tell you so. Anyway, what was FDR to do?"

"I know, I know," Mrs. Boswell said. "He euchred us into the war."

"In a manner of speaking," her husband said. "Now, *there* were the Germans, whom we didn't want to fight, but were a far greater threat to us. Western Europe is part of our traditions, our spirit, our economy. But Japan. Ah, Japan. Those little yellow rats. Monkeys. Rapists. Savages. No problem there. Roosevelt knew he could rouse the electorate to bash them, all right. And he did. No matter whether he did or didn't dream up the Pearl Harbor attack. Sooner or later white America would be delighted to crush yellow Japan. When we did, Hitler came along with the deal. And we licked the Nazis in Europe, which was more important. So you see, 'B' was the war with the Germans—which FDR sneaked in on us. 'A' was Japan—something the country would accept."

"I reject everything you've said," Vangie said. "There was a historic inevitability about the war with the Nazis."

Boswell twirled the champagne glass; he has a positive sensual relationship with his liquor. "Don't be too sure, Evangeline. We've never been in any great hurry to fight fascists. Franco's Spain is fine with us. We tolerate and support right-wing and fascist regimes anywhere we can. I've done business with some of them, and I can tell you they are a shoddy bunch. Still, it's a dollar."

"Now, that is thoroughly disgusting," Vangie said. "Edward, are you sure Senator Hannaford really wants my father to be his Secretary of Defense?"

"They're not too far apart. You know, Hannaford-Western has done a lot of business with Communist countries. Pipelines in the Soviet Union, supermarkets in Hungary. It's *his* way of earning a dollar."

"Yes, that's the awful truth about this awful world," Boswell said, reassembling his limbs and rising as Mrs. Boswell summoned us to dinner.

"Poverty program," Boswell said enigmatically, putting an arm around me, as we entered the dining room, which was a duller, darker green, a depressing chamber with plain mahogany furnishings.

"What about it?"

"Don't you see? 'A' was helping poor people, alleged to be mostly poor whites in Appalachia, where all the publicity photos were taken, press trips, newsreels. Public accepted it. But what did Lyndon really want? He wanted 'B'—helping poor *blacks*, who were far and away the greatest in number and in need. So Congress went along with 'A', but had to swallow 'B.' "

I nodded; he was a man in Hannaford's style, with perhaps a more subtle grasp of the country and its people.

The food was bland—somewhat overdone roast beef, overcooked string beans. What was noteworthy was the wine, a red Bordeaux, which even I sensed was rare stuff. I complimented the host.

"Yeah," Boswell said. "Got it from Rothschild."

"Ah . . . which one, sir?"

"Don't remember. Some Rothschild."

"Baron Someone," Minerva Boswell said.

It dawned on me that they were not joshing. They really did not recall which Rothschild had given them the wine. They were people so secure in their own world, that even Rothschilds did not impress them. Quite the opposite of name-droppers, they were name-ignorers.

"Burke spends a lot of time in France for the Hasluck people," Minerva Boswell said. "He drank so damned much red wine his liver turned to granite."

I could believe it. The tall man had not touched his roast beef, had trifled with his string beans and salad, but had drained his wine glass twice. The fellow had the longest, hollowest legs in Washington; his innards must have been pickled in alcohol.

"Had to take the cure," Boswell said cheerfully, "so's I could get back on martinis. What the devil was that Rothschild fellow's name?"

No one remembered. It was a magnificent display of aplomb—drinking the millionaire's wine, but not remembering his name.

Vangie must have noticed my glazed expression. These people were too much for me, and I am a chap who has been around. The compounding of Minerva Boswell's social status, with Burke's intelligence, wealth and surefootedness in the worlds of Washington and big money afforded them this grace.

132

"Daddy, you are impossible," Vangie said. She'd lit a cigarette and was flicking ashes in her salad bowl—something Fern Hannaford would have frowned upon. I reminded myself to quiz her on Fern's state of mind. With inauguration approaching, I had neglected to follow up on the Deever Plan to revivify the new First Lady. *"Impossible.* You spent three months of the year in France, and you didn't learn a word of French. Not a *bon jour* or a *merci.*"

"You didn't even *try,*" Minerva added.

"Intentional," Boswell said, suppressing a winey belch. "You waltz in speaking the lingo and the French don't trust you."

"But I've been led to believe otherwise," I said innocently. "Don't foreigners admire Americans who can speak their language?"

"Everybody but the French. You come on strong in their language, and they figure you might get a jump on them. They like to think we're dumb bunnies. So I oblige them. They figure if you *don't* speak French, they can fake you out five ways, and they jabber, and grin, and dig each other in the ribs. Meanwhile, you hire yourself a relieable interpreter, and you stay ahead of *them.*"

I declined a long, black Havana, every bit as legitimately Cuban as Angel Lopez Garcia's. Boswell had his sources also.

"I gave up smoking during the censure hearings," I said. "It tended to accelerate my heart."

"Guilty conscience, Edward?" Boswell said.

"No. Nerves."

"That must have been an ordeal," Minerva Boswell said—but without any marked compassion. My head swiveled: she, too, had lit up a Havana stogie and was puffing clouds of cigar smoke into the dim air. I sat befogged amid these three giants, these Anglo-Saxon Barons, and I felt at ease. They had a certain power, a certain right-of-way, and I was glad they were on our side.

"Mr. Boswell, you will have to find us an A and B for the cities," I said. "One of the reasons Senator Hannaford wants you is that he needs to convince Congress to give him billions for housing and schools and job training. That's his B. Where's the A—the measure that the people and the Congress will support?"

Boswell frowned. "May not be any. May have to convince 'em that A and B are the same."

I nodded. "That's what's bothering the boss. He knows he was elected by a third of the voters. And that those who went for Beldock and Upshaw are a single bloc. Hard-working, upright Americans who are furious with angry black faces screaming at them."

Boswell got up from the table. How did he survive? He had eaten nothing. As far as I could gauge, his intake had been two double martinis, a bottle of Bordeaux wine, and a double shot of cognac. Evidently his system burned this as fuel, a sort of high octane to keep those long limbs functioning. Yet he did not behave like an alcoholic. Voice clear, mind sharp, legs sturdy, he led us into a den, another dark green room, and turned on the television for the night news.

The reporter led with the disclosure that Ben would take the oath on the steps of the Lincoln Memorial—no parade, no stands, no hoopla. "A spokesman at the temporary White House says that it is not Mr. Hannaford's desire to take anything away from the Capitol building and from the Congress. But he feels strongly that the symbol of Abraham Lincoln, who led the republic in a divisive, dangerous time, is appropriate."

There would be no inaugural ball, either, the announcer said; and he then read a wrap-up of opinions from editorials around the country. This had proved a popular move. Inaugural balls had become mindless, pointless, expensive, ostentatious crushes of humanity—without rhyme or reason. "The money saved resulting from the cancellation of these events," Senator Sidney Stapp announced, "will be used by the party's urban study group, to complete its research project on ghetto training units . . ."

"Hmmm," Boswell said. "That's sort of a B. But it isn't really a biggie. It's the party's ill-gotten gain. No one can kick about that."

But there was kicking elsewhere in Washington. Senator Gabriel T. Tutt was interviewed. Old Gabe allowed as how he had heard rumors that the President-elect intended to study the defense budget, all 120 billion dollars of it, with an eye to cutting it.

"Ah don't intend to preach to the President-elect befoah he's taken th' oath," old Gabe said, "but he better walk carefully. They is a passel of left-wingers and appeasers around Mr. Hannaford who would lak nothin' better 'n' to cut the guts and innards out of our defense 'stablishment. Godless, atheistic, militant commonism is waitin' to devour us the second we start slashin' and reducin'. I say, moah planes, moah bombs, moah warships, and let Red Russia and the Chinese know we aim to be first, first, first!"

Boswell yawned mightily. This was going to be his mission—the defanging of Gabe Tutt and the Pentagon. He did not seem overly impressed with the ancient hawk. "We'll have a few surprises for old Gabe," the lobbyist said. "He'd better start checking his figures on the Iron Ball. My team has found seven errors in the calculations already, all in favor of the contractors. Something on the order of five billion dollars is all."

Minerva Boswell arched her unplucked brows. "Only five billion? What happened to all those computers Mr. McNamara was supposed to have installed?"

"Yeah, they work. But so do the lobbyists and the retired generals and the admirals." Boswell yawned again. "The defense contractors have this island down in the Caribbean where they send them to work out their deals on defense jobs. Somehow, by the time the ex-general who now works for Sky-High Missiles or whatever, gets to the fourteenth hole with the defense department specialist, the estimate is up by a half a billion dollars."

"Daddy," Vangie said angrily, "are you the right man to be reforming this corruption? You're the man who has negotiated a dozen of these deals! Talk of putting the fox in the chicken coop!"

Boswell winked at her. "Takes one to know one, daughter. Hannaford understands one thing about me. I have no liberal guilt feelings. I've never been Red or left or pink or socialist or liberal in my life. I've never had a moment's worry over whether some bastard like Joe McCarthy or Gabe Tutt or Bates Pendragon or C. C. Pringle would call me a traitor or an appeaser. No, sir, I'm old Moneyman Boswell—"

"Pay-Toilet Boswell, Parente called you," his wife interrupted.

"I'm Mr. America—schemer, conniver, deal maker. And I can do things that an idealistic intellectual like McNamara or the Rostows or the Bundys wouldn't dare. Because, children, nobody calls Burke Boswell an appeaser, or a Comsymp, or anything else. Here I am, folks, the money man. And I can tell all those generals to go climb a tree. And folks will laugh. You wait and see how they'll laugh."

"You are a disgrace!" his wife whooped. "Shame!"

I was exhausted. Exhausted by inhaling cigar smoke, exhausted by these in-group games, by the brash, crude confidences that these WASP inheritors shared. I said my good nights, feeling enervated, but a bit more optimistic about the travails ahead.

Sadly, this optimism was short-lived. Just before retiring, I listened to the all-news radio station for a few minutes. It was now past one in the morning; a bulletin interrupted the basketball scores. Almost asleep, I jerked upright in bed.

". . . three students dead and a dozen wounded in the action. Shortly after midnight, after orders to evacuate the buildings were met with sniper fire, the National Guard attacked in force with tear gas and commando tactics. Large sections of the buildings were destroyed by fire . . ."

I realized what had happened. Under the provisions of President Kretz's Emergency Riot Control Act, Lumumba University—formerly Teachers College—had been cleaned out. The black students and teachers who had set up their separatist school in the old buildings on West 120th Street had been ousted. Three dead, a dozen wounded; four Guardsmen injured. Another Kent State; in some ways, worse.

". . . New York police units mopped up, making 123 arrests, including the rector of the university's *Indaba*, or council, Mr. Kakamba Jones, thirty-one, who recently ran for Vice-President on the Black-and-Tan ticket. Jones said, as he was handcuffed and driven off, that the battle had just begun, and, this is a quote, 'the brothers are nearby and are ready to strike.'"

I thought of awakening Ben; of calling Judge Samuel Moscowitz, newly resigned from the FBI and slated to be our Attorney General; of phoning Fred Goldstein, who had contacts with the New York press and the New York police. Then I decided that I was terribly tired, exhausted and without resources, or any power to change the appalling course of events. Universities had been cleaned out by troops before; the dead, black bodies at Lumumba U. were not the first to die violently on a college campus; and

136

Kakamba's threat was hardly something new. Dazed, I took a sleeping pill and awaited the new day. But it hardly helped: I lay awake thinking of the unending cycle of hate, and murder and unreason. Had I been a religious person I might have prayed for Ben's health and good fortune.

". . . will faithfully execute the office of President of the United States . . ."

A cold, cold day. Or, as the stage instruction in Faust reads: *dreary day*. Above, darkening clouds bumped their way impatiently across the lead-colored sky. The air was charged with an icy mist. I heard the Chief Justice's soft, tidewater drawl and Ben's measured responses.

". . . and will to the best of my ability, preserve, protect and defend the Constitution of the United States."

"So help you God."

"So help me God."

Applause—the sound lost on the cold, wide steps of the Lincoln Memorial. There were no chairs, no scaffolding, no bunting. The dignitaries merely stood in ranks on the great approach to the mausoleum. In spite of Ben's objections, the area swarmed with security people—secret service men by the score, capitol police, and a small army of National Guardsmen, as well as elite units of the Third Infantry Regiment and the Marine Corps. All this was distasteful to the President, but after the Ramada shooting, he had no choice but to bend to Markland's military operation.

There was some handshaking and cheering. The marine band struck up a martial air as Ben moved to the lectern. He had showed me his speech—no more than ten minutes of generalities. I had argued with him about the wisdom of such a brief address, but he was adamant. "People are sick and tired of getting preached at," he said. "Let's do more and talk less."

Around the new President—I found no difficulty seeing him as our chief executive—stood the official family, shivering, wrapped in woolen coats and furs, the leaders of the new government. I liked their looks. It was a solid team, from austere Walter Edgerton, the Secretary of State, fluent in four languages and afraid of no one, to perky, pretty Margaret High McNally, trim in her mink coat, our new Secretary of the Treasury, to youthful,

137

long-haired Charles Gantry, Secretary of Housing and Urban Development (the sexiest man in the cabinet), to huge, black, bareheaded Homer Murphy, Secretary of Health, Education and Welfare, to cranky Abraham Dent, Secretary of the Interior, a good and faithful friend to whooping cranes and alligators. It was a good team, good Americans.

". . . this country is in trouble," Ben was saying. "Why try to hide it? Why invent fancy words to keep the truth from ourselves? We've got millions of poor people, people who haven't had a chance. Mostly because of the color of their skin. We can't change that, but we can change other things . . ."

He was talking the way he talked to a construction gang; Ben would never win any prizes for rhetoric, but he was getting across. Not so much to the Washingtonians around him, the movers and shakers, judges, senators, governors, ambassadors and other elevated personages, but to the ordinary Americans watching him on television. (Coverage, incidentally, was strictly on a "pooled" basis. Mindful of the way Henry Kaspar had posed as a TV soundman with his parabolic microphone masking his gun, the number of TV technicians and gear in the area had been cut down to the barest minimum.)

". . . will need a lot of money. More money than we've dreamed of. I'm a builder. I've worked with money and with materiel and with people all my life. I know what it costs to rebuild a city. And we'll have to raise the money and spend it wisely.

"We cannot pass a law saying, love the black man down the block. But we can create conditions in which people will be more ready to respect one another. I've heard all about black capitalism and 'a piece of the action' and those other phrases. As an old capitalist, I can assure you, my fellow Americans, that black capitalism is more of a comfort to capitalists than to blacks. And when you tell me that the black man wants 'a piece of the action' you'd better be a little more specific. What action? Whose? I wouldn't dare draw up a business contract with a phrase like that in it, so why should any black person accept it?

"We've heard a great deal about private enterprise rebuilding the slums. I'm all for that. I think it's a grand idea. But I still think the elected representatives of the people have to take the lead. Because when you get right

138

down to it, it was private enterprise that *made* the slums. So maybe they aren't the greatest experts in the world on cleaning 'em up, although I surely want their help. . . ."

I turned my attention to Fern Hannaford. She was standing behind Ben. She seemed covered with an icy glaze. There was too much make-up on her face, and it did not sit well on her honest features. I was glad to see Vangie standing next to her holding her arm. I hoped that the young girl was proving a comforter to the First Lady.

"I am not being frivolous when I say to you, my fellow citizens, that there is only one real problem where the poor are concerned. And that is, they don't have enough money. That sounds so obvious we might be out of line for daring to utter it. But it is a fact. Not enough money. We have to get it to them. It won't be easy."

I turned my attention to the key men in the Congress who would be acting on Ben's legislative program. Foremost, and most fearsome, was the Majority Leader, Senator Gage (Honey-Tonsils) Hopewell of Wisconsin. I doubt that he cared for what he heard from the new President. We'd have to deal carefully with old Gage. At his side stood, or rather was implanted, his faithful wife, Rachel, broad-beamed, frizzy-haired, square-jawed, a professional Washington character, full of short answers and harsh judgments, a veteran of a thousand church suppers and Epworth League socials. They were, the two of them, bedrock America, and they and millions like them would have to be swayed.

But we would have friends in the Senate—notably Swinging Sid Stapp, who, as Majority Whip, could be depended upon to run interference for Ben, even if Hopewell might drag his feet. Sid owed Ben a good deal. I eyed the swinger enviously: he was wearing a handsome sealskin fur hat and a fur-collared overcoat. Most senators would denounce their oath of office before so decking themselves publicly; but the Swinger had a certain panache, a certain flair. Sexy Judy, shivering in sable, stood at his side. I made a mental note to meet with her. She had pipelines to the new left, the gurus of the switched-on young people, and I would have to consult with them and see if they would take the pressure off Ben so he could get some action out of Congress.

". . . Russians and Hungarians and Poles and Czechs, and yes, Chinese, are people. They have families, they have children, they have homes, and they have hopes and dreams. I don't like their governments. I detest Communism. I said years ago I would never help a Communist unless I could make money out of him. But these people, and some of their leaders, have understood for a long time that it won't make any sense to destroy the world over ideology. . . . I think there are ways to convince these governments to loosen up on their people. Their citizens are aching for freedom, for air, for comforts, for goods, for a better life. Yes, my friends, the Poles and the Hungarians and the Chinese want these things out of life, every bit as much as the black people in Mississippi and Harlem want them."

Strong stuff. It wasn't what a President was supposed to do at an Inauguration. But Hannaford had his own style, his own methods. I gazed out at the press section. I could see Bates Pendragon, arching his bushy brows and rubbing his he-man's mustache. He and publisher C. C. Pringle, they would not buy that line, not at all.

"I ask you, my fellow citizens to think back to the tragic days of the Vietnam War, that miscalculation for which so many of us in high places, including your President, must share the blame. Let me take one statistic out of that appalling struggle. In the course of the fighting in Vietnam, we lost aircraft valued at eight billion dollars. That's right. *Eight billion dollars* worth of planes, helicopters, bombers, fighters—burned, scrapped, destroyed. I shall not even mention the lives of all the good men who died. But have any of you any idea what we could have done with eight billion dollars here at home?"

I stomped my freezing feet and watched my breath form a wispy cloud.

"Yes, with eight billion dollars, we could have, over a two-year period, doubled federal support for primary and secondary schools—including fifty new junior colleges, doubled federal job and training programs for the unemployed and disadvantaged."

I noticed the disturbance first in the press corps. I could see Lou Parente turning his head; Pendragon rising; beauteous Mona Varnum, the black girl who had been wounded in Ramada City, looking from side to side. And then, straining my ears, trying to ascertain what was drawing their attention over Ben's loud voice on the speaker, I, too, heard the shots.

140

Crack-crack. Crack-crack. Unmistakable. It was small arms fire. Distantly, to be sure, the noises coming from the south, from the black ghetto. Then the noises increased—louder, more frequent. Sirens wailed in the distance, and the people on the steps of the monument turned their heads, and whispered one to another. I watched the secret service men busy with their walky-talkies. The cordon of agents around the lectern suddenly doubled in number, an alert Markland in the middle of the tense group. *Crack-crack-crack . . .*

But if all in attendance were rendered apprehensive and querulous by the explosions—the shots now appeared to be dying down although the sirens continued to ululate across the darkening city—Ben Hannaford ignored them.

"We intend to keep the defenses of America strong," the President was saying. "Your President pledges his intention to work with the generals and admirals who protect our shores . . ."

(This I found beautiful—speaking of the Pentagon patroons as if they were a foreign power, a sovereign entity that had to be dealt with separately; it was Fred Goldstein's touch.)

The undulant wail of the sirens diminished. I strained my ears for any reprise of those disturbing shots, those rude reminders of the state of semi siege under which we now lived. But there was silence; just the insistent humming of the insectlike helicopters hovering above us. And as Ben spoke on—surely the most unique inaugural speech ever made—I ruminated on the disparity between the beauty of the Lincoln Memorial rising in splendor on the banks of the Potomac and the depressing realities of our cities.

"Let me say finally," Ben said, "that I don't for a minute believe that Americans are a mean or a cruel people. We work hard. We get things done. We are ambitious for ourselves and our children and our country. And sometimes the vigor, and speed and determination with which we work tend to run over some of our neighbors. Often they can't keep up, through no fault of their own. I hope this Administration can appeal to everything that is generous and openhearted and openminded in America, and get people to talk things out, work things out, and make a better life available to everyone.

"Isaiah told us that the nation was multiplied, but that

141

joy was not increased. That is exactly our problem. We multiply everything—people, goods, houses, wealth—but we seem to fall short of joy. So let us, my fellow Americans, put aside old hatreds, old grievances, old rivalries, let us start talking to each other again, and create a nation in which 'the ways are ways of pleasantness and all her paths are peace.'"

He'd saved Scripture for the end, and it was effective. The applause was by no means deafening or sustained. It was terribly cold on the marble steps of the memorial, and I am certain that a good share of the dignitaries did not care for his cracks about the defense budget and the defense establishment. I had noticed the chairman of the Joint Chiefs, General Boyd R. Nagel, setting his jaw, when Ben had discussed the eight billion dollars' worth of airplanes lost in Vietnam.

Our hand-picked preacher, a Unitarian named Metcalfe who'd done time as a Vietnam protester, was now at the lectern for the final prayer. He kept it short, as he had promised. A detachment of the marine band struck up "Hail to the Chief," and Ben, surrounded by handshakers and what seemed a platoon of shave-headed secret service men, started to leave. The crowd on the steps lingered, a few people still applauding. I decided to mingle with the audience and gauge reactions. As I walked down the long steps, through the ranks of shivering citizens, Dalton Warfield came to my side.

"Fine speech, hey, Edward?" he asked.

"The boss broke just about every tradition in the book. Someone'll give him what-for for all that talk about money."

Warfield cocked his head. "But that's what it's all about. I got ideals and visions and big plans, just like everyone else. But you got to lay on the bread."

We edged our way through the crowd. Warfield looked positively indigo blue under his black skin. He was a unique man, this Negro social worker, and possibly the bravest man I have ever known. His brother had been killed by a shotgun blast during second Watts; his home and his office were periodically burned; his children suffered obscene threats; his telephone crawled with the vermin and psychopaths who infect our cities; and through it all, he strode serenely, his sad eyes appearing to be stained, his head lowered, his suits rumpled, his huge,

142

black hands dangling at his side. If I were to name the half-dozen most admirable men in America, Dalton Warfield would surely be on the list.

"Hey, Deever!" I heard a harsh voice call. "Hey, Warfield!" It was Lou Parente, hatless in the biting cold, his graying head bent forward, his hands jammed into a sheepskin-lined Mackinaw.

"Not a bad speech from the Master Builder," he said. "But he makes enemies every time he opens his mouth. Who's he kidding with that stuff about private enterprise having *made* the slums?"

"It's only the truth," Warfield said.

"Yeah, but it ain't the way you get votes in this country. Even Bobby Kennedy had to come on with that crap about businessmen and capitalists renewing the slums. I don't think he believed it, but he had to say it. And that stuff about the eight billion dollars' worth of planes lost in Vietnam. Deever, there were guys on those steps today whose only religion is building expensive airplanes and making sure they are shot down."

I nodded. "Maybe the problem is that we've never had a President with the guts to face up to them."

Dalton Warfield shivered. "And maybe we got one now."

Lou Parente's bushy eyebrows rose. "I warned you once, Deever, you better tell Hannaford to watch his step. He barely made it to the White House. Most people don't like the kind of noises he is making."

Warfield shook his ebony head. "They'll learn to like it."

"That's what you guys think," Parente said softly. "Hannaford should know better. He was once on that team—the ones who think they own and operate the show. Well, fellahs, they're still around and they're making plans that your President better worry about."

Cold, cold. The pavement beneath our feet was like pack ice. Were we three miserable Elizas, pursued by the bloodhounds of hate, and fear and the old lunacies that besmirched our national past?

The columnist turned to leave. "Keep your eye on Congressman Ruckett," he said. "I could name twenty others, but you might as well start with him."

He shoved his way through the dispersing crowd; Warfield and I watched him leave, then turned left toward the beckoning White house.

PART II

I never forget that I live in a house owned by all the American people.

—FRANKLIN DELANO ROOSEVELT

At eight o'clock of a chill morning in late January, the line had already formed at the east gate of the White House. Our Americans. Our citizens. At ten the doors would open for the guided tour of the mansion. At noon the tour would end. For two hours the impressive state rooms would belong to the people—the East Room, the Green Room, the Blue Room, the South Portico, the Red Room, the State Dining Room and the first-floor hallways. The people would walk through in respectful silence, look at the historic paintings and furnishings, and perhaps some would be moved to reflect on the travail that had gone into creating these graceful reminders of our brief history.

I had been making it a habit to approach the White House from the east, motivated by some need to look for public sustenance from the people who came to visit the President's home. At times I had the nutty notion that I wanted to address those patient Americans standing in line, eager to have a glimpse of the living past. I wanted to say to them: *Help Ben Hannaford, be generous and patient and act in the best tradition of your countrymen.*

For the truth of the matter was, I was apprehensive. I kept thinking about the nature of Ben's job; the enemies he had; the almost reflexive way, as if responding to unseen stimuli, that our country had become a vassal of the military.

Here I heard the pleasant twang of the Middle West, spoken by a fur-hatted, red-faced man and his chubby wife; there the soft drawl of the South, uttered by a young couple, he in marine corps green, she in a blue woolen coat; there I heard the harsh nasalities of the Bronx or Brooklyn, from a happy family of intense, laughing Jews; or the soft tones of a dignified Negro couple. Our Americans. And yet, and yet . . . Just a third of them voted for Ben Hannaford. Many hated him. Others distrusted him. Some said the scandal of the censure hearings would never permit him to be an effective President. Is it any wonder I had the crazy feeling, on some of these morning strolls from my room at the Manger Hay-Adams (I would live there for a while) to my office at the White House, that I wanted to appeal to them, not only to enjoy their visit to the resplendent state rooms, but to find in their hearts sympathy for the big man now sitting in the oval office in the West Wing?

And there sat the boss—relaxed and thoughtful, devising stratagems to lead the republic back to sanity. Ben was never much of a reader, but he would have laughed aloud at one of James Bryce's chapter headings—WHY GREAT MEN ARE NOT CHOSEN PRESIDENTS. How wrong a historian could be! For if the recent history of the presidency proved anything, it proved that it tended to *create* greatness in its stewards. I make no excessive claims for Ben Hannaford; he was not a visionary or an idealist. But he sensed what was right and what was necessary. And most importantly, his morality was a practical morality. Ideologues rarely succeed in the presidency, or indeed, anywhere else in Washington. There is nothing wrong with ideology, except that it has an alarming tendency to end up at the opposite end of where it wanted to go.

But I banished such thoughts this brisk January morning. It is said that the presidency is what the occupant makes of it. Article II of the Constitution states, with disarming simplicity, "The Executive power shall be vested in a President of the United States of America." But on examination, the great charter is remarkably stingy and vague as to what these powers are. We are all familiar with the list: head of the Armed Forces, the granting of pardons, treaty-making (with the advice and consent of the Senate); appointment of federal officials (the Senate must approve these also); the power to veto acts of Congress; recommendation of measures to the Congress. And the broad command that he "take care that the laws be faithfully executed."

And that is about it. Short. Rather imprecise. A tight
147

bill of particulars for your Buchanan or Coolidge or Eisenhower. A blank check for your Lincoln or your Teddy Roosevelt or FDR or Lyndon Johnson. If I knew Hannaford, he would want to be the latter type of President. But could he? Would the temper of the times give him the freedom he would need?

I kept thinking of the 56 per cent of the people who had voted against Ben. I thought of the rancor and bitterness of the campaign. I thought of that self-perpetuating, self-generating blob, the defense establishment, with its strangle hold on the economy, its snout in the public treasury, its appetites never satisfied, its lobbyists and legislators. And I thought of the resistance of the Congress and a vast section of the electorate. And most of all I thought of my cabdriver, Salvatore Melfi, who would have been happy to shoot down student rioters and send troublesome blacks back to Africa. (As a journalist some years ago had noted, George Wallace awakened one morning and discovered that *nobody* in the United States liked Negroes. In fact, there was a chance that the whole country was *southern.* And in my numbed ears, rang old Sam Rayburn's cruel estimate of so much florid political oratory. It boiled down, Sam said, to three words: *nigger, nigger, nigger.*)

The first person I ran into in the White House press room, where I made it a practice to stop off, was Mona Varnum.

"Can I talk to you a minute?" she asked.

"I can't think of a nicer way to start my day."

Mona Varnum did not smile. She fixed me with a cold eye, blacker than polished onyx. She was a beauty, a stunning, disturbing vision, this café-au-lait girl. Her hair rose bushily in an exaggerated Afro cut, and great golden wheels dangled from perfect little ears. She was not too tall, but of such a slender suppleness, as to give the effect of height. Or perhaps it was her haughty manner.

"I thought I'd tell you that my company is paying the hospital bills," Mona said. "I didn't like the idea of Hannaford doing any favors for me."

"The President acted out of concern for you, Miss Varnum," I said. "My understanding was that United Radio was more than willing to accept his offer."

"But I wasn't." I noticed that her left shoulder was a bit lower than the right—a result of the wounds she had received when the bullets had ripped into her two months ago. But otherwise she seemed healthy. And so beautiful. I had read somewhere—in some high-domed magazine of little influence—that the only solution to America's racial problems was enthusiastic intermarriage and interbreeding of the races. It would never happen in our time, of course, but were it ordained, I would have gladly volunteered if Mona Varnum were named my partner.

"I'll advise the President," I said. "We've all felt guilty that you had to suffer. We appreciate the way you've refused to publicize your role in the assassination attempt."

The iciness of her black eyes, their indifference to my compliments aroused me even more.

"I have no interest in discussing the matter," Mona Varnum said. "What I want to know is, how soon are the people arrested under the emergency law going to be freed?"

Steady there, Deever. For the first time in several years I experienced the erotic urge that signals to me that I am about to get into trouble. But with a *black* girl? A militant, hostile black girl? In a dazzling mental image I saw Miss Varnum naked and supine, skin like a Mark Cross purse, silken and creamy beige. . . . I cursed my own visions, and decided that, thank God, she detested me and would no more succumb to my square Ohio appeals than she would report favorably on Senator Gabe Tutt's latest fulminations against her soul brothers.

"Since this is a new Administration, I have no objection to playing favorites. I don't have to tell you a thing. But we do feel rather special about you, Miss Varnum."

A mocking smile arched her black brows. She had no use for me, no use at all. "I don't want any favors. From you or Hannaford or any of your shifty crew."

"Does that include Mr. Murphy? And Mr. Warfield?"

Pouting, she placed a slender hand on her hip. "Don't try that line. There's black and black."

"I gather. In any case, Miss Varnum, there will be a cabinet meeting this morning, and the President's first order of business will be to instruct the Attorney General to reduce the charges against all the people arrested under ERCA, to stop any further arrests and suspend the state of emergency, which the outgoing Administration claimed to have existed when the campus raids were ordered."

"May I use that?"

"Indeed you may. But no attribution. A highly-placed source will do."

"What if you're throwing me a curve? I recall the Kennedys had a little trick of feeding misinformation to reporters whom they felt had done them dirt. Johnson did it regularly."

"You seem to have more than your share of admirable curves, ma'am. I wouldn't dare trick you. I'm sure you know all the tricks."

If this bit of sexual innuendo had any effect on the black Venus, I was not certain. Satisfied that I was telling the truth, she thanked me not at all, turned her back, and walked into the press room. All administrations play favorites in the press; I'd selected mine.

I crossed the huge lobby of the West Wing, nodded at the secret service men at the doors, and caught a glimpse of Vice-President Verne Sparrier walking briskly toward his small corner office. Ben had announced that the Vice-President would have no staff of his own other than a secretary. For press relations, he would use Fred's people. I rather regretted Ben's decision. Sparrier was a vigorous, ambitious and guileful young man. It might have been better to give him his freedom early in the game. "He'll be happy," Ben said. "He can launch battleships and address fund-raising dinners."

I thought of the immortal Mr. Dooley's view of the office: "The vice-presidency," he wrote, "is not a crime and you can't be sent to jail for it. But it's sort of a disgrace ... like writing anonymous letters."

We assembled in the cabinet room, under the Matthew Jouett portrait of Jefferson. Around the room, other portraits—Andrew Jackson, Daniel Webster, FDR, gazed down at us. At the center of the long table—presented to Roosevelt by Jesse H. Jones—President Hannaford sat, behind him the flag of the republic, the presidential flag and the great seal.

He opened the meeting by advising Samuel Moscowitz to order his staff to start action to begin freeing, in co-operation with the courts, the two-thousand-odd students and other demonstrators who had been herded into stadia, armories and camps, as a result of Hayward Kretz's riot act.

150

"It won't be easy, Mr. President," Moscowitz said. "But we'll do our best."

"We will announce suspension of the state of emergency," Ben said. "And I want a special commission to start hearings, to talk to these kids." He turned to the Secretary-designate of HEW, Murphy. "Homer, you head it up. A small group. Get hold of Senator Henshaw. The youngsters like him. Maybe Dalton can help out."

Vice-President Sparrier shifted uneasily in his seat. "Mr. President," he said, "I would be less than honest if I did not go on record as stating that I oppose these actions, which I am certain reflect your own charitable views. But history teaches us that a revolutionary cabal will wreak havoc unless suppressed."

"We have to take a chance," Ben said. "Can't keep herding people into army camps and old hospitals."

"Why not?" Sparrier asked. "Let them reflect a bit on their acts of treachery against the established order. The American people are fed up with coddling criminal elements, rioters and revolutionaries. These young people represent no one but themselves. The majority of Americans despise and fear them, and applauded President Kretz's brave move to . . . to . . . neutralize them."

"Why not shoot 'em all, Verne?" Homer Murphy asked.

"That is not fair," Sparrier said, reddening. He was still a bit sensitive about the way his National Guardsmen and vigilantes had shot dead over two hundred people during the agony of second Watts. At heart, Verne Sparrier was not a violent man. Quite the contrary, he tended to be cautious and evasive. But events had run away from him in California.

"Hell, they have to be let out sooner or later," Burke Boswell said. "Look, Verne, we can't clutter up the jails and the armories with a lot of unwashed kids. Besides, that law will be tossed out by the Supreme Court as soon as it's tested."

"If I may cite a historical example that is extremely pertinent," the Vice-President said. "I am something of a student of Communism, and I speak with a little expertise in this area . . ."

I could see Homer Murphy bend toward Charles Gantry, and whisper. My ears caught something like: "Here comes the lecture." And lecture it would be; Communism and its diabolical guises were favorite subjects of Sparrier's.

"The liberal government of Alexander Kerensky," the Vice-President orated, "in 1917, decided as an act of clemency to release from prison a horde of Boshevik agitators, including the archconspirator, Leon Trotsky . . ."

"Born Lev Davidovich Bronstein," Fred Goldstein muttered to me.

"A charitable act, yes," Sparrier went on. "But no sooner were Trotsky and his fellow revolutionaries freed, than they began to plot against Kerensky, overthrew him and forced him to flee. As a result of Kerenksy's charity, Bolshevism triumphed and we all know the ghastly result. Those people should have been kept in prison and the world might have been saved this scourge."

There were moments when Ben regretted that he was not an educated, erudite man. Frankly, I doubted if he knew who Alexander Kerensky was.

Walter Edgerton, former Senator Edgerton, the new Secretary of State, came to Hannaford's rescue.

"Mr. Vice-President," Edgerton said, "your references to Russian history are accurate but hardly applicable. When Kerensky released the Bolsheviks in 1917, Russia was ripe for revolution . . ."

"You deny that the United States is not?" Sparrier said quickly. Score one for the preacher, I thought. Goldstein nudged my ribs.

"Yes, but an entirely different kind," Edgerton said.

"Amen," Homer Murphy said.

"The Secretary of Health, Education and Welfare knows what I mean," Edgerton went on. "Russia was a country of starving, downtrodden people, suffering through a war that had destroyed its youth, disillusioned the intelligentsia, ruined the economy. That Lenin and Trotsky and the Bolsheviks, a minor party, were able to seize control was an accident of history, a tribute to the incoherence and slovenliness of their opposition and the corruption of the old order. Whether Mr. Kerensky had let them out of prison or not, there would have been a revolution of the left. It was already underway . . ."

"Ah, you are proving my point," Sparrier said.

"Indeed?" asked the Secretary of State. "How?"

A smile suffused Sparrier's shining face. "Well, I assume

you will say that these radical children and black people are a tiny minority, who could not create a revolution. But you have just proven that that very thing took place in Russia."

"With an important difference, Mr. Vice-President," Edgerton said. "The soil and the climate in Russia were ready for it. The masses were miserable, the vast majority of people, peasants, workers, soldiers, crying for a revolutionary change in society. I say, a *majority*. That is hardly the case today."

President Hannaford shifted in his seat. "By God, I see what Walter is getting at. The kids and people like Kakamba Jones don't have any constituency. The majority of Americans are white and prosperous and they want those loudmouths *suppressed*. It's the truth, Verne. You could turn all those kids loose tonight, and they couldn't start a revolution in Brooklyn. Hell, they can make some trouble. But the people won't tolerate it."

"I have to concur with Mr. Edgerton's estimate of the climate in this country," Moscowitz said. "You simply can't compare it to Russia."

"If there is a comparison," Meg McNally said, turning to Ben, "maybe it's with Germany in the thirties."

"Good God, I hope not," Ben said. "I can't believe that Americans are that mean. I won't. I'm stubborn about it. I've found most Americans will listen to reason. They'll admire a man who succeeds in spite of handicaps. And that goes for black men, yellow men, red men and long-haired youngsters."

Poor Ben. In his bluff, hard-handed way, he believed in goodness and mercy and charity and talking things over. These were decent and tidy things to believe in, of course. But what help could they be to a President faced with an enraged electorate?

Vice-President Sparrier straightened up in his chair. He sat, as is customary, directly opposite the President. He realized he was in a minority around the table. Yet he understood—and Moscowitz and Edgerton and Murphy would have surely agreed—that his attitudes were much closer to the mass of confused Americans than were those of his fellow cabinet members. I had to admire the chesty little jaycee; there was a lower-middle-class courage in Sparrier, and I never sensed it better than when he responded to Murphy.

"Then all I can say, Mr. Murphy," the Vice-President said, "is that some of your people have only themselves to blame for the guns that are fired in Washington, and Detroit and Watts."

"I guess you can say that," Homer Murphy replied. "But you never spent a summer in Harlem or Hough or Watts with the stink and the crime and the rats and the noise. You know, the wonder is that black people *all* haven't gone crazy for what's been done to 'em."

No one spoke for a few seconds. Then Ben took command; the old Ben Hannaford who had ruled the Senate and built cities and airfields and come up the hard way, the fourteen-year-old oil-field rigger, part Kiowa and all man.

"Meeting's sort of wandering around," he said impatiently. "Homer, what you say is so true no one can contradict you. Still, we can't tolerate riots and shoot-outs and destruction. And Mr. Vice-President, I'll take your warning under advisement. If we free these two thousand demonstrators, we'll keep an eye on 'em. I want us all to stop arguing about the past. It's a waste of time. I don't mean studying the past, Senator Edgerton, I mean chewing over it. We all know black people got a right to be angry. But to hell with all that. Let's get the housing and the schools and the libraries built, and let's open up the jobs, and let's give the poor what they need more than anything—money."

"I am not opposed to any of that," Verne Sparrier said swiftly, spreading his hands. "But society must be orderly for all these things to happen . . ."

Goldstein was whispering in my ear. "Goddamn hypocrite," Fred said. "Killed every job training program, every welfare program, every school aid bill in the last three years."

"We'll keep it orderly," President Hannaford said. He turned to Judge Moscowitz. "Get those people out of those damned armories by tonight. Tell 'em the state of emergency is over."

"Mr. President, I must respectfully register my dissent," Sparrier said. "And I pray I shall be proven wrong."

"Your objections are noted, Verne," Hannaford said. He turned to Homer Murphy. "Homer, get with the Urban Task Force and work all day and all night. I need a costing out on the rebuilding plan for the cities. Don't go cheap. Go first class. Give them every dollar you want, and if you're in doubt, double the estimate."

Meg McNally's eyebrows went up. "Really, Mr. President . . ."

"It's all right, Meg. The generals and admirals have been pulling that stunt for years. Why not the poor suckers in the slums?"

"May I remind the President," Meg said, "that the previous Administration has left us with a budget of 220 billion dollars, of which 120 billion is marked for defense?"

Ben held up his huge hand. "I'm aware of that, Meg. But as the old song says, there'll be some changes made." He turned to face Burke Boswell. "Mr. Boswell will be giving the matter of defense spending his earnest attention. We will depend on the Secretary of Defense to trim their allowance."

Meg McNally cleared her throat. "Mr. President, this isn't my direct concern, but it seems to me, we haven't consulted at all with General Nagel or the Joint Chiefs or the congressional leaders on this matter."

Ben got up. I hurried to gather up his scrawled notes, the papers he had left. "Meg, I'll quote you Scripture on that one. 'Surely in vain the net is spread in the sight of any bird.' "

The birds in question, I realized, had huge beaks and strong talons.

Two days later, into the white-and-gold magnificence of the East Room, poured the Daughters of the American Revolution, 1702 of them, be-sashed, be-ribboned, gowned, coiff'd, perfumed, some barely capable of suppressing their hostility. This was to be Fern Hannaford's first public exposure. She had pleaded with Ben to be allowed to cancel the affair. She had shivered a little when my protégé Vangie had explained the ritual, and at last, trembling gently, she consented to the mob-scene.

Surrounded by the fluted pilasters, they trod the parquet floor, a great feminine host, girdle to girdle, blue rinse by white, blond streak by ash-blond, the inheritors of America. A laminated aroma of a thousand scents commingled rose in the heated air—lemon verbena, lavender, sandalwood, attar of roses. A lone man in that swarm of

155

corseted female bodies, I glided about, trying to catch a phrase here and a word there.

"How is the First Lady bearing up?" I asked Vangie. My girl was magnificent—her lank honey-colored hair gold-pinned, her dress a demure dark green, not too short.

"Bravely," she said. "I convinced her to say a few words to the guests. The handshaking doesn't worry me. Fern is physically strong. She'll give them a hard right hand."

"Jimmy Durante used to call it 'the big hello,' " I said. "Although from the looks of this mob, they'd only rate what he termed 'the small hello.' "

They were a grim group. Amid the pastel gowns wandered those discreet, perfectly molded black men who serve in the White House, offering lemonade and cookies (Lemonade and cookies? Was it not the wife of President Benjamin Harrison who became known as Lemonade Lucy? Would our poor Fern be remembered as Fig Newton Fern?) At one side of the famed mahogany Steinway on its three gilt eagles a microphone had been placed. There Fern would have her baptism.

I recalled that there had been some wild scenes in the East Room in past administrations, but I had faith unbounded in the decorum of our DARs. One such hooley, a reception for party workers hosted by Mrs. Lyndon Johnson was described as "an exercise in chaos." The President was kissed and hugged over and over, an 1820 antique lamp was smashed, a social secretary was clopped on the head with a tray, and the ladies wandered at liberty through the state rooms for hours.

Fern looked splendid. She was wearing a simple beige dress, which contrasted discreetly with her blond hair, her clear skin and also with the gold hangings and cream-colored walls of the East Room. Her posture and bearing were magnificent. Head high, the faintest of polite smiles on her thin lips, a slight tilt to her head, she seemed to be at ease as she shook hands with the endless line of gowned women. I stood on tippy-toes and saw before me a sea of flowered hats—ye gods, those paper pansies and cloth carnations, plastic peonies and batik begonias! The heads nodded, bobbed, acknowledged the shake of hand, the wan smile of the First Lady, and moved on, like the great shroud of the sea, in *Moby Dick*.

"Do you realize, Evangeline," I said to the social secretary, "that of these seventeen hundred some-odd ladies here assembled, probably less than ten voted for Ben Hannaford? And of those, maybe half did so by mistake? You are looking into Beldock territory, and a good sprinkling of Upshawville."

I couldn't get my mind off Ben's current problem. His order to the Justice Department had already been enacted. The speed with which the students, blacks and other rioters had been liberated varied from city to city, but most of the people jailed under the ERCA were now free on bail. The state of emergency had been suspended. Moscowitz had issued an appeal to campuses and ghettos around the country to take Ben's charitable act as an earnest of the new Administration's desire to cool the tensions, to talk problems over with the young and the poor and the black, and to put forth a broad program of improvement in the cities. So far, the spokesmen for these groups had barely responded. I realized, of course, that they were by no means unified, that they were a motley congeries of opinions, and that they rarely spoke in one voice. But one might have expected a sign of gratitude from one or two of them.

"I am Mary Louise Cathcart, of Spartanburg, South Carolina, and I believe I once dated your nephew, Jason Cudder," I heard a reedy voice say.

"I am so pleased to meet you and welcome you," Fern responded.

Next. "How do you do, Mrs. Hannaford, I do believe we met at the convention, at the governor's reception? Edna Younghusband, Akron, Ohio."

"Of course, how nice of you to visit."

Next. On and on they marched, these visions in pastel hues and steel jaws. One makes a lot of bad jokes about the DAR, but I think they deserve a good deal of sympathy. They haven't been the same since Eleanor Roosevelt invited Marian Anderson to sing in the Lincoln Memorial after the DAR turned her down on Constitution Hall. It takes a good deal of raw courage to live down a disgrace like that. But then—you recall their stern campaign against that creeping horror—UNICEF? How they urged the boycott of UNICEF Christmas cards on the grounds that— whisper it—UNICEF *helps Communists?* But they were also children, hungry and sick. I recalled the way Jacqueline Kennedy, when informed of the Daughters' hatred of UNICEF and its charitable acts toward starving youngsters in Kenya and sick children in Bulgaria, at once *doubled* her order of UNICEF cards.

"Not too fast, Eddie," I heard a crackly voice say. I turned, as a claw grabbed the tail of my coat. It was the hand of Mrs. Gage Hopewell, old Rachel, wife of our beloved Majority Leader.

"Why, Mrs. Hopewell, how nice to see you."

"You betcha, Eddie." She was hot stuff, Rachel. She had to be, to keep up with Honey-Tonsils.

"This is a lovely affair isn't it?" I tried. "I'd forgotten you were a pillar of the national DAR." The red, white and blue sash crossed her immense iron bosom, like the rally striping on the hood of a souped-up Ford.

"Yeah, a pillar of salt, as your boss would say." Rachel was a character in her own right. She was reputed to be a great comic, a foil and vaudeville partner to her pompously comical husband, but somehow the wit was lost on me.

"I'm sure if the President knew you were in attendance, Mrs. Hopewell, he would have put in an appearance," I said.

"Don't be too sure, sonny."

"Come now, Mrs. Hopewell. You and the senator are very dear to him."

"My sweetie doesn't hold with that business of freeing all those creeps," Rachel Hopewell said flatly. By "my sweetie," of course, she meant Gage.

"The President acted upon sound legal and constitutional advice," I said.

Around me the female whickering and nattering rose; it was amazing how much noise can be made by the rustling of slips, the giggling and cooing and inane chatter of ladies. I had the notion that about a half-dozen double-chinned, cold-eyed women were watching my confrontation with Rachel. After all, Rachel was, next to the First Lady, the most important person in the room.

"Eddie, I have to tell you flat out," Rachel Hopewell said, squinting at me through gold-rimmed bifocals. With her frizzy, blue rinse and the strange pointed hat she wore—her nose was short and beaked—she had the appearance of a barn owl, a terror to rats, mice and small snakes, like me. "I have to tell you flat out, my sweetie

158

didn't care for the way the President made that decision at a cabinet meeting without consulting the Congress."

When Rachel Hopewell said *Congress*, she meant Gage.

"The President felt that was an executive decision," I said. "Inasmuch as the signing of the bill at the last moment by Mr. Kretz was a similar executive decision."

"Don't bull me, Eddie. The Congress enacted those bills. The people wanted all those bearded hippies and Communists slapped into jails until they learn good manners."

"You are so correct, Rachel," a bony woman crowned by what seemed to be a clay pot of gladiolas said. "I think President Hannaford had bad advice. He is one of us, I'm sure, but he has some people around him I don't care for."

"Yup," said Rachel Hopewell. "And he's forgettin' old friends."

I knew what was happening. Under President Kretz, Gage Hopewell, as Majority Leader had been our party's king of the Hill. He was in the opposition party of Kretz, but he had held enormous powers in his hands. It was Senator Hopewell this, and Senator Hopewell that, "Today," "Meet the Press," "Face the Nation," interviews in *U.S. News*, *Time* and *Newsweek*, and every visitor to the Capitol desirous of seeing the Falstaff of the Senate, the chanter of old-fashioned rhetoric.

But now the rules had changed. President Hannaford was of the same party as Senator Hopewell. Gage was still Majority Leader. But he was no longer *Numero Uno* in our party. Not with Hannaford in the White House. It was a strange turn of events, and in a way, a commentary on our two-party system which so often surprises both devotees and its critics. When our party was out of the White House Gage had been a Mighty Lord, Yahweh incarnate. Now that we ruled *both* the Executive and the Legislative, he was smaller potatoes, and that was what was giving Rachel the vapors.

"Who put him up to it? Murphy? Moscowitz?" Rachel pressed. "Turn all those hippies and drug addicts loose, and they'll be raising hell all over the place."

"It was the President's decision, Mrs. Hopewell."

"Yeah, mebbe. But he should have asked my sweetie first."

I excused myself and took a position behind the gilt

Steinway. Rooted in front of a gold drapery, I reflected sadly that the East Room was where both Presidents Lincoln and Kennedy had rested in state after their assassinations. I shivered as a crush of ladies near the mantelpiece threatened President Monroe's candelabra. Vangie left Fern's side to caution the guests about getting too close to the historic bric-a-brac.

Fern's calm face looked with relief toward the end of the long line.

As the last few ladies approached, I noticed particularly a tall, angular woman wearing a straw basket of pink geraniums. Do not ask me why, but I have a nose for disaster. To this day, I am certain, had the would-be assassin, Henry Kaspar, been on ground level in front of the Ramada Stockman's Inn, instead of hiding in the second-story window, I would have spotted him in an instant. There is something about the eyes of these believers. They burn. They know. They have seen the light. And this gangly woman, sailing toward Fern, had that gleam in her hazel orbs.

"How do you do, and welcome to the White House," Fern said pleasantly. I admired her. She looked lovely. She had exhibited grace and charm and had hidden her unease remarkably well.

"I will not shake your hand, Mrs. Hannaford," the specter said in a voice that seemed to rise out of an abandoned mine shaft. "I am Helen Leroy Van Lunden of Muncie, Indiana, and while I honor this house and this room and this republic, I speak for many patriotic citizens who are revolted by your husband's action in freeing traitors who should be shot."

Fern's mouth opened, and she drew back her pale hand. I nodded to Vangie, who shoved her way toward us.

"I think it's about time for your address, Mrs. Hannaford," I said hastily. Gently, I took Fern's elbow. She smiled at me.

"Yes, Edward . . ."

"Please take this as a reminder to you and your husband that most Americans do not agree with his acts toward traitors and revolutionists," the tall lady said.

"Thank you, Mrs. Van Lunden, I'll handle that," I said. I grabbed a sheaf of cards, brochures, envelopes from her, all nicely done up with a blue ribbon. All I could see was the card on top, which read:

"You should read that material, Mrs. Hannaford," said Mrs. Van Lunden. "We who are students of godless, atheistic communism know what happens when one is charitable to their enemies."

"Thank you, ma'am," I said. Vangie, who had arrived at Fern's side, pushed the last few ladies on the receiving line forward, and I grabbed Mrs. Van Lunden's leathery elbow.

"Right this way, Mrs. Van Lunden," I said "I want to talk to you about that literature. I'm a student of Communism myself."

Her eyes glittered with revelation, and she accepted me as a believer. "Someone must tell the President to stop this reckless course. Who are the people close to him who are responsible? Is it the Bilderburg group? Or the Illuminati?"

She was one of them. She had read all the right books and all the right magazines. She trod the earth convinced that internal enemies were conspiring to destroy the republic, and she, Helen Leroy Van Lunden, stood between the nation and the evil ones.

I got her as far as the mantel with the James Monroe candelabra. She kept mumbling about the need for alertness; I quoted Washington as to 'put none but Americans in guard.' " Applause rose around us as I saw Fern approach the microphone, and the ladies settled into jellied, fruit-colored layers around the First Lady.

"Dear friends," Fern said, "I shall be brief, since I have had the pleasure of meeting you all personally. Of course you are all welcome here today ..." She darted a fearful look at Vangie, and Miss Boswell nodded, as if to say, you are doing splendidly.

"You are welcome, because this is after all, the house of all the American people. As that much-loved lady, Mrs. Lyndon Johnson, once wrote ..." Fern's voice was a thin quaver.

And then I heard a noise issue from Mrs. Van Lunden. Escaping steam. A leaky inner tube. The old dragon was hissing. *Hissing!* She was hissing the mention of Lady Bird's name.

"... its furniture, its paintings, its countless mementos make it a living story of the whole experience of the

American people, the habits and the hopes, the triumphs and the troubles and the bedrock faith of our nation . . ."

Beneath Fern's shaky voice, I heard louder and louder, the steamy *sssssssss!* oozing from Mrs. Van Lunden's mouth.

"Please stop that at once," I whispered. "Show some respect for the First Lady."

The outraged eyes fixed me with a basilisk's stare. Gorgon, she would have devoured me with a tongue of flame had she the power.

"I make no peace with traitors," she snarled at me. And smiled.

"It is a subject of great regret to the President that he cannot be here today," Fern said. By now Fern's voice was a ghostly whisper. "But of course he is very much occupied with the problems of government. But President Hannaford sends his . . .

Sssssss. Sssssssss. Ssssssss. The madwoman on my right sizzled on. Grabbing her arm, I warned, "That will be enough. Please come along."

Fern saw the commotion. So did Vangie. Mrs. Van Lunden was resisting, trying to shake loose my grip and hissing louder. Firmly, I led her toward the door, still hissing, still protesting. "I shall hiss that name whenever I hear it," she advised me. Women tittered; some turned away from Fern; others craned baggy necks and double chins to witness the drama.

". . . and so the President and I are very happy that you have come to visit us, and we hope you will come again, for after all, the White House is the home of all the people, rich and poor, black and white, Daughters of the American Revolution . . . and granddaughters of slaves."

I heard this last flourish, written by my friend Vangie Boswell, as I finally dragged Mrs. Van Lunden into the cross hall. Under the eighteenth-century cut-glass chandeliers, I escorted her through the marble columns towards the entrance hall.

"I heard that," she said icily. "I heard that remark about slaves. That is an insult." She spun her dreadful head toward the opened doors of the East Room and let loose a final blast. Fern had finished her address. The applause was less than enthusiastic, and I saw a half-dozen ladies, noses clearly out of joint, come out of the doorway, heads bobbing, voices chirping. Granddaughters of slaves, indeed!

The President was conferring with Walter Edgerton on foreign policy—an area in which Ben, by his own admission, was not too conversant. I hurried to the chief's office.

He was, of course, interested in how Fern's first public appearance had gone, and I told him the truth. She had been brave, and poised, and somewhat pained—and had shown noteworthy courage with the line about the White House belonging to both ancestrally-endowed patriots as well as the descendants of blacks. I praised her performance to Ben, but conceded that she had been shaken by the madwoman's behavior.

"You are quite certain Mrs. Hannaford is all right?" Ben asked.

"Yes, sir. She handled it very well. Miss Boswell is with her now, helping her wish the ladies Godspeed."

"Mr. President, I don't envy what you and Mrs. Hannaford will have to put up with in the way of entertainments these next four years," Edgerton said. "You know what James K. Polk said after witnessing a juggling exhibition in the East Room. He said, 'It was innocent in itself, but I thought the time unprofitably spent.' "

"I'm not so sure," the President said. "A lot of this job is a juggling act. More than ever, Senator Edgerton."

I started to leave. Ben gestured at me to stay. "Listen in, Edward. Mr. Edgerton is giving me a rundown on the state of the world. Maybe you have a few useful ideas."

"It's hardly my area, sir."

"Yeah, it isn't the area of our nation's editorial writers, but that doesn't stop 'em. You read Mr. Pringle's editorials this morning?"

I thought back to those inglorious days when the Paris peace talks on Vietnam had begun, and for months, the participants—ourselves, the Viet Cong, Hanoi, the South Vietnamese—had haggled and traded and carried on like spoiled children over the *shape of the table*. As I recall, it was the Secretary of Defense, Mr. Clifford, who told our South Vietnamese allies to get around the table, any table, and damn quickly, because Americans were getting bloody sick and tired of their sons dying while Asians argued over the shape of furniture. What intrigued me was that now

163

Russian and Chinese diplomats could be every bit as unlearned as ours.

"Still fighting in Mongolia?" Ben asked.

"I'm afraid so. The frontier with China runs twenty-five hundred miles. It's easy for the so-called freedom-fighting guerrillas to sneak across. I have the feeling that the Russians respond with too much force—napalm, heavy bombers, massed artillery. It enrages the farmers and the herders and does nothing but destroy a lot of yurts."

"Come again?" Ben asked.

"Yurts. That is the Mongol word for a peasant tent, or hut."

Ben nodded. "Russians must have taken lessons from our own military. Seems when you get big enough and strong enough, you just assume you have the right to burn and blow up people."

Edgerton frowned. "It won't help their image or their influence in Asia. Incidentally, there is a growing peace movement in the Soviet Union. Groups of writers, intellectuals and young people have demonstrated and circulated petitions against the continued killing. There were mass arrests made outside of Moscow University last week. A group of Mongolian war veterans burned draft cards and denounced Chairman Gromyko."

Edgerton continued his briefing on the state of the world. The joint American-Soviet space station on the moon was functioning although, as anticipated by many scientists, it was largely a gimmick, a toy, a hobby. In Geneva, where the United Nations had been driven from New York by a right-wing cabal some years ago, all was peaceful.

Edgerton picked up another folder. "I hope I am not being overly optimistic, Mr. President, but once the Russians and the Chinese settle the Mongolian war, we may be in for a period of peace. We might even get the Arabs to meet with the Israelis. Ever since the three-day war last year, even the Arabs are beginning to believe they can't have a military victory."

"What about NATO?" Hannaford asked.

The Secretary of State looked a bit surprised. "NATO, sir?"

"Yes. The Six Nations. That Iroquois Confederacy."

I knew what he was getting at. Hannaford believed that the Russian invasion of Western Europe would never

164

happen. Since the death of Stalin, this expansionist dream had been shelved. Old de Gaulle had understood this; so had the Canadians. Britain had all but pulled her troops out of Europe. Of course, we still had Luxembourg. But pleasantries aside, the stand-off in atomic weapons made compact, vulnerable, urbanized Europe a most unlikely battleground. The Russians, of course, would still subvert, throw their weight around, put pressure on weak states and contest us at every point. But a military adventure in Europe was simply no longer in the cards.

"The trouble is the Russians don't provoke us into anything major," Edgerton complained. "Our generals keep looking for incidents, and there aren't any in Europe. Europeans want cars and vacations and less children and apartments. The truth is we don't know what to do with NATO. They've been doing air-pollution studies."

Ben had been listening intently. He had toured the oval office—a copy of Hoban's original "elliptical saloon"—passing by the Shoumatoff portrait of Franklin D. Roosevelt, one of Ben's heroes, the Sully painting of Andrew Jackson, and Gilbert Stuart's "Athenaeum" likeness of Washington. Now he returned to his desk and stood behind the high-backed green swivel chair. Flanked by the American flag and the presidential flag, Hannaford appeared wrestling with some grave, involved matter. For an uneducated man, he had extraordinary powers of concentration, of ordering events and fats in his mind.

"Now, Walter," the boss said firmly, "wasn't there some talk a few years back about a pact, an agreement of some kind between NATO and the Communist group, the Warsaw Pact folks?"

"There was. A logical development. Nothing came of it, because the Pentagon was suspicious. And for that matter so was Marshal Grechko and the Soviet High Command."

"Let's open it up again."

"We can try," Edgerton said.

"We can do better than that, Mr. Secretary," Ben said. He sat on the edge of the presidential desk and folded his brawny arms. There was a mischievous twinkle in his eye. I studied Walter Edgerton's serious, well-shaped professorial head, his pale eyes hidden behind academic glasses, the curved, black pipe smoking furiously as his lips drew on the well-chewed bit. Professor Edgerton, I thought; *You are about to be sandbagged.*

"I am open to suggestions," Edgerton said.

"I have an original one," Hannaford said. "Walter, suppose we tell the Russians we'd like to trade Italy for Czechoslovakia."

"I, ah, beg your pardon, Mr. President?"

"I repeat, Walter. An even-up trade. We give 'em Italy, they give us Czechoslovakia. We take the Czechs into NATO. They take the Italians into the Warsaw Pact."

Edgerton swallowed a mouthful of tobacco smoke and was seized by a fit of coughing. I ran from my seat near the window overlooking the Rose Garden and began to pound his slender back, "Steady there, Mr. Secretary. The boss does these things to me all the time."

"W-w-water . . ."

I went to the President's desk and poured some cold water for the Secretary-designate. He sipped gratefully; his eyes teared; he assembled his shattered professorial parts. "But that's outrageous, Mr. President," he said. "We can't play fast and loose with sovereign states. We can't go around trading them, like green stamps . . ."

"Oh no? That's exactly what we've been doing since 1946. We don't consult governments or people. We just make demands. And so do those buggers in Moscow. Well, here's a trade that makes sense. Hell, if there was once a sentiment toward a deal between NATO and the Warsaw Pact, what better way to crank it up, than to set up a kind of exchange agreement? You know that people-to-people deal. Bunch of Hungarians come over here to look at Grand Canyon and Disneyland. Bunch of Americans go to Budapest to sail the Danube. This would be the same thing. Right off, we wouldn't let the Czechs know *all* our battle plans. Our generals wouldn't like that, even though those plans are moldy and useless and are based on a Russian invasion of the low countries, which I could never understand, since it's always been Germany that invaded them. Let the Czechs in to some neutral meetings—customs of the service, ceremonies, dinners, air pollution, all that guff. And the Russians would do the same for our Italians. Why, the Italians are all over the Soviet Union. Built five Fiat factories. Olivetti. Ignis. Montecatini. I got to hand it to those Eyeties."

Edgerton and I were stunned. Neither of us spoke—me, because it was not my place to speak in such august

166

company, Edgerton because his finely-honed mind simply could not grasp the elemental logic of Ben's scheme.

At length, putting aside the pipe, he found his voice. "But Mr. President ... the opposition to this ... the right-wing ... I mean, sir, the country has been told for twenty-five years about the dangers of Communism and the Russian desire to take over Europe, and now we *trade* them an ally ... we surrender Italy, seat of the Vatican, of the Renaissance, of culture, for, for ..."

"If I may say so, I wouldn't knock the Czechs, Senator Edgerton," I ventured. "An enormously talented people—cinema, literature, art, manufacturing. I think they'd give NATO a certain panache, a certain luster. Goodness knows what improvements the Italians could make in the Warsaw Pact."

"Walter," Ben laughed, "there are no secrets any more. Not since the Russians and ourselves got those monitoring satellites all over the skies. Nobody's got any secrets. Now you go huddle with the Foreign Relations Committee. Talk to the Czech and the Italian ambassadors. We might be on to something."

When Walter Edgerton had left, I walked to the desk. The President had grabbed the telephone and was asking for Homer Murphy. He wanted a complete over-and-under-the-line budget on rebuilding the cities. Hayward Kretz's old budget had been consigned to the dustbin and Ben would start from scratch. "Kretz had his priorities, and I have mine, and they're different," he had told the Budget Bureau chief.

He spun halfway around in the light green chair and fixed a dark Indian eye on me, the eternal patsy. "The boss has some pretty good foreign policy notions, eh, Edward? Not bad for an old rigger."

"You astound me," I said. "The Senate will never permit this crazy experiment. You can't go around trading countries as it pleases you."

"We don't know till we try," the President said. "Might hit a dry hole. Might hit black gold." He tapped the desk. "That reminds me, I want a report from Meg McNally on the human depletion allowance."

"And just how will that work?"

"Easy as pie, son. The oil companies get that 27.5 per cent write-off on the theory that there is a limited amount of oil in the ground. That tax break is surely the biggest swindle since the first three-card monte game in an El Paso carnival. Oil is Holy Writ, Edward. Revealed religion. If there is anything that is the essence of belief in the halls of Congress, it is oil. And a bigger bunch of greedy scoundrels never walked the earth. Know what the average well means to a producer? It saves in taxes alone nineteen times the original investment."

"You can't fight the depletion allowance. Oil, as you have pointed out is the nearest thing to God in Texas and Oklahoma. They get them mixed up sometimes."

"If I can't lick 'em, I'll confound 'em. Look, Edward, the theory behind this tax write-off is that the well will go dry someday. Don't people go dry? I'll talk to Meg McNally about it. Seems to me we have the argument cut and dried. What's good for oil is good for human beings. They get depleted also. Have Cleo set up a session for me tomorrow."

I nodded and started to leave.

"And Edward, get Parente on the phone and leak him that story of trading Italy for Czechoslovakia."

"You don't mean it."

"Mean what?"

"You want to make this scheme public? I thought you were just going to try it out—you told Edgerton to sound out the senators, to talk to the Embassies . . ."

"Hell, let's make it public. We owe the wop a few."

Parente was silent for a moment when I told him about the boss's plan to swap the two nations, even up, and create the roles of "observers" in NATO and the Warsaw Pact. Then he burst into hysterical laughter.

"I love him. I love that big guy. It's . . . it's . . . like at the fights at Madison Square Garden, when each guy's backers get to place a second in the opponent's corner to see they don't put alum on the gloves. Deever, this is the most original piece of foreign policy thinking since Nasser forced the UN troops out of the Gaza strip, thereby permitting the Israelis to kick the shit out of his army."

"Your choice of words on the White House phones is regrettable," I said. "But you can use the story. Just say it is being considered."

"I'll use it and I'll approve, Deever. But lots of other people won't."

"We know they won't like it. But Hannaford feels he can take chances. He's a gambler, Louis."

"Yeah," Parente said. "A gambler. I wish I had enough confidence to bet with him. But I don't like the odds."

After Parente printed his column about the proposed Italy-Czechoslovakia trade and had written with glee, "without a left-handed pitcher or a utility infielder thrown in, and no future draft choices," other public voices were raised against the new Administration. Bates Pendragon wrote:

The thrust of President Hannaford's administration is becoming evident. At home, conciliation of the left and the black extremists, and attacks on property rights. Abroad, a crude sellout of our carefully nurtured defenses against Communist aggression. The President will camouflage all these moves with his cunning disguise. The nation would do well to be on guard. The President now has the brazenness to attempt nothing less than a reversal of America's historic mission as defender of private property and personal freedom.

I tried to ignore Pendragon's attack, but I could not. A sampling of our mail showed that many people agreed with him.

"Mr. President, you will reap the whirlwind in freeing these enemies of the state," a minister in Valdosta, Georgia, wrote. He was to prove a prophet of sorts.

The prophecy was fulfilled in mid-February, on a freakishly warm day, a harbinger of spring. As night settled on New York, Kakamba Jones, Arvid Farbelman and assorted radicals claiming to represent the aggrieved, made their move. Their target was Columbia.

In well-drilled squads, units of no more than a half dozen, armed with home-made Molotov cocktails and a cheap explosive material (gotten from mail-order houses), they invaded the unguarded campus at two in the morning and put the old red and gray buildings to the torch.

I received a telephone call from Judge Moscowitz at 3:00 A.M. The Attorney General-designate told me that the President had ordered him to New York. Both had decided it would be a good idea for me to go too.

169

"The police and the National Guard seem to have it under control," he said wearily, "but the damage has been done—two-thirds of the buildings have been gutted. It was a para-military operation, an act I find hard to forgive."

As I sped out to the airport I recalled that Judge Moscowitz was an old Columbia man himself, a scholarship student from the slums of Brooklyn, and a great football player under the immortal Lou Little. The destruction of his alma mater would affect him deeply. Columbia was no ordinary school, it was *his*. It seemed to me, as I boarded the chartered plane at National (a half-dozen FBI men were aboard along with a few of Moscowitz's top aides) that the judge's world of poor boys on scholarship, Ivy League football games and quiet tree-shaded campuses was a world that had simply proven too good for us.

I was mulling this morbid notion as we later stood at the National Guard command post on the steps of Low Memorial Library, the magnificent classical building on 116th Street, under clouds of sickening smoke. Around us, the blackened structures—Hamilton, Fayerweather, Avery, Schermerhorn, Havemeyer, Philosophy, the Law School—discharged billows of gray-black smoke. Beneath, on the red-brick college walk, fire trucks were jammed against police vans, squads of National Guardsmen patrolled every inch of campus, police emergency units raced in and out of buildings. A litter of files, books, research papers and the impedimenta of the classroom—desks, laboratory equipment, blackboards, formed charred pyramids, sad testimony to the lunatic revenge of the young and misguided.

"How many persons have been arrested?" Moscowitz asked a New York police inspector.

"Very few, Mr. Attorney General. I'd say we've rounded up no more than thirty or forty. It wasn't a mass assault. These were little teams, a handful of people armed with Molotov cocktails and plastic explosives. It was a guerrilla action."

"Have you identified any of them?"

"A couple were on the faculty of Lumumba University. Jones didn't show up, but a couple of his lieutenants. Fellow named Mudonga Smith led the attack on Teachers College. It's an old place and it burned like a cigar box."

Moscowitz sighed. "Students?"

170

The inspector nodded. "A few."

"Was a man named Farbelman involved?" I asked.

"I understand he was here before the burning began. Spoke to a bunch of kids outside the gate on Broadway, then beat it." The inspector laughed grimly. "That's his technique. He gets them roused, then runs. We've never been able to bust him yet."

"That's understandable," I said. "He's a publicity saint. If you jugged him for a day, he'd write a book about it—his three years in Auschwitz."

I made a mental note to track Arvid Farbelman down, which would not be difficult. He was inescapable, a public person of high rank, a self-promoting genius who leered at the world from a dozen magazine covers, spouted opinions on everything, proclaimed his own towering talents endlessly, and was a dear friend of Mrs. Sidney Stapp, our sexy Judy. If I were to be of any help to the President in trying to cool down the irrational children who were now intent on destroying their best friends, I would have to have some entree to their world.

"... close the place down. Impossible to keep classes going ..."

An official of the university, a fussy man in a black Chesterfield coat was talking to Judge Moscowitz. I gathered that the President of the University, Dr. Miklos Voss, had decided that it was pointless to continue the academic year. Already beset with rioting, disturbances and a shortage of classrooms, the university could not cope with the devastation.

"I would hope that Dr. Voss would withhold making such an announcement," Moscowitz said to the man in the black Chesterfield. "I shall advise President Hannaford to provide the university with every conceivable assistance to keep it open. Classroom space will be found. Funds will be supplied. I pledge you this."

The young man in the Chesterfield—he was a public relations person—kept shaking his head. "No, no, it won't work, it won't ... this kind of madness, these hatreds ..." I thought he was going to weep. "You see, I can't see what's left for us today ... we're trapped, trapped in the middle ..."

To the east, at the iron gate, a disturbance had broken out. Blue-helmeted police in jack boots raced across the college walk; sirens wailed; shouts and screams struck the morning air. Our nostrils were clogged with acrid smoke, our eyes teared.

"I suspect the hatred of blacks is less self-hatred," I said, "than an awareness that the world outside the university doesn't want them. The corporations have opened up, and many other institutions, and the government passes laws, but the majority of Americans want no part of colored people—as neighbors, friends, or fellow citizens. They are forced to live with this knowledge and it surely cannot put them in a restful frame of mind."

"But why attack the university?" the young man pleaded.

"Because it is *near*," I said gloomily.

"What recommendations will you make to the President, sir?" Larry Hosmer of United Press asked Judge Moscowitz.

"First, that Columbia, with emergency federal funds, be kept open, if it means setting up portable classrooms in trailers on campus. Use will be made of all available space in the area—the seminaries, the hotels, and so forth. Second, a full investigation of this incident. Whatever federal laws are applicable will be used to prosecute those guilty, and if none are applicable, we will give support to the New York city administration in apprehending those responsible."

"Including the ERCA?" a man from the *Daily News* asked.

Judge Moscowitz looked up sternly. "I cannot answer that. We oppose the measure, but will have to give it further study."

"While Columbia goes up in smoke," Hosmer whispered to me.

Later, Hosmer guided me across the college walk towards the red-brick rear of one of the university buildings. He told me it was the renowned Columbia Graduate School of Journalism.

"Take a look, Ed."

The reporter pointed to a corner of the wall. There, pasted on the bricks, was the white cross on the blue field—the-not-so-secret insignia of some new amalgam of the right wing.

"I've seen them before," I said. "They're big on police cars. Nut groups. What does it prove?"

"They're all over the place," Hosmer said. "Stuck on every building that got hit."

"Well, it could be several things," I said carefully.

"Like?"

"You're pumping me, Larry. But I swear I have no inside information. It could be that the radical kids who did the burning left them as a phony hunk of evidence, so that people would blame the right."

"Yeah, could be. What else?"

"Or it could be that some elements of DOOR, or Save America, joined the Mao-ists and the Crazies for this party."

"Unlikely. They've arrested forty-two people already, and not a crew haircut in the lot. They're all Kakamba Jones's Senegalese mercenaries, or weirdos, or street freaks, or disciples of Farbelman."

"I'm left with one theory," I said. "Some right-wing loonies sneaked in and decided to register their approval. The little white flags are telling us something—*burn Columbia, that's fine with us.* Maybe a hint that they're around, watching, organized and waiting."

"I'll buy that one," the reporter said.

He made a sour grimace, as an ambulance roared through the opened iron gates on Broadway.

I glanced once again at the white cross pasted to the School of Journalism, thanked Larry Hosmer for his help and hurried through the gates. Shoving my way through a shouting mob, I began to search for a taxi.

Assuming that a phone call would only earn me abuse, I decided to beard Farbelman, the literary lion, in his den. I knew where he lived because some years ago, while in New York doing research for Senator Hannaford, Judy Stapp had invited me to a pot party at the poet's "pad" in Greenwich Village.

Considering his preachments of poverty, revolution, antimaterialism, and egalitarianism, Farbelmen lived opulently. His apartment was in a modern apartment building on West 12th Street, the northern reaches of the village, a decidedly bourgeois place. A uniformed doorman tried to stop me but I bluffed my way through the modern lobby that suggested Miami Beach.

The writer lived in a penthouse apartment with an inspiring view of Fifth Avenue. Farbelman earned a good

173

deal of money lecturing on campuses. Recently he had augmented his income with a smashingly successful Off-Broadway play entitled *Crap*, the highlight being a scene in which the cast mimed the acts of elimination and invited the audience to join in. "A new frontier has been reached in the annals of American drama," the critics cried. Farbelman never lost. If attacked by Critic A, Critic B would hail him. Critic B, of course, wanted to be invited to his parties and his summer pad in Martha's Vineyard.

I awaited in the carpeted corridor. The doorman assured me that Farbelman was home. Twice I rang; a third time. Then I heard muffled curses behind the door. Pitilessly, I jammed my finger into the buzzer. At length the door opened and I was confronted by the poet himself, his electric beard sprouting in all directions, the awkward figure bound round in a toxic green kimono.

"Fa Chrissake whaddya think this is, a friggin' doctor's office?" He rubbed his bleary eyes. Bereft of his eyeglasses, Farbelman was hard put to discern anything.

"Good morning, Arvid," I said, assuming my squarest Ohio manner. It helps with finely-honed insiders like Farbelman; let them believe the worst about me.

"Fa Chrissake, get lost. Who the hell are you, anyway?"

"Edward Deever, Arvid. I'm Judy Stapp's friend. From Washington."

Mention the name of a fellow celebrity—*any* celebrity—to Arvid Farbelman, and he is alert, alive. How can he use them? What can he promote? Are they more important than he is? Have they gotten better notices? He conceives of the world as a vast colosseum where he is the king gladiator, emperor and lion, all at once. All introductions are potential contests, and while he saw me as no rival, the mention of Judy's name—after all, she was the wife of the Senate Majority Whip, and a former bedmate—moved him.

"Shit man, say so, come on in."

I entered, following him into a hothouse atmosphere—oriental rugs, baroque furniture, ormolu frames on pictures and mirrors. And the distinctive sweet odor of grass. I'm no prude. I didn't care if he smoked cured camel dung.

"Wait a minute, wait a minute," he said stupidly. We sat opposite one another—Farbelman sprawling on a leop-

174

ard daybed, so that the kimono fell apart and his private parts (of which he wrote regularly, bragging about them, revealing their awesome potency to the world) were exposed. They did nothing for my early morning malaise. "Fa Chrissake, man, you're more than Judy's friend. I dig you now. You're President Hannaford's guy. What a blast. A message from the White House. Man, Arvid has arrived. I'm grooving now. I'm as good as Styron and Baldwin and Mailer and all those finks who made it to the big pad. Should I pack now? Am I invited for the weekend?"

I smiled. It was no secret that Arvid Farbelman, the raging, outspoken, idol-smashing hero of the young, guru to the alienated, had seethed with envy when John F. Kennedy and his wife had studiously ignored him during their brief tenancy in the White House.

"No, I'm afraid the invitation will have to wait. I want to talk to you about what happened at Columbia during the night."

Farbelman shrugged.

"Arvid, I am not a fussy man," I said, "but would you mind covering up your genitalia while we talk? It betrays a contempt for your visitor. How would you like it if I dropped my pants and showed you my rump?"

"No, sweat, man," the poet said. "Don't get uptight. Hey, this is a groove. A call from the Prexy's bag man. Taken any bribes lately, Deever?"

He was torn in two directions. His first reaction was essential Farbelman—celebrity to celebrity. A visit from President Hannaford's aide—hot diggety! But on reflection, he had decided I was just another corrupt tool of the Establishment, and as such, could be insulted.

"Your legendary nastiness will be lost on me," I said. "I'm no second-rate critic, some Cape Cod or Greenwich Village toady who needs your favors."

"Big balls, hey, Deever?"

"Let's move ahead, please. I'm rather tired. That mess at Columbia drained me."

"Yeah. A bad scene. Well, the Establishment asked for it."

I digested this a moment. "What makes you think that Columbia, or any university represents the Establishment? Has it ever occurred to you that more revolutionary concepts have come out of universities than from all your collected poems, and all the plays, stories and novels written by your snotty colleagues?"

Farbelman jerked upright to a sitting position. "Sure, sure. Like ROTC and defense contracts."

"You are more of a fool than I imagined, and something of a knave. No one argues that universities are perfect. They have their failings and they have been guilty of greed and the condoning of brutality, and acquiescence in some dreadful things that government and big business and big labor have done. But over all no reasonable man can help but conclude that they have worked for the public good."

"Nah, nah, that's all irrelevant," Farbelman snarled. "You're out of your tree, man."

"And I suppose you regard yourself as an agent for progress, for good race relations, for human rights, for a good environment?"

"You got it wrong, man. The important thing is for me to realize my potentialities. I live existential. I do things on impulse. I want to create a revolution in the mind of America, by acting out my needs and my wants. I'm more or less where it's at. You dig?"

"And that's why you spoke to a meeting of campus rebels at Columbia last night and informed them it was their duty to destroy the university?"

"Well, like, yeah. If it's on tape, yeah."

"Mr. Farbelman, you can be sent to jail for a long time for that kind of talk."

The poet's beard stiffened. "Fascist. Wha' should I expect from Hannaford's bag man, huh? Come on, Deever. You want me to cop out on the true scene?"

"You people are all alike. You'll raise hell, attack the wrong targets, bully those who can't fight back, out of a moral certainty that would nauseate any rational man—and then you refuse to take your medicine."

"What medicine?" Farbelman crooned. "Look, Deever, a man has to hustle a little. Got a right to my bread."

"I don't understand."

"I mean, like I got a play Off-Broadway. It needs box office. It needed a little promo. So I went up to Columbia and gave 'em speech 2-B, you know, burn the place down—I mean, like figuratively speaking—and I get in the papers, and it helps sell tickets. I mean, a writer has to hustle it up these days or he gets left at the post."

I was silent. With terrible clarity, I saw at last what made him tick. He was Celebrity Incarnate, as much of a public figure as Tuesday Weld or Joe Namath. That was all that mattered to him—*the hustle.*

"Prerogatives of the artist, Deever," he said. "It's like your boss, Hannaford. He hustles. He made his millions, bribes, deals, votes bought and sold. Look what it got him. Prexy of the whole bag."

"But the President has never been concerned with the promotion of himself as a publicity saint. He isn't miffed that he was ignored by the Kennedys."

"Look, whaddya want from me, pal? I mean, okay, I made a speech outside McMillan Theater last night to the kids, and I said maybe the place would be better knocked off. You know, like it's had its day. It's irrelevant, it needs restructuring."

"And you approve of the destruction of the university?"

A baneful look clouded Farbelman's hirsute face. "Don't hang me, man. I'm getting bad vibes."

"I assure you, Mr. Farbelman, I have no tape recorder with me, and I am not representing the FBI or any law enforcement agency. I'm the President's aide, and I need your help."

"Well, like, yeah. You see, Deever, when they burned Columbia, it was a beautiful thing, because it was an *existential* act."

"You use that word all the time. What does it mean?"

He turned his back on me. "Mean? Shit, man whatever I want it to mean. Like *existential.* Something you can groove on. Like it's my bag."

"No, that's no help."

"Well, like it's acting first, on what you feel deep down is the good, and right, and cool and beautiful thing to do . . . and thinking afterwards."

Now I have listened to a good deal of oratorical manure in my life—absorbing the windy blasts of people like Gage Hopewell, or the malevolent mouthings of Lance Ruckett—but I confess I have rarely listened to more twaddle and trash, more fakery and self-inflated poppycock than that with which Arvid Farbelman, now assailed me.

"Beautiful thing. Existential acts. Good Christ, Farbelman, you are a disgrace to letters. I have rarely listened to more fatuous garbage, more despicable gimcrackery."

Farbelman turned, a sheepish smile on his face. "Like it's too early to get sore, man. I mean, you wanna put me down, okay, but admit I swing a big bat. Look, you said you need my help. You wanna rap, let's rap."

"I want you to start telling the students who adore you, to cool it. Lay off. Give Hannaford a chance. He revoked the emergency measures. He's going to enact a civic improvement program. You and your devotees will be pleasantly surprised at the kind of President he is going to be. But he needs help. He was barely elected—"

"Stole it, pal.'"

"—and if he did, count yourself lucky. You'd all be in jail *still* if Smead Beldock were in the White House. Mr. Farbelman, the kids have a lot of good ideas, and we respect their idealism and their desire to make the country more democratic. But in the name of God, pick your enemies more carefully. Every time you riot, you gain more enemies among the great mass of beer drinkers and bowlers and TV watchers out there. You create Levittown killers who would be delighted to shoot all of you in the back of the neck. You have no mass support. You represent a pimple on the ass of the body politic. I must tell you that for all your ideals and high-minded programs, you are viewed with unflagging hatred and shivering fear by the mass of nine-to-five Americans. And they have the vote. You have nothing but your power to disrupt and destroy your own allies, like the universities—"

"And crooks like Hannaford?"

"Yes, damn you. Crooks like Hannaford. You'll realize that someday, maybe too late, when all of us have been rounded up by General Upshaw and his armed White Guards."

Farbelman flopped to the sofa. "Screw off, Deever. You gross me out. I don't jive with squares."

How could I make this loudmouth, this campus Socrates, listen to reason? I recalled that some years ago Farbelman had run for political office—the district leadership of a West Side New York congressional neighborhood. His campaign had been filled with wit and style. But what had he succeeded in doing? Well, he had succeeded in splitting the liberal-left vote, so that a first-rate intelligent *black* man, the favorite, was trounced by a Tammany hack. When this was pointed out to Farbelman, he shrugged, admitted he liked the Negro lawyer and added, "I had to do my thing, like, it was an existential move."

"You are truly disgusting," I said. "I have witnessed high-level corruption in Washington, I've lived with it, but it was innocence compared to your own venality. You suffer from a degrading form of skin-worship. All that matters is I, I, I. No politician could be as shameless as you are."

Far from acting as a goad, my statement appeared to divert the writer. "Yeah, man, you just layed it on me. You're right. That's the artist's bag. That's our hang-up. We have to be corrupt and rotten. Society is, so we got to go it one better."

"Mr. Farbelman, I beg of you for the last time, exhort your worshipers to lay off. Stop shouting and burning and fouling the air just long enough for the President to get his program underway. He's going to cut the arms budget. He's going to change NATO—"

"Shit man, don't NATO me this and NATO me that. I got my scenario all finished for the next phase. Confront. Escalate. Radicalize. Mobilize student power. Get with black power. Hate. Liberate. Fuck everybody."

"You've phrased it rather well. But when the White Guards come for you, don't ask Hannaford for help. We all may find ourselves on the same barricade."

I got up, bone-weary, repelled by the man's narrowness, his tawdry clichés, his refusal to recognize that darker forces than his rag-bag battalions were marshaling their strength. Strange bugles were blowing across the land— and they summoned a better-armed army of militants than his cursing children.

"Too damn early for politics."

I was in the act of picking up my brief case when I heard this new voice—a husky woman's voice. Looking up, I saw Mona Varnum emerge from the bedroom. My Mona, in a white nylon slip, barefoot, nude beneath the snippet of smooth cloth.

"Miss Varnum. Good morning."

She yawned; I was not worthy of an answer. Jealousy turned my face crimson. She had been bedded down with Farbelman. Through my mind raced an old left-wing slogan, "black and white, unite and fight." Mona, Mona—my dusky, satin-limbed love! Having lusted for her, and un-

179

derstanding that it was a lost cause, I raged with inner envy, with bubbling passion. *Farbelman!*

"Deever, you get around," she said. I could not take my eyes from her breasts—firm, up-thrusted. *His left hand is under my head, and his right hand doth embrace me.* The Song of Solomon raced through my mind.

"Hey, Deever, how does your President stand on miscegenation?" Farbelman mocked.

"Knock it off, Arv," Miss Varnum said coolly. She wandered into the kitchen, and I studied the lyrical lilt of her body. *Return, return, O Shulamite, that we may look at thee.*

"Don't look upset, Deever," the poet said. His raw lips twisted into an insolent smile. "I mean, when you get to be number one, you get number one gash."

"You are an impudent son of a bitch," I said. "I happen to respect Miss Varnum. If she chooses to sleep with you, I will respect her choice. But how can you possibly use such language about her? She is a young woman of great dignity and intelligence."

"Ole Mona? Mona? Man, she's got a funky mouth on her like a barrel-house mama. Loves it when I put her down." He shouted toward the kitchen. "Doncha, Mona, baby?"

"Where the hell are the glasses, Arv?"

"Cupboard over the sink, baby."

That she did not know where the glasses were consoled me, but only marginally. Evidently she was not a regular sleeper-in at Farbelman's place. As she returned, sipping orange juice, her Afro'd hair bushier, more enticing than ever, I realized that she was playing the game, the New York game of Celebrity. As a young reporter on the make—ambitious, shrewd, aggressive—she was doing nothing more than what her white sisters would do. Sleeping with Arvid Farbelman was a merit badge of great value to her career.

"Miss Varnum," I said, "I've just made an appeal to Mr. Farbelman to use his influence with students to tranquilize them. Burning down Columbia is no help. There are wicked, miscreant elements in this country who are overjoyed to see the liberal universities put to the torch."

She sat, cross-legged—long, long legs, a tropic tan—on an ottoman. The white slip hiked up her creamy thighs,

180

and I thought I would swoon. *Thou art all fair my love; there is no spot in thee*. "So?" she asked.

"I appeal to you to spread the word among your soul brothers. If Mr. Farbelman and his Larchmont revolutionaries are unable to understand the crisis in this country, perhaps your black friends can. The President wants to help. He *wants* to reorder priorities, as the current cant puts it. He *wants* to restructure society. But he can't do it, if you people keep raising hell."

"Oh, the hell with you liberals," Mona said. "You turn me off."

"You have every right to feel that way. Liberals have played fast and loose with blacks for too long. But stop thinking of Hannaford as a liberal. He's strong and resourceful."

"A crook," Farbelman said.

"Maybe he was—at one time. But he is in the American grain. He can manipulate and operate and deceive a lot of people into doing the right and moral things. Believe me, he is on your side."

"I don't dig him," Farbelman sneered. "He turns me off."

"Neither of you is aware, I gather, that the buildings at Columbia were plastered with stickers showing a white flag on a blue field—the insignia of the White Guard militants, a right-wing activist group."

"You lose me, man," Farbelman said.

"They were giving their approval to the destruction of the university. For all anyone knows, they may have aided the burning. The right is organized, angry, and approve of the way you people are eviscerating the moderates of this country. They can't wait."

"Look, man, I wasn't even at the big bash," Farbelman said uneasily. Had I reached him? Had I permeated that bushy, self-loving exterior?

"I wasn't either," Mona said. Were they both eager to dissociate themselves from the madness on Morningside? Would it occur to them, that vandalizing schools and toppling administrators might bring about their own annihilation?

"Yeah, Mona and me were at Shell Shapstein's blast." He smirked; smug, happy, he was upping me one. Farbelman always missed the violence. He had other engagements—Hefner's blast, Capote's thing, Plimpton's bash.

There was always a public rite with other flesh-worshipers, other names from Leonard Lyons's column. The revolution could wait.

"How gauche of me to forget," I said grimly. "Naturally Farbelman—and his lady of the day—would not miss the social event of the winter. I trust the smoked salmon and the champagne were of Mr. Shapstein's usual high quality. Let Columbia burn and Harlem seethe, all's well with the world so long as our new Lenins and Nat Turners can eat and dine and drop names and deliver choice anecdotes to Suzy Parker. May I use your bathroom? I have to vomit."

"Gets uptight awful easy, doesn't he, Mon'?" Farbelman asked. "The kid's jealous, I guess."

I picked up my brief case and walked to the door. "You have to come to a bad end, Farbelman," I said. "This is the only revolution that has press agents and make-up artists on the payroll. The only revolution that is postponed because of Lennie's birthday party. I'm going back to Washington, where at least the corruption has an innocent charm."

Departing, I saw Mona Varnum—black and comely—studying me with her oriental, exotic eye. Smile, smile, my Queen of Sheba. We had accounts to settle, and I did not mean the hospital costs accumulated during her convalescence.

Engloomed, I returned to Washington to report on what I had learned about the burning of Columbia. A scattered pattern soon emerged. There were arsonous assaults on Swarthmore, Earlham College, three campuses of the University of California—Davis, Riverside and San Diego—and in each instance militant bands of student-guerrillas wreaked their havoc in the dead of night. In each instance the white crosses appeared on university buildings. But no direct connection was made between the arsonists and the White Guard movement. The students denied any involvement with the right; they were "doing their thing," acting "existentially," dragging down the corrupt Establishment.

A few days after my return, I sat in on a small meeting in the President's dining room to discuss the issue that Ben had given A-1 priority: the rebuilding of the cities, and the people of the cities. Present were several cabinet members, Homer Murphy of HEW, Charles Gantry of

HUD, Meg McNally our Treasury Secretary, Dalton Warfield, Senator Maury Eisenberg and Senator Royce Henshaw, chairman of the Labor and Public Welfare Committee.

Around this handsome room runs a panoramic expanse of wallpaper depicting "Scenes of the American Revolution." Under the magnificent eighteenth-century chandelier we dined on guacamole salad and Ramada chili (spicy with small green peppers) and talked at length about plans and projects.

"You wanted a costing out, Mr. President," Homer Murphy said, "and I have one. Maybe it errs on the side of generosity."

"That's okay, Homer," the President said. "We've been shortchanging the cities too long. Folks besides Lockheed and Boeing and McDonnell and General Dynamics got a right to overcharge the government a little. Nobody ever questions the dollar that goes for bombs. Why should we argue over a few extra bucks for schools and housing and job training?"

I had the feeling that Hannaford's simplistic approach would not work. Missionary work of a high order would be needed. So long as riots and burnings ravaged the land, so long as the comfortable white majority and its legions of *lumpen* lower-middle class malcontents would react with horror and fear, we were doomed. No one really had any interest in low-cost housing for Hough, parks for Harlem, junior colleges for the South Side of Chicago.

"Here it goes, Mr. President," Homer said, drawing in his breath. "Support for education—twelve billion. Funding of low-cost housing—ten billion. Income support—ten billion. Hospital and health services—seven billion. Urban mass transport—five billion. Job training—five billion."

"Forty-nine billion dollars," Ben said.

Meg McNally whistled. "It isn't there, Mr. President. Not by a long shot. The director of the budget will go into orbit."

"Dammit, we'll get it," the President said. "What are the estimates for defense for the fiscal year?"

"One hundred and twenty billion dollars," I said quickly. "And that includes seed money for research and development on the MOMSER."

"That's the big one," Ben said, smiling. "The one the

generals tell us can knock off everyone in the world in one big blast."

"It isn't quite that simple," Senator Eisenberg said gloomily. "But that's the idea. If it works."

"If it works," Ben repeated. "If we let them have it."

"Mr. President," Homer Murphy said, "I did some checking on missile systems which are no longer deployed, or never have been deployed, or have been declared obsolete, over the past twenty years. You know—garbage like the Navaho, Snark, Dove, Triton, Plato. All the stuff the generals told us were the last word in deterrence and had to be junked. The total cost was thirty-one billion dollars. I can't think of those figures without seeing in front of me, Lexington Avenue in Harlem on a night in August, with the filth and the stink, and the noise and the depravity."

"Thirty-one billion, eh?" the President said. "For junk."

"Yeah. Junk."

"And in spite of all of it, in spite of all our superiority over the Russians over the years," Senator Henshaw said, "not a single cold war issue has ever been decided on the basis of nuclear hardware. Hungary? We didn't dare drop one. Czechoslovakia? Forget it. They damned Gene McCarthy for telling the truth about Czechoslovakia, but he knew the score. The Russians have their victims and we have ours. Missiles didn't keep Castro from coming to power, and they didn't give us a victory at the Bay of Pigs. Sure, we could have leveled North Vietnam with nuclear warheads, we could have made the rubble of Hanoi dance, but it seems to me there are limits to what the American people and all but the most bloody-minded of American leaders will do."

Dalton Warfield eyed his chili unhappily. I seemed to remember he had a bad stomach, an ulcerated digestive system, probably the result of the harrowing life he had led. "Congress won't buy your shopping list, Homer. Mr. President, it's bleak times. All of us in this room know what the country needs. But the country is listening to Gabe Tutt. And Beldock. And Upshaw. And Lance Ruckett. I sometimes get the urge to join those slum kids and toss a few fire bombs. At anyone. Anywhere."

"That won't help," the President said. " 'The whole head is sick, and the whole heart faint.' Isn't it strange the things money can do in this great nation? Solve everything but clean out the slums and elevate the poor. But by God, we'll do it. I'm tired of being told the money isn't there."

"It is there, Mr. President," said Meg McNally. "But not for the priorities you favor. We're like a wealthy family that spends its income on a four-hundred-horsepower car and a power cruiser, but feeds the children stale bread."

The President turned to me. "Edward, set up a meeting with the Budget Bureau for tomorrow morning. Let's have Meg present, and Secretary Boswell, and Homer and Chuck Gantry. Let's start trimming. We'll perform major surgery on that hundred and twenty billion dollars worth of hardware."

I mulled over the problem, and I decided that part of the answer was, quite simply, that we had been captured by machines, by technology, by hardware. We put our faith in anything manufactured, the bigger, more expensive, noisier and more destructive, the better we liked it. Was there any difference between America's worship of the four-hundred-horsepower hard-top deluxe automobile —and the willingness with which we applauded Gabe Tutt's decision that the country must spend twenty billion dollars over four years to develop that most odious of all weapons, the MOMSER or Iron Ball?

"What makes this thing so tough to handle," Senator Maury Eisenberg said, "is that there hasn't been any conspiracy, any plotting on the part of generals and admirals. Except for a few nuts like Upshaw, our military men are reasonable gentlemen. But they're caught up in this also. The corporations make millions, the competition is fierce, the government throws the money around with a free hand, and everyone gets in on the fun."

"Like Topsy, it just growed," said Meg McNally.

"Watch yourself with cullud folks talk, Madame Secretary," Homer Murphy said, laughing. "Yes, that's the way I read it Mr. President. But there's more to it than just that. You see, the military suffers from a lack of *love*. They know they are often regarded as useless members of society. A farmer grows wheat. A doctor can cure influenza. A contractor can build a road. What can a soldier do? Kill. Oh, it's okay to say they protect the nation, they guard our sacred boundaries. We all know that. Trouble is nobody really threatens our sacred boundaries. We had to go halfway round the world to fight the Vietnamese to find an enemy. Ran out of 'em in Europe. Even all that fuss about Cuba died down. You know—cheer up, they are only ninety miles away. So what? No one invaded Florida. Well, the military realizes they have no reason to exist, no reason you can see, or touch, or understand—like a loaf of bread, or getting over an operation, or riding on a new road. So they want *love*. And when you can't get real love, you settle for money. Know how kids get fat, gorge, when they aren't loved? That's our generals over there in the Pentagon. If President Kretz says okay, develop the Iron Ball for eleven billion dollars, they scream, no, no, we want twenty billion! If Congress says you may develop three Iron Ball satellites, they holler, give us twelve! It's a kind of neurotic greed these people suffer from."

Hannaford smiled at Murphy's analysis. The President had long advanced a theory of what makes the American economy function. It was based on the notion of "controlled greed." That is to say, all Americans, notably the more affluent, were motivated by greed. That in itself could be dangerous to a stable society. Therefore, it was incumbent upon government to *control* greed. A society based on interlocking patterns of Ben's "controlled greed," he felt, was the best kind of society—something for everyone, a little give and take, a trade here, a favor there.

"Homer, it sounds like you are accusing the generals and the admirals and their corporate friends of uncontrolled greed," the President said.

The people around the table, of course, knew about Hannaford's thesis. They laughed uneasily. "Yes, sir, uncontrolled greed," the Secretary of HEW said. "I wish to hell it were a conspiracy. We could handle it a lot better."

"Mr. President, we don't know where to start," Senator Eisenberg said. "I read recently that the Pentagon commands a world-wide force of sixty-two hundred public relations men. They keep over three hundred legislative lobbyists at work full time on the Congress. And their budget for this alone, is over four and one half million dollars. All this is *government* financed. I'm not even getting into what the Boeings and Lockheeds and United Aircrafts and the others spend on getting money out of the public till."

"I'll tell you what the damn thing is," Chuck Gantry

said excitedly, "it's a government within a government. It's a monarchy—Gabe Tutt as king, and all those gold braid boys and brass hats bowing and scraping."

"Somehow the problem always ends up in the Pentagon," the President said. I detected weariness in his voice, impatience. Hannaford had fantastic staying powers, unflagging energy. But now, confronted with the great god, Moloch, the military monster that ate everything in sight, he appeared uncertain. "I called this meeting to get Homer's estimate of fixing up the cities. And we end up discussing the way the military gets all the dollars."

" 'Things are in the saddle, and ride mankind,' " Senator Royce Henshaw commented.

"Who said that, Royce?" the President asked. He was not, like many self-made men, ashamed of his lack of education.

"Emerson, Mr. President."

Hannaford's eyes assumed that dark obsidian look I had seen so many times in the days when he had run the Senate. "Things are going to have to move over for people," he said. "This country has to start worrying about how people *live*, not how they die."

As the meeting broke up, he told me to summon Burke Boswell. He wanted a report on the plan to put the Pentagon on short rations. As I phoned Boswell's office, I began to worry. Could a man referred to as "Pay-Toilet" really take on those fire-breathing sons of Mars?

Vangie Boswell stopped me outside the President's dining room after the luncheon. I noticed she had lengthened her skirts an inch in deference to Fern's modest views. This was a sort of Missouri compromise—the ladies meeting each other halfway. If Vangie would sneak in cracks about granddaughters of slaves in Fern's speeches, fine. But Miss Boswell, in turn, would have to cover a bit more of her thighs.

"Mail on the DAR speech," she said, showing me a sheaf of letters. "*Fantástico.* Ten to one in Mrs. Hannaford's favor."

"Mrs. H. looked pretty shaky to me. Did she recover?"

"She had a bad night after the *confronta*, had to go to bed. Bourbon and two sleeping pills."

"Oh, God." I felt miserable. Was it fair to subject her to this?

187

"Don't look guilty, Edward. You really do act as son, nephew, guardian, butler and alter ego to that family. She's made a remarkable comeback. It's funny what good notices can do for you." She waved the packet under my nose. "As soon as these started coming in, she perked up."

"Thank heavens for all those concerned liberals who write letters."

Vangie led me down the corridor to the small room used by the First Lady as a study. She rapped at the door—it is actually a charming sitting room, adjacent to the bedroom, and Fern's voice responded. We walked in.

"Good morning, Edward. How nice of you to visit," Fern said.

"My pleasure, ma'am."

"Is the President being his usual solicitous self, Edward? Has he sent you to check up on me—to see if I am managing?"

I was stunned. To begin with, Fern almost never made any personal comments about Ben or her relationship to him. They were formal, proud, self-contained people. I think the money had a lot to do with it. Moreover, she made these remarks to me with a pixy-ish smile on her prim mouth. She was, if you can believe it, *teasing* me—and Hannaford—by making the statement at all. I was overjoyed.

"Scout's honor, Mrs. H., he hasn't said a word. Miss Boswell showed me the splendid mail you have received on the DAR reception, and I was so delighted I decided to congratulate you."

"It was a very small achievement, Edward."

At her feet snoozed two of her Gordon setters, huge black, docile beasts. I made a mental note to get some publicity out of them, to use them to improve Fern's image. Dogs were a major item with the American people. Who can forget FDR's Fala? Or the little Russian mutts Khrushchev gave to the Kennedys? Or Checkers of undying fame? Or the Nixons' Irish setter? Fern's Gordon setters would have to make the news columns.

"But you carried it off splendidly, Mrs. Hannaford," I said. "I was near that nutty lady who kept hissing at you, and I was tempted to rush her out of the hall."

Fern looked up from her small, kidney-shaped desk. She was answering letters. A stack of mail lay at her left, and a box of personal White House stationery at her right. I noticed that she was wearing amber-colored eyeglasses. Now for the life of me, I was hard put to recall ever seeing them on her pretty face. She rarely read; she rarely wrote anything; she was an outdoor woman, a horse fancier and dog breeder. Now, bespectacled, she had a new look—a pensive, more confident appearance, like that of a benign librarian. Moreover, there was a crispness in her voice—she did not raise it or emphasize words any more than she did before, but the subtle change was evident—that astounded me.

"Vangie has explained to me that women like Mrs. Van Lunden are part of our nation also," Fern said. "They must be tolerated. Even at the expense of our own peace of mind. We are, after all, representatives of all the people."

"Yes, yes, I couldn't put it better, Mrs. H. ..." Hearing this kind of self-analysis from Fern was the most exhilarating thing that had happened to me in days. Never, never, did I imagine she would assume the mantle of First Lady and accept its symbolic import to the nation. But here, a month after entering the White House, she was ready to seize the nettle—cautiously to be sure—but with a brave hand.

"Some of these letters are not very polite," Fern said. "And I am rather shaken by them. But they shall all be answered ..."

"You shouldn't have to write personal notes, Mrs. Hannaford," Vangie said. "I'm hiring a stenographer today for us. It'll make the work go faster."

Fern smiled, nodding her head. She had assumed a brisk manner that was altogether charming. I decided at once that the White House possesses magical powers to transmute and metamorphose. "Yes, that will be splendid, Vangie. But of course, some letters I will insist on answering in my own hand."

"A good idea, ma'am," I offered. "The President does the same thing."

She ignored me, and I was ecstatic. Had Fern been given to cuss words, I am sure she would have replied: "I don't give a damn what the President does; I'll do it my way." But she merely bent to her writing. There was a large one-volume Merriam-Webster dictionary on a stand next to her desk. This, too, was something I had never seen at Ramada Ranch, or indeed, at the Hannaford's mansion at Potomac Oaks.

I turned to leave. Vangie drew an Empire chair up to the small desk and began to check through a new batch of letters. I had reason to be proud, very proud, of my choice of secretary.

As I reached the door, Fern called out to me. "Edward, your knowledge of White House history is not all it should be," she said.

"What ... Who ... Have I misinformed you?"

"A detail, but you should get your facts straight. You have always been Mr. Reliable to us. I expect better of you."

Oh, better and better! "I'm here to learn, Mrs. H."

She adjusted the amber-rimmed spectacles and took a book from a side table. I could see the title: *The White House: History and Meaning*. "You informed me that Dolley Madison cut out the Stuart portrait of George Washington when the British burned the building in 1814."

"So I did. That's the way I've always heard it."

"Well, let me quote this to you, Edward. 'Dolley Madison gets the credit for saving the painting, but one of President Madison's slaves, a man named Jennings, gave the credit to two other servants—John Suse, a doorkeeper, and Magraw, a gardener. They, it appears, were the real saviors of the portrait of the first President. Mrs. Madison managed to save only a few silver spoons.' "

Fern looked up from her reading and pushed the glasses up on her serene forehead. "I find history absolutely fascinating," she said. "All these years in Washington, I paid no attention to it. But it is never too late to improve oneself."

"Indeed it is not, ma'am." I left the two ladies, anxious to report to Ben on his wife's assumption of command. We had a star in the making, I felt, not an Eleanor or a Jacqueline, but an admirable sort of American woman, who could be a marked asset to the Administration.

About a week later, all of Ben's cabinet appointees were approved by the Senate. We were now bracing for major efforts to get key legislation considered by the Congress. Hannaford had drawn up a dozen major pieces of legislation, but all of them boiled down to two crucial efforts:

1. More money, much more, for the cities.
2. Less money, much less, for the military.

Burke Boswell was ready to start trimming the billions for "defense"; Homer Murphy was refining his figures on funds required for housing, jobs, schools and urban betterment. Soon we would move into the cloakrooms and committee rooms, the hearing chambers and legislative offices which the President had known so well. Matt Fixx and I would be key operatives in dealing with Senate and House—myself specializing in the former, Matt, toward the latter.

"This should be fun," I said to Matthew, as I sat in his small office in the West Wing one afternoon.

"Think so, Eddie?" Matt asked. "I don't. We're not in a one-to-one relationship, any more."

"Really?"

"Our options are limited, I'm afraid. The interface is not encouraging."

"Let me see if I can interpret that," I said. "You are suggesting Ben's prestige with the Congress, no matter how high in the past, won't help him put over an ambitious legislative program."

"The delivery systems are clogged."

"Whose?"

"Everyone's. Most of all the House. Bad action there. We may laugh at the likes of Lance Ruckett, but that corn-shaker means trouble. He'll put a glitch in our interrelationships. Ed, Ruckett is rallying too many soldiers to that strange banner."

"Ah, the Caucus of Concerned Conservative Congressmen, COCCC."

"They intend to obsolete us. He's got people listening to him, and the beloved Speaker of the House, the doddering Mr. O'Boyle of Rhode Island will be no help."

"You really feel Congress is going to battle him all the way?" I asked.

"Ed, they won't give him the time of day. He'll try to pull the military's teeth, and they'll destroy him. I mean it. The House won't listen to any of our proposals, let alone vote the money. Old Rumsford on House Ways and

Means has told his pals already that he intends to examine every single dollar the President requests. Every time he makes a move, they'll scream about that miserable 33.7 per cent of the vote, and say we robbed California." His voice cracked.

"Come on, Matthew, the boss wouldn't go into battle this way. Up anchor and away, Matt. If I knew the Ramada U. football fight song, I'd sing it. This is not the old Matt Fixx I know and love."

"Oh, yes it is, Ed. I've never been much of a gut fighter. I'm not like you or the President. I'm just a nuts and bolts fellow, a guy who understands hardware and how to put it together into a viable system."

"We'll need you, Matt, we'll need you. Senators are fond of you. You're someone they can read. You're no New York wise guy. You are smalltown Matthew Fixx, Ben Hannaford's ace in the hole."

Our legislative aide looked up with a silly grin. "Ah, take the needle out, Ed."

"No needle, Matt. It's how I feel deep down. In my heart I know you're right."

And he was; Matt would prove a winter soldier of the first rank in the perilous months ahead.

The President decided on a multifront attack. On the one hand, a bill of particulars on social legislation, based on Homer Murphy's report, would be presented early on in the congressional session.

Expert testimony to support the Federal Education Bill, the long-term Mortgage and Low Rent Housing Bill, the Guaranteed Annual Wage, the Negative Income Tax, the Industrial and Business Training Measure, and the New Public Works Administration, would be given before such crucial bodies as the Senate Labor and Public Welfare Committee, chaired by our friend Royce Henshaw, the House Education and Labor Committee, the House Public Works Committee chaired once more by a grateful Angel Lopez Garcia, and of course, the inevitable, vital House Ways and Means Committee. Lead-off speakers would include Homer Murphy, Chuck Gantry, Dalton Warfield and other men close to the boss, who had drawn up impressive surveys and charts to demonstrate the urgent needs of the cities and the poor.

But Hannaford was a realist. He understood that the

massive outlay of cash needed to put these programs across would engender equally massive resistance in a weary, recalcitrant Congress.

It angered him to learn that there were no slums in Sweden. Or that no one suffered malnutrition in Israel, or that even in poor countries like Hungary or Italy, poor people were guaranteed medical care all their lives. Why was our infant mortality rate higher than that of seventeen countries? So, the social program was deemed our first priority.

"It won't amount to a hill of peyote buttons," Ben told me, "unless we can cut off the Pentagon's water. Those greedy people have to be stopped. By God, I wrote the book on controlled greed, what makes America go round. But those fellows are advocates of uncontrolled greed, and they have to be brought up short."

Thus, the second thrust of our campaign—a drastic reduction in "defense" spending.

Burke Boswell would lead the foray against the military. He had been meeting with the Joint Chiefs steadily, working a fifteen-hour day, reading, absorbing, dictating memos, despatching experts everywhere, and all the time, smiling, smiling, smiling, never more agreeable.

"Daddy has to be watched most carefully," Vangie Boswell advised me, "when he's at his most charming."

"And I gather that General Nagel and the Joint Chiefs feel they now have a friend at court."

"They adore him. Daddy said the other night that he *spoke their language.*"

We all understood, in our cramped offices in the West Wing of the White House, that our leadership in both Senate and House was not quite what was needed. Congress zealously protected its prerogatives—and it had every right to. And we did not nearly have the votes or support to dislodge the Senate Majority Leader, Gage Hopewell, who, in his sly, slippery manner, was hinting he didn't want the military on short rations. Nor was there the remotest chance of cutting down the superannuated, befuddled Speaker of the House, Emmett Brian O'Boyle of Rhode Island.

Flattery and soft soap, Hannaford decided, were in order. The Speaker was invited to a private lunch in the President's office. Matt Fixx and I were also present. Over our soft-boiled eggs and cottage cheese (the menu in

193

deference to Mr. O'Boyle's frail innards) we sat around a small refectory table and chatted.

Poor old O'Boyle! His hands trembled as he broke his toast. He had difficulty tucking the napkin into his starched collar. Ben nodded at me; I assisted the venerable legislator.

"Why, thank you, young man, thank you. You are the Goldstein boy, aren't you?"

I had been introduced to him ten minutes ago. During my career as Senator Hannaford's aide, I had enjoyed many visits with the Speaker. But I could see his memory was going; he was more to be pitied than rebuked. "No, sir, I'm Edward Deever. Mr. Goldstein is the President's press secretary. It's natural to get us mixed up, since we look alike."

"Yes, yes . . . so you do . . ."

Of course, Goldstein and I do not look at all alike. No matter. One had to take into account the Speaker's age and his long years of service to the Congress, the party, the republic and God. For all of Emmett Brian O'Boyle's good deeds of the past, he was a relic. He was like an ancient, wheezing model-T Ford, still capable of puttering along, propelled by a spoonful of sludge in the carburetor.

"Mr. Coolidge never invited me in here, for lunch or anything else," the Speaker said. His voice was clotted with age and the fungoid coatings of the tens of thousands of cheap cigars he consumed.

"Mr. Hoover had me in here a few times. Of course that was when I was a kid up here on the Hill, and he didn't have much use for kid congressmen." His shivering hand put a match to the black cigar, and I feared that he would burn his long drooping nose, or at least the tuft of white hairs that sprouted from it. But the old fellow managed, and the President and I took a collective deep breath. "But Mr. Roosevelt, yes, Mr. Roosevelt . . . he and I were good friends. Mr. President you know that for a fact . . . wrote about me to his friends. All those New Deal fellows around him—Hopkins and Ickes and Sam Rosenman—they said nice things about me in their books. Yes, they knew, that Congressman E. B. O'Boyle was one of the best friends FDR ever had on the Hill."

"Mr. Speaker, I was reading Hendelman's history of the New Deal last week," I said, edging flattery with sincerity, "and I was delighted to discover that he regarded you as

194

one of the key architects of New Deal social legislation. He says that when you led the party caucus in the House, FDR always felt he could present some new social measure—housing, education, jobs. He says you are one of the most unappreciated congressmen in American history."

Emmett O'Boyle, representing that older generation of warmhearted Irish Catholic politicians from New England, those hard-rock sons of hod carriers and motorman conductors from Sligo and Cork and Wexford, had been a liberal before his time. He would cringe if you called him a liberal. He was uneasy with a lot of the people he found himself thrown in with—radicals, intellectuals, Jews, professors. But when FDR called, he came. And when FDR explained the need for child labor laws and low-cost housing, he listened and he acted. Oh, but that was a long time ago. And the poor Irish for whom Emmett O'Boyle had labored so strenuously were now middle-class and rich Irish with split-level homes in the suburbs of Providence. And the Italians and Greeks and Ukrainians, who had also gone down the line for this faithful old friend of plain people, were no longer sweating out minimum wage laws and federally financed housing. This left only the odds and ends of the lower classes. Blacks. Mexicans. Puerto Ricans. Indians. A handful of the white poor and aged who couldn't fit in anywhere. And for these, Emmett O'Boyle's old Irish heart, while still compassionate, still brimming with charity, could no longer summon up the old fires.

"Fellow said that? Did he? Why son, that's old badadas." Matt Fixx and Ben looked confused. But my ear is a finely-tuned one. Speaker O'Boyle was speaking a pure old Rhode Island dialect. Badadas meant *potatoes*.

"Not so old, sir, that they don't merit retelling," I said.

"Ah . . . yes, yes . . . I try not to talk to those young people much . . . they don't understand . . . anything."

He was ancient. His hair was wispy white, stained here and there with a yellowish hue. He had enormous, pendulous ears, the lobes as extended and loosened as an African chief's. Behind thick lenses his resinous eyes were two tawny blurs. His lips were cracked and shriveled, and he had that disconcerting habit of certain octogenarians of opening and closing them a few times, as if testing them, before speaking. When the shivery words did emerge, and he had concluded his thought, his dry old tongue would dart out, moistening lips for a few seconds. Tea sloshed into the saucer as he brought the cup to his face. He slurped noisily, dabbed at his lips, and then drew fiercely on his stogie. Oddly, the noxious fumes invigorated him—much in the manner in which booze energized Gabe Tutt.

"Mr. Speaker," Ben said—indicating that he was ready to assume command of the luncheon meeting. "I will need your help. You were a great help to FDR. You helped create the New Deal. You stood by Harry, and Ike, and John Kennedy and Lyndon, and you were damned good to Mr. Nixon. I need you now as no President ever needed you . . ."

O'Boyle leaned back and inhaled the praise along with the cigar smoke. I have noted this in professional politicians, especially congressmen. No matter how old they get, how hoary in years of service and how crusted over with experience, they will respond to flattery.

Ben proceeded to outline his program to raise the cities to excellence, to elevate the blacks and the poor, to attend to all the business left undone by a war-oriented society.

"I shall respond, Mr. President," the Speaker croaked, "by saying that I am honored by this briefing. You know I am a man of the common people. I fought for a fifty-cent an hour minimum for the hod-carriers union, when I was a young kid in the state legislature . . . and I know that millions of Americans are in need of help. Well, Mr. President, this is one Yankee who'll stand with you."

Ben patted his spotted hand. "Thanks, old friend."

At that moment, old O'Boyle leaned back in the leather chair, drew deeply on his cigar and discharged a billowing cloud of smoke into the presidential office.

"Yes, sir," O'Boyle coughed. "Yes, sir, social measures will receive first priority in the House. I shall advise the committee chairmen to expedite the President's program."

"I can ask no more," President Hannaford said.

"And, of course, they will want to know costs. We have to know where the money is coming from."

"Mr. Speaker, I'll be frank with you," Ben said. "What I intend to propose in the way of legislation will cost a great deal. But the Budget willed to me by the Kretz Administration is getting a thorough re-examination. We intend to find the funds there, without raising a single tax, or an eyebrow, for that matter."

"Well, I have looked at the Budget you have inherited,

Mr. President, and I must say, I have no idea where the money will come from."

"Mr. Speaker, you know why that is," Ben said. "It is because the military is gobbling up every buck in sight. They absorb seventy cents of every dollar in the Budget. We spend one-fourth of one cent of every dollar on education."

"Those are the grim facts of life," the Speaker murmured.

"Do you really think that those facts are final?" the President asked.

A fluttery hand passed over O'Boyle's brow. He patted down a few silvery strands of hair. Old man's hair; devoid of life and resiliency. "I've never been convinced otherwise. Ever since Communism first reared its head in the world, I've known that we have to insure the peace of the world with arms, and to fight for peace, if necessary."

"We may be overinsured, Mr. Speaker," said Hannaford.

Speaker O'Boyle closed his eyes. When he opened them, he licked at his bloodless lips a few times, and said, "I am not afraid to die, Mr. President. If the showdown comes, and freedom must be defended, I am ready to die. Death doesn't scare me."

I held my itching tongue. I wanted fervently to tell the dodderer that perhaps he wasn't afraid of death because he was eighty-three, sexless, insensate, living out his years surrounded by sycophants, in a gloomy room in the Sheraton Park Hotel. Yes, old O'Boyle was not afraid to die, since his time was about up anyway.

O'Boyle went on: "There is another world, of course. I've never doubted it. I'm ready for it. I believe in the life after death, as deeply as I believe that the wafer is Christ's body and the wine his blood. I have always believed it. So, if this life is a transient period, a mere stop between trains, why be in such despair to leave it? I'm sure God has prepared a better place for us . . ."

It dawned on me—and why I had been so obtuse I do not know—that to understand Emmett O'Boyle you would have to begin with his rigid, innocent, basic, Irish Catholicism. He was, down to his button-top shoes, an Irish Catholic, and there is much to be admired in these people, especially the New Englanders, descendants of victims of the potato famine and His Majesty's Government. Say what you will aout them, they have a fixity of purpose and a moral stance that is worthy of respect.

"I respect your sentiments," the President said. "And there are times when I wish I were as good a Christian. The River Brethren were a lot less convincing on that issue of life after death. I have the feeling that millions of people around the world aren't as convinced as you are. The evidence isn't all in. We haven't had any verified reports of that sweet bye-and-bye. No offense, Emmett. You'd expect nothing less than straight talk from an old colleague, I'm sure. . . ."

Matt Fixx and I suppressed giggles. But the Speaker of the House was not offended. He could kid and be kidded. The President, however, was waxing impatient. I could see the deepening of the lines in his jaw. He spun about in his chair and crossed his legs, moving back from the luncheon dishes. "The Kiowa have a theory similar to your Catholic notions, Emmett," he said. "They believe in a life after death also, that endless field of buffalo and antelope, the dusky maidens, the finest tobacco, and the war games that the Kiowa braves always win. But they keep a little something in reserve. They say that although the world after death is beautiful, it's best to make the most of this one we've got, to keep in training for the next. What's more, if that great hunting ground never materializes, at least you've had a whoopin' and hollerin' time while you were on earth."

"I respect any man's religion," the Speaker said hoarsely.

"As do I," the President said. "Emmett, I will need all the help you can give me in cutting down the Pentagon. I need it badly. We've delayed, and faked, and made excuses about this country's needs, and now we have to pay the piper. Give me your help, Emmett. When I move in to lop a few billion off the defense allocations, stay with me. Keep after Appropriations and Armed Services. They respect you, Emmett. I'll need friends, especially in the House, and I'm counting on you."

Coughing convulsed the Speaker. When he had recovered, instead of drinking the fresh water Travis offered him, he lit another stogie. "I . . . I . . . I . . . ah, I hear it will be more than a few billion, Mr. President," he gasped. "I hear you aim to denude the Pentagon. Cut down on everything. I do hope, Mr. President that you

198

don't reduce our arms so drastically that we are sitting ducks for Red Russian Communists."

Well, there it was again. He didn't fear death, but he did fear Russians. Yet I knew of no Russian that had ever done him any harm, or for that matter any native American Communist, if there were any left.

"I hate to preach to a man about his own faith," the President said warily. "But we have been in touch with Pope Clement, and he is gravely concerned over the proliferation of atomic weapons. His Holiness has informed me that the Vatican will give its support to a de-escalation of the arms race, and that he will help promote new disarmament talks with the Soviet Union. Chairman Gromyko has twice visited the Holy Father in the past year to arrange for diplomatic relations with the Vatican."

One would have expected this intelligence to have moved Emmett O'Boyle. But as Ben spoke, a shifty smile spread across his creased white face. "Oh, those foreign fellows don't concern me," he said slyly. *Foreign fellows?* The heir of Peter, the supreme Pontiff of his own Church? Pope Clement XV was a Belgian, a man of awesome intellect, noted for his tolerance and breadth of spirit. All the new church reforms—birth control, abortion, the lifting of the celibacy requirements for clergy—were products if his vigorous and enlightened tenure as Holy Father.

"Foreign . . . ?" I muttered.

"Why, of course. I revere the Pontiff, that good man, but the Church varies from country to country, although the basic precepts are universal. Still, my vision of the faith goes back to my dear old friend, Pius XII . . ."

Parenthetically, I had worked with many of the progressive young priests of the Catholic Church. No finer, braver, more humane breed of men walk the earth. But the Speaker, while basically kind and generous, was not of their party. He breathed the stale and stationary air of another age.

Ben accompanied the shuffling oldster to the door. "A favor for the boss, Emmett. Get the House to postpone hearings on military appropriations until after the Senate acts. I'd like a full airing of the problem first."

Craft, guile spread across the old man's face. "You have my word, Mr. President."

They shook hands. Matt Fixx walked out with the Rhode Islander.

"I am concerned about our beloved Speaker," the President said. He buzzed for Burke Boswell. "I wish I could convince him of the truth uttered in St. James' Epistle."

"Sir?"

" 'Faith without works is dead.' "

If the meeting with Speaker O'Boyle was a flop, the private session with Senator Hopewell was not much more of a success. Goiterous eyes popping, he intoned: "The military assures me, Mr. President, that the Soviet *Smetana* system will put them ahead, and we may never catch up. Heaven prevent us, dear Mr. President, from being party to such an eventuality. . . ."

"Now, Gage," Hannaford said. "Lots of intelligent people feel that the nuclear race is lunacy, with no bearing on anything, except its power to destroy everyone. Nuclear bombs couldn't win in Vietnam for us, or help us free the Czechs or the Hungarians."

The old medicine man shut his eyes. He wasn't buying it.

I studied Senator Hopewell's ruddy, puffy face, with its fake smile, its charlatan's cunning. Suddenly there raced through my mind a historian's estimate of James G. Blaine, a nineteenth-century scoundrel remembered as "the monumental liar from the state of Maine." The scholar thus described Blaine:

"The perfect politician, he never forgot a name or a friend and always knew how to influence votes and manipulate committees. Yet aside from his personality he made no impression upon American politics except to lower its moral tone." Senator Gage Hopewell, I feared, was a worthy successor to James G. Blaine.

"I want your help, Gage," the President said. "I want you to help me trim and cut and demand an accounting for every dollar given to those birds, and maybe even cut down some of the big items."

"Oh dear, oh dear," Hopewell oozed. "Oh, the angry reaction among my colleagues! Senator Tutt will fight you, Mr. President. And so will many of your friends. Oh dear, the abrasive encounters and the jarring jousts! All those defense jobs—"

"And limitless profits," the President said quickly. "I am

200

damned fed up with these cost-plus deals, Senator. Those people better learn to do business the way I've always done it. Name your price, dammit, and meet it, or take the loss!"

"By all means, Mr. President," he gurgled, "by all means. Yaaaas, we will demand a dollar's value on every dollar spent. To be sure, we are determined to cast a cold eye on the expenditures for every bullet." He paused, and the popping eyes rolled around his ruddy head. "And that goes for all the giveaways and boondoggles that some of our more radical and misty-eyed friends are planning. The Congress will not tolerate wastage of honest folks' tax dollars for costly programs that perpetuate social eeeeeee-vils ..."

Hannaford inhaled; his huge chest expanded, and I had the sensation he would have liked to crush the old wind-bag with it. Ben talked about scaling down the military; the old hack responded by denouncing "giveaways" to hungry children, illiterate blacks, run-down schools. Was there any sanity left in the nation?

"A delightful luncheon, Mr. President," Hopewell said. Waddling toward the door, he grabbed Ben's hand. "We have been through so much, Mr. President, and I am in the Senate to serve you, and to serve the people. They speak to me in the voice of angels, yea, and I listen ..."

"Look out they don't sneak a few devils in on you, Gage," Ben said. "I think you'll find Secretary Boswell's testimony before the committee instructive. Don't close out your options. Think of more plowshares and less swords."

Again, the protuberant eyes rolled and pitched; a pudgy hand went to the side of the flaccid chin. "So hard to do, so hard to do, Mr. President, in a wicked world."

To relax from the fourteen- and fifteen-hour day I was working for the boss (and a seven-day week) I occasionally took Vangie Boswell to dinner. I'd resolved: no sex with this charmer, no more office passion. Burned as I had been by Marsha Treadway Parente, I did not want any broken-hearted wench revenging herself on me at the expense of the Administration.

My caution was excessive. Evangeline Boswell was not a quivering bird. She was tough, confident, pretty, sure-footed, the kind of hard-headed idealist who fears no one. (The Masai, with whom she worked in Kenya, called her

Lioness—because of her utter disdain for savage beasts, polluted streams, rotting goat meat and the tsetse fly.) In fact, I suspect my real reason for not venturing an affair was fear of rejection. I'm a terror at accepting a political challenge, at lying, scheming, arranging, faking, a genius at keeping a poker face when the stakes are highest. (The reader is commended to my cool behavior before the Senate Ethics Committee during the censure hearings.) But I cannot abide the prospect of refusal by a woman. I probably would have been rebuffed by Vangie—if not as a lover, as someone to be taken seriously. This is rather difficult to explain. Quite possibly, Vangie Boswell, long of leg, blond, vivacious, might have agreed to a coupling. However—I was convinced of this—all of our passionate embraces would have been underscored by her own disdain for me and my origins. Maybe I am not being kind to her and underestimating myself. But the truth is, that until a few years ago, I did not know how to hold a *knife and fork* properly when I cut my meat. It took some months of keen practice, of watching better-bred people, to realize that one did not grasp the knife in one's fist or attack the fork as if it were a coal shovel. Ah, well.

"May I confide in the best-looking woman in this restaurant?" I asked.

"You don't confide in people," Vangie laughed. "You test yourself on them."

"Foul!" I cried. We were in Trader Vic's in the Statler Hilton. A six-foot war mask glowered at me. The rattan canoe, dangling over my head, endowed me with a mild case of *mal de mer*. Vangie sipped at a double frosted daiquiri, and I settled for an exotic fruit punch.

"Confide, Edward, confide. I may startle you before the Crab Rumaki gets here."

"Well, I had a terrible case of the hots for Mona Varnum the other day," I said. "I saw her in the press room again, and I had a mad impulse to rape her right there."

"You'd never stand a chance," Vangie said. "Mona regards you as a white, fascist, honky pig."

"I'd agree with her if she'd only give me the same favors she bestowed on Farbelman." I had told Vangie of my interlude with the bearded poet-playwright. "That's it, I think. It's not so much that Miss Varnum turns me on. It's the jealousy that rages inside of me when I think of that fraud Farbelman enjoying her creamy body. Oh, the passion! Island maidens in grass skirts!"

"Careful there, Deever. It's the atmosphere here. All those fake war clubs and thatched roofs."

"No, it's real passion. That fellow who wrote that racial mixture was the answer to America's problems was right. Think of all the new variations. The new thrills. The best part of sex is the permutations it offers, the mixtures, the compotes, the rearrangements of molecules. New connections. New colors. New dazzling displays of derring-do. The old southern slaveowners knew that. Those handsome mulattoes didn't arise out of spontaneous generation or in some test tube. Ah, Mona . . ."

"I've never listened to such nonsense," Vangie said. "Some excuse for wanting to make out with a beautiful black girl."

"On that happy subject," Vangie said, "fill me in a little about our boss."

"Ben?"

"Who else? I know all about that business with the Mexican girl . . ."

"Mexican-American. She is happily married today. Mrs. O'Keefe, lives in southern Ramada. Husband runs a clinic for Indian and Mexican children."

"I don't want testimonials. What gave with them?"

"Nothing. Absolutely nothing. Hannaford was two years younger. He had a crush on Maria Valdez. So did I, for that matter. So did everyone who ever talked to her for more than ten minutes, including Senator Henshaw and Senator Lord."

She sipped her daiquiri through a straw—I seem to recall that a gardenia floated in the pale, iced drink—and her eyes refused to accept my version. "Wow, Deever. Do better than that."

"It's the truth. I was part of the whole thing. I don't think Ben ever kissed her. Not once. Patted her neck or her arm, maybe. He was stunned, thrown for a loop. All his life he'd worked, and built, and made millions, and erected cities and airfields and pipelines, and been faithful to dear Fern. Then—*wham!* Along came Maria with a tinkle of guitar and a whiff of Myrurgia, and the old man was trembling like a sixteen-year-old in a drive-in theater."

"And that was it?"

"That was it. Maria broke it off, left town. Never saw him again. She's got a baby son and a terrific husband."

In the gloom the Chinese waiter came toward us with a tray of erotically perfumed hot towels.

As we rubbed our hands, I saw Vangie's amber eyes narrow. She canted her head. "What would Number One boy say if I told him that his chief still goes in for arm-patting and neck-tweaking?"

Cleo had been right. I decided not to act startled, although I was; and disturbed. "Oh, it doesn't mean a thing. The boss is showing his affection for you. A mild affection, that is. You know, the Hannafords are childless ..."

"I know a tweak, and I know a pinch, and I know when they are fatherly, and when they are not."

"Eat your Hawaiian steak smothered in calla lilies," I said.

"Don't try to change the subject."

"Well, I'd imagine if anyone in the world can handle a President on the make, it would be Burke Boswell's daughter. You've occupied admissions offices, bedded down with Masai warriors, told the Establishment to climb a tree, and now you can taunt the Chief Executive—make him your drooling slave or break his iron heart. How's that for rhetoric?"

Vangie squinted at me. "You sure you didn't work for the Hearst Sunday supplement and not that chain of Ohio newspapers you keep jabbering about?"

"I use fustian because what you are telling me is bunkum. You're around the White House all the time—in and out of my lady's chambers upstairs. And the big fellow is there. You are tall, pretty, smooth-limbed and uncorseted, quite a change from Fern. The boss has never had much time for girls. They would probably sap his powers, his grip on his duties. Okay, he's pinched you or given your nude arm a stroke. Means nary a thing. Zero. It's like Fern petting her Gordon setters."

"Thanks loads, Deever."

"Your womanly vanity would have you believe that the President of the United States is mad for you, and that all this will lead to a sexy scandal that will go down in the history books along with *The President's Daughter* by Nan Britton. Forget it."

She stuck her pink tongue out at me. "Pooh to you,

presidential aide. When I see him *staring* at me, his eyes staying with me, when I cross the room, or gazing longingly at my crossed legs, I know it's more than Big Daddy thinking about the darling daughter he never had."

"And you love the whole idea?"

"Wallow in it."

"Rub yourself with some of that rancid sheep fat that your friends the Masai use. That'll keep him away."

"Seems to me like Joy or Detchema are more in order."

I shook my head in feigned pity. "Ah, Evangeline, how little you know about Ben Hannaford. All that intrigues him is power over men, and governments, and industries. The call of the flesh came late in life to him, and he has never known what to do with it. It scares him a little. I am of the opinion that secretly he was relieved when Maria Valdez ran back to Ramada City and found her young doctor."

"Well, in any case, I'll keep you informed," Vangie said.

"Please do. I'm a splendid confessor."

"I've gathered that. Do women have a mad compulsion to tell you things all the time?"

"Since I was sixteen. I might say, it hasn't helped me in my own pursuit of sex. A hindrance, almost. I'm just the sort of boy girls like to confide in."

Vangie laughed. "I bet. I bet you can be a terror."

"Only under my own rules, which wouldn't interest you."

"And what do you know about Big Ben's rules?"

"Oh, you'd love to have the boss move on up to garter snapping—"

"Never wear them ..."

"—and skirt-lifting, and a few stolen kisses, and some panting and puffing around the desks after you. A little hanky-panky. And wow! Right in the White House! Shades of all the wicked things that used to go on there!"

"Oooh! Tell me about them!"

"Well, you know of course when Grover Cleveland was running for the second time, there was a rumor that he had a bastard child. So the kids would march down the street chanting, '*Ma, Ma, where's my Pa? He's in the White House, ha, hah, ha!*'"

"Something more recent, please."

"No names, please. I am part of the presidency now and I will not spread slanders and gossip about the men who have occupied the White House. They are men, like all other men, and they have their failings, and their needs, and their peccadillos."

"Is it true about Franklin Roosevelt? And the Norwegian Princess? And the girl who was his wife's secretary?"

"Ah, close to home, eh, Evangeline? *Girl who was the wife's secretary.* You almost sound eager for history to repeat itself. One more cyclic demonstration of Vico's theory of events occurring again."

"Mercer . . . wasn't that her name?"

"No secret about it. It's in several books. FDR was a paralytic, so forget about the physical part. But he did need companions, lady friends to talk to him, and soothe him, and flatter him. Why fault a President? It's the loneliest job in the world, and the man who has it is subjected to interminable pressure, to public hatred, to daily decisions and problems. It is a wonder that our Presidents perform as admirably as they do, and with such moral stature. I mean politically and personally."

"More dirt and less theory."

I sipped my bitter green tea. Wasn't there an old movie called *The Bitter Tea of General Yen?* A good title. Vangie was hip on the general yens of Presidents; the vixen was enjoying Ben Hannaford's hesitant hands on her neck and arm. Let her deceive herself. I knew Hannaford. Nothing would happen.

"There was the famous house in Georgetown, where a President, while in office, went for his liaisons. Happily married man. But whenever he found a lady who pleased him, off he was whisked to this well-known Washington bachelor's elegant Georgetown manse, and there he dallied for an hour or so, while the secret service waited nervously outside. The bachelor eventually got married and it cramped the Chief Executive's style. But he still managed."

"No names?"

"No names. Ask other people."

"You know, everything you tell me makes me feel better about our Presidents. They should have their flings. They have a right to get turned on, to groove. It beats sitting around and getting your ears chewed off by people like Honey-Tonsils Hopewell. A swinging President, that's what this country needs."

"It doesn't always work out. It's hard for a man in the public eye. That Georgetown love nest was an exception." I smiled as I recalled a recent bit of Washington gossip. "Oh, they have their problems. Some years ago there was this switched-on Washington hostess type. Big parties. Lots of pizzazz. A certain President got a lech for her, and I am sad to report, they went at it, right in the White House."

"That's what I like to hear!"

"But that was the last time the woman ever got *near* the place. The First Lady's social secretary, one of your predecessors, passed the word out to everyone—and the woman was barred for life from the White House. If she so much as walked by, the guards were to be ready to draw guns and ward her off. And the order stood."

"Poor President."

"Yes, I imagine he felt deprived, and he wasn't the sort of chap who liked to feel deprived about anything. So let that be a warning to you, Vangie. Smile at the boss. Speak to him. Help Fern overcome her shyness and her fits of gloom. In short, be a good and faithful servant, but no more."

I lit her cigarette. The flame from my match cast illuminations on her fine-boned, un-cosmeticized face. A native American beauty, Vangie, the kind of handsome girl found only in this country, home-bred, as truly one of our national products as baseball or Mark Twain or pressure-packed shaving cream.

"Don't think I'd mind," she said softly. "Who ever gets the chance? With a President?" She had stressed the first syllable of the word, drawing it out, the way Eastern Seabord college girls do, in mimicry of those J. D. Salinger characters.

I did not want the boss trapped into anything that would bring him grief, scandal, any knid of impediment to the overwhelming tasks that faced him. Or was I simply a dumb middle western Puritan? Was it possible that a full sex life would make it easier for him?

These musings were interrupted by a hard hand on my shoulder. I looked up in the fire-lit gloom. Lou Parente's swarthy, broken-nosed face stared at me. Amid the Oceanic memorabilia of Trader Vic's, he looked like another threatening mask. A step to the rear—women tended to trail him, like Chinese wives—was my old inamorata Marsha, looking extremely attractive, hair bouffant and reddish-gold, face full of life, and her figure, beneath a black maternity dress, even more so.

"Hiya, Ed. Vangie. You know the frau? *La moglie*. Marsha. Marsha, this is Vangie Boswell, the First Lady's lady."

The girls smiled wanly. It occurred to me that all four of us knew about my long, direful affair with Marsha.

"Will you join us?" Marsha asked. Good for her. She no longer feared me or sought to avoid me.

"We're about to leave," I said. "Early day tomorrow."

"Yeah," Parente glowered. "If I were you, Eddie, you and your boss and all those bright guys he's hired, I'd be up all night. Boy, do you have troubles."

"We're aware of it."

"Lou, I'm dying on my feet," Marsha complained. "Can't you bother Eddie on your own time?"

He called to the captain to seat Marsha and she excused herself. I was delighted by the warmth they showed for one another. The columnist had had a reputation as a hell-raiser; now, he evinced every sign of having become a good husband and father.

Parente edged in next to me. "AP story. Just came in. Read and weep." He handed me a sheet of wire service copy.

Waterbury, Conn., Mar. 22—(AP)—Residents of this Connecticut community voted overwhelmingly today in favor of four issues put to public referendum under a new city law passed last November.

By margins of slightly under three to one, voters approved these items:

1. An end to most welfare payments to unwed mothers.

2. A halt to the voluntary school transfer program, which enabled white parents to send children to ghetto schools.

3. Rejection of federal grants for low-cost housing.

4. Termination of the police advisory commission on minority problems.

The so-called "Waterbury Referendum" was approved by voters last November amid charges that it was a racist maneuver, to prevent any change to benefit the city's small Negro minority. It provides that any public issue before the city can be put to a public vote, and that the results of the balloting are binding. Over twenty-five cities around the country have adopted a similar procedure.

Parente bared his teeth in a ghastly grimace. "It's your America, Deever. The people speak. You hear what they are saying?"

"One town ... one little vote ..." Minimizing Lou's fears, I was nonetheless frightened. He stuffed the AP copy into his pocket.

"Yeah, one town," Parente said. "Reflecting what our citizens feel deep down in their white hearts. I tell you, Deever, the people is a great beast. With fangs and claws. There is only one true function of government, and that is to keep people from tearing each other to pieces."

"No, no, Lou," I said. "It's the strain of the times. Backlash. The blacks suddenly surfaced—and there they were, demanding, shouting, crying out against all the years of abomination. It's more than white people can bear, but it will pass."

"Yeah. Yeah. But not before the walls and the floor get splashed with blood."

He lumbered up from the narrow booth, nodded at Vangie and looked gloomily at me. "When you gonna have some time for me? I got all kinds of stuff for you, if you're in the mood."

"Tomorrow."

I sensed an urgency in the columnist's manner, a heavy pessimism in him. Parente knew a great deal about the country. Like a sorcerer of some kind, he drew me to him; I was impelled to listen.

The following day, on my way to a rendezvous with the columnist at the Smithsonian, I turned on the car radio, to hear what was being said about the Waterbury referendum. To my relief, very little was being said. It was dismissed as an erratic bit of local voting.

As I pulled up alongside the gingerbread eccentricity of the Smithsonian, I caught one last item from the newscaster, that soured the coffee and orange juice I'd gulped at the Manger Hay-Adams.

"Answering charges that his law firm in Wisconsin has made millions of dollars for favors and clients he has arranged for his clients, Senator Gage Hopewell said today, that the charges were 'impertinent, outrageous, insolent, impudent and invasions of his rights as a private person and a United States Senator.' The Majority Leader of the Senate said he had absolutely no intention of making any disclosures about his income, his net worth, or the basis of the wealth that has given him three lavish homes, and a thousand-acre farm in . . ."

I could tolerate no more of this; not with welfare payments being cut in Waterbury.

I found Parente, hiding behind smoked glasses, meandering about the souvenir section of the old museum. He had purchased some hideous plastic dinosaurs for his young son, and was leafing through a picture book about the Smithsonian's famed Doll House.

"Well, Edward Deever, what the hell are you doing here?" he asked.

"Conspiring."

He grabbed my elbow. "You don't wanna see the Ipswich House do you? Or the Pennsylvania Grist Mill? How does Jenny Lind's fan grab you?"

"Not at all. But I read somewhere that Senator Hopewell is considered the most corrupt man in Washington since Daniel Webster. Can you find me one of Webster's old political deals, preserved in formaldehyde?"

"I got better than that."

The columnist steered me through the souvenir shop toward the huge doorway. "Too nice to stay indoors. We will walk along the mall and talk about the prospects of the Washington senators."

As we walked into the dismal gray March weather—the mall was all but deserted at this hour—a small, dark man in a black snap-brim hat and a dark blue raincoat, hands thrust in its pockets, appeared at the crosswalk, and without a word, fell into step. I was the man in the middle.

"Ed, say hello to Augie Baldini. My cousin."

I nodded. "How do you do, Mr. Baldini?"

"Hiya."

He was a slender fellow, about thirty-five, and he gave the impression of great strength beneath the loose coat. Something of the jockey, or the lightweight boxer was evident in his stride and the way he crushed my fingers.

His face, Latin, sharp-featured, was nonetheless bland and dull.

"Here as a tourist?" I asked.

"Nah, nah." Politeness was not Mr. Baldini's long suit; but then again it had never been a hallmark of his cousin.

"Augie is going to tell you a coupla stories," Parente said, as we strolled down the Constitution Avenue side of the mall toward the Capitol. The dome was shrouded in morning clouds; a gray, aimless day.

"Stories?" I asked. "Is that what you get a presidential aide away from his job for?"

"You'll thank me, pal," Parente said.

The tough little man put on a pair of horn-rimmed glasses and removed his hat. His black hair was slicked back and shiny, on the order of Marcello Mastroianni's in *Divorce Italian Style*.

"The republic is at the crossroads," Augie orated, in a shrill, strained voice. "Christian America must make its stand. Stop the riots and the burners. We can take a lesson from Hitler, who might have saved Europe were it not for Roosevelt. The refugees, so-called, from Germany were an alien invasion of Communists and anarchists. Our postwar policies in Germany were dictated by the Communist Morgenthau—looting, hanging, starving defenseless Christians for the benefit of Red Russia. The Declaration of Independence and the Bill of Rights must be scrapped, for they protect traitors. No gun control laws. Decent Americans must arm. We destiny-thinkers must end rationalistic nonsense once and for all, and drive the money-changers from the temple. There were never any concentration camps in Germany. No six million died, just a few traitors who deserved what they got. Bernard Baruch ruled the United States for fifty years. Send Africans back to Africa. Support local police and let them shoot to kill. Hang the traitor Moscowitz. Get the other traitor, Hannaford . . ."

"Stop! Stop!" I cried. "Dammit, Lou, is this what you drag me away from my desk for? When the President wants an urgent report on the status of the Iron Ball System?"

Parente winked at his cousin. Baldini took the eyeglasses off and placed the black fedora on his head. He became his real self—a taciturn Italo-American.

"What Augie got to tell you may be more important

than any Iron Ball," the columnist said. "You see that act Augie went through? That's his cover. Now for Chrissake, Deever, whatever you hear from us today is absolute secrecy. Not a word to anyone. You could get somebody killed."

"Like me," Baldini said indifferently.

"Augie is on my payroll. He's in with Defenders of Our Republic. DOOR is trying to tie the whole thing together. They don't make a move without Augie knowing about it, and telling me. We got tapes, we got papers, we got documents, and we hope to get movies of what the bastards are up to. I'll give it all to you. Moscowitz can sit around and worry about it. Meanwhile, Augie has more to tell you."

"I'm listening."

Furtively, the little man looked around, then began to speak, in a more natural voice.

"DOOR is acting as a parent group to bring the nuts together," Baldini said. "They spent a million bucks on political candidates. Some of it got out. Ruckett got a bundle, but at least he don't hide it. He's on the National Board of Directors. It's got direct connections with the Upshaw-Tutt movement, Save America. DOOR took over the youth group of Save America, kicked out anybody they didn't like, and run it their way."

"What way?" I asked.

Baldini darted a black eye at me. "Meet secretly. Nazi emblems. Nazi songs. Horst Wessel shit. Jewish blood will flow. Cleansing the nation. Next comes Russia. They march and take her over. The kids drill with real guns in basements. They got a slogan, *Was mich nicht umbringt, macht mich starker.*"

"What does not destroy me, makes me stronger," I said quickly. "I've read *Mein Kampf.* But so what? There have always been these small organizations of madmen . . ."

"Small? When it could spend a million on candidates?"

"The secret head of this is a guy named Merton Huckerby, but it isn't his real name," Baldini said. "Hardly anyone ever sees him. He sends out letters, directives. Wrote a book, which these guys use as their Bible, *Near Future.* All the usual crap—war with Russia, cleaning out the materialists, socialists, liberals, leftos, Communists, whoever they don't like. They include feminists and believers in parliamentary democracy. That's Huckerby."

212

"I'm not awed. The FBI knows about these people."

"You can be thick, Deever," Parente said brusquely. "What Baldini here is saying is that once DOOR takes these bastards under their wing, they get themselves a respectable cover. They can get *in*. They're under the big tent."

"I'm still not impressed. We've had these murderous paranoids with us for years. Hannaford isn't afraid of them and neither am I."

Parente grabbed my arm and wheeled us left on Third Street, toward Judiciary Square. Did I see his cousin Baldini (I believed Parente; there was a sort of cousinly bond between them) nod at him, or wink, or indicate that safety lay in a different direction? I could not be sure.

"You don't have any idea how respectable DOOR is getting," Lou said. "Okay, so they're full of nuts. They're also full of money. And they spread it around. Sure, they keep it quiet. The money can be given to candidates through an individual, or a fake front. I don't have to tell you how many ways there are of getting around the campaign fund regulations. You and the Prez wrote the book on that kind of finagling."

I said: "You are saying that DOOR and Save America have become wealthier, more active, and are giving money to right-wing people and causes. Nothing really new."

"Two things are new." Parente was chafing with my bland acceptance of facts. "First, they're hand in glove with one of the vilest bunch of subversive thugs in the country—Huckerby's mob, and second, you'd be surprised if you learned who's handing out the money and who's taking it."

"Maybe I wouldn't be."

Parente dug Augie Baldini in the ribs. "Tell him. Who took money from DOOR last November?"

The columnist's cousin-spy sucked in his breath. "Ready?"

"The suspense is killing me."

"Senator Tutt of Alabama."

"I'm not surprised. He's hand in glove with them."

"Plus the whole Alabama delegation to the House. Every one of them took a bundle. Huckerby brags that he has 'em in his pocket."

I wasn't too familiar with the Alabama congressional delegation, but I knew they had a few wildmen in their ranks. Still, for this out-and-out Hitler-lover, this mad, latter-day fascist to *brag* that he had a state's delegation in his pocket . . .

"Bettenhaus of North Carolina."

This did draw me up short. Stanton Bettenhaus was in the opposition party. Young, handsome, lithe, a former college athlete, he presumed to represent the "New South" in his button-down shirts and seersucker jackets. Actually, he was as black-hearted a reactionary as ever was sent to Washington, voting against any measure to help Negroes or elevate the poor. He was independently wealthy—his family were millionaire textile people—and I wondered why he would bother accepting a few thousand dollars from DOOR. And then it dawned on me: *conviction.* These people believed; and believing, they hung together.

"Sparrier."

Baldini's harsh voice stopped me in my tracks. "Our Vice-President?"

"Yeah. Verne Sparrier."

"I can't believe it."

Parente scowled at me. "Why not, Deever? For a cynical guy, a guy who ran errands for Hannaford all these years, you're innocent. Sparrier took funds from DOOR when he ran for Governor of California and he took more when he tried to cop the nomination in Chicago. Only Hannaford had more money to throw around, and the liberals figured they had to go somewhere, so Sparrier got licked."

"Did Sparrier take any campaign funds from DOOR for the presidential election?" I asked.

"Nope," Baldini said. "They turned the water off, after he decided to go for Veep with your guy. They hate Hannaford's guts. Won't give him the time of day. In fact, they're starting a campaign to prove he stole the election."

"That's no secret," I said.

"But they're making it Number One," Parente said. "These assholes think Hannaford is a sitting duck. Barely elected. Caught in the buzz saw. If he tries to help the *poor*, he gets the middle class sore at him. If he tries to cut the military, he gets the defense industries, the generals and all the workers in Lockheed and United Aircraft and McDonnell-Douglas, on his back. They figure your boss is trapped, baby, trapped."

"Well, he's the President for four years. He's tough. He knows what he's up against."

Parente frowned as we entered Judiciary Square. "I wonder if he does."

Augie Baldini rattled off a half-dozen other senators—men who had accepted donations from DOOR. Erlenmyer, Goodchapel, Owens—many of them run-of-the-mill conservatives.

"Tutt, Sparrier, Bettenhaus, Ruckett, Hopewell and twenty other senators and congressmen have been interviewed on DOOR's radio network," Baldini said. "They cover the country with small radio stations. Send out free tapes."

Parente nodded. "Wake up, Deever. DOOR is a respectable cover. It's got a nice name. Who can get sore at an outfit called Defenders of Our Republic? Even if they got members who drill in back yards with Nazi helmets and pictures of old Adolf."

"Did you say Hopewell?" I asked.

"The old faker from Wisconsin, with the boomy voice," Augie Baldini explained. "Why, that guy is a regular on their radio show, Open Door. Every time they need someone to interview, he shows up. Also, his law firm is a contributor to the DOOR fund."

"Hopewell is too shrewd to get caught in something like this," I said. "These Nazi-type cells in DOOR, and Huckerby's influence, are freakish phenomena. Hopewell, and even Tutt, can't be aware that they are tied in with DOOR and Save America. They can't be."

"Sure, sure, sure," Parente said. "It's new. I have a feeling guys like Hopewell and Goodchapel and maybe even that punk Bettenhaus will clear out when they learn what Huckerby is. They got strong stomachs, but not that strong. But the damage will have been done."

"What damage?" I asked.

"Tying their goddamn destiny thinkers right in to the Capitol, right into both Houses of Congress, shit, let's face it, right into the White House."

"I am certain Vice-President Sparrier would divest himself of any connection with these people if he learns about their association with a neo-Nazi group."

We halted at the corner of Third and Massachusetts.

"Oh, sure, he'll disown them. So will Hopewell. But, like I said, the damage's been done. DOOR can point to all those interviews, those financial contributions and the friends they made got on the Hill like Gabe Tutt and Lance Ruckett and Stanton Bettenhaus."

I was silent.

"Tell Moscowitz and his FBI people I'm sending them a bundle. What does an Attorney General do when he sits in on a cabinet meeting and the guy across the table, your own Veep, once took money from these guys?"

"That was a long time ago, Lou," I protested. "I'm no fan of the Vice-President, but I can't think of him as a storm trooper."

Parente jabbed his cousin. "Tell him, Augie."

"Merton Huckerby says he can take the country over in five years. All he needs is another year of riots in the cities, and maybe an attack on Taiwan by the Red Chinese."

"Your mystery man Huckerby," I said, "is a fake, a fraud and a madman, with no real following."

"Don't underestimate him," Parente warned.

"And don't you, either of you, underestimate Hannaford."

"Yeah, I know all about the big guy." Parente frowned. "Just keep an eye on Congressman Ruckett and his gang. They mean business. Read up on the House of Representatives and the kind of trouble they can give a President."

With that, Parente grasped the small man's elbow, and they turned to cross Pennsylvania Avenue. The columnist hailed a cab, then said to me: "Not a word about Augie. To anyone."

"I know, Lou. Somebody could get killed."

PART III

A decent provision for the poor is the true test of civilization.

——SAMUEL JOHNSON

Burke Boswell, Secretary of Defense, former lobbyist and finagler, had studied the budget for death and machines, and had decided that of the one hundred and twenty billion demanded by the Pentagon, twenty-five billion might be pared. It would not nearly meet President Hannaford's call for forty-nine billion for his urban programs, but it would be a start.

And so we set out to do battle with the Senate Armed Services Committee, chaired by the fearsome Gabriel T. Tutt. Speaker Emmett Brian O'Boyle and the House leadership decided to see which way Tutt and his Senate confreres moved. O'Boyle feared Southerners and their wrath and he did not want the House to act without a reading from the Senate.

I attended a final briefing in the President's office. Secretary Boswell would be our lead-off witness. The man's airy optimism disturbed me. How describe it? Innocence? Naïveté? Or was it nothing more than a false front to buoy the President?

To this day I am not certain about that gangling charm boy, Pay-Toilet Boswell. Was his rosy view of every challenge a product of his shifty legal practice, where he had been paid enormous fees for telling frightened rich men what they wanted to hear? Or was it deep-dyed, an almost religious conviction, a sense that all would go well if everybody persevered? If I had to place him anywhere on the human scale it would have to be at the opposite end of the spectrum from Lou Parente, who morbidly predicted disaster. You would never convince Burke that the coun-

218

try could lie supine under the iron heel of lunatics like Merton Huckerby. Not while Burke Boswell could milk money out of cosmetics manufacturers.

"Go in gently, Burke," the President advised him. "Start by praising the generals. They are the vainest collection of dunderheads in the world. Feed 'em what they want to hear, then sock 'em."

"I always work that way, Mr. President," Boswell said.

I thanked God these two were on our side. When the going is rough in Washington, one needs sneaky, tough-minded men. Ideals are fine, but a shrewd sense of trading, of how to use threats, is much better.

"Burke," the President said, spinning about in his high-backed chair, "keep in mind what those people did to Hayward Kretz. Kretz tried to cut back on the military after all those scandals of the early seventies, and they wore him down. They're a nation within a nation. Not bad men, by no means. But they're like the Blob, that big gooey thing from another planet they had in a horror movie. It oozes along, absorbing people, and money, and the national will. They sat back and let President Kretz complain about overspending, and when he was finished they hollered Communist and patriotism and jobs and profits and what would happen to the whole state of California if we stopped manufacturing missiles. And they beat him."

"Sir, he didn't fight terribly hard," I said.

"No, he didn't," Boswell said. "They didn't have their hearts in it. Hell, his Defense Secretary had been one of the biggest missile contractors in the country."

"Besides," I said, "President Kretz started out as a hawk. He was going to use American arms to police the world, to keep everybody in Sikkim and Gabon safe from Communism. When he realized this was foolhardy, it was too late. He'd already okayed all kinds of Pentagon adventures, including the Iron Ball."

Ben leveled a finger at Boswell. "We got one thing on our side. The people are fed up with high taxes, all this money going for things they can't see. Taxes for social security and better schools is one thing. Taxes for planes you never see, and for nuclear bombs that can't do nothing but kill, don't satisfy folks. Let's play it that way. Less guns, more barbecues."

"I agree," Boswell said. "We see it in the mail. It's not

219

just the liberals and radicals and students and professors who are sick of this waste. It's also ordinary union members and party workers. They're our ace in the hole."

I felt better. If there was one thing Boswell understood, it was self-interest. And if the self-interest of the American people could be aroused, we might get away with our assault on the Pentagon.

"Ace in the hole," Hannaford repeated. "All 33.7 per ent of them who elected me."

"Many more than that, Mr. President," Boswell said, laughing, "many, many more."

The hearings were held in the main caucus room of the old Senate Office Building. This is a most impressive arena—high-ceilinged, the walls decorated with marble pilasters, the windows draped in kingly maroon. There is a long, green, baize table for the senators and their inquisitorial aides, and the usual facing table for witnesses, counsel, and so on. At the sides of the deep room are tables for the press, set at a perpendicular to the senators' magisterial desk. Beyond, are seats for spectators, which, on this April morning, were jammed with a variety of officers.

They were such a decent bunch of clean, intelligent, hard-working and underpaid Americans, these officers, that I had a twinge of guilt over what Burke Boswell and the President wanted to do. If you have ever known any of our service people, they are men of the highest order. That applies even to the higher echelons of the brass, the top cats who order men into battle and lobby for bigger missiles. They are essentially American—modest, honest, capable of being reasoned with, in no way militants or intransigents. But they do, after all, represent a constituency, just as congressmen do. And that constituency is of the opinion that the nation is forever under threat of attack, that we are surrounded, outnumbered, outgunned and friendless. That we maintain a four-to-one superiority over the Soviets in missiles and a twenty-to-one superiority over the Chinese does not modify their fears. In fact, this capacity for overkill, this potency to destroy life on this planet, fills them with other shivering terrors. "Why, it is as simple as this," the generals argue, "when you are as strong as we are, you must be on guard perpetually so that the other fellow doesn't catch up."

To those who would regard such arguments as the ultimate in sophistry, let me say, in support of our generals, that they are not men given to nuances, or subtleties, or Talmudic reasoning. They approach life directly, and with frank and manly countenance. To them, being first means what it says, and one can never be first *enough*. For example, the reader may recall the furor over the last manned bomber program—the so-called "Sky-Broom" or FB-321-A nuclear four-engined intercontinental plane. Long after experts had proven to everyone's satisfaction that manned bombers were obsolete, pointless, wasteful and that the Soviets and Chinese had no plans to build any, and to slowly phase out the planes they operated, the Pentagon insisted on the "Sky-Broom." Why? Well, as the Chief of Staff of the Air Force put it, *"the Russians might change their mind someday, and start building them, so we'd better be one-up."* I did not invent that. It is in the testimony.

"Mr. Chairman and distinguished members of the committee," Burke Boswell was saying, "It is a privilege for me to be sitting here before you as a member of the President's Cabinet. It is an honor I do not take lightly. I've been seen around the Hill a good deal in the past two years, but never with any official government status. Let me tell you all, it's a different feeling, representing the Chief Executive."

Nods, smiles, a chuckle from the senators behind the long table. I looked them over. Smack-dab in the middle, grouchy and sly behind his old-fashioned specs, squatted Gabe. I had last run into him one evening at the Stapps's house in Georgetown. Gabe had seemed almost friendly toward me, perhaps because I had earlier carried the good news that Ben would let him keep his seniority even after he had betrayed the party. But one never knew with Senator Tutt; he was as treacherous as a water moccasin.

". . . of course I have worked for a lot of executives," Boswell said, "in private industry, as you gentlemen know, and I hope I have mastered the knack of keeping an open mind. I come to this job willing to learn, anxious to be taught, and ever-ready to heed the counsels of wiser, more experienced men like the members of this committee and our distinguished military leaders."

Fred Goldstein was seated next to me at the rear of the press section. "That's Boswell," he whispered. "Shmear 'em a little. No matter how much they hear of it, they like to hear it again."

I gave the rest of the committee a fast once-over. It didn't look too ominous. Gage Hopewell had seen to it that he had a place on Armed Services, and the white-ruffed old mountebank might probably be persuaded to side with us. Catch Gabe not cutting himself in on defense contracts, though! We'd have to see to it, that whatever defense cuts were made, they didn't happen in Wisconsin. But there were better men than Tutt and Hopewell among the sixteen committee members—John Tyler Lord of Vermont and Webb Urban of Wyoming. What did disturb me was the preponderance of Southerners on the committee. In addition to Chairman Tutt, I counted ten men from the South or border states. How well I knew the inevitable issue! Yes, save money on defense—but for what? To aid poor black people? Never.

"Now, first of all," Burke Boswell said, "I want to pay tribute to our military men. They've kept the peace of the world these past years. They've seen to it that our shores are secure from attack. Our country has never been more secure nor in a better position to bargain for a lasting peace than it is now. And so much of that security is a direct result of the selfless contributions of our vigilant military men."

"A-men, Mistah Secketary," Gabe Tutt croaked. "Ah hope y'all in the White House keep that in mind."

"It is foremost in our minds, sir," Boswell said, grinning that dopey alcoholic's grin.

"Don' mean to innarupt," Tutt said. "But we been hearin' all kinds of noise from the Executive about cuttin' back."

"Let me assure the chairman, no cutback we recommend will ever endanger the nation," Boswell said. He began to read: "It is the hope of the Administration to economize in certain areas. This is such an old argument that I suspect many of you gentlemen are weary of it. But our economy won't support a military budget of one hundred twenty billion dollars. Dollars spent on bombs are nonworking dollars. They produce nothing. We have to cut down on these expenditures. It's not just a matter of economy. It's a matter of national health."

"Health?" Gage Hopewell interjected. "Excuse me, my dear Mr. Secretary, but what is more essential to health

222

than survival? If we divest ourselves, denude ourselves, discard our shining armor, our raiment of mail, and expose ourselves to the barbarians, what will happen to our health? Yaaaaas."

A chuckle went up from the audience and a few snickers from the press corps. Leave it to old Honey-Tonsils.

"Senator Hopewell, I quite agree that when you're dead, health is no longer an issue," Boswell said. "But the Administration feels that we are more than well-protected from any aggressor. And it feels further that we are approaching a kind of nuclear saturation point that can only mean disaster. We are becoming a war-oriented society."

Boswell kept speaking in that loud, happy voice—the tones he used to disarm federal commissioners and rich clients. It had a soothing effect on the senators. Even Tutt and Hopewell, who had indicated their distrust of Hannaford's plans, leaned back and listened. I understood why. All their professional lives they had dined with, listened to, played poker with, and shared some of their power with the oily Burke Boswells of the Washington scene. He was, in a sense, one of them.

"One in every nine working Americans is employed by the military-industrial complex," Boswell read. "One hundred and thirty thousand firms, large and small, supply goods and services to the military. Every state in the Union and 363 of 435 congressional districts get a share."

"An' thass jus' suits lots of us fine," Gabe Tutt crowed. Oh, it suited Gabe all right. Alabama groaned pleasurably under the weight of the ordnance depots and naval training stations he had lavished on her.

"I am sure the chairman has every reason to be proud of the way he has brought defense industries to his native state," Boswell said.

There was a moment of strain; Tutt did not like to be reminded of the way he took care of his own. For a moment a suspicious look clouded Gabe's furrowed face; but Boswell was grinning at him, as if he were condoning Tutts greed. The chairman smiled back.

"Mr. Chairman, it is the intention of this Administration not to weaken our military, but to make it stronger," Boswell read. "Yes, stronger. I know a little about corporate organization, and I know that the best of industrial bodies can grow fat and lazy when they are overorga-

223

nized. I don't say that our military is all those things. But it shows signs of flab. As we all know, carrying around too much weight can induce heart trouble, diabetes, shortness of breath and mental failings. I don't want a fat, lazy military; I want it lean, tough, alert and healthy."

Goldstein dug me in the side. "Ever see a giraffe skating on thin ice?"

I nodded. Boswell was about to present our case. The senators were attentive. Tutt had closed his eyes. Gage Hopewell was staring at the ornate ceiling.

"The President wants to economize, but only in a manner which will make our armed forces stronger. With this in mind, I should like to review some recent instances of regrettable malfunctionings of our defense establishment. I mention these examples not to point an accusing finger at any person, or any branch, or any system. I do it merely to point out that, like any business, the Pentagon must be asked to operate on a more efficient basis. That's our watchword—efficiency."

Tutt cleared his bourbon-coated throat. One of his secretaries, a good-looking, red-headed woman, artfully girdled and stylishly garbed, approached him with a paper cup of some refreshing liquid. It was assumed to be water. I knew it was a belt of one hundred proof. Her name was Mrs. Whitchurch, and she was one of his seven office and staff aides who had recently spent $7651 of the taxpayers' money touring Europe for the Armed Services Committee.

"Jes' a minute, Mist' Boswell," Gabe gargled. "You sound lak you aim to efficiency and economize our defense outa existence."

"No, sir, I don't." Boswell waved his flapping arms, palms upward, in an odd gesture reminiscent of General de Gaulle. "Our watchword is patriotism of the highest order."

Was he laying it on too thick? I caught an amused expression on Senator John Tyler Lord's aristocratic face. Johnny Lord, a Harvard lawyer, understood Boswell and knew what he was up to.

"Proceed, suh," Gabe mumbled. He sipped his booze; his eyes glazed. My man Boswell would drink him under and around the table any day of the week. In an age-for-weight contest, Boswell would leave him at the starting gate, sniffing his first belt of the day, while big Burke worked his way through a gallon of martinis.

Boswell resumed: "First. Why did spokesmen of the Pentagon lie when asked about the escape of nerve gas in Utah last year which killed seven thousand sheep, four thousand cattle and rendered drinking water poisonous in an area of three hundred square miles? They lied not once, not twice, but, by our count, *fourteen* times. What kind of national security requires spokesmen for our military establishment to tell lies—to Congress, to the press, to the President?"

A shocked silence greeted Boswell's rhetorical question. Suddenly, his toadying had become cruel polemic.

"Whut? Whuzzat?" Gabe snorted. "Whuzzat 'bout lyin'?" It had taken some time for Boswell's purport to reach him. "Y'all sayin' someone lied?"

"It is on the record, Mr. Chairman. It has appeared in every publication of note, including the Congressional Record. Long after evidence was presented to prove that the Army Chemical Warfare Center in Utah had been negligent in testing procedures and had allowed deadly gases to escape, Pentagon spokesmen repeatedly lied, I say, lied, about the incident."

Tutt was stumbling to his feet. "Thass' irrelevant! That has nothin' to do with defense budget! Mistah Seck'tary, this committee got no desire to heah yo' unproven charges!" He fell back into his chair. "Y'all be careful, suh. I warn you, the military people are gon' be given a fair hearin' heah, to answer all those accusations which give aid an' comfort to . . . to . . ."

He wanted to say the *enemy*. This was pure Gabe Tutt. Any attack on the Pentagon was depicted by Gabe and his southern allies on the Hill as some sort of traitorous exercise. But he was facing Burke Boswell.

". . . to . . . to . . . enemies of the finest Americans in the world, our fightin' men!"

"No, sir," Boswell said. "I am paying tribute to them."

"By accusin' them of lyin'?" cried Gabe.

"No, Mr. Chairman, by pointing out that it was only a few misguided people who told those lies, and that the Pentagon's bosses were men enough, a few days later, to admit they lied."

Ah, Burke Boswell. He had every trick in the book. Whenever he repeated the word *lied*, he bellowed it, stretching it out, stressing it, holding it up and rotating it in his hand, like a fish peddler displaying a carp to a bunch of housewives. Tutt had gotten a bear by the tail.

"I don' wanna hear that word lyin' again!" thundered Tutt.

"I believe I've made my point about those lies," Boswell said. The word "lies" came out in three exaggerated syllables.

"Mr. Chairman, I am anxious to hear the rest of the Secretary's presentation," Senator Lord said. "Can't we let him proceed without interruption?"

"I'm gonna innarupt whenever he makes those vicious accusations," Chairman Tutt grumbled. "G'wan."

"Thank you, sir." Boswell turned a page. "Now, the matter of the Sky-Broom aircraft, or the FB-321-A nuclear-manned bomber. The public is asking why they were assured it would cost five and one half billion dollars to develop and produce one hundred of these advanced design planes, when now the cost has risen to seven and one half billion dollars. These can't be called bad guesses, or underestimates. They are signs of dreadful management, a field I know a little about. But we can't get an answer from anyone in the Pentagon. Why two billion dollars more? Why? Can't anyone enlighten us?"

"What answers have you gotten?" Senator Lord asked.

"The only one that makes the slightest sense," Boswell said, "is that the contractor, Vengeance Air Industries in Quake, California, deliberately submitted a low bid. They call this low-balling. They do this with the assurance from the Air Force that the bid is meaningless. That is, they can spend all they want building the planes, because they are guaranteed cost plus a fixed profit of six per cent."

"I have heard that," Lord said, "and I cannot believe what I have heard."

"Ah have heard it, too," Tutt belched, "an' Ah rejected it ten years ago, and Ah reject it naow."

"I am deeply grateful to the chairman for his support," Boswell practically yelled. "Yes, and so is the President. We see eye to eye on the importance of defense. It's just that we want a better defense establishment. More efficient. Up to date. And no more lying."

Goldstein almost fell off his chair. "Jesus, he can't be believed," Fred whispered. "He keeps using that word like a club on Tutt."

226

"Mr. Chairman and distinguished members of this committee," Boswell plunged on, "we want the truth from our generals and the industrialists who contract with them. But I'm afraid the record is a sorry one. We were lied to about Minuteman. We were lied to about the C-5A transport. We were lied to about the ABM. We were lied to about the nerve gas depots. We were lied to about atomic testing in Nevada. We have been lied to about every single major item of defense including the cost of winter underwear for men being sent to fight in Vietnam, in the tropics. It's got to stop. The national budget, the treasury, the American taxpayer is not some great big herd of dumb cows waiting to be milked and milked and milked by the military. I am all for strong defense, but I don't like being lied to."

This speech was so shamelessly blunt, that those who heard it could only sit, mouths agape and ears reddening. I saw the chairman of the Joint Chiefs, General Boyd R. Nagel, a kind and uncomplicated man, who had been known in Vietnam as "Butcher Boyd" because of his predilection for sending men up hills where they could be ground into hamburger by Viet Cong gunners, turn the color of raw pizza dough. He leaned to an aide, a young colonel. Then both began to shake their heads sorrowfully. A gray-haired, scarlet-eared admiral got up and left the room.

"You gonna make a peck o' trouble for yo'se'f," Chairman Tutt warned. Balefully, he leaned over the table and pointed at Boswell. "You givin' aid and comfort to enemies of our soljers."

"I don't think so, Mr. Chairman." Boswell rubbed his lantern jaw. "I think all people responsible to the American public, like you and me, Mr. Chairman, and the military needs shaking up now and then."

"I gon' decide how they git shaken up, and mebbe someone else needs shakin'!"

John Tyler Lord's thin figure jerked upward. "Mr. Chairman, I must register my disapproval of your attitude toward the witness. The Secretary of Defense is not some wild-eyed hippie or radical to be brow-beaten and shouted at. This unseemly affair is going out over television and it will hardly give the people an impression of an orderly proceeding."

Boswell shifted his legs—they seemed to have gotten

hopelessly entangled under the witness table—and waved a huge hand at Senator Lord. "Oh, heck, Senator Lord, I don't mind the chairman letting me have a bit of Old Harry. I have a tough hide, and he can holler at me all day. I think it makes for more honesty."

Goldstein whispered in my ear. "This guy is too much, Ed. You remember what happened to McNamara when the committees jumped on him about the F-111?"

"I do. He *cried*."

Painful, painful that memory. The Secretary of Defense, Robert S. McNamara, that cerebral, automated, creative man, captain of industry, philosopher—*weeping* in front of some raging senator who challenged his cost figures. But never Burke Boswell.

"Mr. Boswell," Gage Hopewell sang, "my dear Secretary of Defense, if I may pose a question, yaaaas . . ."

All heads turned to Honey-Tonsils. The old faker knew how to grab an audience. Let Tutt rave on, let Boswell denounce, let Lord show his Puritan outrage. When Gage was ready to orate, they would no longer have top billing.

"Please do, Senator Hopewell."

"Yaaaas," Gage pumped. "You claim certain distortions of the truth were uttered by the military and their contractors . . ."

"*Lying,* Senator," Boswell shouted. And he slammed the table so that the pitcher of water danced.

"Yaaaaas, that is your charge, at any rate, although I hold dear the probity of our brave men in uniform, therefore . . ."

"So do I, so do I, Senator Hopewell," the Secretary of Defense cried. "I don't say they all lie, I just say it became a way of life, a habit, a way to get around poor performance and graft and overspending, so as to hoodwink Congress and the American people."

"Oh shame, shame, Mr. Secretary," Honey-Tonsils puffed. "An incident here and there, but not, nay, never, a way of life." He popped out his green eyes and I could swear that the absorbent cotton tufts above his ears inflated. "But you, sir, as a private citizen, as Mr. Burke Boswell, did you not, sir, represent Lallor-Hubbs Industries, when they contracted for the data programing units on the Iron Ball system, and did you not submit for them a bid of five hundred million dollars, and did not Mr.

Parente, that newspaperman, claim that your client had falsified its reports and its figures?"

There were smug smiles on the faces of the brass. I saw one high-ranking Air Force type laughing behind his braided sleeve. General Nagel smirked. Two admirals exchanged knowing winks.

"All true," Boswell said. "They acted against my advice. Mr. Parente is correct. Lallor-Hubbs did submit a low-ball bid, with the assurance from Pentagon officers that it would be all right if the system came in for an additional three hundred million. It's one of the reasons I dropped the account."

"Your law firm still represents them," Senator Lord said.

"Former law firm, Senator," Boswell yelled.

I sat in the palatial room, sweating slightly, dazed by what was happening.

"I find it hard to believe that you did not know they were engaged in some jiggery-pokery," Hopewell organed.

"I'm sorry, Senator, I didn't. The darn trouble with these defense contracts is that they are all fakes. And if you find out they are fakes—underpriced, overpriced, padded, juggled, concocted, chock-a-block with hidden or misrepresented costs, there isn't a thing anyone can do about 'em." He opened his cavernous mouth as if to laugh, let his lower jaw dangle in a moronic grimace, then added: "At least up till *now*."

"But Mr. Secretary, how do you explain these liberties that have been taken with the public pocketbook all these years?" John Tyler Lord asked. "Other agencies of government are held accountable. Supreme Court Justices have been forced to resign because of dubious associations. Congressmen have been brought to book. A great senator was censured—"

"Oops. Close to home." Goldstein was whispering at me. "Lord won't win any prizes for diplomacy."

"It isn't hard to explain, Senator Lord," Boswell asserted. "The defense program has always been presented to the Congress and the people as a matter of life and death. No questions asked. No accounting. No checks. No criticism. And money for everybody, money spread all around."

"Too much spreading if you ask me," interjected Senator Webb Urban of Wyoming. Urban was a numbingly

229

dull Mormon elder, a charter member of the Senate's establishment of conservative, rural, older men. One never saw or heard Urban for months on end, and then unexpectedly he would be revealed as a source of strength on major decisions.

"I couldn't agree more, Senator Urban," Boswell responded.

Tutt looked warily down the long table to Webb Urban. One didn't, as Fred Goldstein would have said, *futz* with people like Urban; not even if you were Gabe Tutt.

"Hunh? Hunh?" Gabe barked.

"We are playing fast and loose with the national treasure," Urban said flatly. "There's just so much money to go around, even in a rich country like this." Urban had a gray face, gray hair, gray eyes and wore a sort of cinder-gray suit. His mouth barely moved when he spoke. "I have fought government spending all my life. I have fought it in every field imaginable. I say we are crazy when we insist on cutting a million dollars from a bill to provide job training for poor boys, but keep approving billion on top of billion for weapons we don't need."

"Agreed, Senator," Boswell chortled.

"You both blind to the threat facin' us. Y'all want to denude and isolate this country." Gabe was unsettled. "Y'all doin' the enemies' work for him."

"The chairman should not generalize in that manner," Webb Urban said glacially. "He knows my long record of opposition to Communists and all kinds of radicals. I say we're sufficiently armed. The Russians haven't said boo in five years. And in any case, let's get some honesty and economy and responsibility into this defense business."

Senator Lord waggled his small blond head. "Exactly. There is no money left for anything in the country. The banks don't have a nickel to lend. They are ninety-eight per cent lent out. No wonder interest rates keep soaring. We are destroying the economy with this spending."

Burke Boswell gawked. "If the chairman will permit me, I have something to add to what Senators Lord and Urban are mentioning, because it relates to my next subject, the Iron Ball missile, or MOMSER."

"Here comes the cock-knocker," Goldstein muttered. For some reason Fred always referred to the Manned Orbital Multiple Satellite Entry Relay in that manner.

"Mr. Chairman, the President and I are distressed

about the manner in which the previous Administration presented the so-called 'fact sheet' on this weapon to the public. It was stated that completion of the Iron Ball would cost the nation twelve billion dollars. But a careful reading of the Defense Department's *own* literature reveals that the cost will be closer to *twenty* billion, and even that is regarded as a low figure because it does not include provisions for cost overruns, upgrading, expanding and replacement of spare parts."

"You are sayin' yoah Administration don't wanna spend the money fo' Iron Ball?" Chairman Tutt asked.

"I am saying, sir, we are assessing it very carefully. You see this alleged 'fact sheet' put out by my predecessor, acting on Pentagon advice, failed to include the cost of *warheads* on the MOMSER. That figure alone was two and one-half billion dollars."

"Why this is fantastic," John Tyler Lord protested.

"That is hardly the word for it, Senator," Boswell shouted. "Submitting a fact sheet on a major missile system and leaving out the cost of the warheads is duplicity of the lowest sort. Why, the Federal Trade Commission forces dime stores to be more honest than that. If you sell a flashlight or an electric toy, you are required by law to state on the advertising, *batteries extra*, or *batteries not included in price*. You would imagine that this fact sheet could have had the decency to add a note in small print— *warheads not included in price.*"

"But who is responsible for this misrepresentation?" Senator Urban asked frostily.

"A lot of people," Boswell boomed, "motivated by patriotism and impatience, and maybe fear, and a good deal of greed."

"Y'all better watch yo'se'f," Tutt warned.

"I regret Mr. Chairman, that you feel you have to say that," Boswell responded. The grin bared his equine teeth. "But the fact is that a survey by my office of fifteen weapon systems picked at random developed over the past ten years show that eventual costs were, on the average, 270 per cent over the original estimates. This is wasteful. This is wrong. This is deception. This has got to *stop.*"

"Yaaaas," Honey-Tonsils chanted. "Perhaps so, Mr. Secretary, but I am advised that rising labor costs, harmful strikes, sabotage, and the need for meeting the Soviet threat have caused these price rises. Not some conspiracy by our generals and our industries. Moreover, I am further advised that the costs of miscellaneous hardware, accessories and spare parts for the systems are very high indeed . . ."

"All I can say, Senator Hopewell," Boswell countered, "is that's an awful lot of nuts, screws and bolts. You can buy a lot of gaskets and washers for twenty billion dollars."

There was a snicker from the press table, and some laughing from the spectators. I heard, amid the joyful noises, a healthy *whooop!* from the rear of the room. Craning my neck, I saw the Secretary's rangy wife, Minerva, in the rear row.

" . . . whole question of the Iron Ball is being re-evaluated," Boswell read. "Do we really need it? Is it not an unnecessary escalation? Is not disarmament the path to security rather than endless production of death-dealing systems, which can destroy not only our alleged enemies, but *all* life? Who granted us this terrifying power, and by what right do we use it so freely?" He looked up from his notes. "When I say *we*, I mean the Russians and the Chinese and the French and anyone else who makes these weapons. All of us have a lot to answer for."

"I'll second that notion," John Tyler Lord cried.

"The Chair will not," Gabe Tutt croaked.

Goldstein whispered in my ear. "Old Tutt is scared shitless Alabama will lose the prime contracts on Iron Ball. Gartland Labs in Huntsville are in for half a billion on the MOMSER. Bullitt-Weeks Industries for three hundred million on the goddamn thing. Gabe is counting dollars."

I looked at the committee, studying the faces. What continues to amaze me is not how *bad* senators are, but the astonishingly *high* quality of man that is sent to the Upper House. Lord, Urban, Dierking, were gentlemen of a high order. But even as I cheered myself with this observation, I was sobered by the awareness that too often mean rogues and nasty flintheads rise to the positions of great power.

" . . . to reduce our spending on arms considerably," the Secretary went on. "We will be fair, we will be forever considerate of the nation's security, but we feel that there is no real security from atomic attack, no way to prevent a holocaust except through international agreement. The
232

Russians and Chinese no more want to be wiped out, reduced to heaps of smoking rubble and charred flesh, than do we . . ."

Honey-Tonsils was dozing, his round, scarlet head drooping on his chest; but it was only a trick to dramatize his disdain for Boswell's speech.

"What about old Gage?" I asked Fred, *sotto voce*. "Wisconsin's in for a cool billion in Iron Ball contracts. Talk about controlled greed. The old sneak saw to it that Monitor Consolidated got the big contract on the launching system. And his law firm cuts the pot every time one is signed. Every damn tool-and-die manufacturer in his state got a piece of the Iron Ball."

They had pulled wires, lobbied, bribed, connived and used their small army of retired generals, admirals and lesser ranks to get their snouts into the public trough. At the last counting, there were no less than 3156 retired officers of the rank of colonel or higher, working for "defense" firms, and arranging good will, parties, contacts and general happiness for their employers.

"New approaches to the Russians are being studied," Boswell said, "and Secretary Edgerton will discuss this in detail. Arms talks are our first priority, not arms building. To those who say we will be left defenseless against the Russians, I can only repeat our staggering four-to-one superiority over them in everything from nuclear warheads to police dogs . . ."

Again, there was that ripple of laughter from the reporters and from the public. But the generals did not think it was funny.

"Chrissake," Goldstein whispered to me, "who writes Boswell's material? Art Buchwald?"

"It's not Joe Alsop," I replied.

"I am ready for any additional questions, Mr. Chairman," the Defense Secretary boomed out.

"Ah don' have a question, Ah got some comments, Mistah Seck'tary," Senator Tutt pronounced. "Ah think a lot of enemies of our military have been brainwashin' yo'all in the Executive."

"Oh, pardon me, just for a moment, Mr. Chairman," Boswell yelled. "I left out a few paragraphs about defense mismanagement." He peered at his prepared remarks. "Yes, here it is. When the Air Force was asked how it could account for the one and three-quarters billion dollars overage in the development of the G-208-X all-purpose all-weather nuclear delivery aircraft, it replied, 'inflation, extra spare parts and overtime.' Now I ask you Mr. Chairman, how in the name of common sense can anyone attribute one and three-quarters billions of dollars to 'inflation, extra spare parts and overtime?' I've heard of featherbedding by unions, and chiseling by welfare clients, and all those lazy black people down in Senator Tutt's home state who are said to refuse jobs because they prefer to chisel on welfare, but, gentlemen, there is chiseling and chiseling."

Again, this was an incredible address. But Boswell delivered it with such joy, such oily *bonhomie*, such a sense of eighteenth-hole familiarity!

"We got us a winner," Goldstein said to me. "Half a year ago, this guy was grabbing contracts for every defense plant in the country, had twenty ex-generals on his Christmas turkey list. And look at him now."

"Ah repeat. Ah intend to investigate the source of that repo't yo'all have presented. Ah want to know wheah those sta-sta-sta-statistics come from . . ."

Tutt was grieved. He'd fallen for Boswell's soft soap and flattery early in the hearings. How he must have regretted it!

"Our files, our staff backgrounds, our sources are open books, Mr. Chairman," Boswell crowed. "Not like the secret proceedings of many industrial concerns doing business with the Pentagon."

"He'll go too far," I whispered to Fred.

Goldstein crinkled his freckled nose. "Nah. Boswell's found something he can really believe in besides money. He's no dope. He's got soul. He's looked the whole thing over, and he's committed."

"To what?"

"Life. Living. Keeping the world from getting blown apart."

That would have to be the key to the "whole thing," as our press secretary put it. Boswell had discovered what the radical students, the physicists, the mothers for peace, the academics, the liberal professors and the intellectuals had been aware of years ago. Outsiders all, aliens in Congress, enemies to the Tutts and Hopewells, they had failed, failed, failed. Now, Boswell—and I hoped many more Boswells—saw the truth, saw that unless our course

234

were changed, we would all perish in a mighty flame. I could only pray that he—and Hannaford—could get their views across to the stern-faced men behind the table.

On the way out, I stopped to chat with Minerva Boswell.

"How did you think he did, Mrs. Boswell?" I asked her.

"Average performance for Burke," she said. "He could have brought a little more passion to his presentation, instead of all that cheery bellowing. Good God, he sounded as if he were at the bar of the Stamford Yacht Club, telling dirty jokes to the Regatta Committee."

"But that's what made it so effective. If he'd cried, the way Mr. McNamara did, or got emotional, or sounded uncertain or apologetic, they would not have listened. He spoke to them in their own tongue."

Minerva Boswell cocked her head. "Maybe. But I think he was more convincing when he was arguing for ten-cent pay toilets before the Interstate Commerce Commission."

We were joined by Senator Lord. A socialite, an aristocrat, he was an old friend of Mrs. Boswell's. "Edward," he said, "please tell the President I'm with him down the line. This reappraisal is long overdue. Someone has got to take Gabe Tutt in hand and I think he's found the fellow to do it."

I thanked Senator Lord and hurried through the high white corridors of the old Senate Office Building, only marginally cheered. I'd have been happier if Senator Webb Urban, that austere club member, had told me he liked the plan to cut down the Pentagon. Urban was Senate Establishment, along with Hopewell and Tutt. Young Johnny Lord was something of an outsider—too rich, too Harvard, too intellectual. Still, any ally was a good ally. I drove back to the White House much inspired by Boswell's bravura performance.

"It'll get worse before it gets better, Edward," the President said to me. "Got to get the money away from the generals first. Meanwhile, let's hold on to what we have."

He cheered me up by telling me that the Italian and Czech governments, as well as the NATO allies (the governments, but hardly the generals) along with Chairman Gromyko in Moscow had reacted favorably to the daring national trade he had proposed.

"Something for everyone in that deal," he said. "And the Senate can't do a thing about it. It's all proper under the NATO charter. Anyone wants in, can get in, and that includes Communists. The Czechs are sending observers to Brussels next week."

Europe had become a place where people went to look at museums. It no longer represented much of a threat to anyone. About all people feared in Europe—East and West—were the accumulation of nuclear weapons by the two giants. Hence, anything that defused the situation between NATO and the Warsaw Pact Communist powers was *per se*, acceptable. Oddly, the press, even C. C. Pringle's rags, were generally uncritical on the move. It had been so long since anyone had thought about NATO that most people had forgotten what it was supposed to do.

"Yes, we sneaked that one across," the President said, "And now we got Gabe Tutt shook up a little. Thought our boy Boswell was brilliant."

Agreeing, I said that we should not permit ourselves to be blinded by Boswell's optimism. "Congress is going to battle us every inch of the way," I said. "The House will be worse than the Senate, especially when they see what you and Murphy have in mind in the way of domestic spending."

The President leaned back, and I saw a gleam in his Indian eyes. He was full of the old Hannaford spirit. Maybe the boss would be brought down, but he would come down battling.

"They have put us on notice, Edward," President Hannaford said. "House Appropriations says we don't get a nickel more for the Ghetto Commune Program. Piddling million dollars more. Homer went before the committee yesterday afternoon. They cut him to pieces. Even before we submit the new one, they're cutting back on the old program, the one Kretz okayed."

I was horrified, disgusted, depressed—but not altogether surprised. "Ghetto Communes is one of the best things that ever happened. It's the most successful of Dalton Warfield's projects, how could they—"

"Congressman Lance Ruckett, our placard-swinging friend from South Dakota has a lot more clout than either of us imagined. He's got the committee with him. And he's scared the b'Jesus out of Emmett O'Boyle, our beloved speaker. No, sir, not one more cent for the communes."

"You mean to say we have no support on the Ways and Means Committee?" I asked.

"Congressman Garcia, the old tiger himself, went to bat for the Ghetto Communes," the President said. "Angel did not let us down. But you understand, Edward, he is hardly in favor in the House of Representatives. The poor man spoke fervently for our program, but no one was listening."

It was a direful omen. Ghetto Communes was a modest, experimental program that had proven extremely productive. It was showing extraordinary success in educating and uplifting the most tragically deprived children. Under Secretary Homer Murphy's blueprint, we envisioned a twenty-fold expansion of the Ghetto Communes into every major urban area in America. It would need lavish financing. But now, even before Homer could make his case, the House was intent on *cutting back* the old program, denying a mere million dollars to keep it operating.

The President made a tent of his fingers and touched his lips. "You look distressed, Edward," he said.

"I'm revolted, Mr. President."

"When I was in the Senate, I somehow had the feeling that in the long run, Americans, and their elected representatives ended up doing the right things, even if the road was twisty and turny, and even if it took some fast shuffling of the deck to turn up the winning hand."

"And the right things got done for the wrong reasons."

"That too." Hannaford pounded one fist into the palm of the other hand. He did it not in anger, or frustration, but with determination. "The basis of American life has always been greed, measured out in small parcels. Everybody's greedy, so the function of government and politics, and big business is to control it, use it, spread it around, like manure."

"It doesn't seem to have worked, sir."

"Temporarily, Edward, it hasn't. You see this nuclear thing, and the arms race, and Vietnam, and our global commitments and that fellow Dulles with his rollbacks and holy wars, they muddied the waters, so that greed got out of control. They introduced all this idealism—all these high-falutin' words, notions of freedom and democracy that those poor buggers in the rice paddies don't understand, when all they want is a new bicycle and electricity in the village. Greed got out of control at home—just look at those defense contracts. Meanwhile we didn't realize that greed was the key to those poor countries in Asia and Africa. I don't mean the greed of a few French or English-educated monkeys dressed up in generals' uniforms, I mean the easily satisfied greed of those poor naked suckers in thatched-roof huts. They wanted grain and fertilizer—dammit, the Communists understood this— so we gave 'em something we thought was freedom."

"B-52 raids and napalm."

"Worse than that. We gave 'em ideals, abstractions, slogans. Enough of those will destroy any man's spirit, especially when he's hungry."

There was a discreet knock on the door. Cleo opened it in response to Ben's buzzer, and Fern, accompanied by Vangie, entered. They were smartly dressed in stylish spring coats.

"I hope I am not interrupting," Fern said. "Miss Boswell and I are off to address the Navajo convention at the Statler Hilton."

My eyes blinked. Fern? Addressing a convention?

"That's splendid, my dear," the President said.

"I suspect they'll be a friendlier audience than the DAR," I said.

"A few Red Power militants may show up," Vangie said. "I've already warned Mrs. Hannaford."

"I am not concerned," Fern said. She smiled at her husband, then at me. I had trouble recalling when she had looked so radiant, so young and alert. Fern usually exhibited a rather vacant air. "After all, that is part of a First Lady's job. Edward, as a matter of fact we have received some lovely letters from the ladies of the DAR, apologizing for that disturbed woman's behavior."

"Save 'em, Fern," Ben laughed. "We may need 'em in court someday."

"Mrs. Hannaford didn't want me to brag about her," Vangie said eagerly. "But I have to tell you, Mr. President, she wrote every word of the speech for the Navajo. All I did was supply the information on the Indian Education Bill."

I could see that Ben was moved. And so was I. Fern

238

Hannaford—shy, isolated, a woman immured from the world by money, oil and rich relatives—was coming of age in her late forties. And to think how she had wept at the prospect of occupying the White House!

"I did what you always say, Edward," Fern said, smiling at me. "I kept it simple. I told them what was in the bill and what the President hopes to do for the Indians."

"Best way, ma'am. The way Harry Truman always did."

"By golly, I am proud of you, Fern," Ben said.

"Of course," the First Lady said, "my voice will shake, and I'll miss a few words here and there. It is so awful at the start. I don't know how people in politics do it day after day."

The President took her gloved hand. "My dear, they do it because they're not nearly as sensitive as you are. We're a bunch of insincere clods, that's how we do it."

"I think we'd better get going," Vangie said. "We can't keep the Navajo waiting."

"Certainly not," Fern said. The President kissed her gently.

When they had left, I said, "The First Lady is looking much better. I have the notion she is responding to her duties."

Hannaford was touched. "Yes, Mrs. H. has fine qualities bred in the bone." Obviously, he was delighted with the change in his wife.

We turned to urgent matters. First, I was to drive out to the Ghetto Commune at Potomac Oaks and get some briefing from Dalton Warfield—ammunition for our battle to get the cuts restored.

"Give me your personal reading about the commune, Edward," the boss said. "Then, an errand of a somewhat more delicate nature." He paused. "Some background information . . ."

"On Lance Ruckett."

" . . . nothing unprocessed like FBI files. They'd never check on a patriot like Ruckett anyway."

Parente would know something. I'd call him. Oddly, I felt reassured when I left. When Hannaford began to scheme and plot, I knew, he was ready to move. There was a sordid truth to his thesis—ideals could kill a man, but an understanding of greed and its usages could save us all.

The night before visiting the Ghetto Commune, I watched Congressman Ruckett being interviewed on television by Bates Pendragon.

"The liberal-left critics," Pendragon was saying, "are screaming in their usual hysterical fashion that you, sir, are a racist and a fascist for leading the fight against the Ghetto Commune Program. How say you, sir?"

Ruckett afforded his host and the TV audience a tolerant smile, looking as pure as the driven snow, sweeter than syrup cocillana compound. "That is the typical reaction of liberals when their pet programs are shown to be frauds practiced upon innocent people," Congressman Ruckett said.

His features were small and well-formed—sharp nose, pursed mouth, neat ears. But the eyes disturbed me. They flashed from time to time with sparks of insanity. I know this sounds like hyperbole, an *ad hominem* judgment unworthy of a presidential aide. But I'd read a lot of Lance Ruckett's literature, and the pamphlets issued by his organization, DOOR. Dig deep enough into these burners and you will find an area of unbalance.

"But what exactly did you—and the Ways and Means Committee—find so objectionable about the Ghetto Communes?" columnist Pendragon asked. "After all, our liberal friends claimed it was the answer to every black child's problems."

(Of course we never claimed any such thing.)

"Bates," Lance Ruckett said, "we produced evidence that criminal elements from the slums of Washington were on the payroll of the program. We brought witnesses before the committee who swore that funds for the commune schools were being turned over to addicts, muggers and burglars. I am all for helping the poor, but I am against helping criminals, and I say, when the taxes of honest taxpayers are put to such shameful uses, Congress must say, halt."

"We keep hearing that this was an act of vengeance," Pendragon said. His tones were organ-deep, all man. With lusty vigor he killed moose, elk and bear. Once, he was reputed to have murdered fifty partridges in one morning of shooting. Oh, these idiots who yearn to be Hemingway!

240

"Not at all," Lance Ruckett simpered. "We are concerned with the ghetto people as much as the President and his advisers. Only we refuse to accept the notion that criminals and lawbreakers are the ones to be running things."

"The Administration plans to fight for a lot more money," Pendragon said. "I'm told the President wants that million dollars restored."

"They are in for a battle over every dollar they demand," Ruckett said. "The mood of Congress is such that it will not tolerate boon-doggle socialistic schemes to bribe unwed mothers, drunkards and muggers into behaving. The rule in this country is, if you break the law, you go to jail, you don't get a reward."

"That seems a reasonable view," Pendragon said.

"Let me, Bates, say a few words about the President's legislative program," he went on. "It is not to the liking of many moderate legislators like myself, and my associates in COCCC."

"Mr. Ruckett, you might explain to our audience just what the letters COCCC signify."

"Be glad to, Bates. COCCC stands for the Caucus of Concerned Conservative Congressmen—a group I founded and of which I'm chairman. We are bipartisan. We cover every geographical area of the nation and all income strata. We oppose the drift toward creeping socialism, appeasement of Communism, and the coddling of criminals. We are economy minded."

"Your critics say you are economy minded on domestic programs, like the communes, or aid to education," Pendragon boomed, "but that you are willing to spend billions on defense."

"We accept that criticism proudly. But it needs refining. Like all liberal-left generalizations, it tries to explain too much, and ends up explaining nothing, but distorting our views and misrepresenting us. We say, not one penny for loafers and drunkards and criminals. Examine every tax dollar that goes into these alleged uplift programs to see if it is in fact producing results. If not, cut them off. As for the defense budget, of course we want value for every dollar spent. I know darn well, as you do, Bates, having friends in the military, that they can make little mistakes also."

"Yes, one would not regard them as human if they did

241

not err, considering the magnitude of their task—nothing less than the world-wide defense of freedom."

"Correct," Lance Ruckett said. "I know I'll be pilloried by the liberal commentators for saying this, but I can do no less. I am convinced that these slanderous assaults on our generals are motivated by nothing less than a conspiracy to make us sitting ducks for a Russian nuclear attack."

"Those are strong words, Congressman."

"Strong words are needed today, Bates."

"And do you feel President Hannaford is part of this ... this ... campaign?"

Careful there, Pendragon. The day was long past—at least I hoped so—when a President of the United States could offhandedly be referred to as a Commie-lover. A few nuts were allowed to keep up that drumfire of mad insult. But reasoning people in Washington simply did not buy that hogwash. Not since they jumped on poor General Eisenhower, that most patriotic and honorable of public figures, as a "Communist agent." We almost had to thank the accuser; he'd cleared the air and made such charges suspect and contemptible *a priori*.

"It is my feeling, Bates," Ruckett said, "that the President is being influenced by dangerous men around him."

"Mr. Ruckett, as a journalist, I must ask you to name them. Of course you are not in the House where you'd be immune from lawsuits, but still, if you have evidence of subversion in high places, you should make this information known."

A pause. "Aaaah . . . yes. There is no single person I would name at this time. It is a general atmosphere that I find disturbing."

Pendragon raised an eyebrow. "Hmmmm. Would you include Secretary Boswell's testimony before the Senate in this category?"

"Most certainly. That was a disgrace. A performance rich in slander, misrepresentations and innuendo. Frankly, Bates, it shocked me, and it shocked many of my colleagues in the House."

"Ah, but did Mr. Boswell lie? Did he in fact do the very thing he accuses the military of doing? I notice, sir, that no one has presented any evidence against his charges." Dear old Pendragon! Right-wing he may have been, but in his tweedy, burly way, he knew a story. "For example—in

242

the cost estimates on the MOMSER system—did they lie or not?"

"I say, Bates, that if it is necessary to *lie* to defeat Communism, then let us *lie*," Ruckett said. His voice seemed to spurt out of his constricted nostrils. "I am not afraid to lie, and not afraid to die. And if our brave generals and defense contractors have had to falsify information in order to get the job done better and quicker and to guarantee our safety from the Red monster, then I say, *lie* and get the job done."

"I see our time is running out," Pendragon said. "And thank you very much Congressman Lance Ruckett of South Dakota, chairman of the Caucus of Concerned Congressional Conservatives . . ."

And liar, I thought.

The old Hannaford house, Potomac Oaks, was located in a grove of hemlocks, oaks and beeches, a few miles beyond the Potomac shopping center, on the River Road. It was an enormous place—twenty-seven rooms and fifteen baths on thirty-five acres—a fake Colonial palace, with soaring pillars and hundreds of windows, built in the twenties by a millionaire bootlegger for his Follies girl wife. At least one murder was said to have been committed in its great halls. During World War II, the huge castle served as a training school for Army nurses.

The Hannafords had occupied it throughout Ben's tenure in the United States Senate. On its undulant meadows, Fern had ridden glossy bay hunters, and Ben had often walked across the fields, arm in arm with some Senate colleague whose vote he needed. When the Hannafords left Washington after the censure vote, the house remained unoccupied for a few months. Then, about a year and a half ago, when Congress enacted the Ghetto Commune Program at the urging of our current Secretary of Housing and Urban Development, young Charles Gantry, Hannaford, in retirement in Ramada City, donated the house and the grounds to the government. He had his reasons. He had become fascinated with the whole challenge of rebuilding the ghettos—not just the stones and bricks and pavements, but the *people*. Our old friend, the much-battered social worker, Dalton Warfield, had been called in for advice on the commune program, and he had helped make up Ben's mind.

I could see as I drove in on the dirt road that the government had used the old Hannaford mansion as a central building, and around it, with attractive stretches of greensward in between, had erected a series of prefabricated barracks-style houses. They were painted in pastel shades, and strangely, meshed rather well with the palace standing amid the massive oaks and verdant hemlocks.

It was a mild day. I parked the car, sensing April's warmth from the moist earth. This area is rich bottom land; the river flows its muddy course a few hundred feet to the rear of the old Hannaford home. Birdsong and children's cries; the ringing of a school bell. All these evoked poignant memories of my boyhood in Indian Mound, Ohio.

A dozen black children of preschool age were playing in the dappled sunlight. They were mere tots, little people full of life, laughing, running, singing. Dalton Warfield emerged from the portals of the mansion and waved to me. With him was my dusky princess, Mona Varnum. She wore a beige suit and low-heeled shoes. Around her shoulder was slung a tape recorder. Her Afro bob was bushier, more tantalizing than ever.

"Hey, Edward," Warfield called. "Remember when we met here with the boss after he resigned?"

I explained Warfield's reference to Mona. When Hannaford had quit the Senate, the first thing he had done was to invite Dalton and myself to Potomac Oaks to plan his inner city rebuilding campaign, as a private citizen.

She wasn't impressed. "What's he doing about getting the money for these schools?"

"Pressure. Threats. Magic."

"I wouldn't try to deceive you. Dalton will back me up."

"It's the truth, Mona," Warfield said. "Hannaford wants projects like these as much as you do." He led us across the lawn to one of the single-story prefabricated buildings.

"We'll keep going as long as we can on the funds we have," Warfield said. He didn't sound down-hearted. Dalton had been frustrated, deceived, beaten, denounced and discouraged so often that he simply took bad fortune as the way of the world. He had that casual grace of a true hero.

"Won't the program end?" Mona asked.

"I don't know. We'll keep a few demonstration centers

244

like this one going. But the plan for ghetto communes across the country, that's dead."

We entered the pale-yellow building. Inside, about twenty black children of preschool age sat at tables. Two teachers, a stout, bespectacled black woman of middle age, and a young white man in shirt sleeves, flaunting a fine golden beard, sat among them. They did not work from a desk, but participated with the kids, who were having an arithmetic lesson.

"The whole idea is to saturate 'em," Warfield said. "It's styled on the Israeli kibbutz nurseries. The kids are with us all the time. Sleep here. Eat here. Many of them have no families at all. They all get the same love, the same attention and the same relaxed teaching. We think it works."

The blond-bearded youth turned to a tiny black boy at his right. "Elmo, how much is forty-two, sixteen, nine and twenty-one?"

The tot could not have been more than four. For an instant, his saucer-like eyes rolled about in his ebony face, and then he shouted: "Eighty-eight!"

I was astonished, "Dalton, did you set that up?"

Mona Varnum was equally impressed. "How's that done? Rote? Conditioning?"

"Mona, honey, you a great reporter," Warfield said, affecting an Amos and Andy accent, "but you don' know nuffin' 'bout education."

We watched the classroom group, fascinated. The young white man was moving from table to table, kissing one child, patting another, helping a third with his coloring. Would some Americans, without knowing who he was, have hated him for that scraggly yellow beard?

"You see," Warfield said as we walked out into the thin April sunlight, "we came to the conclusion that leaving these children in the slums was a bad scene. They'd never break the cycle. Sorry about the parents and all that—when there were parents who gave a damn. Oh, they get to visit twice a week. They don't mind. Our feeling is that these kids should remain in the communal schools until maybe junior high."

"It's a deliberate attempt to destroy black families," Mona protested.

"The hell it is, Mona. Get off that militant kick, chick. You're high-class stuff. Bryn Mawr. Big television reporter. Miss Ebony of 1970. You a pretty far piece from these little bastards. Most of 'em got no daddies."

"Yes, I've heard that. Fellow named Moynihan back in the sixties did a report——"

Warfield laughed silently, throwing back his purple-black head. "Oh, *that* cat. Big sociologist. Woke up one morning and discovered most black kids grew up without a man in the house. Did I need a sociologist to tell me that? Man, he was like the fellow who discovered he'd been speaking prose all his life. Or that admiral who did the book showing sea power was important . . ."

We strolled across the lawns, under a bower of oaks, toward where our cars were parked. "Miss Varnum, hit this story as hard as you want," I said. "The President intends to put pressure on the Ways and Means Committee to get the money restored."

"I'll report it as I see it, Mr. Deever," Mona said. "Until you prove to me that the Administration is sincere in wanting to push its urban reforms, I don't see any reason to give you or the President any credit."

We halted by our parked cars. "Miss Varnum, some of you people never seem to understand who your friends are," I said.

"I know too much about you and people like Hannaford to trust you."

"Easy there, honey," Warfield said.

I opened the door of her black Ford. There were press stickers on the windshield. On the seat beside Mona, a box of Kleenex rested, a beige cashmere sweater, a large brown leather purse. I admit it; I'm a fetishist. All of these items rendered me foolishly lecherous.

"If you've got time, I'll let you see Secretary Murphy's blueprint. It hasn't been released, but I promised you a beat now and then."

"Take him up, Mona," Warfield said. "Lockjaw Deever, the reporters call him. You are getting the special treatment."

Mona Varnum's slanted eyes nailed me—distrustful, mocking. "All right. I'll go along."

"Follow me," I said. "We'll do it right now."

I shook hands with Dalton and blasted off the gravel driveway.

Driving along the River Road, I was pained. What

246

could I tell Hannaford about the commune? It was a success; but thousands more, backed by millions more in cash were needed. Well, we'd get publicity on "Today," "Walter Cronkite," the local news shows. TV news was run by compassionate men. No wonder they had been under such wicked assault a few years ago.

Mona's black Ford tailed me along the turnings of the old road. I took the Beltway, then went left on the Washington Memorial Parkway toward the city. As soon as I had crossed the Theodore Roosevelt Bridge some wild impulse took command. Instead of heading to the White House, I drove to my hotel. For a moment I feared that Miss Varnum would see me for what I was, and leave me. But no. She parked her car a few spaces behind mine and we got out.

"Why here?" she asked.

"I live at the hotel."

Tilting her café-au-lait face, she was silent. Sunlight danced on the frizzy tips of her aerated black hair. Gently, I took her elbow and guided her into the lobby of the Manger Hay-Adams.

My two-room suite, luckily, had been made up. I took off my suit jacket, offered Miss Varnum a comfortable chair, and asked her if she cared for a drink. She did— straight gin on the rocks. I wanted only a Diet-Cola.

"Do you drink gin to keep up this stereotype of blackness?" I asked.

"No. I like it."

Her legs crossed; they were superior to Vangie Boswell's. Just as hairless, but of a maddening pale brown luster.

"Miss Varnum, I have the feeling you don't like me very much."

"I'm neutral on the subject of people like you."

"What kind of people am I?"

"A flunky. Errand boy for a big wheel. Hannaford isn't too bad. He's corrupt and self-serving, but he may get something done for the brothers. But as I see it, you're just a paper shuffler."

"Indeed."

"Yeah, Edward Deever. You're an uptight honky, all right."

I answered the buzzer, signed the chit with a too-lavish

tip and took the tray from the waiter. It was no help; he'd caught a glimpse of Mona.

"You usually short-stop room service at the door?" she asked sarcastically. "Or were you reluctant to let him see a black chippy in the Presidential aide's hotel room?"

I set her gin on the coffee table and sat down on the dark green sofa. My motto has always been, why look for trouble?

"I gather that's supposed to reassure me." She drank her gin as if it were Seven-Up.

"Mona ... may I call you Mona?" No response, so I continued. "Mona, I have the feeling you need no reassuring. I have known some beautiful and intelligent women in my day, and the combination is unbearable. Beauty gives them all kinds of prerogatives, and their brains make them fortresses of desire."

She took off the dark glasses. The oriental eyes were half shut. Odd, I could not recall ever seeing the woman smile. "We came here to look at Homer Murphy's urban plans, Mr. Deever. Either get them for me, or stop the chatter. I've got work to do."

"Well, we're making progress. You just called me Mr. Deever. What happened to 'honky'?"

A wicked little smile curled her full lips. "Pretty sharp, aren't you?"

"I know your bag, Mona. Warfield clued me. Bryn Mawr. High-toned black society. I've been to some of those lawn parties and barbecues of the dark hoi-polloi here in Washington. You know something? They're every bit as boring as their white counterparts. I don't blame you for taking on the militant guise. And I adore the hair-do."

"I don't wear it this way to please people like you."

"I think you do. It arouses men. White men. Farbelman—curse that faker—understood. If I were a famous rebel poet, maybe I'd have the gall and the nerve to try. Maybe I will anyway."

I am not very good at this sort of thing. Fearing rejection, I tend to associate only with women whom I know will be easy marks. Marsha Treadway was a perfect bedmate; she gave in easily. And what in the name of Priapus led me to believe that this brown vision would ever give me the time of day—let alone her body?

248

"Gave you quite a turn when you found me with Arvid," she said. "Sort of shook-up Mr. Cool."

"It did. I was insanely jealous. I could have set fire to his beard, the fraud."

"Don't put Arvid down. He's a true revolutionary."

"Arvid Farbelman is a phony, an egomaniacal self-promoter, who has one aim, and one alone—to push his books, his plays, his reputation and his inflated ego."

To my delight, she kicked off her low-heeled shoes. I stared at her stocking'd toes. They curled sexily. "Yeah, go at him, man. Nothing I like better than watching two big white cats go at one another."

"I'll confess to you, Mona," I said. "I want you very badly. The day I saw Hannaford carry you into the Ramada Inn—your shoulder bloodied—"

"And my face *pale*?"

"It was. Let's be candid, my dear. You're paler and fairer than a lot of Italo-Americans and Greeks who vote against low-cost housing for your soul brothers. But be that as it may, I've had this yearning for you. Can't describe it. It's symbolic, mystical—"

"Oh, mother, stop that, man," Mona cried. She finished the gin. "Oh, that awful mystical crap. You been readin' too much Faulkner, man. All that crap about blood and lust and vengeance and how sexy us niggers is."

"Spare me the put-on. I'll accept it from Warfield, but not from you, my Ethiopian princess. Where did you learn to talk like that, from Farbelman?"

"You pretty chinchy on the gin, white boy," she said, lifting her sublime legs on the chair, and tucking them beneath her.

Dutifully, I ordered another double for her, and feeling giddy and in need of sustenance, an imported beer for myself. This time I did not try to hide Mona. I let the waiter enter and place the refreshments on the table. He was a discreet fellow and did not stare.

"I'm furious with you for bedding down with the likes of Farbelman," I said. "He stands for everything I hate."

She was engaged in a series of disturbing body moves on the pale green chair. Now she drew her legs out from under her and rested them over an arm of the chair. I caught a glimpse of that heavenly junction of garter, girdle and stocking, and I thought I would fall away into a dead faint, or perhaps die altogether.

"Yeah, you would hate someone like Arvid. You're the power structure, and he's a threat."

"Nobody is more enmeshed with the grasping, corrupt and self-serving compartments of society than Farbelman. His life is a continual intrigue at preserving his image as national icon—agents, publishers, movie producers, the public, reporters, critics, his adoring handmaidens— Farbelman is an industry unto himself."

"And you, Deever?"

"I'm a functionary of the political system and a lot more candid about what I do than that poet. We ask for no laurel wreaths or marble statues. We do a dirty job, and we try to do it so that more people benefit than get hurt. It's these cursed artists who want nothing but their egos nurtured and inflated who menace the public order."

"Hmmmmm." She digested this a bit. Then, more gin. Her eyes were half shut. "You're not as stupid or square as I figured you to be."

"I tend to surprise people."

"Yeah, I can see that."

Kicking off my black loafers, I got up from the sofa, went to the chair in which she sprawled, and, kneeling beside it, kissed her fruity, gin-scented mouth. She did not shove me away, or move her head, or try to dodge. Triumph!

"Brave little boy," she said caustically. "Gets his nigger whore full of gin, and then sneaks a kiss on them rubber lips."

"I forbid you to talk like that, Mona." My heart was about to leap from my narrow chest. I am the sort of fellow who usually keeps himself under control. But now I was melting, turning into a blob of liquid butter—like Little Black Sambo's tigers. (An unfortunate metaphor, even though I did not verbalize my sentiments to the lady.)

I guided her to her feet. She was not drunk, just a bit sleepy and resigned. "It is my intention to make love to you, Mona Varnum. Long overdue. I'll promise you anything—a journalist's priority with the Administration, a job with the Washington *Post,* the ambassadorship to Somalia. Just don't deny me."

"Go to hell," she whispered in my ear.

We kissed again—longer, my hands now stroking the elegant contours of her body. I guided her to the bedroom. She seemed to shuffle along. We kissed once more at the edge of the double bed; her response was not what it should have been—casual, co-operative, willing, but hardly passionate. There was a "let's get it over with" tinge to her kisses that disturbed me, but hardly dissuaded me.

Mona chose to undress in the bathroom, a disappointment. With the shades drawn, the door bolted, the bed uncovered, I dutifully awaited her. When, after an agonizing length of time, she emerged from the john, like Botticelli's Venus on the half shell, I had to spend a moment steadying myself, absorbing all that beauty—the astonishing symmetry, the gold-brown luster of her skin, the savage adornment of her frizzy crown of hair, a black halo, suggesting the bartered bride of some ancient Ashanti chief. I'd read about these African lords who trade cattle for women. At that moment, enchanted by her long silken and gentle curves, the shivering naked loveliness of her, I would have surrendered every one of Hannaford's prized Black Angus animals for an hour of dalliance.

We embraced. Soon we were in bed. No need to indulge in attempts to recreate the ecstatic joys she gave me. Her behavior was not violent, or barbaric, or unseemly. Indeed, Mona Varnum was more Bryn Mawr than Beale Street in her sexual mannerisms. No matter. I had never felt more fulfilled, more transported, as I covered her narcotized brown face, her tickly black hair, her small perfect ears, with wet quivering kisses.

She spoke not at all as we made love. Not a word. A sigh now and then, a modest cry, a small gasp. Her eyes remained shut. Her mind in seeming sedation, she let her body work. But like a superb natural athlete, she did not strain or contort herself. It all came to her smoothly and effortlessly—each rhythmic move, each caress, each bend of arm or crook of leg.

Enough. Suffice it to say that never in my life had I enjoyed a passion of such lofty quality, of such subtlety and such sublime fulfillment. It was unlike anything I have ever known. All the more noteworthy, because in the crashing moments of climax, we were both subdued, gentle and considerate. I think my problem was one of too great a gift. I had difficulty trying to absorb all of her in my mind, all that chiaroscuro beauty, all that perfection of form and line and texture.

But there was more than that. She was black. I was white. I'm as liberal as the next Washington functionary, but the concept of ravishing a black woman had never seriously entered my mind. When I saw Mona Varnum, I knew it had to happen. Now it had. And it had proved an experience of unbelievable beauty.

"The scars are barely visible," I said. Our love-making over, she had turned on her side. I was studying the marks left by Henry Kaspar's gun. In the dim light I perceived them as two irregular holes, shiny, hard to the touch, oddly striated. "Do they ever hurt you?"

No answer. Was she dozing? I embraced her.

As I tried to revive her lust, she shoved my hand away.

"Mona, dearest, why not?"

"No."

"I have to tell you something. I have never been so passionate in my life. I know now how to solve the race question in America. Let everyone make love to everyone else."

I sought to put my arms around her lean waist. She moved away from me, then got out of bed, and walked to a mauve Queen Anne chair near the curtained window. Primly, she sat down, then lit a cigarette. The match-glow illumined her Nilotic face, and I felt faint. Oh, the perfection of the woman! My eyes lingered on her small, upright breasts, the undulant flanks.

"Why do you get up?" I asked.

"It's all over, man."

"The first round. But I have no appointments this afternoon. We can recreate our first sinful joys again and again."

Smoke streamed from her arched nostrils in twin jets.

"You think so?" she asked.

"Definitely. The President doesn't need me. Not today, anyway. I can tell him I spent the afternoon drawing up his report on the Ghetto Commune Program. With some expert advice from a leading member of Washington's black community."

She turned her head, resting it against the back of the chair. In profile, she might have been some black Nile goddess. The line from brow, to nose, to lips, to chin and then down the elongated neck was of such gracile elegance as to inspire the muse of Homer.

"Where do you live?" I asked. "I shall have to move out

of this place and get an apartment where we can meet with more privacy."

Naked as the Farnese Hercules, I rose from the bed of passion, and approached her, kneeling at her side, resting my head in her lap. With a firm gesture, she shoved me away.

"What's wrong, my dear?"

"Game's over, Deever. That was the first and last time you know me."

I got up and sat down opposite her. "You must be joking."

"The hell I am. Don't bother renting that hideaway where you can drag your black whore. We are through. Quits. End of the line."

"Why? If you let me make love to you once, why not again?"

"Drop it, Deever. I said never again."

As I reflect on the incident, the one and only time I made love to Mona Varnum, I should have been forewarned.

"Ah. I understand. A single act of charity. Back to Farbelman."

Mona laughed bitterly. "Hunh. He's had it, also."

"What do you mean, *also?*"

She got up and stretched, then walked into the bathroom and began to dress. Through the opened door I could hear her matter-of-fact voice.

"It's my bag, I guess. Just once with a white man. Then let him think about it the rest of his life."

So that was her way of getting kicks! "But why? If you like a man, why torture him like that?"

"To hell with all of them," Mona said. "I know what I look like. I know the effect I have on you uptight honkies. Well, I let you try it once, get a taste of it—and then, you can all go to hell, you can all slobber over it, and maybe take it out on your white broads."

She returned in a gauzy lace-trimmed pink slip. I could have ripped it from her and devoured her whole. But I'm a cautious fellow by nature. I'm not a slip ripper or a clothes mangler.

I watched her zipping up her beige woolen skirt, and as she raised her head, I intoned (stealing some of Hannaford's technique) from the Song of Solomon:

" 'Thy nose is as the tower of Lebanon which looketh

toward Damascus.' Mona, you are a cruel witch, a sorceress, turning all your white lovers into swine, like Circe."

She smiled—the first time since entering my room. And it was not derisive. It was almost sympathetic.

"You're worse than a tease," I said. "You are a female demon, a Fury, a siren. You give men a taste of your delights, and then you let them suffer. Is that fair?"

"Is what you folks have done to *us* fair?" She'd buttoned up her suit jacket, and fully-clothed, standing in her sensible shoes, she was Little Miss Reporter again—but as infuriatingly desirable as she was in the buff.

"You can't make yourself a one-woman vengeance committee. It's a hell of a way to extract payment for past sins."

She shouldered her purse, and started moving toward the sitting room. I put on a robe and walked with her. "I told you it was my hang-up," she said.

She seemed a bit glum now that our adventure was over. I tried to cheer her up.

"This actress—famous white society-type—was on location some years ago with your soul brother, the big sexy black Adonis. The two were attracted to one another, but he refused to make the advances. And she hesitated. He turned her on, but nothing happened. She told me later, 'he's a gorgeous hunk of man, and I wanted to go to bed with him, but when it got down to cases, I had to live with the fact that he was black, and I was *yellow*.' "

Mona smiled tolerantly. Not much of a story, but what does one have to say after passionate love-making in the afternoon? I've never come up with any sparkling bit of dialogue for these moments.

"So long, Deever," she said. "Maybe one reason this is the last time for us, is my antecedents are so much classier than yours."

"Ah. An Ashanti prince? A Coromantee king?"

"Hell, no. I'm a Varnum of Rhode Island."

And with that cryptic bit of genealogical information, my swarthy lover winked lewdly at me and departed. I was left with a tender ache in my bones, and a pained longing such as I had never experienced before, nor ever will as long as I live. It was of little comfort that she'd done this disservice to other honkies, including A. Farbelman. I liked to think that I deserved better.

254

President Hannaford's program was going badly, encountering stiffening resistance from the inevitable bloc—racist (or frightened) Southerners and Midwestern conservatives. Many of the senators and representatives who battled us did so sincerely. They lived in a pleasant rural aura of tree-shaded small towns, where every man earned an honest dollar, and no man, except a drunk here, an invalid there, needed public assistance.

"The committee gave Homer another rough time, I see," I said to the President, as we lunched in the small presidential dining room. Only Matt Fixx was with us.

"Henshaw couldn't control 'em," Hannaford said.

"The Senate Labor and Public Welfare Committee is one of the best on the Hill," Matt drawled. "I thought we'd go in there with a one-to-one relationship."

"Homer says it went well until he got around to money," the President said grimly. "Henshaw had them acting as if they'd be ready to move with us on four of the five bills we're proposing."

Matt Fixx checked them off on his white fingers: "federal housing subsidy, elementary and secondary education funding, including the junior college provision, job training and rehab and urban reconstruction, including the Ghetto Commune rider. They didn't seem too interested in the fifth—New Works Progress Administration. But, heck, if we got all the others, we wouldn't need that one. We'd have ignition and lift-off."

Hannaford looked weary. I knew he had been counting on his friends in the Senate, men like Maury Eisenberg and Royce Henshaw and John Tyler Lord to battle for our domestic program. But our allies seemed to be frustrated at every turn.

"Yes, when Homer mentioned the price tag, all bets were off," Ben said. He jabbed half-heartedly at the avocado salad.

Matt Fixx chuckled mirthlessly. "I had to laugh at Pendragon's column yesterday. He claimed that the defense contractors don't really care about building missiles, that the margin of profit isn't that great, and that it's a left-wing myth to say they lobby for the contracts."

Hannaford turned to Fixx. He was on the alert, the old Indian tracker in him reacting. "Say again, Matthew."

"Bates Pendragon, C. C. Pringle's pet columnist, sir. He did a column on how the defense industries aren't a bad

255

lot, but patriotic benefactors of the public, who create a lot of jobs, and who don't make much money."

"Beautiful," I said. "Did Pendragon say why they don't turn down these contracts? Or what they'd be doing if they didn't manufacture Sky-Brooms and Iron Balls?"

"I'm afraid not," Matt said. "He never pursues an argument to the point where it will lose some of the force he wants to get across. Clever old Pendragon."

The President's eyes glittered. "Not all that clever. That's an intriguing argument 'bout the defense contractors, how tiny their profits are. I heard it four days ago at this table from our Vice-President."

"Mr. Sparrier said that?"

"Had facts and figures. All kinds of details on how high-minded and economy-minded the missile makers are. Lots of jobs, low profits."

I was flabbergasted. "You think he was spouting back to you some of Pendragon's nonsense?"

"It's 'tother way around. I have a feeling our Vice-President is in communication with the enemy. After all, he's been one of Pendragon's public heroes for a long time, ever since he turned the machine guns loose in second Watts. Why shouldn't he do him a favor now and then? I don't like the idea of the fellow who is to succeed me if I get rubbed out trafficking with a writer who once called me the Kremlin's favorite millionaire politician."

"Can I be of help, sir?" I asked.

"You can, Edward. Cultivate Vice-President Sparrier. The young man is lonesome in that office I stuck him in. Keep an eye on him. Drop hints. Keep him off balance. I think maybe I'll give him some duties to perform."

"May I suggest one, sir?"

"Please do, Edward."

"They're having another Gabe Tutt Day down in Dog Common, Alabama, the senator's home town. Gabe just arranged for federal funding of a new factory for defense, in Red Dirt County."

"What kind of factory?" the President asked.

"Elastic support items, sir. Trusses, knee-guards, jock-straps. The Chamber of Commerce of Dog Common is dedicating a bronze bust of Senator Tutt."

"Another?" Matt Fixx gasped. Alabama had become a monument to old Gabe—plaques, busts, statues of the old man adorned the state from Huntsville to Mobile.

"Splendid idea, Edward," the boss said. "A fitting occasion for both Senator Tutt and our Veep. Advise Mr. Sparrier he will be our personal emissary."

I had to tread carefully with Vice-President Sparrier. He wasn't my dish of tea, and I had seen little of him since the President had ensconced him in the corner office of the West Wing. His secretary, Miss Culhane, one of those grinning, healthy California blonds greeted me with what I thought was excessive enthusiasm.

As I lingered at her desk, the door to the Vice-President's office opened, and out floated old Honey-Tonsils. I resented Honey-Tonsils' visits to the Veep. The old mountebank had been playing coy with Ben for several weeks—ever since Burke Boswell had given the brass what-for. But his pique with the President did not extend downward to young Mr. Sparrier.

The white eyebrows wiggled as he saw me. "Edward, yaaaas, young Deever himself," Honey-Tonsils chanted. "I have often meant to ask you, dear boy, are you related to Danny Deever, of Kiplingesque fame?"

"You mean, sir, the poem that goes, 'Oh they're hanging Danny Deever, you can hear the dead march play, the regiment's in hollow square, they're hanging him today'?"

"Splendid! Capital! Say, doesn't it make the blood pump faster to recite the old ringing rhymes of the poet of Empire? Yaaaaas."

The old clown! Embarassed at my finding him in communion with Sparrier, he was playing it for laughs. But was I the one being overly suspicious? The Vice-President *is* the presiding officer of the Senate. Sparrier was new to the job, and it would seem logical that he would defer to, and confer with, an experienced senate hand like the Majority Leader. Yet I did not appreciate their huddling. Gage was supposed to be our man. Surely he must have known the doubts Ben had about Sparrier.

"Senator, I'm afraid I'm no descendant of Danny Deever. As I recall, they hanged him for shooting a sleeping comrade, although Kipling never tells us why he shot him."

"Poetic license, dear boy. Waddling, he walked away from me. "Yaaas . . . how does it go on? 'Oh they've taken of his buttons off, and cut his stripes away, and they're hanging Danny Deever in the morning.' "

Miss Culhane buzzed and nodded at me, and I walked in to Sparrier's office. He'd decorated the walls with a gallery of photographs and awards—Sparrier and Hannaford, Sparrier and Pope Clement, Sparrier and the evangelist Jimmy Hubbs, Sparrier and various professional football players of conservative sentiment. There were framed citations from the Elk, the Moose, the Kiwanis, the American Legion, the Freedom Foundation, the Veterans of Foreign Wars and the Ladies Auxiliary of the National Rifle Association. Missing were any plaques, certificates or medallions from the NAACP.

"Ah, Mr. Deever. The President's good right hand."

"Good day, sir."

He fussed with some pamphlets on his desk. One of my skills as an official poke-nose is my ability to read upside down. The veep was reading the Save America Newsletter.

"Those people are after the President's hide," I ventured, nodding at the literature.

"They are rather extreme," the Vice-President said solemnly. "I make it a point to keep track of their positions. It's important to know how they feel."

"I gather there's a good deal of sentiment for that kind of thinking."

"More than I ever thought possible," Sparrier said warily.

I told him of the President's request that he honor Gabe Tutt at the unveiling of the forty-seventh Gabe Tutt Memorial statue in Alabama. Sparrier seemed pleased, even though the occasion marked the opening of a jock-strap factory.

"The President's wish is my command," Sparrier said.

"It will do us good, the President feels, to have the Administration cater to Senator Tutt," I said.

"I could not agree more. For all his failings the senior senator from Alabama is a patriot."

"Mr. Pendragon certainly thinks so."

People like Sparrier dissemble poorly. Is it because they live a life of small fakeries, of pained attempts at sincerity, striving to overcome a congenital lack of candor? When I mentioned Bates Pendragon there was a peculiar fluttering of his left eye. "A lot of Americans think well of him," the Vice-President said.

"Especially all those defense contractors in Alabama."

258

"And the unions down there, Edward."

"Even the ones who don't let blacks in."

Sparrier pursed his thin lips. "I'm aware of the problems. I suppose the President feels I'm a solid conservative fellow for the mission to Alabama. I shall not let him down. Although I do wish you might convey to the Chief Executive that I have other talents besides representing him at dedications of statues."

"Mr. Vice-President," I said, "I am afraid, and surely you know it as well as I do, that the office is a hard one to bear, no matter how it's dressed up. Mr. Dooley once wrote that after the convention nominates the President, everybody leaves for fear one of them will be nominated Vice-President."

"Did he now?" No smile.

"Mr. Dooley also said that people run from the vice-presidential nomination as if from a grand jury indictment. He said that the presidency is the highest office in the land, and the vice-presidency is the next highest and the lowest. He further contended that when Grover Cleveland's Veep, Mr. Thurman, died, the obituaries noted that his declining years were clouded with a great sorrow. He became Vice-President."

"Ahhhh ... just who is this fellow Dooley?" Sparrier was scratching the name down on a pad.

"A humorist in a Chicago newspaper. Mr. Dooley said a man could put in four years comfortably in the job if he were a sound sleeper."

"It seems this Dooley had a good deal to say," Sparrier said frostily.

"Yes, he said that a candidate for the vice-presidency needed to be a good speaker, a pleasant man with the ladies, a fair boxer and wrestler and something of a liar ..."

"Indeed?" Still scratching on his pad.

"Dooley claimed that every morning the Vice-President inquires about the President's health, and when told that the President was never better, he gives three cheers and departs with a heavy heart."

"I would like to know a good deal more about this person. About some of his associations."

This was too good to let ride. I plunged ahead. "It is this Irishman's contention that it is because of our Vice-Presidents, that the Presidents have enjoyed such rugged

259

health. Now let me see if I recall the quote. 'The Vice-President guards the President, and the President, after sizing up the Vice-President, concludes that it would be better for the country if he should live yet awhile.' "

"I believe I am being joshed," Vice-President Sparrier said. "I have the feeling all of this is in a satirical vein, Edward."

"In a manner of speaking."

We exchanged a few more pleasantries. I hinted again at the President's desire to cool down Gabe Tutt. The boss wanted an appraisal from Sparrier as to the mood down in Gabe's district. Suppose all those defense plants were to start closing down? I remarked on how Bates Pendragon's lavish praise of those altruistic defense contractors left the President very cold indeed. Sparrier listened attentively. He was not stupid. He was not a coward. I often had the sensation that he was a lot more humane than many of his backers. Still, a man who had gotten his political start answering an ad in a reactionary rag, the picked agent of the big fruit growers. . . . He'd never gotten over these early associations with mean, crabbed men of great wealth. I was sorry for him; he had potential.

Our seance concluded, the Veep escorted me to his door. "Ah, this fellow Dooley," he said. "Where can I read his column?"

"Mr. Dooley. There was no *real* Mr. Dooley."

Controlled outrage turned him the color of white bond paper. "No . . . no. . . . You mean you invented all those insults?"

"No, no, Mr. Vice-President. Mr. Dooley was a fictitious Irish bartender in the Sixth Ward in Chicago. He was created by a journalist named Finley Peter Dunne in 1890."

"Ah . . . 1890 . . ."

"I'd not bother having the FBI run a security check on him. On either of them. Mr. Dooley or Mr. Dunne."

"Could you find me some of that material? It would make for some nice touches in my speeches to the Bicycle Association and the Girl Guides."

"I'll try, sir. You might want to use this one on the people down in Alabama who are honoring Senator Tutt. Mr. Dooley said he saw great changes taking place every day . . . *but no change at all every fifty years.*"

We moved into May, and our program was becalmed.

Each day I could see the weariness in President Hannaford's swarthy face. In the middle of the night, sleepless, too tired to doze, I turned to Mr. Dooley again, and once, at a bleak 3:00 AM., I read these words:

"A man is old enough to vote whin he can vote, he's old enough to wurruk whin he can wurruk. An' he's old enough to become Prisidint when he becomes Prisidint. If he ain't 'twill age him."

Ben was aging in the job. I saw the shadows under his solemn eyes become deep smudges of charcoal. His hair, once a jet black, flecked with silver gray at the temples, seemed whiter each day.

"The Senate is giving us options," Matt Fixx explained to me as we labored into the night on the housing bill, with Secretary Chuck Gantry and Dalton Warfield, "but it's the House votes all the money. We can get a decent bill through Henshaw's committee. But when we mention the price tab—ten billion dollars—to Speaker O'Boyle and his pals, forget it."

So it went down the line. Ben was determined to battle the military budget on each item, using our formidable allies in the Senate—Henshaw, Eisenberg, Lord, Urban, Stapp—to force the Pentagon to yield ground. They would have to yield some, of course. At long last, disarmament talks were getting somewhere. And Hannaford, in consultation with Walter Edgerton, Secretary of State, had an ace up their sleeve. They planned, as soon as the Russo-Chinese peace talks in Stockholm were concluded, to call for a tripartite disarmament meeting in the same city. "Same hotel, same rooms, same people. We move in and make it a threesome. If the French and British and Indians want in, we open it up," the President explained.

"We are obsessed with China," Walter Edgerton had informed the Senate Foreign Relations Committee. "She has not said boo to Quemoy or Matsu or Taiwan for ten years. Can we not admit once and for all, that China, whether she is Communist, nationalist, republican or monarchical, is a Pacific power also, perhaps every bit as much a Pacific power as we are? Is it not conceivable that China has a right to be a force in that part of the world, so long as she behaves herself within the limits of big power decorum?"

Edgerton proceeded to read off the recent figures on trade with China. The Australians and Canadians were

261

selling them more wheat than ever; the West Germans, our stoutest anti-Communist ally in Europe, were building textile machines for them; the Italians were in there with both feet, making Olivettis and Fiats; even those two stanch anti-Communist allies, and founts of freedom, Spain and Portugal, were trading cork for pig bristles with Peking. The Vatican was negotiating to have some of its churches reopened. Only the Russians, nervous over their protracted "police action" in Mongolia against Peking-directed guerrillas, and still trying to negotiate an "honorable peace," a "troop withdrawal" and a "viable democratic government" in Ulan Bator, were fearful of the Chinese. This led Edgerton—and the President—to the conclusion that it was less politics, or theology, that led to tension between China and the two other great powers, but mere bigness. "It's size, that's all," Hannaford told a meeting of the National Security Council. "Big frogs don't like other big frogs. China's big, and unified for once, and got a sense of mission. Naturally she's going to throw her weight around. What nation doesn't when it gets big enough?"

"But sir," Vice-President Sparrier said, "China is a Communist power. She means to conquer all of that part of the world."

"No, not conquer, Verne," the President said. "Sort of have first shot at it. Same as us. I don't like Communists any better than you do, but if China were being run by Chiang Kai-shek right now, and she was united, she'd be doing the same thing. You know when the Reds took over Tibet and when they invaded India, nobody applauded louder than old Chiang himself."

"We've got to stay strong out there," Secretary of State Edgerton said, "firm, reasonable, in a bargaining position. But we can't make all those Chinese go away by ignoring them or by pressuring their government all the time. The Chinese are a people of immense talent, immense dedication and great capacity for work."

"Sound like Americans," Ben said.

"In many ways they are. And a proud people. Unless we are prepared to annihilate them, I feel we have to start talking to them. Lin Piao has issued some interesting papers of late."

"We'll talk to 'em," Ben said. "We'll be in that hotel room in Stockholm soon as old Gromyko lets us know he's

262

settled his business with them. Yes, we'll be in there with ten good offers."

The prospect of new disarmament talks went over well. Public reaction was better than Ben had anticipated. Walter Edgerton had friends in the Senate. They listened to him when he spoke of the plan for getting the discussions going as an extension of the Soviet-Chinese pact on the Mongolian war. The newspapers—apart from Pringle's chain, which argued in its editorials "no Communist can be trusted, and Chinese Communists are to be trusted only when dead"—evinced an intelligent concern with the spiraling arms race, with the dread prospect of the heavens being filled with manned orbiting satellites, deadly platforms for launching annihilation, the fearful MOMSER system.

There was only the tiniest of protests when Ben selected the distinguished Nobel prize-winning physicist, Professor Seymour Harvey Cohen of MIT to head up the disarmament team. Cohen was a pragmatic, impatient young fellow, prematurely bald, and sporting the most elegant pair of sideburns this side of Greenwich Village. Words tumbled out of his mouth, a mixture of physicist's lingo, Yiddish curses, and Washingtonese. Cohen was utterly unembarrassed by his origins, a long history of supporting liberal movements or the fact that he had been married three times.

"The main thing," Professor Seymour Harvey Cohen brayed to the President, at a high-level session on disarmament, "is we got to enforce on-site inspection of those *fekokteh* missiles in order to determine how many warheads are on each of those lousy things. I mean, Mr. President, we gotta get the United Nations to act with us, to agree to furnish international teams of inspectors to examine every one of those cockamamie contraptions buried in the ground, or on submarines or on the orbiting MOMSERS."

Cohen then outlined a modest approach to the Russians and Chinese: a freeze on deployment of land-based IBMs; limitations on other weapons systems—submarines, manned bombers, multiple warheads, orbiting satellite systems and any other system not yet perfected, such as underground doomsday machines. But he regarded the on-site inspection provision by a United Nations agency as essential.

"Without that, Mr. President," Sy Cohen said, "any agreement on disarmament is like an old bar-mitzvah speech."

We had sent Fred Goldstein down to Dog Common, Alabama, along with the Vice-President, to honor Senator Tutt at the dedication of the statue of the chairman of the Armed Services Committee in front of the Tru-Stretch Elastic Equipment factory, which had just been awarded a contract worth a half a million dollars to make trusses and other elastic items for the Army, Navy, Marine Corps and Coast Guard.

On his return I lunched with Fred and Vangie in the cafeteria in the Executive Office Building. Our purpose in sending Fred down was to keep an eye on Vice-President Sparrier and to report on the mood of the local gentry. What he had to tell us was far from encouraging.

"Boy, they love Gabe in Alabama. NO BUTS, WE'RE TUTT'S, the signs say." Fred sipped his Diet-Cola unhappily. His pale freckled skin had been burned red by the southern sun. "They were out in force, Eddie. Big delegation of guys from NUMB—the National Unions and Military Bureau. Also DOOR and Save America and all of the crowd that worked with Wallace years ago."

"What in the world is NUMB?" Vangie asked.

"What it says. Union guys who don't want military spending cut."

"Grass roots America," I said.

"You know it. Congratulatory telegrams from Senator Hopewell, Speaker O'Boyle, the Director of the FBI and General Nagel. You'd think some of those people would have more pride. The reporters were calling it Jock-Strap Day."

"Let's be honest," I said. "People like those jobs. They like the money. The average Joe doesn't stop to think about the waste and the baloney of defense spending. And if that doesn't bother him, he can't be bothered about the world getting blown up."

"What did Senator Tutt say?" Vangie asked.

"What you'd expect," Fred said. He shoved aside his tuna on whole wheat. None of us had much appetite. "At least he was drunk, so he didn't talk long. Said he was sick of people attacking the military. Said he'd pussonally see to it that not one damn dollar was cut from the military

264

budget, just to feed lazy, dirty people who would spend the money on beer and movies."

"I bet that got a big hand," I said.

"Jesus, those union guys from NUMB went nuts. They wear these funny white hats, sort of like painter's caps. Lots of 'em were carrying big blue and white crosses from Save America."

"And our Vice-President?"

Fred closed one eye and tilted his carrot-topped head. "Verne socked it to 'em. I mean, he did and he didn't. You know, he's a kind of symbol—the tough guy who didn't take any crap during second Watts. He just has to show up and they cheer."

Vangie Boswell agreed. "Don't I remember the convention! He had the hearts of the delegates, that was for sure."

"Yes," I said. "It's a good thing Hannaford had all the money. And a few men who knew how to raid a hotel room."

Vangie looked puzzled. Fred and I grinned, recalling that memorable summer's day when we had photographed Judge Jervis Kickley in the Hotel Overlook.

"Eddie, it's gonna take more than a bribe to get Hannaford what he wants this time," Fred said. "I mean, he's got to convince an awful lot of people. I don't envy him."

"But Sparrier. What about him?"

Fred scratched his head. "I couldn't be sure. He kept saying how national defense was top priority with the President, but that he wanted to make it as efficient as possible, so that there was more for everyone."

"What the hell does that mean?" Vangie asked.

"Nothing really. Sparrier gets that way every now and then. He sounded like a Fundamentalist preacher—full of holy fire. But he didn't knock the boss, not once. Kept telling the folks that the President was thinking of them."

"How did that go over?" I asked.

Fred craned his neck and tugged at his shirt collar. "Like a lead balloon. Every time he mentioned Hannaford, they didn't boo or hiss, they sort of observed a respectful silence."

"Silence?"

"Like for the dead."

Goldstein squinted at me. "Ah, the boss can handle the

Senate. And if we can wake O'Boyle up, we'll manage in the House."

"But that still may not help," I said. "We've got to convince the most important guy of all that we have to stop making bombs and building people."

"Who would that be?" asked Vangie.

"John Citizen. Fellow with the lunch pail and the two Pontiacs."

Three times that week, Burke Boswell tried to cut away at the military appropriation, and each time he was side-tracked. To add to the insult, Gabe Tutt defiantly led his committee in a favorable vote for funds for a useless air field in Alaska. The bill went on to the House.

"Damn Gabe," the President said. "I'll veto it."

"They'll override you, sir," I said. "Money. Jobs. And almost a national compulsion to keep the monster fed."

"I'm not too sure. We have got to end this 'feast of fat things.' "

"You'll need more than your Daddy's Bible to do it."

"It's worth a try, Edward. When I finish with Gabe and Hopewell, the lions shall eat straw like the ox."

And yet, and yet . . . I could not share his stout confidence. The man had a tendency to be blinded by his own courage, his own intelligence, his own sense of power. During the censure hearings, these very virtues had brought him down. But at stake then was only one man's career. Now nothing less than the nation's future was at stake; and I was frightened.

"Hell of a problem," Burke Boswell said to me a few nights later. We were at his gloomy home in Foxhall for an evening of bridge. The President and Mrs. Hannaford were present.

"I think both of us have sensed this, since we know the way the big boys operate." He referred to a few sheets of ruled paper on the coffee table. As he spoke, he imbibed cognac, pouring it freely from one of those musty old bottles. During dinner he had finished a bottle and a half of the rare red wine from "some Rothschild."

"They want it all," the President said.

"And they're getting it," Boswell said, adjusting horn-rimmed glasses on his long face. "Damn, you got to hand it to those sons of bitches. They have a lock on the United States."

"Mr. Secretary, you sound positively radical," I said. "When the college kids, like your daughter, were occupying campus buildings some years back they said the same things, and they were denounced as dangerous revolutionaries."

Boswell's lower jaw drooped. "Kids were right, Ed. They just went about it the wrong way."

"I'm not so sure there was any other way," I said.

The President shook his head. "There has to be," he said. "Go on, Burke, what have you found out?"

"This took some doing, but here it is. Of the twenty-five biggest industrial corporations in America, twenty are among the top one hundred defense contractors. The big guys are in there with both feet."

The President stroked his chin. "I guessed as much. What does that do to our Vice-President's argument—the one he fed to Pendragon—that profits aren't that great in defense contracts, that the corporations do it as a favor to the government?"

"That's a lot of bushwah," Boswell boomed. "Mr. President, I spent two years up here on the Hill lobbying for the big outfits. They love that military money. Sure they do. Because they *can't* lose, Mr. President. The defense industry is the most heavily subsidized in the nation's history. It's state capitalism. Corporate state."

"Fascism," I said.

"In a purely economic sense, yes," Boswell agreed. "The similarities between the way this machine operates, and the way the Germans and Mussolini set up their industries scares the pants off me."

Hannaford was grimmer than I have ever seen him. "And all those fellows who sound off about socialism destroying us," he said, "they get the biggest chunk of government money, is that right?"

"Exactly." Boswell flipped a page. "Defense business, in spite of Sparrier's arguments, is the most lucrative there is for a contractor. Because there's no risk. It's guaranteed. They have these "get well" provisions that ensure a profit, or at least a fallback, no matter how badly they bungle a job."

"And you can't check up on them," I said. "You ask for an audit and they use unverified data."

"Talk about sweetheart contracts," Boswell said. "They cover every angle. Suppose a corporation flops. They can't deliver. They've taken a few billion from the government, but the weapon won't work. They still get out without a scratch."

"How?" I asked.

"Pentagon cancels the deal for the convenience of the government. John Q. Public reimburses the corporation for all expenses. You see, there is a provision for the government to cancel for *default*. The company would get socked then. But it's never used. It's always for the convenience of the government, and the firm doesn't get touched."

"Isn't there something called a 'buy-in' that also keeps the corporations from harm?" I asked.

"Yes, there is," the Secretary of Defense said. "The contractor offers more than he can deliver, maybe lower cost, or a promise to do better than the Pentagon's specifications. Or maybe he promises to deliver before the due date."

"But he knows he can't meet any of these promises, and also that the cost figure is way below estimated cost," I added.

"That's correct," Boswell confirmed. "Technically, he can be held acccountable, but he never is. He knows when he makes these promises about the 'get well' joker. No matter how badly he flops, no matter how rotten the item, or high the costs, those brass hats over in the Pentagon will see to it that he gets well."

The three of us were silent a moment. Meg McNally, our grandmotherly Secretary of the Treasury, sitting out as dummy, walked over.

"Maybe I can help," she said. She sat down next to Ben and he patted her knee—a not altogether platonic gesture. Mrs. McNally, a widow, was extremely attractive.

"Meg, you are the finest-looking Secretary of the Treasury ever to grace the cabinet room," the President said gallantly, "but this business has got us all stumped."

"I'm not so sure we have to be," Meg McNally said. "Let me take a woman's view of it. I don't mean a woman who has been in high finance most of her life, but an ordinary housewife living on a budget, in, say, Stamford, Connecticut."

The three of us listened. Meg was a bright, sharp

person. She'd already initiated a long overdue program of tax reform, one of the most ambitious ever undertaken.

"Now, our typical housewife has a good idea of what the family's income will be for the year. So she sets up priorities, and apportions the income beforehand. Obviously she won't put aside five thousand for a motor cruiser, if Daddy's income after taxes is only fifteen thousand. She keeps the boat in abeyance and takes care of food, mortgage, clothing, the car and so on, first."

"Logical," Ben said. But he looked a bit bored.

"And if there's been a huge, continuing item on the budget—let's say maintenance of a Lincoln Continental that the family unwisely bought some years ago, she just knocks it off. Trade the big car for a Volkswagen or a Ford compact, and save money on gas, etcetera."

"Heck, Meg, you can't make that kind of comparison," Boswell protested.

"Let me tell you what I would do about defense spending," Mrs. McNally said. "Instead of trying to trim it here and trim it there, cut a hunk off the Sky-Broom, and another off the Iron Ball, and maybe close a few airbases and depots, I'd perform major surgery."

"But how?" I asked.

Our gray-haired Secretary of the Treasury got up. "Cut it in half," she said.

"In half?" Boswell gawked.

"Yes," Meg responded. "Right down the middle. We just go to the Congress and the Pentagon, and we say, gentlemen, your budget calls for one hundred twenty billion dollars. You get sixty billion this year. Bring it in for that figure."

Boswell's face looked petrified. Meg got up, straightened her skirt, gave a sexy little wiggle, as if to settle her girdle, and walked back to the bridge game.

"But . . . but . . ." I stammered. "They'll scream bloody murder. I mean, the generals, the corporations, the unions, the newspapers, the patriots!"

The President got up and stood in front of the fireplace. "Gentlemen, I think Mrs. McNally may have come up with something. Burke?"

Boswell, a man to whom nothing ever came as a surprise, a master of duplicity, back-door approaches, a talent for muddying waters and fudging issues when it suited him (he could be a marvel at clarifying issues when *that*

269

suited his needs) seemed stunned by the grand simplicity of Meg McNally's scheme. "Mr. President?"

Hannaford folded his arms and ruminated a moment. "The money's only part of it."

"Why do you say that, sir?" I asked.

"We might win that one. Enough damned mistakes by the military over the years. We'll have lots of support in the Congress. Gabe Tutt doesn't run the whole show. And he knows he's got to give ground, or he won't get a damn thing after a while. Hell, we can walk in with Burke's facts and lots of expert testimony and prove beyond a shadow of a doubt that they can do the job for sixty billion instead of one hundred twenty billion."

"I wonder," Boswell said.

"We could say we'll go somewhere else for our military hardware," I said lightly. "Perhaps the Czechs would sell us tanks cheaper, and the Swedes make good jet fighters."

"That's not as smart-alecky as it sounds, Edward," Boswell added. "I think we'd do better on everything except atomic hardware."

"Dammit, I think I can sell this one. The money end of it, anyway. Jobs'll be lost, but we'll set up a guaranteed wage program. Any man loses a job gets an assured income, and we have this national placement bureau to find him new work. If he's a steam-fitter, and he's been working on missiles, and we cut back, why he goes to work as a steam-fitter building new schools and libraries and hospitals."

"Only you can sell the people on *that*," Boswell said. "That outfit the unions set up, NUMB, they'll battle us down the line."

"I think they'll come around. The beauty of it. Slice the money in half." His eyes moved across the room and stared admiringly at Meg McNally, who had just bid four spades and was examining Minerva's dummy hand. "That's a woman of great intelligence, gentlemen, and I pay her my respects."

It was now Fern's turn to sit out a hand from the bridge game and she walked over to join us around the coffee table. Was it my imagination or had the First Lady been dieting? Her tall, full figure appeared lither. Or maybe she was more expertly corseted than before. Her skirt was several inches shorter than when Ben had taken the oath of office, and there was a rakish flair to the way her wheat-blond hair was set—a bit of a clip here, a curl there, rather different from the usual lacquered style she had favored in Ramada City.

"I was listening to what you said, dear, about cutting the military appropriation in two," Fern said. "I think it is a marvelous idea. It is simple. Ben, you should go on the television and present it right to the people."

I was galvanized. In all the years I had known Fern Hannaford, I had never heard her offer a word of political advice to the boss. She sat back, bred dogs, rode horses and spoke rarely. Now, something had happened to her, and I was delighted. I exchanged a glance with Vangie as if to say: *Well done.*

"Fern, you're right." In the President's swarthy visage I saw resolution, imagination, daring—the old Ben I knew in the Senate, the prowler, arm-grabber and massager, the man of a thousand schemes.

"We'll do it like one of those TV spectaculars," the President said. "Me, and Burke, and Walter Edgerton and Homer Murphy."

Boswell was nodding. "You need one more element, Mr. President."

"What might that be, Burke?"

"Some statement from the Russians that they mean business on disarmament when we start to palaver."

"Good idea. Edward, get in touch with Professor Cohen tomorrow."

"Damn," Vangie said. "Down four."

I tapped her bare shoulder. "Never should have led the Queen of clubs. A bad move. Too *simplistic.*"

"Get lost, Deever," she laughed. We winked at each other. Mine, I suppose was not a flirtation (was hers?) but an acknowledgment of the superb help she was giving the First Lady.

An appalling pattern was emerging in the cities. The Afro Avengers and other black extremist groups—"fed up to here," as a former President had once put it, with a hand parallel to his Adam's apple—had resumed their hit-and-run sniper tactics. Along with the free breakfasts they offered to black children were indoctrinations of white-hatred, admonitions to kill police, all the pent-up anger and bitterness that could only lead them downhill.

"Goddamn you," I heard Dalton Warfield rage at Kakamba Jones on the telephone, as he tried to cool an outbreak of attacks on churches and synagogues, "this isn't Algeria or Vietnam. You damn fools have to understand that all that Frantz Fanon garbage and Malcolm X crap are daydreams. It worked in Algeria because the Arabs were a majority. It beat the French in Vietnam, and it beat us, because we were a minority. But black people are one in ten in this country. You can't make a revolution of one-tenth against nine-tenths. Now go tell those lunatics in the black beards and the lion skins to lay off!"

Even a courageous man like Warfield was getting rattled. The fangs of the majority were showing; the courts and the police were getting tougher. I think it is wrong to impute blame to our hard-working and underpaid police forces. They are in the firing line. They get hit with the first bricks and the first Molotov cocktails. They did not create the slums. They did not invent prejudice. So they struck back. Since the first of the year, 246 people—90 per cent of them black—had been killed not in major riots, but in these sporadic outbursts.

In late April, the black ghetto of Sacramento, California, was ringed with barbed wire and road blocks after a series of sniping and bombing incidents. National Guardsmen checked ID cards of all people entering and leaving. Most blacks thereupon quit their jobs, and all over the state capital, elevators halted, laundries closed down, office buildings remained unswept and undusted, the postal service was cut by half, wealthy suburban matrons had to do their own cooking and the athletic teams of five Sacramento high schools were reduced to a handful of slow and clumsy whites.

"They'll stay in there and stew in their own juice," said Governor William Fancourt, successor to Verne Sparrier. A Muchmore poll promptly showed that this act of seclusion was approved by 82 per cent of the people of California, and that Fancourt was the "most admired" man in the state. Simultaneously, city officials in Sacramento deputized fifty-three members of DOOR, local citizens in pale-blue helmets with white crosses painted on the front.

In a week's time the "Sacramento Formula" had been adopted by seven other cities, including Newark, New Jersey; Waterbury, Connecticut; and Austin, Texas. an-court's motto spread with depressing rapidity: "Let 'em stew in their own juice."

We had become a nation aroused. All the brave loud talk about revolution, and participatory democracy and new scenarios was proving nothing but the brazen mouthings of children. An SDS convention in Chicago drew 600 bearded kids, an Afro Avenger Congress in Hough, Cleveland, 457 angry blacks. And the midwestern regional meeting of DOOR, addressed by Congressman Lance Ruckett, Publisher C. C. Pringle, General Clyde Upshaw, and Bates Pendragon—with telegrams of good wishes from such as Senators Tutt and Hopewell—packed 14,000 into Ak-Sar-Ben Field in Omaha. Eleven thousand more gathered outside to hear the addresses over loudspeakers. Yes, we were getting a revolution of sorts, but not the one that the radical children and the raging blacks had counted on. The visionary kids who had demanded "participation" by all citizens were getting it—with a vengeance.

Lawsuits were, of course, immediately brought in Sacramento, to challenge the city and the state for "sequestering" the ghetto. A California district court ruled that the officials were within their rights, since a state of "insurrection" threatened. An appeal was prepared. Meanwhile the barbed wire and road blocks were doubled to prevent marauding bands of black youngsters from breaking through the barricades. One twelve-year-old boy was shot dead as he tried to sneak out.

"I am scared stiff," I admitted to Vangie. We watched the horror on the evening news in my hotel room. How calmly the nation seemed to be taking it all! It was as if a great collective sigh of relief was being breathed by the nation—the *white* nation. How good a solution! *Let them stew in their own juice.*

"I hate to say it," Vangie sighed. "But it's hard to blame them."

"I know. They made it the hard way, why not the blacks? But all those hard-working Poles and Italians and Irish don't understand that the obstacles confronting Negroes are so much greater. It's no longer our lofty WASP who resists change, it's the fellow with the bowling ball under his arm."

Vangie stretched her legs on the sofa. Lascivious thoughts flickered in me, and died. I lusted for Mona Varnum only.

Parente called me that week. "Don't talk. Just listen. Know the Scott Key Arms? Meet me in Room 817. Use the garage entrance in the basement. Take the service elevator. Knock three times and walk in. Eight-thirty tonight."

That was all he would say. I told no one. Goldstein, Fixx and I spent the day working on Hannaford's television address. We contacted Professor Seymour Harvey Cohen and sent him winging to Stockholm to huddle with the Russians. Hopefully, he'd have some conciliatory word from them to buttress the President's appeal for a huge cut in military spending. All of us were excited, exhilarated. We felt we were moving; Hannaford at the helm.

Lou opened the flaking door on my third knock. The Scott Key Arms was an ancient baroque monstrosity. I have never quite figured out who lives in these obscure Washington apartment-hotels, with their lofty ceilings, superannuated kitchenettes and grumbling toilets. The decor was usually a toxic yellow and sickly mauve.

"Ssssh," Lou said. "Talk low. Whisper."

He was in his shirt sleeves and he was sweating. The huge, shabby sitting room seemed to have been wired for a radio recording session. He pointed to an overstuffed gray chair, whose interior kapok peeked through a hole in the seat. I sat down.

"Put 'em on," the columnist said—and picked up a set of black plastic earphones from the floor. I adjusted the headset and heard a faint humming. Parente sat on a straight-backed chair near a connecting door and put on another headset—tiny plastic receivers, fitting snugly inside the ear. The wire leads from both sets were patched into a black box, a battered piece of equipment full of dials.

The connecting door opened and in walked Parente's cousin, Baldini, the man I had met a month ago during our promenade through the Mall.

"Ready, Augie?" Lou whispered.

"Yeah. Just about."

Augie carried a small tape recorder under his arm. It was a German machine, a Uher. This he set on the sagging sofa, plugged its lead wires into the connection box into which Parente and I were already patched, then tested the action of the machine.

274

I watched Baldini closely. What impelled him to play the spy for his cousin? Money? Dedication? A sense of adventure? I couldn't be sure. But I was intrigued with him. He rarely smiled. There was a brusque, heedless quality about Augie that impressed me. It was as if he understood with pained clarity the sickness of much of the nation, and was determined to play a small part in healing us. In manner, he suggested one of those ill-tempered, irritable old-time physicians who practiced in small towns and slums.

Parente yawned mightily. It was only nine at night, but both of them had the unshaven, grayish look of men who have been awake and hard at work for long hours with no sleep.

"What gives, Lou?" I asked softly.

The columnist put a finger to his lips. "Easy, pal. Don't use names. Talk thick. Like someone else."

"Who are we listening to?" I barely used my voice, forming my words with my lips.

Parente fiddled with the plastic piece in his ear. He acted as if he had not heard me.

"Who, who?" I repeated. The headset weighed heavily on my brow. The earphones had a clammy feeling.

"Nice customers," Parente whispered, grinning idiotically. "Lots of nice customers."

I pointed a finger at the floor. "Here? Right here?"

Still smirking, he nodded affirmatively. Then he glanced over at his cousin. "Gettin' through?" he asked.

Baldini winked at him. Then he left the sofa, knelt on the floor, and began gently to rotate the knobs on the connection box. He handled them with the deft touch of an old communications man.

Voices came through the headset; blurred, mashed.

Parente closed his eyes and put the tips of his fingers on his forehead. He was concentrating, almost like a medium trying to summon up spirits from the vasty deep.

" ... evening, evening ... General ... Congressman ... Mr. Pringle, sir ..."

Oh yes. Oh yes indeed. Nice customers. A collection of them.

" ... never drink, thanks ... little bit of the giant killer ... damned traffic getting over here ..."

The conversation was general, informal, disorganized. I recognized C. C. Pringle's hoarse tones, edged with a kind of paranoid righteousness. I recognized the flat voice of General Clyde Upshaw, presidential candidate of the Save America party. There were a few voices I could not identify. Moreover the electronic wizardry was not of a high order. I'd sat in on these seances before, once at the invitation of the Pentagon; the military went first class, supplying a bird colonel in the Signal Corps to bug, amplify, transmit and record every word at a meeting of an alleged "peace lobby." (The armed forces were good at this sort of thing. Some years ago, I have been told, that likeable fellow Barry Goldwater, a senator from, I believe, Arizona, had at his disposal at a Republican National Convention an Air Force colonel, who at the taxpayer's expense, bugged the rooms of Mr. Goldwater's rivals for the nomination. It was all done in good fun. Everybody had quite a laugh over it.)

There was some more pouring of drinks, some chatter about the prospects of the Washington senators, questions asked about wives and families and travel plans. Then I heard the ministerial voice of Congressman Lance Ruckett of South Dakota, a voice like an infusion of hot oil seeping through everything. I had the sensation that young Mr. Ruckett was right next door and I was hearing him in the flesh.

"Delighted to be here, gentlemen," Ruckett was saying. "Things get a bit tiresome up on the Hill, and I may say depressing, the way subversive notions are accepted. I'm all for old-fashioned patriots."

This was greeted with laughter. Why I don't know. Ruckett guffawed the loudest at his own observation.

"Are these reports accurate?"

Parente's lips formed the name: *"Upshaw."*

"They are, General," Ruckett blared. No mistaking him. "From high sources."

I whispered to the columnist: "Veep."

He moved his head affirmatively. "Or Hopewell."

Fine, fine. The President had not one, but two scorpions pressed to his bosom. Verne Sparrier, that young man-on-the-go might be the pipeline to these fantasts, or perhaps it was old Honey-Tonsils. My own suspicion leaned toward Sparrier. Hopewell was too shrewd an old fox to convey a presidential confidence to such a motley crowd, even though he might agree with them. You had to know Gage to understand him; he was as shifty and as surefooted as a

276

Rocky Mountain goat. I'd read recently, that when confronted with his repeated radio interviews for DOOR, he claimed he had absolutely no knowledge that the patriotic militants were associated with Merton Huckerby's swastika-wearing hoodlums. In fact, Honey-Tonsils humphed, he did not even know such a person as Mr. Huckerby existed. But he would no longer grant DOOR interviews if it developed they were associated with men who fancied swastikas.

"I believe the man has lost his reason," Ruckett was saying. "He is acting irrationally, without regard for the security or survival of the nation."

"Agreed," General Upshaw said.

"And I have heard worse reports," C. C. Pringle's hoarse rumble came through. "We are told that Seymour Cohen, that physicist who, as far as I am concerned was, and still is a conscious member of the Communist conspiracy, flew to Stockholm last night on a secret mission."

There was a buzzing, a tsk-tsking. In my mind's eye I saw a shifting of haunches, a rising of bellies, a rolling of yellowed eyes.

"Only a man like Hannaford would have the colossal gall to engage Seymour Harvey Cohen as a disarmament adviser," someone said.

"Of course, he was cleared," another voice said. It was Bates Pendragon, our he-man. I decided then and there that Pendragon was the most nearly civilized person in the room. He was educated—at Princeton—and wrote books; he could not be all bad. "And Cohen did develop the Fullback Missile."

"You are naïve Mr. Pendragon," Upshaw said. "My informants tell me that Cohen deliberately sabotaged it, that the reason the system was abandoned was because of his tinkering with the fuel systems . . ."

You could not win with these people. If Sy Cohen perfected the "Fullback," its failure could be ascribed to him. If he had *not* worked on it, he would have been accused of malingering. Paranoia appeared to be a sort of sick culture that ran through the national milk supply. It was as inevitable and as ineradicable as mildew in a summer house in Martha's Vineyard.

"It's all of a piece," Ruckett said. He appeared to be the key man. They deferred to him. "This notion of Hannaford's that he can cut defense money in half is part of it, and so is Cohen's trip to Stockholm. He obviously is out to contact the Reds."

"And that, gentlemen, is treason." This was Upshaw again. I could see his straight back, the knife-cut of a mouth, the hard blue eyes. Actually, he was a gentle man who cultivated roses on a modest two acres in McLean, Virginia. "The people seem to have lost their faith, that faith that told us that Communism is an organized conspiracy sworn to destroy America and the free world . . ."

"And China . . . a billion ants . . . a quarter of the world's population, led by a fanatic, ruthless dictatorship, determined to subdue all of Asia, and drive the United States from the Pacific . . ."

Parente made the loco sign—the finger of his right hand rotating alongside his right temple. On the sofa, the discs spun merrily, as the Uher recorded the enlightening remarks of the gathering.

"How does Hannaford expect to get away with this?" Upshaw asked.

"I'm not sure, General," Lance Ruckett replied. "But I can tell you, he won't be able to swing the House of Representatives. Not while I have Speaker O'Boyle's ear. The Caucus of Concerned Congressional Conservatives will battle the President down the line. It's the Senate that worries me. He has friends there. He's led a lot of those older men around by the nose for a long time."

"We have their names," I heard a strange high-pitched voice say. "We have the list."

Again, the shrill womanish voice intervened. "Eisenberg, Lord, Henshaw, Stapp, Mullendore, Furman, yes, we know who they are . . ."

"Right you are, Huck, and we'll get around to that in a moment." Representative Ruckett spoke soothingly.

"I want to discuss it now," the quasi soprano quavered.

"Of course, Huck, of course . . ."

"They are traitors," Huck said. "They are Communists. They are worse than Communists. They are members of the notorious Bilderberg Group and are in the pay of Goldman, Sachs, Lehman Brothers, and the entire Wall Street apparatus, and we know them . . . Stapp, Eisenberg, Henshaw, Lord, DiFalco . . ."

"Okay, Huck. Okay."

Huck. Merton Huckerby, the mysterious leader of the militant wing of DOOR, the fellow who had his elite corps

278

of businessmen drilling with machine guns and grenades in empty lots. It had to be Huckerby, the hidden power, the publisher of *Near Future,* the sworn enemy of feminists, parliamentarians, cosmopolites, socialists and single taxers. I was amazed that Ruckett, Pringle, and the other "nice customers" had let him out of his cage for the meeting.

"I wish to inform all present here," Huckerby proclaimed, "that all your talk of legal and political tactics to stop the traitor Hannaford do not interest me or my legions."

"Well, ah, Mr. H.," C. C. Pringle groused, "we old-fashioned fellows still feel we can get results that way." And why not? I thought. Pringle had rubbed elbows with half a dozen Presidents. He knew how to get favors from them. The second-class mailing privilege was something any self-respecting publisher could understand.

"I reject your methods," Huckerby sneered. "My followers have a simpler scheme."

There was a moment of silence. I hoped that Baldini's roll of tape would not run out as this wisdom was about to be revealed.

"We have them in the cross hairs," Huckerby hissed.

"Now, now," Bates Pendragon boomed.

"I don't follow you, Huck," someone said.

"I shall explain," Pendragon says. "This gentleman is saying that his followers have high-powered rifles with telescopic sights trained on legislators who did not see eye to eye with him."

"Well, golly, Huck . . ." It was Congressman Ruckett's turn to act discomfited.

"The cross hairs are on the backs of their neck," the strident voice persisted.

"Where I was brought up," General Upshaw volunteered, "you looked your man in the face and gunned him down man to man in the street. That was the way in old Arizona. I don't hold with this business of shooting people in the back. I won't hear any more of it in this room, Congressman Ruckett, and you may advise this person to stop that kind of talk."

"Yes," C. C. Pringle grumped, "if this sort of thing got out, it could hurt our campaign."

"You see the way the sentiment goes," Ruckett said. He was a sort of unofficial chairman of the party of patriots. "Huck, we appreciate your contributions to the movement,

279

especially as regards literature and fund-raising. But these comments about people in the cross hairs have got to stop. I suspect they do us more harm than good."

"I shall say no more," Huckerby said. "But when you need my elite corps, they are ready. The guns are oiled. The names are written in a book."

"Well, thanks a lot, Huck," Lance Ruckett said.

Ah, the ice was getting thinner, too thin. There has always been in American politics, a line separating the atrocious and abhorrent from the acceptable. Men in public life honor the line. Even an old terror like Gabe Tutt, or swindler like Gage Hopewell, or a free-swinging radical like Garcia, watched their step. But Huckerby was something else. It scared me that he was included in the meeting. Were we reaching the point where *anything* was permissible, so long as it protected us from Communists, angry blacks and wild hairy children?

"Gentlemen, if you please, let us talk strategy," Ruckett was saying.

"We'll hang Hannaford on this," Pringle said cheerfully. "Every respectable newspaper in the country will damn him."

"Of course," Pendragon boomed, "you must admire the man's flair. Gad, what a bravura touch—cutting their funds in half!"

I had hopes for Pendragon; damned if he wouldn't be with us someday.

"Yes, that's one of our problems," Ruckett said. "Hannaford has a talent for the dramatic move. And he knows how to manipulate and deceive. In addition, I am convinced the Russians are helping him by cooling down their aggressive assaults. Americans are being lulled again. By not attacking the United States, by suing for peace in Mongolia, by agreeing to take Italy into the Warsaw Pact, they prove again they are more fiendish than we imagined. Most diabolical of all, by sending word to the President they are ready to begin talks on disarmament, they are giving America a false sense of security."

"A brilliant analysis, Congressman," someone said.

"Thank you. You see, if they were to bomb Hawaii tomorrow, our job would be easier. They would stand revealed for what they are, monstrous murderers intent on nothing less than the annihilation of the free world. But by delaying this goal, by acting from time to time as equitable men, they have made the American people lazy, relaxed, impatient and, I fear, willing to accept Hannaford's dastardly move."

"You are saying," Pringle rumbled, "that he will have the people on his side?"

"Not if we play our cards right," Ruckett said. "What I suggest is that we make the attack on the foreign and security aspects of his proposal a *minor* part of our campaign. You will not rally enough people on that score. We must do what that biggest traitor of all did, Roosevelt. We must appeal to their pocketbooks."

"I agree," Pringle said.

"Think of what a fifty per cent cut in defense spending will mean," Ruckett said. "Unemployment. Dislocation of families. Loss of cars, houses, all sorts of goods bought on time. Wages down. Prices up. We must reach into every labor union in America, every corporation, every financial organization, and convince them that this act will destroy the economy, will pauperize the American workingman."

"Good notion," Pendragon said. "Southern California will become a desert, a disaster area." He sounded as if he relished the prospect.

"Moreover," Congressman Ruckett said, "we must examine carefully what Hannaford intends to do with the money he takes away from the military. Obviously, he will urge the Congress to enact socialistic, communistic programs, encompassing such pauperizing things as aid to education, federal housing, job training and God save us all, a revival of FDR's wicked public works programs."

"Then Congress must stop him in his tracks," Pringle cried.

"Have no fear, Mr. Pringle," the young legislator said. "My colleagues in COCCC will have some surprises for the President."

Pendragon: "He is a crafty and resourceful man, Mr. Ruckett. He is no dewy-eyed, nit-picking Harvard intellectual. And he *is* the President."

"Presidents can be fools and knaves," Ruckett said.

"And traitors." This gem from General Upshaw.

"Ah, I wouldn't go that far," Pendragon said. "And I warn you again that Hannaford is no ordinary man. He is cunning and devious. Any man of great wealth and ambition, who turns against the sanctity of private property must be watched at all times."

Was he joshing them? Was there a burly humor in Pendragon that had eluded me?

"He stole California," someone said.

"Yes," Pendragon thundered, "and no one could prove it. The man is tough, and shrewd, especially when aroused. Tread carefully, Mr. Ruckett."

"I do not fear him," Lance Ruckett sniffed.

"Rest assured, Lance," the columnist said. "He does not fear you. Or, may I add, anyone in this room, singly or together. And that includes you, Mr. Huckerby, with your telescopic sights."

Over the tangled wires, I heard a mushy, muffled sound. Glasses tinkled, bodies moved. Parente looked at his cousin, Baldini, who sat like a thoughtful gnome on the sofa, watching the brown reel of tape.

Abruptly, as distinct as a rifle shot, all noise ceased in my earphones. I thought at first that my headset or the wiring had gone defective, or that in shifting my legs I had jerked the jack out of Baldini's box. But I saw that Parente's receivers had also gone dead. The columnist yanked the plastic piece from his ear and motioned to me to do likewise. Baldini disconnected the wires. He extracted all four jacks and began to stow his gear in a plaid valise.

"Move, move, Augie," Parente said.

Baldini, sweating, was on his knees, tearing at what appeared to be a main wire that ran under the door that led to the connecting room. Exactly how they had tapped the microphone in the suite where the meeting was taking place, I do not know. But somehow, that cable had been insinuated through a wall, a door, a bathroom window. Now it had gone dead. I knew what was upsetting Lou— perhaps his "nice customers" had gotten wind of the eavesdropping.

"Shit," Baldini muttered. He yanked at the main wire. It resisted. "They got it," he said. He pulled again. There was tension on the other end, as if the wire were anchored, or someone was pulling it away.

"Beat it, Augie," Parente said, as he detached the reel from the recorder and stuffed it into the rear pocket of his baggy tan trousers.

"Lemme give it another try," Baldini said. He tugged at it again.

In the corridor—footsteps, voices. One, unmistakably

was General Upshaw's, the other C. C. Pringle's. I did not hear Huckerby's constricted tones, nor did I get any hint of Bates Pendragon's manly booms.

"Shit and two makes eight," Baldini said. He was holding a ripped end of the wire in his hand. Someone had torn it loose.

"Beat it, kid," Parente said. He gave him the valise. Augie walked to an open window, climbed over the ledge and vanished.

"Lou . . . he'll get killed . . . walking out like that. . . ."

"Nah, nah, he's the human fly. Had a rope ladder strung out there just in case. He'll be in the courtyard in two minutes. They'll never see him."

There was a sharp rapping at the door. "Good Christ, I said, "they're here."

"So what? The President's aide is allowed to visit a newspaperman."

"In the Scott Key Arms, where neither of them lives? And on the same night that the patriots are holding their cabal?"

"It's a free country, pal."

The knocking was louder. "Open up, I say! Open up in there, whoever you are." This was General Upshaw's parade-ground baritone. Hard, cracked, grown husky in service.

"Just a minute, I got to get my pants on." Parente went to the dresser and picked up a 35-mm. reflex camera with a flash attachment.

"Open it, Ed," the columnist said, and planted his burly figure in the foyer, right in front of the door.

"Let us in there," General Upshaw called. "Let us in."

"Is that an order?" Parente shouted.

"You are goddamn right it is, soldier," the general barked.

I pulled the door open. There stood Upshaw in a natty tweed jacket, the hall lights winking on his shaved skull, C. C. Pringle, florid, fat, a rather gentle-looking man.

"Hold it there, folks, you're on candid camera," Parente said. He clicked off a photo. And another. And another. He moved around the two of them swiftly, like a professional, shifting the angle of his 35-mm. camera, raising it, lowering it, getting on his tippy-toes, mumbling the standard bits of cameramen's jargon: "Yup. That's it. Good. Mmm-hum. Nice. Hold. Yup. More. Smile."

It was with a painful effort that I kept from laughing. There they stood, two old men, marinated in their own hatred, blinking and shaking their heads in the repeated flashing of the camera.

"Yes, it would be you, Parente," Pringle said. "And you, Mr. Deever. I am ashamed of you. The President will be shocked when I tell him."

The publisher extended a liver-spotted fist. In it he clutched a tiny black microphone and the ragged end of a cable. "Where is it, Parente?" he asked, smiling. "Where does it go? In the bathroom? The bedroom?"

Parente dropped the camera. "Golly, Mr. Pringle, whatever are you talking about?"

"You sneak, you Commie," General Upshaw said softly. "You were eavesdropping on us."

"Watch it, General," Parente said. "I'll sue you. Deever and I were having a private session. Discussing the aid to unwed mothers bill."

"In the Scott Key Arms?" Pringle asked.

"I always come here," Parente said. "I like the food."

"Give it to me, Parente," the publisher said jovially. "Give me the tape, or whatever it is you recorded here. We know you did it."

"Me? Tape? No, sir, I don't stoop to that."

"Like you didn't stoop to stealing Hannaford's files when he was a senator?" The publisher remained conciliatory. He was in the news game. He knew all about Parente, and he knew it was wise to treat him with care. "How odd that you and the President are now allies. How strange. He is certainly a unique man, once your worst enemy, now your friend. That must have taken a lot of money."

"Now you've gone too far, Mr. Pringle," Parente said. "You have just gone too far. Just for that I'm going to print every word of what went on in your suite."

"I warn you, Louis . . ."

"Warn him, hell," Upshaw said. "Let me handle the son of a bitch."

Parente raised the camera with the flash attachment. "Right now, General? In this room? How'd you like to be photographed with Huckerby, that fellow who has all your enemies in the cross hairs of his rifle?"

"Damned scum! Traitor! Liar! Sneak! Socialist!"

"Now, now, Clyde," the publisher said. He mopped his

beet-red forehead with a handkerchief and placed a restraining mitt on Upshaw's arm. "Louis is a journalist, and he will listen to reason. Now, Louis, give me that tape."

"Sorry, Mr. Pringle."

There were footsteps in the hall. Pringle, who had exhibited a marked calm, a sang-froid, which I found estimable, particularly in contrast to General Upshaw's fury, looked uneasy. "Clyde, tell them it's all right, it's being handled . . ."

The general moved too late. Into the doorway stepped Merton Huckerby and a chubby man I did not recognize. (I learned later he was the Reverend Sand Bewley, a southwestern dealer in faith healing, fundamentalist religion and anti-Semitism.)

"It's all right, gentlemen," Pringle cautioned. Like his underling Pendragon, he understood that there were certain of his troops better hidden from public view.

Click. Click. Click. Parente was taking photos again—Huckerby in a two-shot with Pringle; Huckerby, mouth wide open, eyes staring, in a solo close-up.

"Yup. Nice. Once more. Hold it. That's right. Yeah." Parente was moving around the room like a crazed genius.

"Just what are you doing?" Pringle cried. "How can you possibly hope to do us any harm? These are American citizens."

"Up your cross hairs," the columnist said. "Shove your telescopic sight all the way up, Huckerby, and see if you can shoot your brains out."

I studied Merton Huckerby, for it was the first time I had seen him close up. He was of moderate height, slender, and stood very erect—a tendency I have noted in right-wing zealots. His hair was sandy-red and close-cropped, his eyebrows a magnificent tawny gold, and his creased, lean face—hard nose, full mouth, firm chin—splotched and speckled with freckles the size of nickels and the color of an Orange Julius. His eyes were so pale as to be almost invisible, a boiled-out blue, of less intensity than the piebald markings on his face, so that they tended to disappear into the whites, as if camouflaged. The total effect endowed him with a vacant, eyeless look, the face of a man who did not see the world, and so had to invent fantasies.

"Yes, yes, I'm delighted to meet the enemy face to face," Huckerby said.

"My pleasure, Huck," Parente said. "Read lots about you. I loved that piece about Dachau and Auschwitz, how they were merely places where known criminals got theirs. That was a peach."

"Glad to enlighten you," Huckerby said.

Pringle was disturbed. He knew the limits of dissent. He knew there were some people better left hidden from the light of day. You could use them, and milk them for ideas and money, but they were not quite acceptable. Not yet, anyway.

"Louis," Pringle said, "you and I are professionals and I shall be at your disposal tomorrow to discuss whatever you may have heard . . ." He waved the microphone at Lou.

"There's nothing to discuss Mr. Pringle. And don't offer me an outlet in one of your newspapers. I may be corrupt, but there are limits to what I'll do for a buck."

"Give me that goddamn recording, or notes, or what the hell ever you have," General Upshaw said. He moved toward Lou.

"What'll it be, General?" Parente asked. "Arm rassle? Catch-as-catch-can? Karate?"

It was odd: Huckerby, who had bragged to his colleagues of his readiness to shoot down his enemies, preferably in the back of the neck, shrank against the door. A bloodless coward. No violence for this patriot, thank you.

"Well, General, it has been a long time since I belted an officer, but here goes," Parente said.

Upshaw picked up a heavy glass ash tray and raised it. With a swift move, amazing in a fat man in his seventies, Pringle thrust his arm up and blocked Upshaw. "Please, Clyde, this serves nothing. I must ask you to let me handle this. I am sure that in the privacy of my office, tomorrow morning, Louis and I can resolve this."

"His kind knows only one law," Upshaw said huskily. "I intend to apply it." But he put the ash tray down.

"Scram," Parente said. "Beat it. I've had enough of all of you."

But they did not move. "Okay, that's enough. You guys don't understand English." The columnist went to the phone and asked the hotel operator to connect him immediately with the District of Columbia police.

"Hallo? Police? Yeah, this is Lou Parente. I wanna speak to Lieutenant Sheinblum of the Vice Squad. I was having a meeting in my hotel room here, and four guys busted in. Why? Well, you ask me I think they're fagots. Yeah, four big fags, looking for a good time. Don't ask me. I'm just sick and tired. You tell Sheinblum I don't care to be bothered by old fruits in the middle of the night. I mean, this city is getting to be a disgrace. No wonder the tourists don't want to come down any more. A person can't sit in a hotel room without these homosexual prowlers and perverts forcing their way in and making indecent propositions ..."

There was a mass retreat through the opened door. Parente ran to the window and looked down the three stories into the courtyard. Baldini had made his getaway safely.

The next day I sneaked Parente into the White House, up a back staircase, and up to the third floor, where the guest rooms are located. The Empire Guest Room seemed a good place to meet with the President and with the Attorney General. It is a small corner room, decorated with wallpaper and upholstery featuring scenes from the life of Benjamin Franklin, with the inscription WHERE LIBERTY DWELLS THERE IS MY COUNTRY.

Lou and I sat on the curious bed fashioned after John Quincy Adams' sleigh as he set up the playback on the recorder. The President and Attorney General Moscowitz sat opposite us and listened. All the vicious nonsense spouted at the meeting of patriots was clearly recorded. Ben showed little reaction. But the Attorney General looked grave and made notes.

"I am amazed that they let Huckerby out in public," Moscowitz said. "We have a file on him, and the man is a lunatic. *Near Future,* the Bible of the Defenders of Our Republic, is an out-and-out apologia for the Nazis. In fact, he has bragged that it is the *Mein Kampf* of the American conservative movement."

"There isn't a damned thing we can do until they commit some overt act," the President said. "Nobody can be prosecuted for espousing wicked notions in the privacy of a hotel room."

"That's correct," the Attorney General said.

"Even those threats of Huckerby's? That business about

287

having all those senators in the cross hairs of his rifle?" I was furious.

"We might get some sort of action against Huckerby," Moscowitz said. "But I wonder if it's worth it. As far as we know, for all their loud bragging, we have no evidence of DOOR's militants ever having shot a single person. At heart, they're cowards and yellow-bellies, drilling with surplus rifles."

I did not accept the judge's serene estimate of these people. "May I dissent, Mr. Moscowitz?" I asked. "They may be cowards—but give these people a chance, just the chance to get the upper hand, and they will stop at nothing. I've read the history of fascist movements—Germany, Italy and so on—and while its proponents were mainly disaffected middleclass losers, sneaky lower orders, once they are convinced that they could get away with murder, once they are convinced that the police and the courts would treat kindly with them, they killed with the greatest of pleasure."

President Hannaford stood up and patted my arm. "Steady there, Edward. We're a long way from that."

"Mr. President, I'm going to print this stuff," Parente said.

"Maybe you'd better wait, Louis."

"Sorry, sir. I can't sit on it."

"Do me a favor, son. Let me make my presentation on the TV tomorrow. Let's see what the reaction is. If Ruckett and his mob get rough, then you hit them with that little recording."

Scowling, Parente scratched his lumpy forehead. "Okay. But I can't hold it too long."

The President, pensive, concerned, walked about the room. "Someone's feeding that gang information. It better stop or I'll have to saddle up and ride down a few varmints."

We said nothing; we knew of whom he was speaking.

"It's the ordinary folk who bother me. Not Upshaw or that freckled-face Hitler with his guns. But Ruckett, that corn-fed American boy. He's selling money and jobs and security. People buy that line."

"You overestimate him, Ben," Judge Moscowitz said.

Hannaford shook his head. "Sam, right-wing conspiracies never got off the ground in this country because they didn't offer folks anything in a material way. They

288

deal in fear, lunacy, hate, imagined terrors. The fools who lead them don't understand that people respond to steaks, and beer, and cars and homes—not to devils they can't see. Old Joe McCarthy and a passel of other right-wing nuts never realized this. Ruckett does. That's why he's dangerous."

"I agree with you, sir," I said quickly. "He's scoring points in the House every day. The way things stand right now, your proposed fifty per cent cut in military dollars wouldn't get the time of day."

"I know that, Edward," the President said. "But I'm banking on popular support, the good sense of a lot of Americans. In spite of Mr. Ruckett and General Upshaw and C. C. Pringle, most people don't want to get blown up. They're more interested now in clean air and good schools and less taxes and clear rivers and good police and no riots and a street cleaning department that gets the job done."

Parente packed up the small tape recorder. "I've had my differences with you, Mr. President," the columnist said, "but I never underrated your confidence."

"You sound dubious, Louis."

"Upshaw got a quarter of the vote. Beldock wasn't much better and he whupped you. People want all those things you mentioned. But there's a poison in the body politic, Mr. President, and poisons can have a strange effect on people. Can affect their minds. They might not even know what's good for them any more. They might not be so interested in clean streets and clean water and more roast beef. Maybe they want blood."

"I won't accept that," Attorney General Moscowitz said.

"I sure as hell won't," the President said. He moved toward the door of the small, historic room, with its curious wallpaper depicting the life of Benjamin Franklin.

"I'll hold up on this stuff," Parente said, indicating his taped record of the meeting of super patriots.

"Do that, Louis. Those people will be all over me as soon as I finish that speech tomorrow night. We'll need all the reserve ammunition we can lay our hands on."

In the corridor, Moscowitz looked strangely at Parente. "In your contacts with DOOR, especially the 'Near Future' crowd, have you ever come across a man named Moffo?"

Parente shrugged. "Nope. I didn't think they had any
289

paisans in that crowd. We go more for law-and-order lawyers and judges, Anti-Defamation League of Italo-Americans."

He lied splendidly. Alberto Moffo was his cousin Baldini's *nom-de-guerre*. "Our own men inside of DOOR filed a report on him," Moscowitz said. "I was just curious . . ."

"Glad to hear you're watching them, Judge," Parente said.

"Could I take a peek into the Treaty Room?" Parente suddenly asked. "All these years in Washington, I've never seen it."

"Stick your head in," I said. "I'll give you a light."

Hannaford heard us, and he turned, happy to indulge in a bit of guiding and sightseeing. The four of us stood in the doorway of the elegant Victorian chamber, with its emerald-green walls, ornate chandelier and mirror with surrounding gilt motif.

Parente walked around the old-fashioned room, studying the heart-backed chairs, Julia Dent Grant's desk, the famed Browne and Spaulding clock used by President Grant. At length the columnist paused in front of the E. F. Andrews portrait of Andrew Johnson.

"Old Andy," Parente said casually. "Plenty trouble."

I tried to change the subject. "Yes, this room was chosen by Andrew Johnson as his cabinet room, and was so used until 1902," I said.

Parente looked solemnly at the President. "Yeah, I bet he sat right here, maybe in that crazy swivel chair, and talked about the way the House impeached him. His enemies called him King Andy I."

The word hung, frozen, in the night air. *Impeached.* Why had Parente made such a show of visiting the Treaty Room? Did he actually fear such a development?

"Ancient history, Louis," President Hannaford said. "That's the rusty blunderness of the legislative branch, in case you're hinting around."

"Jefferson called it a scarecrow," I offered.

"Seen enough, Louis?" the President asked.

"Yes, thank you, sir."

I switched off the light and we walked the corridor again. Outside the door leading to the private apartments, the President stopped. He shook hands with the three of us. "Think kind thoughts of the President, gentlemen. Tomorrow, like the Israelites, we will pass over on dry ground."

PART IV

The Senate shall have the sole power to try all impeachments. When sitting for that purpose they shall be on oath or affirmation. When the President of the United States is tried, the Chief Justice shall preside; and no person shall be convicted without the concurrence of two-thirds of the members present.

Judgment in cases of impeachment shall not extend further than to removal from office, and disqualification to hold and enjoy any office of honor, trust or profit under the United States; but the party convicted shall, nevertheless, be liable and subject to indictment, trial, judgment and, punishment, according to law.

—SECTION 3, ARTICLE I,
THE CONSTITUTION

The television director was a young black man from NBC, which had won the coin toss for the "pooled" broadcast from the President's office. Fred Goldstein and I checked some last minute arrangements with him, as the President, and the three cabinet members who would help him present his program, entered the Oval Room and went to their seats.

"You'll like the lighting," the director told Goldstein and myself. "Changed a few things from the way CBS did it."

"Nothing like competition," our press secretary said.

"That wasn't why," the youthful black man said. "Had a problem with your Secretary of Health, Education and Welfare. I had to balance the lighting so's he wouldn't come out purple."

I glanced at Homer Murphy's long, black, noble head, as he sat down in the chair to Ben's right. There was something of the African king about Homer—Cetswayo or Chaka, or one of those great rulers of Benin, depicted in the classic bronze statues.

"We will be on the air in three minutes, Mr. President," the director said.

"We're ready, Mr. Jenks," Ben said. He looked to his right—Homer Murphy, Secretary of State Walter Edgerton, and to his left, Defense Secretary Burke Boswell, ganglier, ruddier than ever, the Treasury Secretary Meg McNally, demon bridge player, and the true authoress of the dramatic plan to control the military.

"Don't worry about cameras, folks," the director said.

292

"I'll have a master shot of the desk and the chairs ready at all times, so it can be as informal as you like. I can always go to the master, but I'll try as much as possible to stay with close-ups of whomever has the floor."

"Fine," the President said. "It will be informal, ad lib, all of us using notes and memoranda."

Hannaford had carefully chosen his *modus operandi*. "I'm what I suppose those psychologist types would call the father figure," he said. "Then we've got Meg—anybody's lovable mother. Then there's Homer, a national hero, the fellow who stopped the Green Bay Packers three times inside the five-yard line. Then there's Walter Edgerton, the university man, everyone's favorite professor. And of course, Burke."

"Of course," I said.

"Yeah, old Burke. The good WASP. You'll find him at every cocktail party in Fairfield County, on the golf course, the yacht club, the Wall Street dining room. How can any man like that be a threat?"

"You've cast it rather like one of those old Warner Brothers platoons in World War II movies," I said. "One of each."

"That's the idea," Ben said.

"One minute to air," the director said. Fred and I wished the President good luck and left the office, hurrying across the West Wing to the press lounge, where monitors had been set up. We would make ourselves available to the White House reporters as soon as the TV presentation ended.

The west lobby was jammed. I saw Mona Varnum amid a group of reporters.

"Good evening my fellow Americans," President Hannaford said. "I'm going to speak informally to you tonight. I've asked some members of my Cabinet to join me. They are, from right to left, Mr. Walter Edgerton, our Secretary of State, Mr. Homer Murphy, Secretary of Health, Education and Welfare, Mr. Burke Boswell, the Secretary of Defense, and Mrs. Margaret H. McNally, Secretary of the Treasury. All shall contribute to this evening's discussion of some plans this Administration has for the nation."

Larry Hosmer of United Press came up to me. He whispered: "Pringle's chain beat him to it. They ran a front page editorial tonight predicting some of what the old man was going to announce. Defense cut. Urban spending."

"Did Mr. Pringle approve?"

Hosmer drew a finger across his throat. "Called it the nearest thing to treason yet attempted by a President in office."

"C. C. Pringle is in for some surprises, Larry."

Hannaford was well into his introductory remarks. He spoke informally, from a set of cards that Fred and I had prepared for him. Ben was not a great speaker. He had none of FDR's beautiful rhythms, or John F. Kennedy's talent for style. I would compare him to Harry Truman at his fighting best—homespun without being corny.

"A few nights ago, Mrs. McNally, speaking not just as our Secretary of the Treasury, but as a good American housewife, pointed out to me that our family budget was out of whack," Ben was saying. The director picked up a shot of Meg, smiling. How could a silvery grandmother like Meg be a coddler of welfare chiselers?

"She was right. We're spending money on limousines we don't need, on fancy hand-crafted shotguns and rifles—when the kitchen sink is leaking and the house needs paint. That's what it boils down to. And to make it clearer, I've come to the conclusion that a lot of those nuclear weapons we are building are nothing but four-hundred-horse-power Cadillacs and Lincolns and Chryslers . . ."

"That's good," Hosmer whispered to me. "Put the knock on all three, so none of them can kick."

"Maybe all we need for defense is that little Ford in the garage. Heck, it does the job. Maybe the missiles we have already do the job—better than most of us know. Secretary Boswell, will you address yourself to that?"

Big Boswell shifted his legs, and his scarlet, loose-jawed face came on to the screen.

"Mr. President, in plain terms we are overarmed. So are the Russians. We know it and they know it. The way things stand there are no winners in a nuclear war. There is no longer any such thing as a first strike. The systems are set up today so that anybody who fires first, gets fired back at immediately. If he aims for our buried silos, they'll be empty by the time his bombs get there. What good would it do him, knocking out a bunch of holes in

294

the ground? Besides, we've got our Poseidon submarines and our manned bombers in reserve. And they have too. So, nobody wins. Everybody dies. The proposed Manned Orbital Multiple Satellite Entry Relay, or MOMSER system, commonly called the Iron Ball, is useless. It can only make the rubble bounce after civilizations are destroyed. We will recommend to the Congress that plans for the Iron Ball be scrapped."

Hosmer whistled. "Was this cleared with Senator Tutt? Or the beloved Majority Leader?"

I didn't answer. I merely raised my eyebrows as if to say—guess again, Larry.

"Thank you, Mr. Secretary," the President said. "That's a saving of twenty billion dollars right there. But as I say, that's just a beginning. For years we have been giving our military people what amounts to a blank check. Now no man in public life respects our generals and admirals more than does your President. But sometimes organizations need an overhauling. For years now, we've coughed up the money for defense, no matter what—no accounting, no checkups, no auditing. That's all going to end."

"What the hell is he up to?" Hosmer asked.

Hannaford went on: "I shall be as specific as possible. The budget for national defense willed us by the previous Administration called for 120 billion dollars for defense, out of a total budget of 220 billion dollars. I shall recommend to the Congress that that 120 billion dollars be cut in half. Yes, by fifty per cent. Instead of a variety of smaller appropriation bills, I shall ask the House and the Senate to authorize expenditures of 60 billion dollars, no more, on national defense. I shall say to Secretary Boswell, here is your 60 billion, now defend us."

There were gasps and shouts from the reporters as Hannaford uttered this outlandish proposal. It was so simple, so unexpected, that half the newsmen in the west lobby thought for a moment he was joking, indulging in some of his frontier humor.

"We have tried, and tried, and tried again to cut down on this defense spending," the President said. "It doesn't work by going at it piecemeal. That, my fellow Americans, is no way to run a government, let alone a business. There is always righteous indignation in the halls of the Congress, when it is discovered that a few thousand dollars in funds for feeding the hungry or training the poor get misused or stolen. I should like to see an equal amount of indignation over the thirty-one billion dollars wasted on useless missiles over the past twenty years."

Hannaford delivered this last bit with a rising inflection, looking right into the camera with his piercing black eyes. The reporters burst into applause.

"That saving of 60 billion dollars is just a starter," Hannaford said. "We've got lots to do, once we get the money away from the bombs and planes and missiles. Think you can handle it, Burke?"

"We'll give it a try, Mr. President," the Defense Secretary replied. "Of course, if we can abandon the MOMSER system, we'll have a real leg up on the job."

I watched the newsmen narrowly. They were enchanted. Even C. C. Pringle's leak of some of the story hadn't taken the edge off Hannaford's presentation. It grabbed them—imaginative, sweeping, humorous, original. What a notion! Was ever a more telling line delivered by a President? *Here's sixty billion; now defend us.*

"There are three parts to my conversation with you tonight, my fellow Americans," the President resumed, after Boswell laced into the military in his charming manner. "There's the matter of reducing these defense costs, that's number one. The second part is what we do with the money we save. I'll turn that aspect over to the Secretary of Health, Education and Welfare, Mr. Homer Murphy."

Homer adjusted his scholarly spectacles and looked at some index cards. "Mr. President, my figures are rough, and perhaps have erred a little on the generous side. They have to do with the rebuilding of our cities, and the people who live in them. Cities are the heart of a nation, and we have let them decay and decline. In place of community, there is crime. In place of humanity, there is anger. In place of creativity, there is filth. As a country of responsive citizens, all of us share in the failure.

"But as you have so often pointed out, Mr. President, money can work miracles, if properly used. A conservative businessmen's magazine some years ago did a remarkable survey of our dirty, crowded, crime-ridden cities, and came to the conclusion that they needed more funds, lots more. In short, the trouble with the poor was that they didn't have enough money. Or, as a distinguished predecessor of yours once said, when people are out of work, unemployment results."

Mona Varnum walked up to us. I couldn't gauge the look in her slanted eyes, hidden as they were by exaggerated granny glasses. But I detected a smile. "You writing Murphy's stuff?" she asked. Ah, the sound of her voice. I quivered. I had to have her again ... and again ... and again. ...

"It's a cinch it's not Arvid Farbelman," I said.

"Funny."

"May I take you to dinner tomorrow night?" I asked. "I never did learn what you meant when you told me you were a Rhode Island Varnum."

"In public?" Mona asked haughtily.

"Of course."

Murphy was finishing his recital of our ambitious plans for the cities. The billions rolled on—twelve billion for education, including an entire new junior college program, ten for housing, ten for guaranteed annual wages.

"Mr. President, these funds are available, provided we halt the unnecessary, unproductive and wasteful expenditures in the name of defense. Our department has examined the national needs closely; all these programs can be financed provided the funds are available."

"Thank you, Homer," Hannaford said. "I'm sure many of you in the audience are saying that this is all a daydream, that we dare not cut in half our spending on defense for fear that the Russians or the Chinese will attack us and defeat us. I'd like our Secretary of State, Mr. Walter Edgerton to speak a bit on that subject."

"Mr. President," Edgerton said, "we have good reason to believe that within the next few weeks, the Russians and Chinese will agree upon a cease-fire in Mongolia. This should lead to substantive peace talks between the two nations, and an eventual settlement of their three-year dispute over that mid-Asian nation. At the invitation of Chairman Gromyko and Prime Minister Tang, we have sent an observer to the talks in Stockholm, not to sit in on the discussions of the Mongolian problem, but to make himself available to the two delegation chiefs in order to discuss guidelines for new disarmament and arms control talks."

Mona Varnum said to me: "I hear your emissary is

297

that physicist cat, Cohen. They'll keep *that* a secret as long as they can."

"Shall we wager on that?" I asked.

I would have won. Walter Edgerton went on: 'The observer we have sent to Stockholm is the eminent nuclear physicist, Professor Seymour Harvey Cohen, former chairman of the President's Advisory Committee on nuclear weapons. His report to us should be available in a few days."

Hosmer whistled softly. "Hannaford's got guts. Cohen is a red flag to a lot of people."

I shrugged. "When we go, we go all the way."

The UP man winced. "And I'd avoid that expression also, Ed. It used to be 'All the way, with LBJ.' And you know what happened to him."

"In short," Edgerton said, "we must accept the proposition that when their own interests, indeed their own survival, are at stake, the Communists may bargain in good faith. Not all the time. But often enough to make it worth while for us to negotiate with them."

The President thanked the Secretary of State, then took over the discussion. "Let me talk about the effect that a cutback in military spending will have on the economy. First, let's look at it from the standpoint of the industries involved. Will it hurt them? Yes, it will. But that's the way of the free enterprise system. Buggy whip manufacturers got hurt when Henry Ford went into mass production. Let me point out that a third of all defense contracts go to a dozen huge firms, whose names are known to you. They are all fine corporations—patriotic and profitable. Put another way, there are about a hundred large companies that do two-thirds of the defense business. But it's those top dozen giants who get the lion's share. Yes, they'll bleed a little, but that won't really hurt them in comparison to what could hurt us by continuing as we are.

"Now, as for those big boys, I'd like to make a few suggestions. We intend to start an incentive program for some of them. We want them to use their capital, and their skills, and their plant, for other things. Let's say corporation X out in California loses a big contract for the engines on the Iron Ball system. Okay, gentlemen, we'll award you another contract—maybe not as big, but big enough to keep you happy—for a water purification project, or a new kind of low-cost multiple dwelling, or a new urban rapid transit system. Let's get some of that famous American know-how and energy directed toward making life better, instead of making death surer. Said what? Lost a 500 million dollar deal for building an airbase? Gentlemen—here's half that amount—and start building hospitals."

"They won't buy that," I heard a man from Associated Press say to a chap from *Time* magazine. "The thing about these defense deals was, they were a stacked deck. You couldn't lose."

"Yes," he replied, "and it'll take an awful lot of schools and hospitals to make up for all that expensive military garbage."

They were right, of course. When a man stopped buying Cadillacs and Lincolns he was left with an embarrassing sum of money for books and medicine and the improvement of his character.

Hannaford continued, "I hear a lot about ethnic minorities. I keep hearing that these good Americans, of Italian, Irish, Polish, Ukrainian and Greek descent—and many other national origins—are the ones who are against helping black people. I'm afraid I won't accept that. I believe Americans are a generous and helpful people. I think what is bothering a lot of these so-called ethnic minorities is that the cities they live in are intolerable. I aim to take all this money ticketed for useless big machines, and use it to make the cities good places to live in."

"Little bit of everything," Goldstein said to me.

"Mr. Murphy, I'd appreciate it, if you would describe the plan we have for areas where defense industries are heavy," the President said.

"Yes, Mr. President. We have made surveys of places like Sunnyvale, California, a town of one hundred thousand which is almost entirely dependent for jobs on the military-industrial complex. About twenty-seven thousand people are employed by three prime contractors with the Defense Department. Under our proposed cutback in defense outlays, about two-thirds of these people would be out of work. We deliberately have taken this as an example, because it is an extreme case. Naturally, unemployment insurance would apply to all such people, and we will propose to the Congress that such payments be doubled . . ."

"Ah," Goldstein said, "there it is. Right thing, wrong reason."

"No, no. Controlled greed."

Goldstein shook his red frizzy hair. "Nah, A for B."

Larry Hosmer nudged me. "Try selling that to the unions. Those guys are cleaning up on double-time and overtime and lunch-hour penalties on those defense jobs. There's so much gravy, everybody gets a little. You stick half those characters in to an honest job, like building a library, and they'll kick and scream."

Hannaford was into his summary now. He ticked off the main points again—a 50 per cent slash in defense spending, a huge increase in outlays for the cities, the guaranteed wage, job training, all the urgent needs of the country, and hopefully, a new effort toward disarmament. It was a three-part program—meshed, interdependent, one part activated by the other.

"I need your help my fellow Americans. I will need the help of the Congress. You must, if you agree with me, and I hope you do, start writing to your representatives and senators and telling them that you want to help this Administration make America fulfill its centuries-old hopes.

"And finally, to those of you who may still be worried about the Russians destroying us, because our military friends have played on these fears for years, let me assure all of you that we are stronger than we've ever been. If we decide to arm more so we can devastate other countries three times over, it's no better than devastating them once. We can, right now, make of the world what the good book calls 'an abomination of desolation.' To devastate thrice, is no greater a deterrent than to devastate once.

"Let us go about our business as a nation and as a people, so that we do not waste our substance with riotous living, and let us heed the old questioner in Luke who asked, 'Which of you intending to build a tower, sitteth not down first and counteth the cost, whether he have sufficient to finish it?' My friends, I'm not afraid about us being able to finish this tower of bombs and satellites and missiles—we can afford anything we want. But I'm worried it may finish us. Let us rather work to end wars and rumors of war, so that we may say in one loud, clear voice—Peace be to this house."

300

President Hannaford looked gravely into the camera. The screen went black, and the great seal of the presidency appeared. An announcer's voice said: "This has been a special broadcast from the White House by the President of the United States."

The silence in the west lobby, crammed as it was with the press, surprised me. I took it as a good omen: Ben had moved them. Of course, the press had never been any real problem for people like us. I had learned in long years of political service, never to gauge *public* sentiment by the editorials in The New York *Times*. As some political cal reporter discovered in 1968, when the Chicago police beat the long-haired children outside the Hilton Hotel, covering the streets with blood, and the bulk of the nation nodded its approval, there was a whole *other* America outside New York City and the editorial pages of tolerant newspapers. The *other* America—devoted to simple solutions, patriotic, good-hearted but fearful of change and challenge and the foreign—was the one Ben had to reach. It remained to be seen if he could.

In my small office I studied the congressional response to Hannaford's address. The headlines, of course, were tremendous, The New York *Times* actually going to an eight-column banner, something it rarely did short of an election.

PRESIDENT ASKS FIFTY PER CENT CUT IN MILITARY SPENDING: FUNDS TO BE USED FOR CITIES IN FIFTY BILLION DOLLAR PROGRAM

And the Washington *Post,* and the Louisville *Courier-Journal,* and the St. Louis *Post-Dispatch,* and most of the big city papers. More importantly, the editorials were cautiously friendly. It was in the smaller cities that we fared less well, and in the chain newspapers, such as C. C. Pringle's.

In a signed editorial that ran in all ten of his journals, the publisher warned the nation:

All those who stand with freedom, and against tyranny must oppose President Hannaford's ill-conceived program. He chooses to ignore the most insidious and

301

gigantic plot in history, the Communist goal of world domination. In so doing, he defeats his entire program.

I sampled congressional reaction. The news had caught up with Gabe Tutt while he was air-borne at the taxpayer's expense, visiting his cotton fields and pecan groves in the delta. (The trip was advertised as an inspection of the Tutt Memorial Military Highway, connecting an obsolete airbase with a shut-down ordinance depot; Gabe always managed a visit to "home folks" when he had the air force to fly him around.) Landing at Washington on his return, Gabe could barely contain his fury.

"This hyeah program of the President cannot and will not pass!" Gabe Tutt fumed. "The Commonists unnerstan' only one thing—nekkid force. I will battle the President down the lahn, in and out of the Congress, and I will rally every soldier and sailor and patriotic citizen to mah sahd! Ah don't accuse the President of treasonable actions, but he has got some damn traitors and appeasers close to him raht now, people in positions to influence him, and they'll be found out, Ah guarantee y'all!"

Gabe uttered this with something less than his usual vehemence. As I studied the comments of other opponents, the notion stirred within me that perhaps our enemies were taken by surprise by Ben's thundering assault on them. What really stopped them in their tracks was Ben's continued harping on our nuclear *sufficiency*—his argument that after a saturation point with death-dealing missiles, there was nothing to be gained by adding and spending until we went broke.

Americans did not like to go broke. They liked to have money. They did not like paying 10 per cent on a mortgage because all the cash in the country was going into useless battleships and needless planes.

How I chuckled when I read the *Wall Street Journal!*

Whatever the merits of President Hannaford's bold plan to halve the defense budget, it has this to be said for it: it confronts fearlessly, and without equivocation, the economic chaos that the military-industrial complex has created. It defies all rational rules of economic health to keep pouring limitless billions into nonproductive enterprises. Civilian industry suffers; the labor market dries up; the natural functioning of supply and

302

demand is impeded; free enterprise is no longer free but a creature of government largess of a distinctly unbalanced nature; and the money and energy needed for expansion dries up to the vanishing point. The economy, the market, the banks, the business community need some fresh ideas, and President Hannaford may have something for all of them in his daring approach to the defense spending problem . . .

Economy. Free Market. Business Community. God, what cant. Ben Hannaford had been talking about nothing less than the blowing up of the world, of the death of every person on the globe, of the end of our civilization. That was why he wanted to stop the nuclear race. But the business leaders had *other* worries. *There was no cash for loans.* Was my boss right or was he not, when he explained to us at great length, that the ruling circles in America were motivated by what he referred to as *controlled greed?*

I checked other congressional reaction. The centers of power seemed unfriendly.

Senator Gage (Honey-Tonsils) Hopewell, Majority Leader:

"I must part with my revered leader on this issue. The Congress will not tolerate such a capricious and emasculating move. One does not disarm, one does not paralyze one's good right arm, one does not simply throw millions of hard-working people out of jobs and shut down factories and bases, on the mere hope, the mere gossamer, wispy, evanescent, diaphanous hope of an accommodation with our sworn enemies."

I loved that phrase *sworn enemies.* Who swore them? Were those black-clad, skinny farmers in Vietnam who kept battling us to the death, for their rice paddies and thatched huts, the *sworn enemy?* I hated Communism as much as any man, and so did Ben Hannaford, but who did all this swearing for us?

We did have some support. Senator John Tyler Lord of Vermont: "President Hannaford has spoken out boldly and I will support him."

In the House we were bitterly attacked. Lance Ruckett, the eager head of COCCC, sailed into the boss. Ruckett was feeling his oats. I'd gotten reports from my spies in the House that he now counted no less than eighty-seven members of the lower chamber as members of his "conservative" group, and that at least thirty others were favorable to their views. He was swinging a big bat, young Ruckett, and he wasted no time in denouncing Ben's plan.

"The proposal to cut the military budget in half is outrageous and scandalous," the South Dakotan told a press conference. "It will denude us, disarm our soldiers and leave us prey to the first-strike capabilities of the Russians."

A reporter asked: "But Mr. Boswell and the scientists say there is no such thing as a first-strike capability any more. That anyone who fires first gets destroyed in the time lapse. The bombs will land on empty holes."

Ruckett was not dismayed. "I have access to other information."

"But what about the President's information? Or the Defense Secretary's?"

The protuberant forehead bulged, the sweaty face glistened. "This would not be the first time that Mr. Hannaford has played fast and loose with the truth."

There were a few gasps from the reporters. Not since Joe McCarthy had a legislator used such language to lay into an incumbent President.

"Are you saying that the President is lying?"

Ruckett grinned. "I refer you gentlemen to the election results in California."

"What do you mean, Congressman?" a UP man asked.

"I'll say no more on that score," he went on. "But I will go on record as stating that the mission of Professor Cohen to Stockholm is a fraud, knowing the man's background, and the way he has failed every test as a loyal citizen . . ."

"He's been cleared four times, Congressman."

"Not by people I trust. He is the last man in the world to be negotiating with the Soviets. Any information he gives the President must be discounted. Seymour Harvey Cohen has not changed since the days his security clearance was lifted."

"Then you favor continuation of the arms race?"

"Yes, I do. The arms race has to make us stronger. As a famous general once pointed out, we can out-invent, out-research, out-develop, out-engineer and out-produce the U.S.S.R. in anything from bean-shooters to the MOMSER system. And we get richer and more prosperous

304

when we do, while they get poorer. Free enterprise can lick socialism any day of the week. Besides, if the President's plan is adopted, we will see suffering, unemployment, anger and despair among millions of America's workingmen. And what about the people who depend on their income—shopkeepers, doctors, service personnel? All will suffer. I want Americans to know that once these great factories of freedom are halted, once the engines stop, not only will we be naked before our enemies—"

"*Sworn* enemies, Lance," I muttered to myself.

"—but economic chaos and human suffering will be rife. I've been in touch with the leadership of the national unions, and they are very upset . . ."

I began to worry. People like Lance Ruckett normally stayed away from unions as if from a plague of boils. What I feared ever since Ben proposed the defense cutback was happening: an uneasy alliance of the far right and the unions. It disturbed me more than any of the congressional reactions; for it portended a mass base, a mass movement, one that had been in the making ever since the civil rights movement of the late fifties. The formula was elemental enough—white workingman, fear of blacks, and now a new fear—losing one's job. And why? For what reason? To shovel millions of dollars into ghettos to support black bastards?

That weekend I saw old Harry Bustard, President of the AFL-CIO interviewed on "Meet the Press." Old Harry—pillar of the New Deal, personal friend to Harry Truman and JFK, and a man who had never found a bad thing to say about Ben Hannaford.

"No, Mr. Spivak," Harry said, chomping his cigar in the corner of his thick lips, wiping his seamed forehead (he was an old steamfitter, an old craftsman), "my people don't like it at all. All them promises about job placement and job training—what does that mean to one of my guys getting fourteen bucks an hour at a missile base? He knows he can't do as well building a library. The President's got to do better than that."

"Do you back the National Unions and Military Bureau?" Spivak asked. "They are distributing leaflets calling for President Hannaford's impeachment."

Cunning old Bustard! He knew he had a tiger on his hands. NUMB was growing in power.

"Well, lemme say Mr. Spivak, the men in NUMB may

305

get a little riled up now and then, and I personally respect President Hannaford, even when I disagree with him, but they got a right to their opinions, and they should be listened to . . ."

The chairman of the Joint Chiefs, General Boyd R. Nagel, who, during the Vietnam misery had earned the nickname "Butcher Boyd," suddenly resigned.

"I do this so that I may more effectively resist the President," General Nagel said. "Holding high office, I can only act upon the President's orders, since I am a believer in the maintenance of civil authority over the military. Now that I am leaving the service, I can help fight the President's ill-advised program. All of this appeasement goes back to the United Nations, anyway, a screen for treason, and a means whereby we will be sold out to the Soviets."

"But don't the Russians ever honor an agreement?" a TV reporter asked.

"Any so-called peace move by them is a trap, a chance to let them catch their breaths for the next round. Their objective has not changed. We must be ready to fight."

"Even if it means blowing up the world?"

"I have no fear of that. If we remain potent and supreme, with a first-strike capacity, they won't lift a finger. Congress should authorize all the money for the Iron Ball, the MOMSER system, tomorrow."

And so he left us; a good old soldier, sincere in his views. After consulting with the Secretary of Defense, the President decided not to appoint a new chairman, but to create—this was Boswell's ploy—a "rotating chairmanship." The head of each branch of the services would be chairman for a three-month period.

We were pleased to note that General Nagel did not suffer financially. Two days after he left his country's service, he took a job at one hundred thousand a year with Cosmic-Strato Systems, a prime contractor, in for about five hundred million dollars' worth of contracting on MOMSER.

Hannaford now warmed to his task. Convinced he had gotten off to a good start in reaching the people, he concentrated on Congress. "We have strength in the dear old Senate, Edward," he told me one morning, "and we lack strength in the House. Let us lead from strength."

A small White House dinner was arranged. The key

guests were our two top men in the Senate—Majority Leader Gage Hopewell, and Majority Whip Sidney Stapp. It was instructive and—in a sense—chilling, to observe the manner in which Ben Hannaford played these two off, one against the other.

Dinner in the presidential dining room was relaxed, conversation was casual. Gage and Rachel Hopewell, and Sid and Judy Stapp all laughed as Ben related the hilarious account of the swift manner in which the Lyndon Johnsons had gotten rid of the Kennedys' French chef. "Fired him so fast," the President said, "his sauce remoulade curdled."

But the small talk ended with the coffee. The ladies remained at the table; Ben invited us to join him in the Lincoln Sitting Room on the second floor. Travis, the Hannafords' suave butler, served coffee (I recognized the pot as part of the famed vermeil collection of a certain Mrs. Biddle) and then wheeled in a cart laden with cognacs and liqueurs.

"That's fine, Travis," Hannaford said. "We'll be here a while."

I detected a hardness in the chief's voice; I suspect Honey-Tonsils did also. Ben had settled into the gold-upholstered armchair. Stapp and Hopewell were on the rather uncomfortable rust-colored sofa. I sat a bit apart on one of the Lincoln Sitting Room's red side chairs.

"Gage, I need your help," Ben said.

"Yaaaas, you shall have it, sir."

"Oh, I'm not sure I will. You don't like the lump appropriation for the military. Or the urban program."

Old Honey-Tonsils' eyes bugged, gleamed. "Grave problems, grave problems, Mr. President."

"Such as?"

Senator Hopewell inhaled the aroma of Courvoisier. His eyes closed. "The mood of the people, sir. They are not, I fear, persuaded of the wisdom of your course."

"Then it is the job of elected officials to persuade them. People like you and me and Sid."

"Yaaaas." I could swear that the cottony tufts at his ears inflated. "But perhaps it is the people who are right. My mail, Mr. President . . ."

Hannaford's jaw twitched. "Don't be too sure about the polls or your mail, Gage. Lots of college kids and blacks and ordinary folks who do their own thinking don't bother writing to you any more. Not the way you've been spinning around."

You'd think the old charlatan would have been insulted. But Hopewell was insult-proof. He was also hard to budge; and as I had feared, we appeared to have lost him. "No sir, no sir," he intoned. "I cannot go against the advice of our military, not while the beast stalks such bastions of freedom as Nicaragua and Formosa, yaaaas."

It was a turndown, a flat turndown. Hopewell was being frank; I had to hand it to him. There'd be no help from our own Majority Leader. There was a heavy pause. I stared gloomily at the Thomas Kelly lithograph of Lincoln and his family, and thought of another President's travail. As I stared, I did not notice Senator Stapp take a small memo book from his blue blazer. (Assuredly not the little book in which he kept the names of his stable.)

"Gage," Swinging Sid asked, "do you know an outfit called McArdle Plastics?"

"Hmmm? Hanh?"

"There was a corporation called McArdle Plastics in Fond du Lac," the Swinger went on, "which last month got a ten million-dollar contract for component parts for the Archer ground-to-ground rocket. Defense Department procurement Order CV-198-A."

"Yaaaas, McArdle, yaaaas. Lovely family. Believe I knew the older McArdle."

"Your law firm certainly knows them," Sid said. "You see, my own law firm did a little digging, at the President's request, because one of our California clients, E & D Extruders were bidding for the Archer contract also. It seems that Merriman, Jacobs, Judd and LeGrange, back in Madison, got a half a million dollars for landing that contract."

Senator Hopewell opened his mouth—a beached mackerel. "Whaaah . . . I daresay this is uncalled for . . ."

"Oh hell, Gage," the President said. "This is just between old friends."

"Agh, agh, let me make it clear, my name no longer appears on the letterhead of my old law firm," Honey-Tonsils said.

"No, but you get part of the profits," Ben said.

"And on this McArdle deal," Sid went on, "my people came up with a check for fifteen thousand dollars made out to you, from the older McArdle, for services rendered."

"A campaign contribution," Hopewell chanted. His skin had turned the color and texture of a Tom turkey's wattles; his eyes rolled about the fleshy face as if seeking escape. "Yaaaas . . . a contribution."

Swinging Sid consulted his little book. "What about the twenty-five thousand from J. J. Mulrooney, Washington lobbyist for Dektatonic Systems, Inc.? Or a check for twelve thousand from Albon Blake, another well-known Washington fixer? How could you be so careless, Senator?"

I could see Hopewell was horrified with Stapp for stabbing him this way. Sid was no bargain himself. He'd played the Washington operator also—a favor here, a contract there—but never on the same scale as Hopewell, and with a bit more discretion.

"We are examining two recent decisions by the Federal Communications Commission," the President said, "in which your hand-picked appointee voted for licenses for two of your law firm's clients, in the face of evidence that neither of these licenses deserved their renewals. Old friend, you had extended conversations with all of the FCC commissioners, and in one case, threatened to have one man indicted for corrupt practices if he didn't vote the way you wanted him to."

"That man had a clear prejudice against my clients," Hopewell huffed. But he was shaken. "Mr. President this is unseemly. We are old colleagues. We are professionals. You and Sidney are not treating with me in a fair and honorable manner."

"But this is all for your own good, Gage," Senator Stapp said. "You see, the liberals are going to get after you when the debate starts on the President's program, and we don't want you to get hurt."

"The President can be a hard man," Gage said. "I wonder, though, I wonder, will the public accept these . . . distortions which my colleague Senator Stapp presents as facts? Perhaps if an attempt is made to blackguard me, it will redound to my credit, and to the everlasting shame of those who seek to destroy me, yaaaaas."

"We won't know till Sid's information is published, will we Gage?" the President asked. "You see, Senator, there have been rumors for years as to how corrupt you are, how your law firm has gotten fat off your Washington career. But nothing in black and white. Now we've got it. It would make interesting reading."

Honey-Tonsils seemed to sink four inches into the Lincoln Sitting Room sofa. His round gut rose as his behind dug deep into the upholstery. He said nothing for a while; the protruding eyes closed, the ruby nose twitched. "Well. Well. That it should come to this." He opened his eyes. "What is it the President wants of me?"

"Support." Ben snapped the word out.

Hopewell pushed his lips forward. "The President asks too much. I believe in my heart that the fifty per cent cut in defense money is a grave error."

Sid Stapp touched his colleague's arm. "But, dammit, Gage, changing your position is nothing new to you."

"Ah, but this cuts deep, yeah, very deep." Yes, he could see all those finder's fees, those ten and fifteen per cent commissions going up in smoke.

"All right, Gage," the President said, "then let me ask this of you."

"I am your servant, Mr. President."

"Stay neutral. Let me fight it out with you on the side lines. That way, none of your clients can blame you. They'll say how brave you were not to go along with the President. Sit this one out."

"Hmmm. Kowf. Hargh. Yaaaas . . ."

"This offer may be withdrawn at any moment," Senator Strapp said lightly. "Take it, Gage."

"I have heard Parente is preparing a series on senatorial connections with defense contractors," I said. "Not on anyone in particular—a general survey. He might just stumble across some of the material Senator Stapp's investigators did."

Honey-Tonsils beamed at the boss. "Neutral, I shall be. Mr. President, I shall refrain. I shall lay down sword and shield—at least on this matter. Yaaaas."

"Private party?" It was Rachel Hopewell's harsh midwestern tones. She poked her frizzy blue-rinsed head around the door. Behind her were Judy Stapp and Fern.

"Business is concluded, Miss Rachel," the President said, rising.

We all moved toward the corridor. "I am never in this hallowed house," Honey-Tonsils gasped, "that I am not inspirited by the grandeur of the republic and the men

310

who serve it. God grant them health, long life and wisdom beyond the conventional."

He could not have been too badly scorched; he could still summon up the organ chords.

Somewhat different treatment was required for the Speaker of the House. Early one morning, Congressman Emmett Brian O'Boyle was invited to the President's office for morning coffee.

Ben exchanged pleasantries with O'Boyle. He then stressed his urgent desire to get his mass military appropriation debated in the House Armed Services Committee and reported out favorably. The Speaker shook his head. Oh, he was having his troubles. Mr. Rumsford on Ways and Means was all for economies, but not at the expense of national security.

The President listened to the old man's breathy voice. In the midst of the rambling conversation the telephone buzzed. Ben picked it up. "Yes, Miss Watterson? He is on now? Fine, fine. And I am assured again that his English is excellent? Good."

Whose English? The Speaker's eyes closed. He seemed relieved that the President would be occupied on a call. Perhaps the meeting would be shortened. Old O'Boyle did not care for these confrontations. He was tired, terribly tired, and he hated fights.

"Good morning, Your Holiness," Ben said. "This is the President of the United States."

I almost fell out of my seat. The Speaker's filmy eyes blinked; his shaking hands rose halfway from his lap, and I thought he would make the sign of the cross or fall to his knees.

"How are you, sir?" Ben asked—warmth, sincerity, a deep interest in the Holy Father's health was evident in his voice. "Good, good. You've met with Professor Cohen. And you and he got along, I gather?"

My head spun. Hannaford had sneaked Seymour Harvey Cohen into the Vatican to get a papal blessing for the arms control talks. All I could think of was an old joke about the way Jewish visitors are supposed to greet the Pope: *"Good yontiff, Pontiff."* (Fred Goldstein explained it to me: "Good yontiff" is a Yiddish expression meaning "Happy holiday.")

I was bursting to grab an extension, but even someone

311

with the nerve of an Edward Deever does not listen in, uninvited, on phone conversations between Popes and Presidents.

"Professor Cohen is a brilliant man," the President went on. "I knew you'd speak his language. By the way, I thought your rulings on birth control, abortion and celibacy last month were courageous and beautifully stated. I'm glad the reaction to it has been so universally good."

Pope Clement, a progressive, had put the moral force of the Chair of Peter behind legalized abortion, where the life of the mother was threatened, or in cases of incest or rape, and he had sanctioned birth control, as well as marriage for priests. None of these reforms had sat too well with the older prelates, or the rigid laity, such as Speaker O'Boyle, but no move had been made to "Impeach Clement."

"Holy Father, an old friend of yours is sitting here in my office, and I'd like you to chat with him," Hannaford said. "He is the Speaker of our House of Representatives, Mr. Emmett Brian O'Boyle, who is a Knight of Malta, a Knight of St. Gregory, and a member of the Order of the Lily, one of the most eminent Roman Catholic laymen in our land. I believe you and he met at the United Nations last year, when you made that fine speech on aid to the poor nations of the world."

O'Boyle's face was the color of pizza dough. He understood clearly what Hannaford's game was.

"Here, use the President's phone, Mr. Speaker," Ben said magnanimously. I helped the old fellow to his feet.

"G-g-good morning, Holiness. Th-th-this is Congressman O'Boyle, and what an honor, yes, what an honor and privilege this is . . ."

Hannaford breathed deeply: he settled back in the high green leather swivel chair and watched Speaker O'Boyle, stuttering, mumbling, his lips pursed as if looking for a ring to kiss. Every now and then I caught a scrap of the Pope's voice issuant from the phone. *Arms control . . . survival of civilization . . . meet the Russians halfway . . . we view favorably your President's attitude . . .*

"Yes, yes, Holy Father, I agree . . . so kind of you, busy as you are, to call, to interest yourself . . ."

My son, this is not an American matter . . . world peace . . . lives of millions of good people . . . the great globe itself . . .

312

"Yes, I shall, Holy Father . . . ah, so good of you to think of me," the Speaker whispered. "I always remember dear Pius XII, when he was a cardinal and came to America, how well we got along . . ."

His Holiness concluded his conversation with O'Boyle. I think some Latin blessing was bestowed on the Speaker's frail head. The President got back on, and wished the Pontiff well on his tour of Catholic birth control centers in Africa.

"Emmett," Hannaford said, "I have never talked to a more reasonable man than your Pope."

"Yes, yes, Mr. President . . ."

"Professor Cohen says their meeting was a great success. Clement is one hundred per cent behind the arms talks. He will advocate total cessation of nuclear production and testing, and an end to all orbiting multiple warhead systems, or any other weapons of mass death."

"Oh, I'm glad, Mr. President. . . ."

"By golly, Emmett, with the Pope guiding you, I want you to show the way to the lost sheep of the House."

"Hmm . . . if you say . . . if you . . . I shall try, Mr. President." Silently, I cursed the seniority system.

"Emmett, whenever you talk to your people, Jack Hexter, and Bill Rumsford, and all the committee chairmen, and the leaders and the whips, bear in mind the wishes and hopes of your beloved Holy Father."

Oh, the scoundrel. I all but expected Ben Hannaford, one-fourth Kiowa Indian, bedrock American frontier Protestant, to make the sign of the cross in front of the befuddled old man.

Hannaford moved ahead. Matt Fixx and I spent long hours with Burke Boswell on the wording of the Mass Defense Appropriations Bill—S. 1098. (The S. signified its origination in the Senate; that job of belling the cat would fall to Senator Royce Henshaw of Montana, sufficiently close to the Establishment, respected, even though he was a college professor, a calm, intelligent man, slow to anger and quick to understand.)

Simultaneously, Secretary Murphy, Dalton Warfield, Secretary Gantry and other members of the Urban Task Force hammered out the wording and financial needs for the vast program for the cities. Again, we had good allies in the Senate—Maury Eisenberg, John Tyler Lord, Jack

Erlenmeyer—and a handful of friends in the House. A curious malaise had settled over the House; the liberal leaders seemed to have gone into hiding. I had the feeling that Representative Ruckett and his boys in COCCC had frightened them.

At times, in those perilous weeks, I wished that I could absorb some of Burke Boswell's breezy confidence. But I was distraught. By nature a worrier and a pessimist—I hide these aspects of character with my brisk manner—I read some foul literature that Lou Parente had sent me and concluded that there were truly no limits to the lunacies of some of our opponents.

IMPEACH HANNAFORD

The President has shown his true colors. He flirts with treason. He is dedicated to the annihilation of this republic, of putting us at the mercy of the Communists. How else can any patriot interpret his criminal attempts to cut down the military?

All of this is of a piece—part of the international Communist strategy that worked itself into high places during the Roosevelt administration in the 1930s, and has remained like a virus in the national blood stream. FDR forced America to fight World War II *on the wrong side,* thereby giving Communism a free path to world domination. The goal of the Communists has never been closer. Our retreat in Vietnam, the sellout of NATO, the machinations of the liberal-socialist cabal in the Vatican, the civil rights movement in America (which is nothing more than a mask for international Communism), all of these are parts of the same bloodthirsty conspiracy. And now the President has succumbed to it.

America can be saved in only one way: *Impeachment.*

This bit of literary grandeur came from the weekly newsletter, a four-sheeted rag called DOOR TO FREEDOM. It was an unsigned front page "editorial." The rest of the issue was given over to quotes from leaders in the military, publishing, the church, industry and labor unions, denouncing Hannaford's tripartite program.

"I know the man. I have known him a long time. He is

intelligent, courageous and at one time was a patriot. But something has happened to him in the White House. The left-liberals have reached him and are manipulating him. People like Seymour Harvey Cohen, and Burke Boswell, and Frederick Morris Goldstein are not to be trusted, yet Hannaford trusts them. The country must act, the people must be aroused."

And who had signed this gem? None other than Ben Hannaford's own nephew by marriage, Fern's brother's son, the multimillionaire oilman Miles J. Cudder!

There were other delicate bits: a crude hint that Hannaford was a homosexual—and here I came in for some publicity:

"Who is Edward Deever? Why is he around the White House so much? Is he more than just an aide, a confidante, a message-bearer for the President? Certain curious aspects of this relationship should be examined. Father-son? Brothers? Or something more sinister and debased? We have access to confidential information which we will release as soon as our lawyers advise us we are on sound ground."

On the back page of the newsletter I found this:

HOW HANNAFORD STOLE CALIFORNIA AND THE PRESIDENCY

Benjamin Bow Hannaford is a usurper. DOOR has irrefutable evidence that he stole California's 45 electoral votes last November. When the time is right, we shall present witnesses and testimony to the effect that Hannaford's agents bribed election officials in the south central area of the city of Los Angeles, rigging election returns to such an extent, that he was able to "carry" California by a few thousand votes over Mr. Smead Beldock. The falsification of voting returns was made possible through the connivance of another member of the left-liberal conspiracy, Representative Angel Lopez Garcia of Illinois, who ran with the revolutionary criminal, Kakamba Jones (a convicted extortionist), on the racist Black-and-Tan ticket. Garcia permitted his returns to be reduced, so as to supply Hannaford with a margin of victory ...

Were they bluffing? How much did they know? I did

not show the vituperative sheet to the boss. He had enough worries; I appointed myself a committee of one to follow the strategies of the paranoids.

Impeachment? Nonsense. This was an extreme act; an act threatened by nuts, outsiders, madmen. I took courage from the historian's assurance that such an act—the indictment of a President for *"treason, bribery, or other high crimes and misdemeanors"*—was only a "rusted blunderbuss that will probably never be taken in hand again." I dismissed from my mind any notion that there were people in the country, enough of them anyway, willing to remove the rust from the blunderbuss, or replace it with a shiny automatic carbine.

As the right railed against us, I looked leftward for support—and was horrified. Noting in the Washington *Post* that a major "new left" rally to unite forces and forge a new program was to be held in New York City, I asked Vangie to join me on a hegira to the city.

It was a good thing I had her along. When, on a warm May afternoon, we reached the Manhattan Center, where the rally was taking place, I found myself barred from entering by a bearded white boy in a yellow dashiki, green love beads and an Indian headband.

"Sorry, fruit," he told me rudely. "No capitalist press."

"I am not a reporter. I am a friend of man."

The youth looked at me balefully—astigmatism, acne, ideals. Ah, the self-deceiving child. He was fuel for General Upshaw's furnaces, grist for C. C. Pringle's mills.

Vangie dug in her leather purse and found a frayed ID card. "SDS charter member, Smith College chapter." She waved it at him. Then she found another. "Peace Corps faction."

He squinted at them. "Yeah. I guess so. What about him?"

"He's my husband."

We walked into the dismal auditorium, redolent of Lysol. The huge, ill-lit hall was about two-thirds filled. I noticed that the blacks had chosen to sit separately. They were by and large bearded, bespectacled, frizzy-haired, sullen. Oh Lord, I have tried to be patient and understanding. I have a generous heart, but don't they know that all they do is harden the iron will of Mr. and Mrs. America?

316

On stage, in front of portraits of Lenin, Mao, Che, Malcolm X, and Patrice Lumumba, sat the key figures, among them Kakamba Jones and Arvid Farbelman. The others, both on the platform and in the audience, were younger—beards, sports shirts, sandals and the odor of total rectitude.

"I think we must address ourselves to the Establishment's latest act of irrelevance, it's deceitful attempt to co-opt the peace movement," Farbelman was saying. "Hannaford is a fox, a sneaky fox, a killer with a smooth manner. We've got to abort his schemes to subvert the revolution!"

A tall Negro man wearing a bandolier stood up in the black section (how those people would have screamed if they'd been relegated to restricted sections of ball parks or movie houses!) and shouted: "You are part of it, honky! You eat their slops and kiss their feet!"

"I resent that, brother Mabonga," Farbelman called back. "I am a soul brother, one of you. I make my stand with Che and Malcolm and all the other brothers."

A derisive cackle arose from the black ranks. They had no use for Farbelman, and in a way, I was on their side.

"I say that the new left coalition represented here must go on record as opposing Hannaford's program. What does it mean to cut defense spending in half? Nothing. They'll find the money somewhere. We demand total, unilateral, complete disarmament! We must rally the unions—"

Unions! Where did a simpleton like Farbelman, self-proclaimed genius, get his notions? Let him tell it to the construction workers!

"—and the poor, and the black, and the Indians, and the young to bring Hannaford to his knees! Better the wolves of the extreme right, as Brother Malcolm X said, than the foxes of the liberals!"

There was applause for this; lots of overfed, smug young punks from Great Neck and Scarsdale, congratulating themselves on their radicalism.

"Why don't they give the President a chance?" Vangie asked me.

"That would be too easy," I said. "And make too much sense. You know, Evangeline, when we are young, we are led to believe that the left has all the answers. They don't.

317

Kids like these, for all their ideals, don't even know the right questions."

" . . . the domestic programs of the Administration offered by lackeys like Murphy and Gantry, Hannaford's stooges, are fakes, deceits, aimed at diverting the revolution! Radicals know that diversions are irrelevant and destructive, and they are to be fought and opposed, as tricks and traps, aimed at lulling the working classes into a sense of security . . ."

I yawned. Vangie joined me in a yawn. Farbelman was the Honey-Tonsils Hopewell of the left.

"And what about the alleged peace mission to Stockholm by Professor Cohen?" Farbelman shrilled. "We know all about Professor Cohen, a merchant of death, the man who designed, for government dollars and under the threats of FBI exposure, the deadly nose cone for the deadliest of our missiles! Some peace envoy! A mad inventor of murderous weapons! So, my fellow delegates, let us join forces—"

"Not with you, honky!" an Afro Avenger called out.

"Make your own protest, white boy!"

The commotion in the black ranks was considerable. I stood up, amid the beards and body odor, and realized that the smooth-skinned soft white children around me, were visibly frightened of their dark allies. Who could blame them? Even the sight of edible Mona Varnum, my black pearl, seated in the front rank of the shouting, cursing Negroes, did not offer me much in the way of comfort.

"I see Mona over there," Vangie said.

"The question is," I said, sitting down, "is she here as a tool of the capitalist press, spying on her black brothers, or is she functioning as an activist, the dark Vera Zasulich?"

"Or Dora Kaplan?"

"She shot Lenin, didn't she?"

"Yes. If it wasn't Maria Spiridonova. Or Angelica Balabanoff."

As I jested with Vangie, playing the game of old Bolshevik lady revolutionaries, I found myself lusting for Mona all over.

"But I love all of you," Farbelman was pleading. "Why doncha love me? I mean, deep down I'm black also!"

"Siddown, honky!"

"Back to your pawnshop, Goldberg!"

"Next time, do it in a synagogue."

Three fearsome-looking blacks were hustling Farbelman away from the microphone. He was no match for them. They came of sturdier stock; no soft hands and pot bellies. And even if he had been as fit as Maxie Rosenbloom in his prime (I use this example to show that Jews also can be tough), he had no will to resist.

"Sure, sure, brothers, whatever you say," the poet mumbled. "You fellows have to realize, I'm on your side."

Yes, they would all end up behind the same barbed wire if they kept at this mad charade. Never was I more convinced of the futility and weakness and aimlessness of their movement.

"To hell with Honky Hannaford!" Kakamba Jones screamed, waving his fly whisk. "To hell with his handkerchief-heads, Murphy and Warfield and those other mealy-mouthed Uncle Toms!"

"Uhuru!"

"That means freedom," Vangie explained. "In Swahili."

"Which," I said, "according to Dalton Warfield, is spoken only in East Africa and was developed by Arab slave traders. So it bears no relationship to these fellows."

"So what? It gives them identity."

Kakamba raged on: he bragged about the burning of Columbia—punishment for not turning over Low Memorial Library to the Black studies program and for providing a "genocidal" program anyway, which "lied about black history."

I glared at Vangie. "Your liberal guilt is showing. Stop making excuses for every act of lunacy and excess committed by these people. I can make more of a case for a Negro mugger in Washington, than I can for an educated man like Kakamba Jones and his followers. If they'd get over their self-hate feelings, and do what Hannaford wants them to do, they'd make it."

"And just what is that?"

"Learn to pad expense accounts. Fake overtime. Demand, demand, demand—but do it the American way, by conniving with other centers of power. Such as the President."

They were almost—not quite—but almost as dreadful as Lance Ruckett's crowd. I say *almost* because they—Jones and his followers—had genuine grievances. Ruckett only had a bellyful of hatred to sustain him. Yet they were equally destructive to progress. It was the old story—the extremes against the middle. What Kakamba Jones and Arvid Farbelman's extremists never learned was that it was a lopsided arrangement. They were a small vestigial organ; Ruckett was an invasive cancer, capable of devouring the body. If the extreme left grew a cell or two, nibbling away at the moderate center, the extreme right, in turn, could ingest an entire organ.

"Tell them, Kakamba!" Arvid Farbelman cried. "Tell them like it is!"

"Shut up, mother-f - - - - r," Jones grunted, over his shoulder. "When I wanna hear from white trash, I'll ask."

"He's right, he's right," Farbelman muttered to a mini-skirted white girl next to him on the stage—a millionaire dress manufacturer's daughter. "We're all guilty, and we all deserve his contempt."

"I say to hell with Hannaford and his Uncle Toms, to hell with his white boss's lying schemes. What is our President, but a lousy peckerwood with a rich wife? A damn oil-drillin', cheatin', lyin' faker. Why his rotten brothers in the Senate didn't even trust him, and he had to be censured. Hah! And now he's President."

"He stole it!" a black girl called.

"Yeah, robbed it!"

Why could they not see? Suppose Ben had worked a little of his rough magic to take California? Could they not understand what he had saved them from? Would Smead (Law and Order) Beldock or General Clyde (Nuke the Chink) Upshaw have been more to their liking?

"Let me say," Arvid Farbelman interrupted, rising and trying to reach the mike, his way barred by four blacks in robes, "that I support every word uttered by Brother Kakamba Jones."

Jones glared at him from the lectern. "Go sit down and count your pawn tickets, Goldberg."

"I don't care how much you insult me," the poet brayed. "I don't care. I love all of you. I confess my guilt for what White America has done to you."

"Yaaah!"

"Die, Goldberg, die."

"Fascist pig!"

"Landlord! Rent gouger!"

Behind the mangling lenses, Arvid Farbelman's eyes turned to a mushy gray paste. His beard trembled. "Okay, okay. I dig you, brothers. Like, I know your problems, and I want to rap with you. . . ."

He retreated; dark laughter rose in waves. I got up, nodded at Vangie and started down the aisle. I'd heard enough. These people—whatever they represented—would be of no help. In fact, they would be one of our greatest problems. They would succeed in convincing a lot of uncommitted, amiable Americans that everything that Lance Ruckett and Gabe Tutt and General Upshaw and C. C. Pringle said about Ben's liberal reforms, his social program, was true. My heart was weary.

In the rotunda I saw Mona walking toward us. The tape recorder slung around her good shoulder. She was sweating and looked harassed but more beautiful than ever.

"A little spying for your boss?" she asked.

"Yes. Frankly, Mona, I didn't learn anything I didn't know before. Your friends' impulse for self-destruction remains inviolate. You know Vangie Boswell, don't you?"

The girls nodded: black head, blond head. Ah, the glory of women. And what a pity, that I no longer had time or energy to pursue them in proper fashion.

"*Ha jambo, bwana,*" Vangie said. More Swahili. She'd been a star in the Peace Corps, I was certain.

A mocking smile lit Mona's mouth. "Isn't that charming. Defense Secretary's daughter speaks Swahili. Yeah, I recall. You were a big Peace Corps cat. Another liberal fake."

Vangie was not offended. "I think you're out of sorts, Mona, because my Swahili is better than yours."

Her Swahili maybe; but not her body.

"Give me a little White House gossip," Mona said. "I'm on the favored reporters list, am I not, Mr. Deever?"

Vangie looked archly at me. She suspected, she suspected.

"Well . . . we are moving into the committees next week. We feel pretty bullish about the Senate, less so about the House. Professor Cohen had a good visit with Pope Clement. He's meeting again with Gromyko tomorrow, and the Russian press is enthusiastic. Homer Murphy thinks that in ten years we can clean out every slum in America, by applying the funds saved from suspension of the MOMSER and other missile and delivery systems. That's a year under his previous estimate."

"Oh, to hell with all that," Mona said. "I want some real news."

"Mrs. Hannaford is getting an award from the NAACP," Vangie offered, with a hint of malice.

"Nowhere. Nothing. She doesn't turn me on. Look, Deever, you know what I'm hinting at."

"I haven't any idea."

"There's a report your esteemed Vice-President is about to resign and work against Hannaford as a private citizen."

I tried to hide my surprise. Verne Latour Sparrier? Our jaycee of Veep? That smooth, preacher-ish young man, who always sensed the main chance, a man who kept his nose clean and his guard up?

"Where did you hear that?"

"It's around. Sparrier, folks say, has had it with your boss and won't back the cut in defense spending. The big people in California—industry and labor—and all the patriots are on his back to step down and start an anti-Hannaford crusade. To join Ruckett and his crowd."

"No truth to it." I tried to control my voice. But it quavered. It may sound odd that a reporter would know these things, when I, the president's aide, had no notion of such a dire event. But good reporters often know more than we do.

"I got it from some brother in Sacramento," Mona said. "Governor Fancourt is close to your Vice-President. The brothers penned up in the ghetto have good sources."

"I'm in the embarrassing position of having nothing to tell you about this. In fact, Mona, I'd appreciate your informing me of anything you learn."

"You sound like you know it's the truth."

"No, no. Mr. Sparrier disagrees with Mr. Hannaford. But his loyalty to him is unquestioned."

Mona sneered at us: a charming sneer. We could all be dismissed—Vangie, me, Sparrier, Hannaford, Governor Fancourt. The meeting appeared to be over. In a swirl and flash of red, yellow and purple robes, leopard skins and yarmulkas, Kakamba Jones and his retinue surged from the auditorium, accompanied by drums.

Kakamba noticed me—pale, white, gray-suited, short-haired, an Establishment functionary.

"Ah, Deever," he cried. The fly whisk was pointed to the space between my eyes. "Deever, I accuse you of the murder last week of Hawthorne Loomis."

"Innocent," I replied. "He was shot by the Sacramento police. And besides, I haven't been in California in two years."

My candor seemed to take him aback. Most whites responded by admitting their collective guilt, by mumbling their apologies. I was deadly sorry for young Loomis, but wallowing in guilt never helped anyone. I steered Vangie toward the street. Behind us the drums thundered. I didn't like their message.

I reported to the President on the ugly tone of the new left meeting in New York and on Mona Varnum's rumor about Vice-President Sparrier.

The attitude of the militant blacks bothered him a good deal more than the story about Sparrier. "Warfield and Murphy and our other friends have got to work overtime, is what it boils down to," he said.

"But their programs are running out of money."

"We'll find it."

"President Kretz cut them to the bone. We've been scrimping and scraping. The ghetto communes are all but shut down. There hasn't been a single low-cost housing unit built with federal funds in seven months. Those junior colleges in the urban centers we wanted to finance—the states aren't interested. They can't come close to getting the counterpart funds."

Hannaford walked about the oval office. "We'll get it. We'll have to get it. Boswell will take Armed Services on tomorrow. He's got new charts, new figures—right out of the generals' mouths. If we can win there, we'll rush the appropriations bills into the House. Pope Clement is about to give our beloved Speaker another honor—Order of the Unicorn, or something. If we can get the money flowing where it belongs, we'll make it."

"And you're not concerned about these reports about Sparrier?"

Ben paused at the globe and spun it. A mahogany table with magazines and newspapers on it stood at its right. Aimlessly, he glanced at the headline in the Washington *Post*.

OPPOSITION TO PRESIDENT'S PROGRAM MOUNTS: HOUSE LEADERS WARY OF DEFENSE CUTS, URBAN PROGRAM

He flipped it over and looked at the Los Angeles *Times*.

SACRAMENTO GHETTO REMAINS BESIEGED: GOVERNOR REFUSES AMNESTY TO LEADERS

"I knew about that business with the Veep," he said casually.

I tried to talk; the words refused to come forth. "You ... you ... knew? He ... he ... is actually considering resigning?"

"Miss Varnum's story is half true. Fancourt out there, who stands well to our Veep's right, wanted him to quit, to head up a national movement to stop me cold. Sparrier is too shrewd to buy that. I had a little chat with him about it t'other day."

"You *what?*"

"I invited Mr. Sparrier up to the Lincoln Sitting Room, and just the two of us talked. I had the dope on Fancourt, and I praised Mr. Sparrier for his good judgment in turning down the Governor of California. Of course, he hadn't quite turned him down, but after I spoke to him, he made a phone call to Sacramento."

"You made a believer of him?"

"Edward, I can't say I blame the Veep for listening to the siren song. God knows I don't represent any power base right now. Even old Harry Truman, at his most unpopular, or poor Lyndon, when things got sticky, had *some* support. I'll be damned if I can locate ours any more. Sparrier knows this. He knows he's got credit with an awful lot of plain folks. He's one of them. But he also knows it's bad medicine to run out on an incumbent President."

"You put it mildly."

"You got to understand Mr. Sparrier. He is a poor boy. He made it the hard way. So did I. But I made mine in industry. By building things you could see—pipelines and airfields and shopping centers. Young Sparrier's dealt in wind all his life. Ran the ball for the big fruit growers. Got paid off by the banks and insurance companies. His itty-bitty law firm had some peculiar clients. The man is all ambition, no substance. And any man who is all ambition, can be handled."

"How did you handle him, sir?" I was sweating.

"I pointed out that I might not survive this ordeal. I was frank with the man. Look, Verne, I said, the way things are shaping up, I may get killed. One fellow tried already but had lousy aim. The next may succeed. And once you're in, you have no worries. They only kill people who want to help blacks in this country. Conservatives are bulletproof. I pointed out I might even have a heart attack. I promised him that if that happened and I'm in the oxygen tent, he'd be allowed to visit me regularly— but no Halloween masks, ghost stories or hollering 'boo!' "

"You didn't."

"Hell I didn't. When I was through with Sparrier, I had him on my side."

"There's an old song Cab Calloway used to sing, Mr. President. 'I'll Be Glad When You're Dead You Rascal You.' I have a feeling Sparrier's secretary is looking for that record this minute."

Hannaford was gleeful. There was a good deal of rascality in the boss, and I respected him for it.

"Yes, he understood that the shortest road to the presidency was through that little office we gave him down the hall," Ben said. "And that fiddling around with nut coalitions and barn-burners never did a man any good. Leastwise if he wanted to be President someday."

"Up to now that's been true, sir. We may be changing."

"I doubt it," the President said.

"There's a lion in the streets, Mr. President. And he's right here in Washington."

"Edward, you astound me. That's from Proverbs."

"I don't care where it's from. Sparrier may change his mind when he studies the nature of our opposition. It's a mass movement, not a nut coalition, as you put it."

Hannaford sat down in his green leather chair. He moved lightly, easily, for a broadly built man in his late fifties. "Maybe, Edward, but lions die also. Try Ecclesiastes."

"Sir?"

" 'A living dog is better than a dead lion.' "

"These lions may prove hard to kill, Mr. President."

"Cheer up, son. You look sorrowful."

"I am. Not that my worries are of any account."

"Well, there's always solace in the Good Book. 'Sorrow is better than laughter, for by the sadness of the countenance is the heart made better.'"

My heart was feeling no better, for all of the boss's Scripture. I even had the sensation he was summoning up those hoary admonitions to buoy his own doubts about what the future held for us.

Without any buzzing from Cleo's outer office, the door burst open and a whey-faced Matt Fixx barged in. Literally, he was shaking from head to toe.

"Mr. President . . ." His eyes bugged, his voice strangled.

"What is it, Matthew?"

"Mr. Ruckett . . . Mr. Ruckett . . . says his group in the House just voted unanimously to . . . to . . ."

"What the hell, Matthew?" Ben asked. "Settle down."

" . . . start impeachment proceedings against you, unless you withdraw the Mass Appropriations Bill . . . said they'd get the votes . . . the votes . . ."

President Hannaford stood up. "Looks like we got us a real fight, boys," he said.

Fred Goldstein burst in. "Everyone wants a statement, sir. Ruckett raised the roof with this one. Do you want anything issued from here?"

The President shook his head calmly. "No. Let Mr. Ruckett and his friends have their innings. People like him never learn their lesson."

The three of us, utterly devoted to this tough, good-hearted man, stood in shocked silence.

"We'll let Congressman Ruckett stew awhile. 'He that diggeth a pit shall fall into it, and whoso breaketh an hedge, a serpent shall bite him.'"

Ah, the hard confidence of the man. I was made of less stern stuff. I saw the pit clearly, and I wondered if we would, in fact, have the power and the guile to shove Lance Ruckett and the dark forces that backed him into the trap he was digging.

We talked no more about it. Ben ordered Goldstein to get the full transcript of Representative Ruckett's remarks. They had been made almost casually, at one of his celebrated "prayer breakfasts." Matt Fixx was despatched to Speaker O'Boyle's office to get a reading on the status of COCCC as a force in the House. I was detained.

"Edward, Mr. Parente might be useful at this juncture. We shall have to learn all about Congressman Ruckett. Perhaps more than we really want to know."

I nodded, gulped back my fears and headed for my office. Was it my imagination, or had Markland, the head of the secret service detail, *doubled* the men on duty in the corridors?

"Mr. President," Larry Hosmer of United Press led off, "Mr. Ruckett keeps saying he'll ask the House to impeach you, if you persist in trying to cut the defense budget in half, and continue to work for arms controls with the Russians."

"It's his privilege to try," Ben said.

We were in the large television room used for press conferences in the basement of the Executive Office Building. The boss did not want to respond to questions about Ruckett's rash threat, but Goldstein and I advised him that it would be bad policy to duck them.

"What do you think his chances of success are?" Hosmer persisted.

"Mr. Hosmer, I make it a practice never to comment on my own personal tribulations. You know what the fellow said who was being rid out of town on a rail: 'If it wasn't for the honor of it, I'd just as soon walk.' "

He got a small laugh with this; not much, but a laugh.

"Mr. Ruckett claims all eighty-seven members of his Caucus will vote for impeachment."

"He needs a majority in the House, as you fellows know. He's about 131 votes short. Can't we get to some constructive questions? Doesn't any of you want to know the details of the Education Bill? Seems to me that Secretary Murphy couldn't get much of a turnout to his last briefing. Don't you care about the billion dollars we will ask for two-year community colleges? Or the billion to extend ghetto communes?"

There was a hiatus; the reporters looked bored. A good bunch, the Washington press corps, but you could not rouse them with such matters.

"Those programs won't get very far, Mr. President, according to your own backers," Whit Krass of the *Post* said, "if you can't get Congress to reduce the Pentagon's funds. Do you agree?"

"I do. That's why Mr. Boswell will argue for a single

blanket appropriation for defense. The evidence we have brought to light on wastage, duplication and mismanagement should work in our favor."

Harry Kavoojian of the Hearst papers was on his feet. "Mr. President, Senator Tutt says that for sixty billion dollars, the Pentagon couldn't defend the state of Alabama. How do you hope to reconcile his views with yours?"

"Persuasion, Mr. Kavoojian. Senator Tutt may be right. After all, he's arranged to give his beautiful state every imaginable kind of military establishment known to man. Might simplify matters if we gave him his own separate defense budget, and let the other forty-nine states depend on my judgment."

There was a titter of laughter. Mona Varnum got up. I must say it was a relief to see her amid the drab ranks of the Washington press corps. We—I say *we*, since I once covered Washington as a newsman—run to rumpled gray suits, clip-on bow ties, bald heads, wash-and-wear shirts and a collective air of disgust. Mona was like a black swan, a hothouse orchid.

"The new left convention in New York has rejected your program, Mr. President," Mona said. "Can you tell us why?"

"Miss Varnum, that is a cause for wonder and concern. To be candid, I don't regard them as new, left or representative of black people, young people, radical people or anything but a fringe that can only make things worse. Talk to Mr. Warfield if you want to know how the black people of America feel about our program."

A man from a Chicago paper asked, "Mr. President, Mr. Bustard said yesterday that the cutback in military production you propose will cause havoc in labor ranks. He says no amount of nonmilitary industrial work can possibly absorb the men who will be thrown out of jobs."

"Mr. Bustard has a point," the President said. "I plead for patience. There will be a period of adjustment. There always is. But I would like every good union member in America, every loyal workman on the assembly line to think less of himself at this moment, than of his children."

"Ruckett was divorced three years ago," Parente said to me, as he tasted his deviled crab and indicated it was delicious.

We were in Hogate's restaurant on the Maine Avenue waterfront. The food is superb, and I have always liked the plain atmosphere. (It was once an iron foundry, later an airplane factory.) But I had little appetite. Not even the luscious broiled swordfish in front of me tempted me.

"That's no help," I said.

"I dunno," Parente said. "She vanished after the divorce. She sued him. Details unclear. Augie is working on it."

"What else?"

The columnist wolfed his fried oysters, stabbed at the coleslaw, washed it all down with Heineken's. "Ruckett's the old story. An outsider who wants to be inside. It's a class war we got on our hands. Ruckett's mother died when he was five. Old man ran a dry-goods store in Mitchell, went broke, tried farming, went broke, ended up managing a Woolworth's in Rapid City. Young Lance was brought up by relatives. Worked his way through South Dakota State and Law School. Small real estate business. State House. Friends with the rich farmers and the court-house crowd."

"A typical American story," I said.

"Yeah," Parente said. He scowled at some notes on yellow copy paper. "Some time during his first campaign for Congress he started taking money from DOOR. He met Huckerby, but they kept it quiet. They started that business of calling up voters and saying, 'Did you know that Herman Lundquist is a Communist?' and hanging up."

"Lundquist, I take it, was his opponent?"

"Liberal type. Old Scandinavian farmer-laborite. He didn't know what hit him. By the time he figured out what Ruckett's telephone brigade was up to, he was licked. You know, the defense never catches up with the accusations."

"That was eight years ago. Ruckett was a kid."

"He's learned a lot." Parente drained his beer. "The oil crowd down in Texas and Oklahoma loves him. A regular speaker at their conventions. He hustles a little also."

"Hustles?"

"Not really a crook," Lou said. "We'd never hang him on his little deals. But it's crummy stuff. Two years ago, the House Un-American Affairs Committee, on which young Lance was serving, was questioning Mrs. Martha Kalsheim, a rich widow who had given some dough to

329

student groups. Innocent and dumb. She was a registered Republican. Anyway, Lance got close to her and dropped hints as to how he might get the committee to go easy if she threw a little real estate business his way. She owned a part of Long Island."

"I don't believe it."

"Augie got the letters on it. Funny thing, Lance never denied it. He claimed Mrs. Kalsheim became a good friend and didn't mind his suggestions. He sees no conflict between his patriotism and the little extras he can earn out of it."

"Nothing you've told me sounds usable," I said wearily. "This man is rounding up signatures to impeach the President of the United States. He claims he has eighty-seven men in the House of Representatives who will vote yea. We can't hit back with stuff like this."

Parente ate his Nesselrode pie with zest. "No. What's lousy is we can't even hit him where he deserves to get hit—those nuts he associates with. They've earned a certain respectability. So what if he meets in hotel rooms with Pringle and Upshaw?"

"And Huckerby?"

Lou nodded. "How about those columns I wanna write on that meeting?"

"Whenever you want to release them. And the photographs."

Parente rubbed his chin. "Photographs. That seems to be one of Congressman Ruckett's hobbies."

"Hobbies?"

"My buddy Lieutenant Sheinblum, vice squad. He keeps track of a ten-room apartment off Dupont Circle which belongs to the Nicaraguan ambassador. Made available to friendly influential Washington types. Like Lance Ruckett."

"Ah . . . ?"

"The ambassador supplies the bed, the linens, the drinks. But you got to bring your own girl."

"So?"

"Sheinblum bugged the room. Lance baby's voice turned up. Crazy recording. Sounded like he was taking Polaroid photographs with his girl. Lance Ruckett in action."

"Oh, for God's sake, Lou, that's no crime."

"I didn't say it was. Who are we to deny a man his jollies?"

"I agree," I said.

"I listened to those tapes, and they're wild. He likes to screw with his clothes on. The girl too. He takes pictures as they go along, one for every stage of dress and undress. Sort of a series. I told Sheinblum to keep the bug in the room."

"And those Polaroids? Can they be used?"

Parente frowned and lit a cheap cigar. The flame illumined the bumps and ridges on his homely face. "Nah, forget it. There are limits. He knows you couldn't publish that stuff. We should be able to get him for the political rat that he is, not for the way he humps."

I sighed. The waiter looked sadly at my plate. "The swordfish wasn't to your liking, sir?"

"No, it was excellent. I'm just not hungry."

"The manager will be happy to get you something else. No charge."

"No, thank you." I paid the check. Parente and I walked out into the mild spring air. The sailboats anchored along the waterfront in the Washington channel suggested freedom, grace, a surcease from the dirty business in which we sometimes had to immerse ourselves.

"What do you think, Lou?" I asked.

"Let's sit tight. I'll spring the columns. Let Ruckett explain why he goes to meetings with a prick like Merton Huckerby."

"And then?"

Parente frowned. I was glad he was on our side. There were times when you needed roughnecks. Gentlemanliness was a much-admired trait in Washington, but it didn't make for winners. I liked the way that professor—Mr. Rossiter, I believe—listed *cunning* as a trait he felt necessary in a President.

"This business of Ruckett's ex-wife," Lou said. "I think it has possibilities."

We strolled along the embankment. "Why does Baldini do this?" I asked.

"Money. I pay him."

"You couldn't pay him enough. Is he really your cousin?"

"Distant."

"I hope he doesn't get hurt."

"Augie can handle himself. Anyway, say a prayer tonight. Not for him. For you and your boss."

We paused as two graceful sailboats drifted by. "You think Hannaford's in trouble?"

"I've thought so since election day. Don't make any bets against Ruckett and his crowd in the House. They smell bad, but they have clout. And money. And, for maybe the first time in fifty years, they got a mass issue—two. Jobs and boogies."

"You sound as if you've lost faith," I said.

"I never had a hell of a lot."

We turned to our cars and left; there seemed little else to say.

I sat with Vangie in my office, and watched her father play a return engagement with the Senate Armed Services Committee. It was nothing short of a miracle that we'd gotten Senator Tutt to bring the bill up altogether. I think Gabe was so convinced that the measure had no chance, and would be laughed out of existence, that he permitted Senator Hopewell (who didn't like the bill either) to talk him into hurrying the hearings along. Honey-Tonsils had gotten religion: so long as Sid Stapp was sitting on those facts and figures about payoffs he'd been getting in Wisconsin, he'd be amenable.

"Now Ah've read thisyeah bill," Senator Tutt said smoothly, "and Ah say hit is an insult, a joke, somethin' that, with all due respect to the President, he don't take very seriously hisse'f."

"I beg to differ, Senator Tutt," Boswell boomed, in that locker room bellow. "The President is behind the slice in military spending one hundred per cent. You'll recall those examples of bribery, incompetence, lying and duplication I brought up last month. That convinced him. That and the way the Russians seem ready to cool off relations with us."

"I quite agree," Senator Henshaw said. "I like the measure."

"Ah do not," Senator Tutt said. "Ah can tell y'all the Joint Chiefs don't lak it one itty-bit. We lost a good Chairman in General Nagel because of this rash move by the Administration, and we ain't gonna find us a military man willin' to serve if this sort of business continues. Who is gonna protect us? Who will be our sword and shield?"

"Mr. Chairman," Boswell thundered, "I can tell you I have had long conversations with the Joint Chiefs and they are beginning to see things our way. We are more than sufficient in atomic arms. There's no place else to go. I don't mean to disparage General Nagel, a great soldier, a hero, a gentleman and a personal friend—"

"Here comes the meat ax," Vangie said. "Beware of my father when he starts complimenting you."

"—but I asked him if the Iron Ball, the MOMSER system would protect us from the Russians and the Chinese. He didn't know for sure. I asked him if they were going to send up Manned Orbiting Multiple Satellite Entry Relays also. He didn't know. I asked him if our current crop of underground missiles, manned bombers, submarines and miscellaneous missiles, could defend us. He didn't know. If he didn't know all these things, who does? I don't blame him for resigning."

"You make a good point," Senator Henshaw said.

"It's time to de-escalate, gentlemen," Boswell said. "We've gone as far as we can in terms of potential destruction. The Russians know it. The Chinese will know it soon enough."

"Commonists never change!" Gabe Tutt cried. "Y'all an intelligent man, Mistah Secketary. Y'all know that!"

"I don't like their politics. I hate their economics. They've made lots of trouble. Once, I suppose they thought they could take everything over, but that's Christmas past. Stalin died in 1954, Mr. Chairman, and nothing's been quite the same."

"Give us some evidence of that, Mr. Secretary," Henshaw said. I noticed that Honey-Tonsils, normally a star of these proceedings, had shut up, crawled into his shell. Neutral, neutral.

"Well, Mr. Chairman," Boswell said loudly—his voice was getting hoarse and his face beet red, and he needed a belt. "I saw a remarkable film the other day of a border clash between the Russians and the Chinese on the Amur River. The CIA made it available to the Joint Chiefs and the National Security Council, after purchasing it from NBC, which bought it for a few hundred dollars in Hong Kong—"

"Commonist film?" Gabe asked.

"Why of course, Mr. Chairman. We have to know what

333

the other fellow, or the sworn enemy, as he is sometimes called, is doing."

"Whut was on thisyeah commonist film?"

"The film showed a clash between Soviet border units in tanks, pushing back a group of Chinese militia—peasants and fishermen armed with hoes, clubs and poles. It was truly amazing. These armored vehicles could have mowed the Chinese down like stalks of wheat with their machine guns and cannon. But they just rode up and down, and the Chinese beat at the sides with poles and clubs and chanted slogans from Lin Piao. It was an instructive scene—the two greatest powers in Asia, belaboring one another with clubs. I have a feeling that's the way people want to settle problems and fight wars. On a small scale. Nobody wants to toss an atom bomb into the men's room of the Kremlin, as your former colleague, a Mr. Goldwater said some years back."

"Mr. Secretary," Senator Urban said in his indistinct voice, "what has all this got to do with the President's proposal that we pass a mass military appropriations bill half as big as the amount recommended by the previous Administration?"

"Simply this, Senator Urban. Here are the two greatest powers in Asia, the Chinese, those one billion fanatical blue ants we keep hearing about, and the Russians with the greatest nuclear arsenal in the world next to ours, and what do they do?"

"I am missing the point," Urban insisted.

"The point is that big nations as well as little people don't want to get blown up. The world wants restraint. That is why we feel secure in reducing arms expenditures at this juncture."

One of our troubles was, there was too much justice on our side. We had too much evidence. The opposition, having no palpable arguments against us, would fabricate, fuss and fudge. And as I had long known, one can get very far in Washington with such techniques.

That night I dined with Homer Murphy and his wife, Ava, in their small apartment on Adams Mill Road. I always enjoyed being with the Murphys. They were among the few black people I knew well, and knowing them well, they never seemed to be black at all. This is not condescension on my part, or a sign that I dislike Negroes.

334

Far from it. It is the simple observation that as we get to know one another, pigment fades and becomes trivial.

The walls of Homer's study, where we sat before dinner sipping beer and watching the TV news, were covered with photographs, art work, citations and prizes reflecting the HEW Secretary's formidable athletic career—All-American at Maryland State, National League Rookie of the Year, five years All-League line-backer, six years as defensive captain of the Washington Redskins.

" 'To the greatest line-backer I ever saw,' " I read, " 'Smead Beldock, Vice-President.' "

"The Veep loved me, especially when I wasn't marching."

"I'm stunned the way we Americans compartmentalize," I said. "We worship a Willie Mays or a Walt Frazier, but are monuments of indifference or worse toward the ordinary black man."

"Celebrity culture," Ava said. "You famous, you okay." Ava mimed the accent. She was tall, black and wore her hair in a neat bob.

". . . gave Secretary Murphy a rough time this afternoon," one of NBC's Washington men was saying. "The committee members wanted to know where the money would come from for the Administration's program. Even if it was available, Congressman Stradella of Pennsylvania asked, would it do any good? Mr. Stradella introduced statistics and photographs purporting to show that federally-financed low-cost housing projects in his state have become slums, because, as he charged, the people who live in them refuse to keep them clean. . . . "

At dinner Murphy grew gloomier. He toyed with his sirloin steak and pushed away the baked potato. I started to feel sorry for him.

"No appetite, hon'?" Ava asked.

"Congress done kilt hit," the Secretary of HEW said.

"Sorry about that. Maybe soul food would help." She cleared the table and walked into the kitchen. They lived modestly. They were careful with the money Homer had earned as an athlete, putting it all into annuities, saving for their boys' education.

"Soul food, hell," Murphy grumbled. "That's an excuse for lousy meat, greasy vegetables, and too much starch. I'm a steak eater."

"At the moment, Homer, you are less an eater, than being eaten."

"I know. It's not the difficulties we got with Congress that's hurtin', it's what's happening to the projects underway now."

"I gathered that." I told him about my visit to Dalton Warfield's Ghetto Commune at Potomac Oaks, and the despair he felt at being forced to close down the program.

The phone rang. Ava answered it, then called from the kitchen. "Hon', it's for you. Dalton. He says one of his IT kids in Brooklyn is in trouble . . . "

Murphy got up from the table, sighing. Amazing, how lightly and easily he moved for a man weighing 265 pounds. "What the hell is eating Dalton, calling me about something like that?" he asked sorrowfully.

"He killed somebody . . . a fireman . . . "

I stared, disconsolate, at the cherry pie that Ava Murphy placed in front of me, recalling a black militant's statement some years ago, that "violence was just as American as cherry pie."

Mrs. Murphy and I looked dully at one another. In the kitchen I could hear the Secretary's voice grow louder and more impassioned. "Dumb son of a bitch . . . that's all we need. We're dead, Dalton . . . "

The day the Industrial Training Program closed in New York for lack of funds, President Hannaford huddled with the Treasury Secretary, Mrs. McNally, Burke Boswell and Homer Murphy.

"Murphy says he needs two hundred million dollars to keep IT and the communes going for the rest of the year," he boss said. "That isn't much."

"It isn't there, Mr. President," Meg McNally said. "It's gone. The well's run dry."

Hannaford looked into the rose garden. Some early blooming tulips brightened the green lawns with splashes of red and yellow. Above them the pink-white blossoms of the White House magnolias formed a feathery pastel arch.

"Isn't there any emergency money we can lay our hands on?" he asked. "Enough to keep the job training program and the communes, at least, operating?"

"I'm afraid not, Mr. President," Murphy said. "We have been switching allocations around since we took office. It's a good thing we have an old friend of yours in the General Accounting Office."

Burke Boswell crossed his stiltlike legs; he was slumped deep in an armchair, and he was stroking his booze-reddened beak. "Too bad this isn't a defense deal," he said. "We always seem to have a contingency fund full of money."

"Said what, Burke?" the President asked.

"Congress keeps filling it up. House appropriations votes every quarter to replenish it. You know, it's sort of a petty cash box. We keep it full for things like getting troops off to some island in a hurry, or to help contractors meet deadlines, or anything that the Secretary of Defense and Joint Chiefs feel needs fast money."

I could see Hannaford's face assume that hard, calculating look that foreshadowed some Hannafordian bit of skulduggery. "Petty cash, Burke?"

"I'd call it that, Mr. President."

"How much petty cash?" Oh, the man understood dollars. How he understood them!

"I can't be sure. There's usually 400 or 450 million dollars in it. Some of it was sneaked into R & D on the MOMSER by my predecessor, without any appropriation for the Iron Ball having been voted. It created a hell of a stink in Congress. It's supposed to be used only in emergency situations."

"Yeah, emergencies . . . " The President was gazing pensively into the rose garden again. "Seem to recall the Pentagon pulled that stunt with ABM way back. Found the money to start the research long before it was approved."

"That doesn't help Industrial Training," Murphy said.

"Now, let's see," Hannaford said, turning slowly in the high-backed green chair. "Let us apply ourselves to this. Does the law setting up IT specify what trades these lads are to learn?"

"No, sir," Murphy said. "Industrial training, that's it."

"Hmmmm . . ." Schemer, schemer. I could see the discs spinning, the gears meshing, the levers operating.

"Now, gentlemen, and Meg, as of today, we are going to issue an executive order, that all young men trained under IT, and hell, let's include the kids in communes, are being trained, educated, prepared, to work in defense industries."

"Oh, come on, Mr. President," Murphy protested.

"It won't work, Mr. President," Meg McNally said.

"Sure it will," the boss said. "Easy as skinning a rabbit. Burke will send me a memo stating that the future of our defense industries is very bleak because of a projected shortage of trained manpower. You know how those projections are worded. By 1985 the Russians will have a three-to-one lead over us in spot welders, paint sprayers and electricians. Point out, Burke, that our survival as a nation is at stake unless we can start now, *today,* training a new generation of technicians to build and maintain our missiles. . . . "

It was ingenious; crafty; essentially Hannaford. He almost had me believing it would work. Boswell, as resourceful as the President, leaped in with both of his size fifteen feet. "Say, that's one splendid idea, Mr. President. May I suggest we could get the funds to keep Homer's junior colleges alive, if I point out the defense industry's crying need for public relations men, also."

"No, not yet Burke," Hannaford said quietly. "That's your *second* memo."

It was done modestly, with no fanfare. Secretary Boswell's memorandum about the projected manpower needs of the defense complex barely rated page thirty-two in the Washington *Post.* It did not make the evening newscasts. When, a day later, the President, acting on Boswell's cry for help, to keep the engines of war functioning twenty years hence, released the first fifty million dollars from the Pentagon's "contingency" fund, there was not the slightest fuss raised in Congress. It all was done so smoothly, and with such unarguable logic (who could argue against investing a few millions in training future defense workers?), that it attracted no attention.

At a meeting of the National Security Council, in the cabinet room, a few days after Hannaford had begun channeling Pentagon funds into ghetto education programs, I noticed that Boswell looked god-awful. His normally beet-root face was the hue of creamed chipped beef, and he seemed to bend at the middle. After the meeting—memorable in that Vice-President Sparrier voiced warnings to the boss about discontent at the Pentagon over the contingency fund—I stopped the Defense Secretary at the door and asked him if he felt all right.

"Little too much of the giant killer last night, Edward. Me and a couple of fellers were rassling at the Army and Navy Club." Wincing, he gulped air, in a grimace suggesting evil doings within his bourbon-coated viscera. I suppose there were limits for even a sponge like Burke Boswell. Then he loped away, all six foot eight of him, to a meeting with the House Armed Services Committee.

"What's with your old man?" I asked Vangie, as I met her in the Cross Hall, on my way to Ben's hideaway in the Lincoln Sitting Room.

"I give up, what's with Daddy?" Vangie asked.

"He looks like death warmed over. I never believed that he was a man susceptible to hang-overs."

Evangeline shrugged. She was carrying an armload of books for Fern. I could read one title: *The Negro in the American Revolution.* "Search me. All I know is he had dinner at the Army and Navy Club."

"That in itself wouldn't make him look so shaky."

"Maybe he watched the 'Today' show this morning. They had films of the big Impeach Hannaford Rally in Indianapolis. Ten thousand people and speeches by Mr. Ruckett and General Upshaw."

"That wouldn't disturb your father," I said. "He laughs at people like Ruckett. Anyway, we're off and winging on Hannaford's latest swindle in the national interest. Did Ruckett mention the diversion of funds last night?"

"Not as I recall. Upshaw and Nagel did, according to the *Times.*"

After reading The New York *Times* and the Washington *Post* on the Impeach Hannaford Rally, and checking the clever items in the "Impeach Hannaford Kit" sent me by Lou Parente, with an accompanying note, I began to sweat a little. The kit contained posters, buttons, bumper stickers, and several leaflets. Among these latter was one entitled *What Is To Be Done?* the old war cry of the anarchists in nineteenth-century Russia. It detailed the *modus operandi* for impeaching, trying and ousting a President. It was scholarly, logical, calm, written in legal language, and had been compiled by "The National Committee to Save America." Its members included Congressman Ruckett, Ben's oilman brother-in-law, Miles J. Cudder, publisher Cosmo Carl Pringle, and a half dozen retired military men, among them, Generals Upshaw and Nagel.

Military men. What the devil had Boswell been up to at the Army and Navy Club that had left him with an all-time record hang-over? I recalled that Travis, the Hannafords' suave butler had a cousin or uncle who worked as a waiter at the Army and Navy Club. I phoned Travis— he and I had always been good friends—and learned that the man was a half brother named Elbert Siddons. Then I called the club, located Mr. Siddons and asked him if he had seen Mr. Boswell at the club. When advised that he had helped wait on the Secretary "and certain other gentlemen," I drove out to the club to chat with Travis's relative.

"There were four in the party, Mr. Deever," Elbert Siddons told me. We walked toward Connecticut Avenue, found a drugstore (not hard to do in Washington; we have more drugstores per capita than any city in the world) and I invited the waiter to join me for a Coke. He was like his stepbrother—pale brown, aloof, articulate, middle-aged, the kind of Negro whose like we will not look upon again after this generation passes.

"There was Mr. Boswell, whom I'd never seen before in person, but whom I admire ever since he made that speech about no segregation being tolerated any more in any defense plant, and General Dudley, Admiral Strang, and General McTaggart of the Air Force. Of course, I know all three of those gentlemen well, since they have been club members many years."

"What took place, Mr. Siddons?"

Elbert Siddons turned his head. "I suppose I can tell you, Mr. Deever. I know about you and the President and Mayor Murphy, what you are trying to effectuate. But we are sworn to discretion. ..."

I marveled at men like Elbert Siddons. Given a different social order, his powers of communication and his natural dignity would have assured him a fifty-thousand-dollar per annum job as a public relations man or a sales executive. Instead, he carted around dishes for dyspeptic generals. "This is an important matter. Unless I judge that the national security is involved, I shall keep anything you tell me to myself."

"Fair enough, Mr. Deever. First off, I try not to listen, since I have no interest in most of the matters discussed by the members of this club. The subjects are not in my field of interest." The black man smiled enigmatically. He

340

was needling me. And he knew enough about me to understand I would appreciate the jibe. (An old Washington chestnut tells about the guide describing the various posh clubs: "There is the Metropolitan Club, where you need money but no brains, there is the Cosmos, where you need brains but no money, and there is the Army and Navy, where you don't need either.")

"I gather they were in a private room?"

"Yes, sir. The corner room reserved for the Joint Chiefs. I was just assisting. Rivers is the headwaiter there. He has seniority."

"What happened, Elbert?"

"A terrible argument developed, Mr. Deever. I have rarely seen General Dudley so angry, or Admiral Strang. General McTaggart was more reserved. Air Force attracts a more sociable sort of person, I believe."

"What were they angry about?"

"This matter of the President using their money to keep the poor people's programs going. They were furious. General Dudley said that the President was playing with fire, risking the nation's security to steal that money and give it to the ghettos. He said we—I mean, *they,* Mr. Deever—would waste it on beer and television and guns."

"Did Mr. Boswell lose his temper?"

Elbert Siddons laughed silently. "Oh no, sir, no, sir. That gentleman is really something, he is really remarkable. He shouted a lot and laughed a lot, but he never once got angry. Even after General Dudley said that Mr. Boswell and the President were selling the country out ..."

"He said *that?*"

"Mr. Deever, don't be hard on General Dudley. He has his worries, and he had an awful lot to drink, three bourbon sours before dinner, and then red wine . . . so maybe his tongue was loosened."

"And Mr. Boswell? When General Dudley said that?"

"He laughed. Sort of boomed it out. Then he challenged them. All three of them."

In the confines of the cold, yellow plastic booth, nursing my Coke, talking softly with this mannerly Negro, I felt giddy, disoriented. What in God's name was Boswell up to. "Challenged . . . ? The Joint Chiefs . . . ? To what?"

"Drinking contest."

"I . . . ah . . . did they accept?"

Elbert Siddons closed his eyes and nodded affirmatively. "Yes indeed, Mr. Deever. Mr. Boswell said he was sick and tired of all those generals and admirals in the Pentagon threatening him and spreading stories about himself and the President, and how they think they are better Americans and better patriots than anyone else. He said he was just as good an American, and he would prove it by drinking them all under, around, on top of, and in back of the table. Now, General Dudley was pretty boozed by now, anyway and he banged the table so hard that the Shrimp Louis danced, and the Cold Salmon Mousse landed in Admiral Strang's lap, and he said, 'Goddammit, no fucking civilian ever out-drank me!' "

"And they proceeded to have this contest?" I asked, incredulous.

"Yes, they did. The admiral said he'd go along, but General McTaggart was reluctant. He said he did not think such an exhibition was in the interest of the services."

"A prudent man. Or perhaps he knew as much about Boswell as I do. Then what happened?"

"Mr. Boswell stood up and made a speech. He said he would out-drink all three of them, and that if he did, they were to shut up, maintain silence, leak no stories to any newspaperman or congressman or anyone else, on the matter of the President's order releasing Pentagon money."

"Elbert, tell me this. You are an observant man who has been around drinkers a long time. Was the Defense Secretary already in his cups when he threw down the gauntlet to the Joint Chiefs?"

Siddons ruminated, rubbing his beige chin. "Hard to say, Mr. Deever. You see, he's a sly fox, that tall man, he's B'rer Rabbit, seven feet tall and just as crafty. I suspect he was play-acting some. Making *believe* he was drunker than he was, to coax the military gentlemen in."

"I understand. We call that coffee-housing, Elbert, or euchring. Mr. Boswell is adept at it."

"Don't I know. He made the rules also. Each contestant got to name his drink, and the quantity thereof, for one round. He called it Boozer's Poker. Any man could raise the ante, and be raised back, and after the betting stopped, the next man named his beverage. This put Mr.

342

Boswell at a disadvantage because he was really in there against the other three."

"I daresay. Who led off?"

"They tossed and General McTaggart of the Air Force won. I don't think he had his heart in this. After all, he is an MIT graduate."

Pondering this cryptic judgment on the waiter's part, I begged him to proceed. Had I not understood Burke Boswell as I did, his powers of alcoholic tolerance, the truly American way in which he sought relaxation through hard stuff, I might have doubted Elbert Siddons's account.

"General McTaggart ordered four half bottles of a 1965 red Bordeaux, an estate-bottled Medoc as I recall. That was easy. Boswell raised him a full bottle, but the other gentlemen did not. So they spent a half hour downing the wine."

"With some food, I hope."

"The chiefs ate quite a bit," Siddons said. "Mr. Boswell ordered me to remove any food from his setting. He said he needed elbow room and did not want to be distracted, even though he had not touched his beef and kidney pie. Anyway, they went clockwise, like in poker, and Admiral Strang was next, and he ordered a double shot of 100 proof bourbon, neat. Boswell did not raise. They all downed that pretty quick. General Dudley was next, and he is a big muscular man, as you know, with a size eighteen neck, and a very red face, and he was drunk already and getting angry. I hate to use such language to you, but he said at one point that the President had brought a bunch of 'fucking socialists' into the Administration . . ."

"What did Mr. Boswell say to that?"

"He said, 'General this is a drinking contest, not a political slanging match, bet or shut up.' Which is what General Dudley did. He asked for tumbler of scotch, water glass full, no ice, no water, no soda, in front of each man. Boswell raised him a glass. I thought General McTaggart would faint. Myself and the headwaiter obliged the gentlemen."

I sipped at my Coke, and I confess that it almost tasted like scotch and damned near turned my stomach.

" 'Drink up, fellows,' Mr. Boswell said, and he downed his scotch like it was mother's milk, one glass after another, and I swear, Mr. Deever, I almost could see the liquor

343

coursing down his skinny throat, the way it looks at the zoo when the giraffe swallows. I'm sorry to report that General McTaggart could go no further. He got up and said that the exhibition was a disgrace and that he would not go along with Dudley and Strang, and they were foolish to have been trapped by the Defense Secretary."

"Mr. Boswell accepted his withdrawal?"

"He got up and shook his hand, and said he regarded General McTaggart as a friend, and that the test of a real man was when he knew he'd had enough, and that all he wanted was for the Air Force to be patient and go along with President Hannaford's program."

"The Chief of the Air Force agreed?"

"Mmmmm . . . a way. He appeared to be nodding his head as if to signify his accord. But then he started to run for the lavatory, and before he made it, he vomited all over the sideboard. Rivers and I spent ten minutes cleaning up. Then we helped him to a private room to sleep it off."

"That left three at the table."

"Yes. It was now Mr. Boswell's turn to bet, and he asked for a magnum of Dom Perignon champagne for each man. He said they had fifteen minutes to get it down. General Dudley took off his tunic and opened his shirt and loosened his belt and raised Mr. Boswell another magnum. There was a delay since we had to get the ice buckets and all, and General Dudley kept getting angrier and saying he didn't give a damn what the President did any more, just so long as Boswell didn't win the drinking contest. I think his pride was hurt. Anyway, they began on the champagne, and after the first bottle, Admiral Strang excused himself and went to the men's room. He went into a booth, and when he did not emerge for fifteen minutes, Chisholm, the men's room attendant got worried. The door was locked, so Chisholm climbed up the wall and he saw that the admiral had fallen asleep on the bowl. Chisholm summoned me. He climbed into the enclosure, opened the door, and we lifted the admiral out, refreshed him with cold water, straightened out his clothes, and laid him to rest in the room next to General McTaggart."

"And then there were two."

"Just Mr. Boswell and General Dudley, who was incoherent and kept saying that Hannaford would get his, that *other* people would see to it that the President got what he deserved. Again, Mr. Boswell ordered the general to button his lip—those were his exact words—and bet. I must say, Mr. Deever, General Dudley is a courageous man. He got through that second bottle of champagne, even though he was weaving, and bobbing and wavering in his seat like a, like a . . . "

"Drunken general?"

"Yes, sir. He had to bet and he ordered a full quart of scotch to be placed in front of each of them, and they would go down the line, drink for drink. No raise from the Secretary this time. My that man was in control of himself. His speech was clear, his voice loud, his eyes in focus. I have rarely witnessed such a performance, and doubt I ever will again."

"I am sure that is the case, Elbert."

"There must have been a dozen of us watching in the private room—myself, Rivers, the headwaiter, Chisholm, the chef, the kitchen help, the hall porter, and the night clerk. We stood in respectful silence, some distance from the table, which had been cleared of everything except the two quart bottles of scotch. Cutty Sark. Fresh glasses were placed in front of General Dudley, who was sweating profusely, and Mr. Boswell, who appeared composed except for a reddening of his face. Before they started to match one another drink for drink, the Secretary turned to the audience—myself and my colleagues, twelve black men—and he said, 'General we have witnesses right here, so no welshing, the way the Army always manages to when it gets backed into a corner.' He said, 'there are twelve good men and true, who will back me up when I say you took an oath, made a gentleman's wager, that you would say no more about the President's use of Pentagon money to keep the poverty programs going.' "

"Did the general respond?"

"He was too far gone, Mr. Deever. He turned his head toward us, and I think he muttered something about his good record on integration and how he had commanded some of the finest black soldiers in the world in Vietnam, and then they fell to. The general matched Mr. Boswell glass for glass. In a half hour they'd drained the quart. Boswell leaned back in his seat, and said, 'My bet.' General Dudley seemed to be asleep on the table. He lifted his head, and I shudder now as I think of his sickly appearance—his cheeks red and puffy, his eyes closed as if he'd been beaten. Mr. Boswell turned to me, and he shouted, 'Courvoisier, Elbert. The old musty bottle, the dark one—one for each of us.' "

"And then?"

"I turned to hurry to the bar for the brandy, when I heard a loud, reverberating crash. I spun around and saw General Dudley lying on the floor. He was finished. Mr. Boswell got up—my, he is a big man—and glided across the room, hardly sweating, even though his skin was like raw steak. Mr. Deever, would you believe, that as he walked past us, the twelve of us, we broke into applause?"

"I most certainly believe it, Elbert. But tell me, were you applauding his talents as a drinker, or his dedication to President Hannaford's program?"

Elbert Siddons winked at me. "Some of both, Mr. Deever, some of both."

This pledge of allegiance from the Joint Chiefs, while unique in its manner of extraction, and encouraging as a portent of Burke Boswell's resourcefulness, did not stop the national malaise. The storm clouds gathered; the wind was rising; and there seemed little we could do to halt the growing unpopularity of the Administration.

There was surprisingly little editorial criticism of Lance Ruckett and his cronies—Upshaw, Nagel, Pringle, Gabe Tutt, all of them heaping opprobrium on the boss's head. It was reasoned by the editorialists, that these extremist groups, these malcontents were "always with us," and while it was proper to keep an eye on them, they could not be taken seriously. Thus, the Washington *Post:*

Mr. Ruckett's strident, well-financed and well-organized campaign to impeach President Hannaford cannot be taken seriously, even though it is cause for some legitimate concern. We must remember that these fringe movements have a long sordid history in American political life, but have always fallen apart because of their own corruption, and the stability of the American democratic system. Movements to "Impeach Roosevelt" abounded in the thirties; President Truman, particularly during the McCarthy heyday and the Hiss-Chambers affair, was threatened with impeachment; Lyndon Johnson was peppered with impeachment talk by both the right and the left during the Vietnam tragedy. None of these movements ever became more than tiresome exercises in slander, threats, paranoid literature and coalitions of the lower forms of animal life in the political zoo . . .

"We are going to see," Lance Ruckett shouted to an Impeach Hannaford rally in a high school stadium, in Bridgeport, Connecticut, for which DOOR bought television time, "we are going to see just who are these lower forms of animal life to whom the intellectual writers of this newspaper refer . . . Well, I don't see any animals. I see good working Americans, policemen, firemen, store owners, housewives, defense plant workers. I wish that smart-aleck writer on the Washington *Post* could be right here this minute and see who our supporters are!"

They roared. They liked it. Young Lance knew how to sock it to them. There was more in this vein. The local chairman of DOOR, a benign-looking supermarket owner then spoke; so did the head of a civil servants union; and a man from NUMB, from Stratford, where defense plants were threatened with layoffs. Then Congressman Ruckett pulled a surprise. I had noticed a young black man with slick "conked" hair sitting on the platform, along with the other guests of honor. This was odd: there was almost never a black face at the Impeach Hannaford rallies.

"Now, one of our supporters from Los Angeles," Ruckett cried. "Mr. Lewis Nesbitt!"

The applause for Nesbitt was restrained, curiously cautious.

"Conservative friends," Nesbitt said, "I was employed as a poll watcher by the Independent Voters Committee of Los Angeles, and I was witness to the depredations committed by the Hannaford people. They bribed. They cheated. They arranged a pact with the forces of Garcia and Jones and as a result they were able to steal the vote in Los Angeles. That man sits in the White House illegally, we will so prove at the right time."

I called Dalton Warfield and asked him if he was watching. He was. "Who is Brother Nesbitt?" I asked.

"Malcontent," Dalton said. "We had to boot him out of the poverty program headquarters. A record of psychiatric unbalance."

"To hell with that," I said as I watched the black man accuse Ben of everything from blowing up voting ma-

347

chines to invalidating absentee ballots. "Does he have anything?"

Warfield was quiet a moment. "If he has, he'll keep it quiet until he can get us in court, or some other official place."

Something in Warfield's manner—hesitation, moroseness, disturbed me.

Larry Hosmer of United Press phoned me with a tip. "Tutt is coming out in favor of impeachment," he said.

"I don't believe it. Not our Gabe."

"That's the word. He's due back from his fact-finding tour of NATO bases this afternoon, and the boys are going to put it to him. Sounds as if he's ready to announce."

I could not believe it. Gabe was a scoundrel, a drunkard, a bigot, a lavish dispenser of taxpayers' moneys in the interests of Alabama and a man who had probably come to hate President Hannaford; but he also feared him. Then I remembered the brutal manner in which our Defense Secretary had sworn the Joint Chiefs to eternal silence, by drinking all three of them into stuporous sleep. Gabe, rollicking about Europe, spending "counterpart funds" on booze, night clubs and ladies, as he dutifully inspected NATO, must have gotten word about the pacification of the Joint Chiefs. It probably infuriated him; and he had decided to take on the President and Boswell on his own—and come out swinging.

Senator Tutt met with the reporters in the press lounge at Dulles Airport.

"Senator Tutt," Hosmer led off, "why did you find it necessary to take a staff of six to Europe with you, when NATO is just about closed down?"

"Ah decide what Ah do, and who Ah take, young man," Gabe said. But he was not wroth—just setting the record straight.

"This trip—not counting your expenses, just your girls—will cost the taxpayers over six thousand dollars. Was it necessary?"

"Mah girls are experts," Senator Tutt gargled, "in everythin'. They know moah about NATO than any pointy-headed intellectual New York socialist. Besides, none of this is yoah business."

"How is the Czechoslovakia-for-Italy trade working out, Senator?" a reporter asked.

348

"We minimizin' it. The NATO ginrals don't care for hit one bit, and we minimizin' hit."

"Senator," another newsman broke in, "your staff of twenty-five have had a total of thirty-eight vacations this year, all paid for by the government. Is that fair?"

"Yeah, Ah think so. We give money's worth on those trips. Inspection, checkin' up on any commonists the State Department maht slip into NATO, or SEATO, or any other of ouah alliances. Yeah, we deliver, not lak the poverty program, or aid to welfare chiselers."

"How do you feel about President Hannaford's use of the Pentagon's contingency fund to keep job training and Ghetto Commune Program in operation until new funds are voted?"

Gabe's rheumy eyes turned to slits. He fingered his white starched collar, and his tongue flicked at his ancient lips. "Ah oppose it," he said softly, almost sweetly. "The President and Mistah Boswell doin' some mahty funny things. That theah money is foah defense, not foah give-away boondoggles. We gon' have a session of the committee soon's I change my Deutscha Marks, and we gon' review the President's interp'tation."

Mona Varnum's lovely head appeared at the bank of microphones, her own pale tan hand thrusting a mike at Gabe. "Senator, Congressman Ruckett is circulating a petition in the House, trying to see what the sentiment is for impeachment proceedings against the President. Would you be in favor of such a move?"

Gabe squinted at my Mona; old lecherous thoughts must have fired his sodden brain. (The overseer and the high-yaller slave. Black poon-tang behind the corn-crib.)

"Waaaall, waaaaall," Gabe brayed. "Ah cain't say, cain't say. Ah disagree with whut the President is doin' in most ay-reas, but Ah reckon we can run him to ground raht in Congress."

"But do you favor a move to impeach him?" Mona insisted.

"Hunh. Hunh. Reckon that isn't none of mah business. 'Mpeachment a matter foah the House, an' the House alone. An' the House, bein' a elected body representin' *all* the people has got to listen to the people. Le's leave hit at that. House is House, and Senate is Senate."

"And the President is the President, Senator?" Hosmer asked.

"Yeah, he is. An' he better start listenin' to those millions o' people who didn't vote foah him."

It was not as bad as I feared. Gabe could not, at this early stage, voice his support of so rash a move as an impeachment resolution. There was too much of the Old Senator in him, too much of the Old Boy in the Upper House.

I offered Mona Varnum a ride back to the city. She demurred. "I've been assigned to cover the Sacramento thing for a day or two," she said.

"Need an assistant? Someone to carry the tape recorder?"

"Forget it, Deever. You know the rules."

"And how I detest them. Once again, Mona? One more time?"

Her slanted eyes mocked me. "Not a chance. Think about it. I like it better that way."

I strolled through the airport with her. She had a few hours between planes.

"What's happening in Sacramento?" I asked.

"The brothers are sick of that concentration camp bit," she said. "Might be a little action. Only black reporters allowed in."

"Keep me advised if you learn anything. I like to think I have a friend at the court."

Again, she disdained my honky attempts at camaraderie. "You try, Deever. Oh, you try awful hard. You know, you might be of some interest to me, if my principles didn't stand in the way."

"Mona, it isn't principle that keeps you from offering me once more the most divine sex any man ever was blessed with," I said as we approached the lounge. "It's your innate superiority."

"Yeah, yeah, you're putting me on . . . "

"No, Mona, you know it. You're Bryn Mawr. Philadelphia black society. You are high-toned and well-bred. And I'm E. Deever, Ohio Normal Institute, born in Indian Mound, Ohio, a grocer's son."

"I see what you're saying. Kind of black snobbery."

"Of course. You're much too classy for me." I helped her with her bags at the counter. She was bound for San Francisco, and then Sacramento for the promised "action."

350

"And you never have told me why the Varnums of Rhode Island are such hot stuff," I said.

She smiled—warmly—with none of that superior smirking she so often used on white swains. "Revolutionary War, Edward. The First Rhode Island Regiment—all black men, freed slaves. One of them was Cato Varnum, a slave of General James Mitchell Varnum, Washington's aide. It's a hell of a story. You give those black buggers guns, you never know what they'll do."

"And what did the First Rhode Island do?"

"Kicked the hell out of the Hessians at the Battle of Newport, and weren't allowed to fight again—ever."

"Ah. I see. Modern parallels. Vietnam, and so forth."

"Yeah, but they're sick of fighting Mr. Charlie's wars. This Sacramento thing is more to their liking. It's going to bust loose, man. Do me a favor and don't tell Mr. President, or Attorney General Moscowitz or any of your liberal superiors. They wouldn't understand anyway."

Emboldened, I looked around, made sure that a few flinty-faced characters were watching, and kissed Mona on the cheek. "I won't. But stay out of range, Mona dear. Remember. Vaseline is no good for Mace or any other gas. It's useless. Carry a wet wash cloth in a plastic bag."

"So long, honky." This last, I felt, was delivered with wry affection. A sort of interracial "Good-night, Chet, Good-night, David."

I watched her graceful figure enter the passageway leading to the giant jet, and responded: "So long, funky." She laughed, and without turning her elegant head, waved her approval of my riposte.

Ruckett raved on. He packed them in—in the Cow Palace, in San Francisco, at Soldier's Field, Chicago, in Mississippi Memorial Stadium in Jackson, and in the Wood Memorial Stadium, Sioux Falls, South Dakota, his home state. The established forces of the country—"the power structure" we hear so much about—had little time for Lance Ruckett, with his smarmy, shiny face, the flashing eyes under the protuberant forehead, and the fetal mouth. But many plain people did.

"Every time there's a gun fired in a ghetto," Attorney General Moscowitz said, "he gets ten more supporters."

The nation's leading lawman and I were driving out to Ramada Ranch for a long week-end of meetings with the

351

President. Around us, on the fabled road Ben had built to his garage, arose new legends, new advices to the people:

IMPEACH HANNAFORD

BACK TO AMERICANISM
GET RID OF HANNAFORD

I noticed that most of the billboards were the ones, which a half year ago, were exhorting the people to IMPEACH MOSCOWITZ.

"I see the boss has inherited your advertising space," I said gloomily.

The Attorney General laughed. "Edward, I'd give anything in the world to let those people have me again as their sacrificial lamb. Anything."

"I'm afraid they want more than a lamb, Judge. They want the bull itself—the biggest, strongest, toughest animal of all."

Heavy of heart, dismayed by the Attorney General's pessimistic advices, I let the billboards and road signs deepen my gloom. One especially succeeded, a re-use of some old Burma-Shave placards:

THE DOOR TO FREEDOM
LIES AHEAD

IMPEACH HANNAFORD
CRUSH THE RED

"It's not quite Ogden Nash," I said to the judge, as we swung into the black-top driveway leading to the sprawling buildings of Ramada Ranch, "but it makes its point."

We walked into the sunken living room—it was late afternoon and the desert sun shot shafts of golden dust-flecked light into the red-brown interior—and greeted the President. He waved at us perfunctorily. He was on the phone, listening intently to his caller. It was a three-way conversation. At the small desk in the corridor, below the stairs, Matt Fixx, our legislative ace, was on the extension, listening in.

"Dammit, Angel, where were our friends? What in hell happened?" President Hannaford asked.

352

They were talking to Representative Angel Lopez Garcia, chairman of the Education and Labor Committee (thanks to Ben's intervention) and one of our few bastions of strength in the House. A slender reed, Angel, and sometimes I wondered why the boss depended on him so much. Garcia, once shrewd and shifty, had become a shell of a man, pariah in the House, tolerated by his colleagues only because he'd licked them in court and still had the power to obstruct.

"What?" the President asked—sounding incredulous. "He fell *asleep?*"

I walked over to Matt Fixx, whose elongated face appeared to have melted into a wax taper, the eyes drooping, the jug ears wilted. "O'Boyle," he said softly, covering the mouthpiece. "O'Boyle fell asleep. Meeting of the House leadership . . ."

"All right, Angel, calm down," he said. "You get with O'Boyle tomorrow, when he's awake, and with Hexter and Barnstable, and see what you can do about controlling the goddamn committee. Get after DiLorenzo and Smales and our other friends, and see can't we get a case against Ruckett. . . ."

Something unforeseen, direful, had happened in the House of Representatives. I suspected what it was. Ben spoke a bit more with Congressman Garcia, then hung up.

"Well, gents, we are in a fight," he said. "Young Ruckett and his people ran one of the neatest end runs I've ever witnessed in long years of service to the republic."

Matt Fixx, who appeared to be shivering, although it was warm in the brick and timber room, loped toward us. "Impossible, sir. I can't believe it, I can't . . . where were our friends . . . ?"

Hannaford tapped the table. "Scared. Or stupid. Or asleep, like the beloved Speaker of the House."

Fern walked in. She looked splendid—tanned, smartly attired in a high-fashion pantsuit.

"Ruckett and some of his boys went to this meeting of the House leadership," the President said, "and raised that impeachment issue. Took everyone by surprise. O'Boyle never dreamed they'd go that far. A hell of an argument took place. Jack Hexter tried to get Emmett to rule them out of order, but the old man seemed confused about the whole thing. Wasn't quite clear what they were up to. Ruckett was arguing that the impeachment resolution

353

deserved a hearing, and that if people like Jack Hexter and Bill Rumsford were so set against it, so sure it was un-American and unpopular, why didn't they let it be taken up by the proper committee? Garcia says Ruckett came in loaded with letters and telegrams and a brand new poll that showed thirty-seven per cent of the people favor impeaching me."

"Gallup?" asked Matt Fixx. "Roper? What poll, sir?"

"Doesn't matter, son," Ben said. "They'll get statistics to back up their position from somebody. It was some new-fangled poll. Some kind of telephone check. Anyway, Ruckett started waving his petitions and his telegrams and his ballots, and then he even got old Walt Prochaska, old labor unions himself, to admit that he was getting drowned in angry letters from that union crowd, whatchamacallem ... "

"NUMB," I said.

"Pretty soon Ruckett had most of 'em convinced that he had a case." Ben got up and strode across the sunlit room. "That's where Jack Hexter made a hell of a mistake, I'm afraid."

The boss was disturbed. Fern's eyes followed his muscular figure, as it paced the room, his voice growing fainter as he trod the bright Navajo carpets. We were all silent.

"Hexter lost his nerve, I'm grieved to report," Ben said. "And O'Boyle fell asleep while Ruckett kept up his harangue."

"It's in-in-in-in-inexcusable!" Matt Fixx cried. "A Speaker of the House who can't stay awake at a time like this!"

It didn't surprise me. Old Emmett O'Boyle was a trial and a burden to us, and had been for a long, long time.

"What did Hexter do?" I asked.

"While Emmett was dozing—not that it would have mattered if the old man had been awake, but it added to Ruckett's strength to have the Speaker asleep—Hexter agreed to let the impeachment matter go to the House Judiciary Committee."

All of us digested this for a moment. Jack Hexter, a decent old Kentuckian, the house Majority Leader, had been bulldozed, intimidated, by Ruckett's letters and telegrams and polls and the testimony concerning union animosity toward the boss.

"I can see why," I said. "The chairman of the Judiciary
354

Committee is our friend Larry DiLorenzo. They'll never get to first base with Larry. He isn't afraid of Ruckett or fifteen like him. He'll kill the resolution the second it's placed before him."

I knew Representative DiLorenzo very well. He was an old-fashioned New Dealer from Brooklyn, a courageous and intelligent supporter of civil rights legislation and social progress. Moreover, I was amazed that Ruckett had suggested this committee. No amount of brow-beating and threats, of organized letter campaigns, would ever get Congressman DiLorenzo—as tough and as outspoken and as cunning at age eighty-three as he had been as a young firebrand—to consider the impeachment motion for three minutes.

"Ruckett knew that," the President said. "And he objected at once. He knew DiLorenzo would wipe the floor up with him. That's where he pulled his end run. While O'Boyle was snoozing, he went to work on Hexter. He promised him support against antitobacco legislation and on narcotics penalties, two things dear to Jack Hexter's nicotine-stained heart. After an hour or so, he had him leaning toward what he wanted—and it wasn't the Judiciary Committee."

"Oh dear, this is awful," Matt Fixx muttered. "He got the House leadership to agree to put it before the Government Operations Committee. He said since they'd already agreed it was worthy of committee consideration, they should at least assign it to the proper committee. Ruckett and his people insisted on Government Operations. Hexter agreed, and so did O'Boyle, after they woke him up."

There was a dismal interval of silence. I understood, of course, what troubled the President—and all of us. The chairman of the House Government Operations Committee was Representative Lemuel Cathcart Suggs of Moulting, Alabama, an aged, befuddled, ridge-runner, a good-natured old prohibitionist and justice of the peace, bound in years of service, of gratitude and a bit of fear, to the leadership of his fellow Alabamian, Senator Tutt.

"There is no point in not being realistic about this," I said. "Lem Suggs will give Ruckett a hearing. He may not be a wild man the way Ruckett is, and he may be beholden to the President, but he's no tower of strength. He'll bend."

"That isn't the worst of it," Matt Fixx said. "Suggs has

agreed to closed sessions when they debate the impeachment resolution."

"And Ruckett is a member of the Government Operations Committee," I said.

"The Speaker must be able to stop this goddamned thing," the President exploded. "Matthew, what can we do to change the old man's mind?"

"Mr. President, he's a lost cause," Matt said. "You know, his home district, Providence, just voted negative on three referenda—no bussing, no more school appropriations for ghetto areas, no more low-cost housing. He's listening to his people also."

"How does that Government Operations shape up?" Ben asked.

Matt Fixx cocked his head, closed one eye, and I knew his alert mind was recalling the list of committee members, party affiliations, political leanings. "There are thirty-three members, nineteen of ours and fourteen of the opposition. Our nineteen include seven from southern or border states, and their fourteen include four. That means eleven who'll probably side with Chairman Suggs—assuming he runs with Ruckett. That's eleven plus Ruckett a maximum twelve votes for the resolution."

"They'll need seventeen to report it out favorably," I said.

"We have darn good support in the committee—Harry Kaplan of New Jersey, and Lewis Smales of Vermont. The swing votes, Mr. President, will be the men with big city constituencies, especially those representing ethnic minorities who are mad as hell—people like Prochaska and Stradella. They're the ones the pressure is on." Matt had stated the problem succinctly and truthfully.

"I can't see people like Fulvio Stradella voting in favor of this—this—damned conspiracy," Attorney General Moscowitz said. "They must understand that in the long run Lance Ruckett represents a destructive strain in America, a strain that can destroy every social gain made since 1933."

"No, they don't necessarily look at it that way any more," the President said. "They got *theirs*. I mean Piasecki's Poles and Stradella's Italians. They got *theirs*, and they don't like being threatened. They are good people. Hard workers. Ambitious for their kids. Don't want war. I can convince them that we should disarm tomorrow and

356

sign a pact with Russia. But I can't budge 'em on black folks, not yet anyway."

"It's a question of how much pressure we can put on Mr. Suggs," I said, "and how much pressure others will put on him."

The President sat down in an old-fashioned wooden rocker. He moved back and forth gently. "Edward, we may be in good shape. We are not yet cast into the midst of the burning, fiery furnace. Lem Suggs is not the same breed of cat as Mr. Ruckett. Say what you will about Lem, he's an old-fashioned populist. Worked closely with Mr. Roosevelt on rural electrification."

"Christmas Past, Mr. President," I said.

We all felt the chill in the sunny living room of Ramada Ranch. It was as if something unspeakable and venomous had been let loose—and instead of responsible men trying to trap and kill the monster, they were propitiating it, feeding it, making concordats and treaties with it. The Alabama delegation may have been largely conservatives, men opposed to civil rights laws, but was it not a baleful change, when they linked arms with such as Merton Huckerby, who, please God, kept those with whom he disagreed "in the cross hairs?"

" 'Strengthen ye the weak hands and confirm the feeble knees,' " Hannaford said. "We're not as naked and un-armed as you all seem to think. Ruckett's got himself a platform with the Government Operations Committee. That's all. Suggs will let him work off some steam, shut him up, make some fudging remarks, and vote it down. And once a movement like that is sunk, it's sunk for good."

"I beg your pardon, Mr. President," Matt said, "but the House radicals kept after Andrew Johnson, over and over and over, until they got a favorable vote in the Judiciary Committee. Nothing stopped Thaddeus Stevens and John Ashley and Ben Butler once they felt they had enough support to unseat Mr. Johnson."

History was not Ben's long suit. He rubbed his chin. "Seems we are a long way from that sort of thing. Besides that thing never got anywhere in the Senate."

Sam Moscowitz cleared his throat. "I beg your pardon, Mr. President, but the impeachment was voted overwhelm-ingly by the House. And the move to *convict* the Pres-ident on the basis of the impeachment findings, which is nothing more than an indictment, was beaten by only one vote. A Senator named Edmund Ross from Kansas voted against conviction, and it was the deciding vote. If he'd switched, Johnson would have stood convicted—on the flimsiest, most vicious and cheaply political bill of particulars ever drawn up againt any man in or out of office. But it was by a single vote that Johnson was spared that humiliation."

Hannaford absorbed this. Fern had drawn closer to him. She was holding his hand. I was amazed to hear her speak. "The President will fight this scurrilous attack on his honor, Judge Moscowitz. We shall all fight it, and God willing, we will overcome it, and will expose the scoundrels who are behind it."

"We're working on Mr. Ruckett's background," I said. "Parente is helping us." But I said nothing else; neither mentioning our spy, Baldini, or Parente's suspicions that the former Mrs. Ruckett might prove helpful if we could locate her and get her to talk. Any man, like Lance Ruckett, who made love with all his clothes on, and seemed to linger over each stage of undress, could be brought to heel with evidence.

"Johnson barely survived the impeachment attempt," Moscowitz said, "and he was never the same after that. But the proceedings did establish one firm precedent."

"What is that, Sam?"

The Attorney General got up and lectured us, something he was good at; he'd taught law for several years at NYU. "The impeachment and the trial in the Senate made clear that impeachment is *not*, I repeat, *not* an inquest of office, or a politically motivated act, something that the House can call into operation any time it gets tired of, or angry with a President. It simply isn't what it was intended to be, no matter how unpopular a President is, no matter how much the polls show the public disapproves of his policies, no matter how much support is rallied in Washington and across the nation."

"You are saying. Sam," the President said cautiously, "that precedent, that the lessons learned then, will prevail. Is that correct?"

"The arguments advanced by Johnson's lawyers are regarded by scholars as the final say on the matter. Impeachment cannot be used as a club, or a threat, or a means to register a vote of no confidence in a President."

358

"Then what is it?" I asked.

"What the Constitution says it is," the Attorney-General said. "A process to indict a President for specific crimes, namely treason and bribery, or other high crimes or misdemeanors."

President Hannaford did not look convinced. A cynical smile curved his wide mouth. "Sam, you keep quoting scholars and legal experts, and constitutional lawyers, as if this country is always guided by reasonable men, who use the past as a guide, who try to settle disputes amicably, who believe in laws, and not in emotions. Like a lot of my intellectual friends, you are too trusting. There's a lion loose in the streets, and he is in no mood to listen to precedent."

"History sided with Andrew Johnson, Mr. President," the Attorney General said. "His role in reconstruction has been reassessed, and his comportment during the shameful proceedings has been given proper perspective. He is considered one of our great presidents today."

"I don't intend to wait for historians to pass judgment on me fifty years from now," Ben said. "I aim to make my mark while I am alive, and to frustrate the rascals who seek to destroy me—and this country."

"I quite agree, Mr. President. I am simply pointing out that no serious scholar believes that impeachment can ever be used again as a political weapon. Your enemies must know that. The Congress knows that. The Supreme Court knows it."

Hannaford shook his head. "Sam, there are moments in our history when we are governed not by laws and precedent and dialogue, but by passion. I don't care if a dozen professors and fifteen law experts built me a case from here to Washington, that there isn't a single issue on which to build a case for impeachment. That this was all huffing, and blowing and threatening of the cheapest order, as low and base as the campaign against Andrew Johnson. It would not stop them. They are convinced they have an issue, just as Butler and that crowd you mentioned were convinced they had an issue—that Johnson was too easy on the South, that he'd conspired with Jeff Davis, or helped assassinate Lincoln, so's he could take over. Lunacy? Sure it was lunacy. But lunatics have a way of sounding logical at certain moments. Awful lot of folks are willing to listen to them, if the going is rough. Mr. Ruckett is working that side of the street."

"He cannot believe he can sway the House," the Attorney General said. "The situation today is not comparable with the situation after the Civil War."

"Isn't it, now?" asked the President.

"No. Things are changing. If we can start your cities program, if we can defuse the international situation—God knows the people are ready for disarmament—we can move the country ahead. Bitterness, yes, but not the kind of vengeful perversity that led the House to try to unseat Johnson."

"What was I elected by, Edward?" he asked. Why he asked me, I don't know.

"Thirty-three and seven-tenths per cent of the popular vote, sir."

"Don't ever forget it, any of you," the President said. "Sam, all your talk about precedents and what impeachment means, and how a President has to commit a big crime before he gets the book thrown at him won't dissuade that crowd of barn-burners if they think they got me licked. Look at what they've done already—ramming the thing into the Government Operations Committee."

"It won't get far," Matt Fixx said. "Even if Mr. Suggs appoints a subcommittee with Mr. Ruckett on it, I am certain the whole committee won't give it the time of day."

"I agree, Mr. President," I said. "The plot is going to backfire on them." As I said these words of reassurance, I'm not sure I believed them. "Ruckett has those eighty-seven zealots who'll follow him anywhere, but they aren't enough, and he's probably got a few summer soldiers in his ranks. We can hit them with patronage threats and a few other things. Besides, Judge Moscowitz is right. Once we get a favorable report from Professor Cohen, I'd suggest we hit it hard—maybe an address to the country about the opening of disarmament talks. We could use some kind of up-date from Murphy on the cities program. Some good news, instead of the kind of thing we are getting from Sacramento."

"That simple, hey Edward?" the boss asked me.

"It isn't simple, sir, but it requires a counterattack. Not on Ruckett's grounds, not in his style. Let him hold his rallies, let him rant and rave. We'll answer him in our own way."

"My feeling is," Fern said carefully, as she poured tea for us, "that that creature Ruckett is waiting for something dreadful to happen that he can blame on *you*, my dear. If it will not happen, he will arrange for it to happen. Cream or lemon, Edward?"

"Cream, Mrs. Hannaford."

"That is a sound observation, Mrs. Hannaford," the Attorney General said. "It is the way these conspiratorial movements work. Faked incidents, or provoked incidents."

The President looked perplexed, straining to reach some conclusion, some formulation. "Isn't quite the same, Sam. Those conspiratorial deals you mention—they are usually minorities, small activist groups trying to swing the majority."

"Are you saying, Mr. President, that this right-wing cabal is more than that?" Moscowitz asked.

"I'm afraid so," the President said. "I don't believe that the majority of Americans want me kicked out, or hate me, or oppose every darn thing I mention. They know all about the rotting cities and the foul air and the danger of too many bombs and nerve gas depots. A lot of 'em even understand that black people need more money. But they're disturbed. They're anxious. They're frightened. Ruckett may just be able to stampede the whole crowd."

"There is sometimes an advantage to being an unpopular President," the Attorney-General said. "One presidential expert is of the opinion that the controversial men are the ones who get things done and who go down in the history books. He drew a comparison between President Truman and President Eisenhower, and he decided that their examples may conspire to prove that the unpopular President, like Harry Truman, is the fellow with the head start to glory."

"That isn't very satisfactory, Sam," Hannaford said. He suddenly turned to me. "Edward, where in blazes is the Vice-President?"

"Mr. Sparrier is dedicating a day-care center in New Bern, North Carolina."

"Set up a meeting with him early next week. You see, gents, all of us think the same way. We need somebody who is a bit closer in ideology to our opponents to help us find the way."

The decision of the House leadership to permit the Government Operations Committee, under its chairman, Lemuel Cathcart Suggs of Alabama, to hear arguments for impeachment proceedings, caused a good deal less of a stir in the press than I imagined. Most editorialists regarded it as self-defeating.

The New York *Times,* for example, advised Congress "to throw Mr. Ruckett's intemperate, vindictive campaign out in short order. It is a sordid, base affair, and it is a reflection on the ineptitude and cowardice of the House leadership, notably Speaker O'Boyle, who has failed to fulfill his duties and has betrayed the head of his own party, the chief officer of the government." There was, the *Times* argued, no case against the President. "The Congress, already begrimed by permitting the campaign to get this far, should reject out of hand any further attempts to impede the President's program."

I sighed. How innocent our liberal journalists were! Lance Ruckett was not trying to "impede" Ben's program; he was after destroying him. Nothing less. And what made them—and the good souls at the Washington *Post,* and CBS News, and *Time* and the *Wall Street Journal*—think that all their reasoned arguments could sway those who had organized against Ben?

Meanwhile, Ruckett and his allies worked shrewdly. They brow-beat Lem Suggs into holding hearings quickly, and they scurried about lining up witnesses. Union officials, neighborhood association spokesmen, police chiefs, firemen, home owners—dead-center Americans, scared stiff of the black man, terrified at the prospect of loss of jobs if the defense cuts went through. The second rank of witnesses would be the spokesmen for the military-industrial complex—General Upshaw and Nagel, and others. (Here they suffered from a glut of talent. Ruckett was like a baseball manager with too many .300 hitters. The country swarmed with former generals and admirals in the pay of "defense" contractors.)

"Why do you suppose Suggs refused to appoint a subcommittee on this business?" I asked Matt Fixx. We were back in Washington, after that dismal week-end at Ramada Ranch.

362

"Self-protection," Matt said. "Suggs is no fool. He's no Gabe Tutt. The subcommittee would have to include Ruckett, and he'd have to stack it with Ruckett's pals, or young Lance would start calling *him* an appeaser and a rubber stamp for the boss. By holding the hearings before a Committee of the Whole, he's got an out. After all, they're thirty-three good men and true, and Ruckett will have trouble swaying them. We've got friends there."

"So you think we look good?"

"Unless something awful happens. Most people don't even know what the contingency fund is. You'll notice, also, Ruckett's shut up about the disarmament talks. He isn't even mentioning Sy Cohen any more. The whole stress is on the rerouting of the money, and the unemployment that'll result from the cutbacks."

"And the California electoral vote?" I asked.

"He'll use that as leverage. Even Ruckett has to understand that whatever happened in Los Angeles happened before Ben became President. And in spite of those paid informers he's coming up with, guys like Nesbitt, it's a bad scene. I mean, it's not an on-going thing."

I wondered. Still, Matt's optimism—and The New York *Times'* call to Congress to toss out the impeachment matter—appeared to be good omens. I must say there were other hopeful signs. Responsible black leaders rallied to Dalton Warfield's side; they cooled it; they talked to their people; they sent their kids to the job training centers and the ghetto communes. Summer was approaching; the traditional season for rioting and blood in the streets.

But apart from the appalling scandal of the Sacramento barricades, most of the cities remained comparatively quiet. To a great extent this was the result of concerted, organized efforts by black leaders and a new coalition of white professionals—university people, social workers, corporation specialists in urban matters, and most markedly, the new activist clergy.

One incident and one individual particularly impressed me, and I made a note of his name. He was a youthful Roman Catholic priest from Waterbury, Connecticut, Father James Francis Ward, and he had single-handedly defused a shoot-out between blacks and whites in his home town, later effecting a shaky truce, and volunteering to serve as mediator between the factions.

Curiously, the conservative press observed a certain

caution. Had Ruckett overreached himself? Were people like Cosmo Carl Pringle wary of his wild assaults? Thus one of Pringle's editorials:

> Mr. Ruckett's move is perhaps the wrong one at the wrong time. It is an understandable reaction to the President's treacherous course. But it would be more to the point to let the Congress conduct a searching, impartial probe first, before moving toward so drastic a step as an impeachment. . . .

Bates Pendragon, my favorite conservative columnist, also danced around a forthright approval of Ruckett. I began to feel that a lot of his right-wing bluster was an intellectual exercise. After all, Pendragon was a graduate of Princeton, a school which some years back appointed a black militant to its Board of Trustees.

The boss appeared to have shaken the gloom he had manifested at Ramada Ranch. After the initial splash of headlines, and television exposure, Ruckett's brash campaign diminished. "It appears," a Washington *Post* editorial said, "that the Ruckett scheme, even taking into account Speaker O'Boyle's inept handling of the affair, will fall of its own weight. Congress has too many important matters on its calendar to be sidetracked with diversionary, mean-minded attacks on the President. Let the Government Operations Committee meet, let Mr. Suggs give these extremists their say, and let the committee consign it to history's garbage dump, where it belongs . . . "

Ah, they were being too cavalier again, too confident in their dismissal of the zealots. These people did not go away; could not be appeased; and they were being listened to. But as I studied the names of the committee members, and as Matt Fixx and I telephoned them, sounded them, talked to their aides, I grew more confident. Perhaps the optimism of the *Times* and the *Post* was justified. Yes, Ruckett would have his day—on the floor of the House, in committee—and then he would vanish, along with his wild, paranoid charges. Just what the charges were to be—strangely—nobody knew.

"If there was a switch I could throw, a damned circuit breaker I could activate," the President said to me moodily one night, as we sat in the Lincoln Sitting Room, going over a list of appointments for the following day. "If we

364

could just sidetrack a lot of people and sort of give them a breather, give them some confidence in themselves and in the country. Hell, we've licked big problems before. There isn't anything this country can't do when it makes its mind up. Why have we stalled on this race thing? Why do we find it so hard to get anywhere?"

I replied that my own theory—one I had read in a novel some years back and with which I concurred—was that *sexual fear* was at the base of the race question. This sort of talk always brought the boss up short. A bit of a prude, Hannaford did not appreciate this sort of speculation. Freud was unknown to him. And modern sex theorists would have shocked him beyond speech. A very square man, I am afraid, but a very decent man.

"That doesn't explain a thing," the President said uneasily.

"I'm not too sure, sir. You have to remember the tradition during slavery and during much of the postbellum period. The rule was this—black women are available to white men whenever the latter want them. It's no secret. All of those good-looking mulattoes over at Howard University weren't created in test tubes. White people have this racist memory—a pleasant one, tinged with guilt, as far as the men are concerned, a jealous and vindictive one as far as their women are concerned."

Ben shook his head. "How does that explain those Poles and Italians and Irish who've deserted our party and call us names? They're not the ones whose great grandpappies had colored girl friends behind the barn. No, Edward, you have to do better."

"I quite agree. But racial myths permeate the whole society. What white America fears is that the black man is awaiting his revenge, that once he gets control, all that will matter to him is fornicating with white women. Now there may be a germ of truth in that. But it takes two to tango, as the old song goes, and there would have to be compliance on the part of white women. As there is already in places like Greenwich Village and San Francisco."

Hannaford, to my amazement, seemed to blush. "Personally, I wouldn't give a hoot, Edward. It's a free country. If a white woman wants to make love to a black man, no one on earth can stop her. You'd think by now people would have gotten over that."

"They haven't. It's beneath the skin, Mr. President. All those people lining up with Lance Ruckett have nightmares of big black bucks raping their wives, mothers and daughters. I have become convinced that the resistance to black progress is a sexual fear. There are other elements to it, but that's the abiding, distinctive issue. Nobody really worried about the Irish, or the Jews or the Italians when they were on the rise. It never occurred to your average middle-class white WASP American that the foreigners' men wanted to bed down with their womenfolks. But the black fellow, well, he's been waiting in the wings all these centuries, mulling over past crimes against his manhood and against his women, and he will avenge it the only way he knows how."

"You believe he wants to?" Ben asked.

"Them as wants to, will try, and either succeed or be rebuffed. What the black man wants is a clean house, a good job, and a chance for his kids. I'm at a loss as to why this seems so hard for us to arrange."

The President leaned back on the sofa and stretched mightily. "Edward, I'm not the man to propose it, and I hope it's never an issue, but let me tell you, that mixed breeds are sometimes the best. Fern's pedigreed Gordon setters and our Black Angus are fine animals, but they're prey to illness and neuroses. Give me a good crossbreed any time. Never suffered a minute for being part Indian. I carry my Indian blood with pride. Gives me a lot of staying power. You know, Edward, there is one thing an Indian could do better than a white man, any white man."

"What is that, Mr. President?"

"Wait. Just set and wait. Maybe that's what we have to do now."

Later that evening, I encountered Vangie Boswell in the West Sitting Hall, that most charming of alcoves with the Mary Cassatt painting *Mother and Two Children*. Fern's secretary was on her way up from the White House library with several heavy volumes.

I stopped her, my own arms laden with notebooks and files, my heart heavy, and read the titles. One was David M. DeWitt's *The Impeachment and Trial of President Johnson*, the other, L. P. Stryker's *Andrew Johnson: A Study in Courage.*

"The First Lady requested them," Vangie said.

"I must say I admire her." I relieved Vangie of her load, and the two of us sat on the beige sofa in front of the window. By lamp light I thumbed through the two volumes. It would be a good idea for all of us to bone up, even though the Ruckett campaign appeared to be running out of steam. Even Gabe Tutt had been equivocal, shifty when cornered at Dulles International Airport a few days ago.

"They're both sort of going into training for this," Vangie said suddenly.

"Both?"

"Well, Mrs. H. is taking this short course in nineteenth-century history, and . . . " She leaned close to me and whispered. "The big man has come up with a serious case of roving hands."

"Quiet!"

"It's the truth. Gave me a big hug tonight, looked deeply into my eyes and said he sometimes wished he'd chosen another career."

I pondered this. How strange. I was witnessing a reprise of what we had gone through during the censure debate—wistful yearning in the boss for a simpler life, in which he could indulge passions he had suppressed because of that puritanical strain. Two years ago it had been Maria Valdez; now it was Vangie Boswell.

"What else did he say?" I whispered—fully expecting Ben to walk in on us.

"Oh . . . just how much he admired me, how he had watched me these months, and how grateful he was for the way I'd roused Mrs. Hannaford's spirits."

"Hugging all the while?"

"No. A squeeze now and then. Then he patted my cheek."

"Facial cheek, I hope."

"Of course, you ninny. He's a gentleman. Eddie, the shyness, the gentleness of that rugged man. It's as if . . . he doesn't know what to do with a woman . . . how to begin . . . "

"He knows, he knows, Vangie. But he won't permit it. Ben is not like some other residents of this great mansion who assumed that they could take whatever they wanted in the way of convenient females. No, not the boss. And he hurts because of it. All of that energy is not expended on legislation, executive orders, cabinet meetings and strategies to confute the Lance Rucketts of our time. There's some left over, and it is rich with the dark blood of his Kiowa ancestors. Beware, Little Redwing."

"I'm as safe with him, dear boy, as I'd be at a convention of interior decorators."

"I suppose you're right. There's a will there, a desire, but the man subdues it. He can't be very happy about these acts of self-denial. Not a man like the boss."

"It must be dreadful to be a man—and want, and want, and want . . ."

"Some of us aren't hung up on sex."

"I shouldn't tell you this," Vangie whispered. "But I encourage him."

"Damn you."

"Oh, he likes it."

I winced. "I'm certain he does. You see, Vangie, the man is in precarium, he's in trouble. That seems to be the pattern. Whenever Ben finds himself backed against the wall he suddenly experiences regrets about the kind of public, vigorous, contentious life he's chosen. He dreams of an easier, hedonistic existence. Secret hotel suites, and long-legged women, whom he can drown in pearls and mink. This is my theory, anyway. This sort of fantasy is common to all eminent men. Some indulge it."

"He's got such big, strong hands," she said moonily.

"And such big, strong inhibitions."

"Sad, isn't it?"

"It breaks my heart," I said. "I bleed for him."

"Edward, that sarcastic tone. You are Mr. Loyalty himself."

"In political matters, yes. As for his personal life. Someday I'll tell you the Maria Valdez story."

"I'm jealous of Maria Valdez. You were really stuck on her. Not to mention Mona Varnum."

"Careful, there, Boswell. You are speaking of a painful, wrenching chapter in my sordid life. The wound has not yet healed."

We heard Hannaford's heavy tread in the hallway. He was calling for me. I had been working on the file on the new Defense Appropriations Bill, some new notions Boswell had wanted included, and he wanted to study it before retiring.

"Back to your mistress, wench," I said. "I expect both

of you to know all about impeachments tomorrow, and have the boss's defense mapped out."

"Edward?" the President called. "Where's that defense file? And what about Gantry's report on the rider to the Housing Bill? Can't find it."

"He'll survive," I said to Vangie. "He always does." I hurried to the President.

Lance Ruckett kept dodging the press, alibi-ing, reluctant to pursue his quarry. "What is Mr. Ruckett waiting for?" Parente asked in his column. "The new model cars?" Goaded by the newspapers and the TV commentators, the young congressman at last set a date for his speech on the House floor introducing his resolution. It was odd: no sooner had he gotten the leadership to assign his move to committee, than he appeared flabbergasted and apprehensive by his own wild success. It was as if the challenge were too great, the opponent too fearsome.

I sat with Parente and Goldstein in the House press gallery as Ruckett shot his opening fusillade. There was a fair turnout—the Chamber about two-thirds filled, a tribute to the interest Ruckett had created. That worried me. Usually congressmen are busy with committee hearings, or ensconced in their offices. But Ruckett had pulled a crowd. I suppose he had a certain hideous fascination. Like Joe McCarthy, you couldn't stop listening, just to see how far he dared go.

The galleries were packed—all 624 seats filled, as were all the seats in the press gallery, where I sat with Parente. Slumped in his magisterial chair behind the walnut rostrum, centered between the two black-and-gold Italian marble pillars, backgrounded by the American Flag, was Speaker Emmett Brian O'Boyle. The venerable Rhode Islander never looked paler, frailer and more bemused. We had talked to him several times since his monstrous *gaffe* in letting Ruckett and his gang pull their end run—wedging the resolution into the Government Operations Committee. And all we had gotten were mumbles, excuses, apologies, and the line, muttered over, and over, "Those people have a right to be heard also, Mr. President . . ."

Ruckett had risen and had been recognized. A podgy man, but with a pouter pigeon's chest, and extravagant gestures of arms and hands? He was wearing a pale gray suit, a white shirt and a dark blue tie. The lights in the lofty ceiling winked on his protuberant forehead; his unbuttoned jacket revealed a young man's paunch, hinting at intemperate habits.

"Mr. Speaker," Lance Ruckett began, "I rise to offer a resolution calling for the impeachment of the President of the United States."

There was applause from the galleries. O'Boyle rapped his gavel. "The Chair will not tolerate any demonstrations of any kind. Officers, up there, get rid of anyone who misbehaves." There was some life in the old Yankee yet.

"Now, I realize the gravity of the statement I have just made," the young congressman went on, "but we live in grave times. I present this resolution with no vindictiveness, with no desire to punish or blackguard any person, but only with the desire to save the republic from its sworn enemies."

"Holy shit," Parente said. "Can he be serious? Can he really expect anyone to go for that line of crap?"

"Take a look at those honest faces across from us, Louis. Those are not readers of The New York *Times* editorials. There has never been a law in this country which states that the citizens are bound to obey the advice of the Restons and Lippmans and Cronkites."

"Tomorrow, Mr. Speaker, the honorable chairman of the House Government Operations Committee, the gentleman from Alabama, our esteemed colleague Lemuel Cathcart Suggs, will open hearings on my resolution. I introduce it today with a heavy heart, but a clear conscience. I am convinced in my mind as are, I am certain, a majority of the American people, that the President, possibly sincerely, and probably because of incompetent advisers—and some worse than incompetent, and perhaps I had better not use the right word—"

In the gallery, I could almost hear the sinister whispering:

"Treason, treason, treason."

"Good Christ," I said to Lou, "we are in the hands of the madmen." This same insane muttering of the word *treason*, I knew, had been a technique perfected by the more addlepated of Mr. Goldwater's followers in 1964.

It was amazing, how calm and free of ranting was Ruckett's voice. He spoke casually, without passion, as if discussing a rider to a rivers-and-harbor bill that affected his home district. I knew he was saving his Sunday-night preaching style for a windup, possibly for the debate that would follow.

"It is important, Mr. Speaker, that throughout the thoughtful and prayerful debate, discussion, dialogue, hearings, that will surround this enormous issue, that we keep in mind that the President was barely elected. That he garnered only a third of the popular vote. That he secured fewer popular votes than Mr. Beldock. And that when Mr. Beldock's votes are added to General Upshaw's, which two gentlemen are, by their own admission, quite close in their patriotic philosophy of government, the President is undoubtedly the least popular, the least desired Chief Executive in our nation's history . . ."

There was a stirring in the great chamber below us. Representative Lawrence DiLorenzo, an old battler, chairman of the Judiciary Committee, was on his feet.

"Mr. Speaker, point of privilege," Congressman DiLorenzo was calling. O'Boyle recognized his fellow octogenarian.

"Will the gentleman from South Dakota yield?" O'Boyle asked.

"Most certainly," Ruckett said.

"Sweetness and light," Lou Parente said to me. "He's going to charm the balls off everyone before he slits Hannaford's throat."

DiLorenzo cleared his throat. He'd been around a long, long time. Former chief lawyer for the Garment Workers' Union in New York, aide to the great Fiorello La Guardia, unreconstructed liberal, reformer, friend to the poor and the underdog, Larry DiLorenzo wasn't afraid of anybody.

"Mr. Speaker," DiLorenzo said, "let the gentleman from South Dakota get to the point. He is here to introduce a resolution of impeachment. I don't want to hear about how close the last presidential election was. That has no bearing on the case. None at all. Mr. Hannaford was elected. He won the electoral vote. The electoral college confirmed his election."

"Thank you, sir," Ruckett said cordially. No, you didn't abuse Larry DiLorenzo with impunity. You watched your step with a cagey old veteran like the Judiciary Chairman.

"Now I shall proceed with my arguments," the South Dakotan said. "Mr. Speaker, it is essential for all patriotic

Americans to keep in mind that we live under constant threat in this country—from within, and from without. Nothing has really changed since Communism reared its poisonous head at the turn of the century. It still seeks to rule the world. But to rule the world, it must bring down this republic, the last bastion of freedom. Do I sound like what the liberal press calls an extremist? I—and my associates—accept that appellation with gratitude. As a great predecessor of ours once said, 'Extremism in the defense of liberty is no vice.' "

There was dutiful applause from part of the gallery. O'Boyle whacked the gavel. Parente scowled. "Why in hell doesn't he have the sergeant show the mace to those ball-breakers?"

"He's afraid of them," I said. But as I said it, I realized that Ruckett's claque, seated across from us, were hardly terrors. The women tended toward frizzy hair sets, rimless glasses, pale cotton frocks. The men favored tan or gray suits, white shirts. A part of Main Street America. They had not read Farbelman and did not go to Judy Stapp's parties; but they were scared stiff, full of the indigestible fried crud that passed for ideology on the far right. Such a diet had endowed them with patriotic cramps, fervent flatulence, the constipation of the righteous. They were more to be pitied than condemned or feared.

"It is my contention, Mr. Speaker," Ruckett went on, "that the President has proven himself incapable of dealing with the threats that face us as a nation. The President has attempted—whatever his motives—to cut down our vast military strength, to discredit our heroic generals and admirals, indeed all of our fighting men, holding high the banners of freedom from Greenland to Thailand. Why has he done this? We can only guess, we can only gauge. But the *whys* of the President's behavior are no longer of moment. He has acted. He is acting. He is threatening. He is using his high office to subvert the nation and to subdue patriots. What is the meaning of that dastardly fifty per cent reduction in our defense budget, other than an invitation to our enemies to conquer us? Why should the Communists rest, when they know we will be weak, ineffectual, shorn of our armor, our sword arm paralyzed, our shield full of gaping holes? But this is what the President has sought—termination of the Iron Ball orbiting missile system, or MOMSER—"

"Talk about MOMSERS," Parente said. "There's the biggest momser of them all down there."

"Yiddish for bastard," Fred Goldstein whispered in my ear.

"—this devious, mischievous act by an incumbent President is without parallel in our history. I impute no evil motives to the President. I do not argue that he has succumbed to the blandishments and sweet talk of the enemy. But I question some of his advisers, some of those who have the presidential ear. Which of us who listened to the Defense Secretary's malicious attacks on our brave generals at the recent congressional hearings, can doubt for a minute that sinister and anti-American forces were behind that testimony?"

Ruckett was warming up. He always seemed to find his true voice—that Bible-bashing, whining, hell-for-leather semi-scream, half way through his perorations. He was getting there sooner than I expected.

"I ask you, Mr. Speaker, what would impel a man like Burke Boswell, wealthy, esteemed by the community, the agent of large corporations, to attack our generals as liars and cheats? What would move a man of such high station, such eminence in the business community to slander great Americans like General Boyd R. Nagel, Admiral Strang and General Dudley, and all the other heroes who guard our sacred shores from their fortress at the Pentagon?

"I shall answer my own question. Two things. Money and ideology. The money comes from the old Wall Street banking eastern Establishment people, the supporters of the United Nations and the Bilderberg Group, the secret agents of Goldman, Sachs, Lehman Brothers and all the others whose names we know so well—"

"By Christ, I thought we'd heard the last of this. Right out of Father Coughlin." Parente was mopping his forehead. "Old-fashioned nut populism. I thought better of Ruckett. I mean in terms of his material."

"—and to whom Mr. Boswell is so much in debt for past monetary favors. But that is only part of it. This same eastern conglomerate of Wall Street bankers has always had a strange affection for Karl Marx and his philosophies. Russia has never been an enemy to them, but a region on which to lavish love, and understanding. So Mr. Boswell has followed this line faithfully, faithful to his money masters, and faithless to this great nation, this

373

great people, who understand the real nature of the apocalyptic beast—"

Ah, he was there, high on his sacred plateau, bashing his Bible, shouting revelation, assigning his enemies to Gehenna and his friends to heavenly Gardens of Eden.

"—and that, Mr. Speaker is the kind of man giving advice and comfort to the President. That is the man determined to strip our defenses!

"In addition, let me cite the illegal and treacherous manner in which the President and his Secretary of State, Professor Edgerton, engineered the trade of Italy for Czechoslovakia in the NATO alliance. Yes, I am sure the President enjoyed a few laughs over his sly move. I am told he is a man with a notable sense of humor. Mr. Speaker, I hope he will still be laughing on the day that Czech spies start feeding our atomic warfare plans to Moscow!"

Parente yawned. "Hasn't laid a glove on Hannaford yet," he said. "Who cares about that crap any more? NATO? Whazzat, Charlie? Defense budget too big? Can't understand it anyway."

"He's getting around to something closer to home," I said.

"I accuse the Secretary of State, Mr. Speaker, of leading the President into a trap that will some day result in the loss of the entire continent to Communism. Because of thirty years of treason, half of Europe is already under the Red flag, and the rest is socialist, which is the same thing. All of this is in accord with the secret plottings of the Bilderberg Group and the Illuminati. Professor Edgerton knows what I'm talking about, and I invite his response.

"But I'm not concerned with the Phi Beta Kappa gentleman, who serves the President. He is a minor figure in this drama of national survival. I am concerned with the man who appointed him, and who now, in concert with other left-wing advisers, such as the Secretary of Defense, turns us away from our historic destiny. It is the President who must be blamed. He and he alone has embarked us on this suicidal course. And that includes the so-called disarmament talks in Stockholm. What a farce! When the Russians have never honored a single international agreement, and have repeatedly broken their word!"

Representative Walter Prochaska of Michigan was on

his feet. Walt was no flaming liberal, but he was a decent old union organizer from Toledo.

Ruckett yielded. A grin illuminated his shiny face; his forehead seemed to bulge as if inflated with holy gas. "By all means, Mr. Prochaska."

"Your attack on the President's foreign policy decisions is so full of generalities and distortions, sir, that I scarcely know where to begin," Walt said.

"Please do me the courtesy," Ruckett said, "of pointing out any misstatement of fact."

"Well," Prochaska said weakly, "you said that the Russians have never honored a single agreement. They've honored hundreds and hundreds including the Iranian troop question, the Austrian agreement, the outer space accord, the Artic and Antarctic pacts, and any number of agreements sponsored by the United Nations specialized agencies such as the FAO, WHO and UNESCO."

"Good for Walt," I said. "Old union guy, good heart."

"And, moreover, Mr. Speaker," Prochaska said, "this business of the Russians not being trustworthy on disarmament is a glib simplification. The whole purpose of the new arms talks is to provide for on-site inspection by neutral experts. Those are the key words. *On site.*"

"I thank the representative from Ohio for these details," Ruckett said cheerfully, "but they are in the nature of details only. I maintain that the enemy has never honored any single *important* international agreement."

Representative Lewis Smales of Vermont was on his feet. He was a weedy, prematurely gray, millionaire, heir to a pulp and paper fortune, and a markedly independent and sensible man. A freshman congressman, he was not afraid of anyone, Lance Ruckett or fifty like him, and while he was in the opposition party, he had a healthy respect for the President. "Mr. Speaker, I must ask the floor," Smales said, after old O'Boyle had recognized him and gotten Ruckett to yield. "This speech by the gentleman from South Dakota is outrageous and irrelevant. He rises to discuss impeachment proceedings against the President. Under the rules of this House that is surely his privilege. But instead of any precise charges, any bill of particulars, anything remotely resembling an indictment, any revelation of acts by the President that render him unfit to continue in office, we get a speech on the dangers of Communism, dangers all of us are aware of, and have been for years. The President's actions in re the defense establishment, and NATO, and the disarmament talks are actions that can be discussed, argued over, and brought before the people and the Congress, if Mr. Ruckett and others disagree with them. They are not remotely related to treason, bribery or high crimes and misdemeanors, and I am still awaiting evidence that they are. I am thankful to the gentleman for his exegesis on the nature of Communism, but I await some facts about the President's evil deeds that require us to sit here and await revelations. Unless the gentleman from South Dakota can be more specific, he is wasting our time."

Good for Lewis Smales, I thought.

"Mr. Speaker, I associate myself with the remarks of the gentleman from Vermont," said Larry DiLorenzo, with a flourish of his white mane: Toscanini on the podium.

There was a stirring on the floor of the House. Ruckett paused, a chubby, vigorous man in his late thirties—what? A successful insurance salesman? A holder of a lucrative farm machinery franchise? Whatever he was, he was a terribly dead-center American. More so, I feared than an old needle trade organizer like DiLorenzo, or a Protestant aristocrat like Smales.

"Mr. Speaker, I accept the criticisms of the two gentlemen in good faith and with an open mind," Ruckett said. He was sweating prodigiously, and he used an old-fashioned, red farmer's kerchief to mop his bulging brow. It was a sort of trade-mark, and his fans knew it—a touch of color on his gray, neutral, surface. "They are educated men, intellectuals, each in his own way, and I am only a country boy . . ."

"When they start with that horse-shit," Parente said, "hold on to your wallet."

". . . yes, a country boy. And sometimes we plain, rural folk, who have been the backbone of America, are more attuned to what is wrong with America, than all the Eastern intellectuals, Harvard professors, inheritors of wealth, Wall Street manipulators, and labor union experts put together."

A reedy voice called out from the gallery: "Tell 'em, Lance!" O'Boyle lazily clacked his gavel.

"Oh, I intend to," the South Dakotan said. "If the gentlemen who oppose me think I am off the mark, that these accusations do not merit an impeachment, let me turn to more present, more immediate matters.

"I refer to the manner in which the President and his aides have given aid and comfort to the revolutionaries and insurrectionists in our cities. No, I shall not shrink from accusing the President of high crimes and misdemeanors, in abetting the violent, murderous, anti-American gangs of hoodlums now terrorizing the cities of America! And I know that as I speak, millions of plain, ordinary citizens—the humble, honest, hard-working, law-abiding folk who make up the bulk of our citizenry, will echo and applaud my words!"

He was rolling now; he had his issue. And I was worried. Lance Ruckett *per se* did not bother me. As I sat in the gallery with Parente and Goldstein, I could not for a minute take his feverish speech seriously. Nor did I expect he would get very far with the House Government Operations Committee, or the House itself. The motion would vanish into the history books, a discredited, unbalanced act. What did bother me, was the considerable army of support that he had rallied to his soiled banner.

"Early in his term, Mr. Speaker," Ruckett said, "the President, claiming he was acting constitutionally, and using his powers to interpret and enforce the laws passed by the Congress, rescinded patriotic actions taken by the previous Administration under the Emergency Riot Control Act, or ERCA. President Kretz opposed this. The outgoing Attorney General opposed it. The Congress opposed it. The people opposed it. But willfully, under the tutelage of his Attorney General, Judge Samuel Isadore Moscowitz, a man whose background includes a dozen court decisions in favor of rioters, rapists, pornographers and Communists, decided that there was no national emergency, that these people had been detained illegally, and that they could be freed. And they were freed. And what happened? Well, we know too well. More riots. More burnings. Columbia University, a school I have not always found to be as patriotic or informed on Communism as I would prefer a great educational institution to be, but which nonetheless served some purpose, burned to the ground. Insurrection in a score of cities—Toledo, New Haven, Waterbury and Sacramento. Thank God for fearless leaders like the Governor of California for saying so far, no further, the line separating civilization from the jungle will be drawn in this city, and those of you who are barbarians may stay in your filth and slime, while we who respect one another's persons and property, will stay on our side!"

There was applause from the gallery again—not just from Ruckett's claque, but from all areas. I found it hard to blame these people. They lived with the fear daily, whether it was real or imagined. Those of us who did not, who took the broad view, who thought in terms of long-range improvements, building cities, schools, hospitals, educating the uneducated, training the unskilled (how dull all of this sounded alongside Lance Ruckett's perfervid ranting) could be calmer, plead for patience and time. Had we run out of time?

"But Benjamin Bow Hannaford, I fear, lacks the insights and the courage of the Governor of California. And so he and his Attorney General, Samuel Isadore Moscowitz . . ."

"What is it with loonies?" Parente asked me. "Always with the middle names. You dig that Samuel *Isadore* Moscowitz? Benjamin *Bow* Hannaford. Lyndon *Baines* Johnson. Robert *Strange* McNamara."

"Makes it sound more evil," I said.

". . . freed those murderers, addicts, rapists, Communists, and let them roam the streets once more, killing, looting, burning, screaming their obscenities at law-abiding citizens, insulting and challenging our policemen, reverting to their foul behavior, secure in the knowledge that there was now a man in the White House who would tolerate, nay, condone, their depredations against decent citizens, and the nation itself!

"I say to you, Mr. Speaker, that such an action by a President, the deliberate misshaping of an Act of Congress, the failure to heed its provisions and enforce it, is a high crime and a misdemeanor, when it results in outrages against the public safety, against the public order, against lives and property! I know there are arguments to be made and I am certain my opponents, men like the gentleman from New York, who has had a long record of fostering liberal legislation, will say that this is a matter for the courts, that if local officials feel that the failure to enforce the Riot Control Act produced bloodshed and violence in their cities, they have recourse to the courts. Normally, I would agree. But these are not normal times.

378

And we have seen, that the knowledge on the part of the organized conspiracy of radicals, the knowledge that there is a President and an Attorney General who will not punish them, jail them, crack down on them, only makes these disturbers of the peace increasingly confident that they can literally get away with murder!"

In a way, I had to hand it to the cocky little fellow. He was pulling all the stops. No pussy-footing for Lance.

"And this is no matter for the courts, for endless litigation, and shyster lawyers and sneaky usages of the Bill of Rights," Ruckett said. "I am a lawyer myself, Mr. Speaker, and I say, yes, let us get this matter before the courts, let us redress the balance. But the President has shown us he has scant respect for the laws of the land, or the courts, or our policemen. Who is to say he will not disregard a court decision on ERCA? Who is to say he will not continue to pursue his goal of liberating criminals and making the innocent pay for his folly? I say, this is grounds for an impeachment proceeding on the part of the House, an indictment of the President, and a trial by the Senate sitting as a court!"

He paused to mop his face; consulted some notes. Larry DiLorenzo got to his feet.

"Mr. Speaker," the New Yorker asked, "is it the intention of the gentleman from South Dakota to offer a resolution or a motion? His speech is filled with misrepresentations, generalities and a variety of abuse directed at the President that is, to my knowledge, without precedent in this House. If he wants to offer a resolution, let him do so, and let him make his case before the Government Operations Committee, where it is supposed to be made."

Speaker O'Boyle cleared his parched throat. His shriveled guts must have recoiled from Lance Ruckett's poison. But he was old and frightened, and he—understandably—was on the side of the police, and the firemen, and the harrassed small home owners in suburban Providence.

"The gentleman from South Dakota does have a right to procede his resolution with explanatory remarks," the Speaker said softly.

"Thank you, Mr. Speaker. I shall conclude my comments with a final charge against the President," Ruckett said, smiling, "and then I shall offer my resolution. I thank the Speaker and the members of the House for their patience and their courtesy, in spite of the objections of a few members"—Ruckett glanced at old DiLorenzo, sitting erect, outraged, his seamed face reddening with anger—"who would prefer to see the truth suppressed, the issues fudged and the unutterable unuttered. Well, here is one country boy, here is one man from the great American heartland, who fears no one and is willing to point the finger at the Chief Executive, not for any personal reason, not because of political differences, not because he is not aware that there exist courts and legislatures and elections in which the course taken by the President can, and will be reversed, but because he holds the President to be guilty of high crimes and misdemeanors . . ."

"He's staying away from bribery and treason," I whispered to Parente.

"Give him time," Lou said, "give him time."

"I come now to another aspect of the President's conduct, which I and my colleagues, who will be associated with me in this resolution, are convinced makes the President a candidate for impeachment by this House. That, Mr. Speaker, is the matter of the diversion of funds, some fifty million dollars to date, and more to come, I am informed, of moneys specifically appropriated in bills passed by this House, by duly elected representatives of the people, supplying emergency funds for our Department of Defense. Mr. Speaker, this fund was not voted capriciously, it was not done to afford a President a plaything, pin money, petty cash, as the President so wittily termed it at a cabinet meeting—"

"How the hell did he know that?" Goldstein asked me.

"Veep," I said. We had been lax with Vice-President Sparrier; the leash had been longer and looser than we had intended.

"—petty cash, indeed! These millions were voted for one thing and one thing alone! The defense of this country! To provide emergency troops and equipment to protect our shores! To make up deficits in other programs. In short, to act as a cash reserve for the Pentagon, and to make sure, Mr. Speaker, that the Communists don't try to pull any fast ones on us, when, in a manner of speaking, we are short of cash. That money served the same function as the handy supply of extra .22 cartridges that any sensible home owner in any American city keeps in his dresser drawer, as protection against the muggers and rapists and criminals outside! That's what it was intended for!

"And what has the President done with it? Well, he has sucked fifty million dollars out of it, with the help of the Defense Secretary, Mr. Boswell, and sneaked that money into a bunch of phony boondoggles and worse, so-called poverty programs that were discredited years ago, and which served only to create more riots and violence!"

"Mr. Speaker, I cannot sit here," Larry DiLorenzo cried, "and listen to these reckless assaults on the President! I beg of you, Mr. Speaker, make the gentleman stick to the point! An impeachment proceeding is no trivial matter. Let him produce his evidence or be still!"

"I have not yielded, Mr. Speaker!" Ruckett shrilled.

"Will you yield, sir?" DiLorenzo shouted—and I thought the old man was verging on the coronary occlusion, so inflamed was his long, Roman face.

"Not now, not now," Lance said, smirking. "I have the floor. I will conclude. All the evidence that the gentleman from New York desires will be introduced at the committee hearings. Let me say now that the President's illegal diversion of funds from the Department of Defense to the so-called poverty program was in direct violation of the Constitution, his oath of office, precedent, the rules of the House, and the will of the people, the sovereign rulers—"

"He's got everything except the Talmud," Goldstein murmured—but Fred was whistling to keep his courage up. We were rocked by the savagery of Ruckett's onslaught. All niceties abandoned, he was steady on course.

"—and that this cunning move constitutes a high crime against the people, a misdemeanor of the severest kind, and that under Article II of the Constitution, he stands liable to impeachment by the House!"

They roared and hooted in the gallery, but the Capitol police were remarkably solicitous of them. The bearded, the blacks, the crazies, the wild kids, who from time to time disrupted proceedings in the legislative chambers, were tossed out without a fare-thee-well. I'd seen obstreperous left-wing lawyers hustled out of committee rooms with half nelsons locking them into pretzels, sputtering and citing through choked larynxes, the Bill of Rights. But the police guarding the public order on that warm day on which Lance Ruckett hurled his challenge were in no hurry to throw people out. After all, these were no enemies of the republic, but her friends. It was all so clear, so plain.

"I therefore do submit this resolution for consideration by the Government Operations Committee," Ruckett said, his eyes shining with the fervor of the anointed. "And four of my colleagues in the House will, when I have concluded, affix their names to it and join me in presenting it to this House for consideration."

We'd underestimated him; we'd underestimated Lance Ruckett and his appeal for too long. We never would again. I knew that as he began to read his resolution.

"Resolved," the young legislator began, "that the House of Representatives impeaches Benjamin Bow Hannaford, President of the United States for high crimes and misdemeanors.

"First. The House charges him with usurpation of power and violations of enacted laws.

"Second. The House charges that he has failed to enforce enacted laws, and has thus fostered violence, bloodshed and insurrection.

"Third. The House charges that he has with deliberation, misused and misinterpreted enacted laws, and has thus fostered violence, bloodshed and insurrection.

"Fourth. In view of these circumstances, Benjamin Bow Hannaford is impeached for the above high crimes and misdemeanors, and his case is referred to the Senate of the United States for trial by the Senate sitting as court, the Chief Justice presiding, as provided for in the Constitution."

The deed was done. A sense of shame and disgust and regret settled over the great chamber. Even Ruckett's plain people were quiet. It is no small matter to utter such words in public, let alone in the House of Representatives. Among the hot-eyed haters there is no hesitancy about putting such venom in print, mailing out reams of leaflets filled with distortions and defamations, of making obscene phone calls, of writing irate letters to more moderate journals. But rarely do the zealots parade their outrage in public forums. They fear rebuttal; they are rendered weak by counterattack. As Sam Moscowitz once pointed out, most of their leaders are cowards at heart, back-stabbers and psychotics, whose sense of justice is limited to shooting people in the back of the neck "through the cross hairs." Rarely, very rarely, did they expose their most stringent feelings to the public. Open debate, dialogue, argument, filled them with consternation. Indeed, their manuals, their guide books, their "impeachment kits" warned them to stay away from public meetings and forums unless they could control them. But now Ruckett had chosen the most open forum in the world. Perhaps it was a good idea to have it out once and for all.

For a moment—as Ruckett sat down, and four or five of his associates in COCCC huddled around him, shaking his hand, patting his back, and Representative Walt Prochaska asked for the floor for a ruling on the assignment of the resolution to committee—I felt confident.

"We'll murder the rat," I said to Parente.

"You hope, Deever."

"He doesn't stand a chance," Goldstein said. "Scares people. Yells too much."

Parente was on his feet. "No chance, huh? Take a look at who's co-sponsoring with him."

Various Representatives were rising to indicate to the Speaker and the clerks that they would be associated with Mr. Ruckett in presenting Resolution H. Res. 988, to impeach the President. I expected people like Sykes Cottrell of Mississippi, and Roger DeVaux of Orange County, California. But I was stunned when John Piasecki of Indiana, good old John, hero to the Poles, Croats, Serbs and Hungarians, once a tiger for social security and labor laws, got to his feet, and joined them. And when Fulvio Stradella, a pillar of the Government Operations Committee, a rather bland fellow from Philadelphia, also joined the sponsors, I felt my stomach quiver, my bowels freeze.

"You see how it's going, pal?" Parente asked cynically. "Stradella's got voters also. Let's get the hell out of here before I puke."

The last sight I noticed on the floor of the House, as Parente, Fred and I wound our way through the press gallery, was the lonesome figure of Representative Angel Lopez Garcia. Sad Angel! I had the feeling that DiLorenzo, Smales, and our friends had told him to stay out of the debate, to avoid entering the lists in favor of the President. We'd managed to get him back his committee posts, his seniority, his back pay—but he was still a pariah. What troubled me was a shivering vision of what the militants had in mind for Ben Hannaford. They wanted to cover him with mud and slime and spittle, to create another Garcia, object of scorn and derision—powerless, abused, isolated.

That night I sat with the boss in the presidential dining room, and Fern and Vangie excused themselves to watch a television documentary on chemical and biological warfare. I found him maddeningly calm.

"Ruckett's through," he said. "Those ranters never last. Let him scream sin and perdition. The Government Operations boys will throw him out after one day of hearings. I talked to Suggs this afternoon."

"You aren't worried by Piasecki and Stradella joining him?"

"No. John Piasecki is a decent sort, but he's frightened. He did this for one reason. Hell of a fight over bussing and integrated schools in his district. Policemen's union warned him—they're checking every move he makes. John called me to apologize. Said the only reason he is backing Ruckett is he knows the move doesn't stand a chance in committee. They'll knock it down, two to one. And that'll end Mr. Ruckett. Stradella told me the same thing."

Was he really that placid? His voice was unemotional. But was he boiling with rage within? To have the holder of the highest office in the world, the most powerful elected official on earth, be subjected to the vile language and accusations of a Lance Ruckett can hardly be a pleasurable matter. A man must long for a rifle and a chance to use it, at times. Or at least the opportunity to employ his fists on those who abuse him. I wondered about Ben. I'd heard stories about him back in his youth, when he was a rugged oil-field rigger, just starting his company. Many a rival, many a union galoot, many a drunk, or smart-aleck driller who cheated him, felt the weight of those fists. How he must have relished the thought of landing one, just one hard right on Lance Ruckett's snoot!

Even when I showed him a new Gallup poll, hardly encouraging, he scoffed, and professed no concern over it. It wrenched me, scared me.

Favor Impeachment	34 per cent
Oppose Impeachment	33 per cent
No Opinion	33 per cent

"That's a first-rate poll, Edward," he said. "We are doing almost as good as we did in the election."

"Yes. That reliable thirty-three per cent of the people. I often wonder, sir, who they are."

"Edward, look happier," Ben said. "This will all be over in a few days. Ruckett will have his innings in front of the committee, and he'll be hanged by his own shabby, shifty case. And once he's down, he's out. He's a yellowbelly, a liar and a sneak, and when he's shown up, he'll quit."

"I wish I could be so confident."

"It's in the nature of things. Americans are not people who like extreme solutions, extreme actions. A lot of 'em don't care for me just now, but the business of up-ending me isn't very appealing to them. In fact, once we knock off Mr. Ruckett, we'll be in much better position to get some of our program through. Almost as if he's giving us the chance for a confidence vote."

"Impeachments were never conceived of in that manner. That's exactly what they're not supposed to be."

"I know. One more example of the right things getting done for the wrong reason."

I was aghast. "Mr. President, are you saying this abominable campaign against you is the right thing?"

"Goodness no, Edward. But the sympathy, and the good will, and the understanding that I shall harvest from this ordeal, will help us in getting things like a housing bill and an education bill through the sullen men in the Capitol. 'All things worketh together for good to them that love God.' Let us love Him, Edward, let us love Him with all our hearts, our souls and might, as the old Hebrew prayer has it."

Ben comported himself magnificently, as the press detailed the mounting campaign to unseat him. Letters and telegrams inundated the Government Operations Committee. Far and wide across the country ranged General Clyde Upshaw, speaking to packed crowds and urging them to let their elected representatives know how they felt about Hannaford. Publisher C. C. Pringle's editorials hailed Representative Ruckett as a new Messiah, clearly presidential timber, a man to be watched and encouraged. I noted with some weary satisfaction, however, that Bates Pendragon was still dancing away from the resolution.

A call from Mona Varnum in Sacramento upset me. Up to that point, Hannaford's confidence had buoyed mine. And so had the vigorous support from most of the press and the television commentators—a decent, fair bunch. But what Mona had to tell me caused me to start worrying all over.

"Deever, I do this as a favor to a good guy, honky though you are," she said. The husky voice suggested midnight indiscretions in thatched roofs on some glittering coral strand.

"Speak, funky."

She laughed—a warm, rippling sound—and I was pained by all the joy I'd never have. Which was just the way she wanted it to be. Still, she was more congenial toward me than ever: there was still hope. "Deever, you are fine for me, just fine, for Mona. Don't mind the collect call do you, whitey?"

"Anything from a professional journalist. What is happening in Sacramento?"

"Friend, I tell you this because it might help Hannaford. He really isn't my breed of cat, but I've been thinking of what you told me. I mean, if we don't like him, we should see who is waiting off stage."

"You're learning, Miss Varnum. Your illustrious ancestor, General James Varnum would be proud of you. Say, he was quite a cat. The man who told Washington to buy up slaves, free them, and make soldiers out of them."

"Most apt, Deever. The soldiers are arming again. Kakamba Jones and Mudonga Smith showed up this afternoon. They were sneaked into the ghetto compound. You should see this mother. Barbed wire ten feet high, armored cars, half tracks. You got to have two different kinds of passes to get in or out. And the brothers—they got what they call a revolutionary council in charge—only black reporters allowed. It's a wild scene, brother, and it stinks. Every day, just about sundown, the shooting starts."

"The papers haven't reported that."

"Governor Fancourt's got a lid on everything. It's not the state police or the local cops. Or the National Guard. They've been pretty good so far. It's those fuckers in white helmets. The White Guards. Some maniac named Huckerby was out here yesterday handing out literature. Little red-headed squirt with big freckles."

"I know him well."

"These bastards have occupied buildings overlooking the compound and they take pop shots at the brothers every night. Thus far there's been no counteraction, but Kakamba held an *indaba* tonight—"

"Indaba?"

"A Zulu word, honky. Means a council. They're organizing the brothers into *impis*—"

"Impis?"

"Zulu, man. An impi is a Zulu battalion, a fighting unit of armed warriors. They had a few guns in this place before the governor sealed it off, but I hear Kakamba brought a big load with him. And some of the old Watts gang are coming up—Afro Avengers, Black Militia. The word is they come bringing not peace, but a sword."

"Mona, you've got to work on them. You've got to tell them to cool it."

"They are long past being cooled, boy."

"They'll make things worse for themselves," I pleaded. "Talk to Kakamba, Mona. Tell him to read up on the Zulu wars. If he has no sense of politics, at least let him develop a sense of history. The Zulu armies were annihilated by the British. They still haven't recovered."

"Man, you talkin' up a tree."

"They'll hang Hannaford," I pleaded.

"Maybe that's what they want."

"Is it what *you* want? Is it what the black people of America want?"

"Cain't say, whitey, cain't say. I figure they're lookin' at it like the Jews in the Warsaw ghetto, the ones who organized a resistance at the end. Don't look for docility, boy, or forgiveness."

"It's not the same, Mona, it's not the same." I tried to explain to her that this nation, for all its failings, was still a place of hope, of experiment, of change, and that we were not *quite* Nazi Germany. We were in pain, and in turmoil; hate and greed were rampant. But it was wrong to give in to them, and it was wrong to make mindless comparisons between us and the bloody dictatorships of Europe.

As we said our good-byes, I found myself in the uncomfortable position of rooting for Governor Fancourt and his National Guardsmen. Let him, I begged some God unknown, keep the blacks penned up, disarmed and neutralized—at least during the hearings of the Government Operations Committee of the House.

PART V

"Well, glory be, th' times has changed since me frind Jawn Finerty come out iv the House iv Riprisintatives; an', whin some wan ast him what was goin' on, he says, 'Oh, nawthin' at all but some damned American business.' Thim was the days!"

—MR. DOOLEY

The committee met in closed session. The press was barred; the press was enraged. This boded well for us. It was as if Chairman Lemuel C. Suggs of Alabama, aware of the awesome job into which he'd been euchred by Lance Ruckett and his COCCC raiders (and the incompetence of Speaker O'Boyle) now chose to conduct his hearings in secret and with the faint hope that they would vaporize and vanish.

It was not a farfetched notion. I have heard it argued that the media—press, TV, radio—tend increasingly to *make* news, to create events, or at minimum, shape their direction and tenor. If the press were barred from the committee meetings, and if all that reporters would receive would be snippets, Suggs reasoned, perhaps the whole sordid mess would disappear. It was not a naïve notion, but it had one flaw. Ruckett and his people would not let it disappear. They would shout, and accuse, and smear, and attack Hannaford—secret hearings or no—and we would be forced to respond. For this reason, and because of the mounting strength of our position, I regretted the decision to keep the hearings closed. We would have benefited by TV exposure. There is something about television that filters through the truth about psychotics like Lance Ruckett. The more he was seen and heard, the less he could be believed.

"Full house," I said to Matt Fixx, as we settled into seats at the rear of the cavernous caucus room. He meant, of course, all thirty-three members of the Government Operations Committee. The seats where normally the

390

press and public sat, were vacant. Only persons directly involved had been admitted—witnesses, clerks, committee aides, various functionaries of the House.

I noticed that a good many members of the House and Senate, using their congressional prerogatives, were in attendance. Ruckett, as a committee member, sat rigidly behind the curved, elevated table. I looked over the other members— thirty-three Americans—and I felt better. Matt Fixx and I had done some nose counting and some analyzing the previous night. According to our secret files, the little index cards we kept on Congressmen, we were in good shape. Men like Sykes Cottrell of Mississippi, Roger De-Vaux of California and bumbling, potato-nosed John Piasecki, terrified of White Guardists and insulted by black extremists, would have to back their co-sponsor of the impeachment resolution with its bland designation, H. Res. 988. But they were a minority. I was further cheered by the flustered, embarrassed look on Fulvio Stradella's face, another Ruckett backer.

"Get a load of Stradella," I said to Matt. "He looks like he forgot his morning Brioschi."

"He deserves to be sick," Matt commented, "for running interference for Ruckett and that mob."

"How do you figure it? Stradella used to be a liberal."

"You read what happened in Philadelphia last week? White labor unions fighting in the streets with black demonstrators. Construction unions are Fulvio's backers. Money and votes, Eddie."

Well, we may have lost Representative Stradella but there was still Harry Kaplan, and Lewis Smales, and a lot of other good men on the Government Operations Committee. Chairman Suggs banged the gavel once—almost silently, as if he'd be just as happy not having the honor— and began to read Ruckett's indictment.

"*. . . he has failed to enforce enacted laws and has thus fostered violence, bloodshed and insurrection. . . .*"

"What kind of reading do you have on Chairman Suggs?" I asked. "Anything new?"

Matt nodded, his ears flapping. "Looks good. The chairman is going to give Ruckett's mob every break—but he'll stay with *us.* Look at the list of witnesses."

I studied the printed list again. Thirty-one witnesses. Not too bad. When the House went after Andrew Johnson, they'd summoned no less than ninety-nine people to testify, almost every one prejudiced against the President. And their list included numerous psychos, fools, knaves and known perjurers. By contrast, the Government Operations Committee appeared to have attempted to strike a decent balance.

"President of National Council of Police Chiefs," I read under my breath, "General Boyd R. Nagel. Spokesman for National Association of Uniformed Firemen. Executives of the National Union and Military Bureau. We the Mothers. Taxpayers Association of Sacramento. Committee of Neighborhood Groups, or CONG, of Waterbury . . ."

"America's middle class on the march," Matt said. "Don't underestimate them."

"I don't. They should be *our* people. They always were, until this race business got out of control."

Chairman Suggs was drawling on, in his hominy-grits voice, assuring everyone that this was not a trial, nor a judicial proceeding, nor an attempt to affix blame, but a hearing aimed at getting information, of determining whether H. Res. 988 should be considered by the House of Representatives.

"How will this work?" I whispered to Matt. "Will Ruckett's crowd call the tune?"

"On witnesses? Suggs decides who gets called."

"Who speaks for the boss?"

Matt shrugged. "You know how B.B.H. is. He is the President, Ed. He can't get down to their level, and he can't have college professors and friends like Burke Boswell coming in here and swinging at these madmen. It's like it was in the Joe McCarthy era. The guy was so poisonous that decent people didn't want to talk back to him."

"And he almost took the country over."

"I don't think so. Eisenhower handled him just right. Let him spout on, let him poison the air—until he choked on his own venom."

No, a President could not appear before House Committees. Nor could he send emissaries to plead his case. I recalled that one of Andrew Johnson's tactics was to ignore the proceedings in the House, to continue to fulfill his duties and to comport himself in a dignified manner. Perhaps that would be our best tactic also. I shivered a little: Johnson had been impeached and had missed conviction by one vote. A damned close run thing.

"You see, Ed," Matt whispered, as Suggs droned on, "we've got friends on the committee. Lew Smales and Harry Kaplan and Hollis Denton won't let Ruckett and Cottrell run away with the show."

No sooner had he said this, than Representative Lewis Smales, that lean, rich, Vermonter was bending across the long table to get Lemuel Sugg's attention.

"Mr. Chairman, I have some preliminary remarks to make," Smales said nasally.

"God bless those Yankees," I said to Matt softly.

"Please do, Mr. Smales," Chairman Suggs said. "It is the intention of the chair to keep these hearings wide open, to give all members of the committee every opportunity to speak and to question witnesses, in short, to examine the matter before us as fully as possible."

"Thank you, Mr. Chairman," Representative Smales said. "I wish to move for an immediate vote by the members of this committee on the germaneness of the resolution."

There was a stunned look on Lem Suggs's plump face. He fiddled with his rimless glasses, and he wet his lips. I glanced at Lance Ruckett. The South Dakotan was nonplused.

"I am not certain I understand the request by the gentleman from Vermont," Chairman Suggs said.

"I will repeat it. It is my contention that on the basis of the resolution submitted by the gentleman from South Dakota and three other members of the House, this committee, or any other committee, or the entire House, has absolutely nothing to consider. The Constitution is precise as to what constitutes grounds for the impeachment of a President. Nothing in the indictment remotely qualifies. We sit here in judgment on nothingness. This meeting of the Government Operations Committee, Mr. Chairman, with all due respect to the House leadership, is about as apropos as a meeting of the Sacred College of Cardinals to discuss the realignment of teams in the National Basketball Association."

Ruckett stiffened in his seat. "Mr. Chairman, I cannot let—"

"I have not yielded," Lewis Smales said curtly. "I move, Mr. Chairman, that the chair immediately poll the thirty-three members of this committee on a motion to dismiss the impeachment proceedings out of hand, on the basis

393

that they are totally in conflict with the Constitution and are not worthy of further debate."

I saw Congressman Harry Kaplan smile, and half nod at Lewis Smales. Three or four others looked at ease now. I noticed a look of surpassing relief on Fulvio Stradella's face. This would get him off the hook. He could go back to his Italians and Poles in Philadelphia and tell them that the committee had done him dirt. Yes, he'd wanted to impeach the President, but it wasn't in the cards this time.

"This is irregular and not in accord with the rules of the House," Lance Ruckett piped. Was his voice shaking a little?

"I remind the gentleman from South Dakota, that I have the right to request a vote on the matter before the committee at any time I so desire." Smales pointed a bony New England finger at Ruckett.

"I associate myself with the gentleman from Vermont," chunky Harry Kaplan said. He was in the opposition party, but he was a long-time supporter of Hannaford's.

"Good God," Matt Fixx muttered. "Smales is stunting. He's red-dogging. Came on with the safety blitz."

"I ask you again, Mr. Chairman, let us have a committee vote *now* on whether the resolution offered as H. Res. 988 is germane, viable, or within the competence of this committee. I will even agree to have us vote on it as it is stated in this true copy issued by the Government Printing Office."

"Without hearing witnesses?" John Piasecki of Indiana asked.

"Yes, without hearing witnesses," Lewis Smales said. "What can they tell us that Mr. Ruckett and his associates haven't already told us? Mr. Chairman, I am sick unto death of these generalities, these imputations of treason and high crimes, without specifics, without evidence, without hard facts. Just look at this tawdry invention!"

Smales held up the printed folder that contained Ruckett's case against Hannaford. "Where does it show that the President has committed any kind of crime? Pray tell, where the treason? *What* misdemeanors? By using the powers granted to him by the Constitution to enact and enforce the laws passed by the Congress? So what if some of us don't like the way he's interpreted some of them? Is that grounds for impeachment?"

"Mr. Chairman," Congressman Ruckett said—and up,

394

up, went his voice, in that Sunday-night shrill. "This is no longer a matter for debate. The House leadership has placed this matter before this committee. We have spent a lot of the public's money and a lot of our own time, getting witnesses to testify. I daresay the public opinion polls, which show that more than one third of the American people favor this proceeding, should also be taken into account. I ask that the chairman call the first witness."

"I shall make that decision, Mr. Ruckett," old Suggs said. He was torn, torn. How tempting it was! Lem Suggs wanted poignantly to follow his conscience and ask for a vote on Lew Smales's motion, and have done with the thing once and for all!

"I will restate my motion," Smales said, in that flat New England voice. "I ask for a vote by the committee on whether or not to consider House Resolution 988."

"It's irregular," Fulvio Stradella said weakly.

"It's unconstitutional," Sykes Cottrell of Mississippi drawled.

"It certainly is not," Smales snapped back.

"Smales is right," Matt Fixx whispered to me. "But Cottrell was using southern gambit No. 2-B. When in doubt, claim that your opponent is acting against the Constitution."

Suggs pursed his lips. I marvelled at the casualness of the scene. An elderly secretary carried paper cups of water to Harry Kaplan and John Piasecki. Lew Smales stoked his pipe and puffed lazy clouds of smoke into the lofty room. We waited. Would it end like this? All of Ruckett's wild schemes and evanescing under the forthright exposure of a man like Smales, a Yankee with a rough sense of justice and a shrewd knowledge of our laws?

"I am troubled, as are many members of the committee," Suggs said, "by the suddenness of your motion. We do have witnesses to hear . . . and the Speaker and the leadership have placed this matter on our agenda."

"I remind the chairman that the Government Operations Committee is his and his alone," Lew Smales said. "As chairman, he can call for a vote any time he wants. He can call three witnesses, or 103 witnesses or none at all. In view of the flagrant bias of this document, the wicked manner in which it blackguards the President, I move for the latter course. We know what these charges are, and what motivates them. We will sit here and listen to a rehash of old prejudices and worn-out slanders, and be none the wiser for it."

Suggs was clearly up a tree. His heart was with Smales; he had never had any stomach for the hearings. He was of that old rural Alabama stock, those good country people, who, for all their feelings on the race matter, were responsive to appeals for fair play and honesty.

As he pondered, and as Harry Kaplan and Fulvio Stradella and Hollis Denton engaged in a colloquy on Lew Smales's motion, I saw Congressman Ruckett scrawl something on a scratch pad, fold it, hand it to the elderly lady—a committee aide who had been distributing ice water. She, in turn, gave it to the chairman. Lem Suggs (as the debate got louder, and the tired phrase "comfort to our enemies" fouled the air) glanced at it, then whacked the gavel a few times.

"The Chair rules that Mr. Smales's motion is out of order. Well, if not out of order, it is premature. The Chair will ask the clerk to call the first witness."

I nudged Fixx. "We lose that round."

Matt did not seem upset. "It was an outside chance. The sad thing is Smales had the votes. If Suggs had put the motion up, we'd be home free. But heck, you can't fault the old man. Why should he abort the mission before it's air-borne? You can't ask a man to destruct his own bird."

"No you can't, Matt." I was itching to know what Ruckett had written to him. I could imagine. Lem Suggs had been having close scrapes with the White Guards and the citizens' councils back home.

Patrick James Hanratty, president of the National Council of Police Chiefs was sworn in.

The committee counsel, a young lawyer named Pierce Eldridge—a colorless, paper-shuffling man with a shaved head and the trim figure of a morning jogger—started to interrogate the witness. I could see the strategy. Ruckett would build a case against the President on testimony from middle-class, and blue-collar Americans, who viewed the national crisis as a product of the boss's policies. It was good strategy. Ruckett would avoid the nuts, the bigots, the out-and-out psychotics. Merton Huckerby and perhaps even General Clyde Upshaw would be kept under wraps.

396

"Yes, sir," Chief Hanratty was saying, "everything got worse after the government let all them people out of the detention centers in February."

The chief was a tired-looking, bespectacled man, with an iron-gray brush cut and a malformed pugilist's nose. It was all there—the fatigue, the bad grammar, the honesty, the confusion. A decent cop. In spite of the failure of Representative Lewis Smales to abort the hearings, I had felt confident. But now, looking at Chief Hanratty's weary, weathered American face, I wasn't so sure. He spoke for a big important constituency—people who believed in thrift, God, the Armed Forces, the flag and hard work. We could not write them off. We did not dare.

"You know what this is going to boil down to?" I asked Matt Fixx.

"Test of credibility?"

"No. Look at that face. The man's honest. He used to vote for FDR. He believes in sportsmanship and fair play. He's right, but then so are we."

"Then what's it going to hang on?" Matt asked.

"Who wins Chief Hanratty over. Ruckett or the boss."

Matt Fixx disagreed. He'd counted heads once more—I could see the notations on his yellow pad—and he'd decided we were solid. At minimum he gave us twenty-one votes against impeachment. "We've got good field position," he said.

"You say that known arsonists were released after the Attorney General issued his rescinding order?" Chairman Suggs asked.

"Yes, sir," Chief Hanratty said. "We had files on four such men, who had admitted starting fires, and we couldn't do a thing about it. They went right out and burnt down the civic center a few hours after they were released. What is a police force supposed to do?"

"May I interject," Lance Ruckett said, bending forward, "that the chief has summed up exactly what these hearings are about. And I say to you, sir, that the policemen of this country will soon, very soon, have a new set of guidelines to assist them in putting down insurrection. . . ."

I yawned. Matt could monitor the hearings. I had no stomach to hear fire chiefs, store-owners associations, house-holders groups, and construction union people, enlisted as witnesses to support Ruckett's attack on the boss.

They were so much better than Ruckett, such basically good people, that I could not bear to see them used so cynically.

The President agreed with my estimate of the situation. "Edward, we have to convince those wage-earning people that a job for the colored man down the street, and a good school for his kids, will benefit *him* also."

"You've tried, sir. The results have not been encouraging."

"We'll try again. Get hold of Meg McNally. Let's rewrite the tax bill, so that the poor sucker in the mortgaged house gets a better break. Let's get us a tax bill that really does something for those people."

I looked sour, unconvinced.

"Anything wrong, Edward?"

"Just everything, Mr. President. We've been in and out and under and around that tax bill, and you know the story. We need every dollar we can lay our hands on. At least until we can get Congress to approve the cut in military spending."

Hannaford leaned back in the high-backed leather chair. His huge hands formed a wooden block under his chin. He was fatigued, enervated, puzzled by the resistance he had encountered. And he was upset by the manner in which his old powers of persuasion, his cunning, his belief in reasoning and trading, had been frustrated.

I found myself wishing he would go on vacation, avail himself of summer White Houses, seaside retreats or mountain cottages, the way other Presidents had. I even wished him a secret, relaxing affair with some young, smooth-limbed temptress. Anything to ease his burdens.

But he was not surrendering to gloom. He had cards to play. As far as the impeachment matter was concerned, he did not seem to care at all. Ruckett and his mob were lice, fleas, as trivial as an itch or a mild rash. He had not referred to them once during our conversation. He was disturbed only by the manner in which the spokesmen for "Middle America"—how I objected to that glib appellation, a phrase coined with warm self-congratulation by a liberal journalist—were emerging as his enemies.

"Edward, find that young priest up in Connecticut who stopped the race riot. Let's set up some kind of commission with people like that—people who can talk to our unhappy white folks."

He was referring to one Father James Francis Ward, a young fellow who had interceded between black rioters and white property owners in Waterbury. I knew he'd be willing to help us, but I wondered whether we were too late for conciliatory commissions.

The impeachment hearings limped along. Soon they appeared ready to run out of steam. After the first three days of testimony, Representative Smales once more called for a committee vote on Ruckett's proposal. Again Suggs politely refused, until all the testimony was heard. He was afraid of Ruckett. I sensed it at the opening session of the Government Operations Committee, and I was convinced of it now. There is something to be said for the strength of people like Ruckett—they threw terror into their opponents. After the second effort by Lewis Smales to terminate the hearings, I phoned Lou Parente to see if he had any information on Ruckett's vanished wife.

"Nope. Also, I suggest you don't ask. It won't help our operative, Mr. Kockalovitch."

He didn't want us mentioning Augie Baldini's name on the telephone. I asked him if he knew whether Ruckett had cooked up a deal with Lemuel Suggs.

"No. No deal. Just fear."

"You mean that mob has cowed the chairman of a major House committee?"

"Suggs is crapping his pants. Remember that note young Lance passed to the chairman? A direct message. It said, *'We'll get you next.'* Suggs is going to have a rough time when he's up for re-election. Ruckett was reminding him. He's gotten Huckerby to threaten the old guy—no more money from DOOR or Save America, or any of the nice customers."

"You've done nothing to cheer me up."

"Stay loose, Deever. So far they haven't laid a glove on you. Those hearings are the biggest bomb since black capitalism. They're so dull, Suggs agreed to open them up tomorrow. Big show for the press and public."

"What does it mean?" I asked. "Why are they going to open hearings?"

"Suggs is no dope. He's frightened, but not stupid. The

way the hearings are going, they couldn't get Hannaford for going through a red light. It was Ruckett and his mob that wanted open hearings, because they were sure they would make Hannaford look bad. But it hasn't worked out that way. Smales and Kaplan are giving the witnesses fits, and guys Ruckett counted on, like Stradella and Piasecki are keeping their mouths shut. So Suggs figures he can act as if he's doing Lance a big favor by opening the hearings . . ."

"So they'll show everyone how flimsy the charges are?"

"That's about it. I give it two or three more days. They'll vote, throw it out, somebody'll wake Speaker O'Boyle up and tell him it's all over, and Hannaford can go back to trying to run the country."

"He'll come out of this stronger than ever," I said.

"Yeah, yeah, I'm sure he will." He paused a moment. "Hey, Deever, you might try getting in touch with your black chick . . ."

"Mona? She's in Sacramento."

"That's what I mean. See can you get her to rap a little. I don't like what I hear from out there."

I tried to telephone Mona at her motel, at Afro Avenger press headquarters, at the State House. She wasn't to be located, so I left messages for her at several places, only slightly offended by a young black man at Afro "press central," who told me to perform an impossible biological feat on myself.

I was at the Boswells' gloomy house a few nights later, watching a special hour wrap-up of the day's hearings before the Government Operations Committee. They had gotten around to a few generals, and as generals tend to be, they were poor witnesses.

"At the time of my resignation," General Boyd R. Nagel was saying, "I was convinced that the proposal to cut defense money in half was a treacherous act, and I am even more convinced of it today. . . ."

"That word treacherous," Representative Kaplan interjected. "That has connotations of certain acts that we normally do not impute to Presidents, whether we agree or disagree with them."

Boyd Nagel's pale face assumed an air of injured righteousness. The former chairman of the Joint Chiefs thrust his jaw forward. "I impute no such thing to the President *himself*. I maintain he came under the influence of evil counselors."

Burke Boswell poured himself a double brandy. It was ancient cognac, amber, clear, satin smooth. "Yeah, he means yours truly," the Secretary of Defense said.

"But let us assume that he had extremely poor advice on defense matters," Harry Kaplan said. The camera panned to Lance Ruckett. He looked apprehensive. The great impeacher did not like the way Kaplan and Smales went after his witnesses. Like the wilder young radicals of the left, people like Ruckett wanted everything their way. "Let's us assume that the proposal to slash the defense appropriation was a poorly conceived one. What in heaven's name does that have to do with high crimes, with misdemeanors committed by a President?"

"That is not for me to say," General Nagel said firmly. "I am a military man, not a legislator."

Lance Ruckett leaped in. "Would you say, General, that cutting back our defense spending to a point where this country cannot defend itself against sworn enemies might be construed as a crime?"

"I prefer not to characterize it." Good for old Butcher-Boy Nagel, I thought.

"That crowd has tried like crazy to get the incumbent chiefs to testify," Boswell crowed. He gargled his cognac. "Yup, I heard they put every kind of pressure on Dudley and Strang and the others to quit their jobs and throw the book at Hannaford. But they're loyal, yessir."

"Now, Boswell," his wife said, "you were saying the other day that General Dudley and Admiral Strang have some mighty odd political connections, and that you were worried they might join the impeachment team."

"Well ... ah ... ah ... that was before I talked to 'em."

Vangie and her mother were both studying the man of the house, with a bemused disbelief. They knew he had been up to something. "What did you tell them, Daddy?" Vangie asked.

"Hell, all sorts of things. You know. Powers of the civilian authority over the military. That sort of thing. Explained Hannaford's over-all concept of defense, priorities, needs of the cities. Got into Clausewitz on war and politics. MacArthur and Truman. McClellan and Lincoln. And even quoted 'em a little Moshe Dayan."

Mrs. Boswell turned her handsome head, stroking back her lank brown hair. She didn't believe a word he had said. "Boswell, that is the greatest collection of non sequiturs I have heard since Gage Hopewell gave the address of welcome to the black Miss Washington contestants. Moshe Dayan! Who are you conning? You did something to those brass hats, and I'd like to know what."

"They're like kids. They can be handled. Their trouble is they only hear what they want to hear from their flunkies. They sort of like me for telling 'em the truth now and then."

On the TV screen, Chairman Suggs was trying to halt a burgeoning argument between Ruckett and Kaplan. Through it, General Nagel sat unsmiling, frigid. It was more good news for us; the military were weak witnesses. Besides, what in the world did Ruckett's vituperative attack on the President for having "failed to enforce enacted laws" have to do with national defense?

"Mr. Chairman, Mr. Chairman," Ruckett was sputtering, "I don't like the way the congressman from New Jersey has been badgering this witness, a distinguished American military hero, who does not have to sit here and take these insults."

"Blame yourself," Representative Kaplan snapped. "You got him into this mess. This is a hearing on impeachment, not national defense. I don't know what this witness, with all due respect to his uniform, is doing here anyway."

"Say, this is grand," Boswell guffawed. "Go it husband, go it bear."

The Defense Secretary was enjoying himself immensely. Not only had he neutralized the generals, but he had bewildered his wife and daughter. Old con man, old courtroom fox.

"Mr. Boswell," I asked innocently. "I understand you had an interesting meeting at the Army and Navy Club recently with some of our top military." The TV résumé showed a new witness, the black organizer, Lewis Nesbitt, who had accused us of vote rigging in Los Angeles.

"Huh? Huh?" The lantern-jawed scarlet face studied me warily. "Where'd you hear that, Edward?"

"I have sources. I understand you extracted a blood oath from certain important officers."

402

"Now what's that all about, Daddy?" Vangie asked.

"Come on, Boswell, tell the truth. What did you do to those poor men?" his wife pursued.

"Nope. Not a word. What I did, I did for my country. All that matters is I got them to keep their mouths shut. They're officers and gentlemen, and I got me an agreement—foolproof."

I could not resist the opening. "Wouldn't you say, Mr. Secretary, that it was more on the order of *eighty-proof?* Or *ninety?*"

He exploded in raucous, clubhouse laughter. How he had enjoyed his entrapment of the military! Drinking them all under the table, besting them at that most basic of American upper-class sports—gluttonous alcoholism!

"Seems as you know more than I'd like you to know, Edward," Boswell said. "But I'll beg you to keep it between us for the time being." He refreshed his brandy snifter. "You can use it when you write the inside story of the Hannaford administration."

"I intend to."

"Which may be the shortest Administration since James A. Garfield's," his wife added. She nodded at the set. "Listen to this one."

Lewis Nesbitt, a cocoa-colored, bespectacled man, was reviewing the manner in which Dalton Warfield had allegedly fixed the voting results in Los Angeles. "Yes, sir, that man was Mr. Warfield, and he was Senator Hannaford's man in LA, and it was him passed out the dollar bills to us poll watchers. I still got mine." And he waved the money at the camera.

"Just a minute, just a minute, Mr. Chairman," Representative Smales said angrily. "I can't let this pass . . ."

Smales tried to back Lewis Nesbitt into a corner. Why, he demanded was a ten-dollar bill that he waved in front of the committee, proof that he had been bribed by Warfield—or anyone else? Did it have Warfield's name on it? His fingerprints?

"I daresay, Mr. Smales, I daresay, I know wherefor I speak," Lewis Nesbitt replied. I knew the type. The true believer. The self-inspired prophet. And yet, he had a certain force, and the committee listened to him with respect. If Nesbitt said that the election had been rigged, the results fixed, should he not be believed? I listened to his cranky testimony, and I had the feeling that many on the committee believed him. And perhaps a majority of the people. Of course, there was always the possibility he was telling the truth—or part of it. Hannaford had never gone into details as to how we had won Los Angeles, and California, and the election. But he had admitted to certain "less than regular" practices. But what of it? Since when had any candidate ever turned down a soiled vote here and there? Did John F. Kennedy recoil from Cook County? Or FDR from South Boston? Did a legion of southern candidates over the decades disown districts where blacks were barred from voting?

"Mr. Chairman, this testimony has no bearing on the impeachment resolution," Harry Kaplan interjected. "This is a different matter. I suspect it is in the province of the Judiciary Committee. I find nothing in the resolution offered by Mr. Ruckett that speaks of election results. I wish to go on record as objecting to this witness's testimony in its entirety."

"I beg the pardon of the gentleman from New Jersey," Lance Ruckett cried. "It has a most direct bearing on it. The frauds involved in the California election—"

"You've proven no fraud," Kaplan said.

"—bear directly on the first charge of the indictment, which states that he is guilty of violation of the law—"

"That is outrageous," Kaplan said. "There is no other word for it. Even if you proved these charges concerning the election, Mr. Hannaford was not even President when they happened. Mr. Ruckett, the traditions of this country are clear, ever since the case of President Andrew Johnson. No President may be impeached for alleged acts that took place before he was in office, or for acts which haven't taken place *yet*. I wish I could get that point across to you, sir."

"I don't need any lessons in the Constitution, Mr. Kaplan," Ruckett huffed. "Let the chairman decide this matter."

Poor Suggs! They'd been after him all right. The trouble with being a good-hearted neutralist like Lem Suggs was that you could not make a stand against militants.

"I must say, Mr. Ruckett, I have a few doubts myself as to the relevancy of Mr. Nesbitt's testimony, but since we have sworn him, and since he has begun his testimony, I think we should let him finish." Suggs nodded at the committee counsel, Pierce Eldridge.

404

"Yes, Mr. Chairman," Nesbitt said stridently, "Mr. Warfield tried to cover these activities, but many of us knew what was happening. The tally sheets from my district, I am certain, were tampered with. It is easy to do ..."

Characteristically, Nesbitt's testimony was sprinkled with phrases like "as a matter of fact" and "as is well known" and "everyone agrees that"—tricks of emphasis that professional witnesses, of the right and the left, employ with much effect.

"Who is this guy?" Boswell asked me.

"A malcontent," I replied. "Former black militant who saw the light. He's the house colored man for a variety of right-wing outfits. Shows up at DOOR rallies and tells it like it is, from his rather special point of view."

Minerva Boswell frowned. "But Kaplan's right. This doesn't have a thing to do with the impeachment charges."

"It doesn't matter any more," I said. "The boss is fair game. I've been reading the history of the Johnson case. The Halls of Congress reverberated with irrelevant abuse, nonsensical slanders. And the damned trouble was, that because Johnson's defenders stuck to the *facts* of the case they were hampered. That's our problem also and Ruckett and his gang know it."

"I wish our President would hit back," Minerva said. "You and Burke keep telling me how tough he is, what a rugged customer. Why doesn't he let loose at these idiots?"

Boswell was at the brandy again. "Nope. Wrong thing for the top man to do. He can't lower himself to their level."

I watched the next witness—the superintendent of public safety of Elizabeth, New Jersey, one Vincent Maniscalco—who claimed that funds from the Industrial Training Program, the emergency money which we had diverted from defense, were being used to teach antiwhite hatred to teen-agers. For all I knew, he was telling the truth. I'd long since graduated from any liberal impulse to make excuses for irrational and self-destructive tactics by black militants. Like many sympathetic Americans, the sight of vandalized schoolrooms and burning libraries no longer filled me with an understanding compassion for the oppressed. I wanted to shake them by the shoulders and cry, *For God's sake stop attacking your friends.*

"That is correct, Mr. Chairman," Superintendent Maniscalco said. "The head of the Training program in Elizabeth is the same man that said he wouldn't be happy until a policeman was killed every day. I heard him say it. He don't deny it. And he got the money for this here program last week."

The camera panned away from the gray-haired witness to a smiling Lance Ruckett. God forgive us, Vincent Maniscalco deserved better than Lance Ruckett. Who was to say we were not at fault for having neglected the Maniscalcos for so long? The camera moved down the row of committee members, and they all appeared solemn and perturbed.

Vangie shifted her legs. I wondered what she was thinking. "Good God, what a moron," she said. "Look at him—murdering the language and furrowing his brow."

Maybe it was my lower middle-class origins that were offended; or the cavalier manner in which this high-born and altruistic girl, could be so blind to what was bugging Mr. Maniscalco and millions like him. "Vangie," I said grimly, "we are all going to learn to have to live with him, furrowed brow, bad grammar, and all."

"You're damn right," Boswell said. "And we better start right now."

His wife sighed. "It may be too late."

I ran a spot check of White House mail, and letters coming in to a few key senators the next day. Cleo Watterson was not encouraging. "It's rotten, Ed," Hannaford's secretary told me. "And it gets worse. I'm pretty good at sorting out the nut mail from the legitimate protesters. And we're getting too much of the latter variety. The nut mail reads alike and is full of abuse. Bundles of it from Dallas and Phoenix and Sarasota. It's always been with us."

"And the other kind?"

"It's up almost forty per cent since we took office. I try not to tell the boss. You know—widow in Scranton, sore because all the welfare money is going to drunken blacks. Retired policeman. Spot welders. It's an urban picture and they aren't happy."

Some phone calls to a few senators confirmed my worst fears. Sid Stapp was cautious, but then admitted the worst. "Ed, it used to be just Orange County that gave us hell

406

on race riots. But I'm catching it from all over California. And it isn't organized, or promoted. It's the voice of the people."

"*Some* of the people, Senator."

"Well, yes. But too many for my peace of mind."

Next I called the offices of Senator John Tyler Lord of Vermont, Senator Alford Kemmons of Nebraska, Senator Harold Erlenmeyer of Iowa and Senator John Kovatch of Pennsylvania, all men more or less sympathetic to the President. All of them had the same painful report: they were hearing from the people, and the people were upset.

Hannaford was in Ramada City with Fern and the key members of the Urban Council—Secretaries Gantry and Murphy, Dalton Warfield, Senators Henshaw and Eisenberg—when the Sacramento crisis reached a frightening, and what was to prove a disastrous climax. I'd stayed in Washington with Matt to keep an eye on the House Government Operations Committee hearings, which were scheduled to conclude early in the week.

As was my habit, I switched on the all-news radio station as soon as I awakened. Under the strain of the last few weeks, I had been plagued with insomnia.

This humid Monday morning I was up at three-fourteen, in time for the sports roundup, which was followed by a recapitulation of major news stories. As I heard the lead item, I recalled the warnings I had gotten from Mona and Lou about something of a grave and violent nature imminent in the barricaded Sacramento ghetto. Apparently it had come. But it was a curious occurrence, if the newscaster's account could be believed.

"... temporary truce had been called between black militant leaders and state and local officials in the black ghetto in Sacramento, California. What started out as an armed showdown, a shoot-out between black extremists and police, ended amicably a few hours ago, when black leaders walked peacefully through the barbed-wire enclosure to a meeting with Governor Fancourt and Mayor Seffert. Here, with details of the story is our reporter in Sacramento, Mona Varnum . . ."

I sat up in bed, turned up the volume, and sipped my milk. Mona's liquid voice stirred no lust in me.

"A little after midnight," Mona reported, "a dozen leaders of the Sacramento black community appeared at the edge of the barbed-wire and steel-beam barricade that had been erected by state police three weeks ago. They included Kakamba Jones, former Vic-Presidential candidate on the Black-and-Tan ticket, Mudonga Smith, his war counselor, and Nat Turner Simms, local chief of the Afro Avengers. All were heavily armed, and displayed their weapons. Among them were the Army's newest high-powered scatter-shot machine guns, antivehicle bazookas, antipersonnel dispersal bombs, and two small antitank cannons. How the arsenal was smuggled into the ghetto is still unknown. But, in the words of Sacramento Police Chief Vardaman, it was enough to start a small war."

"Lunatics, lunatics," I muttered. "They'll get themselves killed."

"There was a tense moment, as the floodlights manned by National Guard units were turned full force on the armed blacks. Members of the White Guards formed a large mob behind the lights, and were ordered to disperse. Half-tracks and armored cars, which had been standing by a half mile from the ghetto, were drawn up in a semicircle around the northeast front of the barricade. Kakamba Jones then spoke over the ghetto's public address system and demanded an immediate meeting with Governor Fancourt. Otherwise, he said, the shooting would start, and he and his people were prepared to die and would take ten Whites for each black man. Here's how it sounded, just three hours ago, when I was in the ghetto, one of six black reporters allowed to witness the confrontation . . ."

The noise on the tape was garbled, mashed—shouts, cries, the hubbub of a large angry crowd. Then I heard Kakamba's voice, challenging, insulting, hurling his defiance at the lawmen across the barbed wire.

We are ready, whitey! We got us the guns and the grenades and the heavy stuff! Maybe you got more, but it won't stop us. We willin' to die, and take lots of you along, and make this place a great big pool of black and white blood. We got us a list of nonnegotiable demands, and we want Mr. Number One, the pig governor himself, Whitey Fancourt to talk with us, here, now and without no soldiers around him!

There was a click, and I heard Mona again.

"After about ten minutes of shouted exchanges across the barricades, Governor Fancourt appeared and agreed to meet in the Powell Motel, around the corner from the
408

ghetto barricade. The governor asked that Jones and his party come to the meeting unarmed, but the blacks refused. And so, just an hour ago, the twelve black men, bearing their weapons, bedecked in bandoliers, grenades dangling from combat jackets and dashikis, walked through the ghetto gate. At this moment they are still in conference with the governor, the mayor and other California officials.

"I have learned that the weapons were smuggled into the ghetto via a secret underground operation, using the sewers and a network of recently dug tunnels, and that they were purchased in the East by Mr. Jones, Mr. Smith and other black leaders . . ."

Mona had a few more details: there was reported to be a detailed battle plan for breaking out of the ghetto and resorting to street-by-street guerrilla warfare, no matter how severely outgunned and outnumbered they would be. Then she concluded her report on a curiously hopeful note:

"In any case, not a shot was fired," she said. "And perhaps this chapter in the national racial crisis is reaching a climax, hopefully a bloodless one. Observers point out that it was not until the blacks leaders threatened to resort to all-out guerrilla war—an organized, planned, well-armed war—instead of the random hit-and-run tactics that have characterized the Sacramento affair, that the governor and the power structure agreed to meet with the blacks. A black youngster—a boy of no more than fifteen, with an automatic rifle slung over one shoulder said to me, 'It show what difference a gun make.' His grammar may have been faulty, but he was expressing the sentiments of every black person in this city. Yes, it show what difference a gun make. This is Mona Varnum in Sacramento."

Was it a hopeful omen? I tried reaching Dalton Warfield, but his phone was busy. No doubt he had been briefed on the events in Sacramento. As the member of the Administration who knew the most about the affair, he was surely trying to learn what the next moves were. I decided the armed truce, the palaver between the conservative governor (no friend of ours) and Kakamba (not much of a friend either) might help us.

I lay awake, listening to the same newscast over and over—no new information was forthcoming, except that the blacks were still in conclave with the governor. A little after seven in the morning I telephoned Ramada and got Goldstein.

"We don't know a damn thing about it. Moscowitz's people out there haven't checked in. Warfield left Sacramento yesterday. He wasn't getting anywhere with Kakamba or Fancourt." Fred sounded as puzzled as I was.

"I suppose we're in the position where we'll take gifts from anyone, even a hard-head like Governor Fancourt."

There was a pause. I could almost see Fred's quizzical, green eyes, his freckled hand running through his carroty hair. "Wouldn't I like to believe it. Peace in Sacramento. The blacks lay down their guns. Kakamba calls on the brothers to lay off, to get with the President. What a dream. Where does that leave Ruckett and his mob?"

"Exactly. I have a feeling we've lucked out."

About a half hour later the phone rang. It was Mrs. H. Calling from the Ramada Ranch.

"Good morning, ma'am. I imagined only Fred would be at work at this hour."

"Edward, much has changed. I find that the early morning hours are the best for clear thinking."

I was reduced to a mumbled agreement. A new estimate of high-born women of wealth from the American South-west germinated in my mind.

"Edward, on this matter of Sacramento, I have some excellent contacts in the black community out there, and I would appreciate you, or one of the staff getting in touch with them *at once*."

The emphasis on *at once* delighted me. And she proceeded to dictate a half dozen names—including some rather wild characters. "Make sure, Edward, that you tell them that the First Lady inquired about the situation, and would appreciate hearing directly from them. You may give them my private number at Ramada, and tell them to call collect."

Goldstein then got on the phone. "I must say, Fred," I muttered, "Mrs. H. is involved. *Engagé*, I believe is the word."

Evidently she was now out of earshot. "You kidding? She's chairman of the New Urban Task Force. City beautification."

"The boss appointed her?"

"Like hell. She *asked*."

The President and his advisers remained at Ramada Ranch. Each day Fred, and sometimes a member of the official family—Disarmament Chief Cohen, or Secretary Murphy, or Meg McNally—would hold an informal press conference. But the boss remained closeted, hard at work on his program, oiling up Senator Hopewell and other congressional powers. I suspect he intended to stay in Ramada until after the House Committee had voted on Ruckett's resolution. The word was now out that a vote was due momentarily, and that the move would be defeated comfortably by at least eight votes.

"That's my guess anyway," Lou Parente said to me, as we took seats in the caucus room, for what was rumored to be the final hearing. It was to be an open session, with pooled television film coverage. A jam-packed audience of press, Washington insiders and congressional aides filled every seat.

Parente scowled. "The wolves are out. They smell blood."

"But you seem certain the committee is going to give Ruckett the boot."

"I dunno. Last few days, there's been a bad wind circulating. Everybody's getting his nuts off attacking your boss. Everyone who's got a complaint has decided Hannaford is to blame."

"That's one thing, but voting for an outrageous, unconstitutional resolution like Ruckett's is another. Give the committee some credit."

"Sure, sure, kid. That's what all the editorials say today."

The press was generally on Hannaford's side. Differ with him, many did. But the Ruckett onslaught had offended most editorial writers.

> ... best service that Mr. Sugg's committee could do the nation would be to record a unanimous vote against Mr. Ruckett's vindictive, political and totally irrelevant resolution.

So said The New York *Times* that I held in front of me on the press table. As I have been at pains to point out, the *Times*, as honest, progressive, and high-minded as it is, often has not the remotest idea as to what multitudes of sober-sided, uncomplicated Americans are thinking.

"Your name?"

"Abe Schwartz, Bronx, New York."

"Your occupation, Mr. Schwartz?"

"Taxicab driver. I'm president of the Independent Cab Owners and Operators Association. Been drivin' a hack for thirty-three years."

Eldridge, the committee counsel, danced Mr. Schwartz gently into the familiar minuet. Mr. Schwartz was fed up. Mr. Schwartz's hackies were fed up. You couldn't get men to drive cabs any more. Why should they? To be robbed, beaten, mugged, murdered? Yes, his men had cheered when the previous Administration had invoked the Emergency Riot Control Act. "An' there shudda been a law for addicts and pushers and all the other scum who are makin' life miserable for us decent people!" Mr. Schwartz cried.

There was applause from the audience. I noticed three of Ruckett's young crew-cut followers leading the ovation for Mr. Schwartz, who normally would have been as alien to them as a Zulu. Suggs rapped the gavel.

Lewis Smales tried to dull the cutting edge of the cabbie's testimony. "Mr. Schwartz, every man on this committee appreciates your dilemma—"

"It ain't a dilemma, Congressman, it's life or death."

"We understand. But do you, and the people you represent honestly believe that your situation will be improved by impeaching the President of the United States?"

Abe Schwartz mopped his lumpy forehead. He had bushy gray hair and clouded eyes—a man who had worked hard all his life, wanted no sympathy, and gave very little. "Look, Mr. Smales, I been a liberal all my life. Roosevelt, Lehman, Harry Truman, La Guardia. I ain't no reactionary. You think the Ku Klux Klan would take me? I got nothing personal against the President. But ..."

"But what, Mr. Schwartz?" Smales asked gently.

"But ... sometimes a good man gets in trouble. Does the wrong things. It's like the President's approach makes *more* trouble instead of improving things. There's people in the cities, Mr. Smales, who aren't *people* any more. They're animals. Ask my drivers. And they gotta be treated like animals. And maybe we need a President and

412

a government that don't kid around any more, that starts arresting a lot of people, and putting 'em away . . ."

Lance Ruckett was affirming the testimony, his fetal head bobbing. Schwartz had been an effective witness, a voice they would listen to. I hoped he had come too late.

Abe Schwartz was excused—a chunky, bowlegged citizen, one of the victims. He had every right to ask for a better life for his children.

"They saved him for last," Parente whispered, "and he was good. When you get Jewish liberals saying the President is a *shtunk*, look out. Anyway, he was the last witness."

Lance Ruckett had gotten up from his seat at the distant end of the table, and was whispering in Chairman Lem Sugg's ear. Eldridge, the counsel, joined them. There was some bobbing of heads. A smile lit Ruckett's sweaty face. I saw Eldridge reach into his brief case for a folder.

"Mr. Chairman, I should like to move that the committee agree that testimony is concluded, and that we proceed to a vote." Harry Kaplan was bent across the table trying to get Suggs's attention.

"I'm afraid I can't entertain the motion now, sir," Suggs said.

"Why not? It was my understanding that Mr. Schwartz was the final witness."

"Well . . . ah . . . the committee, that is your chairman, has decided to hear a few more witnesses before asking for a vote."

"This is most irregular," Representative Kaplan protested. "Why were the members not advised?"

"My apologies, Mr. Kaplan," Suggs said soothingly. "But this matter came up urgently, and the Chair felt obliged to act, using its perogatives as chairman."

Suggs was on solid ground. Kaplan knew it. Committee chairmen in the House or Senate are potentates, despots, lords of their patch of earth. They can do pretty much what they want—as many a frustrated President has learned.

The audience buzzed. There was a sense of anticipation. Suggs got up and waved to the two uniformed Capitol policemen at the door. It seemed—was it my fevered imagination?—that there was a disturbance outside the huge paneled doors of the caucus room. Shouting. The frenzy produced by a sudden sensation. The excited reactions of reporters and cameramen.

The doors opened. Through them marched ten black people— eight men and two women. Leading them was Kakamba Jones in a purple dashiki. Behind him was his "war counselor" Mudonga Smith, who set the style for the rest of the party—form-fitting black turtle-neck sweater, black trousers. And they were armed.

"Jesus Christ," Parente muttered. "A goddamn heavy weapons platoon."

Amid the stunned silence of the committee room, they marched, each holding aloft an ugly automatic weapon— black thick-snouted guns, automatic rifles and machine guns. Around their lean torsos were draped bandoliers of ammunition. From the shoulders dangled fruity clusters of grenades. Never, never, in the history of the Congress, I was certain, had such an affront occurred. And it had apparently taken place with the approval of the chairman!

"It's a goddamn plot," Parente said.

"What do you mean?"

"It's a fix. Fancourt. That law-and-order governor. Some peace meeting. The whole thing was to hang Hannaford. See if Uncle Lou didn't guess it."

"Impossible," I said. I turned to Matt Fixx. "Matt, where the hell is Warfield? I have a feeling we're going to need him."

Matt gulped—he was paler than the white mimeo paper on which he'd been taking notes—and walked to the exit.

A row of chairs had been reserved behind the witness table. The ten armed visitors raised their right fists in the defiant salute. "Long live the black revolution," Kakamba Jones intoned, "and long live the black nation of America and its battle for liberation."

"I ask the gentleman to exercise a little restraint," Chairman Suggs said. "I ask that he wait until he is sworn. Is it my understanding that two of you wish to share the microphone?"

"Yes. Brother Mudonga, our war counselor, will sit beside me."

"Then you will both have to be sworn."

Kakamba raised his elegant ebony head and peered over his gold-rimmed glasses. "We do not recognize the authority of this committee or the colonial government of this country. We cannot take oaths."

414

There was a conference between Suggs and his counsel. Then, of all people, it was Lance Ruckett, who addressed Kakamba in a wheedling manner.

"Mr. Jones, it's our understanding you are appearing here voluntarily, and that you want your testimony to be part of the record. If that is the case, you will have to be sworn."

Kakamba and Mudonga conferred, Afro head to Afro head. I rather liked Mudonga Smith. He was small and wiry and less sinister than the other members of the party. I knew he had a Ph.D. in social work and had once been a valuable member of the urban peace corps. But he had left all that behind to plot the black revolution.

"All right, we will be sworn. But the act does not signify our acceptance of the tyrannical rule of colonial America."

They took the oath. With much clanking of arms they sat down at the twin microphones. Kakamba cradled his automatic rifle in his arms. Mudonga slung his over a shoulder.

"Before the interrogation of these witnesses begins," John Piasecki said firmly, "I want to protest this outrageous display of weapons in the Halls of the Congress. Who, Mr. Chairman, condoned this?"

Lem Suggs scratched his ear. "The Chair made the decision, John. The Chair, acting on advice of committee counsel and staff and some of the membership."

"I wasn't consulted," Piasecki said.

"Nor I," Harry Kaplan added.

"Nobody asked me," Congressman Smales said.

"It's new to me," Hollis Denton said.

"I . . . ah . . . had to act on rather short notice," Suggs said. "Mr. Ruckett and Mr. Cottrell were very helpful. In fact it was Mr. Ruckett who disclosed to me that these gentlemen and ladies had important testimony. Since time was running short, and all of us are eager to conclude these hearings, I agreed."

Parente nudged me. "A tank job. A fix. They're all in on it. That bastard Fancourt. Ruckett. Suggs. And these crazy mystic knights of the sea."

As the committee bickered, as Suggs tried to placate the growing anger of its members—Ruckett and Cottrell were smugly silent during the argument—the audience appeared to fall into a hypnotic trance. All present—and I include Parente and myself, who were inured to Washington spectacles—grew transfixed by the black militants and their lethal arms. They had brought some horrible unavoidable truth into the room.

"Very well," Suggs said after a shouted exchange with Smales and Kaplan, "counsel may proceed with interrogation."

Eldridge leaned forward. "Mr. Jones, please identify yourself and your associates."

Kakamba removed his eyeglasses. His eyes brimmed with hot contempt for everyone in the room. "I represent the black colonized nation of America," he said. "I am paramount chief of the Afro Avengers, a group well known to you oppressors. We seek our own land, bread, housing, schools, justice and peace. And if you pig tyrants refuse to give it to us, we will seize it."

"How do you intend to do that?" Chairman Suggs asked.

Kakamba raised the automatic weapon and pointed it at the carved plaster ceiling. "With this. Chairman Mao has written that all power grows out of the end of a gun. We are at the point where we will follow his advice. The basic tool of liberation is the gun. No political movement of colonial peoples against oppressors succeeds without the gun."

"I am less interested in your political philosophy, Mr. Jones," Chairman Suggs said heavily, "than your recent activities. Can you describe what you have been doing these last four days?"

"I have been lending my presence to the Afro Avenger *impi*—"

"What was that word?" the steno-typist asked.

"*Impi*. It is Zulu for an armed troop of warriors. Such as exterminated the British colonizers under the great Chaka during the Zulu wars."

"Proceed, please," Suggs said.

"I have been in Sacramento, California, aiding my brothers in the concentration camp for black people. The enclosure which the honky governor built and in which he will try to perform genocide on black people."

"Mr. Chairman, I have to interrupt," Congressman Smales said angrily. "I want to ask the witness what his definition of genocide is."

"Race murder," Kakamba said. "Mass slaughter of an ethnic group."

"Do you believe, Mr. Jones, that it is the intent of the governor of California, or of the national leadership of America, to murder all the black people in this country, the way the Nazis killed the Jews?"

"They are doing it already."

Smales shook his head. "You are either a fool or a knave or both, and I must repeat to the chairman that he has made a serious error in permitting such fantastic, inflammatory testimony."

"What difference if they kill us off in gas chambers a thousand at a time, or kill us off slowly by humiliation and oppression and starvation the way you do every day?" Kakamba spoke calmly. It was an old speech of his. But coming now, inside a congressional hearing room, while he cradled the weapon, it had a chilling effect.

"Mr. Jones, when are you going to understand that there are millions and millions of white Americans who want to help black people, who are sympathetic to you, who want to see you enter the mainstream of American life, and that not every single white person is opposed to black aims and desires?"

"They are white. By definition they seek our annihilation. But annihilation is a two-way street." With that he let out an unearthly scream. *"Uhuru!"*

His attendants responded en masse: *"Uhuru!"* And they raised aloft the automatic rifles and submachine guns.

"Shit man, I've seen everything," Parente muttered.

"What precisely were you doing in Sacramento?" Eldridge resumed.

"I held an *indaba*." He leaned toward the steno-typist. "That is Zulu for a war council, honky. At this council it was decided that the time had come for the start of the national liberation of the black colony by means of force. The war would start in Sacramento, since the white pigs had chosen the battle ground."

"What made you think you could win?" Suggs asked. "I mean, there or anywhere else in this country?"

"Oh, we will win," Kakamba said. "Because we are not afraid to die. And we are better armed than you people know. Maybe some of us would die in Sacramento, but it would be the signal for our black guerrillas to strike in every city in America. They are ready. They are trained.

They are armed. No power plant, no railroad, no communications center will be spared. We have studied the national liberation campaigns of our brothers the Algerians, and the Viet Cong, and the El Fatah patriots, and we know that we must succeed."

Harry Kaplan leaned forward. "Mr. Jones, you are one-ninth of the American people. These movements succeeded because the guerrillas represented an overwhelming majority of the population. And your including of El Fatah is an error. Those Arab terrorists have never conquered Israel and never will, because they are a small outside force with no power base within the country. Don't you realize that you don't stand a chance?"

"You better look out, Goldberg," Jones said nastily. There was a collective gasp of disgust from the audience. Harry Kaplan blanched. "All you pawnbrokers and shysters and landlords gonna git themselves a little genocide also. Maybe we finish off what Hitler began."

"Mr. Jones, you are either insane, or so filled with self-hatred that you are no longer rational. I protest again to the Chair, that such abusive testimony be permitted in this chamber. I shall have nothing further to say to this witness or to the chairman." Poor Harry! He'd been a Freedom Rider years ago, and had been beaten up in Mississippi for trying to desegregate lunch counters.

"I associate myself with Mr. Kaplan's remarks," Lewis Smales said. "I am overwhelmed with disgust by this witness's attitude and choice of words—"

"Words gonna end soon, guns gonna talk," Jones mocked.

"—and I would like to advise him that right here in Washington there are thousands and thousands of intelligent, respected black citizens, who have made it up through the ranks in the service of their government, successful, diligent people, who would not touch him with a ten-foot pole."

"Yeah, yeah. Oreos."

"I beg pardon?" Suggs asked.

"I think he said Oreos," the committee counsel said. "Some kind of chocolate cookie, isn't it?"

"Yeah. Oreos." Jones smiled. "Black on the outside, and white on the inside. That's what those middle-class Uncle Toms are. They'll go, too, when we start the revolution."

To relieve my misery, I found myself staring at the two

women. They were pungently attractive—lean, firm-breasted, dusky maidens. Gold hoops dangled from their black ears; their hair rose in an areated bushy crown. I could have possessed them both, surrendering my bleached body to their umbrous embraces. Or was it Mona I craved? I forgave myself my divagations. The truth of the matter is, the bombast of revolutionaries, particularly self-deluded militants like Kakamba Jones, are in the long run, boring, deadly soporific. Once they have shocked you, and once you realize that they are mouthing masturbatory fantasies, there is nothing worth listening to. Hence my lickerish thoughts.

"Can you tell us more about your visit to the Sacramento ghetto last week?" Eldridge asked.

"Man, I told you. We came to discuss battle plans."

The counsel consulted his notes. "Did you bring anything with you in the way of arms?"

Kakamba turned to Mudonga Smith. "*Maulana,* respond."

"Excuse me," the steno-typist said. "Isn't the gentleman's name Mudonga?"

"*Maulana* is an honorific title in Swahili." Jones did not look at him as he explained.

"Jesus Christ, they'll drive me up a wall. All of this on film. And on the television tonight. It'll guarantee that Upshaw and Tutt get elected next time out." Parente did not say what effect the witnesses would have on Hannaford's efforts to calm the racial situation, to help black people, to unify the nation. But it was implicit. Both of us understood. I wondered whether Matt Fixx had found Dalton Warfield.

"In order to give the Sacramento brothers a fighting chance against the occupying troops of colonial America," Mudonga said, "against the pig cops, the beasts of the National Guard, the honky murderers who call themselves White Guards, our *indaba* succeeded in smuggling into the *boma* the following items."

"What the hell is this?" Lou asked me. "Why are they admitting?"

"I have my suspicions."

"Two dozen Katchkalnikov automatic rifles, with a thousand clips of ammunition. Two dozen Thompson automatic submachine guns, with seven hundred clips of ammunition. Fifteen M-21 semiautomatic rifles with seven hundred clips of ammunition. Two thousand fragmentation grenades. A hundred Browning automatic rifles with tripod stands and five hundred clips of ammunition—"

Mudonga kept reading—a housewife's shopping list. Was he lying? Was this all a hoax? It was certainly partly true. We had the evidence before our eyes. Whenever the war counselor mentioned an item, one of the delegation would hold aloft a weapon.

"In addition, the *indaba* has arranged the purchase and delivery of a dozen antitank bazookas with sufficient rockets, and assorted small mobile artillery pieces, mortars and satchel charges. These will be stored in our secret arsenals and not immediately given to the brothers in Sacramento. Beyond this, we are not desirous of revealing further acquisitions, except to state that the program is continuing."

Chairman Suggs drew in his breath. He seemed hesitant to go any further. Eldridge looked at him, as if for a cue.

"And it is your belief," Lewis Smales asked patiently, in his constricted, New England voice, "that this accumulation of weapons will succeed in improving the lot of black people in America? Is that what you believe?"

"Without any doubts," Kakamba replied. "We are ready to shoot and kill for what we want."

"Mr. Jones," Smales said, "I think it is time we stopped calling you people extremists or militants or black patriots or anything else. There is only one word for you. *Fascists.*"

"We been called worse."

"It is not the label that should bother you," Smales said. "It is what it represents. You have become as evil as your oppressors. All the excuses in the world cannot justify this brutal madness that has seized you. I am sorry for you. I will say no more."

There was a hiatus. Suggs appeared confused. Committee counsel and chairman conferred again. As they did, Lance Ruckett called across the table to them. "Mr. Chairman, I have some questions for the witness."

Relieved, Suggs told Ruckett to proceed.

"Mr. Jones, or Mr. Smith, whichever of you wishes to respond," the young man from South Dakota began, "how were these weapons purchased?"

"With cash," Kakamba shouted. "American Yankee money."

420

"I understand," Ruckett said. "But where did the money come from?"

"From the United States Government."

"Here it comes," Parente whispered.

"The government?" Ruckett asked. "Please explain."

"We got us a check for one hundred thousand dollars from the United States Treasury, and we used it as we saw fit." There were grins and nudges among his followers.

"You say *us*. I am not clear on that. Who was the check made out to? To the Afro Avengers?"

Kakamba chuckled. "No, not yet. We'll be hitting you up for reparations soon enough, man. This was a check to the New York Industrial Training Office, to which I am a paid consultant."

"Industrial Training," Ruckett repeated. "That is the government agency under the Department of Defense that is known as IT. Is that correct?"

"Yeah, that's it. IT. Set up to train black children in defense trades."

"When exactly was this check delivered to the IT office in New York?" Lance Ruckett asked crisply.

"I got it here, folks," Kakamba said. He took from a black brief case a photostated sheet of paper and held it up. Then he passed it across the table to a clerk who took it to Suggs.

"Dated June 17, payable to the Industrial Training Office, New York City. Treasury Check number 178 AG 5789 BX." Suggs read the information indifferently, as if the dull recital of numbers might cover up the enormity of the slander.

"Now this payment," Lance Ruckett said, "was a *special* payment, was it not, an emergency dispensation, because the IT program was short of funds?"

"If you say so," Jones said.

"I do say so. I know the history of it. As does every member of this committee and every knowledgeable person in the United States. This check for one hundred thousand dollars came out of the Defense Department's contingency fund. It was issued as part of a mass of payments authorized by the Secretary of defense, Mr. Burke Boswell, acting on direct orders of the President of the United States. Its avowed purpose was to keep the IT program and other alleged antipoverty programs functioning because Congress had refused to renew the funding of many of them. If I have made any incorrect statements, I ask the other members of the committee to correct me."

No one spoke. Suggs, his voice quavering, took up the questioning. "You are saying that this check, which was issued to implement industrial training of young men in New York, was used to purchase weapons? Is that what you are telling this committee?"

"That is what I am telling this committee and the whole United States. We're *takin'*. We're takin' what's *ours*. You give us money, we gonna buy guns. And when we get enough guns, we will take our land from you and set up the black nation."

"This is outrageous," Harry Kaplan said. "This testimony has no bearing on anything. It is provocative and inflammatory and utter hearsay."

A shouting match erupted. Lance Ruckett was banging the table. Kaplan was on his feet, running toward Chairman Suggs. The black smiled. They were enjoying the spectacle of whites at each other's throats.

"Mr. Chairman, I ask you to order the gentleman from New Jersey to take his seat and let me continue," Ruckett shrilled. "I am by no means finished with my interrogation of Mr. Jones."

Kaplan retreated. Suggs nodded at Ruckett. The young legislator leveled a finger at Kakamba. "Mr. Jones, correct me if I'm wrong. The office of Industrial Training in New York was given a check for one hundred thousand dollars, emergency money to keep the program going. This money came out of the Defense Department and its dispensation was authorized by the Secretary of Defense and the President himself."

"You said it, man."

"And you say that as consultant to the IT program in New York, you then used part of that sum to purchase weapons."

"That is correct."

"How did you manage that?"

Kakamba giggled. "Mr. Ruckett that is no problem. The brothers who got signing powers, who can pay out the money listen to me. Ain't nothin' better than a government check to buy guns. And you folks all know how easy it is to buy *anything* that kills. Why, some of you people been making certain for years that any American can buy

422

any kind of gun he wants any time he wants, if he can pay for it. We actin' like good patriots, like your friends in the National Rifle Association and the hunting clubs. Ain't no law says we can't buy anything we want. Like these fine Soviet-made Katchkalnikovs."

"Mr. Jones, this is very important. Was any member of the Administration, that is, of the government, and by that I mean, the Executive Branch, was any person *aware* of what you intended to do, or did in fact, do with the IT emergency allocation?"

"Yes."

"Who was that person or persons?"

"I know of one for sure, and maybe others, of who I ain't sure."

"Who was the person who, to your precise knowledge, was aware of your plot?" Ruckett asked.

"Mr. Dalton Warfield."

A murmuration rose in the packed room. "Who is Mr. Warfield? Identify him."

"He is a black man. He is a special assistant to the President of the United States. He is a member of the Urban Task Force."

Mudonga leaned to the microphone. "The brothers call him Mr. Uniform Tango."

"Say again?" Chairman Suggs asked plaintively.

"Uniform Tango," Smith repeated. "That is military phonetics for U.T. Uncle Tom."

Ruckett resumed. "Tell me the circumstances under which Mr. Warfield knew about your plan to use this government money to buy weapons."

"Ole Warfield came to New York three weeks ago. We had dinner at the Malcolm X Memorial Gardens in Harlem. He told me that the IT money was coming through, thanks to President Hannaford's generosity, and his kind heart, and his concern for black people."

"Were those his exact words?" Ruckett asked.

"Well, I dress them up a little. Warfield may have said it different. He wanted me to spread the word with the black community that the President wanted to do nothin' but good for black folks, and therefore they'd come up with all this extra bread."

"Bread?" asked Suggs.

"Money."

"What else did Mr. Warfield say?"

"Oh, he rapped on and on, the way he does, like all them Oreos, how he expected that the brothers would now behave themselves and act like good citizens and learn to be carpenters and electricians and data programmers, and get themselves jobs with Lockheed and United Aircraft and Boeing and help the country move ahead, and there'd be more bread comin' on for education and houses, once the President got the Congress to stop spending all them billions on nuclear bombs and such."

"And what did you say to this, Mr. Jones?" Ruckett asked.

Kakamba stiffened in his seat. He pounded the metal butt of his automatic rifle on the tabletop, and everyone gasped. From menace he switched to smooth contempt. "No sweat, beasts. It's loaded, but the safety is on. We been trained. Yeah, the brothers are trained and ready to move. Lock your doors. Own a police dog. Stock up on shortwave radios and canned goods. The fire next time, pigs."

"I repeat the question," Lance Ruckett said. "What was your response to Mr. Warfield?"

"I told Mr. Uniform Tango that we were through listening to soppy liberal promises. We had enough of Industrial Training and Head Start and birth control clinics and poverty programs. We goin' to make the decisions, and make 'em our way. The black sub-nation of America was about to become the black nation. And how is a nation born? How was Israel born, Mr. Harry Kaplan? I tell you how. With guns. With bullets. With grenades."

"You told this to Garfield?" Suggs asked.

"I did. I told him we would accept his money from the Defense Department with pleasure, and with no thanks. And that we would use it not to train nice sweet-talkin' tax-payin' welders and electricians. But to buy guns. To buy power. To create us the Black Nation."

"What did he say to that?" Ruckett asked.

"Nothin'. He just sat and looked droopy, the way Warfield always does."

"He did not protest?" Suggs asked.

"Nope. Oh, maybe once he tried to tell me I was wrong. I don't think that errand boy for Hannaford took me seriously. They never do. They never have. Well, you better start takin' us seriously now."

424

"Mr. Warfield did not try to dissuade you?" the South Dakotan asked.

"Nope. Kept shakin' that dumb Uncle Tom head, and sayin' he couldn't believe I'd be that stupid, and besides there were other people in charge of the IT Program in New York, who would not listen to me, and he'd get to them." Kakamba raised his gun again; the others followed him. It was an unbelievable dream; those strong, ebony arms, thrusting upward.

"You see how he got to them," Jones shouted. "That bunch of burrheads, those scaredy-cat social workers, they listened to me! They listened to the voice of their African tribal gods, the unavenged blood of the Congo, the Coromantee and the Zulu."

Parente was shaking his head. "Boy, they worked hard at this one. All of them. Ruckett, Fancourt, these *schwarzer* madmen."

"Did Mr. Warfield tell you that he intended to convey your threat to use government funds to buy weapons to the President, or anyone else in the Administration, such as the Attorney General?" Ruckett asked this with slow emphasis.

"Why, sure he did," Jones answered. "He said he was going to run right back to Washington and tell his Big White Daddy about us. Yes he did."

Parente leaned toward me. "Now he's lying," the columnist said. "All the crap up to now—maybe some truth in it. But this business about him telling Hannaford, that's a lie. Look at the guy's face. He's telling them— *I'm lying, and what are you gonna do about it?*"

Lemuel Cathcart Suggs shifted his plump body. He looked exhausted, abashed. "Mr. Jones, did you ever see Mr. Warfield after this meeting? And did he in any way indicate to you that he had spoken to the President about your intentions?"

Kakamba's eyes became feline slits. "No. Not again. I think I scared Uniform Tango. You see, people like Warfield are afraid of people like me. They know I am the future of the black nation, and they are the dead past."

Eldridge, the committee counsel, looked at Suggs. The chairman indicated to him to take up the questioning.

"I think it might be wise to recapitulate some of this testimony, Mr. Jones," he said. "You say that Mr.

Warfield met with you in New York to tell you that the IT Program, to which you were a paid consultant, was to receive one hundred thousand dollars in emergency funds?"

"Correct."

"You then advised Mr. Warfield you would use the money to buy weapons?"

"As we did."

"And that Mr. Warfield did not try to stop you?"

"Not with enthusiasm."

"Nor did he try to stop the payment of this money to IT."

"See for yourself, man. Look what we got with it."

"And Mr. Warfield said he would tell the President, and other members of the Executive Branch of your intentions."

"Yeah, he sort of warned me. In so many words."

"Did you have any further communications from anyone in Washington—anyone representing the President, or any cabinet member, or any special assistant, warning you *not* to use the IT allocation to purchase guns?"

"Nothing, man. Silence. Old Warfield vanished after I put him on notice."

Lewis Smales called across the table to Suggs. "Mr. Chairman, this testimony is a lot of unsubstantiated rot. It is garbage, manure, a compost heap of hearsay. I demand that Mr. Warfield be called immediately so that we can get *his* version of any meeting with Mr. Jones, and find out what took place. All we know for certain is that the IT Program in New York received one hundred thousand dollars to keep going, under the Defense Secretary's perfectly legal and constitutional use of the department's contingency fund. We know that. We also know that Mr. Jones and his colleagues have purchased a lot of guns and ammunition and grenades and smuggled some into the Sacramento ghetto. What happened between those two provable events is nothing more than hearsay, the word of this witness. I object to the manner in which this testimony has been given, and the attempt to blackguard the reputations of Mr. Warfield, Secretary Boswell, and the President of the United States."

Harry Kaplan took up the counterattack. "I want to ask Mr. Jones this. After he and his associates appeared on the barricades in Sacramento, armed to the teeth, a truce of some kind was effected with Governor Fancourt and police officials. Is that correct?"

"Yeah, Goldberg."

Suggs winced. "I caution the witness to observe a modicum of civilized behavior in this chamber. Rude and abusive language directed at the committee members or other persons will not be tolerated."

"Thank you, Mr. Chairman," Congressman Kaplan said. "Mr. Jones's use of racial innuendo is more to be pitied than condemned. I come of an old and embattled ethnic background, and I have never found it necessary to indulge in self-hatred and self-delusion to make my way in the world. Perhaps with experience, such wisdom will come to Mr. Jones. I would like to comment that in my view, he does not speak for the vast majority of black Americans, not by a long shot, not for the Dalton Warfields and the Homer Murphys and all the dedicated, courageous and intelligent black people, laboring to improve their lot, and to make America a better place. I will excuse his rudeness, and I don't give a tinker's damn whether he has the guts to answer the blunt question I am about to put to him."

Jones did not like this. For the first time, I saw him look faintly ill at ease. Behind his gleaming eyeglasses, he betrayed a moment of uncertainty. Was the arrogance, the glib boasts of murder, nothing but a mask for fear?

"Mr. Jones," Harry Kaplan said, "Governor Fancourt has never been a friend of the black militant movement. Indeed, he has hardly ever had a good word for moderate groups like the NAACP. Some might call him a cautious racist. Yet he refused to press charges against you and your armed friends, he made no attempt to disarm you, he did not denounce your smuggling of guns into the ghetto, and I am advised by newspaper reporters in California, he saw to it that you and your attendants were given safe conduct, so that you might appear before this committee, guns and all. How do you explain this?"

"Why, man, maybe we see eye to eye on some things."

"Some things?" Kaplan pursued. "Last week you referred to Governor Fancourt as, I quote you, 'a white honky pig, a corrupt old cracker, who'll get his when we are ready.' Did you make that statement?"

"Yeah, yeah."

Parente grinned with satisfaction. "Go get him, Kaplan." He grabbed my arm. "Harry's got the goods on him. Fancourt and the rest of this crowd—Ruckett, DOOR, the Save America lunatics—they rigged this with Kakamba. The crusher. They think they'll get Hannaford. I smelled it the minute this minstrel show began."

"Please tell me, Mr. Jones, whether this is an accurate quotation. It is attributed to you and it appeared in the San Francisco Chronicle four days ago. 'One of these days the black nation will read in the paper that Governor Fancourt has been shot dead by a black execution squad, while skinny-dipping in his private swimming pool, and that the killers have fled without a trace, and then the black masses will understand the basic truth of our program of liberation.' Were those your words, sir?"

"Yeah, man."

"Mr. Jones, how could you say these appalling things about Mr. Fancourt, and then sit down and parley with him, talk him into letting you keep your weapons, and with a maximum of secrecy, permit you to fly to Washington and bring your troupe of performers into this room, so you could slander the President of the United States?"

There was an explosion of applause from the audience.

If Jones and his aides looked irked—I could see them fussing with their gear, slinging arms, adjusting the grenades—Ruckett was no less upset. I knew what was about to happen. The blacks, realizing that Kaplan had seized the advantage, would get up and walk out. It was standard strategy. Once the debate started shifting against them, they walked. They had learned it from the new left students, and had even turned it *against* white new left groups, with dazzling effect.

"Just a minute, just a minute, Mr. Chairman," Lance Ruckett was crying. "I don't like the tenor of Mr. Kaplan's remarks. He is charging some kind of conspiracy between the governor of California and our witnesses, and he is hinting that the committee is involved in it. I don't like this sort of sneaky assault—"

"Sneaky!" Kaplan cried. "You are the biggest sneak of all, with your phony impeachment resolutions—"

"Gentlemen, gentlemen!" Suggs cried.

"I will not be silenced," Lance Ruckett brayed. That Sunday-night Bible-bashing voice asserted itself. It rode roughshod over Kaplan, Suggs, the rising babble in the crowded chambers. And the cameras kept whirring away, recording the shameful scene.

"I say I will be heard!" Ruckett shouted. "This testimony is crucial and vital and bears directly on House Resolution 988 impeaching the President! We have proven without doubt that the President is guilty of high crimes and misdemeanors, that he has knowingly and willfully aided an armed conspiracy against the republic by providing funds for the purchase of deadly weapons, that his assistants have known of these conspiratorial deeds and have reported them to him, and that he has done nothing at all to stop this Communistic, revolutionary, anti-Christian plot to destroy our replublic, and I further charge—"

As he raved on, the blacks got to their feet, saluted all in the room with clenched fists and marched down the aisle toward the rear doors. "—I am not frightened by Benjamin Bow Hannaford, or all his paid stooges in government, and his lackeys in the press, and the liberal conspirators who cover up for him, and excuse his malefactions and schemes—"

"I demand that that man be silenced!" Lewis Smales shouted. "Mr. Chairman, run this committee as a proper committee, or adjourn it—"

It was a single shot, but it sounded like a 105-mm. cannon. And it *was* an accident, as was proven later. But the noise, the sharp explosion resounded like a TNT blast in the crowded room. Women screamed. People leaped for cover. The three uniformed Capitol policemen and the half-dozen FBI men, whom Suggs most judiciously had posted around the hearing room sprang toward the file of departing blacks. But it was only an accident. A black girl had tripped. Unfamiliar with the carbine slung on her shoulder, she had neglected to lock the safety catch. A single bullet had been fired.

"Everybody stop!" one of the FBI men shouted. "Don't move, don't move. No one leave!"

The bluish haze of gunsmoke cleared. The sobbing, convulsed girl began blubbering how sorry she was.

"Jesus, Mary and Joseph," Parente said to me. "I thought for sure the revolution had begun." We stared at the ceiling. A chunk of plaster dangled from it, where the stray bullet had impacted.

"Clear the room at once, clear the room," Chairman Suggs said huskily. "Everyone out, everyone. Press, members of Congress not on this committee, everybody. Clear the room."

"I move for adjournment, Mr. Chairman," Smales said.

"The Chair is not ready to entertain motions to adjourn." He banged the gavel. "Clear this room at once."

Stunned, bewildered, the crowd began to move out of the double doors, behind the ten gun-bearing witnesses. Parente and I followed.

"Who gave you permission to bring arms into the committee room?" a man from the Associated Press was asking.

"No one gives us permission, honky. We do what we want."

Kakamba Jones and his people had formed a double row in the marble corridor, arms folded, faces hostile behind their dark glasses.

"Was it Suggs? Was it Ruckett?"

"There were no deals made. We decided to testify. And here we is." He uttered the solecism deliberately, smirking at the man from the Washington *Star* who had asked the question.

"What can you accomplish by it?" Larry Hosmer asked. "You may succeed in getting the President impeached."

"What do we care?" Mudonga Smith said. "He ain't our President. He's the *pig* President. We got no use for him, that big, liberal millionaire. You suck-asses must know how we feel. It's the liberal pigs, the phony two-faced, lying accommodators we aim to bring down. We don't hide it. We got no use for Hannaford, or Warfield, or Murphy or any of those cats."

"Mr. Jones, do you agree with that?" a New York *Times* man asked.

"In spades, beast."

"You'll end up with Mr. Sparrier as President. Didn't he turn the National Guard loose in second Watts, where over two hundred of your people were killed?"

"Yeah, now you coming on," Kakamba said. "That's what we want. Get it out in the streets. Only this time we'll *see* who has more guns and who is more ready to die. We'll see about guerrilla raids in every damn white city. Better a cat like Sparrier who says, come on, shoot it out, boys, than a fox like Hannaford who keeps sweet-talking us while he's plotting genocide."

430

"You may get Upshaw as President someday," a girl from ABC offered.

"Better him too. We do these things with a lot of thought. Trouble is you honkys can't think our way."

Lou Parente edged to the front rank of the jostling, churning mob of newsmen. He was in range of the TV cameras. "What'd they pay you Jonesy?" Parente asked casually.

"Hi, Louis. Pay me what?"

"Pay, *pay*. You never did anything except for money in your life. They got lots of moolah, man. They got all the bread, brother, and you know it. Save America. Defenders of Our Republic. DOOR. Mr. Huckerby and all those oil people who give him money. Congressman Ruckett, their Number One man in the Congress. For sure they paid your expenses. And maybe something extra for the pension fund, hah, Jonesy?"

"End of press conference," Jones said. All over the country people would see the newsfilm that night, and again, and again, and again, the lying, outrageous testimony, involving the President in a maniacal plot that had no sense, no future, and not the slightest chance of ending anywhere but in the violent death of innocents.

"Who made the check out, Jonesy?" Parente called after him. "Huckerby? DOOR? You play around with those people, they'll squeeze you dry like a lemon and throw you out, pal. Get smart, Jones, Hannaford is the best friend you people have."

There was no response. Black fists aloft, the Afro Avengers, displaying guns and grenades, marched through the hallowed halls of the House.

"Dumb bastards," Parente said. "I'm through making excuses for every goddamn thing they do. I've had it with them. Deever, you better go see your boss and fill him in. These guys may have succeeded in doing what a hundred jerks like Huckerby couldn't do."

The mob of reporters and photographers around the caucus room began to thin out. Some raced for telephones; two men were talking into tape recorders; a TV film crew was changing magazines in their 16-millimeter Auricon camera. Parente and I lingered, wondering if the committee would issue a statement. He doubted it. Smales, and Kaplan, and Denton and our other allies would put powerful pressure on Suggs to resume hearings,

431

to call Warfield and other Administration people to refute Jones.

Suddenly the doors of the committee room opened. The policemen formed a cordon around a group of congressmen. Then, with slow, vaguely direful steps, all moved toward the cameras and microphones.

I saw Chairman Suggs, pallid and distrait; Ruckett, sweating prodigiously; Fulvio Stradella; John Piasecki; Roger DeVaux; and Sykes Cottrell. Suggs had a paper in his trembling right hand.

"What the hell?" Parente asked rhetorically. "What gives?"

The reporters came together again, a clot of jostling bodies. Poor Suggs! He seemed to have shrunk, to have vanished into his rumpled gray suit. I could not see his eyes. They appeared to have liquefied behind his eyeglasses.

"I—I—I shall read a statement in behalf of the committee," he said in a muffled voice, "and that will be all. I cannot speak for other members of the committee, but at the moment I am not prepared to answer questions."

Lance Ruckett was standing behind Suggs, and somewhat to his right, and I had the feeling that the young man was somehow propping the chairman up.

"The chairman wishes to announce," Lem Suggs said, "that the House Committee on Government Operations has recorded its vote on House Resolution 988, submitted by Messrs. Ruckett, Stradella, Piasecki, Cottrell and DeVaux. The vote on the motion, which was taken at the conclusion of this morning's testimony, was seventeen in favor, sixteen opposed, and the resolution is thus reported out favorably and is referred to the House of Representatives."

With that, the reporters broke and ran. Suggs turned away and stuffed a handkerchief against his withered mouth. Lance Ruckett stepped forward. "I shall be glad to answer any questions," he said.

Harry Kaplan and Lewis Smales and a few of our other allies were standing in a group to one side. Kaplan was white with rage, and Smales's hungry New England face was crimson. "Mr. Smales and I have a few things to say also," Kaplan said shakily.

My heart beat frantically at my rib cage. I turned to Lou. "You stand in for me, Louis," I said. "Give me a call in an hour."

As I walked down the corridors of the House Office Building, I could hear Ruckett's invasive voice. Oddly, now that he had his victory, he was sounding reasonable, a moderate man, who wished even his enemies well.

"We realize this is a serious matter, a matter of national import," Ruckett was saying, "and so we intend to ask for open and wide-ranging debate in the House."

"Do you have the votes right now to impeach the President?"

"I would say, Mr. Hosmer it is close. Very, very, close. But I suspect the course of events *outside* the House will determine the result as much as will the debate."

He was a knave, possibly a nut, and a schemer. But he wasn't stupid. All of us in the White House—and especially Ben Hannaford—had been underestimating him, and the irrational, vengeful forces he symbolized, for too long a time.

Dalton Warfield, Matt Fixx, and I watched the helicopter land on the White House lawn. We had been together all morning awaiting the boss's return from Ramada City. None of us had had a chance to talk to him since the unbelievable seventeen-to-sixteen decision of the House Government Operations Committee to approve the impeachment resolution and refer it to the House for debate. But we had chatted with Fred Goldstein in Ramada.

"He acts like they haven't done anything," Fred said. "Told us he couldn't be bothered, that it was a freak, and that we control enough votes in the House to knock it for a loop."

"But, dammit, Fred, isn't he aware that even if the House throws it out, it's an enormous setback for his program?" I asked.

"You know B.B.H. He says he isn't going to win any popularity contests anyway, so why worry about seventeen congressmen who don't like him? Full steam ahead, he says—all stops out on the defense budget and the cities program."

"I can't believe it," I said to Fred. "Where in heaven's name is our support coming from? Who is on our side any more?"

Our press secretary had afforded himself an out-of-character snicker. "The boss is betting on his old friends in the Senate. He's wheeling and dealing and twisting arms and collecting old debts like you never saw. Had Gabe Tutt on the phone for a half hour yesterday. I think they're working something out on Boswell's fifty per cent cut. Maybe a third off, like bargain day. Promised Gabe that no matter what, Dog Common, Alabama would get that military garbage disposal plant. Honey-Tonsils flew down here and smoked the peace pipe. If Gage will push the community control package through, he'll see to it that the FCC looks kindly on Gage's brother's bid for the new UHF television station in Madison. Sound familiar?"

As we watched Hannaford's purposeful figure debark from the helicopter, I marveled at the man's resiliency. So what if the polls showed that a third of the people believed he *should* be indicted and tossed out of office? So what if the frenzied black militants were determined to make common cause with the extreme right and bring down a moderate President? He moved across the White House lawn, waving to us, chatting with Burke Boswell, who had accompanied him, as if he had not a care in the world, that his Administration was as free of turmoil as Calvin Coolidge's.

We all greeted him, and then followed him toward the West Wing. We had been alerted that he wanted to get right to work.

"Dalton. Edward. Matthew. Seems I can't leave town without you fellows getting me stuck in a cactus patch."

"We are sorry, Mr. President," Matt Fixx said morosely. "We are all to blame."

Inside the oval office, Cleo Watterson had ordered coffee. We sat in an informal group—Hannaford not behind his desk, but on the chintz-covered rocking chair—and discussed the grievous situation. Boswell, as undismayed as the President by the House Committee's vote (I had come to the conclusion that his optimism was in his genes) left, advising us that he had a few generals to straighten out about some useless tank.

"All right, Dalton," Hannaford said. "Stop looking so glum. What happened?"

Warfield sighed. A helpless rage inundated me. That an intrepid, honorable man like Warfield could be vilified and deceived by a scoundrel like Kakamba Jones—in league with the Rucketts and the Huckerbys!—almost convinced me that there was no justice in the world.

"Mr. President, a lot of it was like Jones said. I did

434

meet with him in Harlem. I told him how you and Mr. Boswell were going to keep feeding the city programs from the Defense Department, and that we wanted his co-operation in seeing that the money was used properly and that the IT operation, and all the other antipoverty agencies not only keep going, but got *more*. I knew he pulled a lot of weight. The kids listen to him, wild as he is."

"All right," Hannaford said. "You did the right thing. Now, Dalton, did he say to you he was going to use the money to buy guns?"

Warfield's mahogany face, that patient, brave face that mirrored so much tragedy, appeared to melt and droop. "Mr. President, he did and he didn't. You can't ever tell just what in hell Jonesy means. I have known the man a long time, and I'm never sure what he's saying or what he's after."

"That is because he doesn't know himself," I said.

"Maybe, Ed. But it sure gives him an advantage." Warfield opened his black hands. "He kept telling me that he wasn't going to say thank you to the President or anyone else, and that he and his friends had taken over IT in New York and a few other outfits, and he'd decide how the money would be used . . ."

"Then he lied to the committee," Matt Fixx said.

"The way he testified it was a lie, but there was some substance there. I warned him not to do anything crazy. You know, there have been charges in the past—Chicago, where that white minister got in trouble, and Newark— where poverty funds were misused, a few bad actors got their hands in the till and used the money to buy dope or guns. It's awful hard to stop that, but we try. Anyway, Jones knew what I meant. He said, he'd buy what he wanted to buy, and that included the means of liberation."

"I'd say he made it pretty clear," Fixx said. "When Jones talks about liberation, he means guns."

"I know, I know," Warfield said miserably. "Mr. President, if it will help you, I will resign. I think I've done you a disservice, and I am ready to quit. Why not lay the whole mess on me?"

"Hell no, Dalton," Hannaford said firmly. "I won't have the Philistines making sport of Samson."

Warfield smiled with embarrassment. " 'Suffer me that I

may feel the pillars whereupon the house standeth, that I may lean upon them.'"

"That won't be necessary, Dalton," Hannaford said. "You haven't been blinded, or shorn of your strength, and the House won't be brought down. Not the House of Representatives or the White House."

The biblical banter bothered me. Was Hannaford using the story of Samson less as an analogue of poor Warfield's fallen state—or as a metaphor for his own grievous situation? Samson he had been to us, and to millions; and now the Philistines, the Rucketts and the Cottrells, and the vengeful mobs, would cry for his blinding.

"Dalton, why didn't you convey this to me?" the President asked. "Jones was a Vice-Presidential candidate once. A man like that can be dealt with. Paid off. His greed can be controlled. Give him an A for a B. If he threatened he was going to buy machine guns, why there were ways of diverting his zeal."

"Mr. President, I did not believe him," Warfield said. "Nor did I wish to burden you, what with your other problems—the defense budget and the legislative program going so badly. I thought Jones was bluffing. I thought if he did start, it would just be a piddling little matter. I never dreamed he'd line up with the wildmen, because he's always kept his options to the power structure open, he's always had a deal going with the police, and as you say, he can be bargained with. But I guess he's quit."

"I understand, Dalton." The President looked as if he'd had enough of the discussion.

"In defense of Dalton, Mr. President," I said, "none of us here, and none of our sources on the coast, or our friends in the press ever dreamed that Fancourt and his crowd would cook this thing up with the blacks. It came out of the blue."

Hannaford pursed his lips. "You're right, Edward. Out of the blue. I intend to regard it as a mischance, a steer turned loco. I'll ignore it. I'll depend on you people to make sure the House throws it out. Emmett O'Boyle owes us a favor or two."

"I hear he's been in church several hours a day ever since the committee vote," I said.

"He's got a lot to confess," the President said.

"Mr. President, the Speaker will be no help," Matt Fixx

said. "The House leadership has voted to ram the Ruckett resolution through in a few days. The Rules Committee is meeting this morning, and it's guaranteed that they'll put it at the top of the calendar."

"Any indication of *how* they'll report it out?" I asked.

"O'Boyle and Hexter and Rumsford want the House to sit as a Committee of the Whole. Debate will be limited to eight hours, four of them controlled by Suggs, and the other four by the ranking opposition member, Smales. The House is bound to accept this formula. Ruckett will probably open debate for the majority, and Smales or Kaplan for the opposition."

The President folded his hands. "Doesn't sound too bad. What does your last count show, Matthew?"

Young Fixx opened his mouth, gasped for air, then tried again.

"Well, sir, when Ruckett made his speech in the House, when he introduced the resolution, we were over a hundred and fifty votes to the good."

"And now?"

Matt swallowed. His ears jiggled. "It . . . it . . . isn't nearly an accurate count."

"Approximate," the President said testily.

"A-about a hundred to the good, sir. I'm afraid that after that circus in front of the committee, and that gun going off, we lost some support."

Hannaford closed his eyes. "It isn't the embarrassment of this thing, or the slander, or the lies or the pressure that bothers me," he said. "It's the way it's holding up work that's got to be done."

I was twisting and turning on the small, uncomfortable sofa. I had known Ben Hannaford a long, long time, and I knew that one of his failings as a public man was this very cockiness, this self-assurance. The man could not conceive of failing, or of being undone by brutal adversaries. (In candor, this was probably a result of his own nature—he himself could be brutal when necessary.)

"You look out of sorts, Edward," he said.

"Mr. President, you must hold a press conference, as soon as possible, perhaps tomorrow, and strike back at these liars. We cannot sit around acting as if House Resolution 988 is a freakish error, or something that happened when everyone was looking the other way. No matter how many lies Jones told, no matter how outrageous the attacks on you, they do reflect a national malaise. I urge that all of us mount a counteroffensive at once. Shall I talk to Fred about clearing time with the networks for a press conference tomorrow?"

Only I dared talk to the President like that. And he appreciated my directness. But he wasn't ready to accept my gloomy analysis. I almost sensed that he relished biding his time, planning a careful and ultimately devastating response—one that would scatter his enemies like chaff.

"Edward, that can wait. Dalton, fine. Let him talk to the press all he wants. Tell 'em the truth, just like you told me. The proper thing for the President to do is to ignore this dirty business. I have a country and a government to run, and that's my first priority."

"You are making a mistake, sir," I said boldly. "You'll have no country to run if you permit these elements to get the upper hand."

"They won't," the President said. "The executive family has been authorized to start the counterattack. In fact, it gets underway at the Sheraton-Park Grand Ballroom in a few hours. National meeting of the Four-H Clubs of America."

I blinked. "Four-H Clubs? Is the Secretary of Agriculture going to defend you?"

"Mrs. Hannaford is speaking. Threw out her planned address last night and wrote a brand new one. A history lesson for the youngsters. Might be worth hearing, Edward."

With that suprising bit of information the President got up and began to take off his jacket. He did not intend to let so piddling a matter as an impeachment deter him from moving ahead. Perceiving our glum faces, he admonished us:

" 'Come, and let us go to Gilgal, and renew the kingdom there.' "

Leaving, I asked Warfield about the quote.

"Samuel," Dalton said. "Just before they made Saul the King of Israel."

"Is that a good or bad omen?"

"It's not too apt," Warfield said, as we walked down the corridor of the West Wing. "You know what happened to Saul. The Philistines killed him and hung his body on the walls of the city."

438

I shuddered. "Dalton, let's not carry these biblical parallels too far. You and the boss can trade these *begats* and *selahs* without me from now on."

When I reached the Grand Ballroom of the Sheraton-Park, Fern was already into her address to the young farmers. I scanned the huge room for a familiar face, and saw Vangie Boswell standing to one side of the dais, near a side entrance.

"Have I missed anything?"

"No, Mrs. H. is just warming up. She's giving them a history lesson. The story of President Andrew Johnson."

"How inspirational. Opening gun in defense of his Administration. How ... how ... how in God's name did the First Lady ever agree to this?"

"Those who do not learn from the errors of the past," Mrs. Hannaford was saying, "are condemned to repeat them. I would hope that the people of our nation, and especially you young people, will learn from the mistakes of the past ..."

She looked grand. Fern was one of those tall, stately women, a bit full in the bosom and round in the rump, who maintained a firm bodily vigor as they aged. They did not sag or run to flesh around the middle or succumb to bad posture.

"Historians have asked, why was President Andrew Johnson, the man who succeeded Abraham Lincoln, impeached? Why was this severe action taken against this humble, honest figure, who had tried to hold the shattered Union together after the Civil War? After all, impeachment is not a light matter. It has only been attempted once in our history—"

"Maybe twice," I muttered to Vangie.

"—and it is today regarded as a dangerous and irrelevant procedure which solves no problems and leads to no constructive goal. Why then was President Johnson impeached?"

"Help from you?" I said.

"I wrote some of it," Vangie replied. "It wasn't easy. The trouble is, we *wanted* to sympathize with Andy Johnson, and point out that impeachment was a dirty political act. But it wasn't easy. He wasn't all that smart or pleasant a fellow. And let's face it, Ed, he didn't care too much about letting black people vote."

Oh, there were subtleties on top of subtleties. The

radical Republicans had sought to wring Andy Johnson's neck because they were convinced he was conspiring with the South, that he was a racist who did not want the Negro to achieve equality in the southern states. (A simplification; they had other reasons for seeking to overthrow him, but there is much truth in what I've just said.) And now, we had come full circle. Ben Hannaford, another border state President, for trying to bring equality and hope to black people, for trying to enact laws which would give the blacks their long overdue rights, stood in danger of the only impeachment since Johnson!

"Why impeachment?" Fern asked. She adjusted a pair of elegant glasses and studied her notes. "Why this vengeful political act against an incumbent President? Let us, my young friends, examine a few theories. One notion advanced by the historians is that the radical Republicans regarded Mr. Johnson as the last obstacle standing in the way of Republican domination of the defeated South. But the truth of the matter is, that at the time of the impeachment—and there were three separate attempts to indict the President—Mr. Johnson had already been bound hand and foot by the radicals in Congress, and was in no position to thwart their political aims.

"There is a second theory. This one argues that the men seeking to unseat President Johnson regarded the campaign as a long-range corrective measure, an opportunity for Congress to weaken the entire institution of the presidency, and reassert itself as the predominant force in Washington."

This was good stuff. It was history, writ plain, clearly stated, delivered in an interesting manner. I was so delighted with Fern, with her emphatic reading of her speech, with the dignity of her person, that I paid scant attention to the audience. Now, as I cast my cynic's eye over them, I understood why she had selected these scrubbed, healthy, innocent, uncomplicated farm children as the audience before whom she would open a counterattack. These were some of the Americans we had to win over. These were the people we needed—not Arvid Farbelman and Kakamba Jones and the raging outsiders, nor indeed the militants of the far right. It was the vital center we needed. And these youngsters, the children of center, were crucial to us—and to the nation's future. I knew them; I had come from Indian Mound, Ohio; I had faith
440

in them. They were not subtle, or complex, or militant people. They could be talked to, they could be reasoned with, and, like their parents, they were not mean or vindictive or bloody-minded people.

"Both of these theories are interesting," Fern said. "First, that the Republicans, by impeaching Mr. Johnson, would capture the southern states, and secondly, that they would elevate the Congress to a position superior to the President, one in which they could keep him under their control forever.

"But alas, these theories are full of inconsistencies. The bases of Republican strength was in the North. Their leaders, in their more lucid moments, understood that their hold in the southern states was a precarious hold—you young people all recall the stories of the carpetbaggers.

"So the question remains—why impeachment? I have read a great deal on the subject, for reasons which all of you, my young friends, have probably guessed—"

There was a nervous laugh from the audience, a titter, a few guffaws, and then the tension eased, and the assemblage of milk-fattened youngsters broke into a wave of laughter and applause.

"As you can see," Fern said, smiling at them, "I have learned some of my husband's talent for straight talking and plain speaking. We are, after all, country people."

More applause. I scowled at Vangie. "That line couldn't have been yours, Miss Boswell. And if it was, our friendship ends right now."

She pinched my forearm. "Pure Fern Cudder Hannaford. But don't knock it. The woman is a natural politician, Ed. All these years I think Big Ben's bluster kept her quiet, afraid to open her mouth. But she knows all the moves, all the tricks."

"I think that it is a mistake, as some historians have maintained, to regard the impeachment of President Andrew Johnson as a rational act in pursuit of group or national interests, in pursuance of specific political or legislative changes. It was not that at all. Rather, I have concluded that the impeachment of Mr. Johnson must be viewed, in the words of one historian, as 'a towering act of abandoned wrath, wholly detached from reason.' Let me repeat those words, for I think they sum up a great deal. *'A towering act of abandoned wrath, wholly detached from reason.*' If we view the impeachment in those terms, little else is needed to explain it, for what the nation experienced in those tragic times was nothing less than 'a state of unwholesome madness.'

"To quote the historian again, 'the moral air of the nation's politics had become heavily poisoned.' It is only fair to say, that Mr. Johnson, a proud man, an unbending one, had contributed to this, by provoking Congress in petty ways. But none of his acts, not by the remotest stretch of anyone's imagination, constituted grounds for impeachment—either as treason, bribery or other high crimes and misdemeanors.

"The frenzy aroused by his opposition, the spiteful anger, the unreasoning hatreds were out of all proportion to the President's acts. History students among you will recall, the only specific charge on which they were eventually able to hang their motion, was that the President had violated something called the Tenure of Office Act, by attempting to replace Secretary Stanton—a difficult and contentious man—with a secretary of his own choice. Was that treason? Bribery? A high crime? A misdemeanor? Even many of the radical Republicans were forced to admit that the pretext was flimsy. But they were gambling on a national sickness, a national hatred, the divisions and disputes growing out of the Civil War, to unseat the President. And, they all assumed it would be easy, very easy indeed."

First Ladies were not supposed to get down on the mat with their husband's adversaries. But here was Fern, sleeves rolled up, chin firmly outthrust, hurling the challenge. I could have hugged and kissed her.

"I am not here to defend President Johnson or President Hannaford," Fern said. "My husband hardly needs me to defend him. But I would be derelict in my duties as an American citizen, proud of her country's heritage if I did not use this forum to make known my own views on this subject. For as many of you have guessed by now, although the cause of the proceedings against Mr. Johnson and against Mr. Hannaford are dissimilar, and President Hannaford—as far as I *know*—is still sitting in the White House and looking after the country—"

Applause washed over her; there was loud laughter, pounding of the desks, a display of support and sympathy that astounded me.

442

"So, I trust no further parallels will be necessary," Fern said. "But to conclude the history lesson, let me remind you, that the Senate, by the margin of one vote, acquitted Andrew Johnson, after a disgraceful trial, which dragged on interminably and did nothing but expose the flimsiness of the radicals' charges. Many a senator, and editor, and public figure, who had cheered the assaults on Mr. Johnson, about halfway through the trial, began to have second thoughts about the affair. Well, my friends, let's hope that *this* mean-spirited and ill-founded attack on another President, doesn't even get that far!"

"We've got us another Eleanor Roosevelt, Vangie," I said. "They'll have to start assigning political reporters to cover the First Lady, instead of the woman's page writers."

"They have already," Vangie said. I looked at the press section to the left of the long, be-flowered dais, and I saw Larry Hosmer, and Burt Vadim, and Ted McPhelan, and a few other political writers. Fern had arrived. I also saw Mona Varnum. I made a note to query her about Sacramento.

"—and I'd like to conclude with some reference to Mr. Johnson's last days. He died in obscurity in 1875, seven years after his impeachment and trial, a humble and plain-spoken man. The bulk of the mourners at his funeral in his home town of Greeneville, Tennessee, were the plain people for whom he had labored—farmers, mechanics, tradesmen. For several years his grave was unmarked. Then, his family, at their own expense, placed a simple shaft of marble over it. On it was carved a hand, resting on the Constitution, and the words, 'His Faith in the People Never Wavered.' "

The cavernous room was silent. Fern had not only learned her history, she had learned the art of performance.

"For is that not one of the great attributes of a President? To cherish an unwavering faith in the people? I assure all of you here, that the President of the United States—at this very moment, in this time of crisis—is not losing one iota of faith in the people of this country. Thank you, very, very much."

Oh, how she roused them. The youngsters were on their feet—cheering, clapping, whistling. I turned to Vangie. "If

443

the House of Representatives were composed of Four-H Club members, we'd be home free."

I followed Vangie through the swarm of strong, young bodies—boys in narrow jackets, girls in knit dresses, the Americans we needed on our side—to the edge of the dais, where Fern was accepting the plaudits of Four-H Club officials.

The First Lady spied us and waved. "Magnificent speech, Mrs. H.," I said. "The President will want a copy of that for the official presidential files."

"A *carbon* copy," Fern said sweetly. "The original is for my *own* file." She turned to Vangie. "Dear, will you please get in touch with that nice man at NBC about 'Meet the Press'? I'll take the first Sunday they have available. And would it be unfair to offer ourselves to 'Face the Nation' on a first-come, first-served basis?"

Secret weapon? She was Hannaford's shock troops, ranger battalion, Green Berets and Palmach, all in one Nieman-Marcus-suited package!

But I was not happy with the way the rest of our counteroffensive was going. Dalton Warfield held a press conference to take the edge off Kakamba Jones's testimony. I am obliged to admit it was a failure. The trouble was Warfield was too honorable and modest a man to contend publicly with a demagogue like Jones. Malcom X, in one of those sharp insights that relieved his otherwise malformed view of the world, once remarked that fanatics and extremists always have the edge over compromisers and rationalizers. They hit hard, and fast, and are not afraid to lie and distort and hurt people. Dalton Warfield, perhaps the bravest American I have ever known, was too good for the wicked world of Washington. He could not lie. He could not dissemble. He could not twist the truth. Had he met with Kakamba Jones at the Malcolm X Memorial Restaurant? Yes, he had. (That, sad to state, produced the big headlines: WARFIELD ADMITS MEETING WITH JONES—as if the meeting alone constituted proof of Jones's delirious charges.)

"Did he tell you he was going to take the IT funds and buy weapons?"

"Not exactly. Not that way." My stomach shivered. Warfield was telling the truth—but it sounded equivocal. "He hinted he'd use some of the money for liberation.

Liberation he kept repeating, and I warned him to play it smart and not try to rob the funds, but to let IT use 'em for what they were intended—industrial training for the kids."

"Aren't you aware, Mr. Warfield, that Mr. Jones uses the word liberation as a euphemism for armed rebellion, for insurrection?"

"He uses words however they suit him. Look, I tried to tell him not to, and I didn't think he'd carry out the threat. You know, he makes lots of threats, and if you check on them, you'll find ninety per cent he never carries out."

The reporters snickered. They found it hard to accept Warfield's innocence. "And you didn't tell the President?"

"I don't make it my business to bother the President with these ups and downs of the civil rights movement. He has got the peace of the world and the welfare of the whole country to worry about."

"Did you tell anyone?"

Dalton inhaled. No, the man could not lie, he could not fake, he could not play the role of deceiver. We were being defeated by honesty.

"I told Secretary Murphy and Secretary Gantry."

Worse and worse. I could see the headlines even as Warfield spoke. WARFIELD TOLD TWO TOP CABINET MEN OF AFRO PLOT.

"Did they suggest any move to stop Mr. Jones and his group?" a friendly reporter from the Newark *News* asked.

"They felt as I did, that Jones was bluffing, that he'd never go ahead with that fool thing. Besides, he never said *exactly,* in so many words that he was going to steal the funds to buy weapons. He kept saying liberation, liberation . . ."

"Mr. Warfield, did anyone make any notes at that meeting? Is there a tape recording of it? Or were there witnesses?"

"No. There were just myself and Jones. The meeting didn't last more than fifteen minutes."

"Assuming that Jones never did tell you in so many words, that he was going to buy guns and smuggle them into the Sacramento ghetto, do you doubt now that he did just that?"

"I'm sure he did."

"Then how can you—and Mr. Murphy—and the President—justify involving people like Kakamba Jones in poverty programs, giving them responsible jobs, and access to government money?"

Poor Warfield! I saw his black eyes glaze. No matter what he said, no matter how he tried to explain his relationship to Jones's crowd, it would sound dreadful. What had been imprinted, burned, tattoo'd in people's minds were those photographs and newsreels of armed blacks in the hearing room. No amount of explanation could erase those frightening images.

"You fellows know as well as I do, that when you work in the cities, you use anyone who has influence there. Jones has done a lot of jobs for the poverty program. It's nothing new. The street gangs in Chicago worked out a terrific adult education setup. Muslims in Los Angeles, for years, have helped us run a day-care center. Same thing with Jones. Sure, it's a calculated risk. Sure, you take a chance. But he gets across to people, the unreachables, the ones who need the most help, and we're glad to get help . . ."

The reporters were silent a moment. Bates Pendragon, who had been sitting in the back of the room, heavily tweeded, even though it was an insufferably hot and humid Washington day, suddenly boomed out.

"Really, really, Mr. Warfield. We have all read Mr. Jones's best-selling books and articles and his interviews in the press. He makes it very clear that his aim is armed insurrection and the murder of the white policemen and white officials and anyone who stands in the way of his bloody goals." Pendragon was on his feet. "How in the name of all that is holy, sir, can you solicit the help of such a person?"

Pendragon almost sounded sorry to have to embarrass Warfield. But the question was a fair one. I could have asked it myself.

"Mr. Pendragon, I know about all those statements Mr. Jones makes, and I've talked to him about them at length, and all I can tell you is, that with men like Jones, you have to pay attention to what they *do*, not what they *say*."

"A risky game, is it not, Mr. Warfield?" the columnist asked.

"I suppose," Dalton said. "But that's exactly what the people in Mr. Nixon's administration kept telling us—

don't pay no mind to all those conservative things we *say*—just look at our record."

"Hey, Dalton," Lou Parente said, sounding exasperated, "is it the same? I mean, what Nixon's administration did—a deal here, a change there, a guideline for this state, an allocation for that. That's the way things work in this country. Not with machine guns and automatic rifles."

Even Parente, who respected Warfield enormously was impelled to contest his leisurely view of the affair. Public men have their limits, their capacities. Poor Warfield was worn out, a man so used and misused that his strength was eroding, his will to pursue the battle weakened. "Lou, any man who has been shot at as much as I have, has no use for that sort of stuff. What I say is not intended as a defense of Jones and his people. Sure, he bought guns. Sure, he got them to the Sacramento ghetto. Sure, he makes threats and wild statements . . ."

"Pretty good reason to lose him," Parente interrupted.

"Yeah, but look at what's happened. Hasn't a single shot been fired there since he did. Not a bullet. The White Guards have left. The cops and the National Guard are quiet. And what's more, the governor is talking with the blacks. Talking. Maybe the whole thing'll blow over."

"You're saying maybe Jones's tactics will have been the reason?" a girl from *Look* asked. "Aren't you agreeing with him, then, that power grows out of the end of a gun?"

"No. I'm just looking at this one situation. Nobody's been hurt in Sacramento in the last few days."

Dalton was telling the truth. His evaluation of the temporary peace, the renewal of dialogue in the California city was accurate. We hardly realized how his words would haunt us in the days ahead.

"It's got me faked out," Matt Fixx said. "We are actually in a one-to-one relationship with the Senate."

We were sitting in Matt's tiny office in the basement of the West Wing. On the wall was Matt's private chart showing the progress of our legislative program. On a dozen major bills, the chart showed inked-in blocks, denoting progress, but only on the Senate side. The House was for the most part, a vast white area—stasis, paralysis, sloth, indifference.

"The good old Senate," Matt said, "the dear old Senate."

"You have to remember, Matthew. It's Hannaford's old home. He is one of the distinguished alumni."

"Don't I know it. Look at that chart! It is not to be believed. We haven't aborted once. Not a single destruct activated. Even Gabe Tutt has been sounding almost civilized. Boswell had him to dinner at the F Street Club again."

Boswell. Was it not written in the good book, that any man who could booze as much as that, connive, brag, boast, scheme and earn lots of money for corporations, *had to be a patriot?*

"Gabe is starting hearings again, and Boswell swears he's ready to work out a compromise—one-third markdown in the defense budget and a new watchdog agency to review contracts. I'm grooving on that one, Ed, grooving."

"Any hang-ups?"

"In the Senate? None that we won't be able to dance with."

I let Matt's Washingtonese—that clumsy mixture of space jargon, hippie talk and pro football argot—stew in my head for a while, as he reviewed the progress in the Senate. It was amazing. It was almost as if there were two governments. In the House, Ruckett's poison, the fearful stampeding of the Government Operations Committee, the threats and coniving of COCCC and its allies—NUMB, DOOR, Save America—and the mad acts of the Afro Avengers, had created what Fern's historian aptly called a state of "abandoned wrath."

Soon, the House, sitting as a Committee of the Whole, would meet to debate, modify, rewrite and consider H. Res. 988. And they would vote. In the meantime, they had atrophied, withered. It was the reliable old Senate, that exclusive club of one hundred tribal elders, the deacons, the Sanhedrin, the teachers of righteousness, who were moving the country.

"You're an optimist, Matt," I said. "Back in the early seventies, when the assaults on the military began, a day didn't go by without a new scandal in Pentagon waste, graft, incompetence, lying and worst of all, masterplanning for mega-deaths. And what happened? The generals got every dollar they asked after the shouting was over."

Matt raised an eyebrow. "Ah, but we're in another ball

park now, Ed, another ball park. The name of this game is *reform*."

And he proceeded to outline for me how the President's urban programs were moving through the Senate Labor and Public Welfare Committee, how friendly the Senate Interior and Insular Affairs Committee had been toward our antipollution bill, how intelligently the Senate Finance Committee—under Majority Leader Hopewell's prodding—had begun consideration of Ben's tax reforms, the one aimed at taking pressure off our beleaguered lower middle class.

"Nothing but good news, eh, Matt?" I asked.

"The whole thing is a gas. We're in orbit. Docking will take place any moment. And wait till Professor Cohen drops his peace bomb in a few days. Red China wants in on peace talks. I tell you, Ed, I am tripping without benefit of acid or speed. We're grooving."

It would have been nice to share his optimism. As for myself, I could think only of the House of Representatives, who, very soon, would hear the rancid arguments boiling around "the great act of ill-directed passion."

There was a top-secret meeting of the House leadership that night—six of the powers, the President, and no one else. Not even me. Not even Matt Fixx.

I made it my business to be loitering in the corridor when the meeting ended. Out of the President's office—did they look grim? harassed? worried?—came Speaker O'Boyle, Majority Leader John J. Hexter, Larry DiLorenzo, the chairman of the Judiciary Committee, Lewis Smales and Harry Kaplan of Government Operations and Bill Rumsford, the chairman of Ways and Means. Most of them were older, slow-moving, slow-speaking men, grown gray and worn in the service of the replublic. I saw a few reporters emerge from the press room and head for them. Speaker O'Boyle held up a withered hand and shook his frail head; there would be nothing said, nothing at all.

I followed them out on to the portico. It was raining lightly, a warm, misty July rain, typical of Washington. The White House lawn was preternaturally green, as if sprayed with coloring agent. As the old men shuffled off, working their tired limbs into raincoats, fussing with black umbrellas, I walked after Harry Kaplan, the youngest, most outgoing, most approachable of the group. Goodness, they were old people! O'Boyle seemed to move in a trance; he leaned on John Hexter's arm.

"How did it go, Mr. Kaplan?" I asked. "Are we all set for the big show tomorrow?"

The labor lawyer responded with a characteric Jewish shrug of his thick shoulders. "Who knows, Eddie?"

"But we have the votes, don't we? Ruckett's crowd can't believe they can ram this through with some contrived act of terror, the way they did in committee, do they?"

"We got the votes, kid. My momey, not to mention my future, is on the big guy. I think we're safe."

"Think?"

"Okay, I *know* we're safe." Kaplan walked away.

I stood alone, letting the soft warm rain cover me, and I had a desire to be a child again, roaming the green meadow in back of my father's grocery in Indian Mound, Ohio, a commander of white and yellow butterflies.

Seated again in the press gallery next to Parente—Bates Pendragon was in back of us—I scanned the morning editorials. It was the first day on which the House of Representatives, sitting as a "Committee of the Whole" would consider H. Res. 988 impeaching the President for "high crimes and misdemeanors."

I suppose I should have taken heart from the pro-Hannaford editorials in The New York *Times* and the Washington *Post* and the St. Louis *Post-Dispatch*. But as I had long ago learned, the good sense of editorial writers is not always mirrored in the corridors of power.

"Here they come," Parente said. "The saints go marching in." Speaker O'Boyle was shuffling toward his high chair of authority. Various clerks and officials of the House were taking their places at the long dark tables to the right and left of the rostrum. Most of the congressmen had arrived. They stood in casual groups, chatting, laughing, visiting. A few sat in thoughtful solitude, sobered and saddened by their task.

"Get this show on the road," Lou muttered. "Look at Ruckett. I swear the little fink has grown three inches since he got that committee vote."

It was odd. The young man from South Dakota actually seemed taller, broader. Maybe it was the new navy-blue suit he was wearing, or the breezy manner in which he strode the floor of the cavernous chamber, whispering to

Lem Suggs, chuckling with Sykes Cottrell, grabbing at his other co-sponsors, exchanging pleasantries with opponents like Larry DiLorenzo and Hollis Denton. As ever, I was reassured by the casual, Rotarian nature of the House. It was a good place, a reflection of the national temper. But whether that boded well for us, I was no longer certain.

"Try this one," Pendragon said. He handed me a folded copy of C. C. Pringle's Baltimore newspaper. All of Pringle's chains ran the same editorials on national and international affairs. The publisher himself wrote most of them. "It might balance those you've just read in the *Times* and the *Post*."

"Why thank you, Bates," I said. The man was almost friendly.

Pringle's editorial was entitled: *Without Fear or Prejudice*. It was mild in tone, but it hit hard, and I had to admit that it was closely argued. I sensed that the line of approach taken by the publisher would be used by the advocates of impeachment. It would be a hard one to rebut.

The heart of the matter, as Mr. Ruckett and Mr. Cottrell kept stressing at the committee hearings, is whether the President should be held accountable for the misuse of government funds for the purchase of weapons to be used in an armed insurrection against legal authority. Evidently, the committee believed this to be the case. So do we. So do many Americans, who are not bigots, racists, phychopaths or professional haters. The issue is simple; the facts are plain. The president and the Secretary of Defense rerouted Defense Department funds to sustain a specific training program in the ghettos. These funds were then illegally used for the aiding of armed rebellion. Whether the President did or did not have direct knowledge of this is immaterial. Indications are that he did. But surely some of his cabinet officers and aides knew about it. Incredibly these executive assistants appear to have condoned the rebellion against authority . . .

"And how do you feel about Mr. Pringle's views, Bates?" I asked the columnist.

Pendragon patted his thick mustache. "I'd have phrased it a bit differently." He frowned. "This impeachment brouhaha, you know, I've never been keen on it. Early on I advised against it. It seems to me a vote of censure, a resolution on the sense of the Congress, might have been more in order . . ."

"Where the hell was he when we needed him?" Parente said to me.

The Speaker, fussing at his high desk, whacked the gavel and called the four-hundred-odd representatives to order. Suggs had to make the next move. The gentle old Alabamian was on his feet and was recognized.

"Mr. Speaker," Lem Suggs said, "I move that this House resolve itself into the Committee of the Whole House on the State of the Union for the consideration of the resolution, 988, to im-im-im-"

A fit of coughing convulsed Chairman Suggs. Psychosomatic, I was certain. One does not lightly pronounce the word *impeachment* on the floor of the House. Suggs had voted in favor of the Ruckett resolution, but he had done so with a gun held to his head. Parente claimed he had proof that DOOR and Save America had threatened to destroy his career and expose him as a race-mixer. I had seen old photographs of Lem Suggs as a young congressman, standing by FDR's side, helping Roosevelt frame early farm legislation, rural electrification, flood controls. I understood why the old man was coughing now, his eyes brimming with tears, his body doubled in a paroxysm.

". . . to impeach the President of the United States."

There was a motion to second, there was a swift, almost inaudible voice vote. Then the Sergeant at Arms, responding to a nod from Emmett O'Boyle, removed the mace, the revered ebony rod, crowned with globe and eagle and symbolizing government authority, from the tall, green marble stand at the right of the Speaker's desk. This signified that the regular session of the House had ended. Then he placed it lovingly on the white pedestal to the *left* of the Speaker's desk, to indicate that the House was now meeting in committee.

Some preliminary fencing was taking place. O'Boyle, now prepared to relinquish his seat of authority to Congressman William Rumsford, the aged, respected, and acutely intelligent chairman of Ways and Means. (This again is traditional when the House convenes as a "Committee of the Whole"—the Speaker steps down in favor of another member, whom it is his privilege to select.)

452

I watched the two white-thatched oldsters conferring briefly, and my gaze wandered about the august chamber, the biggest legislative room in the world. Outside, at the entrance, stood the statue of Will Rogers, in accordance with the cowboy-humorist's jest that when he died he wanted to be "where I can keep my eye on Congress." It is a huge room, and a peculiarly American one—the walnut rostrum, the black and gold marble columns, the flag, the gilt faces on the rear wall. On the face of the rostrum are carved wreaths and the words—*Union, Justice, Tolerance, Liberty and Peace*.

I should say something concerning the philosophy of "the Committee of the Whole House." It is an extremely vital and eminently democratic mechanism, and it is invoked for about 90 per cent of all major legislation. It is important because detailed, searching examination of bills *already acted upon by standing committees*, takes place when the House so sits. Each section of a bill, or resolution, is considered in turn, and votes are taken on each. Moreover, votes on these sections are almost always by voice vote, standing vote or "passing through tellers." No representative has to answer "yea" or "nay" and have his vote recorded.

The usual procedure in a session of the Committee of the Whole, is for the chairman of the standing committee— in this case Lem Suggs—to "control" four hours of debate, while the ranking minority member is also allotted four. These recommendations, sent down by the House Rules Committee are always adopted without discussion— as they were now, with Mr. Rumsford replacing O'Boyle and acting as Speaker pro tem.

Lance Ruckett would lead off for the impeachment resolution, although it is usually the job of the chairman to open debate. But Suggs had no stomach for speaking in defense of H. Res. 988. He was willing to defer to Ruckett.

The next step is for the clerk to read off each paragraph of the bill or resolution. Any representative may then offer an amendment to the bill. Now the action is fast, expert and professional—the democratic process at its dazzling best. Proposed amendments are debated in capsule speeches which can last no longer than five minutes. After brief argument, a vote is taken. Then on to the next paragraph; amendments are offered; the crackling debate ensues; the members vote again. I stress that not only can *amendments* be offered during this period, but a member can move to reject an amendment altogether. Such a vote is final; the amendment is dead. If an amendment is accepted, however, it remains merely a *committee* decision; said amendment cannot be written into the final version unless the House approves it.

After the measure's final paragraph has been read, and all amendments have been voted up or down, the committee "rises," its work done. The House now has the report of the committee before it, and it reconvenes in formal session. A roll call vote, in which every member's name is called by the clerk and he must respond can then be demanded, so that members who hid behind the anonymity of the committee's voice votes, must show their positions, on every amendment.

Opponents of the measure now have one last refuge, before the final vote. They may move to "recommit" the bill by sending it back to the originating committee, perhaps with instructions that it be changed. Again, a roll call is in order on a motion to recommit, and every man has a chance to declare himself. Motions to recommit, I hasten to add, are almost always beaten down, and all that remains is for the full membership of the House to pass or defeat the measure. This can be done by voice vote, or, on the demand of one-fifth of the representatives present, by roll call vote. In major matters of legislation, the latter is almost always employed. Roll calls are splendid time-wasters, mind-changers and vote-stallers. But most importantly, it is a way of making each man declare himself *publicly*, particularly those congressmen who are ashamed of their vote and would just as lief not be recorded.

As I reviewed this procedure in my mind, I realized that the President's allies in the House had a tough problem confronting them. It was this: the vagueness of H. Res. 988, the violent language, "the towering act of abandoned wrath," all these would make it difficult to offer amendments. How does one "amend" a charge that the President of the United States has "fostered violence, bloodshed and insurrection?"

Matt Fixx and I had discussed this early that morning, before Matt took up his listening post in the House anteroom, where he and his staff could be close to our allies. "Committee debate," Matt said, "presupposes something

454

to be debated, points to be discussed, ideas to be amended. This monstrosity is just a bad trip. You can't debate it, you can just kill it."

"You're right," I said. "None of our people will want to offer to amend a resolution that accuses the boss of usurpation of power and violations of the law. What is Smales going to do? Ask that they amend it to read 'occasional' usurpation of power, or 'minor' violations of the law?"

"That is why, Ed," Matt said icily—he was a frail and anemic young man, but he was courageous, and I liked him more the longer I knew him, "that is why it has to be all or nothing. This lump of space garbage has got to be obliterated, crisped. We can't accept *any* resolution, because that admits guilt. The President is emphatic about it."

We were in Statuary Hall, the semicircular corridor lined with breccia marble Corinthian columns and with the bronze and marble statues of great patriots, lawgivers, eminent Americans.

"Unfortunately, that gives the bastards an advantage," I said uneasily.

"How so, Ed?"

"No matter how critical a man can be of the Congress, it is a reasonable place where real issues are debated. This Ruckett resolution is sheer madness. It's an outrage against sanity. So it can't be amended or debated. It can only be thrown out."

"Ed, I can't accept that." We stopped in front of the statue of Thomass Hart Benton of Missouri.

"Some of the fence sitters, border state friends of the President, southern moderates, may offer amendments to tone down the language, but you know that neither Ruckett's gang nor our people will tolerate them. We can't start agreeing to amendments that say the President stands indicted for minor crimes and petty larceny."

"I'm aware of that. But I'm confident we'll lick the whole thing. Once the Committee of the Whole winds up debate, there'll be a vote—probably in the exact words in which the Suggs committee reported it. I know we can lick them. O'Boyle is waking up, at long last. He wants that nuclear reactor in Pawtucket very badly."

Matt Fixx and I had engaged in that discussion an hour ago. Now the drama was to begin. I glanced at the floor of the House. A positive tension was evident; an unheard

455

humming; an invisible brightness; the drab tans and grays and browns of the chamber charged with unearthly light. The majority and minority leaders and their aides had taken their seats at the small tables. At larger tables, on the aisle, sat the "floor managers" of the rival factions for the debate—Sykes Cottrell of Mississippi for the impeachment faction, Hollis Denton of Oregon, in behalf of the President.

"Here we go," Parente said. "For all the marbles."

Lance Ruckett, as originator of the resolution, was recognized by William Rumsford, who had taken the chair over from Speaker O'Boyle. The young man got to his feet, fussed with the papers on his desk and proceeded to speak. He was learning. His voice was low and well-modulated. There would be no hellfire from him today.

"Mr. Speaker, I do not approach this assignment with enthusiasm or with vindictiveness, or any sense of satisfaction . . ."

"*Managg'*," Parente muttered. "We got the humble act."

". . . the resolution we present here, to the Committee of the Whole, the resolution passed by your Government Operations Committee is a momentous one. We have not acted lightly. We have not acted passionately. We have not acted in precipitate fashion, as the liberal press has charged. No, gentlemen, we have weighed the evidence, heard the witnesses, listened to expert testimony, and we have come to a sobering, but absolutely obligatory remedy for the sickness eroding our national character, our viability as a nation. The seventeen members of the Government Operations Committee who voted for impeachment are not heedless, vengeful or destructive men. Mr. Speaker, we are thoughtful and prudent and cautious men. Men who have a more accurate knowledge of what ordinary Main Street Americans are thinking than do the intellectual editors who write for The New York *Times* and the Washington *Post*, or the Harvard and Columbia professors who lecture us on the powers of the presidency, or the alleged malfunctionings of democracy. For it has always seemed to me, Mr. Speaker, that these Eastern intellectuals, are for the popular will only when it coincides with their own notions of what is good for the country!

"Contrariwise, when the people, the wage-earning, tax-paying, church-attending, God-loving, family-rearing, non-rioting masses of people make their wishes known in a way that *offends* these high-and-mighty arbiters, they decide that there is something wrong with democracy, that the system isn't effective, and perhaps some kind of mysterious elite, some cabal of fiercely intelligent snobs knows better.

"Mr. Speaker, nobody knows the needs of the country better than the people. And we of the Government Operations Committee, we seventeen who voted for Resolution 988, the resolution to impeach the President of the United States, did nothing more than follow the will of the people, as it was expressed to us, not in editorials in The New York *Times*, or in Harvard classrooms, or on CBS News, at meetings of the Foreign Policy Association, but as expressed to us in our letters, in the public opinion polls, in our conversations with our constituents and in that marvelous way in which the will of a sovereign people makes itself manifest to its elected representatives."

"Rather impressive," I heard Bates Pendragon intone in back of me. Parente held his nose.

"What is H. Res. 988?" Lance Ruckett asked. "It is a statement of facts which have been evident since the present occupant of the White House came to power. And what are these facts? They are, the incontrovertible proof that the President has usurped the powers of the Congress and has violated the enacted laws and so grievously misinterpreted them, as to create the *opposite* effect of that intended by these laws. Instead of order and stability, we have reaped violence, bloodshed and insurrection.

"Yes, those are the words of our resolution, and we do not intend to modify them. Day after day, our committee heard the testimony of law-abiding Americans—police officers, firemen, union officials, taxicab drivers, housewives—emphasizing the ravages of crime and civil disorders in our cities. Disorders, Mr. Speaker, which were encouraged by the President's refusal to enforce the Emergency Riot Control Act. This is not a matter for debate. The record is clear. The sworn testimony is available to everyone. Are we to deny these Americans *their* day in court? Are the lawbreakers the only ones who have a right to the law's protection and the caresses of the press?"

"He's got a new speech writer," Parente whispered.

"No, he turns this stuff out himself," I said. "It's too good. It's on the nose. He's got his finger on the lower middle-class pulse. And let me tell you something, Lou. I'll never underestimate those people again." I cursed our own myopia and lack of foresight that we had not listened to them, as much as we had listened to the aggrieved blacks. For now many of them were listening to the Lance Rucketts.

Ruckett was into the text of the resolution now, defending it, analyzing it, doing a shrewd job. It was a dreadful piece of work, this libelous thing called H. Res. 988, but he was making it sound reasonable.

"Now, what does the committee mean when it says that the President fostered violence, bloodshed and insurrection?" the young man asked the attentive chamber. "Mr. Speaker, it means just that. We are not clever television editorialists who twist the facts. We are average Americans. Violence means just that. We all know what bloodshed is. And insurrection is a simple word with a precise meaning . . ."

It was evident to me that the strength of the resolution was its very *weakness*. Having been through DeWitt's classic work *The Impeachment of President Johnson,* I saw the stunning similarities between Ruckett's attack on Hannaford, and the eleven malevolent articles that the House concocted to impeach old Andy. Senator Buckalew, a supporter of Johnson's, had written:

> . . . its *strengh* consists in its weakness—in the obscurity of its charges and the intricacy of its form. Considered in parts, it is nothing—the propositions into which it is divisible cannot stand separately as charges of criminal conduct or intention; and considered as a whole, it eludes the understanding and baffles conjecture. . . .

Small comfort! The House, acting on the eleven articles drawn up by the Judiciary Committee, and under the prodding of intransigents like Thaddeus Stevens and Benjamin "Beast" Butler, had impeached Andrew Johnson, and he had been saved from conviction by one vote in the Senate! Ah, I told myself, this cannot happen to Ben Hannaford.

Our supporters were starting the counterattack. "Mr. Speaker," Lewis Smales said, in his Yankee drawl, "I should like to ask the gentleman from South Dakota, is he not troubled by the vagueness of the resolution?"

"Not at all, sir. I find it most specific," Ruckett replied.

Smales fussed with his old-fashioned rimless glasses. "Well, sir, as I read it, there is no specific charge in the resolution relating to a precise act of bloodshed, just a repetiton of a general charge, which is hardly good legal wording. Why does the resolution not include exact times, places, occurrences proving that the President, and no one else, not his aides, or special assistants, or cabinet officers, or local officials of any kind, but the Chief Executive of the nation, fostered such appalling acts?"

"We've got a few tigers on our side also," I said, turning to Pendragon.

"Don't futz with those Vermont Yankees," Parente said. "He's about to cut Ruckett's balls off before young Lance is even started."

"I remind the gentleman from Vermont," Lance Ruckett said, "that the committee hearings, in which he participated, heard evidence from dozens of good citizens—firemen, policemen, taxicab drivers—about the increase in crime and violence—"

"I don't mean that," Smales said. "I mean something that would stand up in court as a high crime or misdemeanor. Evidence that the President supplied the weapons and the motivation and the encouragement to lawless persons. In dealing with a matter so grave we have a right to demand evidence."

Sykes Cottrell of Mississippi, who was scheduled to be the opposition's second speaker, got to his feet. He was a spare ruddy man, with thinning sandy hair, an affluent farm machinery dealer who fancied himself an expert on constitutional law. He was a worrier, Cottrell. I looked up his record once. Way back, when he'd started as a freshman congressman, after a term in the state legislature, he might have been described as a moderate on the race issue. But the pressures had been too strong.

"If Ah may, Mistah Speakah," Cottrell said, "Ah too was on the Gov'ment Op'rattions Committee, and Ah should lak to respond to the gentleman from V'mont."

"I am anxious to hear an explanation as to why the resolution is so formless, so unspecific," Smales said. "I fought this matter in committee. Were it not for the near riot that took place the other day, the atrocious emotional atmosphere which the chairman permitted, the parading of guns and grenades before a legislative body, I doubt we'd be sitting here today."

Lemuel Suggs stared at the eagle in the House chamber ceiling. He knew that Smales was telling the truth.

"Ah happen to disagree with the gentleman from V'mont, but his remarks do lead me to an important point," Sykes Cottrell said. "Mistah Speakah, the gen'man asks about *specifics*. Whut, Ah ask, whut, could be moah specific than guns and the threats of murder that we heard the other day, from the mouths of people who used government funds, funds auth'rized by he President, to buy 'em? How precise does he want us to git? Does he want us to wait until those revolutionaries blow up the country?"

Parente's eyes were shut. He grabbed my knee. "Smales got him," he said. "That ridge-runner walked right into the trap. Watch the Yankee trader closely. He just sold him the wooden nutmeg. Now he'll make him pay double for it."

"Does that answer the gentleman's question?" Ruckett asked. "May I resume my address?"

"Not quite," Lewis Smales said. His bony fingers scratched at his gray thatch, a head grown hard and calloused in sixty New England winters. "I heard that testimony. I saw the machine guns and the grenades and the ammunition clips, and I listened to the ravings of Mr. Jones and his aides, and the threats of violence, and I was as outraged as you gentlemen. But my question is this. If you were so all-fired impressed by that testimony about power growing out of the end of a gun, and the way the President's aides knew about it all, and presumably the fact that the President himself knew—which I don't believe for a minute—why, gentlemen, didn't you write the whole shebang into the resolution?"

Ruckett cleared his throat. He'd been sand-bagged. He and Cottrell had walked right into Smales's rabbit trap. Old Vermonter, old Green Mountain boy, he had them where he wanted them. "The answer, sir, is that the charge includes many *other* misdemeanors on the part of the President," Ruckett said weakly. Now there was a disbelieving, disturbed buzz on the floor. The galleries also reacted, a murmuration that seemed to say *Oh, come on, come on.*

460

"Full of crap and he knows it," Parente said.

I could see our old friend, Congressman Angel Lopez Garcia, still one of our supporters, shaking his head. I saw his lips form the words, "Holy Jeez."

"Many *other* misdemeanors?" Smales pursued. He had been a tough commissioner of public safety, I was certain. "How many, Mr. Ruckett? Five? Fifty? Where? When? Show me the police reports. Find me evidence of acts of violence, bloodshed and insurrection fostered by the President. I shall keep asking you until I get an answer! Why does this resolution not include a *specific* charge about a *specific* act, or acts? If you are so convinced that the Sacramento ghetto incident, the arming of black extremists and the threats voiced by these people, are directly attributable to the President, why have you not chosen to place these alleged facts in your bill of particulars?"

We all knew why. Any specific charge could never be proven. It was a case of Kakamba Jones's word against Dalton Warfield's. And in any court, by any standard, our man would prevail. Moreover, even if every word Jones said had been the truth, the attempt to link Hannaford with the lunacy in Sacramento could not succeed.

Ruckett and Cottrell were head to head, whispering at the long table where the authors of the resoluion sat. In the hiatus, page boys scurried about with paper cups of water and messages. One sat at the side of the speaker's rostrum, calmly picking his nose. In a front row seat, Emmett Brian O'Boyle, temporarily removed from his high magisterial chair because the Committee of the Whole was in session, was fast asleep.

"Mr. Speaker," Ruckett said. "My colleagues and I will develop this point later on, in our prepared remarks. The gentleman from Vermont is understandably impatient. But we ask him to bear with us."

"Mr. Speaker," Lewis Smales said irritably, "I have asked a simple question, and it requires a simple answer. Why doesn't the proposal to impeach the President cite the matter of the Sacramento ghetto, naming names, places, dates, and events, in lieu of the fuzzy, shapeless charges presented?"

"Go get him, Smales," I said to Parente.

"Wait, wait, they got Harry Kaplan in the wings. I'll say one thing for Hannaford. He got shrewd lawyers."

"I repeat, Mr. Speaker, we will develop this matter in

461

due course," Ruckett said. His skin was turning scarlet; his ears were crimson.

Harry Kaplan was on his feet. "Mr. Speaker, I should like to ask the gentlemen arguing in behalf of the resolution, do they intend to offer amendments to articles three and four of House Resolution 988, amendments that would satisfy the questions raised by the gentleman from Vermont? It would be an easy matter. Instead of the vague language, a direct charge could be made that the President of the United States bought, or sanctioned the buying of guns for an extremist group. That's all that would be needed."

"Mr. Speaker," Ruckett said tautly, "it is not our intent to reveal our plans for the resolution to Mr. Kaplan or anyone else. We are arguing for the resolution as it stands. At the moment no amendments are contemplated. Why should they be? We drew up this resolution. We, with the guidance of the committee chairman, our distinguished colleague from Alabama, heard evidence, debated the issue, and voted in favor of it."

"In an atmosphere that was a disgrace to the House," Harry Kaplan said. "An atmosphere contrived to frighten, sway and inflame the public and the committee members—"

"Mr. Speaker, advise the gentleman from New Jersey that I have said all I wish to say on the phrasing of the resolution, and I should like to resume my prepared remarks." Ruckett was trembling slightly.

"Proceed, Mr. Ruckett."

Kaplan and Smales sat down. They shook hands with their eyes. They had scored heavily. The blurred quality of the resolution may have been a source of strength in that it could not be closely examined. But this was true only when exterior circumstances were sufficiently exacerbated so that emotions were ascendant. In the calm atmosphere of the House, it would prove treacherous trying to defend the extreme wording. Under attacks by men like Kaplan and Smales, and Hollis Denton, the resolution could be shown to be something less than a contemplative, meticulously crafted work.

"Dark and evil forces are at work in America today," Ruckett said, resuming his prepared comments. "They hide behind smiling masks. This civil rights movement. That mothers-march-for-peace. All sorts of groups, pro-

462

fessing to do good, to elevate the poor, to renew the cities. But it is instructive, Mr. Speaker, to examine what sinister forces are behind these movements. Are we not horrified to hear that Martin Luther King was a tool of the international Communist conspiracy? But he *was*. It has been *proven*. Oh, he was not aware of it. He had not the slightest idea how he was being used by the satanic forces of irreligion . . ."

Some congressmen turned away. Gamey, smelly stuff. Ruckett had been unnerved by Smales's thwacking attack on the resolution. I had the feeling he was ad-libbing. What did the memory of Martin Luther King have to do with the case?

"When in doubt," Parente said to me, "holler Communist, and when in real trouble, holler Communist nigger."

"I see the dubious expression on the faces of the gentlemen from Vermont and New Jersey, my esteemed opponents in this debate. Yes, Martin Luther King, considered one of the mildest, most peace-loving, of the civil rights leaders, was nothing more than a cat's-paw for Communism. The Communists will tell you as much, if you choose to listen. And why was he killed? He was killed by the Communists because he was no longer of any use to them, and had given signs of becoming aware of their mastery over his program . . ."

Angel Lopez Garcia got to his feet—fat, sweaty, rumpled. I felt a rush of pity for the congressman from Chicago, the old battler for the underdog. In the old days, he would have gobbled up Lance Ruckett as if he were a *chili and queso tostada*. But the times had changed; the Ricketts raved on, in and out of Congress. Garcia mopped his forehead and walked toward the rear door. He'd hear no more slanders. I marveled that the rest of the House sat lumpishly and listened to the South Dakotan's fulminations.

"You may ask, Mr. Speaker, what Martin Luther King, his career and his mysterious death, have to do with our resolution. I mention them, sir, only to give us some historical perspective, to, as it were, set the scene for the events that have occurred since the President of the United States took office last January on the steps of the Lincoln Monument. . . ."

One of the press gallery attendants came down the steps

and called softly to Lou Parente. He had a phone call outside.

"Heard enough of this garbage," the newspaperman said. "Have to fumigate the place when that hay-seed Goebbels is finished." As he lumbered up the aisle he called out to Pendragon. "Pleased with your friends, Batesy? Proud of the people who read your column?"

But there was no response from Pendragon. A sodden pall had settled over his robust face, as if he were wondering how he had ended up in bed with rascals like Lance Ruckett and villains like Merton Huckerby.

Ruckett and Cottrell would conclude their presentations that day. They would probably use two hours of the four allotted to them by the Rules Committee. By prearranged agreement the anti-impeachment speakers would have the next two hours. My guess was that the debate would then be broken off until tomorrow, at which time the remaining four hours would be consumed. Then would come questions, answers, further debate and finally the reading of each paragraph of the resolution, and the opportunity to offer amendments.

In the press room I encountered Mona Varnum. She had been sitting on the radio-TV side, and I had not noticed her.

"Hello, dark and secret love," I said, *sotto voce*. "Can whitey carry your tape recorder?"

"No thanks, Deever. I make it a point not to be indebted to Establishment spies."

Lechery melted my knees. I'd have traded all, my birthright, my lofty post as the President's confidential man, my white skin and my cool detached blood, for one more night of passion with Mona.

"Mona, dear girl, I've always been aware of that. What bothers me is the degree of your indebtedness to people like Kakamba Jones and his lunatics."

The stoic mask, that supremely aloof face, betrayed a moment of unease. "I don't run with that pack, Ed," Mona said. "But if I did, I wouldn't apologize to you or any other Charlie."

"I'm sure of that. But you were there. What happened? How did that truce come about? Why did Fancourt agree to talk to Jones and his guerrillas—and let them keep their guns—and let them off scot free, to show up in Washington, where they could give the committee all it

464

needed to vote for impeachment? What do you know about it?"

"Don't bug me, man. I'm a hard-working reporter for a network. Keep my nose clean. No editorializing. You know how the FCC is about us electronic journalists."

I grabbed her slender wrist. "Listen, Mona, I can't believe that you approve of what's going on here. I know you've always looked upon the President and those of us who serve him as a collection of cynical politicians, of self-serving Establishment types, worried about profits and big business and corporations. I keep telling you that you're mistaken. What your involvement was in Sacramento I don't know—although you were inside the ghetto, and you did have an in with the extremists."

"Oh, you rap too much, Deever. I'm in no mood for it. I have a piece to write."

"Not so fast. If you won't tell me what kind of sneaky deal was cooked up between the black militants and the right wing, at least tell me what's next on the agenda."

"Next?" She was getting upset.

"Yes, damn you. Where is Jones, and Smith and the rest of that mob?"

"I don't keep tabs on 'em. Kakamba went to New York. Smith too. They've done their bit. They're through. The scenario doesn't call for them to participate any further."

"Typical," I sneered. "They raise hell, then run. What about the others?"

"I don't know for sure." She started to walk away.

"The earth just didn't swallow them up. They walked out of the hearing and vanished."

"Black magic."

"Not funny, Mona. What are they up to?"

"They're back where they belong. With the brothers in Sacramento. They're watching and waiting, man. They're not through yet."

"How in hell did they get back in with all that military hardware?"

Mona Varnum shrugged and pulled loose from my grip. I was bothering her. Whatever her association with the extremists—*fascists*, Harry Kaplan had accurately called them—she was no longer so sure she sympathized with them.

"They got ways. Maybe they were smuggled back in in

465

a laundry hamper. Or a load of watermelons." And her lithe figure walked by me.

As I headed to a telephone to call the Attorney General's office and see if Judge Moscowitz knew anything about the whereabouts of the avenging black angels, Parente came hurrying toward me.

"Listen," he said, "I just talked to Baldini."

I had forgotten about Parente's cousin, the furtive man who was his secret operative, electronics expert, spy in the right-wing camp, all-around daredevil.

"Does he have anything we can use?" I asked.

"Not much," Parente muttered. "Only the former Mrs. Lance Ruckett."

"What? Where?"

"Take it easy," the columnist cautioned. "I'm getting on the three-o'clock shuttle to New York. You take the four-o'clock plane. There's instructions on this where to meet me. I dug up some stuff on Sykes Cottrell, but that's for light reading on the flight. See you in New York."

He walked away from me, glowering at a young man from *Time* who had tried to eavesdrop.

"Say, Cottrell is raising the roof in there," the young man said. "He's got your boss guilty of everything from miscegenation to ballot box stuffing."

I had an hour or so before leaving for the airport, and I entered the press gallery again, standing at the rear and trying to scheme up an underhand counterattack. *The right things get done for the wrong reasons*, Ben Hannaford used to say. Was Mrs. Lance Ruckett a wrong reason?

". . . it will be argued," Representative Sykes Cottrell of Mississippi was saying, "that the mere failure to enforce the laws does not constitute a high crime or a misdemeanor. But, Mr. Speakah, what if such failure to enforce laws on the part of a President results in bloodshed and violence? Are we not justified, then, in holdin' him guilty, along with the revolution'ries?"

Outside, I called Judge Moscowitz, but was told he was conferring with the President. Nor could any of his aides enlighten me on the whereabouts of the "liberation" forces.

Air-borne, the great jet circled over the magnificent city I loved so much. Below, the white monuments gave me assurance. We'd come out of it. Hannaford was too much in the American grain—yes, his faults as well as his virtues —to be rejected. Whatever I could do to help him survive, no matter how coarse and cruel it might be, I would do. The Washington monument, a dazzling pillar of gray-white stone, pointed its finger skyward, as if to direct my thoughts to a more lofty level. But I was in no mood for elevation. Parente and I had to roll up our sleeves and do some dirty work. It would not be a new experience for either of us.

Slumped at the rear of the jet, I read the sheet of yellow note paper that Parente had given to me in the House press room. At the top were scrawled some instructions. *Prince Albert Hotel, W. 27th St., Room 809.* That would be Augie Baldini's hideaway, I guessed—the standard obscure room hiding an obscure woman.

Below this, was a type-written résumé of some data Parente had collected on Cottrell. I gathered Lou had hoped it might aid us in our counterattack. It was juicy stuff, but before I'd finished it, I knew it was useless; when I had to read to the end of the paper, I saw that Lou had come to the same morbid conclusion.

Cottrell. Pillar of the church, honorable congressman, foe of pornography, soft-spoken gent, expert on constitutional law. Has three times intervened to get special favors for his farm machinery dealership. Knocked out all competitors on bidding for contracts for state prison farm at MacKennaville; branched into heavy equipment and road-building business, and made $278,000 sale of graders and earth-movers to federally-financed rural road improvement program by tossing out other dealers' bids. All of a matter of record. His law firm got fat fees for representing state's richest farmers in lawsuit against fed. gvt. lawsuit, which they won, over land reclamation. Result: dough for Cottrell's firm; reclaimed land at a cut price for fat-cat cotton and peanut growers; dispossession of several hundred black farmers in the delta. Cottrell has his finger in all and makes money without even trying.

"Will you pay by cash, check or credit card?" the hostess asked.

"All three," I said. "No, sorry, ma'am. I didn't mean that." I found a twenty and resumed my reading of

Parente's depressing report. After listing all of Cottrell's outrages, deeds that we could publicize and use to discredit him, I saw a handwritten comment by Parente—one with which I was in full accord.

Good stuff, but forget it. Can't use any of this against Cottrell. Won't cut any ice with public, press or Congress.

If Parente's report on Cottrell did nothing to cheer me up, the cab ride from Kennedy Airport to the Prince Albert Hotel was even less heartening. The headline in the New York *Post* read: HOUSE DEBATES IMPEACHMENT, CLOSE VOTE SEEN.

"Throw him out on his ass," my cabdriver, one Milton Blum, volunteered.

"Who?"

"Hannaford. I voted for him. But to hell with him now."

"Why do you say that?"

"He's for the boogies, that's why. Everything for the boogies."

"That isn't quite accurate," I said. "The President is trying to improve the lives of many Americans who work for a living. Don't you know about his tax proposals—that would benefit people like yourself? Or the urban program, to build more schools, and parks and low cost housing—not just for black people, but for all our cities?"

"Look, Jack," he snarled, turning an angry gnome's face on me, "I don't care what they call it. We suffer."

The three-lane highway was being squeezed into two. A police car blocked the right-hand roadway, and the traffic was jamming up. As our cab approached the bottleneck, another taxi, driven by a Negro zoomed in ahead of us.

"Lousy spade," Milton Blum grumbled. "Goddamn gypsy boogie."

"Gypsy?"

"Yeah, gypsy cabdriver. He's got no license. No medallion. City's full of them. Against the law, but try to find a mayor who'll stop 'em. Black bastards'll kill us all."

I had read about the unlicensed cabs driven by blacks and Puerto Ricans, but the name "gypsy" was new to me. "But aren't they operating because you licensed fellows refuse to pick up colored people or go to Harlem?" I asked.

"Screw 'em," Blum rasped. "Screw 'em. We don't pick 'em up because they'll cut our throats."

For a while, as we crept along in heavy traffic, I was silent. "And you really believe that President Hannaford should be thrown out of office, that all this violence is his fault?"

"He ain't helped it, Jack. Yeah, I'd like to see a tough guy like that Sparrier in there. He took care of 'em in California a few years ago. Couple hundred dead, that's the language they understand."

The cab grumbled ahead. Looking out to the right, I saw why the traffic was being routed into two lanes. A file of green and white New York City patrol cars filled one lane, along with several police "Black Marias" and three ambulances.

Beyond on the land bordering the highway, rose an immense, endless construction project—high-rise apartments, three-story apartments, an unfinished complex of stores, parking areas, unpaved streets. A sign informed me:

AIRPORT CITY: LOW-COST HOUSING PROJECT

A COMBINED PUBLIC ENTERPRISE

City of New York—State of New York

Distantly I saw a file of white pickets walking around one of the soaring skeletal armatures. Evidently no work was going on. The picketing had stopped construction.

"Beat the shit out 'em yesterday," Blum said with satisfaction. "When those boogies showed up to picket, the guys on the job hit 'em with bricks and rocks and buckets of piss. You know what? The cops cheered. Didn't make a pinch. The airport workers union came out and brought coffee and cake for the guys. Finally the cops arrested fifty people—all boogies. That's what we need, brother. I'm gettin' so I love cops."

After all we had been through, I suppose I should have been inured to this sort of thing. But I wasn't. As Hamlet put it, all occasions did inform against us. High on the scaffolding around the apartment fluttered huge banners.

469

SPARRIER FOR PRESIDENT

HE'LL HANDLE THEM
* * *

THEY BURN: WE EARN

I lasped into a pessimistic silence and did not respond when Blum said, "Ship the bastards back to Africa. That's where they belong. Know what I mean?"

I knew.

Parente answered the door. As I crossed the threshold into the dingy room, the odor of disinfectant in the corridor merged with an aroma of a pungent perfume.

Augie Baldini was stretched out on a sofa—it was a small two-room suite—listening to a transistor radio. He nodded at me. Baldini did not talk much. He looked smaller, darker, more enigmatic than ever.

"I tell you the truth, Ed, I haven't figured out how to play this hand," Parente said in a low voice. "We got the broad. The question is now, what the hell do we do with her?"

From the adjoining bedroom, the woman I took to be the former Mrs. Lance Ruckett walked in.

"Ed, meet Carla Foraker. The ex-wife of Congressman Ruckett. Carla, baby, this is Mr. Edward Deever, of whom you may have read in my column and elsewhere."

"How do," she said.

"A pleasure, Mrs., I mean Miss Foraker."

"That was part of the divorce settlement. I had to use my maiden name. Lance insisted."

"I see." She sat down, daintily on the edge of a maroon brocade chair and smoothed her skirt. "The way Mr. Parente had been talkin' I almost expected the President himself to walk in."

"Miss Foraker," I said, "the President is not even aware of your existence, or that I am meeting with you. Whatever occurs here, whatever is said, is a matter that concerns only the four people in this room."

Baldini had his magic tape recorder spinning somewhere, perhaps in a closet, or in the next room. Where the microphone was, I couldn't be sure. In any case, I wanted everything on tape. I glanced at Augie—as if asking *where is it?*—so that I might project my voice in the right direction. Parente's spy yawned and arched his eyebrows toward a hideous turquoise lamp on the end table next to the sofa.

"Yes, I understand," Carla Foraker said. "An important man like Mr. Hannaford . . . and someone like me . . ."

The former Mrs. Ruckett was, I judged, in her early thirties, but there was a curious mixture of maturity and adolescence in her face that made it difficult to pinpoint her age. She exhibited a kind of young-old amalgam—not entirely unattractive—that one often sees in the snub-nosed faces of servicemen's wives in supermarkets. I could see Carla Foraker Ruckett, elevated on her white wedgie shoes, her sassy behind and thick thighs sausage-tight in lavender stretch slacks, her ash-blond hair piled high in a bouquet of curlers. I saw her frowning, sullen eyes narrowed, lips pale, pushing a cart laden with canned corn and frozen TV dinner, through a supermarket in Fort Dix, New Jersey, or Victorville, California. And yet she was by no means without a sexy, provocative quality.

"You're lookin' me over like I was auditioning," Carla said uneasily—but with a friendly smile. Her teeth were uneven; I realized that I liked her, and why my heart went out to her. She was so much like me—a child of the *lumpen* lower classes of the American heartland. Her hair was combed in an attractive page boy—a style I hadn't seen since the late forties, and her pale green suit was a trifle shoddy. I had a pang of sympathy for her.

"Well, in a sense you are, Miss Foraker," I said.

"I explained to Carla already what this is about. I think she understands." Parente was pacing the small room, his arms folded, his pugnacious face scowling.

"Don't I ever. You want the dirt on Lance."

"In a manner of speaking, yes, Miss Foraker," I said. "We are dealing with a serious matter. The campaign against the President led by your ex-husband has been a wicked one. Unfortunately a President cannot strike back in the same way."

"But his assistants can, right?"

"Yes, Miss Foraker. But you must understand that Mr. Parente and his employee do not work for the President. They do this in the interests of American journalism. Myself, I'm another breed of cat. I'm here for the President, even though he hasn't the faintest idea what I'm up to."

"Okay. I'll talk. Anything to get back at that dirty, four-flushing, sex maniac of a son of a bitch."

Up to now, her language had been decorous, her voice restrained. Now the mood changed. She was like the wife of a master sergeant stationed at Wiesbaden, a sulky American girl, learning that her hubby had been keeping a blond *fräulein* in an apartment outside the base.

"Ruckett spreads joy wherever he goes," Parente said. "She's told me some beauties."

"If Miss Foraker doesn't mind, I'd like to hear it from her. I won't take any notes, I'll just listen."

Miss Foraker crossed her legs—the knobby knees, faintly bruised, were in keeping with my vision of that supermarket Venus—and lit a cigarette.

"Lance really wasn't such a louse at first," Carla said. "And he wasn't a crook either. From what I hear, he still isn't. Just in little ways like lotsa congressmen. But I mean, he's had chances to make big hauls from corporations, and it really doesn't interest him."

"I've gathered that," I said. I knew why Ruckett was not among the major thieves in Congress. He was a small-timer, a cheap John. "Your ex-husband has pretty much kept his nose clean as regards financial matters. Of course he's never wanted for extra funds, being on the national board of the Defenders of Our Republic. A well-oiled operation."

"Don't tell me," she said. A bitter smile twisted her thin lips. "Didn't I get sick of those goddamn Texas oil millionaires and their snotty wives. I kept tellin' Lance they were using him, sucking up to him because he'd run their errands. And the way those women with their Texas accents and diamonds and minks looked down their snoots at me. I had it up to here, honestly."

My heart bled for Carla Foraker Ruckett. Knowing the brutality of people like Miles J. Cudder—the First Lady's predatory nephew—I empathized with anyone who had to associate with such grasping boors, and worse, had to suffer their snubs.

"I guess you know all about that," she said. "How Lance financed his campaigns with lotsa oil and gas money, and how he really made DOOR a going thing. I mean, that maniac Huckerby, he was running it into the ground

472

with his long-range rifles, threatening to kill anyone he didn't like. Lance was smarter. Lance shut him up, and made DOOR respectable. Lance gets invited to Harvard and Stanford to speak. Nobody would invite Huckerby. Not even to a funeral. What a creep."

She was reinforcing what I had believed about Ruckett all along—he was not stupid, not by any means. He'd gotten his mitts on an endless source of money, and had found *issues*. While the idiot right-wing had been shrieking about fluoridation and sex education in the schools, and the international Communist plot, and assorted paranoid issues, none of which the American people cared about, Ruckett shrewdly understood that the only issues you could move *masses* of Americans on were *race and money*.

"I guess you know most of this political stuff," Carla said. "Mr. Parente said what you want is about the divorce."

"Tell us anything you think is interesting, Miss Foraker," I said. "It's all useful."

A chain-smoker, she lit up again and filled the room with smoke. Her mouth curved in a vengeful smile. She was getting ready to jab the knife into her former husband.

"Lance is a bastard," she said. "I mean, he's a little nuts, but that's no excuse for what he did to me. Also, one of his problems is he's got a tiny thing. You know, underdeveloped. Heck, I used to tell him, 'Honey, that's nothing to be ashamed about. It's not the size of it, it's how you use it.' "

"Very well put," I offered. Was I blushing? "In high school, our basketball coach used to tell us, 'it's not the size of the boy in the fight, it's the size of the fight in the boy that counts.' But I'm no expert."

"Hmmm. I dunno, you look like you know something about everything."

"No, I'm a political man. That's all."

"So was Lance, but that didn't keep him from wanting it five or six times a day. Mostly with our clothes on. That was his idea of fun. Sometimes with our coats on in winter. I always had to keep my clothes on."

"That by itself is surely no crime." I sounded sympathetic.

"I had no complaints those first few years we were

married." A lascivious smirk wrinkled her cheeks. "I was a match for him, all right. He knew he was in with a champ."

Parente's dark eyes almost popped from his head. As for me, I had trouble keeping a straight face. Carla Foraker was, in H. L. Mencken's phrase, "as magnificently unruffled as a grass widow at her third wedding."

"Well, anyway," she continued, "after about five years, after Lance was in Congress, and we were living in Washington, I guess he figured he needed other girls to stimulate him. I caught him with two chambermaids, in a motel outside Memphis, when we went down so Lance could speak to the American Legion. I cried a little and screamed a lot, and he cried also, and said he couldn't help it, that he was overactive, and had no control over himself. But with *two*?"

"It's known as a sandwich," Parente offered.

"Hmmm. I guess that's supposed to be funny." She stuck out her tongue at Parente—an unmistakably provocative gesture—and I realized that I had assumed the role of kindly father-priest-older-brother. Parente, if he wished, could play the part of lover.

"Well it got worse. He kept saying I didn't satisfy him, that I wasn't responsive, and I took my clothes off too fast. I got sick of his crazy ideas. I like to be comfortable, but that madman, making me change dresses and slips and panties, and what-all, I got fed up. And the way he boasted all the time, about what hot stuff he was."

"It must have been difficult," I said.

"I guess I got less interested and began to show it. For a man who thought he was the greatest stud in the world, I suppose this was sort of a blow. Once I fell asleep in the middle of it. He wouldn't talk to me for a week."

"But kept making love to you?"

"Oh, sure. One thing had nothing to do with the other."

"This was how long ago?" I asked.

"About three years. Lance was in Congress. But he did an awful lot of traveling and lecturing. We were on the road all the time. Golly, he made a bundle giving those speeches. I had to laugh. They always opened with God, the flag, Christ, prayers, hymns. And there was Lance thinking of nothing but the next round—with me, or with one or two others."

"Now you say you knew about his cheating, his need

for women, and yet you didn't protest, you didn't threaten him with divorce?"

Carla pursed her lips. "I got sore a few times, but I still liked him. Lance can be very sweet. And let's face it, we ran in some pretty high circles. I mean, I didn't like those Texas oil ladies, but the men were nice. Real sports, some of them."

"But what led to the divorce?" I asked.

"Oh. The divorce. Well, it's all in the papers, Mr. Parente has copies of the proceedings."

"If it would not embarrass you, I'd like to hear it from you."

"I couldn't care less. It was when he started forcing me to watch him do it with other women. So I'd learn a few things."

"I beg your pardon?" Now I *was* blushing.

"What I said. Lance would get these dames, and I'd have to sit in the motel room and *watch* them."

"Ah, sort of a visual aid?"

"Yeah. As if I hadn't been a match for the squirt. I want to tell you it's no fun for a young woman who takes pride in her own good looks and her own sexiness. It was a goddamn insult."

"You are so right, Miss Foraker."

"God damn him anyway. Who the hell did he think he was anyway? There I'd sit, in the corner of the room, and there he'd be on the bed, him giving the orders, hollering at me to watch, to learn something, so I'd know a few things. And Christ, the collection of floozies and tramps he did it with—carnie dancers, barmaids, a lady rodeo rider, niggers, Mexicans and one, I swear, was an Albino."

"Excuse my frankness, Miss Foraker," I said hoarsely, "but were you ever invited to join in? Or did you offer to participate?"

She raised her plucked eyebrows in a display of hauteur that was not without a certain dignity. "Excuse *me*, Mr. Deever, but I have moral scruples. I was raised in a strict Methodist house. Yeah, the first few times Lance would ask me to join in, but I had absolutely no desire to. I let him know it too."

"You say this went on for six months before you got angry enough to sue for divorce. Why did you wait so long?"

Carla blew a cloud of smoke across the room at me. I

475

had the feeling it was a protective screen, like the ink thrown out by a squid, or the gases emitted by insects. "I guess I loved him. I kept hoping we could put the pieces together again."

Yes, she had loved him. Only a deep love, betrayed, could bring her to Parente and me with this squalid tale.

"And you say that what you have told us is a matter of court record? That Mr. Ruckett did not contest this?"

"That's right."

Parente waved a sheaf of Xeroxes at me. "It's here. Ruckett and his oil friends tried to rob the files a coupla times, but some editor out in South Dakota who hated Lance's guts got copies of the originals and stashed them away in a vault."

"Miss Foraker," I said, "we do not, at the moment intend to publicize this information, and we probably never will. But we may confront Mr. Ruckett with it. As you know, he has, through threats and connivance brought us to the brink of a catastrophe. We may have to use dirty methods to bring him to heel. I am sure you understand."

"Yeah, yeah, I know what it's all about. Heck, I was a congressman's wife. I danced with President Kretz. There was a real gentleman. And he liked me too."

I could see that old Hayward Kretz would have. Carla was pretty, innocent, tough, with that faintly worn look of the sexy American midwestern wife.

"We may also have to ask you to confront Mr. Ruckett," I said.

"Hunh?"

"Oh, we'll be present. Just to see him again, perhaps in a hotel room. With no performing ladies present. Would you mind?"

She frowned. "I swore off that little bastard once and for all. Frankly, he gives me the creeps."

"It may be necessary. It may not."

Augie Baldini yawned, got up and walked into the bedroom. The tape reel was probably ready for changing.

"Lou, I believe I have no more questions for Miss Foraker," I said. "Will she be reachable in the next few days?"

Parente nodded. "Yeah. Augie is looking after her. They'll be in New York if we need them."

Baldini returned and told Miss Foraker that he would take her to dinner. She excused herself to comb her hair.

"I don't know," I said. "I don't know what we can do with it."

Parente scowled. "Neither do I. It's too putrid. I mean, there are limits. Even with the court testimony, the papers would lay off."

With a heady whiff of perfume, Carla Foraker returned from the bedroom, shook our hands and walked toward the door with Baldini. "All the time I was talking to you," she said, "you know, it's like I realized Lance was *two* people. He could be sweet and charming and kind. You should have seen him campaigning. And the same way with me. But then that fire would come into his eyes, and it seemed like he hated everyone, and was suspicious of everyone, and wanted to burn everything to the ground. Crazy, isn't it?"

When they had left, I said: "She supports a theory of mine. All these political weirdos, left and right, have some deep psychological injury, some failing of the normal emotional processes. On the left, it manifests itself in drugs, especially among the kids and the blacks. On the right, among these native American militants, the root of their problem lies in sexual frustration, in too much, too little or, as in Mr. Ruckett's case, a raging need to experiment."

"You mean because that guy is undersized the whole country has to suffer?"

"It's not inconceivable. The tsarevitch's hemophilia helped bring on the Russian revolution."

"I thought Lew Smales was brilliant," Judge Moscowitz said. "He made Ruckett and Cottrell look like the small-timers they are."

The President nodded. "We will have to do something good for Vermont when this mess is over. I never knew I had such good friends up there in New England."

We were sitting in the White House Library on the ground floor, Attorney General Moscowitz, myself, the Majority whip, Senator Sidney Stapp and President Hannaford. The President had suggested we meet there after dinner to discuss the progress of the impeachment.

"Listen to this," Moscowitz said. He opened the worn copy of DeWitt's *The Impeachment of President Johnson,* the signed copy I had located among the twenty-seven hundred volumes in the White House Library, where we

477

now sat. "From the Republican minority report on the impeachment charges. 'A great deal of the matter is of no value whatever. Much of it is mere hearsay, opinion of witnesses and no little amount of it is utterly irrelevant to the case.' Comparatively a small amount of it could be used on a trial of this case before the Senate."

"That's good, that's damn good," Hannaford said.

Moscowitz and I exchanged smiles. "I'll say it's good," I said. "Lewis Smales thought it was good enough to use it in his speech to the Committee of the Whole." I waved the transcript of the days' proceedings. "Word for word, it's in there."

"That's a smart Yankee," Hannaford said appreciatively.

"Where he really bombed them was on the legal aspects," Moscowitz said. "Smales kept challenging them to cite the laws that had been violated by first, freeing people under ERCA, and second, releasing the defense money for the poverty program. He had them there. Ever since the Johnson case, the courts and the Congress have agreed that no offense, except those named in the Constitution—treason, bribery, and provable high crimes and misdemeanors—are impeachable, and that even these acts, must be indictable, not under common law, or public opinion, but under an existing statute of the United States. Smales is a hell of a lawyer."

The President got up from the caned chair and began to pace. He paused to stare at the five oil portraits of the Indian delegation that visited the White House in 1821. Did he feel a surge of his aboriginal blood, a stirring of that stoic courage that served him so well?

"I'm sure, Sam, we have the best lawyers and the best legal arguments on our side," Hannaford said.

"Mr. President, we'll have them if this mess ever gets as far as the Senate," Sid Stapp added. "But I'm assured by Speaker O'Boyle and Jack Hexter that will never happen."

Hannaford shook his head. "I would agree with you, Sid, if it weren't for the emotional binge the country's on. We're all prisoners of our skins."

"Mr. President, the arguments of men like Smales must have their effect. Many people will listen to them. The press, the media, the academic community—they're on your side."

Hannaford laughed. " 'But by the grace of God, I am what I am.' They didn't line up with me a few years ago."

The Attorney General took off his heavy-rimmed eyeglasses and wiped them. "A lot of us had our doubts. You've won over a lot of people who didn't care for you."

The President tapped the top of the large green table. "I suppose that's grounds for optimism. I'm not concerned that the House will get a majority to impeach me. We'll win that one. And if through some freak, some lunatic mischance, it ever gets to the Senate, there is not the remotest possibility that they can get up a two-thirds vote."

"Amen," Senator Stapp said.

"What does bother me is the cloud of suspicion, the doubts, the whispers, that'll remain after this blows over," President Hannaford said. "I'll be like poor old Harding."

"A bad comparison, sir." I was outraged. "You're not like that bumbling newspaper publisher at all."

"Edward, I don't mean in terms of politics, or the presidency. It's the bloody lies. They whispered nigger at Harding all his life—that dirty rumor of his alleged colored ancestor, which nobody ever proved."

Moscowitz shook his leonine head. "Listen to what Lew Smales had to say. 'The history of the words in the constitutional convention that framed the Constitution, as narrated by Madison, seems decisive of the controversy. The original proposition submitted was to make the President removable on impeachment and conviction "for mal or corrupt conduct" or "for malpractice or neglect of duty." Afterwards, the clause was modified so as to read, "for treason, bribery and corruption." This was finally confined to "treason and bribery" alone.' "

"I'm sure Congressman Smales was on sound historic ground," the President said. "But do you honestly think these legalities, this history lesson will sway the public? I tell you, Sam, I'm more concerned with those thirty-one per cent who think I should be tossed out than with the House of Representatives."

Only Sam Moscowitz could have lectured the President as did the Attorney General. "Mr. President, it is not like you to lose faith in the people. They may make some wrong turnings and be driven by their emotions from time to time, but under bold leadership, they will opt for the right course."

"True, Sam. But I am afraid we are living in a time when, as Paul put it, 'evil communications corrupt good manners.' "

"I don't deny that," the Attorney-General said. "But listen to Lew Smales's history lesson. He said: 'When after being so amended, it was taken up once more for consideration, Colonel Mason voted to add 'maladministration'. That sound familiar?"

"Dammit," Sid Stapp said, "Smales had them there! It was as if they were turning the clock back two hundred years—to standards that were *rejected* by the founding fathers!"

"Exactly," Moscowitz said. "Listen, 'Madison, objecting that so vague a term would be equivalent to a tenure during the pleasure of the Senate, Mason withdrew the word and substituted "other high crimes and misdemeanors against the state," which was agreed to, and on the general revision the last three words were deleted as superfluous.' "

"Then he concludes," the Attorney-General went on, " 'so that if any construction of a constitutional provision by resorting to its origin and gestation was ever valid, the phrase "other high crimes and misdemeanors" used in the Constitution must be held to mean only such malfeasance in office as constituted at common law a high crime or a high misdemeanor of a kindred grade, respectively with treason or bribery.' "

"That lays it out clearly," Senator Stapp said.

Moscowitz chuckled. "Yes, it does. Just as Mr. DeWitt did over sixty years ago in his book *The Impeachment of President Johnson*." The Attorney-General held up the volume. "Smales lifted it right out of here, but he was gentleman enough to cite the source of his arguments when the debate ended."

"Kaplan did a good job also," I said. "When Cottrell asked him whether the President's action would lead to civil war or a race war, he really let fly."

"Also from DeWitt," Moscowitz said. "There's nothing like a good source, as any lawyer can tell you." He scanned the transcript. "Ah, here it is. 'Mr. Kaplan: Is the gentleman from Mississippi saying we should impeach the President for what he may do in the *future*? Do our fears and suspicions and prejudices, by themselves, make a President guilty of high crimes? If we cannot arraign him for a specific crime, for what are we to proceed against him?' "

"I'm sorry I missed it," the President said. "Too bad a man isn't allowed to sit in on his own trial." I could see what was bothering him. In his years in the Senate, Ben Hannaford had been the king of the floor—wandering, chatting, patting backs, tugging at lapels, joking, dispensing favors, putting down enemies. It irked him that he could not walk on to the floor of the House chamber and speak in his own defense—instead of depending on Lewis Smales and Harry Kaplan to do it for him.

"I'm sorry, sir, it doesn't work that way," I said mischievously. "Speaker O'Boyle would faint dead away if you showed up. If you glared at Ruckett, he'd shrivel."

"But what a temptation it is, friends." The President rubbed one huge fist into his palm. "Yes, I would love to go into all the world and preach the gospel to every creature."

When we had reviewed the day's debate in the House and made optimistic predictions about the forthcoming vote, I was driven to the Manger Hay-Adams by Judge Moscowitz.

"What did you learn from the former Mrs. Ruckett?" he asked me.

I almost choked, then tried to be casual. "It was supposed to be secret," I said.

"Edward, it helps to be the former boss of the FBI. I have some contacts myself. The fact of the matter is, I'd asked for a little check on the lady myself. Poor thing, I'm afraid friend Lance did not treat her very well."

What was I to say? I supposed it didn't matter. Moscowitz could find out anything he wanted to know. "I learned very little, sir."

"Edward, whatever you do, do it carefully. I think we'll come out of this all right."

"I do too, Judge. It's just that Lou Parente and I felt the need for a bit of insurance."

The Attorney General stopped his car in front of the hotel. "I suppose they'll wind up the reading of the charges tomorrow," he said.

"And they should vote in a day or two."

"By which time we can all breathe easier."

I opened the car door. "Good night, Judge," I said.

"Edward, tell me what you think of this legal team—myself, Mr. Boswell and young Fixx."

"Three of the smartest, sir."

"I suspect we can handle anything the House throws at

us in the way of prosecuting attorneys. Good night, Edward."

As I entered the lobby, I realized what the crafty lawyer had been saying. They had already drawn up a panel of defense lawyers in case the impeachment got to the Senate for trial. Suddenly the unpalatable necessity of enlisting Carla Foraker as a pawn in our desparate game against Ruckett loomed larger.

I sat once more in the press gallery with Lou Parente and Bates Pendragon and watched the House Committee of the Whole conclude its debate on the impeachment resolution. All arguments having been heard, the clerk was now authorized by the Speaker pro tem, Bill Rumsford, to read off the paragraphs of the resolution, the now famous "H. Res. 988", and ask the members if they had any amendments to offer.

"It is the sense of the House that Benjamin Bow Hannaford, President of the United States, is impeached for high crimes and misdemeanors . . ."

We waited. No one asked for the floor.

"What I expected," Parente said. "You can't amend lunacy, you can only fight it."

"That's right," I said. "None of our people will want to change it. They want to kill it. And Ruckett's crowd wants it the way it is, not a word changed."

"Look, look. Rumsford's got a customer."

It was Angel Lopez Garcia, on his feet, waving an unlit Havana cigar. "Mr. Speaker, I should like to move to amend the first paragraph of House Resolution 988, if you please."

"Chair recognizes the gentleman from Illinois."

"Thank you, sir."

Garcia still had a clown's talent to command attention. That was Garcia's tragedy: his vain foolishness, his shiftiness, had betrayed him, had annulled what would have been a career marked with honor and accomplishment.

"Mr. Speaker, I don' like this resolution. I have been quiet all the time, because better lawyers, like the gentleman from Vermont and the gentleman from New Jersey been arguin' in defense of the President. Lemme tell you somethin'. I ran against the President las' time, and he don' need my defense. He can handle his own defense. He is, as we *latinos* say, *muy toro*. I wanna say to you, Mr.

482

Speaker, that President Hannaford is a match for all 435 of us sitting here today, and he's specially a match for people like you—"

With that, Garcia, whom I suspected was half shot, pointed a finger at Lance Ruckett. "Yeah, you, Mr. Gentleman from South Dakota—"

"The member is out of order," Rumsford said. "The gentleman from Illinois is out of order. Those personal remarks are out of order and have no bearing on the debate."

"Mr. Speaker," Garcia said, "I rise to offer an amendment. I should like to offer thees amendment to paragraph one, and it reads as follows. 'It is the sense of this House that Benjamin Bow Hannaford, President of the United States, is to be commended for his courageous and imaginative efforts to end injustice, poverty and discrimination in the nation.'"

Rumsford blinked. "That is all?"

"Tha's it, Mr. Speaker. Clear as that. I theenk it only changes the meaning of the original slightly. But ees more accurate my way."

The press gallery laughed; some applauded. But the members of the House found nothing humorous in Garcia's attack. Satire is lost on most legislators; especially when they are the butts of the joke.

"I am sorry, Mr. Garcia, but the Chair must rule that such an amendment is not an amendment at all, but a contradiction of the sense of the resolution, and cannot be entertained."

"Excuse me, Mr. Speaker, why not put it to a vote?" Garcia asked.

"Bad, bad," Parente muttered. "His clowning won't help Hannaford. Some of these yokels will figure your boss put him up to it."

The Speaker of the House roused himself from semi-slumber and tottered to the rostrum. He, Rumsford, Majority Leader Hexter and the House parliamentarian conferred.

Rumsford called for order. "The Chair rules that the amendment offered by the gentleman from Illinois is in order and will be subject to the usual rules—arguments of no more than five minutes in duration."

"Thank you, Mr. Speaker. May I presen' my case for the revised paragraph?"

"Proceed."

"Now, Mr. Speaker, what is thees resolution, as it stands, but an attempt to cut the President down? And why do these people wan' to cut him down? I tell you why. Because he is for the underdog. He is for black people. He is for brown people. He is for poor people. Tha's all. It got nothin' to do with usurpation of powers or misuse of laws or bloodshed. We had bloodshed and violence in the ghettos long before Mr. Hannaford become President. He is tryin' to end it. Why can't you people see that? But lots of us right here in this room like the country to be the way it has been. A white country for those who got money and jobs and a future. And a black country for those who don't. I know. I been there. President Hannaford is sayin', change it, make it better, give people a chance. And so he made enemies. Tha's what this resolution is, Mr. Speaker—revenge. Throw it out and praise him for the good job he is doin'!"

Garcia spoke with emotion and verve, and some of the gallery viewers applauded him. But the speeches opposing his amendment cut him to pieces. Unlike a shrewd lawyer like Smales, he could not defend himself. And the capriciousness of his "amendment" made it impossible for the majority of the House to side with him.

When the brisk debate ended—the House is at its best when these amendments are offered, debated and voted upon—the speaker pro tem called for a voice vote.

"On the amendment offered by Mr. Garcia," the tally clerk called. "All in favor say 'aye.' "

There was a sparse response of affirmative voices. No more than a handful would go along with Garcia's half-joking thrust.

"All in favor say 'no.' "

A great roar went up.

"The motion is defeated," Rumsford said.

And so, they proceeded paragraph by paragraph, to read the resolution.

No one rose to offer an amendment to the second and third paragraphs of the resolution.

"Third paragraph," the clerk intoned. "The House charges that he has, with deliberation, misused and misinterpreted enacted laws, and has thus fostered violence, bloodshed and insurrection."

"Usually there's battle royal to see who can offer the first amendment," I said to Parente.

The columnist grunted. "Nah. Not on this abortion. Nobody wants to touch it. And it doesn't pay to kid around the way Garcia did. I love him but nobody thinks he's funny any more."

Across from us, in the radio-TV section of the press gallery, I saw Mona talking to a young reporter. Then she got up, and despite the crucial moment that the debate was reaching—it was possible that the impeachment vote by the House in *regular* session was imminent—she walked up the aisle to the press room.

I wiggled past Parente, and ran up in back of the gallery. Mona was walking toward the offices used by the broadcasting people.

"Anything I should know about?" I asked her. "People don't run out on an impeachment vote unless it's important."

"Tip from the coast. A shoot out in Sacramento."

"Serious?"

"Nobody knows." She turned to the lad who had summoned her. "Frank, you cover the debate for me. I'll take the call."

I had my suspicions. And she had her contacts. "Mona, please let me know what's happening."

"I doubt it's anything. The honkies pump shots into the place regularly and the brothers shoot back."

I raced to the press gallery in time to hear the clerk read off the last paragraph. ". . . is referred to the Senate for trial by the Senate sitting as a court, with the Chief Justice of the United States presiding, as provided in the Constitution."

"The Chair will entertain motions for amendments," Rumsford said.

Representative Lawrence DiLorenzo of Brooklyn, chairman of the House Judiciary Committee, a weathered old battler for liberal causes, was on his feet. He brushed back his crown of white hair.

"Mr. Speaker," Larry said in the tones of a road-company Rigoletto, "I rise not to offer an amendment to the last paragraph, but to offer a substitute amendment, that would replace all five articles of the existing resolution. I am informed I am within my rights."

I perked up. DiLorenzo had planned this carefully.

"There is some question as to whether that is proper procedure," Rumsford said. "Are you offering an amendment to any paragraph?"

"If the Speaker prefers, let me state it this way," DiLorenzo said. "I move the striking of the first four paragraphs of House Resolution 988, and the amendment of the last paragraph."

"Shrewd old bird, Larry," Parente said.

"Proceed."

"It reads as follows, Mr. Speaker," the old man said. " 'Recognizing the widespread civil disorders and discontents now current, the House resolves to request of the President an immediate conference of legislative and executive leaders concerned with urban matters, said conference to have as its goal the reduction of violence and bloodshed and the forestalling of insurrectionary movements, and the restoration of harmonious relationships between the legislative and executive branches, so that the nation may benefit from the combined wisdom and prudence of both.' "

Ruckett was on his feet; he was recognized. "Now, Mr. Speaker, I respect the years of the gentleman from New York, and experience and knowledge of big city matters. But whom is he trying to fool? The amendment he offers is no amendment at all. It is subterfuge. It is a diversion. He talks about reducing bloodshed and violence. And that, quite simply, is the proven responsibility of the President for the crimes that are taking place daily in the cities of America!"

DiLorenzo was scarlet with rage. "Mr. Speaker, the gentleman from South Dakota is talking through his hat. I have lived and worked in New York City all my life, and the tragedies and crimes that beset us today have a long, sordid and painful history. We cannot undo four hundred years of injustice in a decade. We are bound to make mistakes and wrong turnings. Tempers will be frayed, reputations smeared, baleful words exchanged. What the President has tried to do is reduce this fevered atmosphere. He has tried to get them to talk to one another. All revolutions breed militants, violence-ridden men, who will not be appeased. I detest them as much as you do, sir. But to lay the blame for the turbulence, the dead and wounded, the burning store and the vandalized school at the feet of the President of the United States is a wicked simplification, an act of thickheaded vengeance.

"Hence my substitute resolution, replacing paragraph five. I beg of my fellow members of the House, with whom I have labored for so many years, to act charitably and constructively and lay aside their understandable grievances and frustrations."

DiLorenzo was effective. I saw the gallery spark with interest; people nudging one another. On the floor of the House, Roger DeVaux, a suave, sun-tanned young man from Orange County, California, got up to respond in reasonable fashion.

A House page entered from the giant double doors at the back and walked toward Ruckett, handing him a slip of yellow paper.

When De Vaux had concluded, Ruckett asked to be recognized.

"Mr. Speaker, I listen to our opponents go on and on about conferences, about discussions of urban problems, all the pious, well-meaning, soft soap we have listened to these years, and I sometimes wonder how they have the gall to go on feeding us this," Ruckett began. And in a move reminiscent of the late scourge of the Senate, Joe McCarthy, he held aloft a half sheet of yellow paper. "I have here in my hand a bulletin issued by the United Press five minutes ago, Mr. Speaker, and it speaks more eloquently of the need for us to act courageously and swiftly in indicting the President and his Administration. I shall read it."

Ruckett's chest swelled. He passed a hand over his thinning brown hair, and his eyes were wide with satisfaction. "It is marked 'bulletin.' And it reads thus. 'Sacramento, Calif., July 9. Shooting broke out again today in the barricaded Sacramento ghetto. The California capital was rocked by small arms fire for about a half hour, as black militants inside the barbed-wire enclosure and state police exchanged shots. The National Guard sealed off a twenty-block area round the ghetto. No official reports were issued by the governor's office or by police. But the firing was heavier than usual. There were no reports of casualties.'"

Young Lance looked triumphantly across the aisle at DiLorenzo.

"Mr. Speaker, the gentleman from South Dakota is

playing an old and disreputable game," Larry DiLorenzo said. "It is no secret to the members of this House that there is violence and gunfire in American ghettos, where pent-up hatreds are erupting. We are aware of that. Does the gentleman intend to supply us with a running commentary on civil disorders? Has he set up a private line to the United Press and Associated Press, and is it his intention to start a congressional news service to keep us apprised every time some ghetto militant takes a pot shot at a policeman, or a police officer cracks the skull of a rioter? Is that what he intends to do?"

There were a few nervous laughs. But Ruckett did not find anything humorous in DiLorenzo's attack. I could begin to feel one of those seachanges of sentiment. Perhaps the DiLorenzo amendment might pass.

"I appreciate the humorous comments of the gentleman from New York," Ruckett said. "But I find nothing funny about revolution, about the declared intent of armed radicals to shoot down civil servants. May I remind him that the situation in Sacramento is a special one, that the guns those people are shooting at policemen and citizens and National Guard soldiers were purchased, on the sworn testimony of a black leader, with funds supplied by a federal agency of the government, funds illegally released by the President, and that the President himself was aware of this situation. Does that clarify matters for the gentleman? Does he now comprehend why I cite this new outbreak of rebellion in California? Or does he care to make further clever remarks about my interest in news developments?"

"Mr. Speaker, I resent the attitude of the gentleman from South Dakota and the tone he is adopting. I have made what I believe to be a sound point. This House cannot be swayed by bulletins. The work of a legislative body must be deliberate, thoughtful and carried out in an atmosphere free of emotion and hysteria. I have spent a half century in the House, and I have never known of any worth-while measure being passed in such an atmosphere. Now may we proceed to further debate on my proposed amendment to the last paragraph?"

A page entered the chamber again and walked to Ruckett with another yellow sheet of what I guessed was additional wire copy. The congressman studied it, but did not rise to read it.

488

"Very well," the Speaker pro tem said. "We shall proceed to a voice vote on the amendment offered by the gentleman from New York."

Under the rules of the Committee of the Whole, one-fifth of the membership can demand a roll call vote. No one on the floor so moved. Our supporters had no enthusiasm for DiLorenzo's amendment, and our enemies were determined to kill it quickly.

"All in favor say 'aye,'" intoned the clerk.

There was a hesitant, mashed response; clearly no majority.

"All opposed say 'nay.'"

The response was loud and conclusive, but not overwhelming.

"The amendment is defeated."

Rumsford looked about the great chamber to see if anyone had anything to add. The resolution to impeach had been debated by the Committee of the Whole, had emerged unscathed, and would now move on to the House in regular session.

"The Committee of the Whole having completed its work, the Chair asks all members to rise, to so signify."

Amid a shuffling of papers, moving of chairs, mumbles, coughs, exchanges of small talk, the members rose. The Speaker of the House would now take over the rostrum from Rumsford, since the House was reconvening in regular session. He dragged his tired body to the carpeted steps and ascended slowly, shaking hands with Rumsford, who whispered advices in his ear, and bracing the Speaker's back as if to keep him propped up.

As they spoke, the sergeant at arms removed the mace from the white pedestal and returned it to the tall green marble stand. this symbolized the change: the House was in regular session.

"Zero hour," Parente said. "I wonder if O'Boyle will let 'em vote now. If he's got any sense he'll knock off."

"You think that will help?" I asked.

"Yeah, it's a bad scene down there. Getting ugly. Hannaford's home free, by thirty, forty votes. It could get close if Ruckett keeps reading bulletins. Every time some *schwarzer* fires a gun, you guys lose a congressman."

"We lose more than that, Louis."

"House Resolution 988 stands unamended," Emmett

O'Boyle said. "House will come to order. Come to order please, gentlemen."

There was a conference taking place at the long table at which sat the resolution's "managers"—Ruckett, Cottrell, DeVaux, Suggs, Piasecki, Stradella, committee counsel Pierce Eldridge, and a group of congressional aides.

A similar meeting was taking place at the opposition table. Lewis Smales, Harry Kaplan, Hollis Denton and our other backers were engaged in debate. I had a notion what their next move would be. Like Parente, they feared the atmosphere in the House. They did not appreciate Ruckett's injection of news bulletins into the debate.

"Mr. Speaker," Lewis Smales called.

The Vermonter was recognized. "Mr. Speaker, in view of the inflammatory comments made by the gentleman from South Dakota, and in view of the closeness of the Government Operations Committee's vote on this resolution, a margin of a single vote, achieved, I am convinced, by the intimidating performance put on by an extremist group and in view of the President's repeated appeals for a cooling of tempers, I move that House Resolution 988 be recommitted to the Government Operations Committee for further discussion, and for possible amendment."

There were angry cries from the managers' table. They must have foreseen this. But they felt they were riding the crest of the wave. If the resolution were sent back to committee, Hannaford was capable of cutting off their water. He'd neutralize the Sacramento affair; he'd turn the Attorney General loose on Kakamba Jones and discredit him.

"Mr. Speakah, this is evasive and typical of the opponents of this heah measure," Sykes Cottrell said. "There are no amendments to consider. The House made short shrift of the amendment offered. The Committee of the Whole has agreed on the wording of the resolution. Let us vote now."

O'Boyle cleared his throat. "The gentleman from Vermont is within his rights. Any member can move for recommitment of any pending bill. I ask the gentleman from Vermont if he wishes to withdraw his motion, or has he moved to recommit House Resolution 988 to the Government Operations Committee?"

"I have so moved, Mr. Speaker."

There were shouts of "second!"

490

O'Boyle rapped for order. There was nothing Ruckett could do about this. A motion to recommit is not only proper, it is almost always used as a last-ditch effort to thwart a vote. And the points raised by Smales were sound ones.

I saw Eldridge, the committee counsel come flying through the House doors with a sheet of wire service copy in his hand. The group at the "managers'" table gathered around him.

"What the hell are they up to?" asked Parente.

"Mr. Speaker," Lance Ruckett called. "Before a vote is taken on the proposal to recommit our resolution to the standing committee, I am impelled to impart some late information to the House, information which bears directly on the decision we are about to make."

"I must object, Mr. Speaker," Lewis Smales said. "The gentleman from South Dakota is determined to make a farce out of these deliberations, by injecting a running news story into the debate for dramatic effect—"

"I have not yielded!" Lance Ruckett cried. "Mr. Speaker, there is nothing irrelevant about rebellion and murder, not when it relates directly to the indictment we have drawn up against the man responsible."

"I beg of you to restrain the gentleman," Smales pleaded. "There are no charges in the resolution, nothing that connects the President with acts of violence in the city of Sacramento or anywhere else!"

"The gentleman from South Dakota had the floor, he will proceed." O'Boyle blinked and sighed. Too much, too much for him. He was happier when Rumsford had been in the chair.

"Mr. Speaker, I have in my hand another piece of wire copy from the United Press, and in spite of what the gentleman from Vermont says, it bears directly on the subject under debate. I shall read it, for it speaks more eloquently of the matter at hand, than any of the legal nit-picking, the nice Nellieisms, the subterfuges and tricky diversions of our opposition."

Ruckett braced his feet, placed his left hand on his left hip, held the paper at half arm's length and began to read. "This latest advice is headed 'bulletin first lead,' and it is date-lined Sacramento. It states: 'Six policemen and ten black militants were shot dead today when an attempt to break out of the Sacramento ghetto was crushed. The blacks, armed with automatic weapons and grenades, launched their attack with sporadic sniping a little after dawn. An hour later, in response to police firing, machine guns and at least one small artillery piece were used.' "

A horrified silence encompassed the chamber. Several reporters left. I grabbed Parente's knee. "Good Christ, they'll hang him now."

" 'Governor William Fancourt announced that the insurrection had been suppressed, and that National Guard units had taken over from the badly mauled Sacramento police force. All the fatalities occurred when a bus load of specially trained riot police approached the front gates of the enclosed area to reinforce units that had been on duty all night. Concentrated fire from automatic weapons and a shower of grenades struck the vehicles. In addition to the six officers killed, four others were wounded.

" 'A mass assault on the barbed-wire enclosed by National Guard units resulted in the surrender of the armed units inside the ghetto, who were identified as members of the Afro Avengers and other black extremist groups. The death toll of ten was an approximation. Several dozen of the guerrillas were said to have been wounded in the counter attack, in which tear gas, automatic weapons and antitank rockets were employed.

" 'At the height of the battle, a dense cloud of smoke hung over the city. Considerable damage was done to buildings surrounding the area. The actual fighting lasted for over an hour, between 8:30 and 9:45 AM, PST. Shortly after 10:00 AM, Governor Fancourt announced that resistance had ended, and that the leaders of the revolt had been either killed or taken into custody . . .' "

Ruckett stopped. "Now, Mr. Speaker, I should like all the members of the House, and particularly our opponents to pay close attention to this last piece of information in the United Press dispatch."

His clarion voice, as invasive as hot oil poured in the ear, rose and fell in the cadence of the Sunday-night hellfire preacher.

"Listen, I say, to this evidence, this proof, that what we urge the House to do, is the right thing," Ruckett said. " 'The names of the six police officers killed are as follows: Sgt. Alton Demarest, 51; Sgt. Wayne Husserl, 44; Patrolman Dario Colucci, 23; Patrolman Jack Joe Reedy, 24;

Patrolman Andrew Taverner, 28; and Patrolman Heywood Post, 26.' "

Ruckett waved the paper aloft. "Proof, do you want? Evidence? You ask for specifics, for details? Well, here they are, gentlemen, here they are, here are your specifics. I say, throw out this motion to recommit, withdraw it, sir, if you have a shred of patriotism or honor left, and let us vote on the resolution now!"

"I need no lessons in patriotism from you!" Smales shouted.

"Yes you do! And I'll give them gladly!"

Shouting erupted in a half-dozen places. All of the managers were on their feet, yelling. Smales and our other backers returned the verbal fire. Some members were crying to O'Boyle to adjourn. One of them, Majority Leader Jack Hexter, walked to the rostrum and began to plead with the Speaker. The hubbub increased. O'Boyle rapped for order. No one listened. Then, summoning up his failing strength, the Rhode Islander rasped out: "The House will come to order. I say, come to order." No response. Then: "Sergeant at arms, restore order."

No one heard him. Smales and Kaplan strode over to the managers' table—fists were shaken, insults traded, and some rude shoving took place. Now a third group, self-appointed peacemakers, led by Bill Rumsford, tried to intercede between the warring factions. Was a punch thrown? I couldn't be certain. But it looked as if several members were restraining Hollis Denton of Oregon. At that moment, O'Boyle muttered something to the sergeant at arms. With deliberate movements, this functionary then lifted the mace from its pedestal. Standing to the right of the rostrum, he now held the mace forward and aloft— "presenting" it to the House. High, high, he elevated the thirteen silver girt rods of ebony, crowned with the silver globe and eagle.

"*Mama mía*," Parente gasped. "I finally saw it. They did it. They presented the mace."

Oh, it was magic. Call it what you will—bone-pointing, fetishism, witchcraft—it worked. As soon as the disputing, shoving men saw the raised silver eagle, they stopped, some of them in mid-curse.

"Too bad," Parente said. "Harry Kaplan was winding up to let Ruckett have one on the chops."

"Sergeant at arms will return the mace," the Speaker

493

croaked. His rheumy eyes were closed. His liver-spotted hands were palsied. "The Speaker deplores the display of emotion. There is important business to be done, and the House must proceed with its business in orderly fashion."

"Mr. Speaker, there is a motion before the House," Smales said politely.

"I am aware of that. The clerk will proceed with a voice vote on the motion to recommit House Resolution 988 to the Government Operations Committee."

This time there was no mistaking the sentiments of the House. We didn't stand a chance. Not after the way Lance Ruckett had so shrewdly exploited the tragedy in Sacramento to pour salt in wounds, to raise the temperature of the membership. The *ayes* were enthusiastic, but lacking in substance. And the *nays* on Smales's delaying tactic were clearly in ascendance.

"Lou, they're moving right into a vote," I said nervously. "O'Boyle can't let them get away with this. Not with tempers the way they are. Not with the ghosts of those six dead policemen crying out for vengeance."

"O'Boyle slumped deep in his chair. Cottrell and De Vaux, Ruckett's lieutenants, were on their feet. They apparently had more details on the bloody events in California, and wanted to make sure that every sordid detail was read into the record, that every shot fired in Sacramento would ensure one more vote for impeachment.

But the Speaker did not recognize them. Instead, he began to maunder into the microphone, his sleepy voice acting like a sedative on the outraged members.

"Mr. Speakah, I move that we put House Resolution 988 to a vote!" Sykes Cottrell shouted. "The House has made clear its sentiments—the members have indicated their opposition to the move to recommit! Let us take the bit in our teeth and move on!"

For a long time, too long, old O'Boyle had been cynically manipulated by the Southerners. They alternately flattered him, threatened him, confused him, ran errands for him and kept him insulated from his old liberal friends.

"Move on, I say, Mr. Speaker, move on!" Cottrell shouted.

O'Boyle's lizardlike eyes swept about the chamber. In saurian fashion, his shriveled tongue flicked at his parched lips. Something was touching him.

494

"The Chair feels that the emotions engendered by the reading of news bulletins on the floor of the House, while not in violation of House rules, has made it impossible for debate to continue, or for any vote to be taken at this time."

I prayed fiercely for the good health of Emmett Brian O'Boyle. Was he recalling that telephone conversation with Pope Clement?

"Mr. Speaker, there is no reason why we cannot vote now—" Ruckett was on his feet, waving his sheaf of wire service paper at the rostrum.

O'Boyle yawned. It was time for his nap. Not the little catnaps he stole in the House, but the two-hour snooze in his princely suite.

"Chair will entertain a motion to adjourn."

Like a train of firecrackers, the motions were made, seconded, and the gavel came down with a crack of finality. "House stands adjourned until Monday at 10:00 AM."

It came as a relief. Perhaps even some who were against us wanted the weekend recess. It was not absolutely sure they could have won. Given an extra two days, they would labor frantically to harp on the bloody tragedy of Sacramento.

"If that doesn't get O'Boyle into Heaven," Parente said, as we made our way up the stairs to find out what had happened in Sacramento, "nothing ever will."

"I hope he makes it," I said. "He saved our necks, at least for the weekend."

That night the President went on television to discuss the Sacramento tragedy. It was not one of his better performances. Hannaford, as I have pointed out, was not a spellbinding speaker. Ben was what he was—a blunt, direct millionaire, a builder, a doer, who was effective with a small group of legislators, or friends, or visitors, but tended to grow rigid and neutral when confronted with the impersonal TV camera.

I knew he was agitated. We had hoped to score a resounding majority against the impeachment resolution. Now, the horror of Sacramento would color everything. And although Matt Fixx still insisted that his nose count showed we were at least two dozen votes to the good, we realized that we were in a different ball game.

The President did not mention the impeachment proceedings. As he had done all along, he rested on the dignity of his office.

Hannaford listed some achievements of the Administration, a sort of dessert, a reward for good behavior. But as Matt and I watched the TV screen in his small office, we both felt that no amount of cheery news about the low level of unemployment, the release of funds for low-cost housing, the imminent disarmament talks in Stockholm, or the promise of the Senate Armed Services Committee to look favorably on Boswell's compromise proposal on the defense budget, could soften the national anger.

"We've got urgent problems in this country," the President said, "and nothing is accomplished by Americans shooting one another. I don't care who starts it, or who ends it, or who gets killed. It's wrong. It diverts us from our job as citizens—building a better country for ourselves and our children, and serving as a model to the rest of the world. These hatreds and fears and jealousies that express themselves in terms of guns and grenades and blood in the street have nothing to do, absolutely nothing, with the duties of being an American . . ."

When the boss had finished, Matt and I sipped Cokes in his office. In front of us were stacks of AP and UP copy and some special reports from the Justice Department and Dalton Warfield's contacts in Sacramento. None of them boded well for us.

"What's wrong, Ed?" Matt asked. "You look spaced out."

"The boss. He's got me worried. He hasn't found his A and B—you know, the bait, the sugar-coating that makes the public accept the bitter pill."

"He will. He's not a man to be strung out for long."

"And for the life of me, I can't think of any wrong reasons to get the right things done. I'm stumped, and I think he is also."

"Why do you say that," our legislative aide asked.

"He didn't quote the Bible once."

It was past midnight when Larry Hosmer of the United Press called me with news that was, in its way, grimmer than anything we had heard in the last twenty-four hours.

"We're moving a piece in a few minutes on the trunk

wire," Larry said. "The national conference of police chiefs is organizing a march on Washington."

"What?"

"It started with the buddies of those guys who were killed in Sacramento, and it's spreading all over the country. They figure the blacks and the peace kids did it and got results, why can't they?"

"March . . . ? When?"

"Monday. They'll start piling into Washington over the weekend. Cops, firemen, unskilled workers, house owners, the whole bunch. They've got all the union locals, the ethnic societies, the taxpayer groups, the bowling clubs, the volunteer firemen associations, it's the damnedest thing I ever saw. We ran a spot check of communities to see if they knew, and they were way ahead of us. Everybody in Staten Island and Cicero is going to be here."

"Everybody who isn't black."

"That's the size of it. They say it will be peaceful, orderly, no speeches, no meetings, just a march. Up and down the Mall, around the Capitol, the White House, to let the leaders of the country know how they feel."

"The leaders know already."

"I guess they do." Hosmer yawned. "Look, Ed, people like us, the power structure, or its errand boys, we got to stop snubbing these guys in lumber jackets and black shoes. They vote also. They pay taxes. And you know how many there are? Some sociologist figured about eighty-five million is all. That's a lot of unhappy Americans."

"Who's ignoring them?" I asked. "I was born in Indian Mound, Ohio, and my father was an impoverished grocer."

"Chicago says it'll send twenty thousand people . . . unions are organizing bus loads right now."

I relayed this information to Fixx and Warfield, and called Goldstein's office to make sure the copy kept coming to us in our basement command post.

"Monday," Matt Fixx said hollowly. "The day the House votes on impeachment."

"It will be an interesting interface," I said. "Four hundred and thirty-five men casting votes on whether to indict the President, and a quarter of a million outside, offering silent advice."

"Any suggestions?" asked Warfield.

"I think Hannaford has to issue a statement welcoming

them to Washington, sympathizing with them, and telling them that they aren't forgotten," I said.

Warfield knotted his mahogany brow. "I haven't given up hope, men. You know an awful lot of those people liked FDR, and Harry Truman and the Kennedy brothers."

"And too many dig Lance Ruckett today," I said.

"But that's just why we got to pay them some mind," Warfield said, "and get them on the team again."

We seemed powerless. Events were playing hell with Hannaford's blueprint. I thought of Thomas Wolfe's lament: *We are lost here in America, but we shall find our way.* When? I wondered.

Parente summoned me early the next morning. I was to meet him at a motel outside of Rockville, Maryland. "You and me and a congressman," he said, "and a young lady."

Dressing, I heard off-key singing in the street. They were singing "God Bless America." This cheered me up. Some years ago, one of the more cracked patriotic groups had sought to ban this lovely hymn, as well as "White Christmas," charging that they were diabolical substitutes for, respectively, "The Star-Spangled Banner" and "Silent Night." Was it not curious, a leaflet mailed from Sarasota, Florida, asked, that the author of both these songs was *Jewish?*

Outside the hotel were parked two charter buses with Illinois license plates. The singers lolled around one of them—a half-dozen men in yellow construction helmets. I knew them well. They could have come from South Boston, or south San Francisco, or Astoria or Bay Ridge, or Charlestown or Parma or Downey. They were sipping beer from cans, at nine in the morning, and they seemed self-conscious, overly exuberant, as if to hide some smoldering shame.

"Here for the march, fellows?" I asked.

"You bet," one of them said. He had a moon face, a blunted nose, and a warm smile. "Somebody got to do it."

"Do what?" I asked.

"Tell the government what the people want."

"Well, have a nice time in Washington, fellows," I said. "I guess you got here early for a little sight-seeing."

"Yeah," the stocky man said. "It's our country also."

498

"It surely is," I said, and walked toward my garage, pondering the unarguable truth of what he had said.

The Meadowlark Motel had a decaying look—the kind of jerry-built place that starts to peel and crack one week after opening its doors. I knocked on the door of number 16. Parente opened it.

We talked about the march on Washington. As I sipped coffee, Parente went to the closed door of the adjoining room and called in. "Carla baby? You ready?"

"In a minute, Mr. Parente."

"Ah," I said. "A copyrighted Parente confrontation?"

"What can we lose?"

Nothing, I decided. We were in desperate straits. Anything was worth trying. So, we waited. A radio newscast engloomed me even further—already the army of the frustrated was on the march, their cars and buses bedecked with American flags. Stickers reading REMEMBER THE *PUEBLO*, and THESE COLORS DO NOT RUN, and SUPPORT YOUR LOCAL POLICE, I HAVE A DREAM TOO: LAW AND ORDER, and the one I liked best, WHEN GUNS ARE OUTLAWED, OUTLAWS WILL HAVE GUNS!

There was a knock at the door. Lance Ruckett was standing in the hot morning sunlight. Up close, he always seemed smaller. I think it was the way he used his body, his gestures, that gave him him an elastic quality, a capacity to grow before your eyes, when he spoke on the floor of the House or in a packed arena.

"Perhaps we can conclude our business right here in the open," Ruckett said. "I would prefer not to come in."

"Mr. Ruckett, I promise you that the room is not bugged. I will make no recording of you—this time."

"You cannot be trusted, Mr. Parente."

"I know. But neither can you. That's why I asked Deever to be here."

Ruckett poked his bulgy forehead into the room and saw me sipping my coffee. "Ah, I see. From the very top. From the President himself."

"Yup. We go first class." Parente opened the door wider, and Ruckett, after a moment's hesitation, crossed the threshold.

"That is amusing," the congressman said. "You say that neither of us can be trusted, and yet you invite one of the
499

most suspected men in Washington, a known perjurer and briber."

I smiled at him. "Congressman, I haven't said a word about the money you take regularly from certified maniacs like Huckerby."

"No, but Mr. Parente has in his column. And, I am pleased to note, these slanders have had no effect on my campaign to rid the country of the international socialist who now occupies the White House."

"Ruckett," Parente said plaintively, "that horseshit goes down fine with the Richmond, Virginia, chapter of Save America, but we know you for what you are. Can't we lay off that crap and get our business done. Sugar and cream in your coffee?"

"Both, thank you. Two sugars, please." Ruckett sat down.

"Okay, let's get down to business," Parente said.

"I fail to see what business we have to contract."

"You will in a minute." Lou rapped on the door of the adjoining room. "Ready, dear?"

The door opened and Carla Foraker, the former Mrs. Lance Ruckett entered the room. I studied Ruckett's glossy face: he had self-control. He got up, grinning, and bowed from the waist.

"Carla, my dear," he said. "How nice to see you."

"Nice seein' you, Lance, hon."

They were made for each other. Carla had not let me down. Her brown hair was in a mass of metal curlers the size of beer cans, the whole apparatus held in place with a chartreuse scarf. She had no make-up on, and she was wearing a pair of hip-hugging, tapered, lemon-yellow slacks and a purple sweater. Her shoes were high white platforms. Everything but the supermarket cart.

"This is touching, Mr. Parente, this reunion with my former wife," Ruckett said. "But it is without point, and if that is why you brought me here, I shall leave. I am addressing a mass rally of the national unions and military bureau at the Mall in an hour. I suggest you both come, for a better understanding of the minds and hearts of work-a-day Americans, the people who do *not* read your column, Mr. Parente, or go to elegant lunches at the F Street Club, Mr. Deever."

Yes, he suffered the slings and arrows of eternal snubs. Lance Ruckett could become President of the United

States tomorrow but he would still feel left out, ignored by Wall Street lawyers and university deans.

"Calm it, Lance," Parente said. "Siddown and have some more coffee. Look, we've had some talks with Carla. We've read the divorce testimony, and we have a copy of it."

"I am unmoved. It is a pack of lies. It has been discredited."

"You agreed to it," Lou said.

"He sure did. He had to agree to it, before I'd let him go."

Ruckett's eyes were almost closed. The mocking smile, the smile of a man whose rigid view of life endows him with unshakeable confidence, bothered me.

"Now, Lance," Parente said, "how would it sound to all your church-going, God-fearing, antipornography supporters to know that their fearless leader puts on sexy exhibitions in hotel rooms, for the benefit of his wife?"

The smile became a grin. "You would not dare."

"I've done worse than that in my time, Lance. And to people a lot bigger than you."

"You would not dare."

"It would make a half-dozen columns, the stuff I got here. Imagine, the leader of America's moral rebirth, posing for dirty postcards in hotel rooms around the country."

Carla was not enjoying it. Nor was I. But Parente had a strong stomach.

"Try me out, Lance, push me a little. I'll run the first column tomorrow, so all the marchers on Washington can read about their plumed knight."

Ruckett's aplomb was staggering. "I take it, you seek a *quid pro quo.*"

"You guessed it."

"Blackmail."

"Why yes, that's the exact word," Parente said.

"And what makes you think I would agree to this vile arrangement, when the very survival of the republic rests in my hands?"

"Jesus, Lance, you haven't changed at all," Carla said angrily. "God almighty, he's always the one standing between the country and . . . and . . . destruction."

"You never did understand me, my dear," Ruckett said.

"Yeah," Parente growled. "In or out of bed. Whaddya say, Lance, you ready to listen to my proposition?"

"You had better do some listening to me. What makes

501

you think that no matter what you threaten me with, you can undo the inexorable march of justice in this land? You are too late, Mr. Parente. The deed will be done. Your President will be impeached on Monday, and in short order he will be found guilty by the Senate and thrown out. We will triumph. We will set the nation aright again. No amount of threats can move me now. Even if I gave in to you, it would not stop the march of destiny. Things are out of your hands, Mr. Parente. They are in the merciless but just hands of the American people, who are converging on Washington to make clear their disgust with the conspiracy of revolution. Yes, they are coming by the thousands to make their imprint on our times and to overthrow the traitor. . . ."

His breath control was superb. He'd said this on one gulp of air. Now he ran short of oxygen and had to stop for a refresher.

"I get the message," Parente said. "Christ, you people are like the Communists. You'll bore us to death before you murder us all."

Ruckett got up, hitched his belt, shoved his jaw forward, and started to leave.

"You haven't heard my offer," Parente said.

"I am not interested."

"You're right, Lance. I can't change the committee vote, or the vote by the Committee of the Whole. But the House will vote Monday morning. You're licked there. The way I see it, you're at least twenty votes short, in spite of Sacramento. Once you get beat, you're through. You can only go downhill. You and your whole goddamn movement. Those guys marching in the streets in construction helmets and police badges aren't bad guys. I know them better than you do. They'll come around. They'll settle down. They'll do the right thing. They're a little unstrung these days, and I don't blame them. But they'll get fed up with your brand of poison. Hannaford's a lot smarter than you, or Gabe Tutt, or Huckerby, or Pringle, and he'll make his peace with them. And you'll end up selling tax-free bonds to old ladies in De Smet, South Dakota."

"What is it you want of me? I haven't all day."

"I want this." Parente stood up. His voice was softer, appealing. "I got the goods on that bastard Kakamba Jones. He took money from DOOR to stage that horror movie in front of the Government Operations Committee.

Seeing as you are on the National Board of Directors of the Defenders of Our Republic, you must have known about it. I have proof that one of Huckerby's agents—I got his name and I got photostats—passed money to Jones out in Sacramento, to arrange for that *schwarzer* to bring those gun-toting freaks into the hearing and concoct that story about the President knowing how the guns were bought with IT funds. It was a lie, all of it. But it never would have meant anything unless Jones could stage that show in front of the committee. That's how you people got your seventeen-to-sixteen vote, and that's why Hanna-ford is in trouble."

"I know nothing of any such arrangement with Jones," Ruckett said.

"You're a big man with DOOR. They're your people, Lance."

"I cannot be responsible for every member of the organization. They are patriots. That's enough for me."

"Don't wiggle off, Lance, I accuse you and your patriotic associates of conspiring with the Afro Avengers to impeach the President. I want you to get up on the floor of the House when O'Boyle bangs the gavel on Monday morning and announce to the members that the testimony of Mr. Jones before the committee was a pack of lies, and that Mr. Jones was paid off by your superpatriots."

"And if I refuse?"

Parente pointed to Carla. "We start running the private sex life of Congressman Lance Ruckett in installments. I might even sell the rights to *Good Housekeeping*. Or a television series. " 'I Love Lance.' 'What's My Congressman?' The possibilities are unlimited.".

"Mr. Parente, your sense of humor is as uninspired as your talents as a blackmailer."

"Let's hear it, Lance. You make that speech on the floor of the House, and I'll lay off. Otherise, you can start figuring out what to tell the Ladies Auxiliary of Save America in Muncie, Indiana, when you talk there next week, for your usual fee of one thousand dollars."

Ruckett was shaking his head. As much as I detested the man, I understood that there was a psychotic courage in him that had to be respected. "I do not fear you, Mr. Parente, not at all. I am aware of the network of wealth and power you are serving, but I will not be deterred. I will not make any such speech, on the floor of the House, or elsewhere. As the Duke of Wellington put it to a blackmailing prostitute, *'publish and be damned.'* "

With that, the congressman spun about and walked out of the room. Parente looked at me, not altogether upset. "Well, we tried."

"I'm sorry," Carla said. "I forgot how stubborn he is."

"Yes, he is," the columnist agreed. "You can take the curlers out of your hair, Carla. I got your plane ticket in my pocket."

While she was dressing, in the other room, I said to Parente: "That business about Jones taking the money to scare the committee. How'd you dig that up?"

"I didn't," Parente said. "I made it up."

"What? You were bluffing?"

"I figured if I could shake Ruckett up a little, I might go to work on Jones. You never know with him. I think he *was* on the take. Augie says someone saw Kakamba with one of the DOOR organizers. And even if he didn't, Jones is unpredictable. He might decide that it suited his purposes to say he lied about the guns and about Warfield." Lou made a sour face. "Deep down, Jones doesn't believe in anything. That's his problem."

"And ours."

"One of ours."

Parente was looking out the motel room window. "Jesus, look at them. Three bus loads checking in. Cleveland chapters, national unions and military bureau. The bone and sinew of the country."

President Hannaford issued a statement that night welcoming the marchers to Washington. Fred Goldstein and I decided against his going on television; it would seem a grandstand play. The marchers were now calling themselves the "Supporters of the Six." I knew about Herbert Hoover appearing at an opening day (or was it a World Series) in 1932 at the height of his unpopularity during the depression and being roundly booed. Hoover had undergone the ordeal with his usual Quaker dignity, but he had never recovered from the insult. The public shaming of a President is a painful thing; and the raucous noises emitted by baseball fans that warm afternoon were a grim prelude to his defeat at the polls a few months later.

"We welcome you to Washington," Hannaford's proclamation read, "and we join you in mourning the six brave policemen, and all victims of unreason and violence. Washington is the city of all the people. It belongs to all of us. It symbolizes our best hopes. Americans are distinguished by their capacity to improve the world in which they live, to solve problems, to find better ways of working things out. You good Americans who come here today to pay tribute to the memory of those courageous civil servants, are in the advance guard of our countrymen who can bring about the changes needed to make America a better place. It will not be easy. There will be more anger, and more argument, and more dislocations.

"It has been said that many of you who come here to register your distress with the violence that has ravaged our cities are forgotten Americans. This Administration does not intend to forget you. Your contribution to this country is immeasurable. All Americans are in your debt. No, you are not forgotten. You will be remembered with tax relief, better schools, better medical care, more parks and libraries and recreation facilities, but most of all, with cities and communities that are peaceful and pleasant and productive. But for these gains to be made, the President will need your help. We are not indifferent to your complaints. We know about the economic and social problems of the wage earner, the workingman, the civil servant. And as you march peacefully through the streets of this city, this city which is *yours* in the truest sense of the word, look upon it as a place of hope, of achievement, of desire. The building of America is a job never finished. I ask for your help in building it. Faith without works is dead, the Bible tells us. I appeal to you good Americans, you fathers and husbands, who have built this country, fought our wars, paid the taxes, raised children and been generous neighbors, to have faith in the future of America, and to perform those vital works that make this nation the hope of the world."

Fustian? Corny? I suppose so. Hannaford had written it himself. We hoped it would calm them. Sometimes you could tell angry Americans that they were really grand fellows, reasonable men, and capable of honorable deeds, and it would almost work. I recall, years ago, as a boy, seeing Adlai Stevenson, looking uncomfortable in an American Legion cap, addressing a convention of paunchy, bespectacled, distrusting legionnaires. They started by staring at him, tight-lipped, suspicious, hostile. It was the time of Joe McCarthy, whom they dearly loved. Here was this patrician, intellectual, crypto-pinko, coming at them with his highfalutin' English. Adlai was everything they despised. I don't recall what exactly Stevenson said to them, but he told the truth. He asked them why they automatically opposed every bit of liberal legislation; why they fought so vigorously for endless special favors, for veterans, why they were opposed to progress. They listened. And by God, they applauded! Not quite the ovation they gave Joe McCarthy. But they applauded.

On Sunday, the President met with Walter Edgerton, Burke Boswell and his disarmament adviser, Professor Seymour Cohen. The most broad-ranging, optimistic arms talks were to begin that week in Stockholm. A Chinese delegation led by Chairman Lin Piao had agreed to attend as "observers."

During the night I was kept awake by the noise of drunken demonstrators below my window and in the corridor. The laughter was loud and embarrassed, the singing off key, a stew of harsh and grating sounds. In the morning, I found a four-sheet newsletter under my door. In an unusual display of courage, the Defenders of Our Republic had affixed their name to the last page, as well as Merton Huckerby's. They were getting more confident. Huck was usually kept in his cage.

Today, courage is demanded of the House of Representatives. Treason must be punished. The republic must be saved. The Socialist-Communist cabal, the Wall Street conspirators, the university traitors and black criminals who have dictated national policy and made a captive of President Hannaford (a willing prisoner!) must be struck down. It is in the power of the House to do so, and those congressmen who fail the nation in the hour of crisis, must be ready to pay the price of their cowardice. Let them look out their office windows. Let them look from the windows of their cars as they drive to Capitol Hill this morning, and see an angry America on the march. Yes, gentlemen, you will be accountable to these millions of Americans if you fail to answer the ringing of the Liberty Bell. . . .

I folded it and put it in my coat pocket. Huckerby and

506

the worst elements in DOOR and Save America had latched on to a mass movement. Many of the outraged Americans parading in Washington had no use for Merton Huckerby. But that would not stop Huckerby from exploiting them and claiming them as his own.

Just before I left my hotel room, I had a call from Congressman Walt Prochaska of Ohio. Prochaska represented an "ethnic" working-class district in Toledo. He'd been fence-sitting all along on the impeachment issue. In his heart, he admired Hannaford. But his constituents had been at his throat. The city had had a riot in May.

"Ed," he said, "I got to tell you this. The President should know. And tell the Attorney General. I can't reach him."

"What is it, sir?"

"Some son of a bitch, some whispering bastard called me at home this morning and said if I didn't vote to impeach the President, they would have me in the cross hairs of the telescopic sight."

"They use that expression all the time."

"It took me a few seconds to figure out what they were saying. That is a threat against the life of an American congressman, and I am going to raise a stink on the floor."

I thanked Walt. I knew why he had been called. The enemy was hitting at the waverers, those not yet committed. But I decided there was no point in bothering Hannaford, or Judge Moscowitz. With two cups of black coffee to sustain me, I decided to forego my usual morning constitutional across Lafayette Park to my office in the White House. Hailing a cab, I told the driver to go directly to the House side of the Capitol.

"They gonna have a damn big crowd," the driver said. I squinted at his ident card. HENRY DESPARD. A tidewater man? A Virginian or Marylander? Thin, sun creased, bespectacled, well mannered.

"Would you like to be marching with them?"

"They got a point. But it ain't all Hannaford's fault. If they stop and think a bit, they'd realize hit."

The cab moved slowly through the phalanxes of marchers. Construction helmets predominated—yellow hard hats. There were also American Legion caps, VFW caps, and the civilian version—the white union cap. It was a smiling, tranquil crowd, and hardly a mob bent on vengeance.

Were they faintly contrite, regretful that they had come to the lovely city, with such mean thoughts? My heart went out to them. They put gold stars in the windows, and signs reading WELCOME HOME, DANNY, and apart from the blacks and Puerto Ricans and Mexicans, they supplied the nation with the bulk of our soldiers. They cheered the Marines. They adored John Wayne. They worried about "the new element" moving into the neighborhood of two-story, one-family homes, sided with fake brick and green-painted lumber. Long hair and drugs offended them. They nurtured beer bellies from long contemplative hours at the corner saloon. They lived in hope of the big score at Aqueduct or Rockingham Park. Vaguely, they hoped for something better for their children, but didn't do much about it. Their wives tended postage-stamp front lawns, minuscule back yards, and they knew nothing about air and water pollution, NATO, the Middle East, pop art. The words "kinky, trendy and kinky" were unknown to them. None of them ever read The New York *Times* or gave a damn what it said. Nor did they care much about the quality of education in their local schools, unless occasionally stirred by a few true believers against sex education or left-wing propaganda in the textbooks. (Why is Jefferson mentioned more often than Hamilton?)

I got out of the cab, and as I did, noticed a large group of men moving toward the steps of the Capitol. Newsreel cameramen and TV units started toward them.

Demonstrators appeared to be carrying huge boxes. Others bore giant placards.

"What the heck are those?" I asked the cabdriver.

"Coffins. I seen 'em t'other side of the park this morning."

They were indeed coffins. The men bearing them moved in slow cadence. I heard muffled drums: a Legion post, no doubt. And as the group drew nearer, stepping lethargically in the hot, morning sunlight, I counted six coffins. Six coffins for six dead policemen. On each was painted a name—the six men killed in Sacramento. (There were no coffins for the dead blacks.) I read the names: DEMAREST. HUSSERL. COLUCCI. REEDY. TAVERNER. POST.

The pallbearers moved in measured steps to the beat of the drums. Massed American flags appeared on either side of the six oblong boxes. There was also an honor guard—

paunchy men, in quasi-military uniforms, carrying old bolt-action rifles, the kind used only for ceremonial purposes.

As the somber parade went by, I turned to a stringy man wearing a cap with the words: MILLWRIGHTS LOCAL AFL-CIO, IRONTON, OHIO on it, and asked: "They don't really have the bodies in those, do they?"

"Nope. But we damn well should have brought 'em."

Vangie was waiting for me in the press gallery.

"How is everything at the White House?" I asked. "All calm?"

"They're both magnificent," she said. "The President suggested Fern go to Ramada until this is over, but she wouldn't hear of it. She's visiting the Industrial Training School in South Baltimore. She said she hopes the reporters ask her about the vote. She has a few things to tell them."

"And the boss?"

"I didn't see him. But he's the same as ever. Acting as if all this never happened. My father was at the office early this morning, and I could hear both of them shouting."

"At each other?"

"Oh, no. At the generals. Something about nerve gas shipments, and the Army telling lies again."

Larry Hosmer joined us and we walked into the press gallery and took the reserved seats. "How does it look?" I asked the United Press man.

"I was going to ask you the same thing, Ed."

"I used to think I could gauge the political temper of the American people, but I've given up. I may end my life as a dirt farmer in southern Ohio."

"Hexter said this morning they'll beat it. By at least twenty votes."

"It keeps going down," I said morosely. "But of course, Jack Hexter is a conservative fellow." I asked Hosmer if he'd heard anything about threatening phone calls to fence sitters. Larry had not and was inclined to doubt that the "House managers"—whatever one may have thought of Mr. Ruckett—would countenance such tactics.

"That's the trouble, Larry. They are not bad guys. And those union members and policemen outside, with their flags and honor guards and coffins are not bad guys either. But there *are* bad guys who'll creep in and run the show if we aren't careful."

"Yeah," the newsman said. "And may be running part of it right now."

The House was called to order by Speaker O'Boyle. Now that they were in regular session, he was at his high desk, trying to concentrate on the thankless task ahead of him. Below, at the side of the aisles, at the long tables sat the "managers" of the impeachment resolution—Ruckett, Cottrell, DeVaux, Stradella, Chairman Suggs. At our table, I saw Smales, Kaplan, Denton—joined today by Matt Fixx, slumped deep in his chair, his eyes glued to the huge glass and bronze oculus in the ceiling of the chamber.

"The House will proceed at once to a vote on House Resolution 988," Speaker O'Boyle said.

Prochaska was on his feet. Good for him, I thought. He was a gutsy little fellow, Walt. "Mr. Speaker, before we vote, a point of privilege, if you please," the Ohioan said.

"The gentleman from Ohio realizes that debate on the resolution has been concluded, and all amendments voted down."

"I am aware of that Mr. Speaker. But I am impelled to make a statement concerning the situation in Washington today."

Sykes Cottrell was up. "Mr. Speaker, if Ah may, Ah have some comments to make. Ah simply feel the House should express its welcome, its heartfelt welcome to all those patriotic Americans, those good people, peacefully making their will known to us, in the best 'merican tradition . . ."

"I did not yield, Mr. Speaker," Prochaska said. "But since the gentleman from Mississippi raises the question, I agree that I welcome the Supporters of the Six, and respect them. That isn't what I wanted to mention. May I proceed, sir?"

O'Boyle nodded.

"Mr. Speaker," Walt Prochaska said, "last night I received an anonymous telephone call in which the person calling warned me that unless I voted in favor of the resolution before the House, I would find myself, and these were his exact words, 'in the cross hairs of the telescopic sight.'"

There was a roar from the gallery—horror, disbelief, derision. It was the same kind of roar I heard at the

510

Republican convention in 1964 when Nelson Rockefeller, in his finest moment, accused his right-wing opponents of obscene phone calls, threats, roughhouse tactics. There is one curious thing about the intransigents of left and right. They resort freely to vile tactics, but they don't like being told about it in public.

"Mr. Speaker," Lance Ruckett cried. "I resent this attempt to sway the House! I don't say some irrational person may not have made such a call to the gentleman from Ohio, but we all get these phone calls, and if we are men, we ignore them! I get them all the time from the Communists and socialists. I'm willing to bet that if we could trace that call, the one that has bothered the gentleman from Ohio, we'd find that the Communists were behind it! It's an old trick of theirs. They murdered John Kennedy, and tried to blame it on conservatives, they—"

"Mr. Speaker, I won't be lectured to," Prochaska said. "I've been getting threats like this for a long time. And they don't come from Communists."

Belden Hastings of Illinois, another man I had marked as a fence sitter, got up to say he'd gotten the same call. And so did Charles Peacock of Colorado. But Ruckett talked them all down. By the time the angry scene was gaveled into silence, he had made a convincing case. First, he argued, he and his fellow managers could not be held responsible for the acts of inflamed citizens, and for a handful who were unbalanced. Wild threats and abusive calls were part of public life, Ruckett argued. He even had the colossal gall to quote Harry Truman about the perils of the presidency: "If you can't stand the heat, get out of the kitchen."

"Oh, mother," Vangie Boswell sighed. "He is too much."

"His brand of fun seems to be paying off. It's amazing, though."

"What is?" she asked.

"How familiar are the tactics of Ruckett's crowd and your own young building occupiers. When they accused the SDS children of burning a liberal professor's files at Columbia, and of committing other desecrations against scholarly places, the kids immediately snapped back that 'the New York police did it'."

"Bigot," she whispered. "Fascist beast. Establishment fink."

Our lighthearted dueling was only a diversion to keep our spirits up. An ugliness, a sense of abandoned revolt was in the air.

"The clerk will call the roll on House Resolution 988," O'Boyle said.

Members returned to their seats. I saw Larry DiLorenzo sitting in his chair, straight-backed, an old Roman senator full of years and honor. I saw Garcia, our fallen angel, who but for his greed and vanity could have been as effective a voice as Larry. I saw the tough-faced, decent men representing the so-called "ethnics"—Piasecki, Prochaska, Stradella, Trypokowski, Vatsoulas, Stenek, Abbate, Mamula, Nagurny, Machinski—and I worried about them.

A roll call in the House takes about twenty minutes. That's as fast as they can do it, and it assumes that no time will be wasted running after missing members, rousing those who do not vote the first time around, and so on. The roll is called twice. Members who miss both calls can then stand in the well of the House and signal to be recognized to vote. I had the feeling that we might have to await the votes of a handful of fence sitters who would decide which way to jump after they'd gauged the temper of the majority.

"There's 433 of 'em," Hosmer said. "One vacancy by death, and Pulsifer of Texas. He's in the last stages of terminal cancer. They even tried to see if he could get up here, but the poor guy is comatose."

I mulled the figure. Four hundred and thirty-three. They would need 217 votes to lick us. Was it possible? Were the outraged men in the streets in front of the Capitol, bearing the empty coffins symbolizing their dead buddies, going to decide the fate of Hannaford—a President who, if given the chance, would have been the best friend that working and lower-middle class people had had since FDR? Ben Hannaford's formula—the "A" of more dollars in white pockets, to get them to agree to the "B" of long overdue assistance for blacks—had not worked. The equation had fallen apart because of "C," the bloated Blob, the monster of the Pentagon that had gobbled up the national treasure. Ben had not been given a chance. He and Boswell and Murphy and Meg McNally had barely started. When—and how—could they start again?

"Mr. Aadlund."

"No."

"Off to a good start," I said to Vangie. "We're ahead one to nothing."

"Optimist. Jens Aadlund is a farmer-laborite from up-state Minnesota. He's got no blacks to worry about. Just good-natured Swedish farmers."

"Mr. Abbate."

"No."

A good sign: Frank Abbate was from San Francisco. He had the big city blues, but he was turning away from impeachment.

"Mr. Adcock."

"Yes."

"No surprise," I said to Vangie. "One of the Alabama delegation, reputed to be in Huckerby's pocket."

"Mr. Ammons."

"No."

"Mr. Arricale."

"No."

John Arricale was from Boston. He was the second big city "ethnic" to stay with the President.

"Mr. Babich."

There was a pause. I watched Costic Babich, who represented a district heavy with Croats and Slovenes in Illinois. He raised his gray head and pronounced: "Yes."

The clerk repeated it. It had a resonant, painful sound. Hosmer, busy marking his tally sheet, raised his eyebrows. The ranks of industrial city representatives had been cracked.

After about four minutes, the vote was tied at forty-one to forty-one. The south and the border states were almost unanimous in voting in favor of the Ruckett resolution. And that area called the "Sunland" by a bright young political expert, the fellow who cheerfully wrote off the blacks and advised them to go elsewhere for their strident needs, was rejecting Hannaford. Southern California, led by co-sponsor Roger DeVaux, was backing the resolution, as well as Arizona. Nevada and New Mexico. But we held firm in the Middle West, the Pacific coast, New England and the Middle Atlantic States. The final result would hinge on the votes of the industrial cities, the grimy, smoky conglomerations of two-family houses and corner bars, of neighborhood softball teams and Holy Name societies. For the life of me, I could find no pattern. We seemed to be holding more than we lost.

"Mr. DiLorenzo."

"No," Larry boomed.

"Mr. Dobbs."

"No."

Booker Dobbs was a black man from Milwaukee.

"Mr. Dockery."

"Yes."

Bad, bad. Francis X. Dockery was a Boston South Sider. Normally he was on our team. But he'd attended the rallies against bussing and for more police dogs. The message had gotten through.

"Mr. Dunstable."

"Yes."

No surprise; a routine Virginian.

"Goddamn." Hosmer whistled. "It couldn't be tighter." The vote stood at sixty to fifty-eight, against H. Res. 988.

Vangie shivered. "I don't know if I can take this. It's awful. All those people, elected by the people, saying they want to kick out a President because he tried to solve the race problem . . ."

"It's a bit more complex, Evangeline," I said. But was it? Had Sam Rayburn summed it up with his estimate of southern oratory—*nigger, nigger, nigger?*

"Mr. Hexter."

"No." Good old J.J.! Good old tobacco farmer! He was one of the rare border state congressmen who were staying with us. Kentuckian, conservative, he knew a little about the balance of powers, and the powers of the Presidency.

"Mr. Hubbell."

"No."

Caleb Hubbell, a Maine man. The New Englanders were standing firm.

"Mr. Kaplan."

"No!" Harry Kaplan shouted.

"Mr. Kubenik."

"Yes."

Michael Kubenik of Erie, Pennsylvania, was bowing toward the marchers outside. They were his people.

"Mr. Leverage."

"No."

514

Surprise! A vote from an Oklahoman. Amos Leverage—a good man, an advocate of Indian rights.

We were now halfway through the voting. It had taken an amazingly short time. There were hardly any absentees.

Hosmer showed me his tallies. I had stopped recording them. The pen had trembled so badly in my hand that I had given up, crumpling my tally sheet. "Neck and neck, Ed," the UP man said. "You're still leading. By the huge margin of 121 to 119. I think there was one guy who didn't vote so far. Machinski of Indiana."

"Mr. McAvity."

"No."

"Mr. MacAndrew."

"No."

"Mr. Madderley."

"No."

"It's a runaway," I said to Hosmer. "Look. We're ahead by five."

My euphoria was short-lived. Suddenly, a rush of positive votes had us even again. It was the old story—an immovable bloc of southern and border votes—with a few exceptions, such as the delegation from Ramada City, mavericks like Leverage of Oklahoma.

"Mr. Piasecki."

Poor old John! He's been a White House confidante at the start of the term. Now, with the hot breath of his voters on his neck, he had no choice. "Yes," he mumbled. He turned away, resting his forehead in the palm of his hand.

"Mr. Prochaska."

"No," Walt shouted. He was furious. Goddamn their cross hairs and their phone calls!

"Mr. Stradella."

There was a pale, weak, fluttery "yes" from Fulvio Stradella; he had satisfied the enraged construction workers of Philadelphia, where stood Independence Hall and the Liberty Bell.

"Mr. Strange."

"No."

"Mr. Suggs."

"Yes." Old Lem; he had died a thousand deaths.

"Mr. Sutphen."

"No."

"Mr. Tandy."

"Yes."

"Mr. Teas."

"Yes."

"Here we go," Hosmer said. "The homestretch. It's a dead heat, Ed. I have it tied, a flat-footed tie, 189–189."

"Mr. Wayland."

"Yes."

"Mr. Waxman."

"No."

"Mr. Wham."

"Yes."

"Mr. Wigley."

"Yes."

"Mr. Wojacki."

"Yes."

Mr. Wooster."

"No."

The press gallery was on its collective feet. On the floor of the House, each member sat forward as if hypnotized. No one moved around. The public galleries appeared to be frozen.

Hosmer mopped his forehead. "I can't stand it."

"How do you think I feel?" I had a sudden rush of confidence, some old Hannafordian optimism, the feeling that we'd win, that we could not lose.

"Mr. Zaring," the clerk intoned.

"Yes."

"Good Christ," Hosmer moaned. "Tied again. Two hundred and fifteen apiece."

There was a pause of such deathless silence, such a total absence of noise, that it terrified me. It was the soundlessness of oblivion, of the far reaches of outer space where no life stirred.

"Mr. Zwan."

This was Ed Zwan, an amiable, dumb lawyer from Schenectady, New York. God knows what went on in his uncluttered mind at this dreadful moment. He looked up—a round-faced, balding man with a potato nose and muttered: "No."

The clerk repeated the word. Then he looked at Speaker O'Boyle.

"On House Resolution 988. Ayes, 215. Nos. 216. Two not voting."

We were not home free—not yet. They needed 217 to pass the resolution. They had 215. Two members had not voted on the first ballot. One was Ludwig Machinski of Indiana. The other was Haynes Fearon of West Virginia. They were marginal cases. All I knew about Fearon was that he had voted against the coal miners' interests on a bill to tighten mine safety requirements.

Thus Fearon bothered me. He was one of those bright young chaps who had discovered that legitimate grievances of the white worker could be channeled neatly into prejudice. As for Ludwig Machinski, I knew nothing about him; nothing at all.

"It's like the end of a pennant race," I said to Vangie. "Any combination of two votes wins for us. They only need one."

The clerk was well into the second roll call. This time, it went swiftly, with no delays, and as far as I could ascertain, no changes. When the clerk read off Fearon's name there was no response. Nor did Machinski answer. They were both, I suspected, somewhere in the Capitol, wrestling with their consciences.

Once more Ed Zwan's name was called; once more the anchorman voted in the negative.

"On the second roll call," said the clerk, "Yeas, 215, Nays, 216, two members not voting."

They appeared like a bridal couple approaching the altar. Through the center doors and down the aisle marched Haynes Fearon of West Virginia and Ludwig Machinski of Indiana.

Fearon was a slender man, too well dressed for a fellow who represented coal miners. His dark blue suit was sharply tailored and he wore one of those white tab collars and a thin, dark blue tie.

"Know anything about him?" I asked Hosmer.

"Inherited money. Princeton. So-called new breed of congressman, but watch out."

The clerk was conferring with O'Boyle. Suggs got up from his slumped position at the managers' table and joined the discussion.

"Machinski?"

Hosmer shook his head. "Hasn't had an idea in his head since he came here. Represents a suburban district of Indianapolis, small factories."

O'Boyle nodded at the clerk, who turned to his tally sheets.

"Mr. Fearon."

And there they stood—two Americans, with the nation's future on their shoulders.

"Yes," Fearon said.

There was a massive gasp from various points on the floor, a troubled murmuring in the press gallery.

The vote was deadlocked at 216.

"Mr. Machinski."

I looked at Machinski. He was one of those men destined to be ignored and unheard during his tenure on the Hill. It was his first term. I doubt that he'd be re-elected. He was of moderate height, moderate build, a man of about thirty-eight or forty, prematurely gray, crew-cutted, clean-featured, running to fat, wearing amber-hued eyeglasses.

In the dread silence, Representative Ludwig Machinski of Indiana stood in the well. With the light bouncing off his eyeglasses, they turned his eyes into two orbs—sightless neuter.

"Can he refuse to vote?" Vangie asked.

"No. Not once he's here."

I thought I saw Machinski's mouth open; then close.

"I am sorry, Mr. Machinski, but I did not hear you," the clerk said politely.

Once more the congressman opened his mouth. It seemed, that like "Casey at the Bat," "a thousand eyes were on him"—although with press, public and the House, there were well over two thousand.

And then we heard it. A sound like the first faint crack when on Judgment Day the earth begins to split.

"Yes."

The clerk, in a booming voice, repeated the vote, drawing it out. "Yeees."

There were no shouts, no applause, no whistling. Only more silence, then some shifting of behinds and legs on the floor below, some rustling of papers.

"On House Resolution 988," the clerk said, "the vote is 217 in favor, 216 opposed. The resolution is passed."

"Oh dear, oh God," Vangie muttered. "I never believed it would happen." I saw her eyes turned red. They brimmed with tears.

I thought bitterly, let them see how the country goes

without someone like Ben. God save us all, if things kept running down, Sparrier would be ruling us.

And still that awful silence commanded the House. The public galleries seemed frozen. There was minimal movement in the press gallery. And apart from a small conference at the rostrum—the Speaker, John Hexter, Lem Suggs, Bill Rumsford—the congressmen seemed to be cemented to their seats.

"With the approval of the membership, the Speaker and the House leaders have appointed Mr. Suggs and Mr. Stradella to be a committee of two to advise the Senate of the action this morning."

There was a hasty voice vote; the decision was approved.

O'Boyle, all praise to him, had voted against the resolution. Unlike the forgotten Speaker who voted for Andrew Johnson's impeachment, and in the historian's words, "rushed forward gratuitously to pillory himself in the gaze of all coming generations," he had backed the boss. Now he was ready to adjourn the session. But he noticed his old colleague, of the New Deal era, and he recognized Larry DiLorenzo.

"Mr. Speaker, I realize it is the wish of the Chair and the members to adjourn after this astonishing session," he said. Tall, white-maned, he towered over all of them—Machinski cringing and sweating in his seat, head lowered, Ruckett, chesty and eyes agleam, Suggs, staring dully at the oculus, Stradella, whispering to Piasecki, perhaps both of them wondering what had happened to America. But there'd been no surrender from Larry DiLorenzo. In his last run for office, Pulaski-Day picnickers in Bay Ridge had hurled beer at him and cursed him as a "nigger-loving wop." He'd barely been re-elected. But he would not compromise.

"Mr. Speaker, the House has committed a rash and vengeful act," DiLorenzo said. "We have surrendered to emotion, to blind hatred and to our own cowardice. I grieve for my beloved House, for my beloved nation, and for the Constitution. But I do not grieve for the President of the United States, for he is a courageous man, a patriot and a fighter. I tell you now, Mr. Speaker, I shall be at his side when he fights this scurrilous act of weak-willed, revenge-seeking men, and we will beat the living daylights out of you, in or out of court!"

With that, O'Boyle adjourned the session. There was still no applause, no cheering, no disturbance. There had been this same gravelike quiet when the House vote on Andrew Johnson was recorded.

Vangie and I wandered on to the Capitol steps. The crowd of marchers, the endless sea of white faces—a policeman told me they estimated them at over two hunderd thousand—stretched far back into the greenery of the Mall. They seemed to have covered every open space. And they were silent. They did not move. Many held transistor radios to their ears, and they all knew that Hannaford, by a single vote, had been impeached. Was that not what had brought them to Washington? Had they not—not *all* of them, but most of their leaders—said they had come to the capital to teach him a lesson? So the lesson had been taught. But I saw no smiles, no dancing in the hot and humid streets, heard no singing. Rather I saw a multitude of shame-faced, heavy-set, helmeted and capped American males, the good people who patrol the streets, build homes, deliver milk, put out fires, repair automobiles, and keep the country going; people who had every reason to be on Ben Hannaford's side as they had, for the most part been on FDR's side, and Harry Truman's, and Jack Kennedy's, and Lyndon's.

"It's eerie," I said to Vangie, as we wandered through the clotted, sweating mob. "It's the damnedest thing. They're stunned. They didn't believe it would happen. If we could poll them right now, I bet they'd want the House to undo what it did."

Across the Mall we walked. The protesters rested beneath trees, in groups around benches, around ice-cream vendors. I heard no one shout, or cheer, and once, as we passed by the Smithsonian, I saw three burly men in yellow helmets chase a fringe crackpot, an American Nazi party member, a youth with an insane pinched face, bearing a sign reading: HANG HANNFORD. GAS JEWS.

"Get lost you little bastard," one of the workmen cried, and threw a rock at the retreating heir of the Third Reich.

As Vangie and I passed the Washington Monument on Constitution Avenue, I saw a large group of men in blue union caps standing around an orator. I recognized the
520

speaker as Harry Bustard, the President of the AFL-CIO. Harry had the stub of a dead cigar clenched in his crooked mouth. His steamfitter's local cap was pushed back on his furrowed head, and he kept spitting as he spoke.

"What the hell," I heard him say, "what the hell, it isn't what we wanted. I mean, I made that clear to O'Boyle and Suggs and the rest of that crowd in there. . . ."

None of his partisans commented. He'd been dragooned into supporting the march by the extremists of NUMB, that liaison of union men and military contractors, who had their knives out for Hannaford and Boswell. But Bustard had never had his heart in it.

"It wasn't what you wanted, Harry," I could not resist calling to him. "But you got it."

"Hey, Eddie," the union chief called. "Tell the boss we're with him. Most of us. I mean, killing those cops, it got people upset. But we don't want him out. Do we, guys?"

There were murmurs of assent. But at least two or three men cried: *Throw the bum out. Let him go to the niggers.*

"Well, if you get your way," I said, as Vangie and I left, "I hope you enjoy Mr. Sparrier as President. He once said that the labor union movement was begun by Communists and hadn't changed much."

We elbowed our way through the mob of reporters in the lobby of the West Wing. I had nothing to tell them. I had no idea when the President would have a statement. I saw Mona Varnum's exotically beautiful face, and I sensed a bit of shame in it. It was amazing, truly amazing, how so many people who had had no use for Hannaford, who had been quick to criticize and ridicule him, were now wondering whether they might be facing someone, some philosophy of government rather more indigestible than Ben's.

"Anything, anything at all, Ed?" a man from the *Post* called.

"Sorry, Al. I'll see Goldstein in a minute, and he should have a schedule for you."

As I made for my basement office, I bumped into Vice-President Sparrier. He had been more under wraps than usual, and I had forgotten about him—except at such times as I entertained the shivering possibility of the Senate convicting Hannaford.

"Edward, this is appalling, absolutely appalling," the Vice-President said. We had met on the stairs. Now we paused.

"It is, Mr. Vice-President." As long as I live I will never forget the look on his handsome, tightly controlled face. It was the damnedest, most incredible, most *evident* admixture of heartfelt sorrow and unbridled joy. The poor, transparent man! He was terror-stricken by what had happened in the House. After all, he was part of the executive family. More and more, Ben Hannaford, in his forceful way, was making a *mensch*—as Fred Goldstein said—out of this petty, ambitious friend of airplane manufacturers and restricted country club savants. Sparrier was learning all the time. Free enterprise and private property and mealy-mouthed generalities about church, God and the flag were no substitutes for a program, for compassion, for understanding, and for the intelligent courage that high office demanded.

"I am on my way to the President's office," he said. "He has summoned us, and I suspect he will want you there also."

I turned around, and followed him up the stairs to the corridor outside the West Lobby, and then down the hall toward the boss's office.

"I want you and all of the President's intimates to know, Edward," Sparrier said, "that I stand four-square behind the boss. I mean it, Edward. I don't deceive myself. I have never been close to him. But I shall make my stand with him. And if I am hesitant about saying this to him, I ask you to do so for me."

"It shall be my pleasure and my privilege, Mr. Vice-President."

Lord, Lord. As he said these words, I was convinced he was searching his heart and his conscience and speaking truly. But he still could not stifle a flutter of excitation. Was it my fevered imagination? Or was he battling against that flame of ambition that flickered in his bowels?

"Thank you, Edward. Perhaps in this time of testing we shall all get to know one another and respect one another a bit more." And he put his arm around me!

"I hope so, sir. You remember what Mr. Dooley said."

"Indeed I do."

522

"He said that the Vice-President, on rainy days, calls at the White House and begs the President not to go out without his rubbers. He has Mrs. Vice-President knit a shawl to protect his throat against the night air. And if the President has a touch of fever, the Vice-President gets one himself. He even gets the White House doctor on the phone, and he asks whether he can do anything for the President—"

Sparrier interrupted me. "Like drawing his salary? Or appointing the postmaster of Indianapolis?"

"You know it! I'm impressed." My estimate of Sparrier, was rising by the minute.

"You taught me a little lesson in humility that day, Edward. I have become a Mr. Dooley fan."

Outside of Cleo Watterson's office, a group of weepy, handkerchief-sniffling girls had assembled.

Cleo's gray head appeared in their midst. She was angry. "Stop that blubbering!" the President's private secretary commanded. "And put those handkerchiefs away! I'll fire any girl that cries in the President's office. You—Selena—cut that out! At once! Let's see a smile!"

Selena was a very black girl in a mini-skirt. She seemed convulsed. But she stopped her sobbing.

"Good girl, Cleo," I said. "The boss wouldn't tolerate that sort of thing for a minute." I spoke to the girls. "Now cheer up, girls. You will learn that our President is at his best when he's in a fight. The rougher the fight, the meaner he gets. It'll make things more interesting around here."

Inside the oval room, we stood in a semicircle around the President's desk, as he talked on the telephone to Majority Leader Hexter. "Good enough, Jack," he was saying. "That will give us plenty of time. Same bunch that drew up the resolution are going to prosecute me, eh? Well, they don't sound like such tough hombres. Jack, many thanks for all your help, and thank Emmett for me also."

I swallowed. *All their help.* Hexter and O'Boyle had been pillars of Jello-O. But at least they had not voted for impeachment.

"Everybody relax," Ben said, rising from behind the desk. "Dalton, don't look so miserable."

Warfield was standing to one side, his mournful black face a mask of self-inflicted guilt. He was convinced that

523

his dealings with Kakamba Jones had brought the President down. We all knew otherwise.

Hannaford was flanked by Fern—looking grim and drawn—and several cabinet members, including Meg McNally and Homer Murphy.

"Mr. Vice-President," Hannaford called out. "You come stand here with us." He paused slyly, and the Indian eyes crinkled. "You may just have to get used to this side of the desk."

The President said this with such good nature, with such warmth, that the tension broke. We all roared—secretaries, aides, cabinet officers, even the dour Professor Dent, Secretary of the Interior, who valued ocotillo plants above people.

Sparrier laughed also, and it was an honest laugh. He crossed to the opposite side of the room. "Mr. President, I hope that I shall never occupy that chair under these shameful circumstances. I wish to state to you, sir, and everyone in this room, that I shall support you and fight for you. Benjamin Bow Hannaford is my President, and my boss, and I am on his team. I wish to make that perfectly clear."

We applauded him thunderously. What insurance he had just taken out! Maybe he would be our President one day. And maybe those of us in the room who never quite trusted him, would learn to work with him.

"Why thank you, Mr. Vice-President." Hannaford folded his arms. Was I imagining it, or did he look *better* than a few days ago? It was truly amazing. Struggle invigorated him. I honestly felt he appeared less weary, that he stood straighter. "Ed Deever and Matt Fixx have been making a history scholar out of me. And in reading about the way Andrew Johnson was impeached, I was impressed with what he had to say when he learned about it." Hannaford picked up a book from his desk.

"I marked it here. 'I think many of those who have voted for impeachment feel more uneasy as to the position in which they have thus placed themselves than I do, as to the situation in which they have put me.' "

We cheered. "That's the truth, sir. I was on the House floor and in the cloakroom afterwards. They can't look each other in their faces," Matt said.

"Now let me state that we are going to lick this thing," Hannaford said. "I think our mistake has been in staying

524

aloof from it. I did that out of respect for the House, and because I thought that indictment didn't stand a chance. I was wrong. But we're in the fight now, and we will get the Senate on our side, and get it there overwhelmingly! It isn't going to be enough to get a close call. We've got to swamp 'em. We've got to smite the Philistines hip and thigh, so that the Senate will rise like one man."

"Amen! Amen!" a windy, resonant voice pronounced. Senator Gage Hopewell had entered the office. His round face glowed. His eyes were ready to pop from their sockets. "Yeah, we shall smite your enemies under the fifth rib, sir! The Senate will stand fast!"

"Why thank you, Senator Hopewell," Ben said. "But just a little faster than when they censured me."

We roared again. Hopewell blushed. Hopewell, long one of Hannaford's supporters, beneficiary of a hundred favors from the boss, had voted to censure him during that crisis. But the President, at the moment, was in a forgiving mood. He needed every vote he could get.

"I enter this contest to redeem my honor with hope, little bitterness. It was my bad fortune to get caught up in a wave of national strife, just as it was Andy Johnson's. But we'll win this, and we'll come out of it stronger than ever.

"That's all I want to tell you. Except that Presidents have been on the spot before. The good ones, the effective ones, the ones who understand the power and dignity and meaning of this great office are the ones who overcome and prevail. Let me tell you about a man I loved as much as any I have ever known, President Harry Truman. In 1948, when I was a young fellow, I watched Mr. Truman on television when he made his acceptance speech at the convention. The poor man had been disowned and denounced by just about everyone. Liberals and conservatives in his own party were furious with him. A few had tried to get General Eisenhower to run as a Democrat and replace him. They said he didn't stand a chance against Mr. Dewey and his slick team of big operators. Joe McCarthy had been after Harry Truman's skin. And there stood Truman, as true an American as any that ever lived. And next to him was another man I revered, Senator Alben Barkley of Kentucky, running as his Vice-President.

"It was a great moment, friends. Because all over America people were convinced they were looking at a
525

beaten man, a loser, a man rejected and despised by the majority of his countrymen. And do you know what Harry did? Why he looked those people in the eye, all those frightened ones, the doubters, the haters, and he shouted, '*Senator Barkley and I are going to beat those Republicans and make them like it!*' "

This time I led the applause. Gage Hopewell was guffawing. Sid Stapp was wiping tears of laughter from his eyes. The girls were ecstatic. Fern offered a prim, knowing smile.

"And beat them he did. Harry Truman has been my idol for years, friends, and we shall follow his brave example, and be as confident and courageous as he was."

Matt Fixx's eyes lit up as Hannaford recalled Truman's glorious victory over the odds, and to the astonishment of all of us, he burst out: "Give 'em hell, Mr. President!"

That, of course, was the famous battle cry of Truman's supporters when the old campaigner took to the hustings. And it never failed to rouse the crowd.

"That's what they shouted at Harry, Matt," the President said jovially. "And you know what he responded?"

"No, sir, I don't recall."

"He said, 'I just told 'em the truth, and they thought it was hell.' " The President held his arms out. "Now, all of you do your jobs a little bit better, work a little bit harder, and above all, be polite, generous and openhearted to any senator who comes your way. Even Gabe Tutt."

We gave him a deafening ovation. With the issue joined, the challenge made, he was ready to do battle. I almost felt sorry for his enemies.

When the meeting broke up, Cleo informed me that Burke Boswell wanted to see me urgently at the Pentagon. It had to do with organizing Hannaford's defense for the trial in the Senate.

As ever, I was amazed by the informal atmosphere in the Pentagon. It has been described as a fortress, a monstrous castle of evil deeds, but it is not that at all. One gets in there very easily. I did not even show my White House ID card, nor did I identify myself. I merely nodded at the sergeant at the information desk and proceeded toward the Defense Secretary's office.

I was brought up short by Burke Boswell's booming voice. I had entered the anteroom to his magnificent office. Master-Sergeant Cayetano Gomez, a regular army man who was Boswell's aide, advised me that the Secretary was conferring with Admiral Strang and General Dudley.

But conferring was hardly the word.

"Goddammit, Admiral, you people are telling lies again about those aircraft carriers!" Boswell's voice exploded. The door to his office was half opened, and his echoing blasts shook the walls.

"The Secretary appears to be perturbed," I said to Gomez.

The master-sergeant pursed his lips. "Mr. Deever," he whispered, "the old man is eatin' ass like it was steak."

I had never heard the indelicate army expression, but it admirably summed up the nature of Boswell's ragings.

"Now look at this report, Admiral! Your office okayed this nonsense! How can you justify it? 'In some sixty wars or near wars since 1946, the United States had not lost a single aircraft carrier.' Admiral, that is a lie and a cheat and something that the Navy should be ashamed of! I asked you six times to give me a list of all these mysterious wars or near wars. When you did, look what I found out. These naval battles included twenty-two alerts at sea in which no enemy was present. Also showing the flag to the Laotians who have no coast line and damn little navy! The Zanzibar riots, when the enemy, whoever the hell he was, could not have sunk a canoe! The so-called protective action off Guatemala, which has no navy, and the quarantine of the Seychelles island, which has no bombers, and the two-day blockade of Yap, which has no navy, no bombers and two thousand people in grass skirts. Now what kind of way is that for a big nation's Navy to talk? *No carriers lost!* Jesus Christ, Admiral, you'd have to be a magician to lose one of those barges in any of those actions!"

"I resent this, sir. I do not have to listen to it."

"You'll listen, Admiral. Carriers are obsolete. They've had it. No one builds 'em, not the Russians, or the Chinese, or the English, or the French. They're toys. They're playthings. They're luxuries. And they cost too much. If I do any one thing before I leave this job, I'll see to it you get one billion dollars less this year for carriers."

There was a pause. Sgt. Gomez's dark eyes rolled upward. He'd never heard a naval chief talked to that way.

"You may be leaving this job sooner than you realize," we heard Admiral Strang say coolly.

"Is that so, Admiral? Because the President is under fire? Well, don't count on it. Don't count on it one bit. Or do I have to challenge you people to a contest again?"

Gomez looked at me, confounded by the Defense Secretary's question. In a second the admiral emerged from the inner office. He did not look overjoyed.

"Okay, General Dudley, let's get into this nerve gas business," I heard Boswell shout, "I don't like it a bit."

"Mr. Secretary, this was a case of misunderstood orders. A lower echelon failed to comprehend properly your order."

"General, I hope you won't be offended by my question. But what is it about chemical and biological warfare that brings out the worst in you folks?"

You folks. This was pure Boswell. A couple of dads talking about the schedule for the scout troop that fall.

"I do not appreciate your comments, Mr. Secretary."

"Don't you now? Come on, General, be a sport. Look me in the eye. Let's talk about those secret shipments of VX gas that your men in CBW pulled off. I know all about them. I think you knew. And you haven't done a thing to stop them."

"The men responsible will be reprimanded," Dudley said.

"I want more than a reprimand. I want them replaced. And if I hear of one more of these cross-country shipments of VX, that nerve-paralyzing crap, that poison you people love to manufacture, and stockpile and ship through cities and towns, against the wishes of the Congress and the President and the Secretary of Defense, there'll be hell to pay. I'm not kidding, General. I've about run out of patience with some of you birds."

We'd gone from *you folks* to *you birds.* I had the feeling that Harry Truman never talked to General Marshall that way.

"That's all we need," Boswell said. "That's all we need is for some of that murderous stuff, that VX—I know what it can do to human beings in a minute or so— to get diffused into a populated area. They'll blame it on the President. So just watch it."

"I shall do so, Mr. Secretary. The colonel who made those shipments will be relieved. He will probably resign

528

as a result, and we will again have to pay the price of abusing our finest officers."

Boswell reared back at him. "Now what in hell does that mean? You trying to scare me, Dudley? You saying he'll go join up with Upshaw and Nagel and the rest of those ball-breakers? Well, let him. And let me tell you something. We know all about those retired officers and their connections with DOOR and Save America. I hear tell your old boss Nagel is making speeches around the country saying now that we've gotten rid of Hannaford, they'll be able to control Sparrier for three years, and then there won't be any need for elections. They'll take over and run things the way they want."

"I have no part of such talk."

"Good for you, General. But if you do talk to General Nagel, or Upshaw or any of those other sulking Achilles, tell 'em Hannaford is going to be around a long time."

"I have made it a point, sir, not to become embroiled in politics."

"Fine. Now just stop your CBW experts from *lying*. Stop 'em from lying to me and to the public about those VX shipments and those GB tests. They lied about Utah, they lied about Hawaii, and they lied about Alaska. Hell, it's bad enough the way they toss that deadly crap around the country, without their lying about it. That'll be all, General."

Dudley, a handsome, mild-mannered man, walked out of the office; his eyes were iron gray and they stared ahead as if embedded in glass. He did not see me; he did not see Sergeant Gomez.

Boswell's soaring frame loomed in the doorway. "Come on in, Edward. We got some plotting to do." His breath was a fruity bourbon; it parted my hair.

"Little of the giant killer, Edward?" he asked, pointing to a decanter on his burnished desk.

"No thanks, Mr. Secretary. Not when I'm plotting. It reduces my talent for sneakiness."

His laughter boomed about the spacious paneled room. "Yeah, we got a lot of work ahead. First off, the defense lawyers will be me, the Attorney-General and Matthew Fixx. I'll do most of the talking. Matt will work on the briefs. The judge will be the brains behind the whole thing. It's too bad Sid Stapp won't be able to join us, but he's required by his oath to be part of the court."

"I see no danger of their getting that three-fourths vote," I said. "Unless something unforeseen happens. Another Sacramento, another bloodbath. But I feel that the boss has to win big in the Senate, if he ever hopes to get his program underway. If the opposition comes up with a majority, even a losing majority, it will be a defeat for us."

"Right you are, Edward. Now let's look over that impeachment resolution and see how we can tear it to shreds on the floor of the Senate."

I spent the night studying the details of the Andrew Johnson case. I tried to learn something from the maneuverings and arrangements, the rules ordained by the Senate, the limited role assigned the Chief Justice, and found that it was too much for me to absorb. Over a hundred years later, we faced different problems, a different nation. Polity and policy had changed vastly in the century-plus gone by.

In one of those odd coincidences, as my mind turned toward Samuel Moscowitz, the erudite Attorney General, who with Boswell and Fixx, would handle the President's defense, the phone rang, and the judge himself spoke.

"Do you know a man named Moffo?" he asked.

"I don't believe so, Judge."

"Little dark fellow. He was a member of Defenders of Our Republic, and a few other far right organizations."

Baldini. Parente's cousin. I decided to divulge nothing on the phone. What I knew I would tell the judge tomorrow in person, in his office.

"Parente might know something, Judge."

"I tried his house, but Marsha said he's been out of town for several days and can't be reached. She thought he was in New York but she wasn't certain."

"What about Moffo do you want to know?"

"He was murdered this afternoon in Chicago. He got off a plane from Rapid City, South Dakota, and was apparently tailed by a car from which someone with a high-powered rifle blew his head off. We had an agent following him, but there wasn't a chance of catching whoever did it."

Augie Baldini was dead. I put a few things together. South Dakota. He had escorted Carla Foraker back to her home town and was returning east. They had broken his

530

cover. They knew that he was not Angelo Moffo, right-wing militant, representing some fictitious Italian-American community of patriots.

"Judge, let me check my files, and I'll call you tomorrow. And maybe I can locate Parente and find something else out for you."

"Many thanks, Edward."

I turned on the all-night, all-news station. There was no report on the death in Chicago of A. Moffo or A. Baldini.

An impeachment is a process of such rarity, such an outlandish quirk, that the rituals tend to be provisional, arbitary and subject to day-by-day votes and conferences of the two Houses. Above all, it is a congressional show. And so is the trial. It is Congress against President; Congress acting as guardian of the people against the executive. Thus the shameful charade proceeded, each step more disturbing, more dreamlike than the next.

Two days after the impeachment vote of 217 to 216, the House's two-man committee of notification, Lem Suggs of Alabama and Fulvio Stradella of Pennsylvania, appeared in the Senate and formally notified the Senate that impeachment had been voted, and served on them a copy of the House resolution.

Lou Parente came back from his secret trip to New York. He was unable to barter, buy or bludgeon information from Kakamba Jones. "Goddamn jerk," the columnist said, as we ate cracked crab on his flagstone patio in Bethesda, on a sweltering evening. Marsha, huge, laden with child, filled our glasses with cold Lowenbrau.

"Will Kakamba ever learn?" I asked.

"I doubt it. Spends his evenings making threatening calls to Jewish storekeepers. That's his idea of black revolution."

We talked about the mysterious murder of Augie Baldini. The papers had run little about it: a freak accident, some crank with a gun.

"You think it was one of those people who talk about the cross hairs?"

"I can't prove it," Lou said, lowering his voice. "But I got my suspicions."

My skin prickled.

"I know what you're talking about," Marsha said. "Lou, why won't you ask for police protection? I know about

Baldini and what happened to him. You have a family to worry about."

Parente shrugged. "Ah, those jokers don't scare me. I'm like Dolci in Sicily, the reformer. He gives the Mafia fits but they won't touch him. Too well known. Same with me. I'm a lousy celebrity."

I was silent, admiring the man. Would I ever have such courage, to confront America's public monsters and tell them to go to hell?

He lifted his stein. "To Augie, Ed. One hell of a guy. *Arrivederci, paisan'*."

PART VI

Few nations have solved so simply and yet grandly the problem of finding and maintaining an office of state that embodies their majesty and reflects their character. Only the Constitution overshadows the Presidency as an object of popular reverence, and the Constitution does not walk about smiling and shaking hands.

—Clinton Rossiter,
THE AMERICAN PRESIDENCY

After a week of preparation—the House managers had prepared their case, as had the President's defense—the Senate convened to effect a miraculous metamorphosis. The one hundred good men would enter their hallowed chamber as senators, *and lo!* touched by the magic of the Constitution, they would emerge winged, multicolored and gracile, from their hardened cocoons as a *court*. But what were they? Judges? Jurors? No one was quite sure. No matter. They would sit in judgment. And if two-thirds of their number decided that Ben Hannaford was guilty as charged by 217 members of the House, they would throw him out.

I was back in the press gallery for the grand show, the public undressing of a President. A newspaper editorial of the Andrew Johnson era, had suggested that it was not clear whether the Senate would succeed in convicting the President, or *the President in convicting the Senate*. A good point. "The brilliant array of counsel retained by the President," the writer noted, "are not likely to come before the Senate in any very apologetic attitude."

As I looked down at the Senate, I realized that Hannaford's counsel was a potent team: Boswell, Moscowitz, Fixx. Against the House managers, Ruckett, Cottrell, Suggs, DeVaux, Piasecki and Stradella, they would quickly establish their command presence, their knowledge of Constitution and government.

"It must be borne in mind," the nineteenth-century editorialist had written, "that the strict rules of legal testimony do not apply in impeachment trials. New testimony can be brought in at any time. Special pleading is allowable. It is a sort of loose and popular court, consisting of fifty or sixty judges. Counsel, accordingly, cannot be tied down to petty technicalities, must have a free range over the whole field. Just think of it. Somebody will get impeached badly. There is little doubt about that."

Vice-President Sparrier, presiding until the Chief Justice of the Supreme Court would replace him, thus signifying the change from Senate *qua* Senate, to Senate as court, sat upright in his high chair. Banishing churlish thoughts about the young Californian, I found myself murmuring to Larry Hosmer that I never saw the Veep looking so well.

"Just be thankful he isn't presiding," Hosmer said. "Or that he gets to vote."

I was about to divulge Sparrier's words of allegiance to Hannaford, when a reverent hush descended upon the Senate, and all the legislators rose. We in the press gallery, and the public, also stood up.

The Chief Justice was entering. A portly, dignified man, he appeared to sail, borne on the winds of wisdom gathered in his black judicial robe. On either side of him walked six of the deans of the Senate, a committee of honor, to escort the Chief Justice to the chair of authority. There was a moment's hesitation, and then people began to applaud. It was not loud or emotional applause, but was in keeping with the solemnity of the occasion, and the splendid appearance—and admirable record—of Chief Justice John Laurens Early.

Early had been a middling conservative Federal Judge in the Circuit Court of North Carolina, when the previous President, Hayward Kretz had plucked him from anonymity and appointed him Chief Justice. President Kretz was also a North Carolinian, a diffident newspaper publisher whose family had extensive interests in cotton mills. A kind man, Kretz was nevertheless a do-nothing President, a master at obfuscation, of fudging issues, of sweeping problems under the presidential rug. Liberals cried out in anger when John Laurens Early was appointed and approved by the Senate. He met all of the Senate club requirements—southern, courtly, moderate-to-conservative, honest. To quote H. L. Mencken, they regarded Judge Early in the same manner in which the acidulous writer memorialized Calvin Coolidge: *"He had no ideas, and he was not a nuisance."*

But the Supreme Court can change a man mightily. (As can the Presidency, or indeed any office of public trust in our amazing land. The somnolent become alert; the indifferent, passionate; the cautious, daring.) Kretz, who thought he had appointed a neutral Southerner soon discovered that he had a reformer on his hands, a loose constructionist, a man with a profound sense of justice, and fair play. Soon, the era of the "Early Court" was proclaimed—to the delight of civil rights advocates, and the despair of the Bourbons. President Kretz, surely no bigot, was dubious about bussing and scattered sites housing and was known to have murmured to a confidante: "That was the worst darned appointment I ever made."

Had President Kretz known a little about Early's ancestry, he might have been less surprised. Judge Early's maternal ancestor, John Laurens, was one of colonial America's most intrepid battlers for the enslaved Negro ever to emerge from the South, or anywhere else. Known as the "Chevalier Bayard" of the Revolutionary Army, young Colonel John Laurens had come under the influence of Rousseau in Geneva. A libertarian, a humane and beloved figure, this South Carolinian aristocrat, at the age of twenty-four, was an aide to Washington and distinguished himself in several campaigns. Beyond his military achievements, he was the South's most ardent and eloquent advocate of freedom for the slaves, whom he called "this unfortunate body of mankind." Young Laurens was ahead of his time. In the South, he met with resistance everywhere, especially when he urged the liberation of slaves to serve as soldiers. Tragically, he died at the age of twenty-nine in a skirmish with the British.

Thus John Laurens. Understanding this unique American, one might have had an inkling of the character of the ancestor with his name. As I have indicated, Early was an activist Chief Justice: no flaming liberal, but a wise and tolerant captain who saw the course clearly and kept the good ship of the high court "steady on."

Big-boned, heavily fleshed, Early possessed the natural dignity of the overweight. His face was almost flabby, with ruddy pendulous cheeks and a thick nose. His eyes were a soft brown, and he wore his gray hair long, in a thick fall over his forehead. He spoke slowly, and was known as a man who never lost his temper.

The dramatic moment now took place. Sparrier, smiling

eaily, vacated his chair, shook hands with the Chief Justice and motioned to him to succeed him. But before Judge Early could be seated, he had to be sworn in.

"I see Early lost on that one," Hosmer whispered to me.

"It seems so."

There had been a report that Early had objected to the Senate's decision that he had to take an oath. Early had argued that he was the presiding officer of the court. Tradition had it that no oath need be administered. But the "rule" stood, and now Associate Justice Dennis Mara administered the oath.

". . . so help me God."

"I've heard of swearing on a stack of Bibles, but here it is," Hosmer said. Pages were scurrying about distributing Bibles—one to each member.

"The Chief Justice is even up," I said. "He won on *that* one."

It appeared that the senators—as jurors, judges, whatever—would now take *their* oaths *en masse*. Early had preferred this, over an endless parade of one hundred people, each repeating the same words until the ceremony lost all meaning.

"Gentlemen," the Chief Justice said softly, "I attend for the purpose of joining the Senate of the United States in forming a court of impeachment for the trial of the President of the United States. Will you all place your left hands on the Bible and be sworn."

Pages and various aides were at the side of each senator's desk. The holy books were held aloft; the senatorial hands were placed on them; the senatorial hands were raised.

". . . and do impartial justice according to the Constitution and the laws," the Chief Justice intoned.

A hundred voices responded: "And do impartial justice according to the Constitution and the laws."

"So help you God."

"So help me God."

It was chilling, awe inspiring, a drama that beat anything on any stage, anywhere in the world. What did those protesting kids know about participatory democracy? We *had* it; and they were not aware of it.

The sergeant at arms then proclaimed in a loud tremolo:

"Hear ye! Hear ye! Hear ye! All persons are commanded to keep silence on pain of imprisonment while the

Senate of the United States is sitting for the trial of impeachment against Benjamin Bow Hannaford!"

"Imprisonment?" I asked Hosmer.

"Gabe Tutt insisted on that one," the UP man said. "He's worried about pinkos and leftos in the gallery."

"The impeachment managers will be seated," John Laurens Early pronounced.

"Here they come," Hosmer said. "The secret six."

Through the great central doors trooped the prosecutors—Ruckett, looking cocky, Cottrell, at home in the biscuits-and-gravy atmosphere of the Senate, DeVaux, the Orange County patriot, a West Coast advertising agency president, a miserable Lem Suggs, stooped and aged, and the two big-city men, Fulvio Stradella and John Piasecki.

They walked to a long oak table to the left of the rostrum, where stood six large armchairs. Behind them, was a second row of chairs for their aides and advisers.

"Counsel for the President may now be seated," Early said.

Through the doors came our defenders—Burke Boswell, loping unsteadily with the rolling gait of a running guard, and Matt Fixx, drooping, pale, his gray sharkskin suit looking a size too big.

"Why don't you people buy Fixx a decent set of threads?" Hosmer asked. "Poor guy looks like he gets them at the Salvation Army thrift shop."

"Strategy, Larry. Senators don't dig mod clothes or sideburns. Matt is one of theirs—down to the tailoring and the golf-club tie clip."

Our lawyers settled into their chairs, at a counterpart table, to the right of the Chief Justice's chair. Early then ordered the clerk to read the rules of procedure.

When this formal business was concluded, Lance Ruckett rose. I had heard that the anti-Hannaford group had wanted Lem Suggs to lead the debate. Suggs was much like a senator—an older, gentle fellow. But, thanking them for the honor, the chairman had demurred. Ruckett was more than willing to accept the task.

At once it became evident that this quasi trial with its jerry-built rules, would be a sticky affair. It would require all the skill and diplomacy of the Chief Justice to keep it from heaping ridicule on Congress.

"Your Honor," Ruckett said, "I raise this question not only in behalf of my associates, but the entire membership of the House." Ruckett looked up at the public galleries, where many of the congressmen were seated.

"Proceed, Mr. Ruckett."

"Your Honor, I ask the court why the accused is not present."

There was an embarrassed murmuring on the floor. I knew why. The words *the accused* did not sit right. They were rude. They stank of a certain nastiness and vengefulness that did not go down well with the courtly men of the Senate.

"The President," Chief Justice Early said softly, "is not required to be present at his own trial."

"If is please the court," Ruckett said. "Why is that the case?"

"Precedent," Early said. "The court has seen fit to honor the traditions established in the only previous impeachment of a President, Andrew Johnson. Mr. Johnson, on advice of counsel, did not appear. Mr. Hannaford, whether on advice of counsel or by his own choosing, will not appear, and the court honors his decision."

I whispered to Hosmer: "Worst kept secret in Washington. Hannaford was all for wading in here with both fists. Boswell and Moscowitz decided it was wrong."

"They have a point," Larry said. "There's only one President, and you can't make a mug out of him."

"Are we to conclude, Your Honor," Ruckett said, "that a different set of rules governs the conduct of a President?"

"In a manner of speaking, Mr. Ruckett. He is the living symbol of the nation, the highest elected official. Let me suggest to you that in excluding the President from these deliberations, we do so out of respect for the *office*, no matter what our feelings may be about the incumbent."

Ruckett digested this a moment. Sykes Cottrell tugged at his sleeve. The South Dakotan conferred with the Mississippian, and then resumed. "Your Honor, the managers, as elected officials themselves, appreciate this reasoning. But as we have maintained in committee hearings, and as we shall *prove* at this trial, there is grave doubt, there is serious question that Benjamin Bow Hannaford was ever elected President of the United States—"

A rising moan of derision rose from the press and from the public galleries. "*That* old record," I heard a man from the *Post* mutter in back of me. "They won't quit."

"We shall introduce new evidence, new witnesses to prove that the state of California was illegally awarded to Mr. Hannaford. I maintain, that since there is serious doubt that Mr. Hannaford has the right to be in office, he should pay proper respect to this court and appear here to answer the charges against him, as would any accused!"

Ruckett stepped back, hands on his hips. He felt he had scored. I saw Gabe Tutt nodding his head. Evidently Gabe thought so also. For a moment the Chief Justice was silent.

"I repeat, Your Honor, in view of these questions concerning the last presidential election, I urge that the court reconsider, and that the papers of impeachment be served once more on the President, and that he accept the Senate's invitation to appear."

I wondered what Early would do. It was a throbbing moment. Under the rules drawn up for the trial, the Chief Justice could rule on points of law—but, and it was an enormous *but,* if any senator objected to a ruling, it could be put to a vote of the one hundred jurors!

Burke Boswell got to his feet.

"Look out," I warned Hosmer. "Here comes the clean-up hitter."

"Mr. Boswell?" Early looked almost relieved.

"Your Honor, I should like to ask Mr. Ruckett," the Secretary of Defense bellowed, "would it be fair to say that he, and his associates do not recognize Mr. Hanna-ford as President of the United States?"

"Ah . . . I . . . ah . . . I suppose he is . . ."

"But you claim he stole the election. That he was elected illegally. And that you'll prove he shouldn't be in the White House."

"That is correct."

"Then you *don't* regard him as President."

"I . . . ah . . . until such evidence . . . that is . . ."

"Simple answer, Mr. Ruckett, yes or no. You've said it to the press many times, that he's a usurper who got where he is by rigging the vote in California."

It dawned on Ruckett now that he was in a fight, a fight to the death. The glaze of confidence dulled on his young face. Ruckett was whispering to his colleagues.

"Here's what you said, Mr. Ruckett," Burke shouted. "Here it is, in the Washington *Daily News.* Quote. 'I don't even regard him as the President any more. He never has

540

been. He was never elected.' Unquote. What could be clearer?"

"Yes, I said that," Ruckett said. "I meant it, ah, in a metaphorical way. Technically, Hannaford is President, but—"

"Actually he is not? Legally he is not?"

"Ah . . . I stand on what I just said, Mr. Boswell."

Boswell seemed to grow six inches taller. His gaunt figure loomed over the Senate chamber, and he thundered at the prosecutors:

"Gentlemen, if that is the case, if Mr. Ruckett and the rest of you, and I suppose a lot of Mr. Ruckett's associates in COCCC, are of the mind that Mr. Hannaford is not, I repeat, *not*, the President of the United States, how, how, I ask, in heaven's name, can you impeach him?"

Laughter burst from the galleries, from the Senate floor. The Chief Justice looked annoyed and banged the gavel.

"I'm not joking, Your Honor," Boswell thundered on. "I am serious. A different court, one whose composition I cannot begin to imagine, must be organized and convened for the trial of a pseudo-President or an anti-President, to borrow a useful phrase from the Roman Catholic Church. The Constitution says nothing about trials for usurpers. Only for honest-to-goodness elected Presidents. They don't even say anything about Vice-Presidents. If you folks who oragnized the impeachment, who drew up the resolution, who produced the alleged evidence and so-called witnesses, are convinced that he is *not* President, then, gentlemen, we have got to start all over. Your Honor, I leave the matter with you."

Ruckett sat down; another whispered conference took place.

"What is it you wish me to rule on, Mr. Boswell?" asked the Chief Justice. A furtive smile turned the corners of his lips. He knew Boswell from way back. The tall man had been a trial lawyer before the Supreme Court for dozens of greedy corporations. Such training endows a man with infinite slyness.

"I think the managers have to be asked by the court, Your Honor," Boswell said, "whether they regard Benjamin Bow Hannaford as President of the United States. If they don't, we are in trouble here, and the impeachment, this trial, this entire proceeding is illegal and irrele-

541

vant, having no basis in the Constitution. If so, I will move to ask the Chief Justice to declare a mistrial."

"But you regard him as *your* President!" sputtered Ruckett. "We're impeaching him as *your* President!"

"Ah, but not as *yours?*" Boswell persisted. "Come on, Mr. Ruckett. Maybe you've polled your 87 members of COCCC. Or maybe you've even polled the 217 members who voted to impeach. Tell us how many of them agree with you, and Mr. Cottrell, and Mr. DeVaux, and Mr. Suggs, and you other gentlemen who say that Mr. Hannaford is *not* President. Because if he isn't, you can't impeach him."

"In view of the point raised by Mr. Boswell," the Chief Justice said, "the court is impelled to put the question directly to the managers. Gentlemen, do you regard Benjamin Bow Hannaford as the President of the United States, or do you not?"

Lem Suggs was on his feet. As committee chairman, he outranked the others. But he had settled into the background. "Your Honor, I speak for the members of the House Govenment Operations committee, now acting as managers of the impeachment. We all regard Mr. Hannaford as the President."

"As of this moment," Ruckett added.

"How about tomorrow? Or yesterday?" Boswell shouted.

"How about 3:15 P.M. this afternoon? Or 4:00 A.M. Tuesday morning? I don't know what Mr. Ruckett means by '*as of this moment,*' Your Honor."

The Chief Justice nodded. "Does Mr. Ruckett wish to withdraw those qualifying words?"

The air-conditioned atmosphere of the chamber, redolent of dry-cleaned dacron suits, tobacco and Aqua-Velva (did some Washington wag once describe the Senate Establishment as a notch above the Aqua-Velva After Shave Club?) filled Ruckett's chest and he resembled a blowfish stroked into inflated ecstasy. "I . . . withdraw . . . them . . . Your Honor."

"Why, thank you, Mr. Ruckett. Now that we are all in accord as to who the President of the United States is, I imagine we can proceed." Boswell grinned—that wide-mouthed, disarming grimace.

"Mr. Ruckett, if you please," Chief Justice Early said.

"Thank you, Your Honor. I shall restrict my opening arguments to a review of the events leading to the vote in the House of Representatives, and shall reserve for our witnesses details and added evidence of the case against the President. . . ."

In addition to making a bloody fool out of Ruckett and his colleagues, Boswell had underscored that for all their hatred of Hannaford, they had to concede he was the President. In so doing, he'd cut the ground from one of their favorite arguments—that he was never elected.

Ruckett droned on. But some of the fight was out of him. It was round one, and we'd won on points.

Parente's column the next day told me what he had been after on his secret trips to New York. It also indicated he didn't have much to go on.

The inmates are now running the asylum. That is a charitable way of describing the lunatic minuet being performed today on Capitol Hill. The impeachment of the President, on charges so flimsy, so wild, so inexact, so outrageous, charges based on rumor, innuendo and the testimony of a shabby professional agitator, liar and con man, is a chapter in American history that will take a lot of explaining in future textbooks.

Even if the Senate swiftly and overwhelmingly absolves President Hannaford, as they should, making a merciful end of this clownish charade, the bad odor will linger on, thanks to vindictive and ambitious men like Lance Ruckett and Sykes Cottrell, and the cabal that supports them in and out of the House. *View from the Hill* has long pointed out the connections Mr. Ruckett has with DOOR, Save America and other unsavory groups. He has met with, written articles for, taken money from, and praised publicly, the psychotic schemer Merton Huckerby, that outspoken admirer of Adolf Hitler and Benito Mussolini. As far as we know, Ruckett has never disavowed his friendship with Huckerby, although he prefers to mute it. After all, a man who teaches the *Horst Wessel* song, the Nazi anthem, to teen-age boys, hardly is fit company for even a reactionary congressman.

But that is only part of the Ruckett story. On top of his warm friendship with the extreme right, Lance Ruckett has developed a curious affection for the extreme left, notably its black extremist variety, in the

person of Kakamba Jones. It was Jones's testimony that stampeded the House Government Operations Committee into its shameful seventeen-to-sixteen vote for impeachment. How did Jones manage this? How did a black militant, a crackpot fascist, discredited by every respectable black leader, manage to walk into a House Committee with his gang, armed to the teeth, and scare the pants off thirty-three congressmen, while detailing a lurid tale of arms being supplied to the Sacramento ghetto by the President's aide, and with the President's knowldge? Well, it is an old story, this sordid business of extreme left and extreme right plotting against the middle. It is what happened in Germany in the thirties, a perverse cooperation of Communists and Nazis, against a democratic government. This column will have more information to disclose shortly on the secret dealings between Kakamba Jones and the militant right.
. . .

That night I telephoned Parente. "How about that additional information you promised? Want to tell me? Or Boswell?"

"I wish I knew. That sneaky bastard Jones. I was close to buying him off. One more nudge. Then he clammed up. He's too busy sending his storm troops into Brooklyn to vandalize Chassidic synagogues. What a hero. I'd like to rompo his *coglioni*."

The debate dragged on. Opening arguments were heard. Judge Moscowitz spoke for the defense. He was a superb advocate. The senators listened. Increasingly, it seemed the trial would be nothing more than a replay of the House hearings, both in committee and regular session.

Then, as I pondered ways of getting to Kakamba Jones, I got a call from Judy Stapp.

"Hey, Ed. Feel like taking a lonely broad to New York this weekend?"

Judy is in her forties. But she looks ten years younger. She detests Washington. Snubbing the city, it has snubbed her. Judy feels left out, and she returns the compliment. To her (odd in a San Francisco girl) New York is Nirvana, a glittering flesh pot of intellect, genius, and pot parties. Judy is very high on what she calls her "thinky, trendy crowd."

544

"Judy, I would love to, but I am bone-weary, running errands for our distinguished counsel."

"This might be more than a pleasure trip."

"In what way?"

"Farbelman is throwing an End-of-the-World Party, to celebrate Hannaford's downfall. That crazy dingo, Kakamba Jones is the guest of honor."

How New Yorkish! How truly indicative of the selfish, skin-worshiping indulgence that passes for wit in Gotham! Farbelman, of course, was Arvid Farbelman, the bearded guru of the new left. He was the megalomaniac who'd experienced Mona Varnum's satiny limbs before me. And an End-of-the-World party! How dandy! Kakamba Jones as guest of honor? Why not?

"I'll be delighted," I said. I paused and thought for a moment. "May I bring Lou Parente?"

"And how. He's always good for a fist fight."

"Many thanks, Judy. I think Lou will enjoy this sort of respite from his labors."

In response to demands from the press, the President held a news conference after the first few days of the trial. The East Room was jammed with reporters.

"I have one announcement, gentlemen," President Hannaford said. "The disarmament talks will open in Stockholm next Monday. The Chinese will attend as observers, which for all practical purposes, means they are participating. Your questions."

No one cared about disarmament.

"Mr. President, there's a report that a wealthy group of southwestern millionaires have approached the Vice-President and asked him to announce his support of impeachment. Is that accurate?"

"You'll have to ask Mr. Sparrier."

"We did."

"What did he say?"

"He denied it."

"Son, that's good enough for me. Mr. Sparrier is understandably reluctant to discuss the incident. His exact words to those people, one of whom was Mr. Cudder, were 'I'll see you damned first.' "

"Mr. President, there is a report that an approach was made to you through a group of senators in your own party to replace some of your cabinet members, namely

545

Mr. Murphy, Mr. Boswell and Mr. Edgerton, and that if you did so, they would guarantee an acquittal."

"There was one such approach," Hannaford said. "But it was made by your colleague Mr. Pendragon, and not to me, but to Mr. Goldstein, sitting over there, and it was rejected out of hand. I informed Mr. Goldstein that if this sort of thing continued I would have to start insulting people."

"Have you considered resigning, Mr. President?"

"Absolutely not. I've just gotten used to the job."

"Has anyone suggested it?"

"Lots of folks. Mr. Pringle's newspapers have been suggesting it for a month."

"Mr. President, do you feel any personal resentment against the men who led the impeachment—Mr. Ruckett and Mr. Cottrell and the others?"

"Goodness, no. Why, the First Lady reminded me this morning we are due to hold the congressional reception next week and we will be obliged to invite a lot of those folks who voted to kick me out. I hope they'll attend. After all, the White House is everybody's house."

Parente was hesitant about coming to New York with Judy Stapp and me for the End-of-the-World party. Marsha had experienced false labor pains the night before. But they had hired a nurse to stay with her, and Lou agreed to make one more attempt at Kakamba Jones.

"Two things my kids won't be allowed to be," Parente said, as we rode the cab from La Guardia airport to Greenwich Village. "Reporters or politicians."

"You love your work," Judy said. She patted his knee.

"Hands off, Judy. In my condition, I'll faint."

I was in a sullen mood. I regretted leaving Washington, where I had a hundred chores, to track down a mountebank like Jones. To relieve my morbid frame of mind I played my dismal game: *Ask the Cabdriver*. This one was John Reardon, an elderly Irishman.

"How do people up here feel about the President's trial?"

"Who?"

"The President. Hannaford. You know, he's on trial."

"Ah, b'Jesus, I thought they'd convicted him already. Had his hand in the till."

"No, no. That was when he was a senator and he was censured. That was three years ago."

"Same sort o' thing, I guess."

Parente's hooded eyes mocked me. "Don't look so sad, Deever. That kind of ignorance may save you people yet."

I detest New York parties. I detest the people. I don't understand what they are talking about, I do not smoke pot. I drink very little. The women snub me. The men insult me. I can't help it; I stand there in my narrow gray suit, white shirt and maroon tie, my sideburns short, my dark hair slicked down with stay-comb, my white face impassive, and clearly I am an *ausländer*.

Not so Judy Stapp. She wore a kind of short coat of mail, all links and baubles, over a pink body stocking. The clanking metal contraption ended perhaps two inches below the crotch. Luckily, she had splendid legs for a woman in her early forties. Her face was painted in circus white and red, and her voice rang with a harsh jangle of ambition and lechery that had attracted so many lovers. However, Judy had one rule. She only bedded down with famous people, only with the with-it, trendy, thinky, kicky, kinky crowd of whom she was charter member, a sort of duenna in Dior.

"Clank, clank, clank," Farbelman intoned. "Clank, clank, clank. It's Judy Stapp, the senator's concubine. With two bodyguards."

Judy introduced us. Farbelman, in a haze of bluish, sweetish smoke, was pleased to see Parente. He was another celebrity, and the poet began measuring Lou for size. This was standard Farbelman.

"Man, you are a big ginzo," Farbelman said, circling Parente. "Why in hell don't they give you the Pulitzer prize?"

"They don't like big ginzos," Lou said. "But I understand they're very high on bearded Hebes from the Bronx."

"Tough monkey, hey Parente?"

Lou looked angrily at Judy. "Jesus, do I have to listen to this shit? Where's Jones?"

Farbelman noticed me. "Ah, Deever. Hannaford's pratt boy. You were here once.. Friend of Mona's. I hear she's quitting her job and going to work as minister of information for the Afro Avengers. Smart move. Get off that Establishment kick and start grooving with the brothers."

"Yes, the *brothers*," I said. A young girl, whom I gathered was nude, except for two green leaves pasted on her nipples and a third glued to her crotch, glided by me. Somewhere a rock trio was affronting my ears.

"Tell me. Farbelman, have the brothers called you Goldberg lately? Have they promised to kill all the Jews in Israel when they join forces with their glorious Arab brothers? What the hell is wrong with you idiots? I have more respect for the Chassidic Jews who organize defense committees to keep Kakamba Jones's lunatics from burning their Torahs. But that wouldn't bother you. You are too busy playing anarchist, mouthing banalities, and supporting any outrageous *Jacqueries*, especially if it comes on in black face."

"Yeah, yeah, Deever." Farbelman was wobbly. "Well, that big crook, that mother-loving boss of yours, that hick millionaire, that shit-kicker Hannaford is getting his."

"I was certain you and your pack of rats would cheer when Hannaford was impeached," I said. "The generals are already bragging that there won't be *any* elections next time, that Sparrier will be the last President. They have their own ideas. You'll end up in the same concentration camp with me, and by Christ, I won't have any part of you."

"Talky little fucker, isn't he?" Arvid Farbelman murmured. "Shitman, Judy, where'd you latch on to this creep?"

"There he is," Parente said, turning away. "Rochester in drag."

Kakamba Jones, in a swirl of orange robes, emerged from an inner room. Lou shouted at him: "Jonesy! Jonesy, baby!"

Kakamba saw us. He ogled Judy Stapp and joined our group. *"Hajambo keena bwana."*

"Non rompere mi coglioni, Kak," Lou said. "You know Mrs. Stapp?"

"I have met the lady." I noticed this in Jones: a stiff formality in the presence of Establishment ladies. "How is your esteemed husband, the good senator?"

"He gets by," Judy said. "Why don't you ask about the President?"

Kakamba's mouth opened wide. Now he was playing Sambo, another role. "Ah. The big fox. Yes, the big fox will be run to ground by the hounds. Good. Then we'll get the wolf. Better the wolf than the fox."

"And after the fox the tigers," I said.

"To eat Little Black Sambo?" Jones snickered. He jabbed me in the short ribs with his fly whisk.

"Isn't his robe gorgeous?" Judy Stapp asked. "I dig that orange silk. Where's it from, Mr. Jones?"

"Japan. You see, the poor Africans, our brothers, have no textile industry. The colonialists destroyed it, to keep them in bondage, so we must buy our clothing."

Parente was impatient. He grabbed Kakamba's beads (lions' teeth?) and moved his face forward. "Look, Kak, this is all fascinating, but let's stop the crap. You know I been after you for almost a week. And you know what for."

"Yes, yes. To betray my trust."

"Balls, your trust. I knew you when you were one of the smartest social workers in West Harlem. Okay, so you got sore, you got fed up. But you're no goddamn good to anyone. Any man who threatens old Jews in Williamsburg, better take a good look at himself. And besides, you should watch your step with them Chassidim. They'll put a Hebrew conjurer on you and turn you into a pumpernickel, you dig?"

"Unhand me, wop."

Judy looked worried. She took my arm, whispering. "I don't like it. They'll start a fight."

I shook my head. "No. They understand one another."

"Kak. I want you to come to Washington with Uncle Lou. And you can tell me who paid who off, how come Fancourt and these other ridge runners were so sweet to you, and how you told lies to the House Government Operations Committee. Then you can do the same thing in front of the Senate. It's nothing to be ashamed of. Back in Joe McCarthy's day there was some guy, some professional witness who made a career out of exposing Communists to the FBI, and Fighting Joe, and a lot of other creeps, and then turning up and admitting it was all a lie. It never did him any harm. He became a high-priced writer."

Kakamba threw his head back. "No, no, wop. I do not think so. Nothing. Not a word. Let them hang the great honky pig in Washington. He is worse than the generals and the Kluxers and the Birchers. He is much worse because he sweet-talks us."

"You are a dumb bastard," Parente said. "Dumber than I thought."

Farbelman, a young girl on each arm—they could not have been over eighteen, nubile, blond, lanky college kids in mini-dresses—walked toward us. "Group grope time. Everybody in psychedelic chamber for organized games."

He turned his fuzzy-wuzzy head toward the bedroom. Through the opened door I saw multicolored lights flashing. I have never understood the artistic values, or even the erotic qualities of these inane games with lights. They give me a headache.

"Ah yes. The group grope. I shall participate only to show my contempt for all of them." Jones pulled away from Parente and sashayed away.

"Excuse my ignorance," I said to Judy Stapp, "but what is a group grope?"

"A goddamn bore," Sid's wife said. "They lay around on couches, smoke pot, watch those lights, listen to space music, and freak out."

"I mean . . . do they . . . ?"

"No, not usually. But there's a lot of fondling and grabbing and kissing. All very community-minded."

"Participatory democracy?" I asked.

"Yes, if you can stand it," Judy said. She shook her mane of Coca-Cola-colored hair. "Most of them have BO and bad breath."

A brutal look came over Parente's face. He grabbed Judy's arm. "Listen, kid. You wanna help me? Go in there and get on a bed with Jones."

"I will like hell. I choose my own."

"This is for history, Mrs. Stapp. The senator will forgive you. Keep Jones busy. Love him up. Just a little. Don't be surprised if I show up. On the other side of the divan. Go on. Judy, it's for your country."

Judy Stapp looked at me, as if appealing the decision. "Ed . . . ?"

"I think I know what Lou has in mind. Greater love hath no woman, Judy."

She smiled with the cynicism of an art dealer. Judy was still a looker at forty-two. "Okay, bright boys. But if it gets too sticky in there, forget it." She clanked off in her short coat of mail, then turned. "I don't groove on these crowd scenes."

"What the hell," Parente said. "It's worth a try." He

grabbed the naked girl wearing the three leaves. Pasties, I believe they call them. "Wanna career in show business? My name is Lastfogel. I can get you on Ed Sullivan, if you're co-operative."

Receiving no answer other than a vacuous smirk, he dragged her to the bedroom.

Lead-footed, I found an easy chair in a study off the living room. In the darkness, I sipped at a Coke and watched a fat man with a spade beard, whom I knew to be a critic for an insider's magazine, attempt to fondle a Chinese girl with a pneumatic bosom sheathed in black silk.

"Wake up, Deever. Let's get the hell out of here." Parente was shaking me. I must have dozed. Yawning, I got up. The sweetish odor of pot permeated everything.

"How was your group grope?" I asked. "Educational?"

"It beats scrabble."

I followed Lou into the hallway. Slyly he took from his suit jacket two objects.

"Keys," I said. "And a wallet."

"Kak's own. Lemme tell you, it was no easy job getting my mitts under that goddamn orange robe. That Judy Stapp. She sure came through."

We headed for the door. Judy could take care of herself. As we did, the girl with the three leaves came wobbling toward us, her bosom jiggling.

"Hey, Lastfogel, or what the hell ever your name is. What kinda crap is that, splitting out on me? Whaddya, straight or something?"

"You deceived me," Parente said sternly. "You ain't naked. You are wearing a body stocking. If it's one thing I hate, it's a tease."

She came upon us, her breasts shaking with anger. "Like hell. I wanna go on the 'Ed Sullivan Show.' Besides, you hardly touched me."

"Can't help it, lady," Parente said. "I'm really a big faggot."

We fled. I took a cab to La Guardia Airport and Parente, warning me that this was his job, and his alone— a mission fraught with special risks—took a taxi to Morningside Heights where Jones had his headquarters.

In the press gallery a few days later, the excitement was less over the repetitious debate, than over Senator Gabriel

T. Tutt's drunken outburst outside his office. I had not been there, but several reporters, including Mona Varnum had, and I got an account of what had happened. Senator Tutt had been receiving a delegation of Alabama ladies, representatives of the United Women's Auxiliaries of DOOR, when his aide, Eustis, the fellow I'd met at Gabe's dirty movies some months back, had come in and whispered something in his ear. At that point, Tutt, in a scarlet rage, his scrawny neck throbbing, his eyes blazing, had shouted out:

"God damn, he will be convicted! Ah gon' vote to convict him, and Ah gon' see that every friend Ah got in the Senate does also!"

As soon as he had apologized for his profanity, the senator dismissed the ladies, summoned his favorite newsmen, and made the announcement formally: he had reached the conclusion that President Hannaford was guilty as charged. The breach of etiquette was shocking, an outrage. That Tutt was stewed (at ten in the morning!) mattered not. The old sidewinder was clear of mind.

"We figured out finally what it was," a young man from *Newsday* told me. "It was that rider to the Military Appropriations Bill. The one for sixty million dollars for Southland Aviation down in Alabama."

"Forgive me. I've never even heard of it."

"Gabe kept it a secret. Even from most of his colleagues on the Armed Services Committee. This damn thing wasn't even requested by the Pentagon. It's for a plane that won't even be used by our own Air Force, just some piece of hardware that Southland intends to sell to the Egyptians so that the Israelis can shoot them all down. Tutt rammed it through the committee and got it stuck to the bottom of the bill. He was convinced he was home free, and then Boswell, acting on the President's order, lined up *his* people on the committee and they tossed it out. I think Senator O'Gara carried the ball for the White House. He told Tutt the committee would be damned if it would subsidize arms peddling, especially when there wasn't enough money for schools. That's why Tutt went into orbit, and that's why he blasted Hannaford."

We leaned forward as debate resumed. The lawyers had concluded opening arguments. Now witnesses were being called. It had a dreamlike air. The accused was not present. The hundred judge-jurors interrupted frequently.

552

The austere man with his fat-cheeked, almost womanish face sat in the presiding officer's chair. The same accusations were heard. The same charges were hurled by Ruckett, Cottrell and DeVaux.

The House managers' strategy was evident. They would try to prove Hannaford guilty of "high crimes" on the basis of the rioting that followed the rescinding of the ERCA arrests and the release of the detainees. This was a general charge, one they would have trouble with. The second charge would be the Sacramento affair, the smuggled weapons and the six dead policemen. They had dropped all references to Ben's having stolen the election; Boswell had faked them out on that. Having compelled them to concede that he *was* the President—how else could he be impeached and tried?—they now had to avoid any intimations that he held office illegally.

A portly man in a gray suit was being sworn as a witness. He had a massive, gray-thatched head, and an air of professorial dignity.

"Voss," I heard a newsman say. "President of Columbia."

"Defense or prosecution?"

"Defense."

Dr. Miklos Voss proceeded to tell the court that he was a native of Budapest who had fled his country during the Hungarian Revolution of 1956. A leader of the intellectual community, a foe of the Stalinist tyrants who ruled the country, he had been a framer of the famous "fifteen points" that had led to the establishment of a coalition government of liberal forces, the government which was ruthlessly crushed by Russian tanks and guns.

"Dr. Voss," Boswell asked, "your university was among the casualties of the riots that followed President Hannaford's order to release the prisoners detained under the Emergency Riot Control Act, was it not?"

"Yes, sir," said Voss. He had an engaging Hungarian accent, but his manner was not notably Hungarian. That is to say, he was no professional charmer. In his sixties, stooped, saturnine, Dr. Voss was a scholar. "But we have recovered. Much of our classes now take place in temporary buildings, but we did not interrupt the academic year."

"At the time, did you agree with the President's order

to release those people in the prison camps on Ellis Island and elsewhere?"

"I did."

"How about right now?" asked the Defense Secretary. "Do you still feel he did the right thing?"

"I do."

"Why would you say that, Dr. Voss? After all, a great university was almost destroyed. Students and faculty were beaten by the police. Would it not have been better to keep all those people under lock and key, the way the previous Administration had arranged it?"

"I was jailed," Voss said, "for six years by the native fascists of Hungary and by the Nazis. I was jailed for five more years by the Communists. I am something of an authority on political prisons. I assure you, Mr. Boswell, and members of this distinguished court, they are not conducive to civilized society, to human progress or to human happiness."

"But suppose a country is teetering on revolution, that agitators have announced their intention of seizing power? Should not people like that be jailed promptly?"

"No, sir."

"You prefer to have them running loose, so they can riot and burn and destroy places like Columbia?" Boswell persisted.

"Running loose, if you wish to phrase it that way, yes," the educator said carefully. "We must take these risks in a free society, Mr. Boswell. I am prepared to take them. I have been in jail too long to be eager to jail others. There are local laws and local officials and local conditions that must be applied in these cases. I, for one, prefer to give protest the largest possible arena in which to function."

"Even if it means the destruction of your university?"

"I accept the risk. There is a grave danger in having outcasts in a democracy," Dr. Voss said. "In them are the seeds of rebellion. The nature of a democracy, is that it must be a mosaic of all the people, offering something to all of them. Outcasts may be of many natures—black men who are humiliated, young people who are asked to die for causes in which they cannot believe, or white working-men who watch the falsehoods of a luxury-loving America on their television screens every night, but cannot afford a vacation or an operation for their wife. Here, Mr. Boswell are the seeds of revolution. The riots and the wicked
554

attacks on universities and liberal educators are disgusting, and I deplore them. But they are surface manifestations of a bone-deep infection in the body politic."

"Then as far as you are concerned, Dr. Voss," Boswell said, "as one of the victims of the disorders that followed the amnesty, you think the Administration did the right thing?"

"I do."

Roger DeVaux asked for the Chief Justice's permission to cross-examine.

"Dr. Voss," DeVaux said, "what party do you belong to?"

"Party? I am an independent."

"No, I mean, when you were in Hungary."

"Ah, in Hungary. I was a socialist as a young man."

"Socialist. That is, a Marxist."

"Yes, that would be correct. We derived from Marx. The Social Democratic Party of Hungary, to be precise."

"An off-shoot of which formed the Bolshevik or Communist party in Russia, correct?"

"That is also correct. But in Hungary, we were a separate party, we did not preach revolution, and we were opposed to the Communists for years. If you know my background, you will know that I led the fight against the Stalinists, and helped establish the first democratic government in—"

"Stalinists," DeVaux repeated, cutting him short. "That implies a *variety* of Communist. Can we conclude then, Dr. Voss, that you did not fight *other* Communists, non-Stalinists? That your so-called democratic coalition government included Communists?"

"But of course it did, sir. That is why it was a coalition."

"But Communists? Many of them?"

"Some."

DeVaux fussed with his tie, tucking it into his jacket, and turned to face the senators. "I leave it at that, Your Honor. This man, who tells us it was all right for Communists and left wingers and extremists, agitators freed by the President, to burn down Columbia, is a man who cooperated with Communists."

"*Liberal* Communists," Dr. Voss said softly. "And it was a true coalition—Small-Holders, the Catholic Party, the Social Democrats."

"The details do not matter," DeVaux said. "This man co-operated with them once, and he co-operated with them when they burned his univeristy down. If I were the trustees of that so-called liberal university, I'd want to know more about his past."

"The trustees, sir, consist of alumni, students and members of the West Harlem community."

"Naturally," said DeVaux. "People like you, and universities like Columbia deserve what they get."

"How interesting for you to say that," Voss said.

"Why is it so interesting?"

"It is exactly what my mail from the organized hate groups of the right said. The ones who pasted white crosses on our buildings when we were attacked. They, too, Congressman, felt we deserved our fate."

DeVaux started to speak, then stopped.

"But I suggest to you, sir," the educator said, "the intellect survives. The power of the free mind lives on. Inquiry, the search for truth, these go on."

Some youngsters in the gallery applauded—a thin sound in the vast room.

That evening I was summoned to the President's office to review the trial. There had been a disturbing occurrence that afternoon in the Senate. Gabe Tutt had moved to override one of Early's rulings on some particularly gamey evidence submitted by the managers. This was Gabe's prerogative, under the confusing rules of procedure; a simple majority was all that was needed to set aside any ruling by the Chief Justice. (The same crippling rule had applied at Andrew Johnson's trial.) Tutt's move was defeated, fifty-seven to forty-three; but we were stunned that forty-three senators, in effect, had cast their lot with Hannaford's opponents.

"What about that business today?" Ben asked us as we entered. Senator Stapp, our top man in the senatorial "court," was present. He had, before we entered, evinced curiosity about Judy's trip to New York; but he did not know about our game with Kakamba.

"Some of Tutt's friends thought they'd test the Chief Justice," Sid said.

"Some test," Hannaford said. "Forty-three votes against him? And me, by inference. Cold comfort, Sid."

"It's a long way from a two-thirds majority, Mr. President," I said.

"Too close, too damn close. We've said all along we've got to whup 'em and whup 'em good. So most of the damage done in the House can be canceled out. So we can move ahead in the Congress and get the money where it should be."

"We'll fight it all the way, sir," Stapp said.

The President was quiet for a while. He turned in his swivel chair and I saw his square, handsome face in profile. Looking out across the White House lawn, he appeared pensive. Hannaford was a man of action; these moods did not sit well with him.

"Where'd we go wrong, Sid?" he asked.

"On this impeachment thing?"

"No. The whole business. Not just this Administration. But the country, these past twenty years or so. What happened? Why's everyone so mad at everyone else? I looked at those marchers. Here they were wanting to hang me."

"Not quite, Mr. President," I offered. "I walked among those people. They were embarrassed, after the House voted. I could tell. Harry Bustard is still apologizing."

"I think," Stapp said, "they want recognition. They feel no one listens to them. They feel left out. We talk a lot about the blacks, and the wealthy have theirs made, but these people sense that their government has let them down. High taxes, beef costs too much, no money for medical emergencies, crowded highways, schools falling apart."

"But dammit, Sid, I aim to correct as many of those things as I can. With the military's money, and with a Congress on our side, we could work on every one of those problems."

"You and I are aware of that Mr. President," Senator Stapp said. "But we—and the Administrations that preceded us—didn't do a very good job of convincing the people."

Hannaford cocked a dark eye. "And that brings up a mighty sore point with me. Never really understood it until I got this job. I was always prone to believe that the more you democratized a country, the more you got people to vote and take part and know how decisions were made, the more liberal the country became. Like those long-haired kids yelling about—what do they call it, Edward?"

"Participatory democracy."

"That's it. I'm not so sure any more. About twenty years ago, a Chief Justice said if you put the Bill of Rights to a popular vote, it might lose. And it might still lose. I have a hunch that Joe McCarthy just might have been elected President. Democracies, even when they get to be more democratic, tolerate an awful lot of racism, violence and downright meanness. Sid, what's the most reactionary group on the Hill?"

"The House. It almost always has been."

"Darn right. And look how it's elected—one man, one vote. Pure democracy. The Senate's miles ahead of 'em, and it's less of a democratic institution. There are so many fine men in the Senate—brave, honest men, like Eisenberg and Henshaw and Lord and O'Gara. But the *most* progressive departments of our government, those who have done the most and worked the hardest to help the poor, the black, the weak, well hell, Sid, and Edward, you know the answer."

"The Presidency, of course," Senator Stapp said.

"And the Supreme Court," I added.

"That's right. And with the electoral college and the fact that a President can be elected by a mighty thin margin—not to mention the Court which is not democratic at all, but *appointive*—it means that the *less* democratic arms of government are the lost liberal. Now how do we explain all that?"

"If I may, sir," I said, "it goes back to your concept of controlled greed. I'm not so sure that greed is always that well controlled. It is often uncontrolled, and running wild. We learned that in 1929. And we're learning it every day in terms of the graft, and gluttony, of the military-industrial people. And it has a way of trickling down, of infecting a society. So we get a public that's jealous, fretful—not to mention all the legitimate gripes that those marchers have."

"You paint a grim picture, Ben," Stapp said.

The President barely heard him. "All this guff we listened to these last ten years or so. From Presidents and politicians and candidates, about forgotten men. Most of that was to soft-soap a lot of white people who were full of self-pity and bad tempers. Oh, they had complaints. But instead of looking to the complaints, the people who ran things kept telling 'em they were the salt of the earth. All

558

that manure about law and order—who is against law and order?—was a trick to keep 'em from realizing the government wasn't doing a thing, about schools, or slums, or pollution, or *peace*. And pretty soon people realized it was a fake. The blacks wouldn't go away. The dirty streets and the filthy rivers wouldn't clean up magically. There still wasn't enough money around to build homes and schools because it was going into planes and bombs."

"Perhaps it was what the people wanted," I said.

"I don't think so," Hannaford said. "And what if it were? Suppose a majority of the people wanted black skulls cracked and didn't give a damn if the cities were pigstys and the rivers full of garbage and the schools falling apart and the highways strangling? Suppose they did? I tell you what has to happen then. The President has got to lead! Like Uriah, he has to be in the forefront of the battle. A President can't nod his head and satisfy every stupid and brutal notion that the majority decides is what they want. Even if what he does is damned unpopular, and he catches hell for it, and he's called traitor, red, Communist and plain old son of a bitch! If he is President, he must do the right things, and to hell with what he's called."

"Let me be candid, Ben," Stapp said. "That is what you tried to do. And you were impeached for it. Two hundred thousand white people, the ones who used to be the backbone of our party, came here to approve of the impeachment."

"I know that, Sid. And if you think it is going to stop me, you don't know me as well as I thought you did."

Stapp shook his head; the light glinted on the silvery waves. "Ben, I'd go easy if I were you. Lay low. Oh, I know, I know. You have your concept of the Presidency ... the President has to take the lead, set the example, make the policies, do unpopular things. The activists against the cautious men. But sometimes the country will not accept change. We're finding that out."

"You want me to take the middle of the road, hey Sid?"

"That's right. Where it's peaceful and quiet."

"And no grass grows. Just go on letting black people get more miserable and more desperate and more murderous? And letting the military grab every dollar in sight to satisfy their fears and their hates?"

"Ben, liberal senators and congressmen have been trying to clip the military's wings since 1969. It fails all the time. With all the proof, all the evidence, all the truth on their side—the Pentagon still gets every dollar it wants, and on the most scandalous things, at that."

"Because the Presidents didn't take 'em on. Sid, this job needs a scrapper, a battler. Let me tell you this. When the Senate gives me that overwhelming vote of acquittal that I need, when the people calm down a little, I'm going to put on a show that'll make 'em think of FDR and his hundred days. I'm not Warren G. Harding, dammit, or any other of those pussy-footers, and I won't turn the country over to Lance Ruckett and Gabe Tutt and Gage Hopewell."

"I'm sure you won't, Ben," Stapp said.

"Moses may have been meek above all men on the face of the earth," President Hannaford said, "but he got the Israelites over to dry ground."

Outside his office, I asked Senator Stapp how it looked in the Senate.

"Bad," the Swinger said. "We can lick this business. I never doubted it. But if that vote follows the one today on Tutt's motion to override the Chief Justice, Hannaford will never be the same. As thin as our mandate is now. . . ."

"What can we do to help him?" I asked.

Senator Stapp's sleek face—he was eternally boyish, the man in a men's cologne ad—furrowed. "Be damned if I know. In the old days, we'd spread some patronage, make a few campaign contributions, twist a few arms, call in a few debts. But the rules have changed."

"I guess they have," I said. "But, as Mr. Micawber said, something may turn up."

Normally I abstain from sleeping pills, or any form of barbiturates. I sleep; and then I am hung over for two days. But after a long session with Fixx and Goldstein, following the meeting with the President, my mind was buzzing with stratagems, plots, schemes. I had taken not one pill, but two, and the telephone must have rung three or four times, because I was dreaming of the fire bell at the old Indian Mound volunteer fire department when I managed to open my eyes and take the phone off the hook.

"Ed? Ed?"

Stupefied, cotton-mouthed as I was, I recognized Mona Varnum's sensual voice.

"Whah? Whah?" The clock on the end table advised me that it was 3:30 AM, the hour of lost hopes and shattered dreams. "Mona . . . ? What are you . . . ?"

"Listen, white soul brother. I hope I'm still among the favored members of the press."

"Barely. Just barely."

"I got a call from our news room. The AP ran a funny one about fifteen minutes ago and then killed it. Listen carefully."

I yawned—for about ten seconds it seemed—while Mona read the news item.

"It's datelined Louisville, Kentucky. Here it is. "Police in Louisville reported tonight that the explosion of an Army shipment of chemicals had caused casualties in Browning Junction, Indiana, about thirty miles west of here. The area has been cordoned off by Army and local police. Six or seven people were reported injured.' "

"That's it?" I asked.

"The AP sent a message ten minutes later killing it. You know—one of those lines reading KILL, KILL, KILL, and then reminding you that it was a mandatory kill, in big letters. Which means the report is wrong, or else pressure is being put on by the Army to keep it quiet."

"Have you called the Pentagon press information office?"

"Yes. There's a sergeant on duty, and he don't know from nothin'. Refused to wake up any important press people."

I sat up in bed. The sleeping pills retaliated by rendering me dizzy. "I don't think I can do anything about it, Mona. No one's told me. It probably is a false start. Maybe there was an explosion. Happens all the time."

"Listen, Ed. There is a town called Newport, Indiana, where they store some of the worst poison gas this country makes."

"Indiana is a big state, sweetie. Besides, there are firm orders not to ship that stuff anywhere except if needed to fight a war. And it's never shipped through populated areas. Go back to sleep."

"Do me a favor."

"Why should I?"

"Wake up Boswell. Ask Boswell to find out."

"I will not. The poor man is busy defending the President. He's exhausted. I can't bother him about some AP report on an explosion that probably never happened. Be a good girl, wait till morning, and call me again. I'll try to find out for you when my head clears up."

"Can I do something to help clear it?" Her voice took on a feline purr.

"You could. But in my condition it might kill me. And Hannaford needs every friend he has."

"Okay, Mr. Charley. But if Mona learns that this is a real news story, and she misses out because of your laziness, watch out. You don't even get to hold my tape recorder."

I thought no more of the AP report and fell into a hard sleep.

In the morning I got one of the PIOs at the Pentagon, a civilian, named Valentine. He was wary of my questions.

"Look," I said, "I'm calling for the President. I would suggest that in spite of the Pentagon's dim view of Mr. Hannaford, they are obliged to respond to queries. Was there not an accident or an explosion last night in southern Indiana? And why was that first report on the AP wire knocked off?"

None of the morning newscasts carried anything on the story, nor had the "Today" show had any report. And if it had happened in the middle of the night, it would have been too late for morning papers.

"I have nothing on it, Mr. Deever. There was some sort of minor accident there, but we aren't sure what."

"Man, you represent the greatest military force in the world. You people have over four thousand press agents. Why can't someone make a phone call?"

"I'm trying to get through right now, Mr. Deever. I'll call you."

"Are you sure some uniformed fellow isn't sitting on you, Valentine?" I asked acidely. "Civilian to civilian, this is a presidential aide speaking, and I want a report."

"I promise you, sir, you'll have it the second I get word."

He was lying. I can tell when people lie to me, especially government people. They are too obliging, too ready to please.

562

As I entered the press gallery, Senator Stanton Betten-haus of North Carolina, a young ally of Gabe Tutt's, but a lot slicker ("an attractive candidate" was how the press referred to him), was requestiong that the senators be polled to override another of Chief Justice Early's rulings.

"What's up?" I asked a lad from the St. Louis *Globe-Democrat*.

"Early's getting tough on them. He just told DeVaux that they'd better start introducing evidence bearing on the charges in the impeachment. All this crap about how lousy things are in the cities is interesting, but hasn't anything to do with Hannaford's alleged crimes."

I looked down at the floor. Was it my imagination, or did I detect an uneasiness, a revulsion on the part of many of the chosen one hundred? They seemed to be lying around, lounging, indifferent, impatient. *Get the damned thing over with,* seemed to be the unspoken consensus.

". . . and I move for a poll of the membership on the ruling," Bettenhaus said.

"Under the rules established for this body," Early said, "I have no choice but to agree. But I suggest to the senators that if we are to pause for these votes on every ruling by the presiding officer, we shall be at this business for a long time. It is my impression that not only the President, but the Senate itself, and the nation, desires a conclusion of this trial."

"That may be so, Your Honor," Senator Bettenhaus said, "but it is the feeling of many of us that justice must be served—no matter how long it takes."

Early betrayed not a flicker of emotion. He ordered the clerk to proceed to call the roll. There were sighs of annoyance from some of the senators. I saw Maury Eisenberg throw up his hands in disgust, get out of his chair and walk over to Webb Urban.

As the roll call began, I heard two reporters in back of me talking.

". . . seven or eight dead . . ."

"AP says it was some kind of chemical spray . . . southern Indiana . . ."

I flew from my seat, raced up the aisle, and into the press room. On the spike next to the AP printer, I leafed through the yellow carbons of the most recent news items. In a few seconds I had located it.

BULLETIN

Louisville, Ky., July 15—(AP)—At least seven people were reported dead today and fifteen hospitalized as the result of the accidental explosion of a shipment of lethal nerve gas in southern Indiana.

The material, described by a Pentagon spokesman as VX, one of the deadliest of gases stored by the Army, was released when a private car smashed into a parked Army truck outside a diner.

The accident took place at Browning Junction, a crossroads about fifteen miles west of Louisville, Kentucky, in Harrison County.

Police gave the time of the crash as about 2:15 AM, EST.

The dead were said to include three persons in the automobile and three or four soldiers.

The entire area, a mile square around the scene, was closed off. Special decontamination units from the Army nerve gas depot at Newport, Indiana, were rushed to the scene immediately after the accident, and were said to have removed all traces of the gas.

The gas VX is described as a slowly evaporating liquid of extreme toxicity, which can cause death by paralysis in less than a minute. It is absorbed by vegetation, so that an area infected with it can remain lethal for a long period of time.

MORE

I turned to the elderly press room attendant. "Anything else moved on this?"

"No, Mr. Deever. Same story on the United Press."

Holding the sheet of wire copy in my hand, I went back into the press gallery. They were calling the roll on Bettenhaus' motion to overrule the Chief Justice.

"Mr. Kemmons," the clerk tolled.

"No."

"Mr. Kovatch."

"No."

"How is it going?" I asked a girl from *Newsweek*.

"About the same. I think you might pick up a few votes. I don't think they'll ever overrule Early. But that

564

isn't what they want any more. They just want to show there's an awful lot of senators who don't like the President. Have you seen this?"

She gave me a four-page newsletter. It was the most recent issue of DOOR TO FREEDOM. It was headed, A PROGRAM FOR PATRIOTS.

Barring some Communist or African outrage on the national scene, it appears that Benjamin Bow Hannaford, the usurper in the White House, will manage to squeeze through his current trial for murder. This treacherous man has spread his millions around and threatened senators and played his usual game of deceit and bullying.

But even if the Senate fails to muster the courage to punish the traitor and throw him out of office (we refuse to use the word "President" in connection with him) the way has been charted for concerned conservatives and their allies. Hannaford will come out of this so discredited that he dare not run again. Even if he does, the conservative majority is growing. It has been shown that there exists a vast, dedicated majority of antiliberal forces. No longer does a candidate have to toady to the blacks, the intellectuals, the press, the universities, the welfare chiselers, the pornographers, the radical clergy, the Wall Street clique.

The next election will see a patriot on the order of General Upshaw, or General Nagel, or Congressman Ruckett, carrying the banners of victory. Hannaford and his liberal-radical-Establishment conspirators are finished forever, no matter how the Senate votes . . .

"Makes my flesh creep," the girl said. "I never believed these nuts, but they make it sound so logical."

"Mr. Mullendore."

"Yes."

"Mr. Nordlinger."

"No."

As the vote proceeded, I saw one of Boswell's aides come on to the floor and walk to the defense table, and speak to the Defense Secretary. Boswell assembled his lanky frame, whispered to Sam Moscowitz and strode out of the Senate chamber. I ran out, and hurried downstairs.

Several reporters were talking about the deaths in Indiana.

I caught up with Boswell at the side entrance of the Capitol, as he awaited his limousine.

"That business in Indiana," I said. "Is that why—?"

"Yep. I warned 'em, and I warned 'em. And now this. Hannaford just found out, and he went up the wall."

The chauffeured Lincoln pulled up. Boswell and I got in and we sped off to the White House.

When we reached the President's office, we found we had been preceded by General Dudley, acting chairman of the Joint Chiefs and a youthful colonel with a shaved blond head, steel-rimmed eyeglasses, and the crossed retorts of the Chemical Warfare Service on his tunic lapels.

"Burke, we got us a mess here," the President said.

"I'll say we have," Boswell glared at Dudley.

General Dudley tapped the arm of his chair. "There was a mix-up in orders, sir. Our people at Newport misunderstood my last directive on shipping VX."

"Hold it, General," the President said. "What in hell is VX?"

Dudley cleared his throat. I could see why he'd brought the colonel along. An expert. And possibly a patsy. "Colonel Widnall can explain it better than I can, Mr. President."

The Chemical Warfare man clasped his hands on his brief case. "This gas, VX, sir, is one of our most effective agents. It is an extremely sophisticated defensive weapon . . .

"Sir, VX has the viscosity of motor oil, but when exposed to the atmosphere it can turn a target area into a no man's land for days. The gas is absorbed by vegetation, and the grass, the plants, the trees remain deadly. A remarkable item."

"Just dandy," Boswell said.

"We categorize VX as a *persistent* agent, far more effective than our other nerve agent, GB. Among the attributes of a persistent agent is its capacity to penetrate protective clothing and masks. A lethal dose of VX is about one milligram, less than one-fiftieth of a drop. That is a truly high level of efficiency."

We had succeeded in producing machines instead of men. As the Russians had. As all superpowers do. I was certain that Colonel Widnall was a good family man, a church-goer, a patriot, a foe of pornography, an intelligent scientist. But he'd been scooped out; he'd been cored. Nothing beat in his chest. In place of a heart, lungs, viscera, he had a set of test tubes, Erlenmyer flasks, crucibles, retorts and pipettes. As he resumed his lesson in "nerve agents" I watched the President's dark passionate face. The natural ruddiness was giving way to shadows denoting a profound, unforgiving anger. His wild ancestors had worshiped the buffalo, slept beneath pure skies, inhaled the free air of the prairie. And here before him sat this young dealer in chemical death, bragging of his "persistent" agent which could kill in drops of one milligram.

"We store VX at Newport, Indiana," the Colonel said. He was unaware of the rage discoloring Hannaford's face. "We manufacture very little of it, since our inventories are high, more than enough to counter any enemy attempt at a sneak nerve gas attack."

"How does this agent of yours kill people?" the President asked.

"It's fairly complex," Widnall said. "It inhibits a vital enzyme in the human body called ACHE. This enzyme is needed to control muscle movements. The VX stops the production of the enzyme and the body loses control of its own muscular movements. In effect, the body strangles in its own vital organs. Death can take place in less than a minute. Voluntary muscles become paralyzed. Involuntary muscles lose their capacity to activate and deactivate nervous stimulations. The pupils of the eye, the bladder, and the alimentary canal constrict. The penis erects. The tear and saliva glands secrete. The heart slows. Death itself is usually caused by asphyxia following paralysis of the respiratory muscles."

General Dudley crossed his legs. "One of the virtues of these agents," he said, "is their adaptability."

"That a fact?" the President asked. I had never heard his voice so strained.

"Yes, sir. We can use VX in a variety of shells, rockets, warheads. Also, we've tested them in guided missiles, spray tanks and land mines."

"Yeah, I seem to recall, those tests you lied about in Hawaii were with sprays." Boswell was slumped deep in his chair.

"Mr. Secretary," Colonel Widnall said, "we had to cov-

567

er up in order to keep the population from getting worried."

"We also," Dudley continued, ignoring his aide, "have a new thousand-pound bomb that carries seventy-six small dispersal bombs and can disperse the VX in tighter concentrations."

"We call them bomblets," the colonel said.

"Bomblets," the President repeated.

"The shipment involved in this, ah, unfortunate accident," Dudley said, "was of small standard one-gallon spray tanks, which had been requested by Benning."

"All right, let's have the report," Boswell said curtly. "Now that we know what VX is and what it can do."

The colonel opened his brief case. "I'll do this chronologically, Mr. President," he said. "There was only a single truck involved, a standard Army six-by-six loaded with a dozen crates of the basic VX spray tank for shipment to Fort Benning. In addition to the driver and the relief driver up front, there was an accompanying Jeep with three enlisted men, carrying decontamination emergency equipment—plastic sacks, protective clothing, gas masks, sprays, and atropine capsules, which have proven effective as an antidote.

"The two vehicles stopped at about two-twelve this morning, at a diner at a place called Browning Junction, off the main highway to Louisville. The standard procedure is to keep one man on guard duty. The two vehicles had just stopped, in the parking area outside this diner—it's called Clark's Eats—when a civilian vehicle in which three persons were riding, made a sharp turn off the highway exit, came up the service road, and, apparently trying to swerve into the parking area of the diner, smashed into the six-by-six.

"The car in question was a stock racer of some kind, and our reports indicate that the three men within were drunk. They were all killed by the agent, not the accident, and autopsies are pending. Someone in the diner saw the car speeding into the lot, saw it smash into our truck, and concluded that only someone inebriated could have driven that way. The parking area is well lit."

"You say the three people in the car died of the gas?" Hannaford said.

"Mr. President, it was a freak. An absolute freak. The vehicle had an exceptionally heavy custom-made grille, with a lot of heavy steel in it. It struck the side of the truck, smashed open one of the crates, and one of these one-gallon tanks I mentioned cracked open and began to diffuse in droplets. It was absolutely a million-in-one shot, Mr. President."

"And some of this poison got on them?" Boswell asked.

"We've verified that. Our special decontaminating units have everything under control. The area is safe now, but we are keeping it quarantined for at least a week.

"The three soldiers in the Jeep were also sprayed with VX and although they made an effort to decontaminate themselves, the tank was spraying gas with great force. There were two soldiers in the cab of the truck, and when the crash occurred, they leapt out and ran toward the diner. It never occurred to them that one of the tanks could have been shaken loose and have been pierced. The VX is odorless and colorless when it evaporates.

"People in the diner began to come out, and soldiers ordered them back in. At that point one of the men took it upon himself to start decontamination, as soon as he saw the seriousness of the accident. While one soldier dragged the dying man to safety to the side of the diner, the other man raced to the Jeep and got out a plastic sack that is used to retrieve and neutralize dispensers or contaminated objects, and without regard for his own safety, extracted the tank which was still spraying gas in aerosol droplets, wrapped it in the plastic cover, and set it in a clump of bushes."

"How is he?" the President asked.

"He's dead, sir," Colonel Widnall replied.

"It was an act of high heroism," General Dudley said. "I am going to recommend the highest possible posthumous award for that young man."

"Yes," the colonel agreed. "He not only saved the lives of all the people in the diner—there must have been ten or eleven—but many in the town itself. There's a cluster of stores and homes at the crossroads, a small community. The whole place would have been saturated with VX."

"And the other soldier?" Boswell asked.

"As soon as he dragged his buddies away, he put on a protective suit and mask and special gloves and secured the land mine. Then he got out the decontaminating sprays and went to work. I think we've got it under control."

569

Hannaford's eyes were closed. "We've been asking for this, Burke," he said. "Who is to say next time it won't be seven dead, but seventy?"

"Few heads are gonna roll," Boswell said, glowering at Dudley. "A few of you people are going to have to shape up, General. I want all the names of every officer in the Pentagon, in Newport and in Fort Benning, and anywhere else, involved in this thing."

"You shall have them."

"Let me assure you, Mr. President, that this was an absolute freak, a one-in-a-million shot. Normally these spray tanks will not go off unless they are subjected to extreme pressure, or unlocked. There is a possibility that the item that went off was defective."

"Gentlemen, it wasn't that spray tank that was *defective*," Hannaford said. "It was something defective in our lives and our society. And if you think I'm through fighting it and turning this country away from death and machines and the ruination of the land, you're wrong in your estimate of Benjamin Bow Hannaford."

"Mr. President, I support you on your social program and I always have," General Dudley said. "But the country cannot be left denuded. If *they* produce nerve gas and biological agents, we must also—"

"Hell, General," Boswell said. "I've seen the intelligence reports. We've got more of these lethal gases than the rest of the world put together. Name your poison, we can kill whole cities with it."

"So can they," the colonel said.

"And we all get killed," the President said. "Can't believe a nice, educated boy like you wants that. Or that the Russian generals do." Hannaford spun about in his chair and looked out the window. "I think we need some decontamination of the soul, gentlemen. That's a lot harder than cleaning up a mess of—what'd you call it, Colonel?"

"It's VX, sir."

"I'm concerned about security on this matter, Mr. President," General Dudley aid. "We tried to kill the story, to keep it out of the papers, but some reporters from Louisville got wind of it . . ."

It confounded me. The blindness of these people! Candor was the general's armor. He was not remotely aware of what was infuriating the President and Boswell! *Securi-*

ty concerned him. Then I got a glimmer of what was in his martial mind. As far as many of them in the Pentagon were concerned, Hannaford was a plucked chicken. Impeached, vilified, discredited—did they have to fear him any more?

"No, no," Hannaford said softly. "You misunderstand me, General. I want this story told to the people. I want them to know what happened. As soon as that area is clean, let the press in."

"I'll see to *that*," Boswell growled.

"Let me make my position clear," the general said. "I hate these weapons. They are sneaky. They are unmanly. It isn't what I was taught about warfare at West Point. I'm aware of the revulsion they create. But when the country's survival is at stake, I am forced to go along with them."

The intercom on the President's desk buzzed. It was Fred Goldstein. He had new information on the tragedy. The President asked him to come in.

"The death toll is higher than seven," Fred said, as he approached the President's desk, reading from his notes. "Some of that aerosol spray got into a front yard and three members of a family were discovered dead this morning."

"Persistent agents tend to persist," the colonel said.

"An officer down there, a CW guy, got us the names of the four dead soldiers. He says if that guy who ran out to retrieve the tank and wrap it up hadn't done so, there could have been twenty or thirty more dead. He lived just long enough to secure it, so his buddy could finish the job. There's some eyewitness stuff that's pretty hard to take."

Fred's squinty green eyes looked at Hannaford. "Mulford, the GI who covered the tank lived for a minute and a half after the stuff got on him, crawling and screaming, until he choked to death."

"What was the boy's name?" Ben asked.

Fred looked at his notes. "Mulford. Pvt. Moses Mulford, of Redpath, Texas. Nineteen. Son of Mr. and Mrs. Adam Mulford."

General Dudley stiffened in his chair. "He'll get a medal and a hero's burial. I shall see to that. Mulford. Sounds like he was a *good old country boy*."

The phrase offended me. These words—*good old country boy*—refer to a variety of hard-drinking, straight-shooting, southern rustic. Years ago, when it was revealed that the Army's top noncommissioned officers had run a network of graft in their private clubs, they were defended by various generals as "good old country boys."

Fred Goldstein, of course, knew what the words signified, and he turned to General Dudley. "I don't think so. Mulford was black."

Back in my office, Parente called me from Washington General Hospital. Marsha had just given birth to a baby, their second son, a healthy eight pounds, three ounces.

"My sincerest good wishes to mother and father," I said. "What will you name the little fellow?"

A growling noise issued from the phone. "Wayne Carson, for Chrissake. Those Methodist relatives of my wife's in Watertown. The next kid is gonna be Rocco Angelo, for my people."

"In any case, Lou, let's hope the kids grow up in a world free of VX."

"Beautiful story. You got anything new?"

"A soldier named Moses Mulford, a nineteen-year-old black boy, was the hero."

"Poor bastard. They'll give him the big funeral. Gabe Tutt will make a speech how he likes some niggers especially when they're in the army and get themselves killed neutralizing nerve gas spray tanks."

I told him how grim the President had been at the meeting I had just attended.

"Tell the big guy to cheer up. I delivered a bundle of stuff to Moscowitz, and a surprise witness."

"Ah . . . a fellow in a purple dashiki?"

"Go watch, Ed. It may be the best show in Washington since Schlesinger jumped into the swimming pool."

Yes, Parente had delivered. As I returned to the gallery, I saw Kakamba seated in the witness chair to the side of the rostrum.

The Attorney-General was interrogating him. Kakamba had forsaken his robe for a paramilitary rig—black turtleneck sweater, a medallion, black form-fitting trousers, black boots. I liked him better in dashiki. The Senate, unlike the Government Operations Committee, had invited him disarmed. He was a lot less menacing in the chamber,

572

a solitary black figure surrounded by the white Establishment.

"Mr. Jones, do you have direct knowledge that President Hannaford knew that you had bought weapons with Industrial Training funds?" the Attorney General asked.

"Hunh?"

"Direct knowledge."

"Whazzat mean?"

"It means were you present when the President was told about it? Or do you know of any letters, or any record of such advice to the President?"

"Just what Warfield said."

"And what did Mr. Warfield tell you?"

"What I told the committee. Warfield said he was gonna warn Hannaford."

Chief Justice Early's face reddened. "I must caution the witness to observe some element of respect toward the Chief Executive. He is referred to as the President, or *President* Hannaford."

"He ain't my President."

"He is, Mr. Jones. He is *our* President."

Moscowitz resumed. "Mr. Warfield has denied that he ever told the President, in so many words, of your threat because he did not believe you. At any later time, did he tell you otherwise?"

"Nah. You know Warfield. He talks in circles."

"He did not talk in circles when he said that he never said any such thing to the President."

Kakamba leaned back, threw out his narrow chest. "He told him, he told him."

"But you were not present at that alleged conversation," Moscowitz said.

"Well, man, I don't git invited to the White House."

"But you have been, Mr. Jones, many times. I've been to meetings with you right in the President's office."

"That was when I was a Vice-Presidential candidate and the big man had to listen to me. Now I am only a bad nigger."

Chief Justice Early spoke patiently. "Again, Mr. Jones, I caution you to temper your language."

Jones shifted about in the witness chair. "I don' recognize this Senate, this court, that President. Nothin'. I represent the black armed forces of revolution."

As yet, nothing new had emerged from the interrogation. About all that was being achieved was a further discrediting of Jones as a loud-mouthed troublemaker.

"Mr. Jones, who is the Reverend Sand Bewley?" Moscowitz asked casually.

"Hunh?"

"Sand Bewley. That is spelled, S-a-n-d, first name. Second name, B-e-w-l-e-y."

"Never heard of him."

"He is a minister. He is pastor of the United Christian Militant Church of Scobeyville, Oklahoma."

"Don't run with no honky preachers."

"Perhaps you know him in one of his other jobs. He is chancellor of Kape College in Scobeyville."

It was difficult to tell what Kakamba's reaction was. Behind his outsized dark spectacles, his eyes were invisible. A consummate actor, he could hide his emotions, assume different guises and mannerisms with admirable skill.

"So you have never met the Reverend Bewley?" Moscowitz asked. "And you have never heard of Kape College."

Jones shrugged. He was cautious. "Man, we rap with lots of white cats. Maybe someone talked to this Booley once. I ain't sure."

Something came into sharp focus in my mind. *The fat man in the Scott Key Arms the night Parente and Baldini bugged the room where Ruckett, Pendragon, Pringle and the detestable Huckerby held their meeting.* A fat man in a dark suit, smirking, standing behind General Upshaw. A hellfire fundamentalist quasi-nut, leading southwestern organizer for DOOR, Lou said.

"Mr. Bewley is an important figure in an organization called Defenders of Our Republic, or DOOR," Moscowitz said. "He has frequently recommended that the President be hanged."

There was a horrified buzzing in the chamber. Lance Ruckett was on his feet. "Mr. Chief Justice, I resent these insinuations about DOOR, a patriotic organization of which, as is well known, I am a national director. I know Mr. Bewley slightly. I do not agree with everything he says. I am not aware of his ever having said what Mr. Moscowitz claims he said. And besides, none of this bears on the case. I don't think it unfair of me to ask Mr. Moscowitz if he feels responsible for the leaders of the

574

Communist party in this country who have praised his so-called liberal approach to the laws governing sedition and treason. If he chooses to besmirch patriots with unproven associations, I think I can ask him that."

Moscowitz was blandless itself. He was an old courtroom veteran. "Mr. Ruckett, I have never once accepted the plaudits of Communists. These were matters of law on which I ruled. I would give the same protection to fascists and black extremists. As Franklin Delano Roosevelt once said, 'I have not sought, I do not seek, I repudiate the support of Communism, or any other alien ism.' Are you prepared to renounce Reverend Bewley?"

"This is off the mark, off the mark, Y'Honor," Sykes Cottrell said, attempting to rescue Ruckett.

"I agree, Mr. Cottrell," the Chief Justice said. "Mr. Moscowitz, Mr. Bewley's background may or may not be relevant. If it is, please make that association clear to the court. If not, I ask you to abandon that line of questioning."

"Yeah, man. Lemme go home." Jones jerked up in his seat.

Moscowitz, who had been pacing in front of the witness chair, now returned to the table. Matt Fixx shoved a slip of paper at him.

"Mr. Jones, do you recognize this paper?" The Attorney-General held it in front of Kakamba.

"Hunh? Nope."

"But you should, Mr. Jones. It is a photostat of a check for five thousand dollars made out to you. It is signed by the Kape College Foundation of Scobeyville, Oklahoma. It is drawn on the Cattlemen's Bank of Dry Springs, Oklahoma."

"So whut? We gits lots of financial help from white cats. The guilt bit."

"I am sure you do. But why should a college run by Sand Bewley, a man who has advocated the shipment of black Americans to Africa, and the arming of white vigilantes to combat civil rights marchers, why should such an institution be so generous to you?"

"Beats me, man."

"One year ago, Mr. Bewley was quoted in *Time* magazine as saying that forty of his old army buddies, armed with burp guns, could stop the entire black resistance movement. I repeat, why should such a man give you five thousand dollars?"

I offered a silent prayer to Judy Stapp and Lou Parente. The group grope at Farbelman's had cost Jones his keys and his wallet; and would now cost him a good deal more.

"You regard this, then, as a routine contribution?" Moscowitz pursued.

"You said it, man. Charity. Reparations. You know about this reparation bag, don't you? We hittin' the synagogues now."

"Then how, Mr. Jones, shall we explain this letter on the official stationery of Kape College, in which the Reverend Sand Bewley thanks you for your co-operation, and allows that it was a pleasure meeting you in Sacramento, and that he feels you and he see eye to eye?"

"Fake!" Jones shouted. "Forgery! It ain't the first time! The damn FBI works for *you*, man. Those people can forge anything. They forged you that letter."

Moscowitz ignored him. He turned to the Chief Justice. "Your Honor, I should like to read this letter and have it inserted in the record of this trial."

"Proceed, Mr. Moscowitz."

"I object, Your Honor!" shouted Lance Ruckett. "The Attorney General has confused his job as law enforcement officer with his functions as a defense lawyer for an accused man!" He looked toward his allies in the Senate.

Gabe Tutt wobbled to his feet. "Y'Honor, Ah move that the senators be polled, the roll be called on yoah motion to permit readin' of that letter!" A great shout of *nos*, of angry cries, arose. I was astonished to see frosty Webb Urban, Mr. Senate Establishment, on his feet and *shouting*. "To what point, Senator? You cannot win that vote and you will delay these proceedings. The letter will be read anyway. It will be released to the press. Let us, in God's name, move ahead!"

Gabe Tutt sat down. Webb Urban was not a man lightly defied.

Moscowitz began to read. "This letter bears the insignia of Kape College, Scobeyville, Oklahoma, and is dated June 19. It is quite short. It reads: 'Dear Mr. Jones, I trust the arrangements are satisfactory to you. It was a pleasure meeting you in Sacramento and I am delighted with your co-operation. Although we differ on many

576

things, I am sure we are united on the urgency of getting rid of a certain high-ranking person. Perhaps this should be the last written communication between us. Sincerely, Reverend Sand Bewley.'"

"Fake, forgery, lies," Kakamba Jones sneered.

"Yes, a fake," Lance Ruckett shouted. "Forged."

"Ah," Judge Moscowitz observed, "the two of you appear to be in agreement, which is the point I have been trying to make. Your Honor, the entire case of the prosecution is based on a conspiracy between the forces of extremism in this country. There *is* a great deal of fakery involved here, and it concerns the concocted charges against the President of the United States."

The Attorney General held up the letter and the check. "Here is the evidence, gentlemen. Mr. Jones and the bigots of the right plotted the Sacramento incident and the nasty testimony in front of the House Government Operations Committee. No amount of denials, outraged protests and charges of forgery can obscure the evidence."

As I left, Congressman Ruckett was on his feet and shouting about "socialist plots," and "paid informers," but I had the sensation he was losing his grip—on himself and on his following. He was perilously close to incoherence.

Mark Sullivan's estimate of Daughtery, Warren G. Harding's corrupt Attorney General came to mind as I thought of Lance Ruckett: *"He lived by a code of his own; if his code did not happen to be identical with the world's conventions, so much the worse for the world's conventions."*

"I assume Sam is after that Bible-basher," the President said. "He deserves a chance in the witness chair."

"Unfortunately, sir, the Reverend Bewley has disappeared. Officials down at Kape College say he is on an extended tour of religious sites in the Holy Land."

We were having dinner in the President's dining room at the west end of the second floor of the White House. There were just four of us at the American Federal table—the boss, Fern, Vangie Boswell and me. Fern had done the cooking herself—Mexican food, which she prepared with culinary skill.

"We may never need him," the President said. "I have got to do a big favor for Parente, Edward, and for Mrs. Stapp."

Fern blushed. I imagined Hannaford had told her my story of Farbelman's brawl, and the manner in which Parente had picked Kakamba Jones's pockets. ("And it wasn't easy," Lou had told me. "Christ, you try fumbling around inside one of them Zulu robes that the bastard wears. I think he thought I was a broad, or at least queer." This morsel I had *not* repeated to Hannaford.)

"You might send him a present for his new son," I said. "Marsha had a baby early this morning."

Fern and the President were delighted. Marsha Tread-way had once been our chief mail clerk; the same young lady who had (it seemed eons age) stolen secret corre-spondence from our files and touched off the censure. She'd long been forgiven.

"I wish them all well," the President said. "Funny, how everything changes in time. Fern, buy them something real fine."

Mr. Hannaford nodded. Vangie complimented her on the chili with green peppers.

"My dear, this is one of the most relaxed evenings I've had in many weeks," Hannaford said. He looked at his wife with profound affection.

"Shouldn't say this in front of someone so young and pretty as Mrs. H.," Hannaford said lightly, "but I sort of feel as if you two are our kids tonight. . . ."

"I am not offended, Benjamin," Fern said. *Benjamin?* He had always been "the senator" or "the President" or "Mr. Hannaford" or "my husband in front of third par-ties. The sound of his Christian name on Fern's lips rocked me. Soon he would be plain old "Ben."

As we sipped coffee—Vangie moved lithely around the table, a mini-skirted and panti-hosed blond houri serving us—the President got down to business. I had been ordered by him to prepare a file on the nerve gas tragedy in Indiana; it had been on his mind all day.

"Boswell is firing a few generals," the President said. "And anyone who authorized that shipment is going to do a little sweating. I think we may get some mileage out of this terrible thing."

"Yes, I think we can, sir," I said. "Another case of the right things getting done for the wrong reasons."

Vangie shook her blond hair. She'd never understand us. "Isn't it sickening?" she asked the First Lady rhetori-cally. "The way good things happen?"

I opened the manila folder of new clippings, notes, transcripts of phone conversations. "Mulford was an enlistee, nineteen years old. He is the oldest of nine children. His father, Adam Mulford, is a cotton farmer, owns a small place, which he works with his brother, Jacob. The Mulford boy had graduated from Sam Houston High School, where he was a B student and a substitute on the football team. It was an all-black school, although it had been four times ordered to desegregate. That's about it."

"Nineteen," Hannaford said.

I held up a newspaper photograph of Private Mulford. It had appeared on the front pages of the afternoon papers. *The Hero of Browning Junction,* it had been headed. A slender black face stared at us—wide liquid eyes, a blunt nose, heavy lips. Pvt. Mulford wore a brimmed garrison cap and a serene expression. He seemed to have made his peace with the Army.

"You wonder what motivated the boy," the President said. "I know a little about those Negro farms in Texas."

"And Ramada," Fern added.

"Yes dear, and Ramada." Hannaford shook his head. "Lifetime of being called Nigger. Higher prices for seed and farm equipment. Bad schools. No future. Worst of all the contempt and ridicule and humiliation. I know what makes black people so angry. It's not the things they can see and hear and touch. It's the knowledge of what goes on in white people's *minds*. What's being *thought* about them. And here's young Mulford, nineteen, a child, giving his life to save a white community."

The President was thoughtful; his eyes were almost shut. " 'All these things worketh God oftentimes with man, to bring back his soul from the pit,' " he said softly. "Maybe there'll be a lesson in Mulford's death."

"Better a lesson than *mileage*," Vangie said tersely.

"Edward, what about the other lad? The one who survived?"

"Also a private. His name is Costa Velastos. Greek-American family from Camden, New Jersey, twenty years old, draftee, high school graduate. Father owns a tailoring shop." I glanced at my notes. "He's been hospitalized in Louisville for shock, but he seems to be okay. In fact, he's going to the funeral in Redpath this Thursday, with an honor guard of men from Mulford's outfit, the 2189th Chemical Warfare Supply and Maintenance Company."

Fern was setting her spectacles on her nose. She studied her husband's furrowed face.

"Benjamin," Fern pronounced, "you must go to that boy's funeral."

"It wouldn't look like grandstanding would it?" he asked all of us. "Taking the play away from that boy and his folks?"

"Not at all," Fern said. "You must go there. You must show this country what it owes the Mulfords, these people who have done America's hardest and dirtiest work and gotten such little reward."

I threw in my contribution. "His parents would be honored. I spoke to the preacher, a Mr. Russell, the pastor at the Mount Sinai Baptist Church of Redpath, and he said they all voted for you."

Hannaford sighed. "Well, we can't *lose* any more voters. We got to be friendly with anyone who's for us."

"Benjamin," Fern said, "you need not be so cavalier. I have heard it said that when Mr. Eisenhower was President, some people advised him to go to Little Rock during the school integration crisis, and lead those black children into the school by hand."

Ben sighed. "Fern, Eisenhower had a lot more public support than old thirty-three-per cent Hannaford."

"All the more reason to attend the boy's funeral. You have nothing to lose."

The President laughed. "Yes, I'll do it. And for Miss Boswell's benefit—I see the outrage in her face—I'll do it with all my heart, as well as my political instincts. Young Mulford deserved better than that terrible death. Maybe we can make it up to him and his folks."

Fern raised a finger. "Benjamin, I suggest you not only attend the funeral, but deliver the eulogy."

Hannaford turned to me. "Edward, call the preacher down there and see how he feels about this, how the boy's parents feel. Get Goldstein to call the networks. And Edward . . ."

"Yes, sir?"

"See can you arrange for them to hold it in prime time, about seven o'clock in the evening. CBS and NBC won't mind if we pre-empt them."

"Shall do, sir."

Leaving, I saw Vangie clap a hand over her horrified mouth.

The trial of the President was about to conclude. All the witnesses had been heard. There remained only the closing arguments. Busying myself with the arrangements for our trip to Redpath, Texas, and Private Mulford's funeral, I was unable to attend the final session of the "court of impeachment," the one that would be followed by the crucial vote. But I got a running account of it from the AP, and my friends in the press.

Boswell began his summation by paying tribute to the Senate, the Chief Justice, the House managers. He was especially flattering to the prosecutors.

"Gentlemen," the Defense Secretary said, as a wide smile distorted his toothy mug, "you came here with good instincts. You had the good of the country at heart. You love your country. You oppose violence. By golly, so do we. It shouldn't be so hard for us to see eye to eye on the issues confronting us. But I think we've all let our emotions run away with us. It's time to stop throwing nasty words and accusations around, and resume the dialogue. You know, Your Honor, after the disaster of the Andrew Johnson impeachment, a farce and a mummery, a trial in which not one jot of evidence was introduced to buttress the charges against *that* President, a student of American history might have assumed that such a carnival, such a display of prejudice and bad temper and petty jealousies might be avoided in the future.

"Such has not been the case. We've seen a Johnson trial all over, only worse. The two specific cases raised by the gentlemen from the House concern the Emergency Riot Control Act and the executive order redirecting the Defense Department's funds to train youths for defense jobs. In neither instance has the prosecution proven, not by the remotest stretch of anyone's fevered imagination, that the President of the United States had any desire, intent, or wish to touch off new demonstrations, and in the second instance, to arm and encourage black militants to rebel. I remind the court that the Sacramento ghetto was closed in, shut off from the rest of the city by local fiat and local police. The Administration has worked diligently to defuse that situation and dozens of others across the country.

"But what is most damning to your case, gentlemen, is the proof introduced by counsel for the President, establishing that the alleged complicity of the President in furnishing arms to the militants, is a fraud and a lie. Oh we do have a conspiracy. It is a conspiracy of paranoids, of wildmen. The mysterious Reverend Bewley, whose ordination papers I should very much like to examine, has vanished. We're looking for him. And we'll get him, no matter how industriously he is engaged in visiting the shrines of the Holy Land. I'm amazed, Your Honor, amazed, that the learned managers haven't started their search for this signer of checks. If they are so certain he never did bribe Kakamba Jones, and conspire with him to lie and slander the President, if they're so convinced of his innocence, why aren't they out looking for Sand Bewley? And why were they so reluctant to cross-examine Mr. Jones? He's a great talker. He likes to rap with people. But what did we find from the managers' table across the way? Silence. A prodigious silence.

"Speak up, gentlemen," Boswell declared. "We confronted Kakamba Jones with the evidence of his sordid dealings with Mr. Bewley, with Kape College, and that patriotic group, the Defenders of Our Republic. And yet, Mr. Ruckett, and Mr. Cottrell, and all you other fellows from the House have said nothing. It's as if you believe there is no Sand Bewley, that he never gave Mr. Jones five thousand dollars to concoct his lies. I hope you are all proud of this wicked mess. I hope you are."

Boswell looked at poor Fulvio Stradella when he said this. The Philadelphian had been behaving as if he wanted to hide, to run away from Cottrell, DeVaux and Ruckett.

"Nothing's been proven here. Not a thing. The House Resolution is a mess of inflammatory nonsense. It is garbage. It is junk. I know 217 members voted for it. I know why they did. They were maneuvered into it by the exploitation of fears and hatreds. I grieve for those dead policemen in California and for their families. I also grieve for the dead black people in the ghetto. We listened, and listened and listened to the previous two Administrations babble on about law and order, as if anyone in their right mind isn't for law and order. But law and order seemed to apply only to blacks who committed street crimes. Fine, let's put an end to that. For some odd reason, all this fuming about law and order never applied to school officials who daily violated the laws of the land, or to labor unions that illegally locked out black people, or police forces that beat up black prisoners behind jailhouse doors. No, Your Honor, I saw no vigorous prosecution of *these* broken laws, these disorders. Do we wonder that black people entertain doubts about our standards of law enforcement?

"Well, Your Honor, Benjamin Bow Hannaford inherited this mess. And as President, he intends to *change* it. Maybe all of the members of the court are not appreciative of the President's *modus operandi* and his policies. But I doubt that any one of them has misgivings or uncertainties about his courage. So he acted. He is still acting. He is trying to right century-old grievances. To depict these presidential actions as conducive to violence and bloodshed, is a malformation of motives and purpose that stuns the reason. It is a deed of petty, bitter men, men who have given up on their country, and seek nothing but a nation controlled by privilege—and white skin."

"They swallowed it," Larry Hosmer told me later. "They didn't like it, but they took it from Daddy Long-Legs."

Boswell's next arguments were perhaps even more unpalatable to the one hundred anointed. "Many thoughtful Americans," he said, "are concerned about these proceedings. I am aware that the Constitution provides for the impeachment and trial of a President. But scholars contend that the words 'high crimes and misdemeanors' mean just that. A President cannot be impeached or brought to trial for political reasons, even though that is precisely what has happened here. If I were a United States senator, I'd think about it a bit. Once the presidency is vulnerable to wild and intemperate assaults from any demagogue in Congress, we're in serious trouble. Nor can the House arbitrarily decide what is or isn't a criminal act by a President. That is truly subversive."

Lance Ruckett's eyes were frozen.

"At the heart of this affair, Your Honor," Boswell went on, "is the question of the Constitution and what it means to us. The decision of the House to pass this resolution, I assert, is a clear case of the Congress placing itself above the Constitution!"

"Shame! Shame!" shouted Gabe Tutt. "It's people lak you an' Hannaford who desecratin' the Constitution!"

He was ignored. "It is my belief," Boswell said, "that the American people, when they are in a calmer mood, will not be satisfied with these events, unless they are prepared to admit that the Congress is indeed above the

583

Constitution. Let me show exactly what I mean, by precise examples."

Now I understood why he earned those staggering fees from cosmetics manufacturers.

Boswell went on:

"It is hardly necessary for me to point out to so distinguished a body, that Acts of Congress, not warranted by the Constitution are not laws. Let us take the case of a law believed by the President to be unwarranted by the Constitution, such as the Emergency Riot Control Act—passed by the Congress, signed by the *prior* President, and hence not subject to veto by the incumbent. Now it would seem to me, Your Honor, that the President has the duty to execute this law precisely as if he held it to be constitutional—*except in the case where it directly attacks and impairs the executive power confided to him.* In that case, it is the duty of the President to disregard the law, so far as is necessary to bring the question of its constitutionality before the courts.

"In the case of ERCA, there was a wide variance of rulings in the lower courts. Hence, the President was not only within his rights in granting of amnesty, he was fulfilling his oath of office.

"And indeed, Your Honor, how can a President fulfill his oath to preserve, protect and defend the Constitution, if he has no right to defend it against an act of Congress, like ERCA, believed by him to have been passed in *violation* of it? Therefore, it is evident that the President had a right, and was under the highest obligation to rescind the mass arrests, the suspensions of bail, and the other excesses of the Emergency Riot Control Act, since he did so not in disregard of the Constitution, but with the belief that the act was unconstitutional. And we are advised that the matter is being brought before the Supreme Court in precisely the orderly manner which our forefathers envisioned. Plainly, what President Hannaford did, was the proper and peaceful, if not the *only* proper and peaceful mode of protecting and defending the Constitution."

It was a brilliant argument. Boswell had turned the entire issue of constitutionality around. But he was not finished with them yet.

"As for the second charge, or at least the charge

brought forth here in the court, but not specified in the resolution," he went on, "what can be said in defense of it? It is so farfetched, so much the product of minds in full intellectual retreat, that I find it a task to discuss it. Are we to believe that the President woke up one morning and decided to give guns to militant groups, that they might murder policemen? I could cite you endless statistics on the number of ghetto youths who are now receiving helpful training with the funds that the President released. Was some of the money stolen by a rabble rouser with a long record of provocations? Yes, I am afraid that occurred. And perhaps he bought arms with the money. Gentlemen, the answer would seem to be, get after that miscreant and punish him. But what has happened? This same firebrand after showing up in Sacramento with his arsenal, is invited to a palaver by the governor and then he surfaces before the House Government Operations Committee, armed to the teeth and boasting how he stole the funds, bought the guns, all, presumably with the President's benign approval.

"We heard Mr. Warfield deny this. We saw the evidence of Mr. Jones's connivance with the most outrageous elements of the lunatic right. And still we sit here and ponder the case. Your Honor, this whole mess should have been thrown out the first day this court convened.

"I shall beg the indulgence of the court, all the estimable members of the Senate, as I speculate on one of the reasons for both the impeachment and the trial. I see in it an attempt by elements in our troubled society, men motivated less by humanity and tolerance and understanding, than by a fearful compulsion towards greed and privilege, to have done once and for all with a President who will do battle for the poor and the black and the powerless. That is about as candidly as I can put it. I make no apologies. Let us be done with checks and balances, these militants cry. Abandon the Bill of Rights! Suspend civil liberties! Limit protest! Suppress dissent! Build more prisons! Oh, we have heard those siren songs. We have heard the chanting right here in this chamber, and we have heard the choraling—with greater volume and less harmony—in the House of Representatives.

"But let those who weary of liberty take heed. This narcotic dream of an orderly, obedient, closemouthed,

585

static society, can turn into a nightmare. In 1834, before the Senate of the United States, Daniel Webster warned his colleagues in these words:

" 'The first object of a free people is the preservation of their liberty, and liberty is only to be preserved by maintaining constitutional restraints and just division of political power. Nothing is more deceptive or dangerous that the pretense of a desire to simplify government. The simplest governments are despotisms.'

"Your Honor, during the debate on Andrew Johnson's impeachment," the Defense Secretary said, "the issue came up, what if he were found guilty? What punishment would be meted out to a convicted President? No one seemed to know. The Constitution isn't explicit. It merely states he is subject to punishment, according to law. I think perhaps we should have discussed this a bit. I know that some of Mr. Ruckett's backers, including Mr. Huckerby and the Reverend Bewley have said outright that the President should be hanged. They keep talking about all these army veterans armed with burp guns, and all the dirty liberals, like myself, and some cabinet members who are in the cross hairs of their rifles.

"In Andrew Johnson's case, Congressman Boutwell wondered what punishment was appropriate for a guilty President. In a remarkable prediction of the space age, he told the hushed court of a vast space in the heavens which the uneducated call 'the hole in the sky.' In that cold, dark place, Boutwell explained, 'the Great Author of Celestial Mechanism had left the chaos which was in the beginning.' And then, with a straight face, Boutwell suggested that once Johnson were convicted, 'he could be heaved upward through atmosphere, stratosphere and space to disappear forever in the great hole in the sky.' It's in the record of the trial, Your Honor. As James Thurber said, you could look it up."

The Senate exploded in laughter.

"Your Honor, I won't scoff at Congressman Boutwell's ingenious plan of disposal for American Presidents convicted and deposed by the Congress," Boswell went on. "I think that the managers should give it careful study. When the time comes, assuming the President is found guilty, perhaps Mr. Ruckett himself will volunteer for the job of conveying the master criminal to the launching pad at

586

Cape Kennedy. There, before the all-seeing eye of nation-wide television, Mr. Ruckett could wrestle the President into a new Gemini capsule, and as a final patriotic act toward his country, volunteer to be blown into outer space, where they could become a new orbiting set of twins, a celestial reminder to Presidents to behave themselves and not stick their hands into such matters as jobs, schools, housing, conservation, discrimination, and the building of a decent society." Boswell paused then looked across the room at Senator Tutt. "Why, we might even arrange for the distinguished chairman of the Senate Armed Services Committee to introduce the appropriations bill for this new space flight, the hardware for which, quite naturally, would be built in the state of Alabama."

"Ever seen one of these?"

We were aboard the presidential plane, cruising easily at thirty thousand feet through cloudless skies en route to Austin, Texas.

Markland, the head of the secret service detail, was showing me an enameled lapel button, about an inch and a half in diameter. In white letters on a pale-blue field, was the single word: RESIGN.

"No," I said. "But I know what it means. Where'd you find it?"

The security agent sat down next to me. "One of the boys picked up some nut outside the airport distributing them. He had bundles of that rag OPEN DOOR on him. We couldn't hold him, so we just took his name and grabbed a few of these."

"It's their new angle," I said. "They've given up on getting two-thirds of the Senate on their side. Not after the way Boswell chopped them up."

Markland's face, the face of a lawman, was impassive. I had always suspected he was not wholly in sympathy with Hannaford's program, but loyal cop that he was, he never uttered a word about politics. Was that not the essence of the efficient secret serviceman?

"Mr. Pringle is running a front page editorial on the subject," I said. "I'll say this for the President's enemies. They're co-ordinating a lot better." I showed him the newspaper.

587

HANNAFORD MUST RESIGN

It appears that the Senate, acting with less than the required courage, will not vote to convict President Hannaford. As we have long known, President Hannaford is a tough, intelligent man. He has allies. He has money. He has resources. And it is only fair to state that his battery of high-priced corporation lawyers proved to be as slick and as devious as their boss. In truth, the House managers of the prosecution, no matter how dedicated and patriotic, could not match the legal maneuverings and historical examples cited by the defense. So it now appears that a two-thirds majority of the senate voting for conviction is unlikely. But there is a good chance that the resolution will muster a majority. The roll calls already taken show anywhere from thirty-nine to forty-eight senators voting with the anti-Hannaford forces. What does this mean for the country? It means deeper divisions, more violence, more rivalries, even if the President is acquitted. Therefore, let Mr. Hannaford heed the sense of the House, the sentiments of many in the Senate, and the clear voice of the people, and step down. The Pringle newspapers urge their readers to bombard the White House with letters and telegrams. One word is all that is needed: *Resign.*

"Strong stuff," Markland said. "My guess is this will make the boss all the more determined to stick it out."

"You know him better than I thought," I said.

I am ever amazed at the speed with which our television networks can act. I've never been in agreement with those critics of the left who say they are licenses to print money, or those of the right who accuse them of being liberal conspiracies run by an eastern clique. They are, by and large, useful and productive entities, and they supply many public services.

In a field behind the small white clapboard church, baking beneath the merciless Texas sun, stood a dozen huge vans filled with sophisticated gear—tape machines, transmitters, the intricate cameras, the "dish" to send the signal back to Austin—all the refined technology which brought events into American living rooms, and which could, if ever used intelligently, make us better people. I am an eternal optimist.

It was a solemn occasion. The Mulford boy was dead. Any lesser man than Hannaford would have been accused of capitalizing on the tragedy for his own political benefit. But Ben's sincere interest in the lad was evident to all. No one—least of all the black people of the small farming community—doubted that he was there to dramatize his political and social beliefs, and to influence the Senate as it prepared to vote. But what of it? He came with a rugged honesty, a sense of identification with their hopes and dreams.

The minister of the Mount Sinai Baptist Church was a Reverend Russell, a slender, bespectacled man wearing an NAACP button in his lapel. As we stood on the dirt path to the church, surrounded by a throng of several thousand people—townsfolk, black and white, the press, our own party, the military honor guard and a horde of police including a few enormous Texas Rangers in wide hats—I experienced what a novelist once called an "epiphany." By that, I think he meant a sudden revelation, a swift insight, almost mystic in nature.

Beneath that broiling desert sun, with the yellow dust of Texas choking my nostrils, my body sagging after the long ordeal of the impeachment and trial, I felt *hope* surge through me like a refreshing sea wave. I had the notion that these people, especially the white people, who came to honor Private Moses Mulford and to see a President pay tribute to the farmboy-soldier, were not, by any stretch of the imagination wicked or cruel or greedy people. But they needed forceful leadership of the highest moral order. At this juncture in their brief history as a united nation, they needed it more grievously than ever.

"Your daddy was a lay preacher," Reverend Russell said. "I am afraid you will show me up with your knowledge of scripture."

"I don't think so," Ben said. "He wasn't ordained. I use the Bible mostly to give my political opponents a little religion. You probably are a much better Old Testament scholar."

The black man smiled. "Not really. My field was Social Psychology and the Dynamics of Rural Communities."

I saw the cameramen move away in a churning group, saw the TV cameras swing their probing snouts around, and on the macadam road across a field of stubble and stunted cacti, seared and brown in the summer furnace of the Texas plain, I saw the cortege.

Two mules, led by a man in coveralls came first. On the white-painted, flat-bed wagon rested the simple casket, covered with an American flag. Behind, in several cars were the members of Mulford's family, and his buddies, from the 2189th Chemical Warfare Company.

As we watched, Fred Goldstein came up to the President with a young white man in uniform, and two older people.

"Mr. President, this is Private Velastos," the press secretary said. "He was Mulford's buddy. His parents, Mr. and Mrs. Velastos."

"Good to meet you, son," Ben said. He shook hands with them. Our ethnic minorities, our so-called "forgotten Americans." Yet they had come to Redpath, Texas to honor the black man. Velastos was the man who, after the Negro had covered the cylinder, had donned the protective suit and secured the container.

"Costa tells me," Mr. Velastos said, "that was the bravest thing he ever saw a man do, to give his life like that for his buddies."

The casket was removed from the wagon. Eight soldiers, five white, three black, moved up the dirt path with the burden. From inside the church an organ played and a choir sang.

"Just a closer walk with Thee,
Grant it, Jesus, if you please . . ."

The dark, vibrant voices filled the air. There was grace, and hope and decency in those voices. More than we had any right to expect.

Private Mulford's family approached us. The father wore a black suit, Mrs. Mulford a black dress. There was a line of children behind them. A stocky white man in a tan suit was walking with Mrs. Mulford. He introduced himself as Mayor Smoot of Redpath. Hannaford shook hands with all of them.

"A brave boy," Hannaford said. "I want to ask you to forgive the United States government for this. He did not have to die."

"We are honored you are goin' to speak," Mr. Mulford

590

said. "We know what you tryin' to do. You, and Mr. Murphy and the rest. We know."

The pallbearers had entered the opened doors. We followed them. Inside, the flag-draped casket was set on a catafalque in front of the altar. The pews were packed, and I was glad to see many white faces and many uniformed men, including several officers of company grade. Again, the singing rose in the air.

> "I am weak and Thou art strong,
> Jesus keep me from all harm . . ."

"And it came to pass," Reverend Russell began, "when Pharaoh had let the people go, that God let them not through the way of the land of the Philistines, although that was near. For God said, 'lest peradventure the people repent when they see war, and they return to Egypt.' But God led the people about, through the way of the wilderness of the Red Sea. And the children of Israel went up harnessed out of the land of Egypt. And the lord went before them by day in a pillar of cloud, to lead them the way, and by night in a pillar of fire, to give them light to go by day and night. . . ."

We rose as the choir sang:

> 'I shall not be, I shall not be moved,
> I shall not be, I shall not be moved,
> Just like a tree that's planted by the water,
> I shall not be moved!"

"The eulogy will be delivered by the President of the United States, Mr. Benjamin Bow Hannaford."

Ben rose from the pew. The worshipers saw a broad-shouldered man in his late fifties, Indian blood shadowing his square face. How gray his hair had become! It was almost a frosty white. The congregation rose, but none applauded. Suddenly I found myself crying.

Ben walked to the pulpit. His huge hands grasped the sides of the lectern. I wished I could have seen him on a TV monitor. I had the feeling he had never looked more impressive. Mentally I made a note to have Fred Goldstein get us the videotape for a White House screening.

"Mr. and Mrs. Mulford, Reverend Russell, family and friends of the deceased," the President said. "And also, the millions of Americans in the quiet of their homes watching this solemn ceremony. I wish I could make some ennobling inspirational speech about the death of Private Moses Mulford, aged nineteen. I wish I could say to his parents and his brothers and sisters and his friends that he died for freedom, or that he died in a noble cause. I am afraid that is not the case. Moses Mulford's death, my friends, is less important than his life. And it is his life I want to talk about, for there is an object lesson in it for every one of us.

"I don't minimize the heroism of Moses Mulford's act. Very few of us would have acted so bravely. His parents tell me that Moses was that kind of boy. He liked to help people. He was kind to his younger brothers and sisters. When he saw the necessity for action, the deed that would save many lives in that little town—he responded. As have responded his black brothers on hundreds of occasions in our history. My fellow Americans, I am humbled and filled with a shameful sense of inadequacy the more I learn about the black man's contribution to our progress as a nation. I will make no apologies to anyone for talking about it.

"It has been said by one of my predecessors that above all, the presidency is a place of *moral* leadership. Beyond all the practical demands of the job, the defense of the nation, the material well-being of the citizens, the maintenance of laws, there is one overwhelming duty that the President has. And that is to rally the people behind those moral imperatives which are the cement of a civilized society. A President cannot stand aside from moral crises. He cannot make believe they do not exist. He cannot ignore injustice and hatred. We cannot paper over disunity. And as all of you know, my friends, we are not a united nation today.

"It is not this President's intention to stand aside from them, or paper them over or ignore them. And that's why I am here as the guest of Mr. and Mrs. Mulford. For the story of Moses Mulford's brief life should be a painful reminder to us about the moral imperatives facing America.

"Let me tell you about that young black man who died a terrible death to save people he didn't know. He did not stop to ask how many black people lived in Browning Junction. That didn't concern him. But I'm a curious man.

592

So I asked. There are two black families in that little Indiana town, out of a population of 253. And there was one black man in the diner outside of which the accident took place. He was the cook."

Standing on the dignity of his office, he had refused (as had Andrew Johnson) to subject himself to the rancorous trial. But now he had found his platform; he had found his arena. And when I heard him identify the Negro in the diner with the four-word sentence, *He was the cook,* I knew this was the old Ben Hannaford, the tough and shrewd man I had esteemed all these years.

"I don't think Moses Mulford paused to ask himself how many black lives he would save as against how many white lives. He was motivated only by honor, and courage, and a spirit of self-sacrifice that should fill many of us with humiliation. The preacher of Ecclesiastes tells us, 'Rejoice, O young man, in thy youth; and let thy heart cheer thee in the days of thy youth, and walk in the ways of thy heart, and in the sight of thine eyes.'

"But young Mulford never had a chance to walk in the ways of his heart. But in the few years he spent on this earth, and in his death, I find a lesson for us. It is not a very pleasant lesson, and I am aware that as I talk about it, I may offend some of my fellow citizens. No matter. As the Bible says, 'let us hear the conclusion of the whole matter.'

"Moses Mulford was born in a wooden house ten miles from here, on the fifty acres of hard earth farmed by his father. Two children who were born to the Mulfords before Moses, died in infancy of some undiagnosed fever. You see, there is no hospital near their home. No hospital that will take care of black people, in any case. Nor is there a doctor in the area who can make house calls, let alone a pediatrician. We honor the free enterprise system, and we respect the American Medical Association, but where were the doctors when the Mulfords' children died?

"In Moses's home, the diet was mostly beans and bread and drippings. There was never enough milk to go around, especially after the other children were born. His mother, whose dignity makes me wonder how people who have been so ill-treated can look at us with a mite of tolerance, suffered from anemia as a result of childbearing. But she did her household chores. She kept her children clean, and sent them to the local school. It is an all-black school. The local authorities here have found ways of bypassing the Supreme Court decision of 1954. It wasn't too hard. Private schools for whites. Lower school budgets for the blacks. They call that a 'middle of the road' approach.

"There were never enough books or enough teachers or enough motivation in that school. Most of the Mulford children quit after the eighth grade. There was no bus service to get them to the Redpath High School, so they didn't go. Moses, the oldest boy, finished the eighth grade. But he didn't learn much. He helped his daddy on the farm. He sometimes worked for a white farmer with a thousand acres in cotton and a subsidy from the federal government. Moses could drive a tractor when he was thirteen, and run a cultivator, but his reading and writing were poor.

"When Moses was sixteen he went into Austin to see if he could be trained as a tractor mechanic. He knew a lot about them. Well, he might get some training under a federal program, if he waited awhile, but nobody would hire him. And the union wouldn't help out. In fact they would see to it, he couldn't be hired. They didn't want black men competing.

"So young Moses joined the Army. Volunteered. And while the Army runs a pretty fair and square operation, promotion was tough for a black man with no education and few skills. But he didn't complain. Moses didn't talk much. He was raised to respect his elders. Yes, my friends, I wonder sometimes how our black people have been so patient, so dignified, so co-operative. I know all about law and order, and the crime rate in the cities, and the extremists, and maybe we've had a little bit to do with creating those conditions also.

"We didn't do much for Moses Mulford did we? Maybe we assumed he didn't care, or was too dumb to know the difference. That's an old habit of ours where black men are concerned. Back in the Revolutionary War, there was an entire Negro regiment formed in Rhose Island, slaves who were freed and trained and armed. They licked the tar out of the Hessians at the Battle of Newport, and then they marched into oblivion and out of the history books— no pay, no advancement, not even a kind word. Until a few years ago, you'd never know there had been a First Rhode Island Regiment, or thousands and thousands of other black men who fought and died in our struggle for independence.

"I wish I could say we've changed. But when I study the facts of young Mulford's life, I wonder. But maybe he's dramatized the issue for us. Maybe we can learn something about ourselves from the circumstances of his life and his death. With all my heart I wish he had been spared, the way the angel stopped Abraham's knife at the altar."

Hannaford paused. There was a sound of weeping. Mrs. Mulford was being comforted by her husband. Two small boys were sniffling. The President opened his Bible.

" 'And Abraham stretched forth his hand, and took the knife to slay his son. And the angel of the Lord called unto him out of heaven, and said, Abraham, Abraham: and he said, Here am I. And he said, Lay not thine hand upon the lad, neither do thou any thing unto him: for now I know that thou fearest God, seeing thou hast not withheld thy son, thine only son from me.' "

There were cries of *Amen*. I saw Fern dabbing at her eyes. Many in the congregation were crying.

"But we have not listened to the Lord, my friends," Ben said. "We have failed to stay our murderous hands. We have no sacrificial altars, but we have giant machines and substances of death, and we kill our Isaacs. We, the Presidents and senators, and generals, and industrialists and workers, we build the altars. The Hebrew sages tell us that God's intervention with Abraham marks a turning point in mankind's history, the end of human sacrifice and the covenant between God and man, the dawn of civilized society. But how much have we learned from the old Hebrews?

"As your President I have tried, and I am trying now, to keep us from putting our Isaacs on the altar. Our young people deserve better than that. For the death in battle, the death from bombs, is only part of the evil in the world. We face the death of rotting cities and fouled air and stinking rivers. And we insult the Lord and his works when we permit these. Americans, don't deliberately break the covenant. But the complexities of modern life have confused and angered many of them. It's time we saw the goals clearly. I hope young Mulford's death will help us along the way."

Hannaford raised his head. He was going to scripture

again. I could tell by the fire in his eye. But he knew the passage by heart, and he closed the book. " 'Return, oh Lord, how long? And let it repent thee concerning thy servants. Oh satisfy us early with thy mercy; that we may rejoice and be glad all of our days. Make us glad according to the days wherein thou hast afflicted us, and the years wherein we have seen evil. Let thy work appear unto thy servants and thy glory unto thy children.' "

The President walked down the rickety steps. Reverend Russell nodded at the choir, the organ sounded its solemn chords, and the plangent voices rose in the heat-heavy church.

"We are climbing Jacob's ladder . . ."

I have never heard such a sound in my life. It shivered me with its resonance, its courage, its affirmation. It was as if the united voice of America was telling the President that they understood.

The next morning I was back in Washington. In the anteroom to the press gallery, a lanky blond man, gaunt of face, accosted me. "Mr. Deever? I'm Father Ward. From Connecticut."

I shook hands with the new member of Warfield's Urban Council. Of course I remembered him—the priest who stopped the Waterbury riots.

"Do you think you could get me into the press section to watch them vote?" he asked.

Somehow his clerical presence cheered me up. "It's tight in there, but we're both slender. You share a seat with me."

Inside, I introduced Parente to Father Ward. We sat amid the hushed, tense reporters and waited for the Senate court to come to order.

"Here it comes," Lou said. "Big Casino."

The Chief Justice entered. "The High Court of Impeachment is in session," the clerk announced.

"If there is no further debate," Chief Justice Early said, "the clerk will call the roll."

Lester Goodchapel, perhaps the dumbest man in the Senate, rose to ask whether their responses would be "guilty" or "not guilty" instead of the traditional "yes" or "no." This had already been agreed upon; Lester had forgotten, and Early politely affirmed the decision.

"Vote, vote," Parente muttered. "Bettenhaus and Tutt and a few other hardheads tried to ram through a separate vote on each paragraph. But Stapp and Henshaw argued against it. Looks like they dropped that one."

So tense was I, so cold, that I could not respond. I stared down at the Senate—that mystical, worshipful, symbolic council of tribal elders. Once more Ben Hannaford's fate rested with them.

"Mr. Abbott."

"Not guilty." Willard Abbott of Delaware. One of our regulars.

"Mr. Allerdice."

"Not guilty." James Allerdice of Oregon was a close friend of Congressman Hollis Denton, who'd been a stout ally on the Government Operations Committee.

"Mr. Arnold."

"Not guilty." This drew me up short. Huntley Arnold was a flinty law and order man from Tennessee.

Father Ward, sharing the upholstered seat with me, made the sign of the cross.

"I thought radical young priests aren't sold on the power of prayer," I said.

"Can't shake the old habits, Mr. Deever. Goodness, we're off to a grand start, aren't we?"

I explained to the pastor that we did not need merely a victory but an overwhelming one. On the way to the Capitol that morning I had seen those cursed RESIGN posters all over the Mall.

"Mr. Bettenhaus."

This was a big one. Stanton Bettenhaus was North Carolina cotton mill money. He had contributed to Save America and DOOR, and for all his Ivy League, button-down modernity, he was an immovable reactionary.

"Guilty," Senator Bettenhaus said. But he did not sound exuberant.

"Screw," Parente muttered.

"Mr. Brady."

"Not guilty," said Emmett Brady of Massachusetts.

"Mr. Byram."

"Not guilty. A surprise: Byram was a conservative from Virginia.

"Looks pretty good," Parente said. "Maybe we win big."

"Mr. Chambers."

"Guilty." Ah well, Mississippi.

I checked my tally sheet after the next few votes. We were down through the first twenty names, one-fifth of the Senate, and the count stood at fifteen to five for acquittal. It could have been better.

"Mr. DiFalco."

Up rose little Henry DiFalco of New Haven, an old friend of ours. He was a courageous mini-senator, father of seven children, grandfather of eleven, a descendant of those industrious Italians who built the New Haven Railroad and stayed on in the pleasant state of Connecticut to run filling stations, bars, bowling alleys, supermarkets and city governments.

"Your Honor," Senator DiFalco said, "it is my understanding that under the rules of this court, any senator may be permitted to explain his vote. Am I correct, sir?"

"That is correct, Senator DiFalco."

Parente edged forward. Father Ward and I felt each other's bodies stiffen. Something was in the wind.

"And it is also my understanding that that provision implies the right of any senator to yield when the roll is called, to another member of the court, for the purpose of voting."

"That is my interpretation of the rules, Senator."

Below, I studied Congressmen Ruckett, Cottrell, and DeVaux. They did not look overjoyed.

"Thank you, Your Honor," Senator DiFalco said. "I yield to the senior senator from Wyoming."

"Whatever they dreamed up," Lou Parente said. "Here it comes."

Webb Urban of Wyoming got to his feet. He was the Senate incarnate.

"Your Honor," Senator Urban said, "I am convinced that a continuance of this vote serves no purpose. It will only serve to further split the legislature, weaken the executive, and divide the people. I believe in opposition, and checks and balances and criticism and dissent. But this trial has gone far enough. The reaction to the President's address yesterday, as I read it, the national sentiment in favor of much—not all, I say—but much of what he said—"

"You votin' or makin' a speech?" Gabe Tutt gargled. "You gon' vote, vote! You gon' fillibuster, filibuster!"

Urban peered over his bifocals across the chamber at

598

Gabe's minatory figure. "I thank the senator from Alabama for reminding me of my duties," Urban said drily. "My vote, Your Honor, is not guilty. I now resume my explanation of my vote.

"I have disagreed with the President many times. I shall continue to do so. But this entire affair is demeaning and destructive of orderly government. Passion ruled, not reason. We have had our debates. We have listened to the arguments. We have grown weary and ill-tempered hearing the same charges over and over."

"You finished? You finished?" Gabe Tutt shouted.

Urban ignored him. "I feel, sir, we have had enough of rancor and anger and bitterness and name-calling. Let us get this thing over with. It never should have gotten this far. The violence in the streets blinded many of us to the reasonable, thoughtful, prayerful processes whereby government gets its jobs done. I say it is time to return to those processes.

"I therefore move, Your Honor, as an extension of the explanation of my vote, that the Senate, by voice vote, and with no further calling of the roll, render a unanimous verdict of not guilty, and acquit the President of the United States of all charges embodied in House Resolution 988."

The galleries exploded. Applause, cheering, whistling cascaded from above—even from the seats where the visiting members of the House sat.

Ruckett was on his feet. "Your Honor! This is irregular! The court cannot make these arbitrary decisions!"

But none of his fellow managers were having any part of the protest. I could see what was happening. Had the roll call continued, Hannaford would have won by a good-sized majority— perhaps two to one. But the thirty-odd men who voted against him, who had found him guilty, would have suffered a good deal of nervous sweating during the remainder of his term. They knew all about Hannaford's long memory; his strength; his determination. Since the acquittal verdict was assured, why not, reasoned the elders of the Senate, get it over with swiftly and surgically.

John Tyler Lord of Vermont and Maury Eisenberg of Illinois quickly seconded Urban's motion.

I had to hand it to Lance Ruckett. Of course, I had always thought him a bit insane. The gleam in his eyes,

599

the set of his jaw, the ranting voice when he roused himself—these were more than mere quirks of character. As the clerk began to read Urban's motion, Lance got up, with nary a look to right or left and marched stiffly out of the chamber.

Parente sucked in his breath. "Poor jerk. You don't futz around with the United States Senate like that."

". . . will signify by saying 'Not guilty.' "

The roar was like a monstrous breaking wave—relief, joy, freedom.

". . . by saying 'Guilty.' "

Silence. Then, a low hum, a relieved muttering, a laugh here, a chuckle there. Senators rose and talked informally. I saw Sid Stapp and John Tyler Lord walk over to Burke Boswell and pump his hand. The tall man looked as if he were ready to buy drinks for the entire Senate, bend elbows with them all day, and booze them all into a stupor.

"The court will entertain a motion to adjourn," John Laurens Early said.

In his aristocratic southern blood, I told myself, ran the spirit of his noble ancestor, John Laurens, the 'Chevalier Bayard" of the American Revolution.

"Power of prayer, Mr. Deever," Father Ward said, as we got up amid the agitated reporters. In the public galleries, people were still cheering, whistling.

"No. The prevalence of common sense. And maybe some feedback of national guilt."

It was past midnight. We stood on the balcony of the South Portico, the one that Harry Truman, ignoring criticism, had built anyway.

"I tell you, Edward," the President said, "I feel like King David after the Israelites recovered the Ark of the Lord. They played before the Lord on all manner of instruments made of fir wood, on harps, psalteries, timbrels, cornets and cymbals."

Below us and around us, the gemlike lights of the city sparkled brilliantly in the indigo-blue summer night—the Washington Monument, the Lincoln Memorial, the Capitol, all the imposing structures, the enduring reminders of our past. Harry Truman had been gratified when the Kennedys' English nannie had told him how much the Kennedy children enjoyed the view from his balcony. "I'm glad somebody likes it," Harry had said.

"And if I were a frivolous sort, Edward," the President went on, "I might just dance a bit."

"Dance?"

"Why, of course. You know that King David broke into a buck and wing when the ark came home. Girded with a linen ephod, he leaped and danced before the Lord. For some reason, one of his wives, Michal, a snooty sort, despised him because of his fancy stepping and scolded him."

"My dear," Fern said, as she joined us on the balcony, to look at the magic city, "if you started to twist and turn and do whatever it is the young people do, I could not mock you."

For a moment I thought these two Titans might actually begin to dance on the curving balcony of the South Portico. But, no. They just held hands. A strange marriage. One must not speculate too much on the private lives of kings, princes and Presidents. But love, or something akin to it was surely present.

"Mr. President," I said, as we took one more look at the glittering lights around us, "would you say that the vote in the Senate today was a case of the right thing happening for the wrong reason?"

"Of course, Edward. That Mulford boy had to die a horrible death. That was a terribly wrong reason. I had some misgivings about intruding on his family's sorrow. But I think they understood."

"They did, Benjamin," Fern said. "I had a long talk with Mrs. Mulford. Those people are aware of what you are doing. They know who are their friends."

Hannaford frowned. We walked through the silent corridors of the White House. "I suppose that lad, giving his life to squelch those poisons, those lethal chemicals we're so intent on producing, made a lot of people think. Senators aren't stupid, Edward. Sometimes they even have a conscience, and are motivated by nothing more than the moral imperatives of a situation, just the thing you wrote about in the eulogy."

"More often than we suspect, sir."

"That's why I've never been so hopeful as I am now," the President said. We followed Fern's queenly figure toward her sitting room. She had ordered tea for the three of us, a mild celebration to mark the end of a triumphant day.

"Nothing's going to be easy," I said. "They're still after you. They'll scream for you to resign. Save America says it's sure it can knock you off in the next election. Generals Upshaw and Nagel were quoted tonight as reaffirming their convictions that there won't be any presidential elections next time around. They've got their own plans. And Kakamba says he was framed—by you, by me, by Moscowitz, by Parente, by anyone he can think of."

"Edward, I cannot be discouraged by bad news. We're moving, son. We're moving away from this damned economy of death to an economy of life."

"Swords into plowshares again?"

" 'Many shall be purified and made white and tried; but the wicked shall do wickedly; and none of the wicked shall understand; but the wise shall understand.' "

Travis, the Hannafords' butler, entered, pushing an elegant tea wagon. Fern dismissed him. She poured.

"Edward, read me that passage from that professor's book once more," the President said.

I took my dog-eared paperback Rossiter from my pocket. It had been a good companion during our ordeal.

" 'The presidency is a standing reproach to those petty doctrinaires who insist that executive power is inherently undemocratic; for to the exact contrary, it has been more responsive to the needs and dreams of giant democracy than any other office or institution in the whole mosaic of American life. . . .' "

Hannaford closed his eyes. An uneducated man, an unread man, he had a shrewd understanding of the way of the world, of what was right and necessary. And he listened to my reading, not in a vain and self-aggrandizing spirit, but as a man of tolerance and warmth, eager to learn, to grow, to work, to serve his country.

" 'The American people,' " I continued, " 'who are, after all, the best judges of the means by which their democracy is to be achieved, have made the presidency their peculiar instrument. As they ready themselves for the pilgrimage ahead, they can take comfort and pride in the thought that it is also their peculiar treasure.' "

I closed the book.

"That is beautifully stated," Fern said. "And undeniably true."

"A peculiar treasure," Hannaford said wryly. "Never quite thought of myself in those terms."

"It isn't you the professor is saying it about," the First Lady said quickly. "It is the *office*."

"Right you are, my love," the President said. "But let me indulge myself a little. On this night, anyway."

Fern smiled tolerantly. I wondered what her oil-well relatives thought of her now.

"And tell me this, Mr. President," I said, "do you still believe in the powers of controlled greed?"

He sipped his tea. "I guess I do, Edward. It's a cynical philosophy for a President to entertain, but I'm afraid we've got to recognize it. The only thing I would say, now that we've passed through the fiery furnace again, is that it's got to be controlled a hell of a lot more."

"I'm glad you feel that way. Less for Gabe Tutt, more for Amos Mulford. Is that the idea?"

The President stroked his square chin. I saw the humorous glint in his eyes. "You know what Moses said, son."

"I'm afraid not, sir." We were playing the old game. I knew he was back in form, ready to take on the whole crowd—generals, oil gluttons, racists, union bosses.

" 'When thou beatest thine olive tree, thou shalt not go over the boughs again. It shall be for the stranger, for the fatherless and for the widow. When thou gatherest the grapes of thy vineyard, thou shalt not glean it afterward; it shall be for the stranger, for the fatherless and for the widow.' "

Nothing would come easily. Nothing would happen overnight. But the President would keep battling. And knowing Hannaford as I did, I knew he would give us strength, and the will to get the jobs done.

The men who held the office, the professor had written, *recognized the true source of the power and were ennobled by the knowledge.* How true this was of Benjamin Bow Hannaford, I thought, how gratifyingly true.

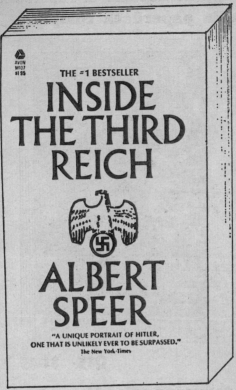

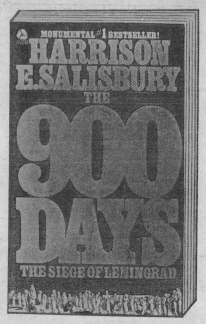

Avon the New Leader in Paperbacks

the Senator
DREW PEARSON

The big bestselling novel that really takes you inside!